W.I.T.C.H.

Will Irma Taranee Cornelia Hay Lin

Part VII. New Power Volume 3

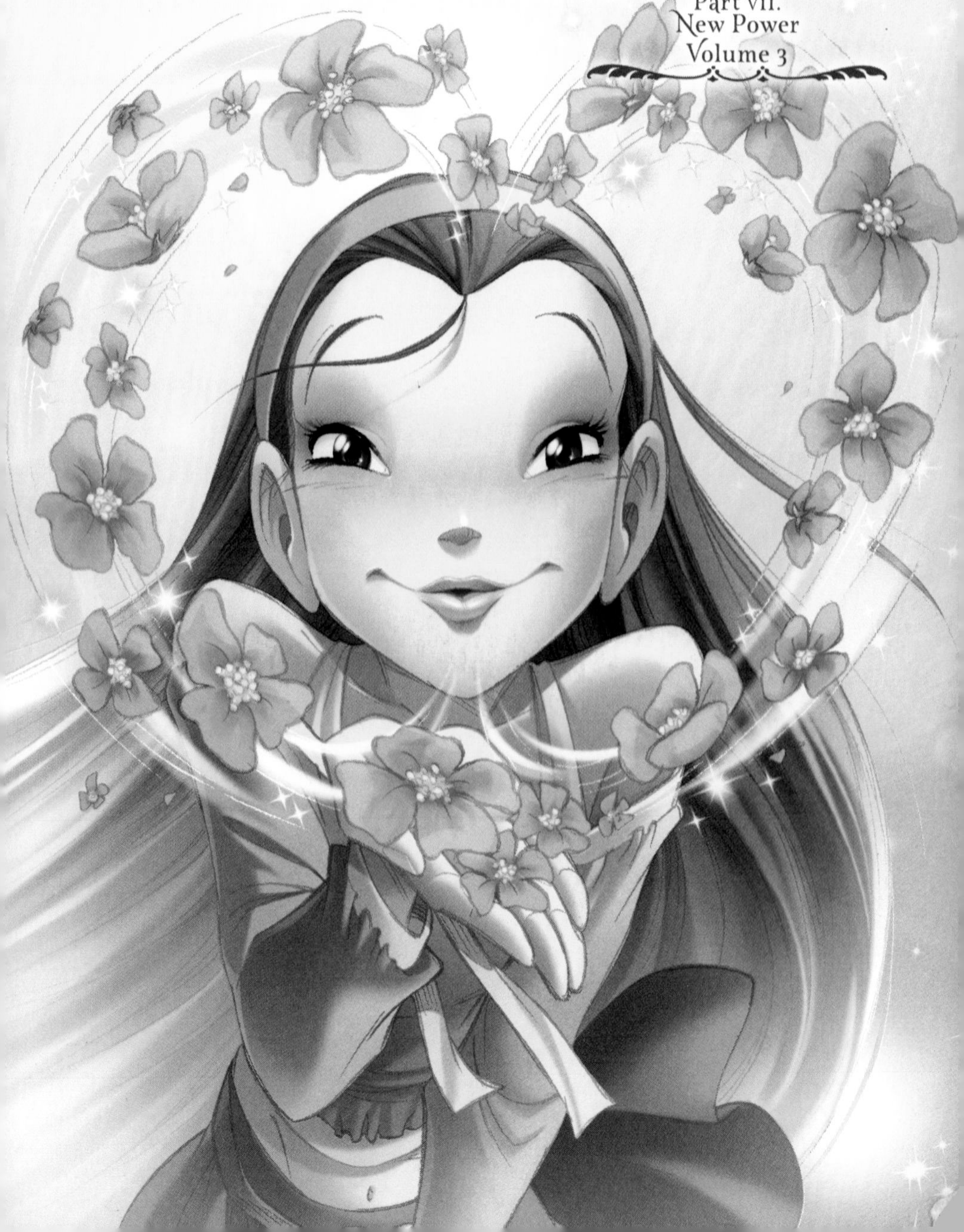

W.i.t.c.h.

Will Irma Taranee Cornelia Hay Lin

Part VII.
New Power
Volume 3

CONTENTS

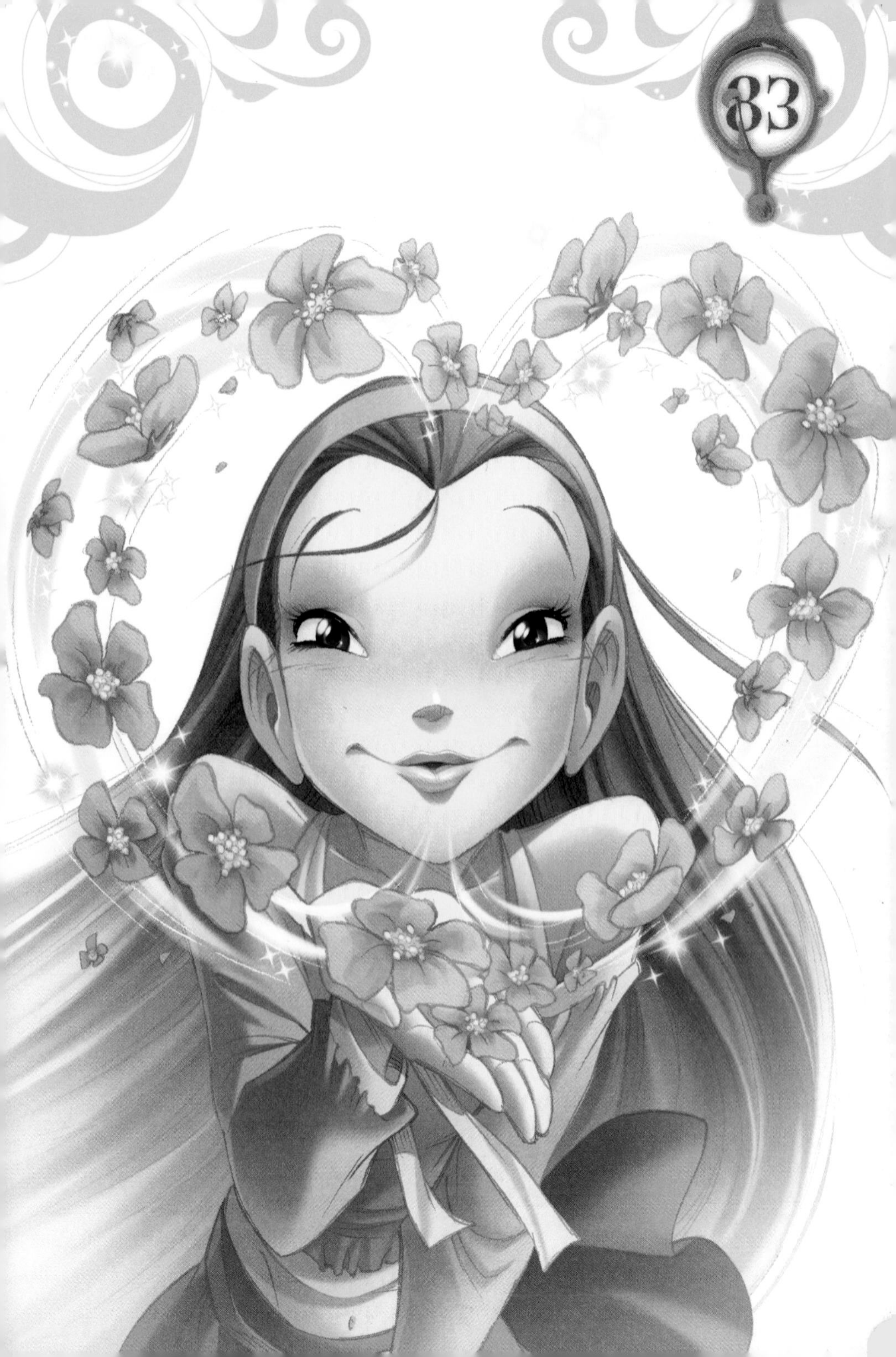
33

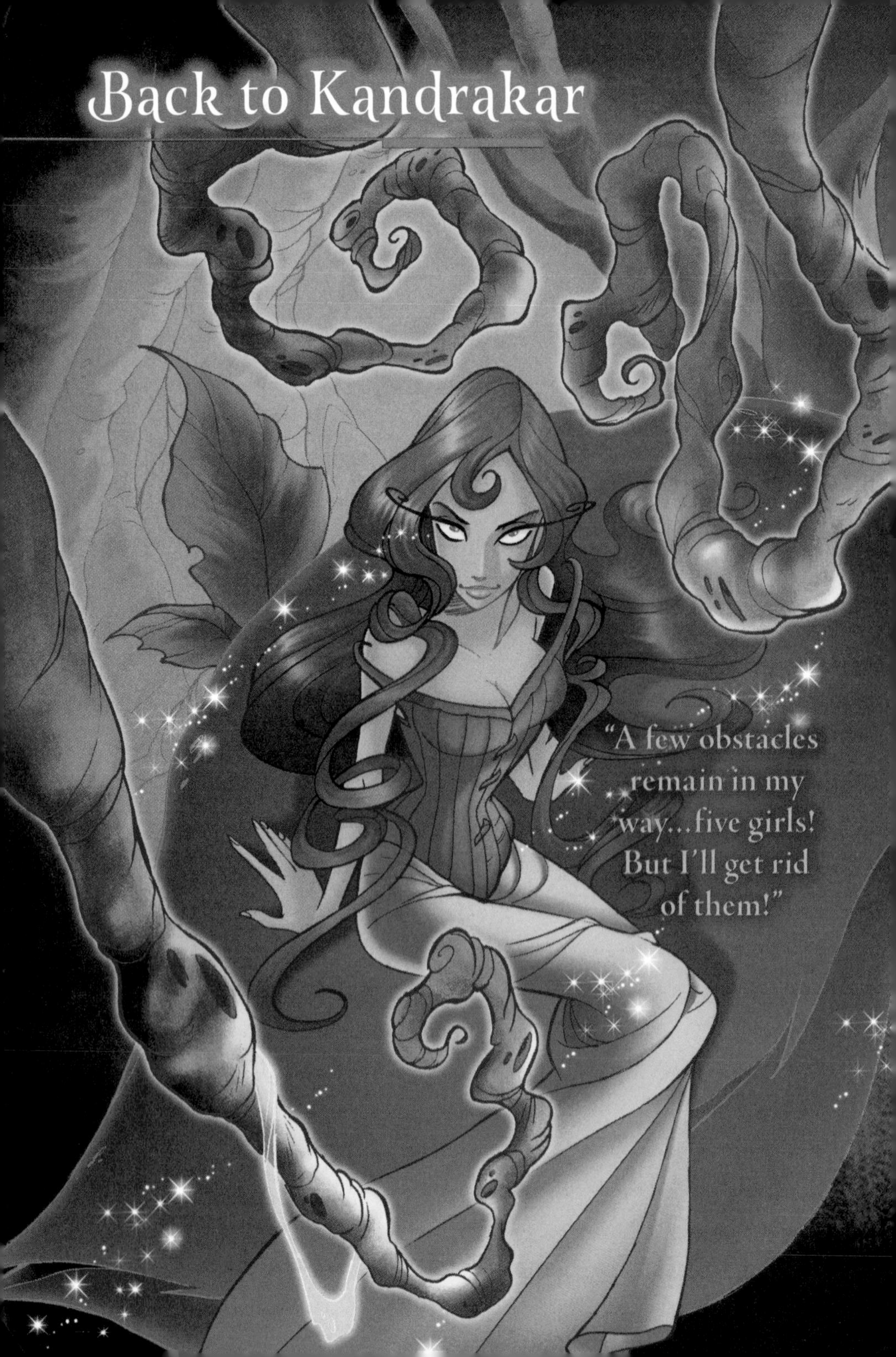
Back to Kandrakar
"A few obstacles remain in my way...five girls! But I'll get rid of them!"

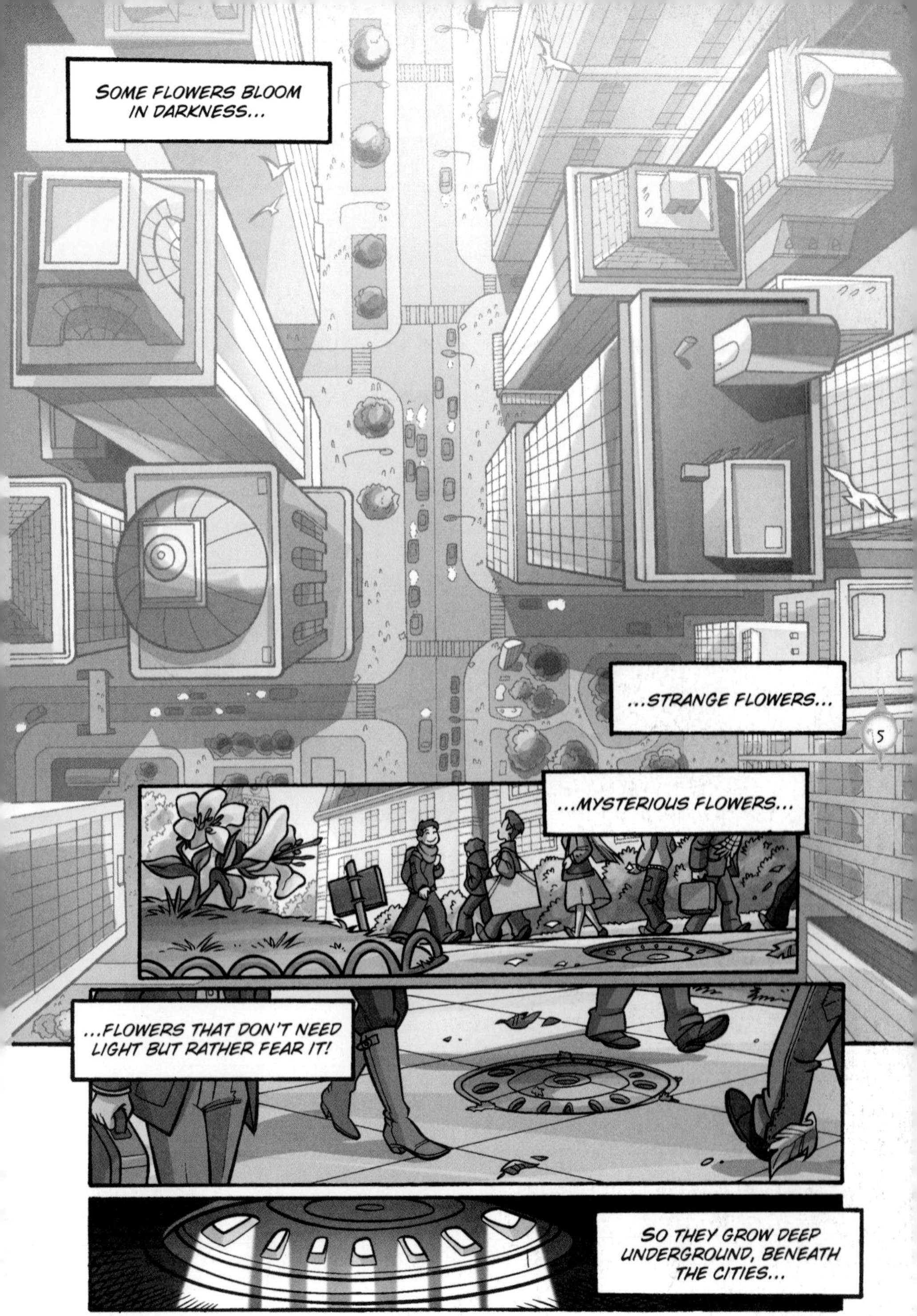
SOME FLOWERS BLOOM IN DARKNESS...
...STRANGE FLOWERS...
...MYSTERIOUS FLOWERS...
...FLOWERS THAT DON'T NEED LIGHT BUT RATHER FEAR IT!
SO THEY GROW DEEP UNDERGROUND, BENEATH THE CITIES...

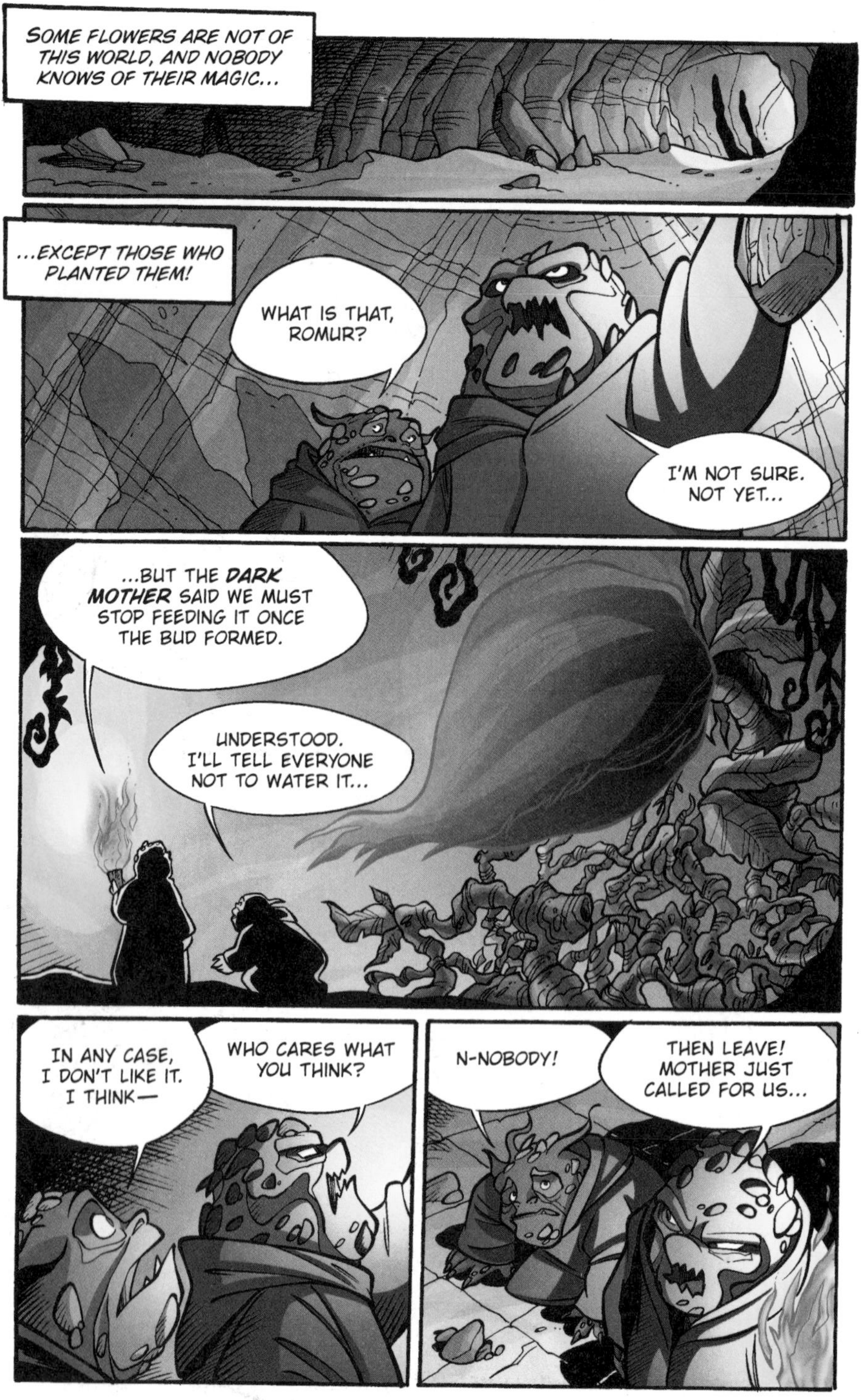

SOME FLOWERS ARE NOT OF THIS WORLD, AND NOBODY KNOWS OF THEIR MAGIC...
...EXCEPT THOSE WHO PLANTED THEM!
WHAT IS THAT, ROMUR?
I'M NOT SURE. NOT YET...
...BUT THE DARK MOTHER SAID WE MUST STOP FEEDING IT ONCE THE BUD FORMED.
UNDERSTOOD. I'LL TELL EVERYONE NOT TO WATER IT...
IN ANY CASE, I DON'T LIKE IT. I THINK—
WHO CARES WHAT YOU THINK?
N-NOBODY!
THEN LEAVE! MOTHER JUST CALLED FOR US...

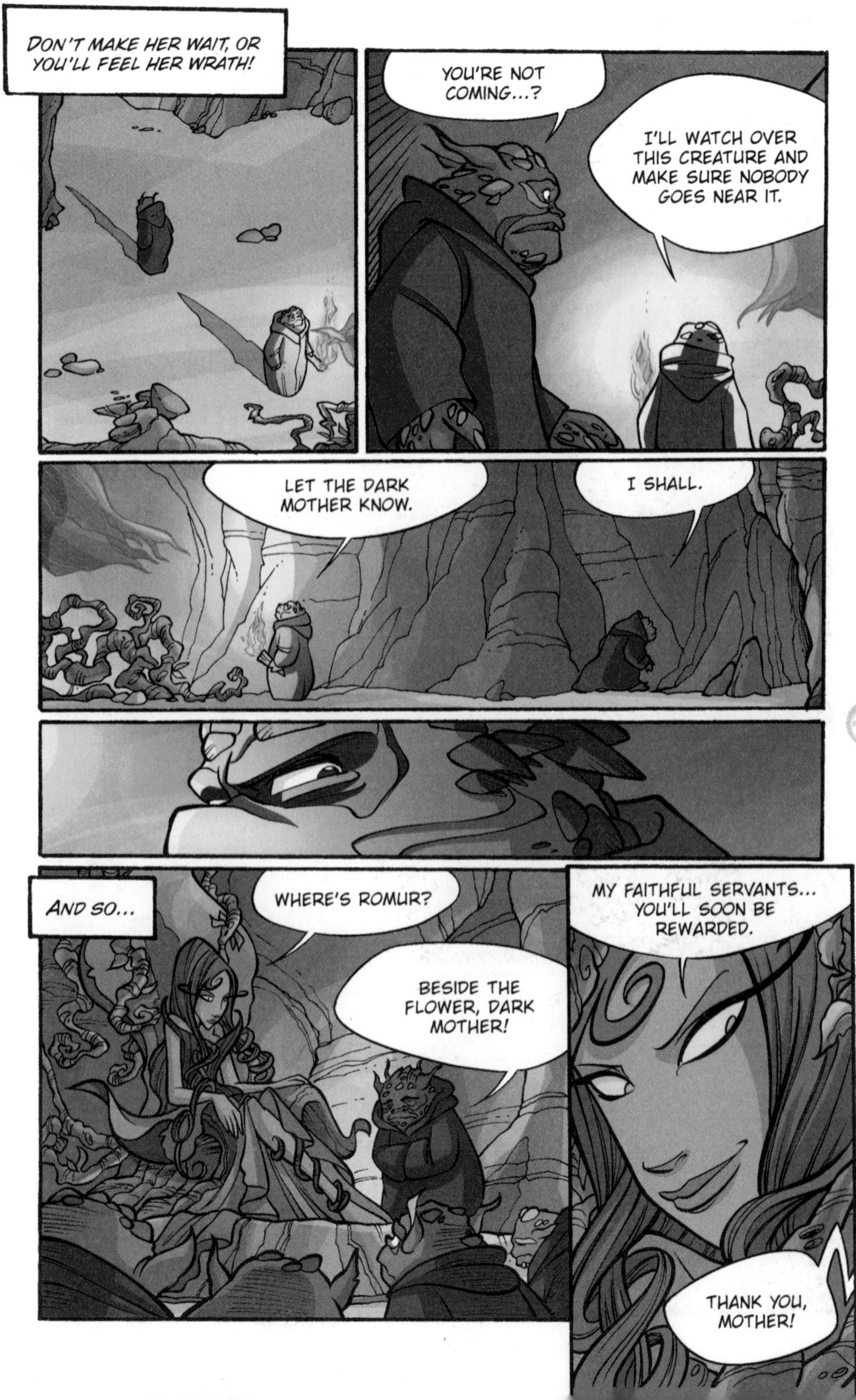
DON'T MAKE HER WAIT, OR YOU'LL FEEL HER WRATH!
YOU'RE NOT COMING...?
I'LL WATCH OVER THIS CREATURE AND MAKE SURE NOBODY GOES NEAR IT.
LET THE DARK MOTHER KNOW.
I SHALL.
AND SO...
WHERE'S ROMUR?
BESIDE THE FLOWER, DARK MOTHER!
MY FAITHFUL SERVANTS... YOU'LL SOON BE REWARDED.
THANK YOU, MOTHER!

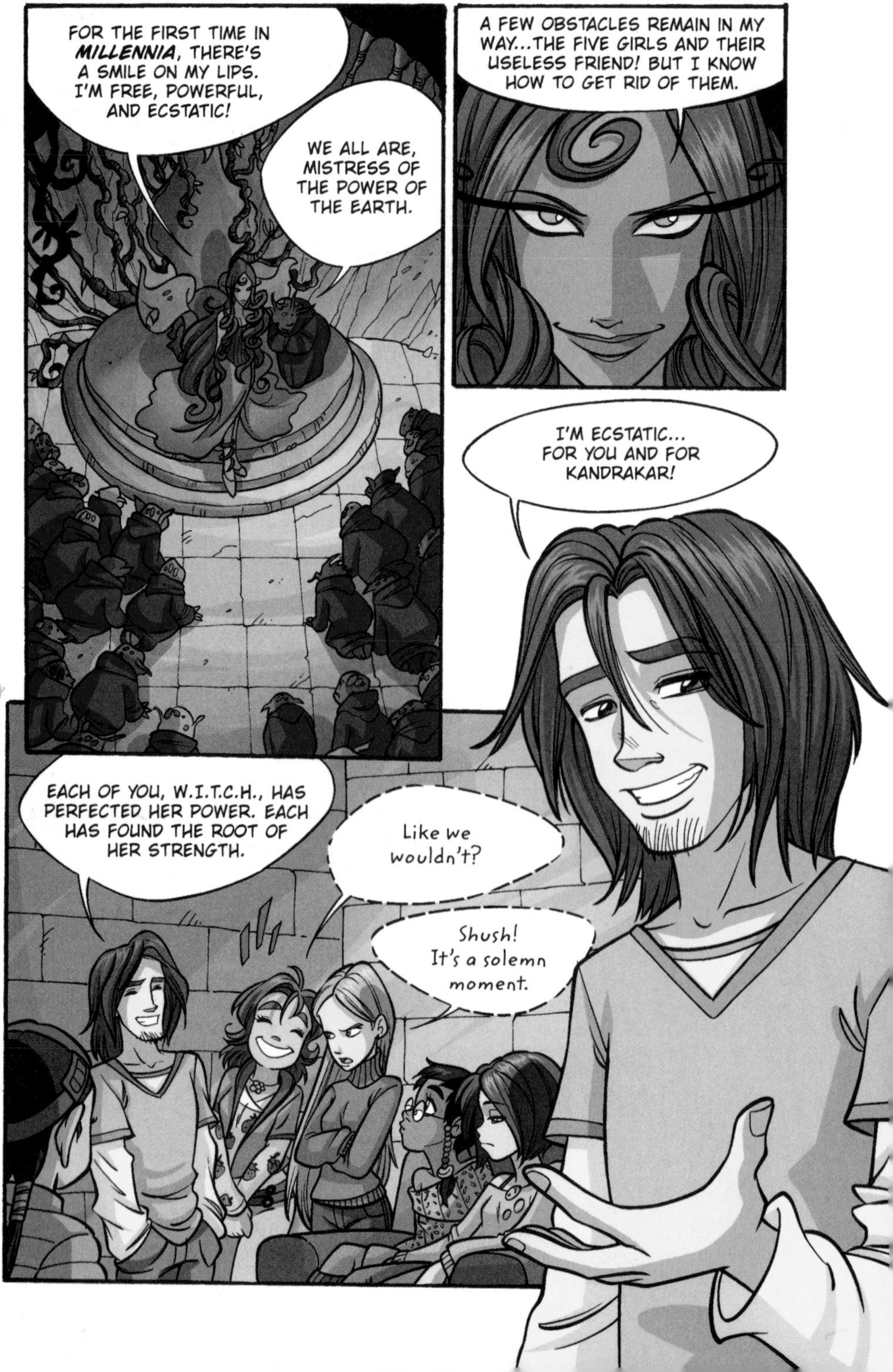
FOR THE FIRST TIME IN *MILLENNIA*, THERE'S A SMILE ON MY LIPS. I'M FREE, POWERFUL, AND ECSTATIC!
WE ALL ARE, MISTRESS OF THE POWER OF THE EARTH.
A FEW OBSTACLES REMAIN IN MY WAY...THE FIVE GIRLS AND THEIR USELESS FRIEND! BUT I KNOW HOW TO GET RID OF THEM.
EACH OF YOU, W.I.T.C.H., HAS PERFECTED HER POWER. EACH HAS FOUND THE ROOT OF HER STRENGTH.
Like we wouldn't?
Shush! It's a solemn moment.
I'M ECSTATIC... FOR YOU AND FOR KANDRAKAR!

IRMA, THE POWER OF *WATER* IS CRYSTAL CLEAR TO YOU!

CORNELIA, THE POWER OF *EARTH* WALKS WITH YOU LIKE A FRIEND!

I KNOW—I CAN FEEL IT!

HAY LIN, YOU RULE OVER THE *AIR*!

TARANEE, YOU AND *FIRE* BURN WITHIN EACH OTHER.

WILL. THE POWER THAT BINDS THE ELEMENTS IS IN YOUR HANDS. HOLD IT TIGHT AND STRENGTHEN YOUR BOND WITH YOUR FRIENDS!

YOU'RE OUR STRONGEST LINK— THE MOST RESPLENDENT JEWEL!

AND YOU, THE GUY WHO SAID HE LOVED ME? WHAT ARE YOU *TO ME NOW*?

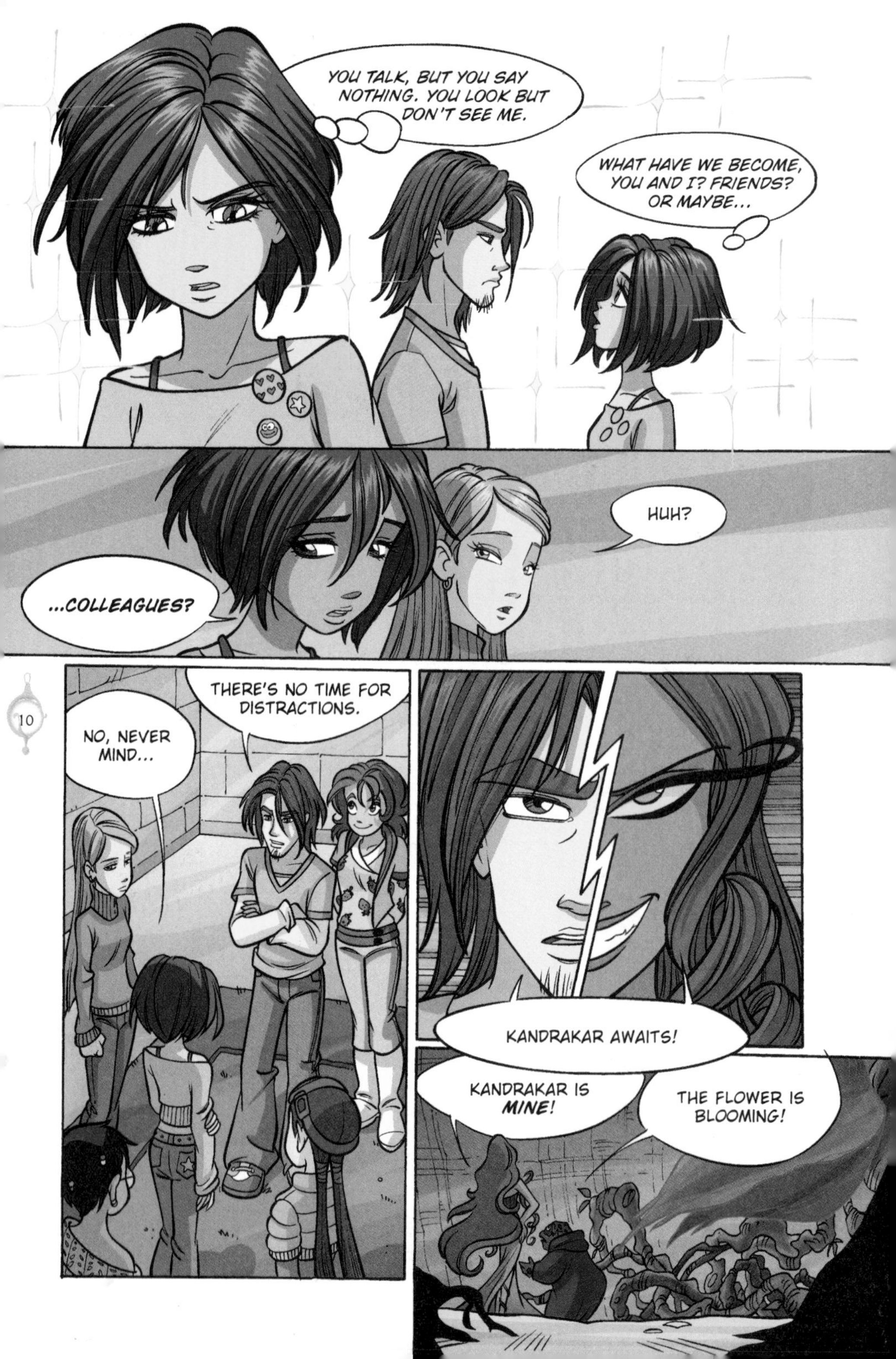
YOU TALK, BUT YOU SAY NOTHING. YOU LOOK BUT DON'T SEE ME.
WHAT HAVE WE BECOME, YOU AND I? FRIENDS? OR MAYBE...
...COLLEAGUES?
HUH?
NO, NEVER MIND...
THERE'S NO TIME FOR DISTRACTIONS.
KANDRAKAR AWAITS!
KANDRAKAR IS MINE!
THE FLOWER IS BLOOMING!

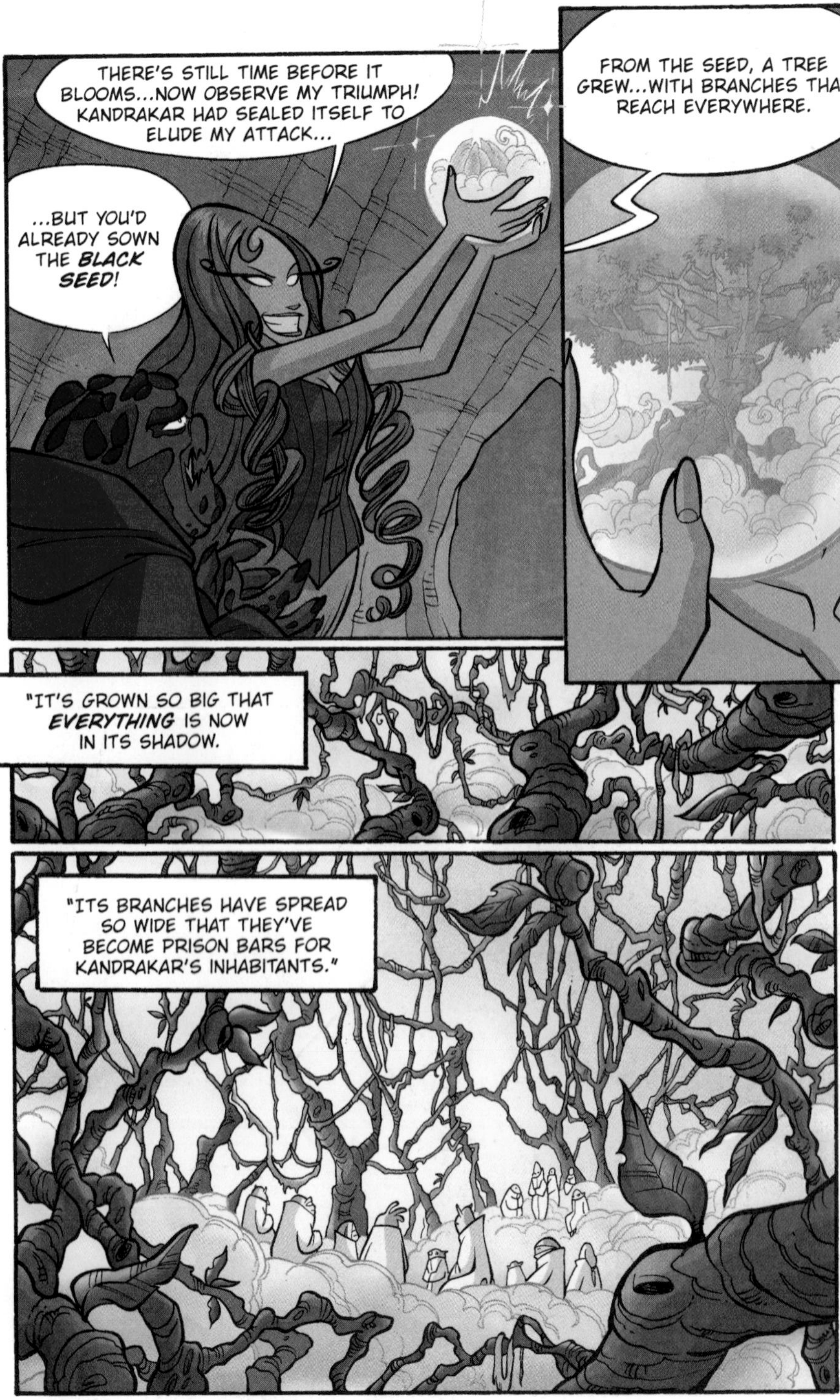
THERE'S STILL TIME BEFORE IT BLOOMS...NOW OBSERVE MY TRIUMPH! KANDRAKAR HAD SEALED ITSELF TO ELUDE MY ATTACK...
...BUT YOU'D ALREADY SOWN THE ***BLACK SEED***!
FROM THE SEED, A TREE GREW...WITH BRANCHES THAT REACH EVERYWHERE.
"IT'S GROWN SO BIG THAT ***EVERYTHING*** IS NOW IN ITS SHADOW.
"ITS BRANCHES HAVE SPREAD SO WIDE THAT THEY'VE BECOME PRISON BARS FOR KANDRAKAR'S INHABITANTS."

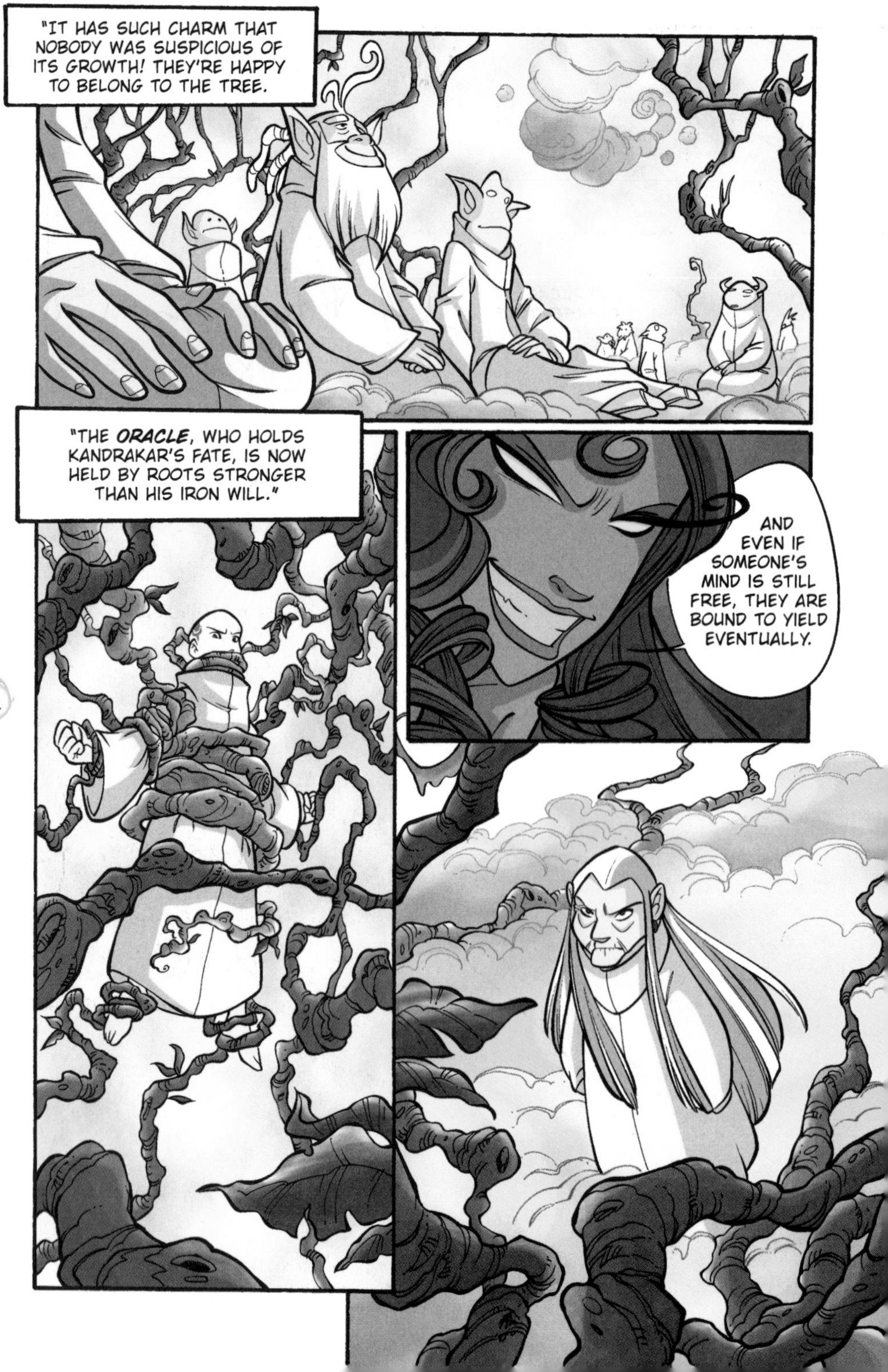
"IT HAS SUCH CHARM THAT NOBODY WAS SUSPICIOUS OF ITS GROWTH! THEY'RE HAPPY TO BELONG TO THE TREE.
"THE *ORACLE*, WHO HOLDS KANDRAKAR'S FATE, IS NOW HELD BY ROOTS STRONGER THAN HIS IRON WILL."
AND EVEN IF SOMEONE'S MIND IS STILL FREE, THEY ARE BOUND TO YIELD EVENTUALLY.

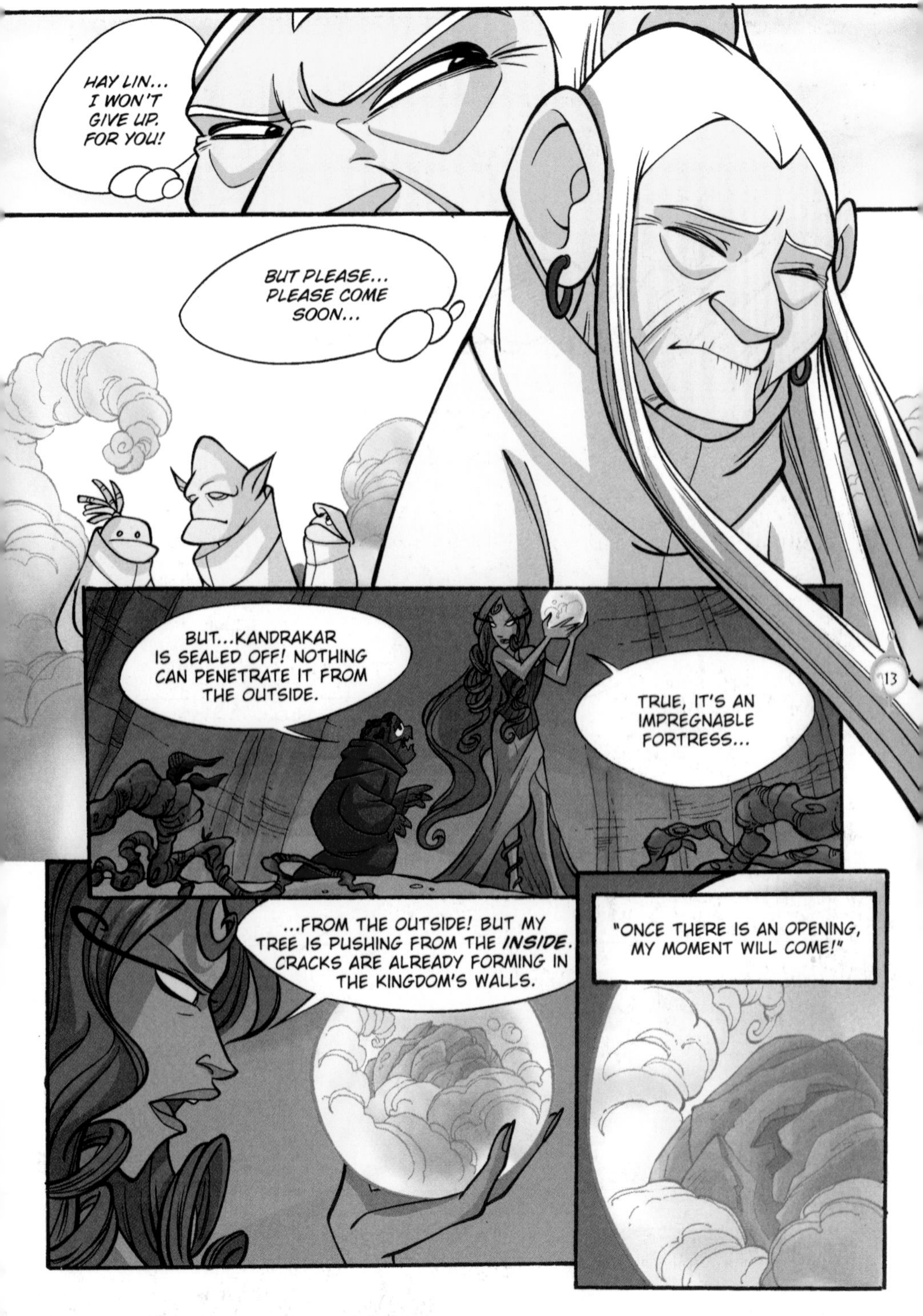
HAY LIN... I WON'T GIVE UP. FOR YOU!
BUT PLEASE... PLEASE COME SOON...
BUT...KANDRAKAR IS SEALED OFF! NOTHING CAN PENETRATE IT FROM THE OUTSIDE.
TRUE, IT'S AN IMPREGNABLE FORTRESS...
...FROM THE OUTSIDE! BUT MY TREE IS PUSHING FROM THE *INSIDE*. CRACKS ARE ALREADY FORMING IN THE KINGDOM'S WALLS.
"ONCE THERE IS AN OPENING, MY MOMENT WILL COME!"

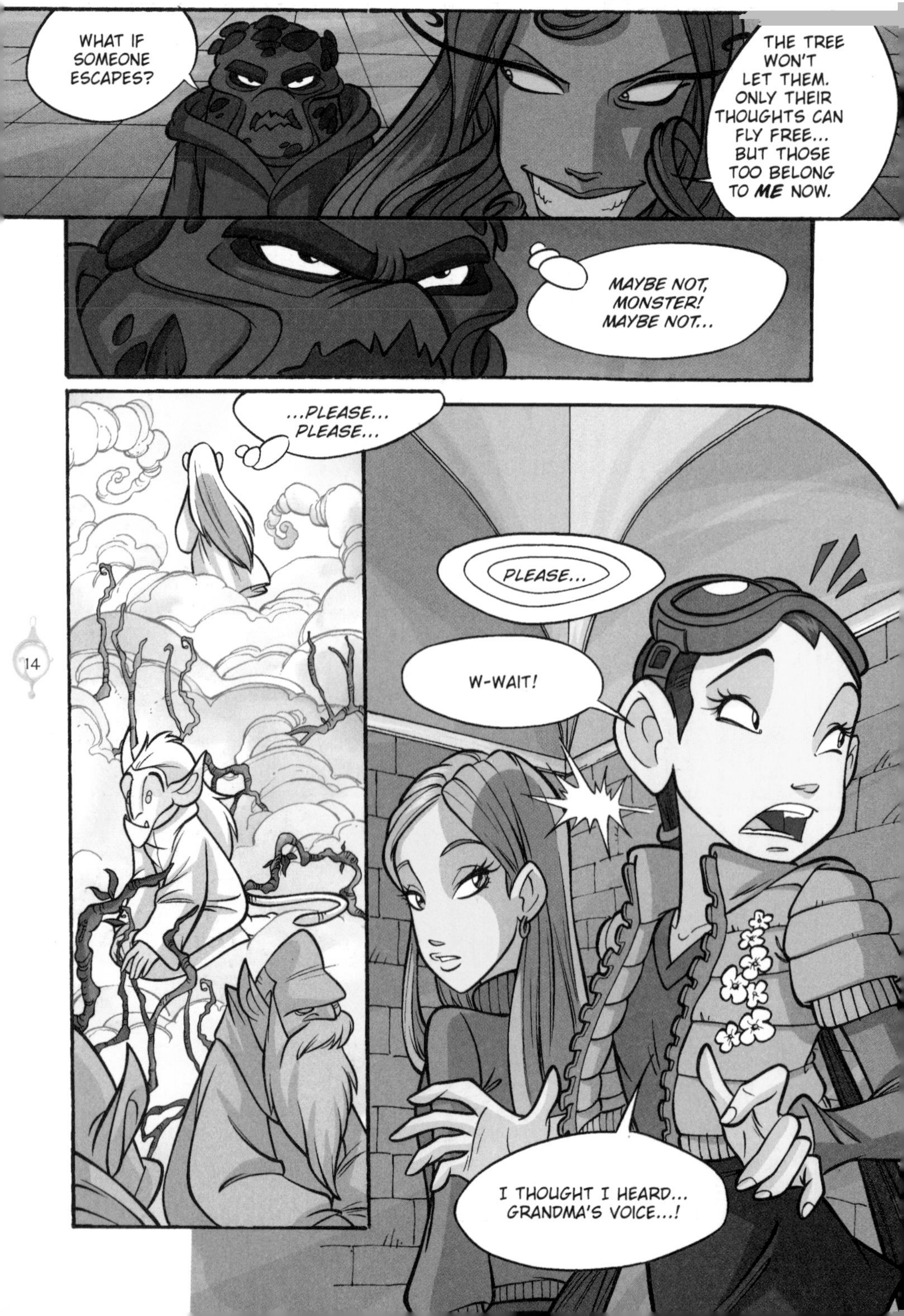
WHAT IF SOMEONE ESCAPES?
THE TREE WON'T LET THEM. ONLY THEIR THOUGHTS CAN FLY FREE... BUT THOSE TOO BELONG TO **ME** NOW.
MAYBE NOT, MONSTER! MAYBE NOT...
...PLEASE... PLEASE...
PLEASE...
W-WAIT!
I THOUGHT I HEARD... GRANDMA'S VOICE...!

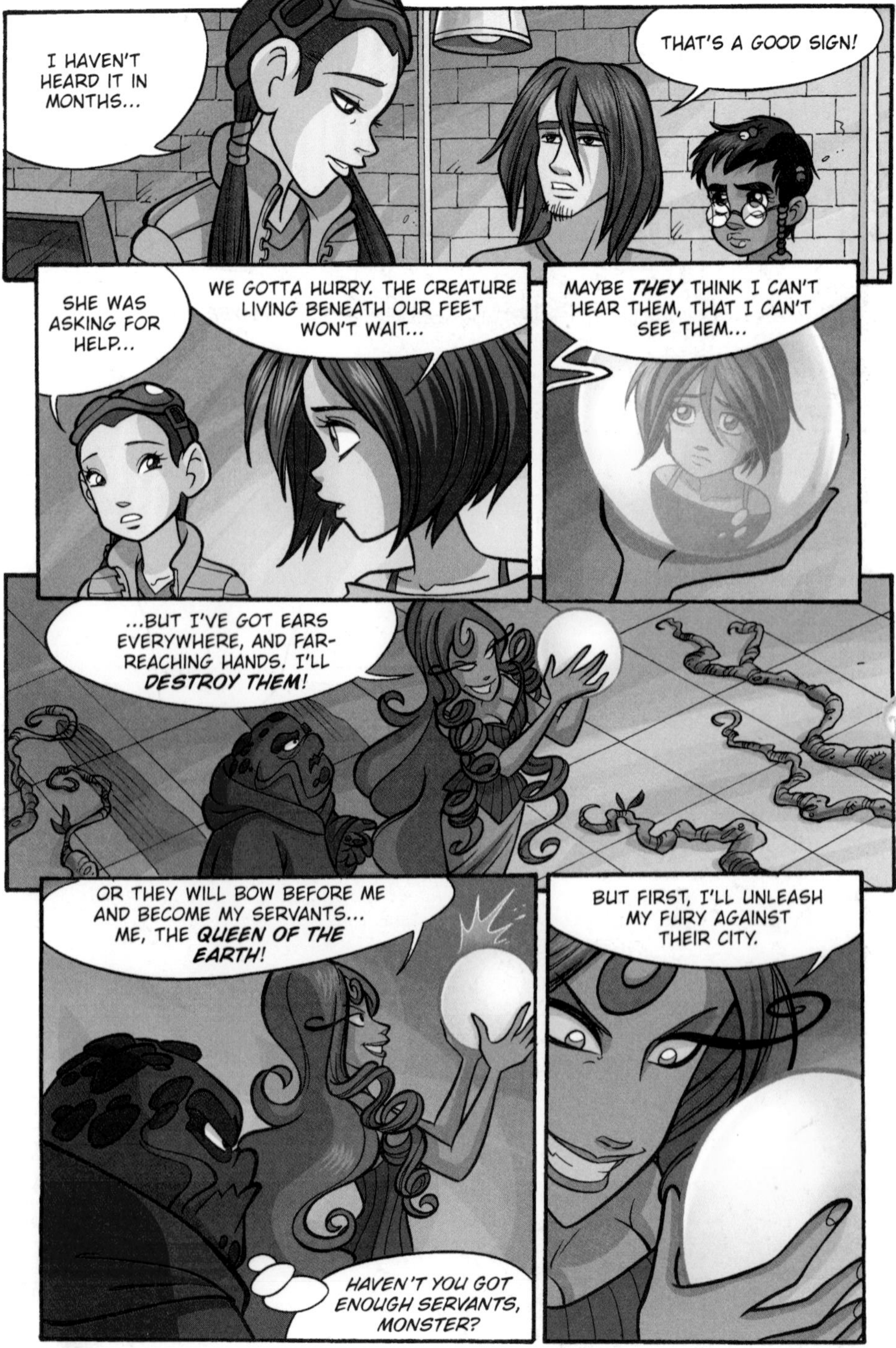
I HAVEN'T HEARD IT IN MONTHS...
THAT'S A GOOD SIGN!
SHE WAS ASKING FOR HELP...
WE GOTTA HURRY. THE CREATURE LIVING BENEATH OUR FEET WON'T WAIT...
MAYBE THEY THINK I CAN'T HEAR THEM, THAT I CAN'T SEE THEM...
...BUT I'VE GOT EARS EVERYWHERE, AND FAR-REACHING HANDS. I'LL DESTROY THEM!
OR THEY WILL BOW BEFORE ME AND BECOME MY SERVANTS... ME, THE QUEEN OF THE EARTH!
HAVEN'T YOU GOT ENOUGH SERVANTS, MONSTER?
BUT FIRST, I'LL UNLEASH MY FURY AGAINST THEIR CITY.

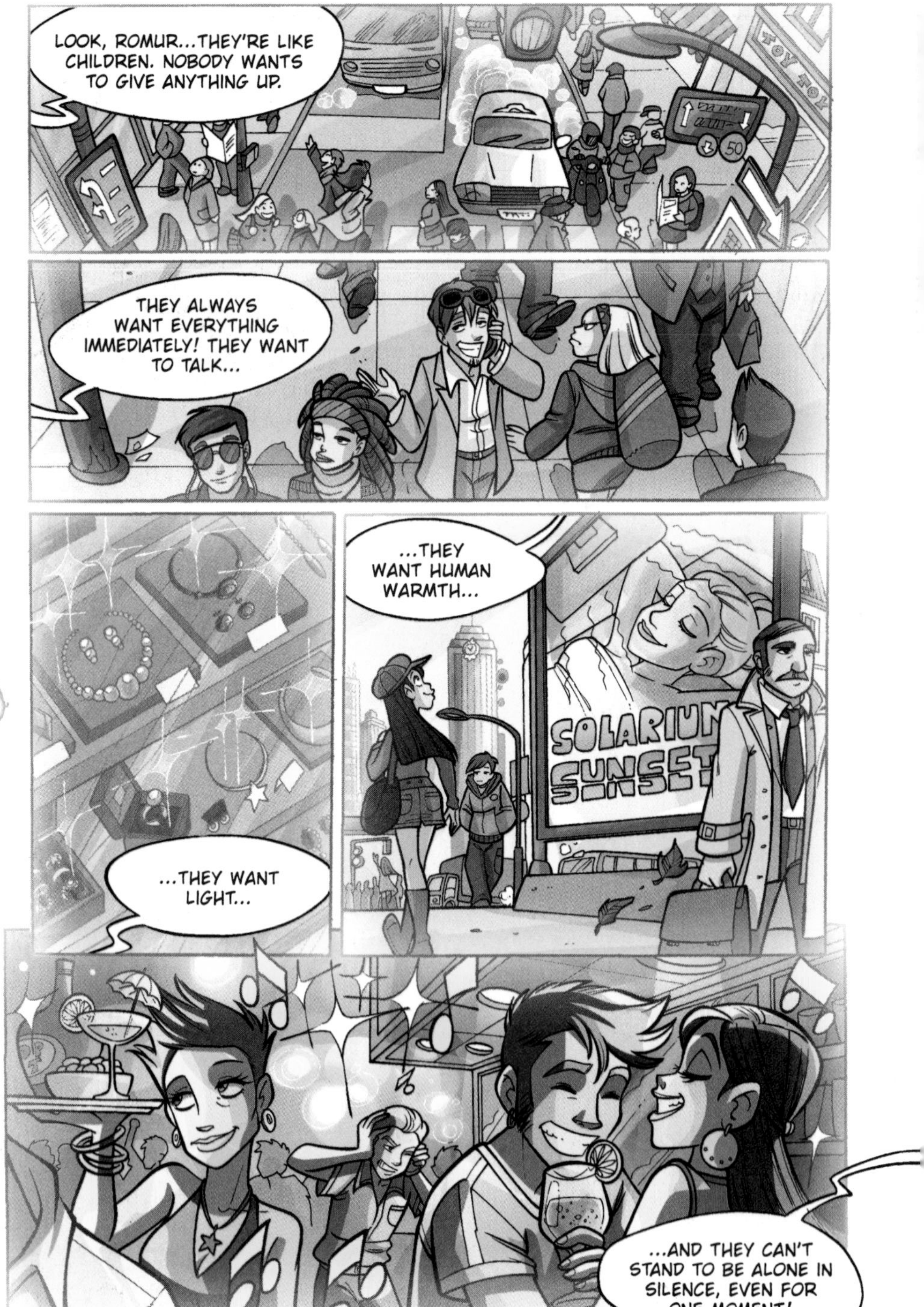
LOOK, ROMUR...THEY'RE LIKE CHILDREN. NOBODY WANTS TO GIVE ANYTHING UP.
TOY
50
THEY ALWAYS WANT EVERYTHING IMMEDIATELY! THEY WANT TO TALK...
...THEY WANT LIGHT...
...THEY WANT HUMAN WARMTH...
SOLARIUM SUNSET
...AND THEY CAN'T STAND TO BE ALONE IN SILENCE, EVEN FOR ONE MOMENT!

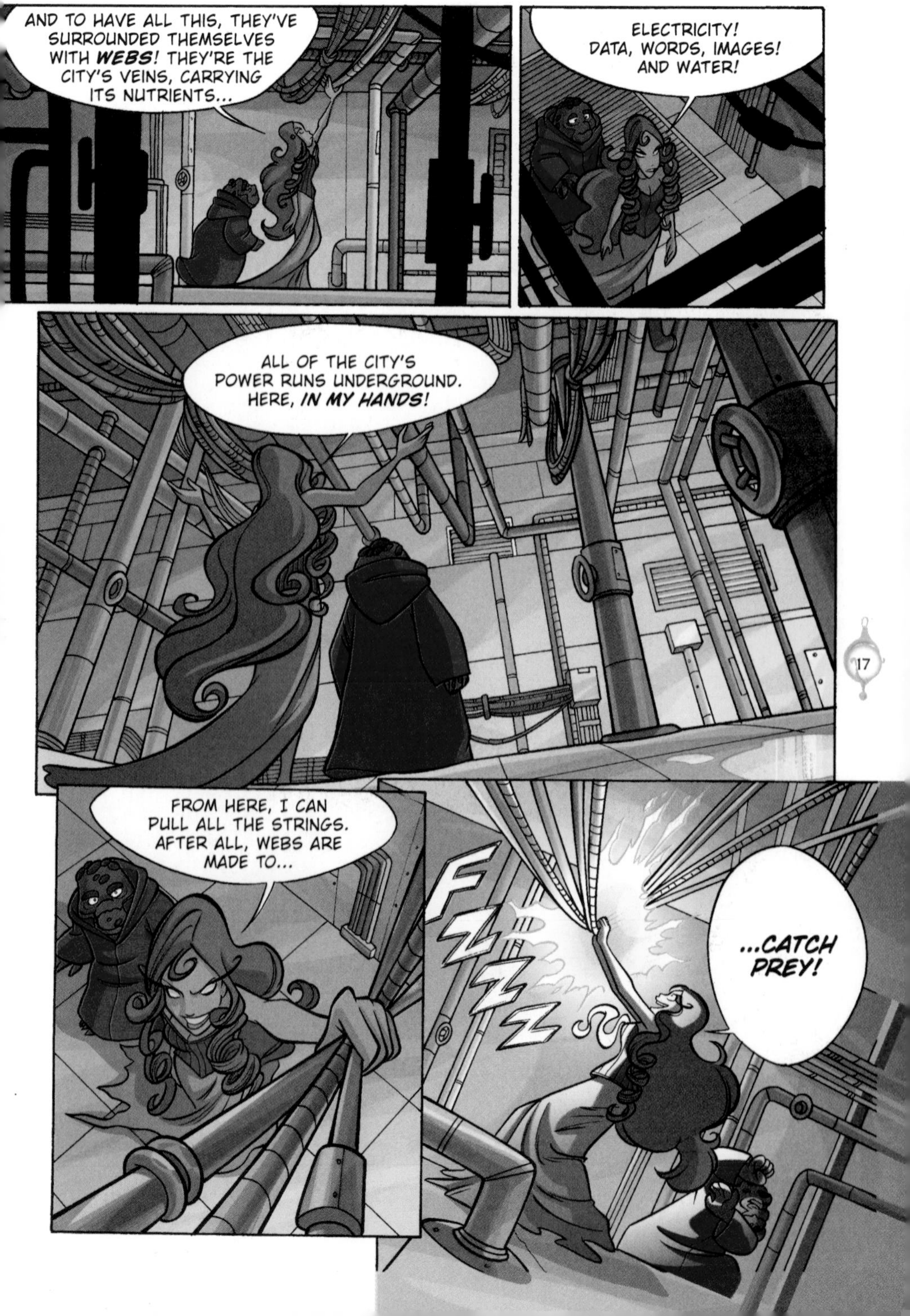
AND TO HAVE ALL THIS, THEY'VE SURROUNDED THEMSELVES WITH ***WEBS***! THEY'RE THE CITY'S VEINS, CARRYING ITS NUTRIENTS...
ELECTRICITY! DATA, WORDS, IMAGES! AND WATER!
ALL OF THE CITY'S POWER RUNS UNDERGROUND. HERE, ***IN MY HANDS***!
FROM HERE, I CAN PULL ALL THE STRINGS. AFTER ALL, WEBS ARE MADE TO...
FZZZZ
...CATCH PREY!

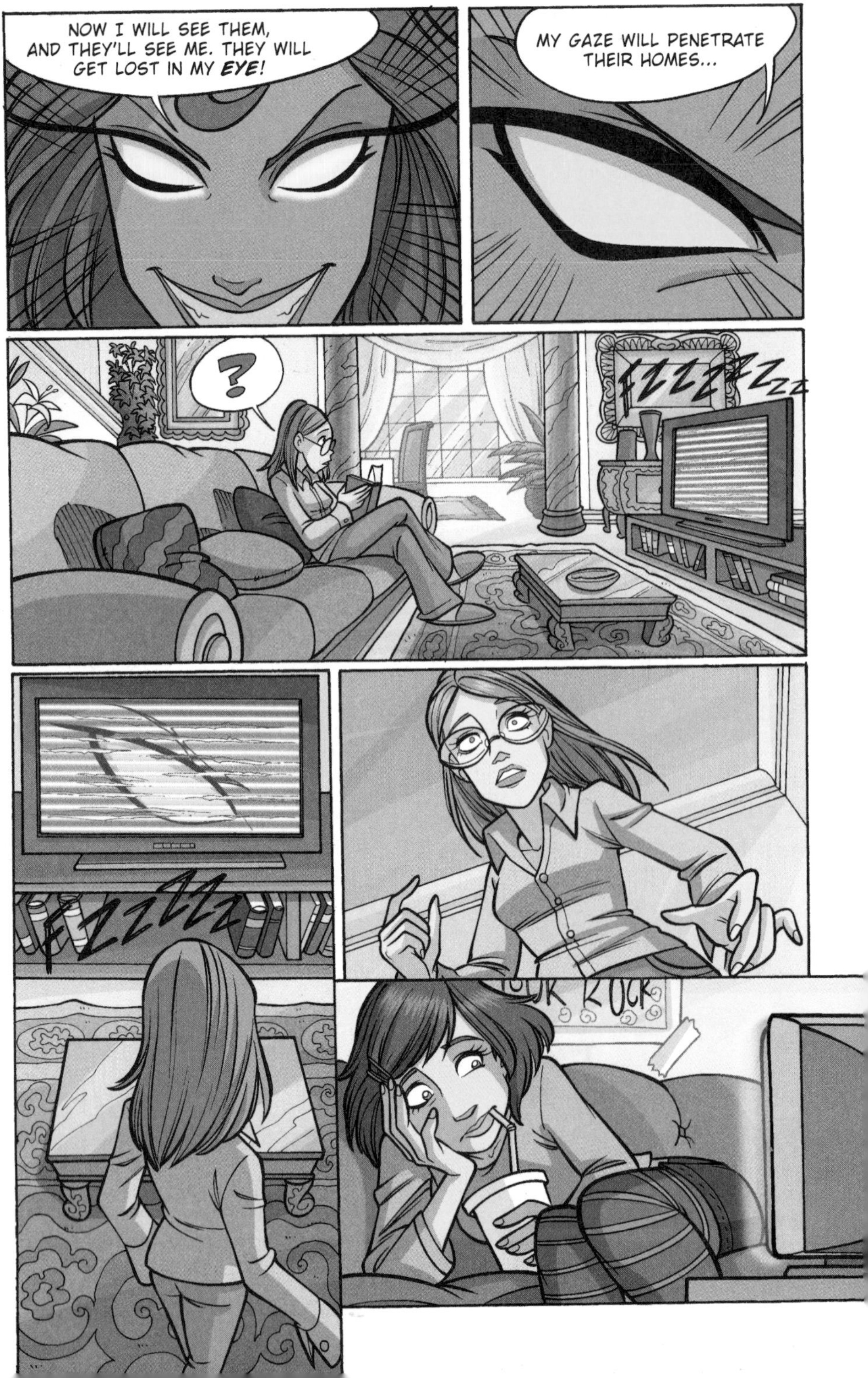
NOW I WILL SEE THEM, AND THEY'LL SEE ME. THEY WILL GET LOST IN MY *EYE*!
MY GAZE WILL PENETRATE THEIR HOMES...
?

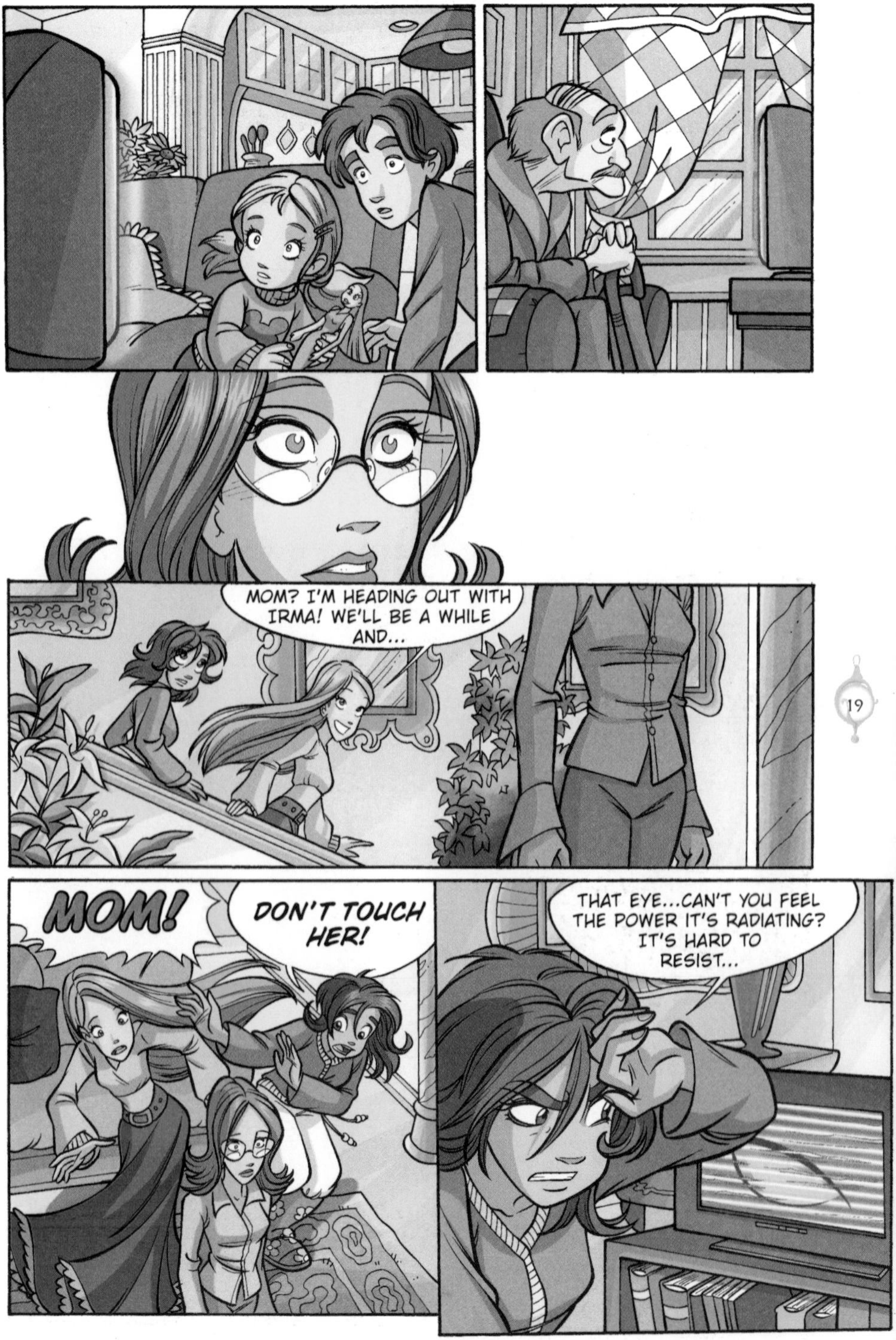
MOM? I'M HEADING OUT WITH IRMA! WE'LL BE A WHILE AND...
MOM!
DON'T TOUCH HER!
THAT EYE...CAN'T YOU FEEL THE POWER IT'S RADIATING? IT'S HARD TO RESIST...

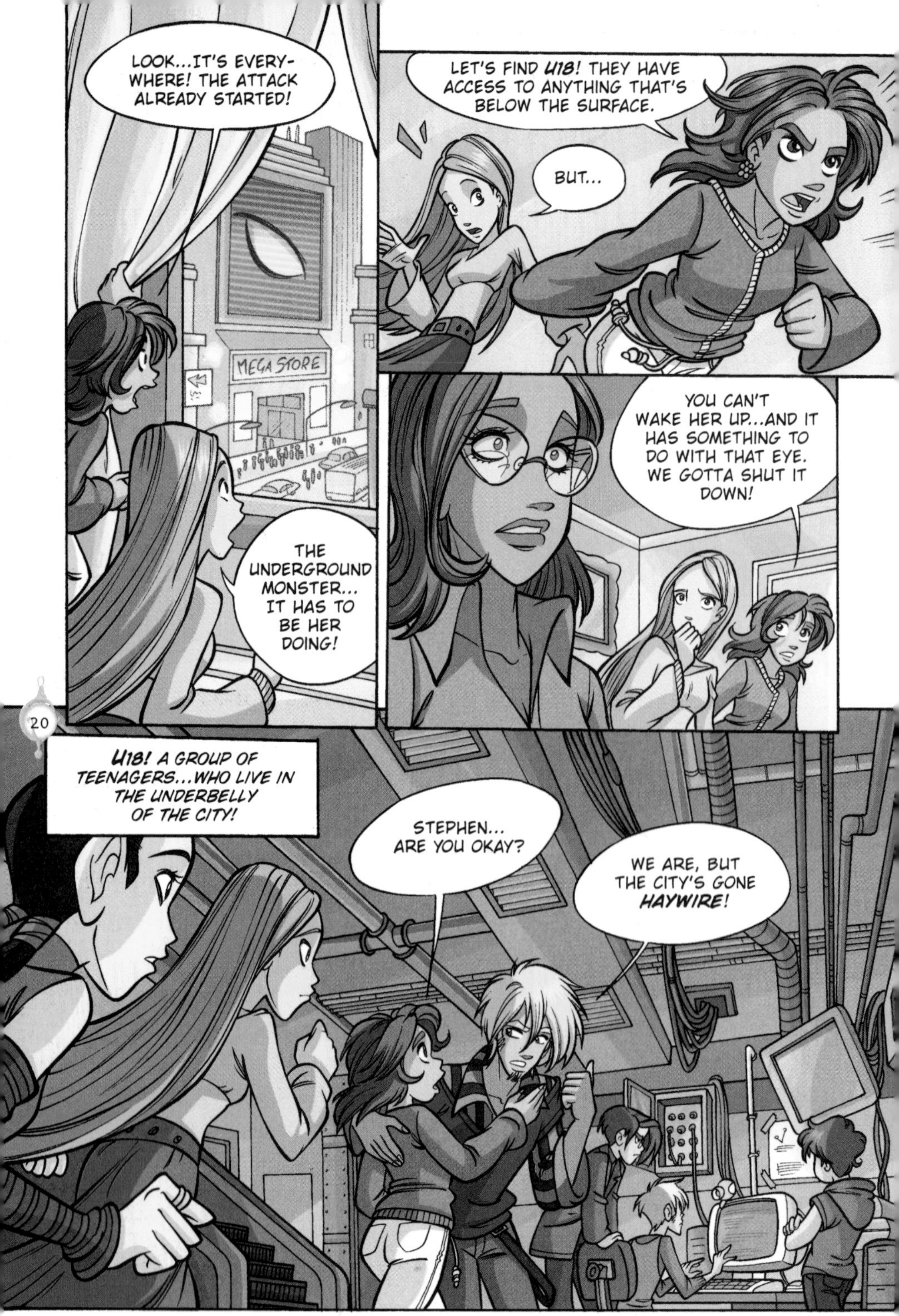
LOOK...IT'S EVERY-WHERE! THE ATTACK ALREADY STARTED!
MEGA STORE
THE UNDERGROUND MONSTER... IT HAS TO BE HER DOING!
LET'S FIND U18! THEY HAVE ACCESS TO ANYTHING THAT'S BELOW THE SURFACE.
BUT...
YOU CAN'T WAKE HER UP...AND IT HAS SOMETHING TO DO WITH THAT EYE. WE GOTTA SHUT IT DOWN!
U18! A GROUP OF TEENAGERS...WHO LIVE IN THE UNDERBELLY OF THE CITY!
STEPHEN... ARE YOU OKAY?
WE ARE, BUT THE CITY'S GONE HAYWIRE!

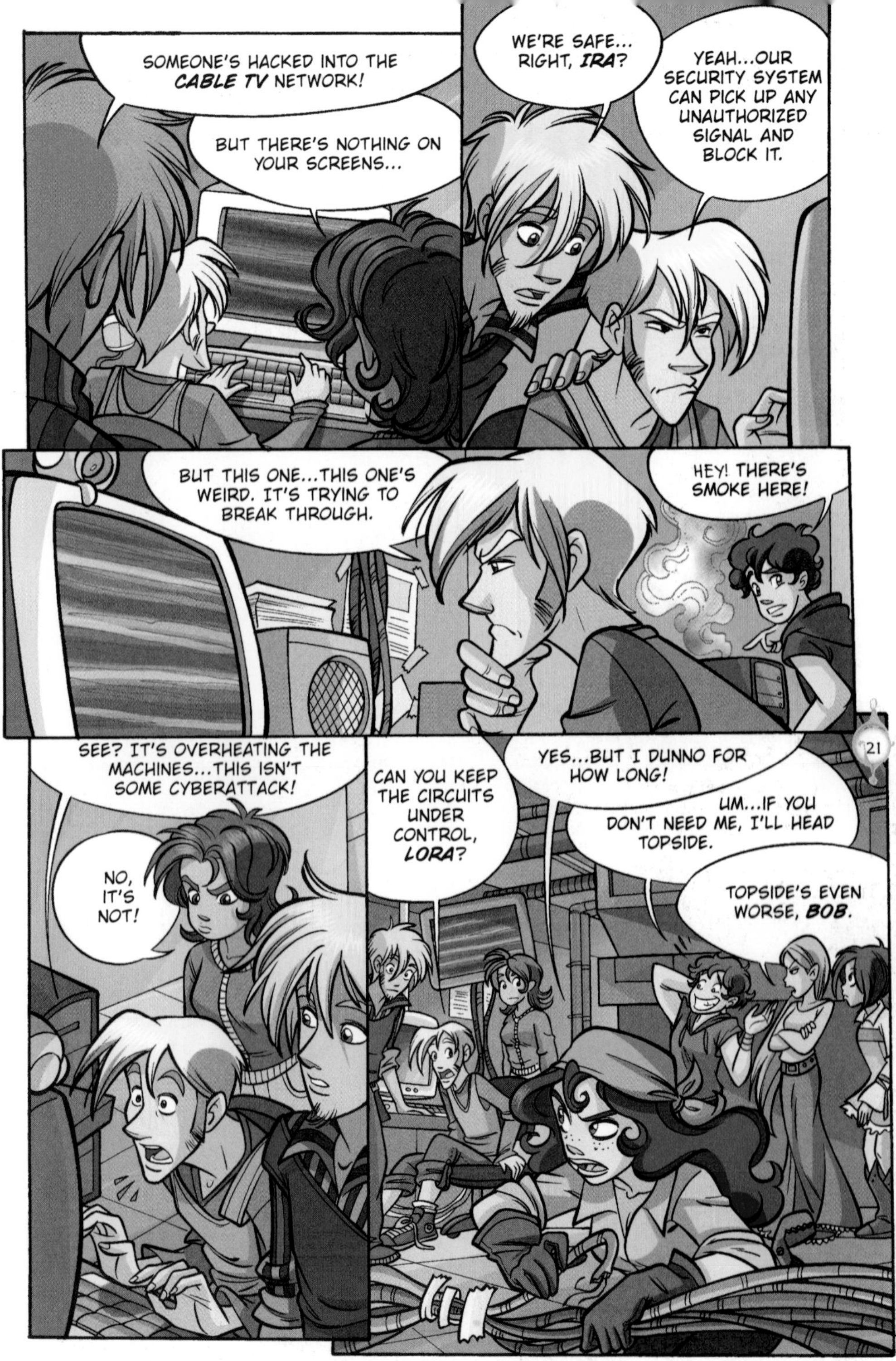
SOMEONE'S HACKED INTO THE CABLE TV NETWORK!
BUT THERE'S NOTHING ON YOUR SCREENS...
WE'RE SAFE... RIGHT, IRA?
YEAH...OUR SECURITY SYSTEM CAN PICK UP ANY UNAUTHORIZED SIGNAL AND BLOCK IT.
BUT THIS ONE...THIS ONE'S WEIRD. IT'S TRYING TO BREAK THROUGH.
HEY! THERE'S SMOKE HERE!
SEE? IT'S OVERHEATING THE MACHINES...THIS ISN'T SOME CYBERATTACK!
NO, IT'S NOT!
CAN YOU KEEP THE CIRCUITS UNDER CONTROL, LORA?
YES...BUT I DUNNO FOR HOW LONG!
UM...IF YOU DON'T NEED ME, I'LL HEAD TOPSIDE.
TOPSIDE'S EVEN WORSE, BOB.

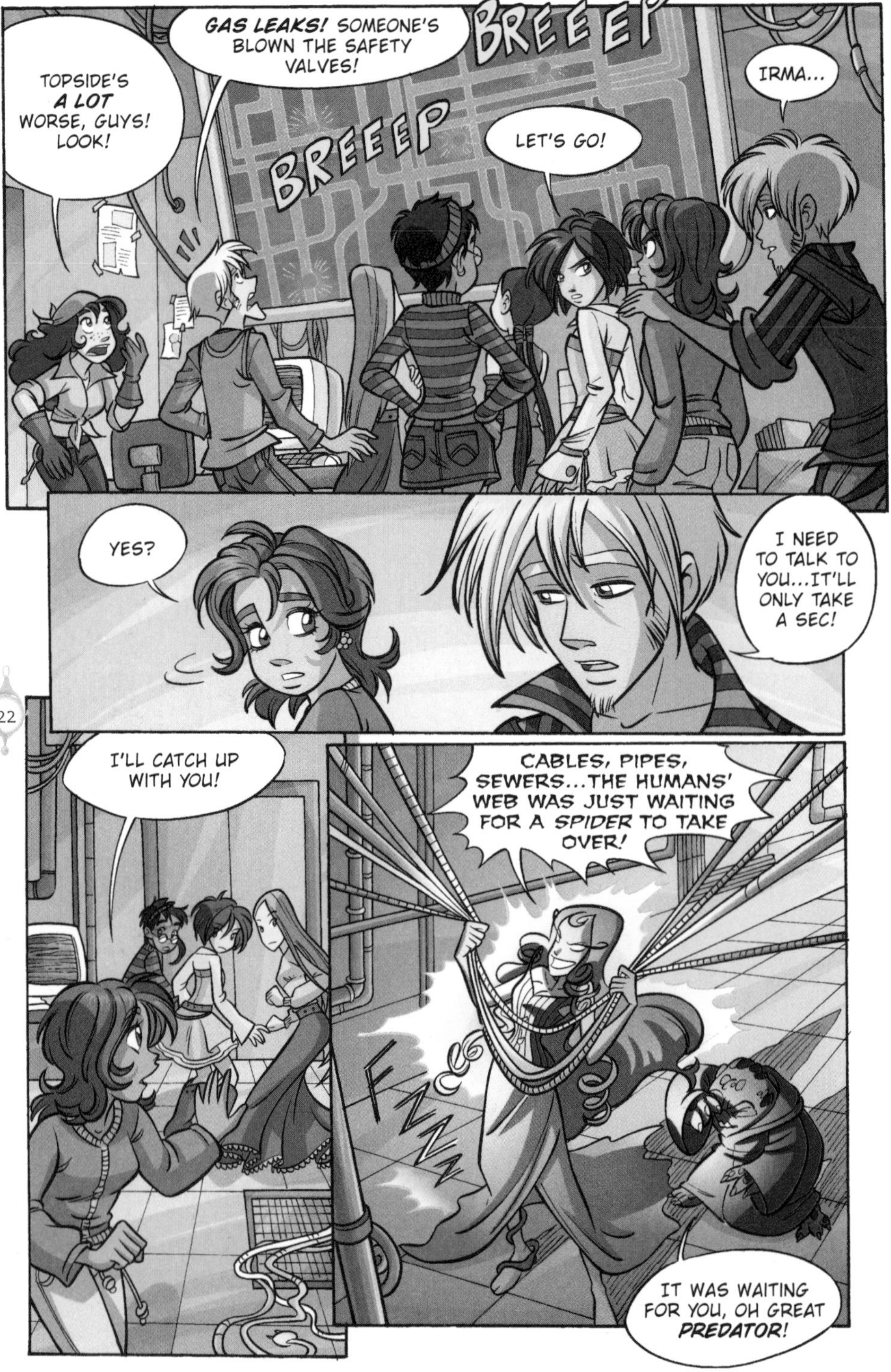
TOPSIDE'S **A LOT** WORSE, GUYS! LOOK!
GAS LEAKS! SOMEONE'S BLOWN THE SAFETY VALVES!
BREEEP
BREEEP
LET'S GO!
IRMA...
YES?
I NEED TO TALK TO YOU...IT'LL ONLY TAKE A SEC!
I'LL CATCH UP WITH YOU!
CABLES, PIPES, SEWERS...THE HUMANS' WEB WAS JUST WAITING FOR A *SPIDER* TO TAKE OVER!
FZZZ
IT WAS WAITING FOR YOU, OH GREAT **PREDATOR**!

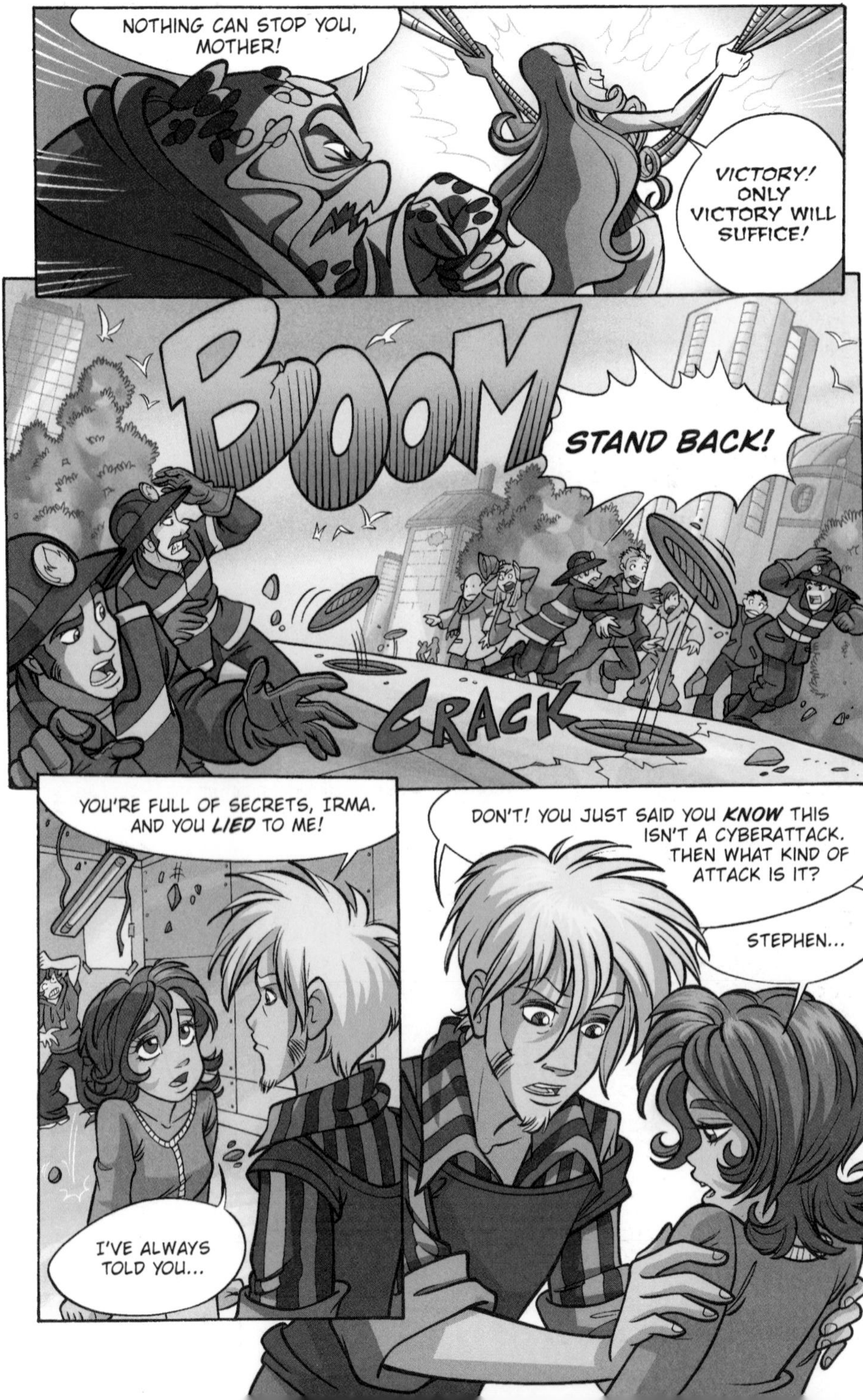
NOTHING CAN STOP YOU, MOTHER!
VICTORY! ONLY VICTORY WILL SUFFICE!
BOOM
STAND BACK!
CRACK
YOU'RE FULL OF SECRETS, IRMA. AND YOU LIED TO ME!
I'VE ALWAYS TOLD YOU...
DON'T! YOU JUST SAID YOU KNOW THIS ISN'T A CYBERATTACK. THEN WHAT KIND OF ATTACK IS IT?
STEPHEN...

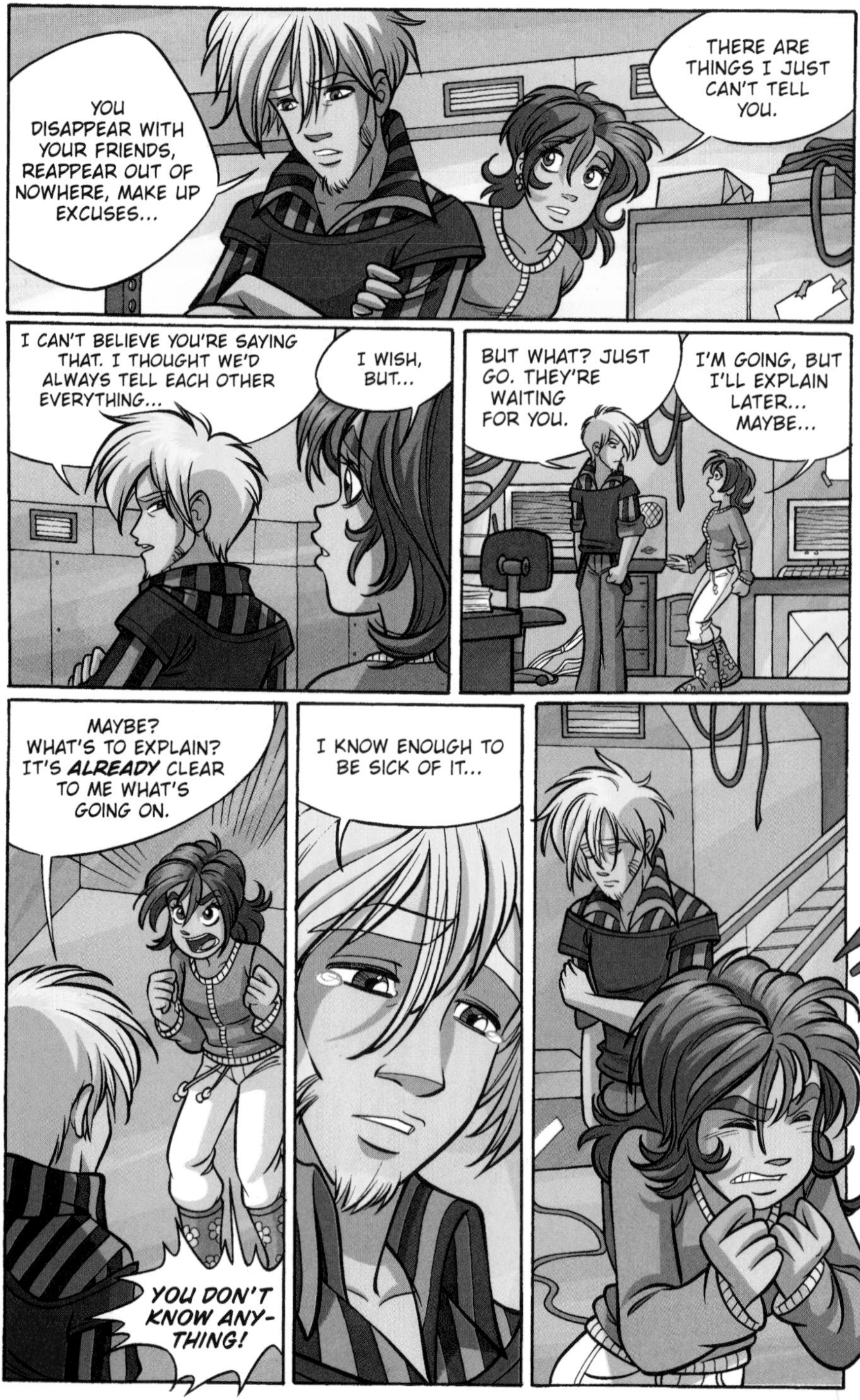

YOU DISAPPEAR WITH YOUR FRIENDS, REAPPEAR OUT OF NOWHERE, MAKE UP EXCUSES...
THERE ARE THINGS I JUST CAN'T TELL YOU.
I CAN'T BELIEVE YOU'RE SAYING THAT. I THOUGHT WE'D ALWAYS TELL EACH OTHER EVERYTHING...
I WISH, BUT...
BUT WHAT? JUST GO. THEY'RE WAITING FOR YOU.
I'M GOING, BUT I'LL EXPLAIN LATER... MAYBE...
MAYBE? WHAT'S TO EXPLAIN? IT'S ***ALREADY*** CLEAR TO ME WHAT'S GOING ON.
YOU DON'T KNOW ANY-THING!
I KNOW ENOUGH TO BE SICK OF IT...

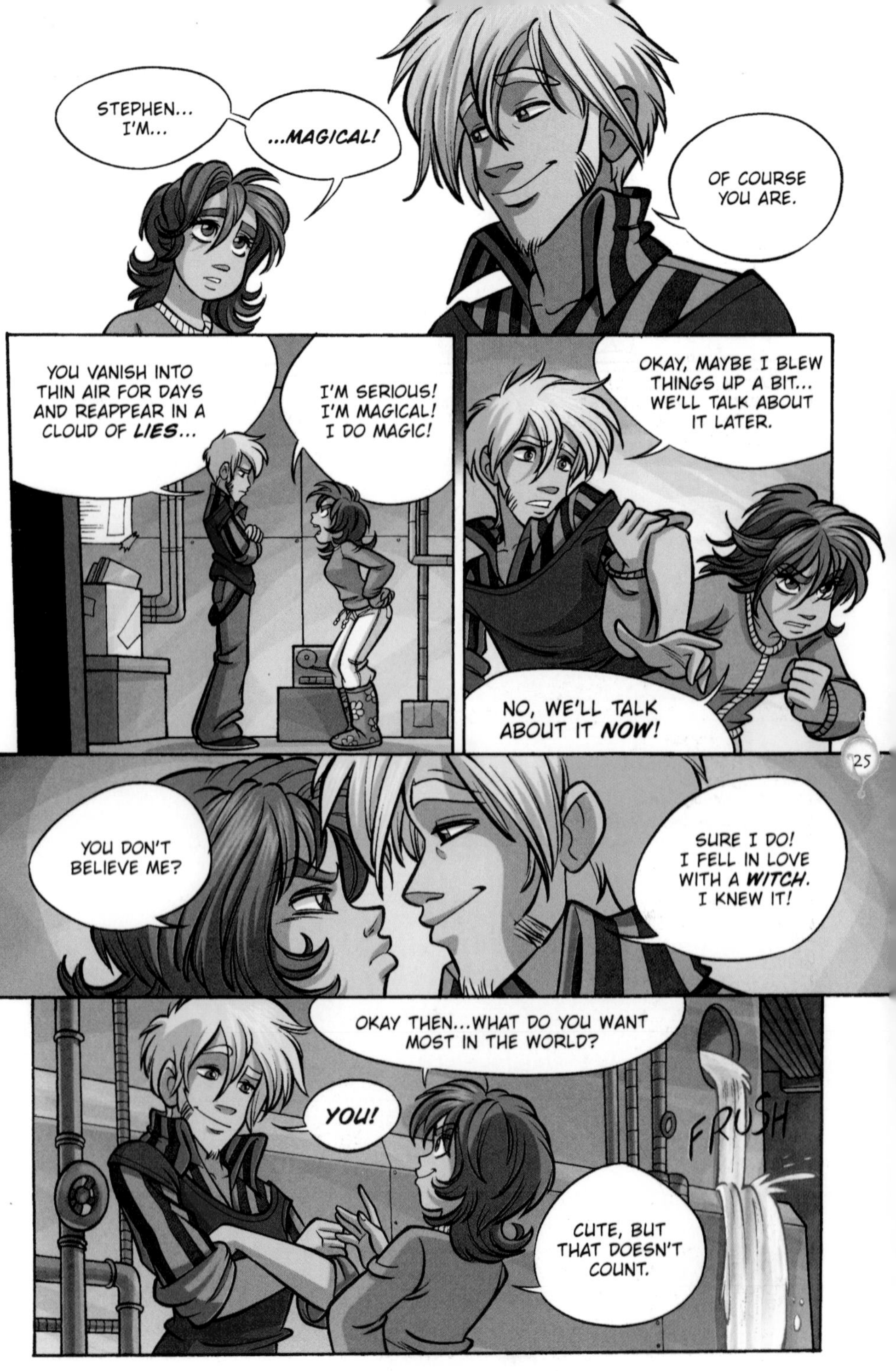
STEPHEN... I'M...
...MAGICAL!
OF COURSE YOU ARE.
YOU VANISH INTO THIN AIR FOR DAYS AND REAPPEAR IN A CLOUD OF LIES...
I'M SERIOUS! I'M MAGICAL! I DO MAGIC!
OKAY, MAYBE I BLEW THINGS UP A BIT... WE'LL TALK ABOUT IT LATER.
NO, WE'LL TALK ABOUT IT NOW!
YOU DON'T BELIEVE ME?
SURE I DO! I FELL IN LOVE WITH A WITCH. I KNEW IT!
OKAY THEN...WHAT DO YOU WANT MOST IN THE WORLD?
YOU!
FRUSH
CUTE, BUT THAT DOESN'T COUNT.

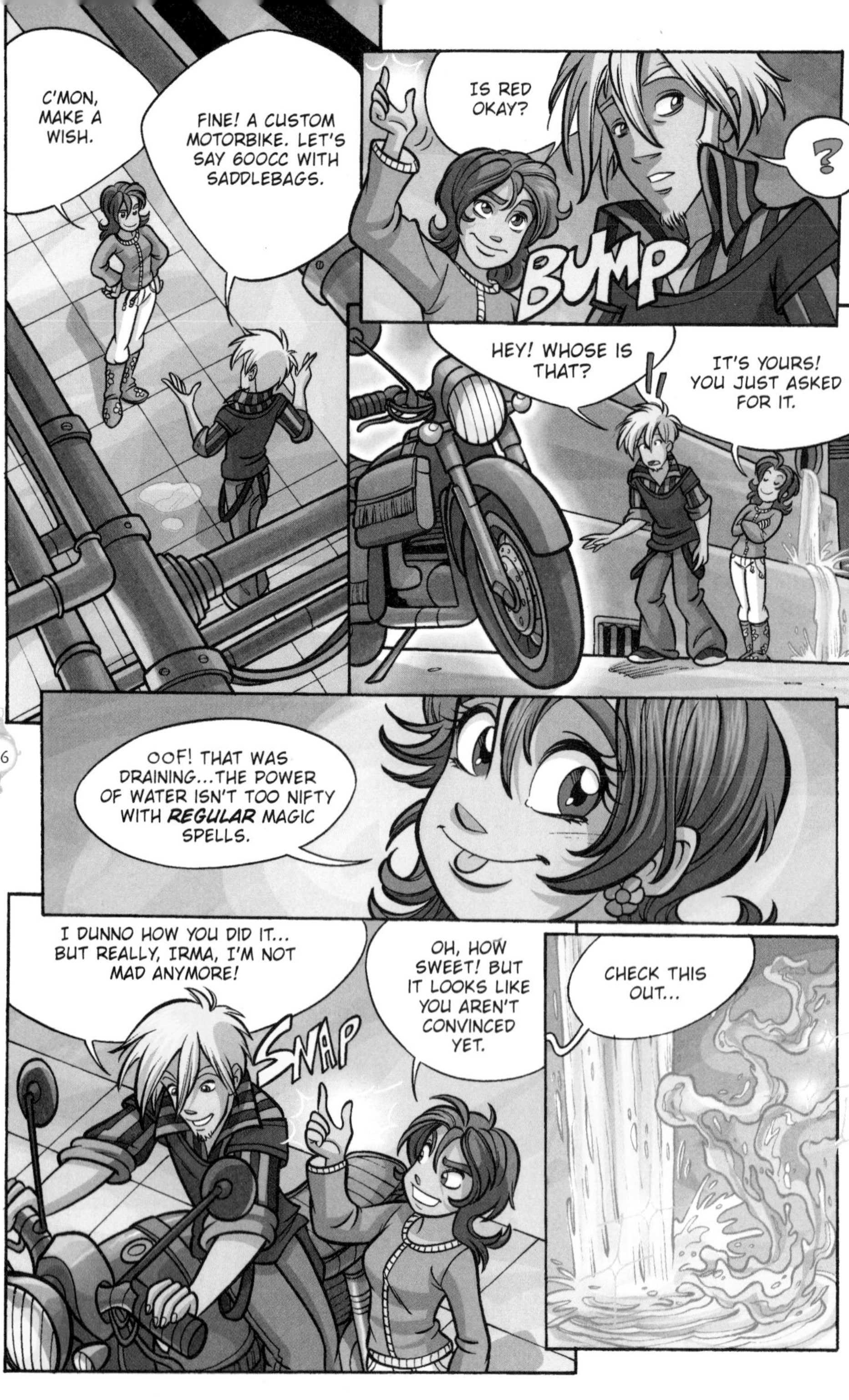
C'MON, MAKE A WISH.
FINE! A CUSTOM MOTORBIKE. LET'S SAY 600CC WITH SADDLEBAGS.
IS RED OKAY?
?
BUMP
HEY! WHOSE IS THAT?
IT'S YOURS! YOU JUST ASKED FOR IT.
OOF! THAT WAS DRAINING...THE POWER OF WATER ISN'T TOO NIFTY WITH REGULAR MAGIC SPELLS.
I DUNNO HOW YOU DID IT... BUT REALLY, IRMA, I'M NOT MAD ANYMORE!
SNAP
OH, HOW SWEET! BUT IT LOOKS LIKE YOU AREN'T CONVINCED YET.
CHECK THIS OUT...

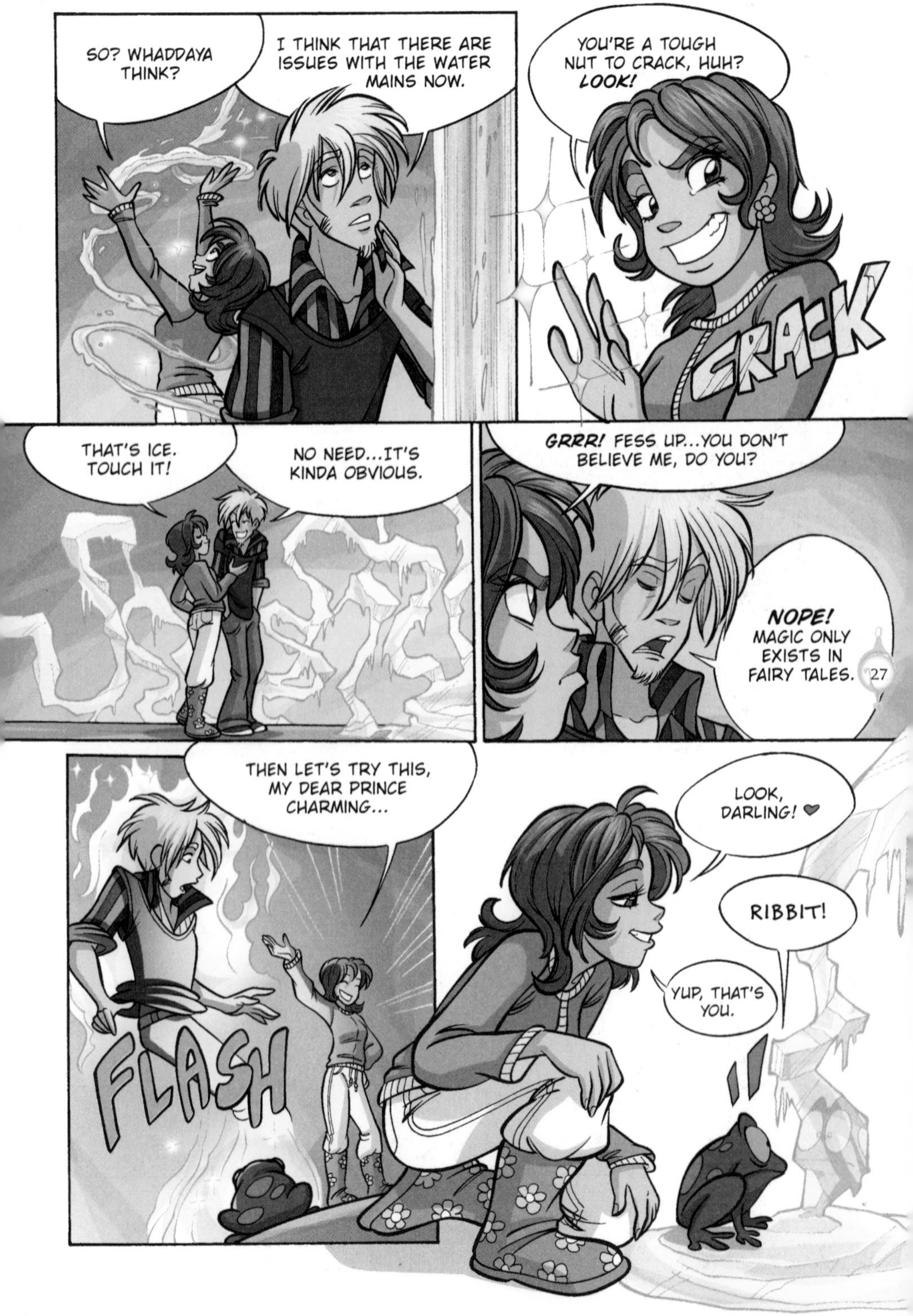
SO? WHADDAYA THINK?
I THINK THAT THERE ARE ISSUES WITH THE WATER MAINS NOW.
YOU'RE A TOUGH NUT TO CRACK, HUH? LOOK!
CRACK
THAT'S ICE. TOUCH IT!
NO NEED...IT'S KINDA OBVIOUS.
GRRR! FESS UP...YOU DON'T BELIEVE ME, DO YOU?
NOPE! MAGIC ONLY EXISTS IN FAIRY TALES.
THEN LET'S TRY THIS, MY DEAR PRINCE CHARMING...
FLASH
LOOK, DARLING! ♥
RIBBIT!
YUP, THAT'S YOU.

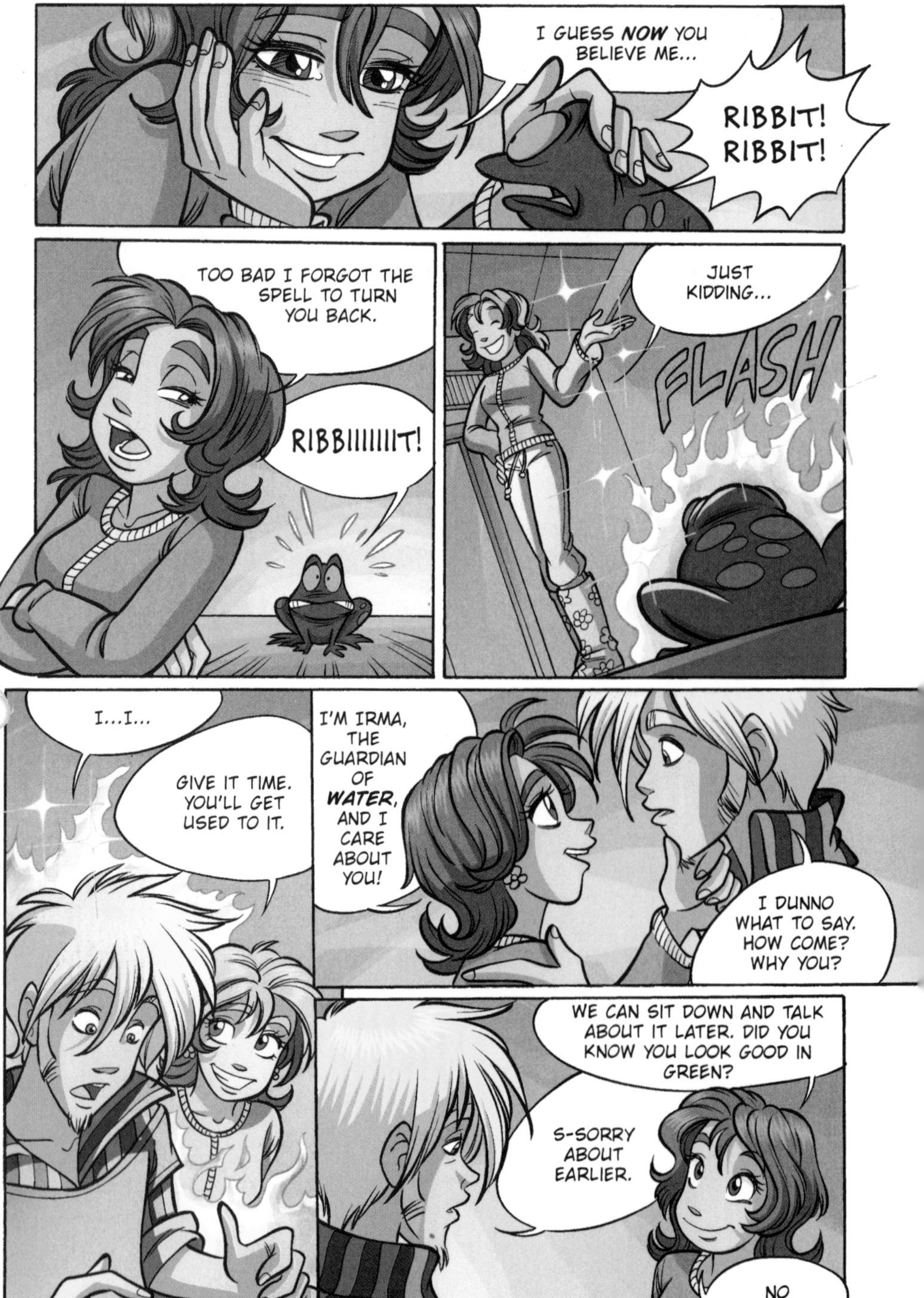
I GUESS *NOW* YOU BELIEVE ME...
RIBBIT! RIBBIT!
TOO BAD I FORGOT THE SPELL TO TURN YOU BACK.
RIBBIIIIIIIT!
JUST KIDDING...
FLASH
I...I...
GIVE IT TIME. YOU'LL GET USED TO IT.
I'M IRMA, THE GUARDIAN OF *WATER*, AND I CARE ABOUT YOU!
I DUNNO WHAT TO SAY. HOW COME? WHY YOU?
WE CAN SIT DOWN AND TALK ABOUT IT LATER. DID YOU KNOW YOU LOOK GOOD IN GREEN?
S-SORRY ABOUT EARLIER.
NO WORRIES!

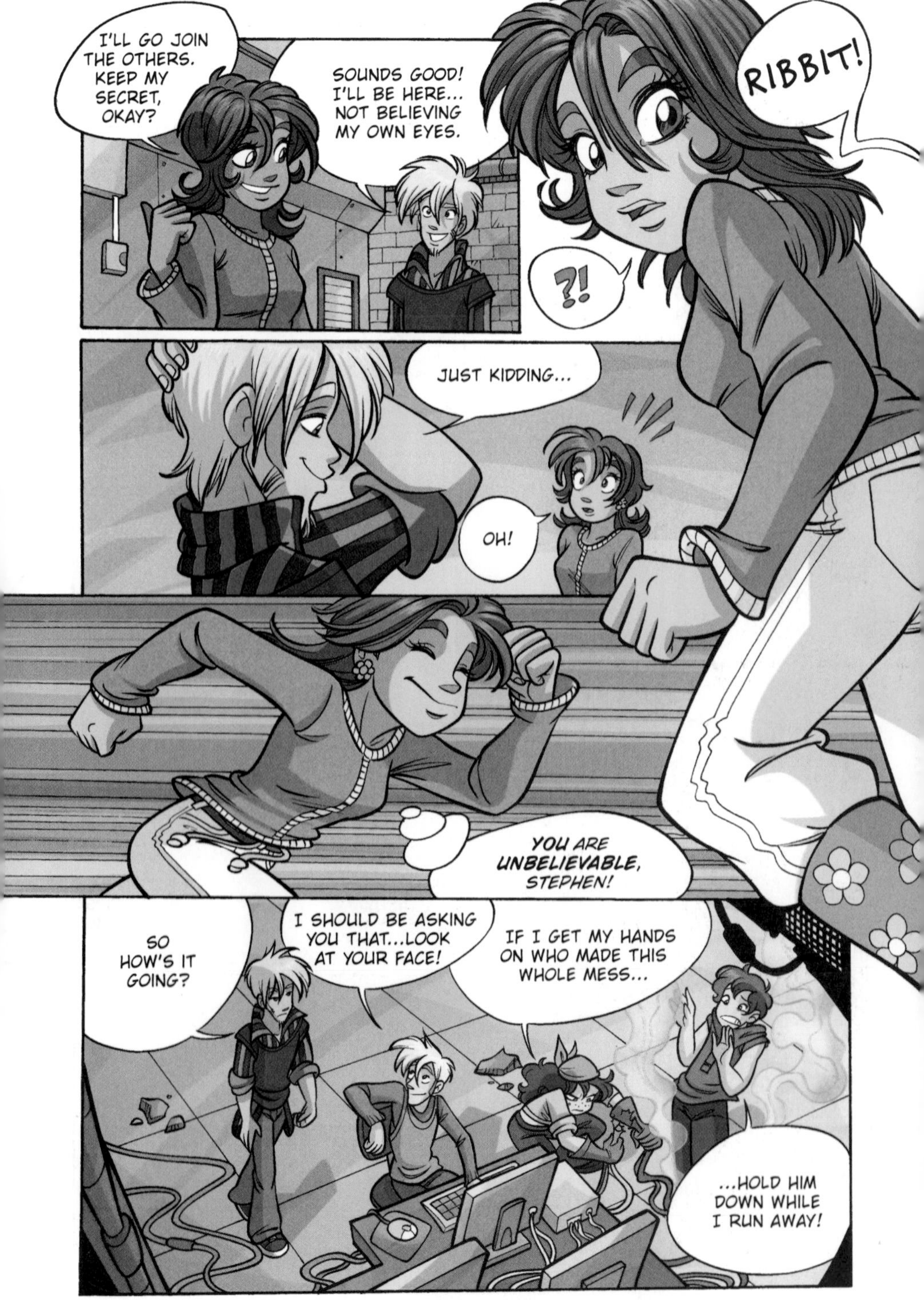
I'LL GO JOIN THE OTHERS. KEEP MY SECRET, OKAY?
SOUNDS GOOD! I'LL BE HERE... NOT BELIEVING MY OWN EYES.
RIBBIT!
?!
JUST KIDDING...
OH!
YOU ARE UNBELIEVABLE, STEPHEN!
SO HOW'S IT GOING?
I SHOULD BE ASKING YOU THAT...LOOK AT YOUR FACE!
IF I GET MY HANDS ON WHO MADE THIS WHOLE MESS...
...HOLD HIM DOWN WHILE I RUN AWAY!

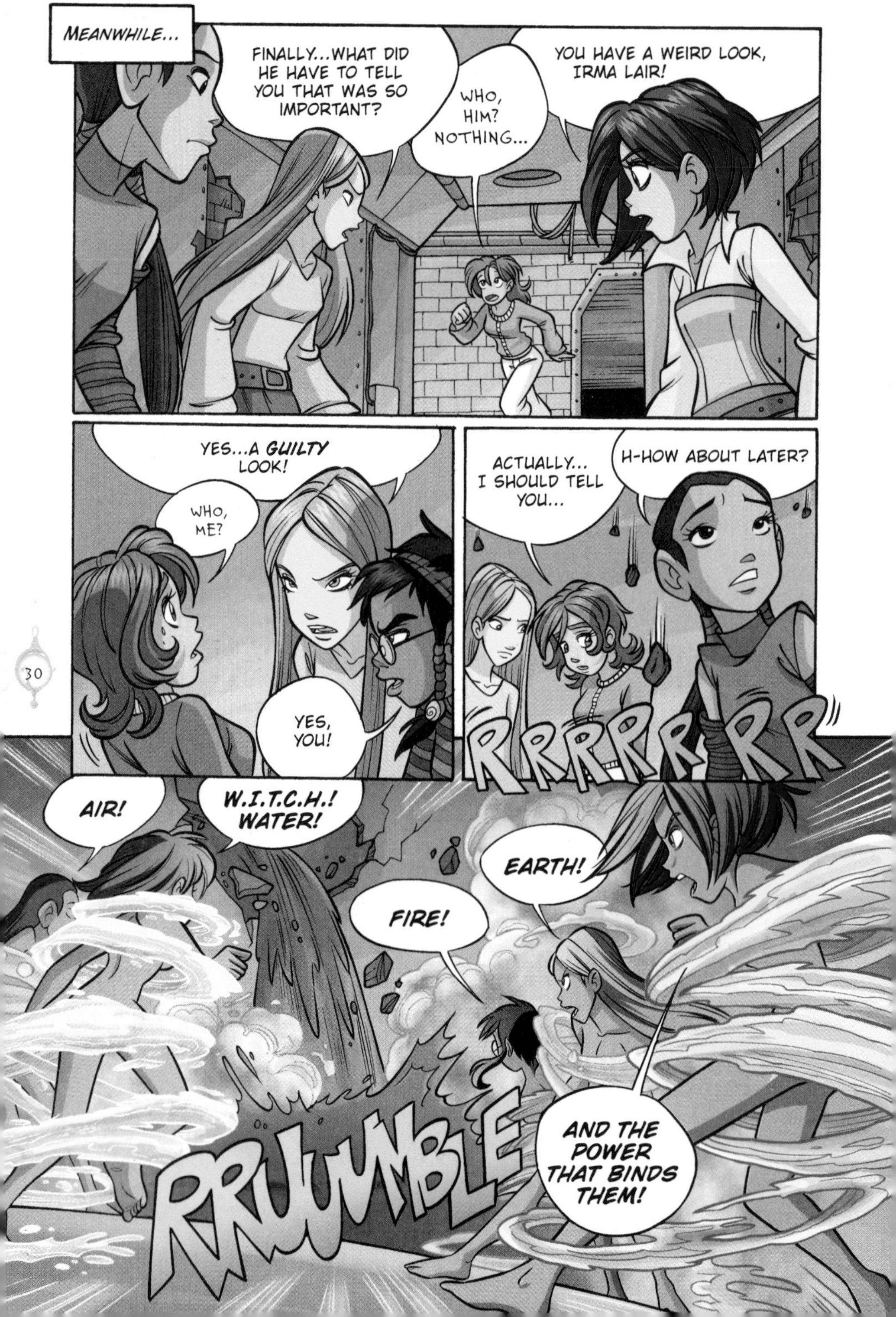
MEANWHILE...
FINALLY...WHAT DID HE HAVE TO TELL YOU THAT WAS SO IMPORTANT?
WHO, HIM? NOTHING...
YOU HAVE A WEIRD LOOK, IRMA LAIR!
YES...A GUILTY LOOK!
WHO, ME?
YES, YOU!
ACTUALLY... I SHOULD TELL YOU...
H-HOW ABOUT LATER?
RRRRRRRR
AIR!
W.I.T.C.H.! WATER!
EARTH!
FIRE!
RRUUMBLE
AND THE POWER THAT BINDS THEM!

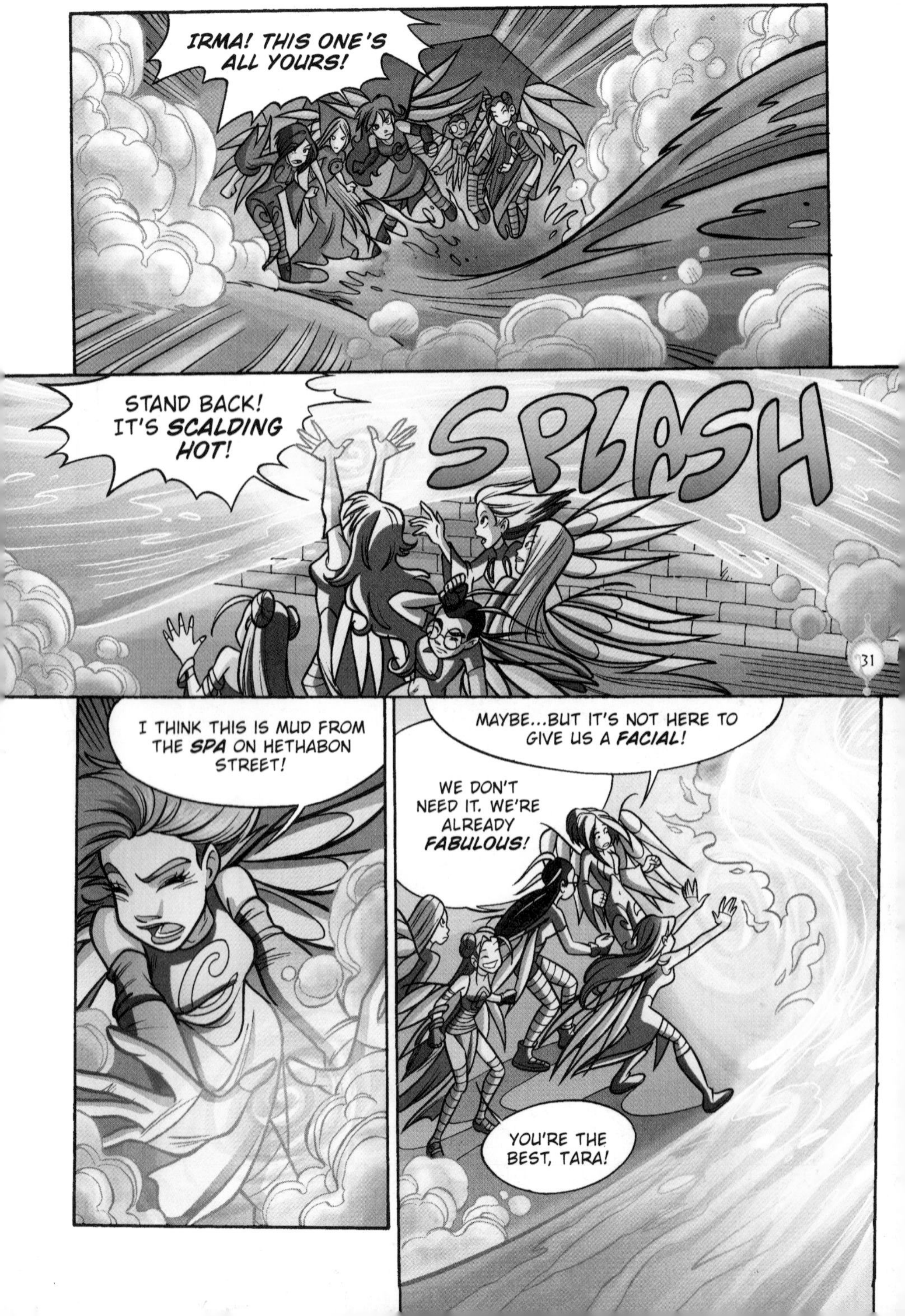
IRMA! THIS ONE'S ALL YOURS!
STAND BACK! IT'S SCALDING HOT!
SPLASH
I THINK THIS IS MUD FROM THE SPA ON HETHABON STREET!
MAYBE...BUT IT'S NOT HERE TO GIVE US A FACIAL!
WE DON'T NEED IT. WE'RE ALREADY FABULOUS!
YOU'RE THE BEST, TARA!

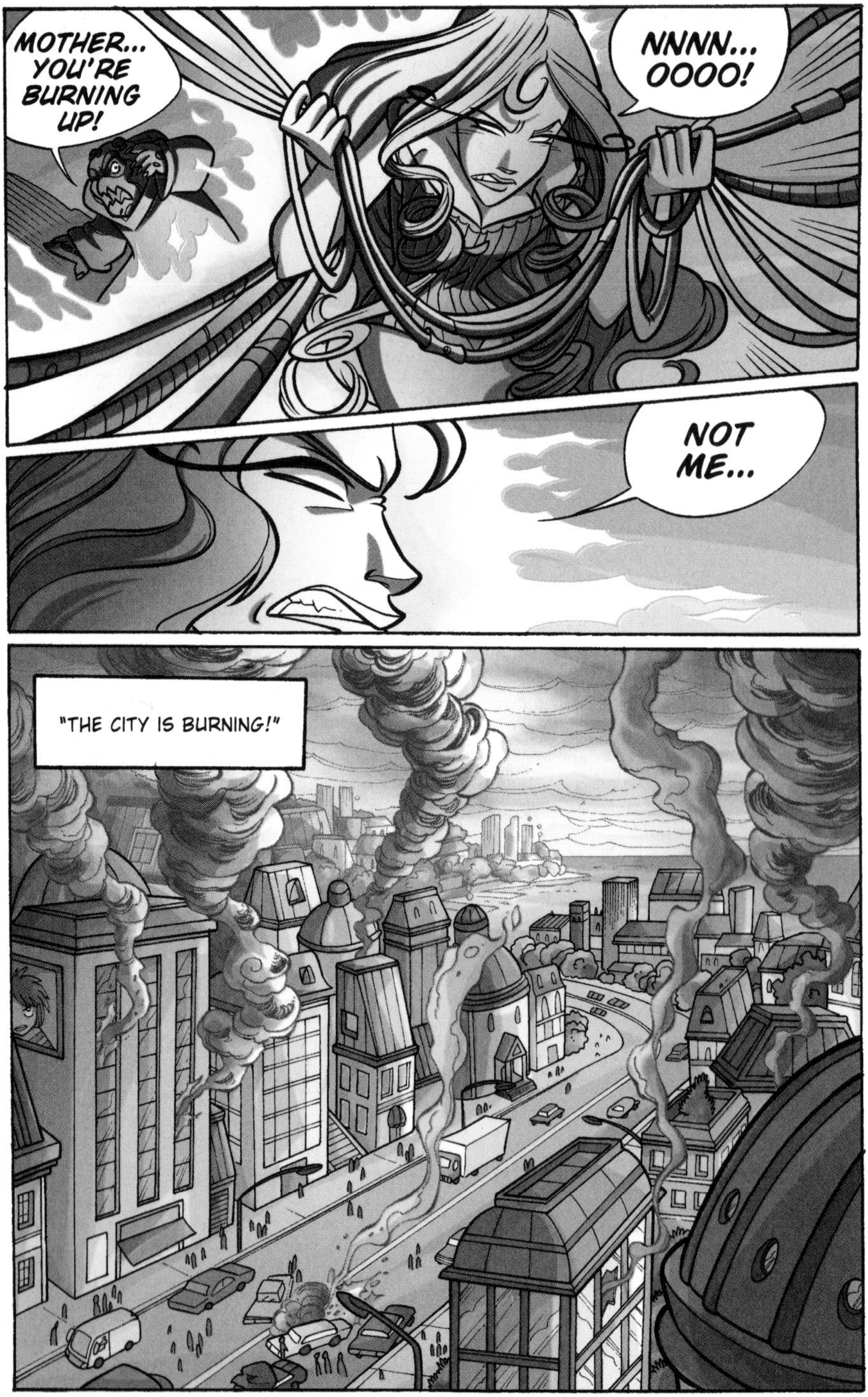
MOTHER... YOU'RE BURNING UP!
NNNN... OOOO!
NOT ME...
"THE CITY IS BURNING!"

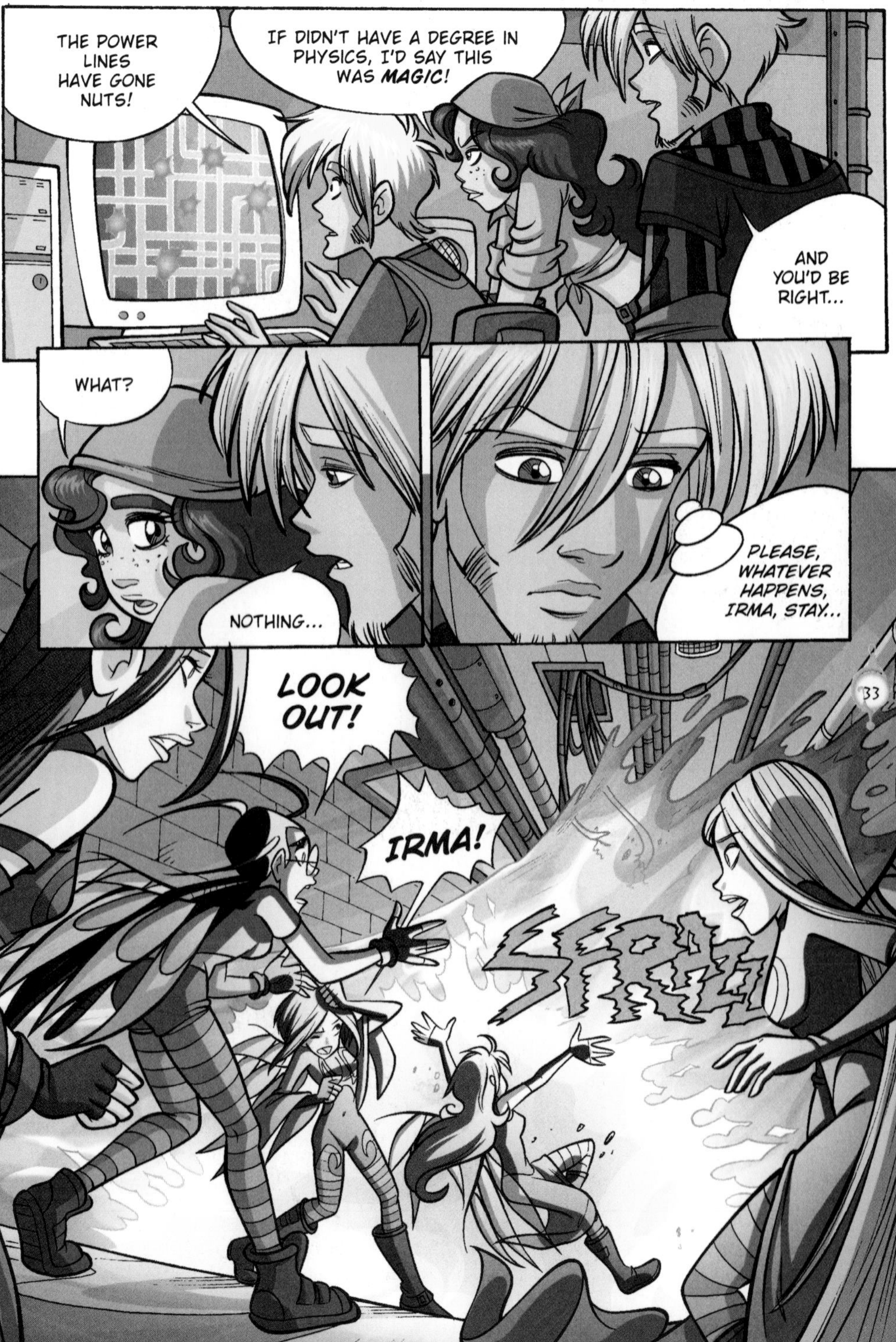
THE POWER LINES HAVE GONE NUTS!
IF DIDN'T HAVE A DEGREE IN PHYSICS, I'D SAY THIS WAS *MAGIC*!
AND YOU'D BE RIGHT...
WHAT?
NOTHING...
PLEASE, WHATEVER HAPPENS, IRMA, STAY...
LOOK OUT!
IRMA!

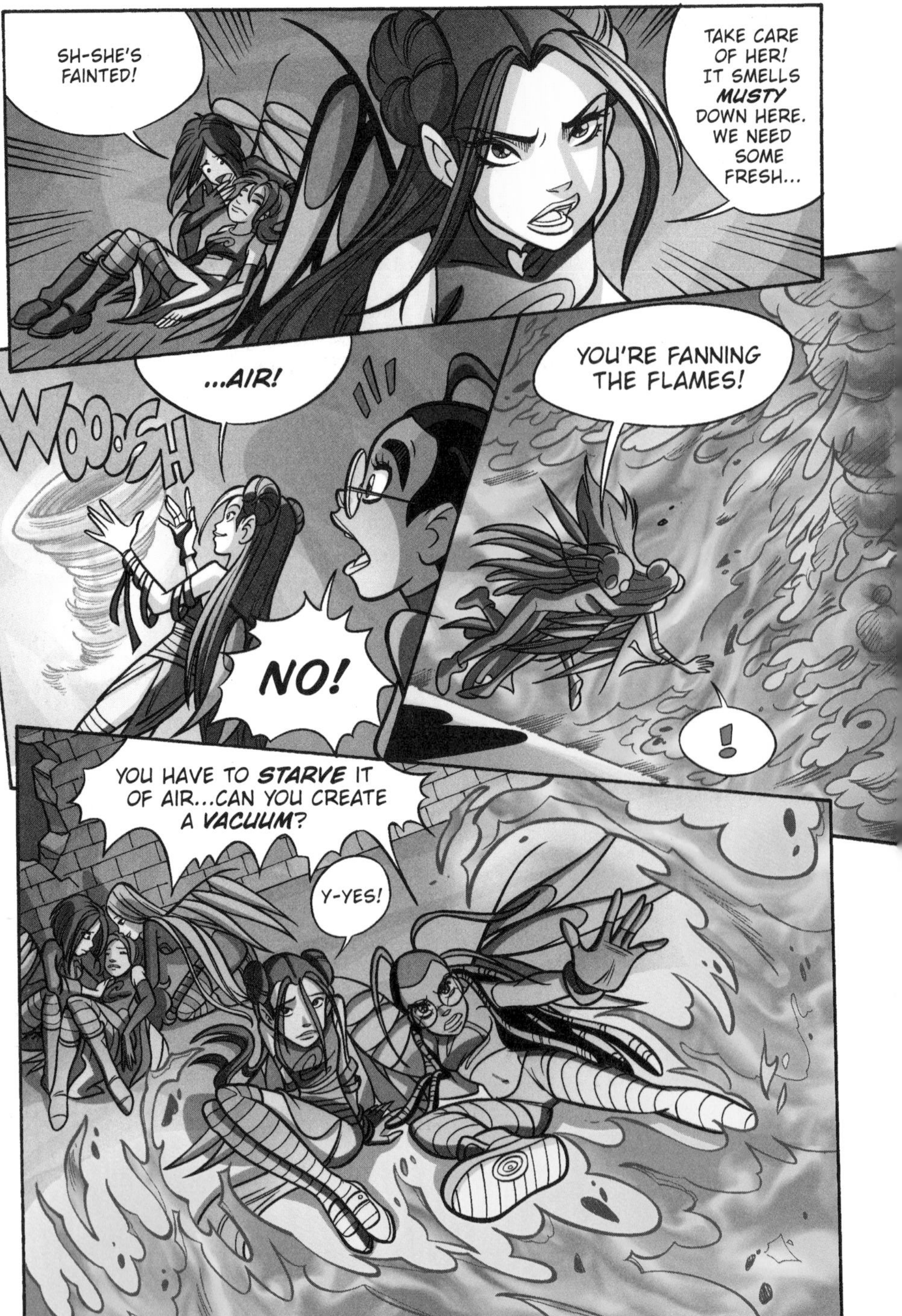
SH-SHE'S FAINTED!
TAKE CARE OF HER! IT SMELLS MUSTY DOWN HERE. WE NEED SOME FRESH...
...AIR!
WOOOSH
NO!
YOU'RE FANNING THE FLAMES!
!
YOU HAVE TO STARVE IT OF AIR...CAN YOU CREATE A VACUUM?
Y-YES!

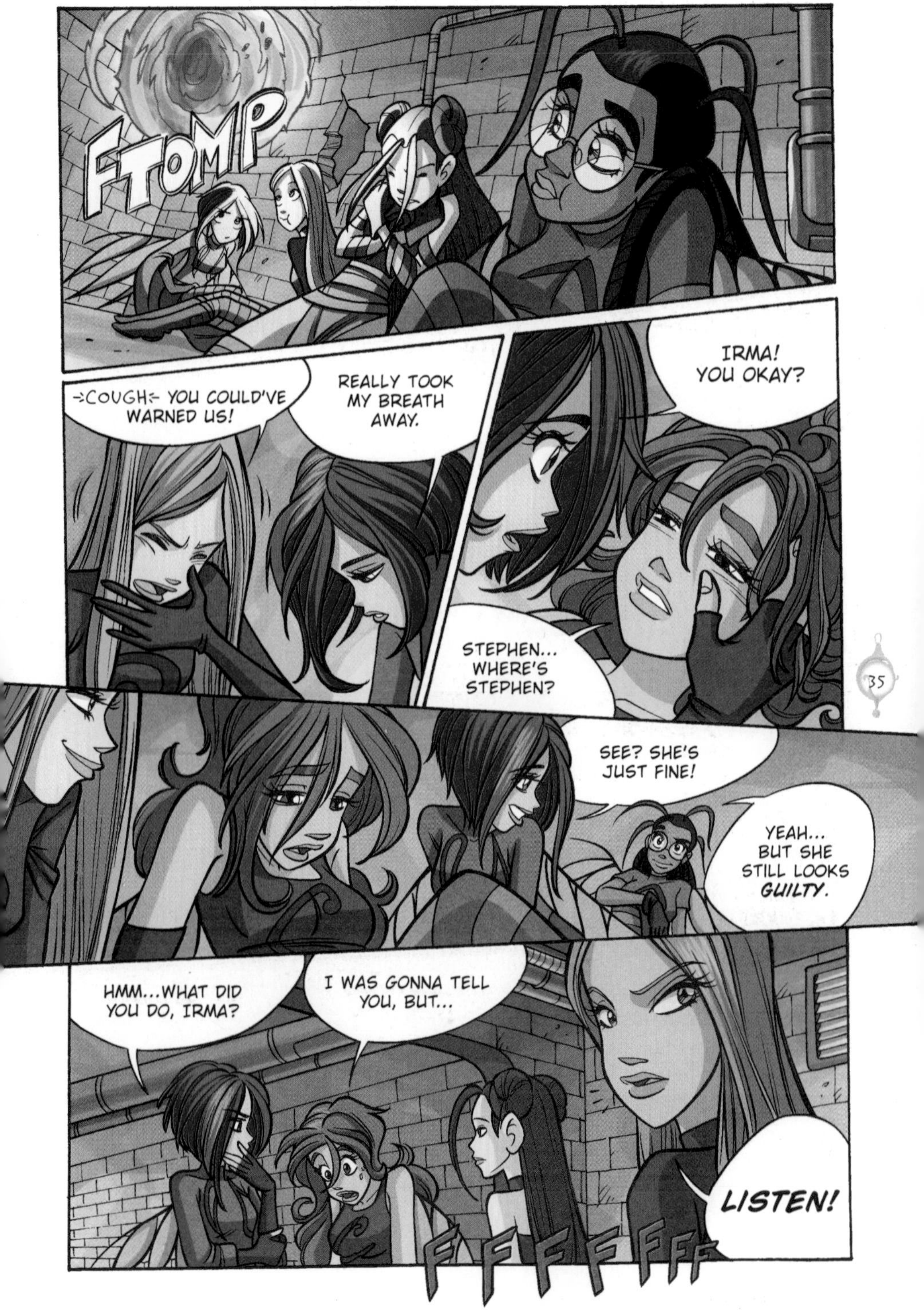
FTOMP
⇒COUGH⇐ YOU COULD'VE WARNED US!
REALLY TOOK MY BREATH AWAY.
IRMA! YOU OKAY?
STEPHEN... WHERE'S STEPHEN?
SEE? SHE'S JUST FINE!
YEAH... BUT SHE STILL LOOKS *GUILTY*.
HMM...WHAT DID YOU DO, IRMA?
I WAS GONNA TELL YOU, BUT...
LISTEN!
FFFFFFFF

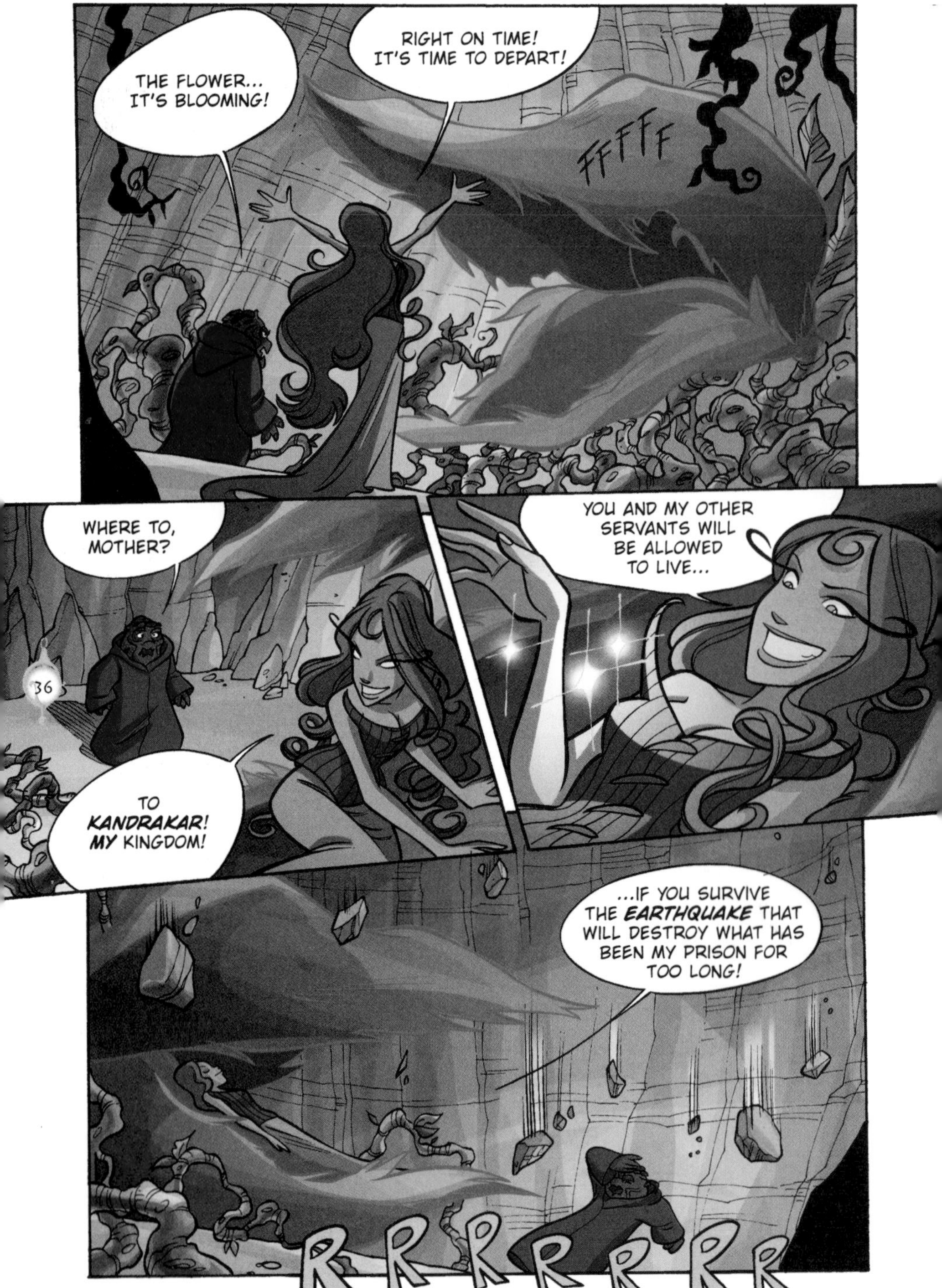
THE FLOWER... IT'S BLOOMING!
RIGHT ON TIME! IT'S TIME TO DEPART!
FFFFF
WHERE TO, MOTHER?
TO KANDRAKAR! MY KINGDOM!
YOU AND MY OTHER SERVANTS WILL BE ALLOWED TO LIVE...
...IF YOU SURVIVE THE EARTHQUAKE THAT WILL DESTROY WHAT HAS BEEN MY PRISON FOR TOO LONG!
RRRRRRRR

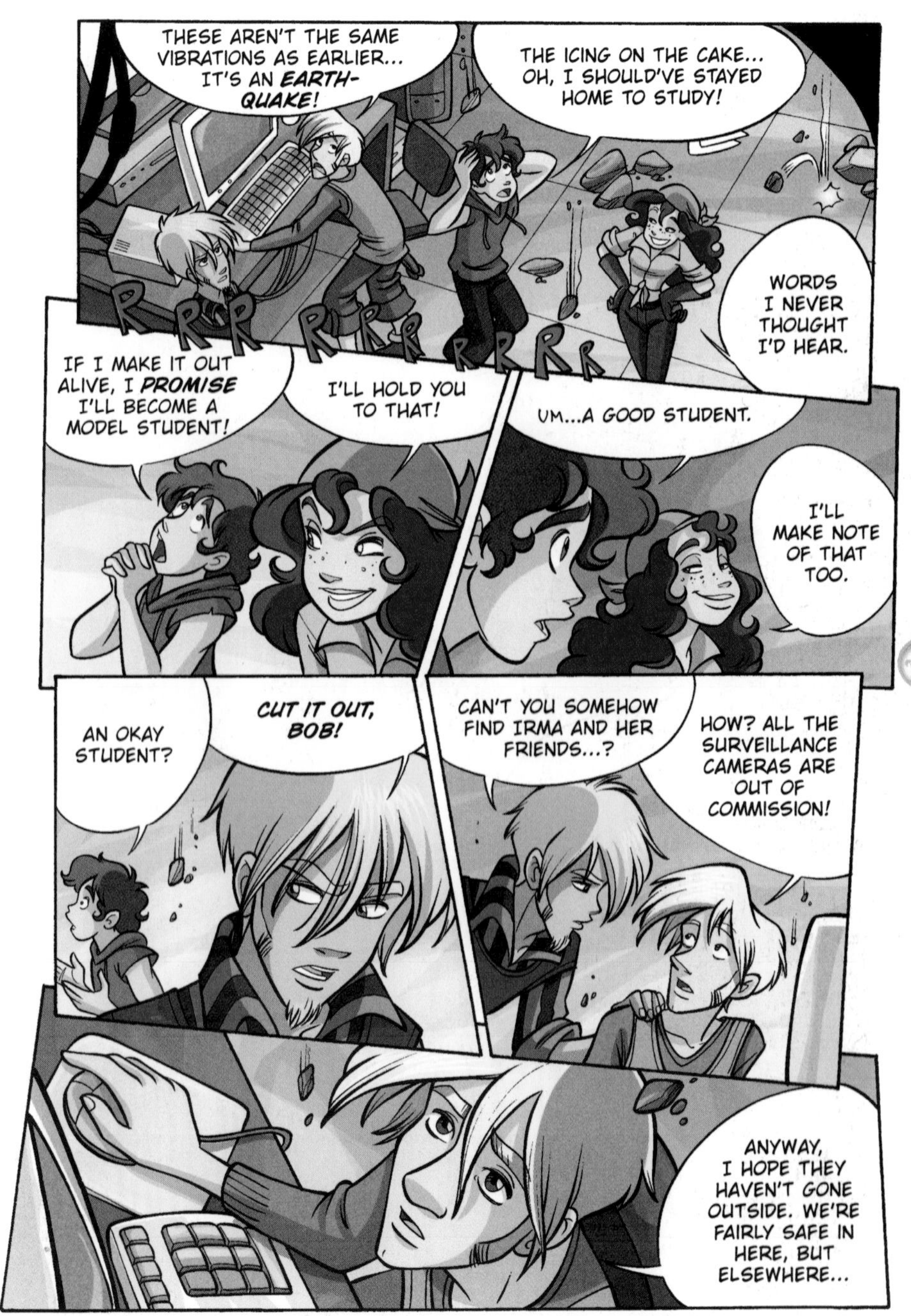
THESE AREN'T THE SAME VIBRATIONS AS EARLIER... IT'S AN EARTH-QUAKE!
THE ICING ON THE CAKE... OH, I SHOULD'VE STAYED HOME TO STUDY!
WORDS I NEVER THOUGHT I'D HEAR.
RRRRRRRRRRRR
IF I MAKE IT OUT ALIVE, I PROMISE I'LL BECOME A MODEL STUDENT!
I'LL HOLD YOU TO THAT!
UM...A GOOD STUDENT.
I'LL MAKE NOTE OF THAT TOO.
AN OKAY STUDENT?
CUT IT OUT, BOB!
CAN'T YOU SOMEHOW FIND IRMA AND HER FRIENDS...?
HOW? ALL THE SURVEILLANCE CAMERAS ARE OUT OF COMMISSION!
ANYWAY, I HOPE THEY HAVEN'T GONE OUTSIDE. WE'RE FAIRLY SAFE IN HERE, BUT ELSEWHERE...

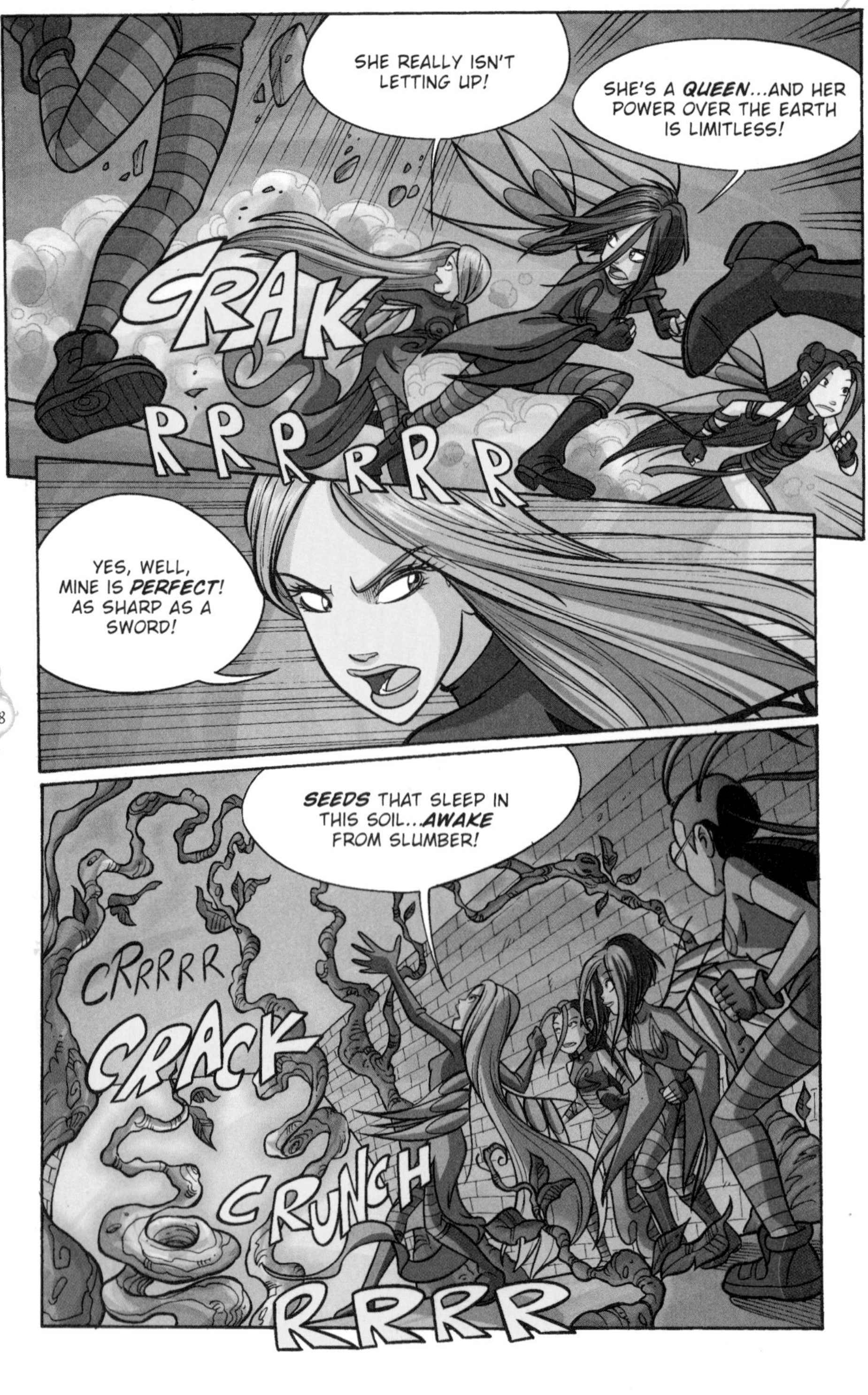
SHE REALLY ISN'T LETTING UP!
SHE'S A QUEEN...AND HER POWER OVER THE EARTH IS LIMITLESS!
CRAK
RRRRRR
YES, WELL, MINE IS PERFECT! AS SHARP AS A SWORD!
SEEDS THAT SLEEP IN THIS SOIL...AWAKE FROM SLUMBER!
CRRRRR
CRACK
CRUNCH
RRRR

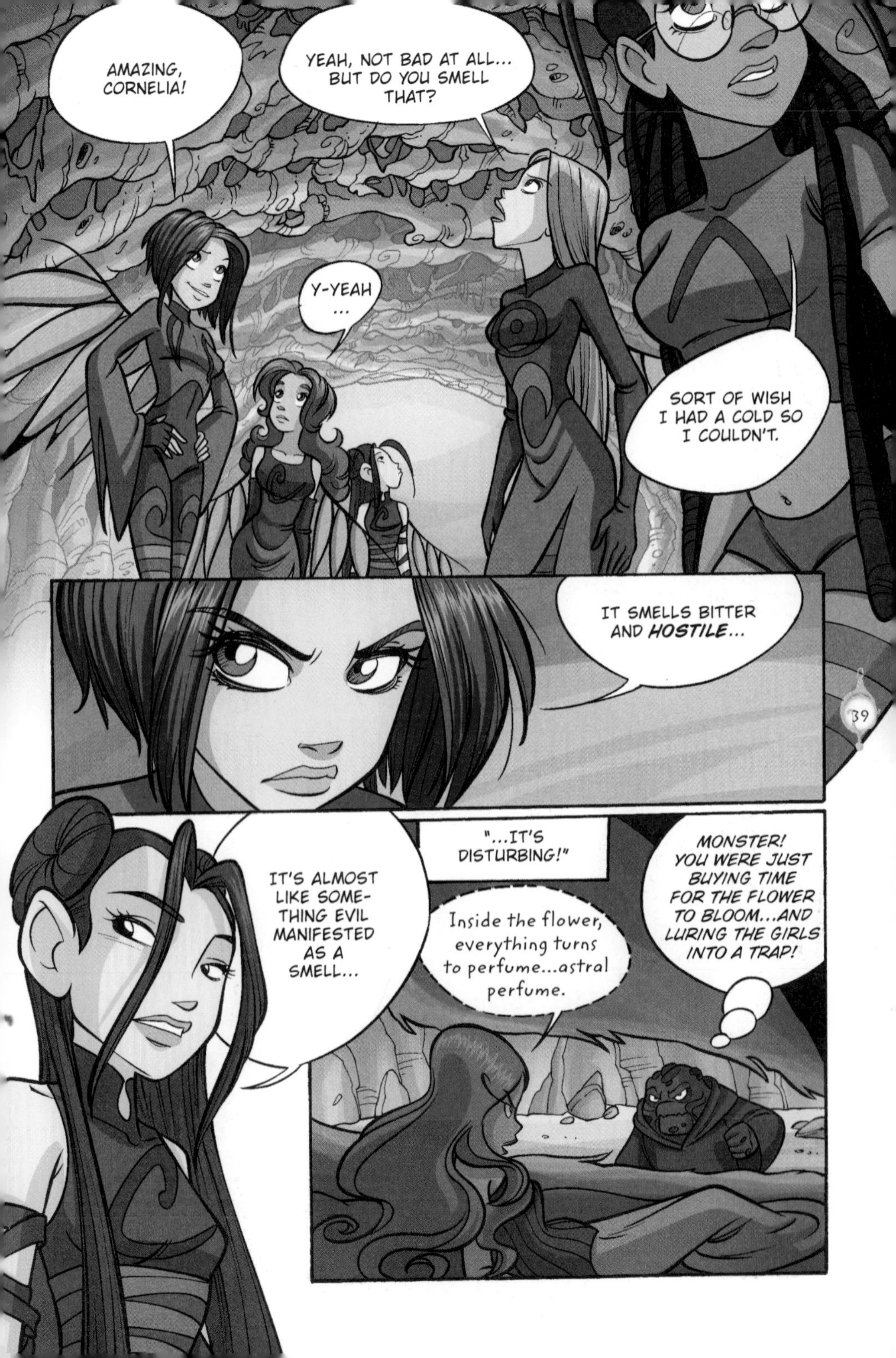
AMAZING, CORNELIA!
YEAH, NOT BAD AT ALL... BUT DO YOU SMELL THAT?
Y-YEAH ...
SORT OF WISH I HAD A COLD SO I COULDN'T.
IT SMELLS BITTER AND HOSTILE...
IT'S ALMOST LIKE SOME-THING EVIL MANIFESTED AS A SMELL...
"...IT'S DISTURBING!"
Inside the flower, everything turns to perfume...astral perfume.
MONSTER! YOU WERE JUST BUYING TIME FOR THE FLOWER TO BLOOM...AND LURING THE GIRLS INTO A TRAP!

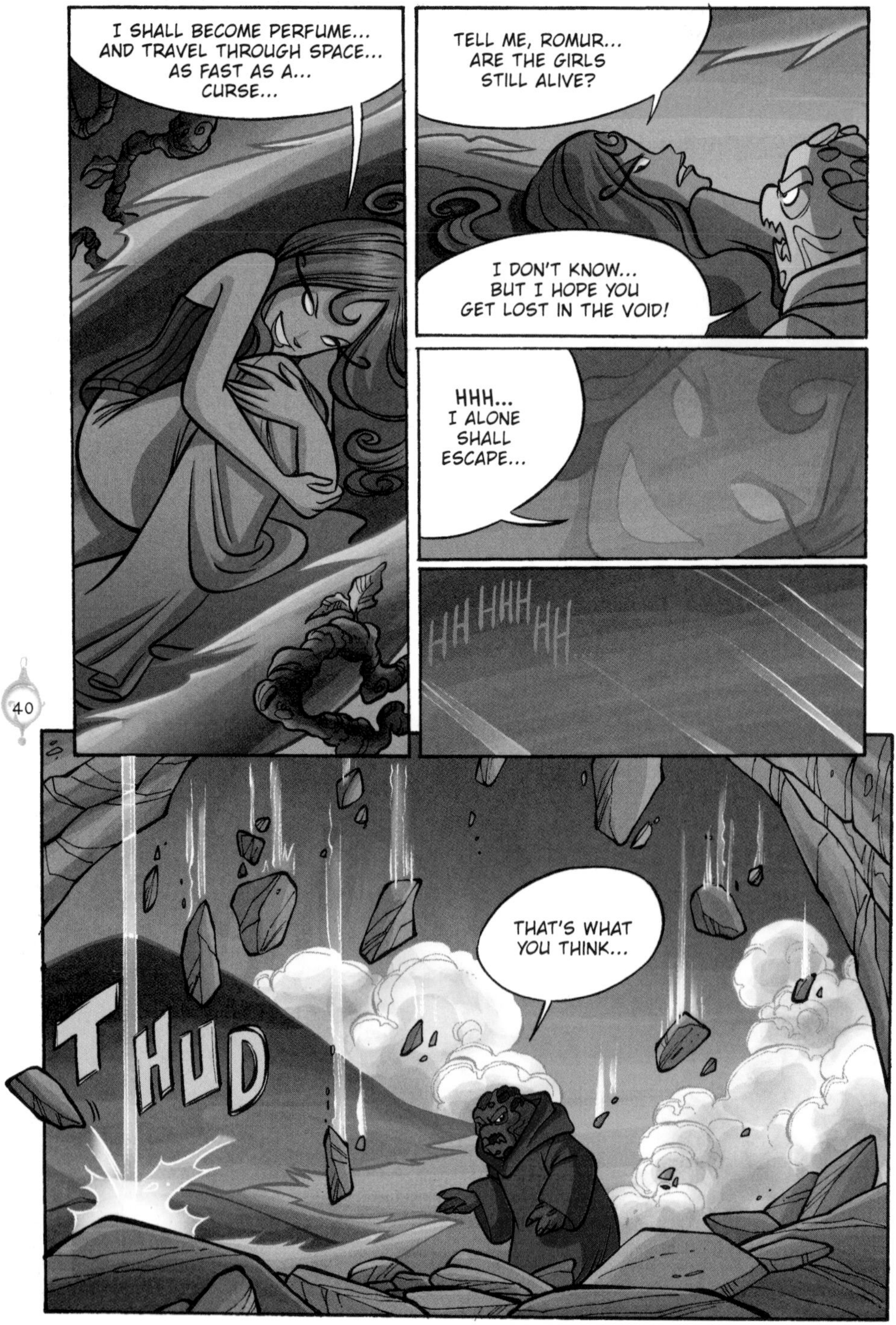
I SHALL BECOME PERFUME... AND TRAVEL THROUGH SPACE... AS FAST AS A... CURSE...
TELL ME, ROMUR... ARE THE GIRLS STILL ALIVE?
I DON'T KNOW... BUT I HOPE YOU GET LOST IN THE VOID!
HHH... I ALONE SHALL ESCAPE...
HHHHHHHH...
THAT'S WHAT YOU THINK...
THUD

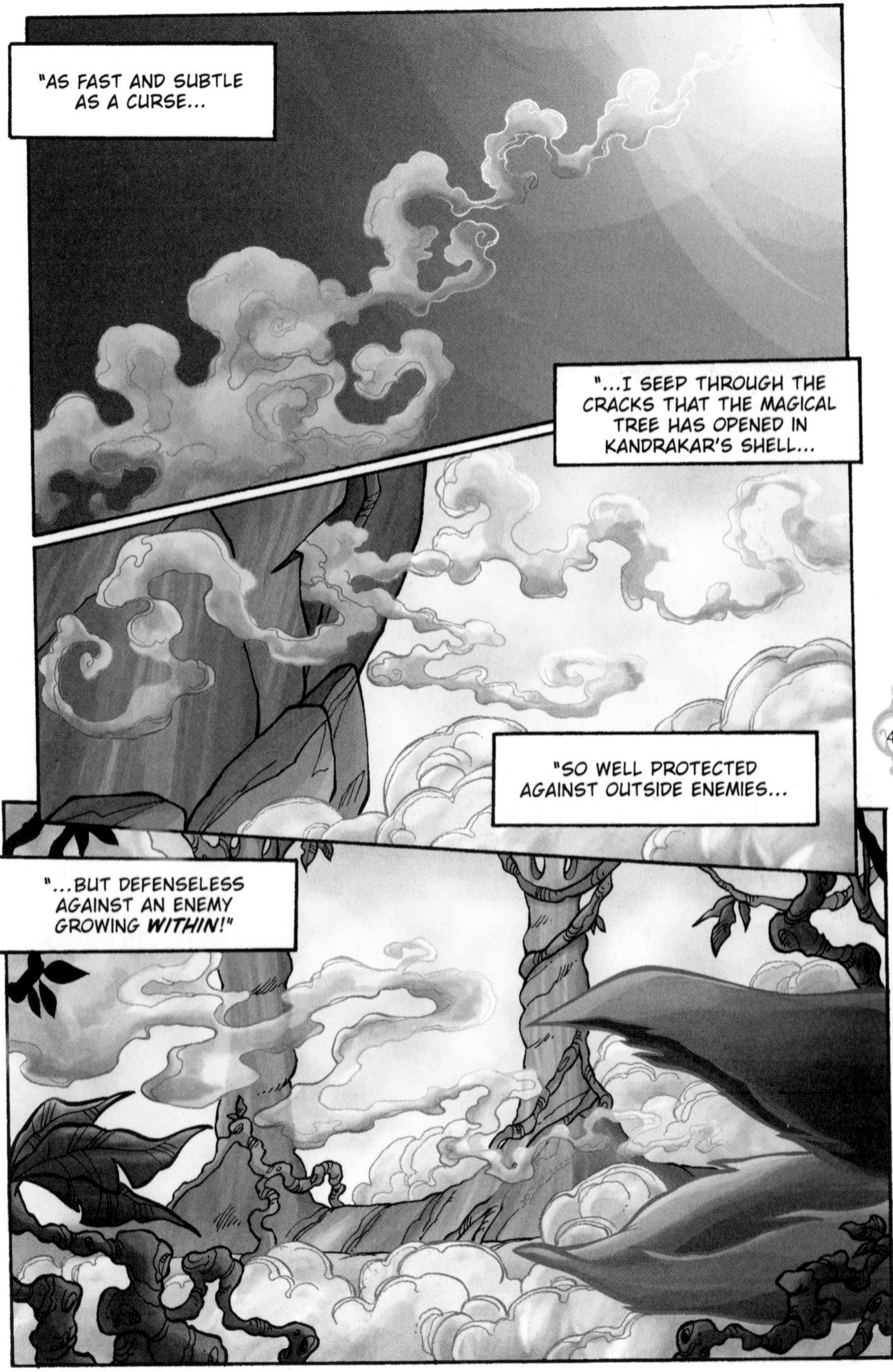
"AS FAST AND SUBTLE AS A CURSE...
"...I SEEP THROUGH THE CRACKS THAT THE MAGICAL TREE HAS OPENED IN KANDRAKAR'S SHELL...
"SO WELL PROTECTED AGAINST OUTSIDE ENEMIES...
"...BUT DEFENSELESS AGAINST AN ENEMY GROWING ***WITHIN!***"

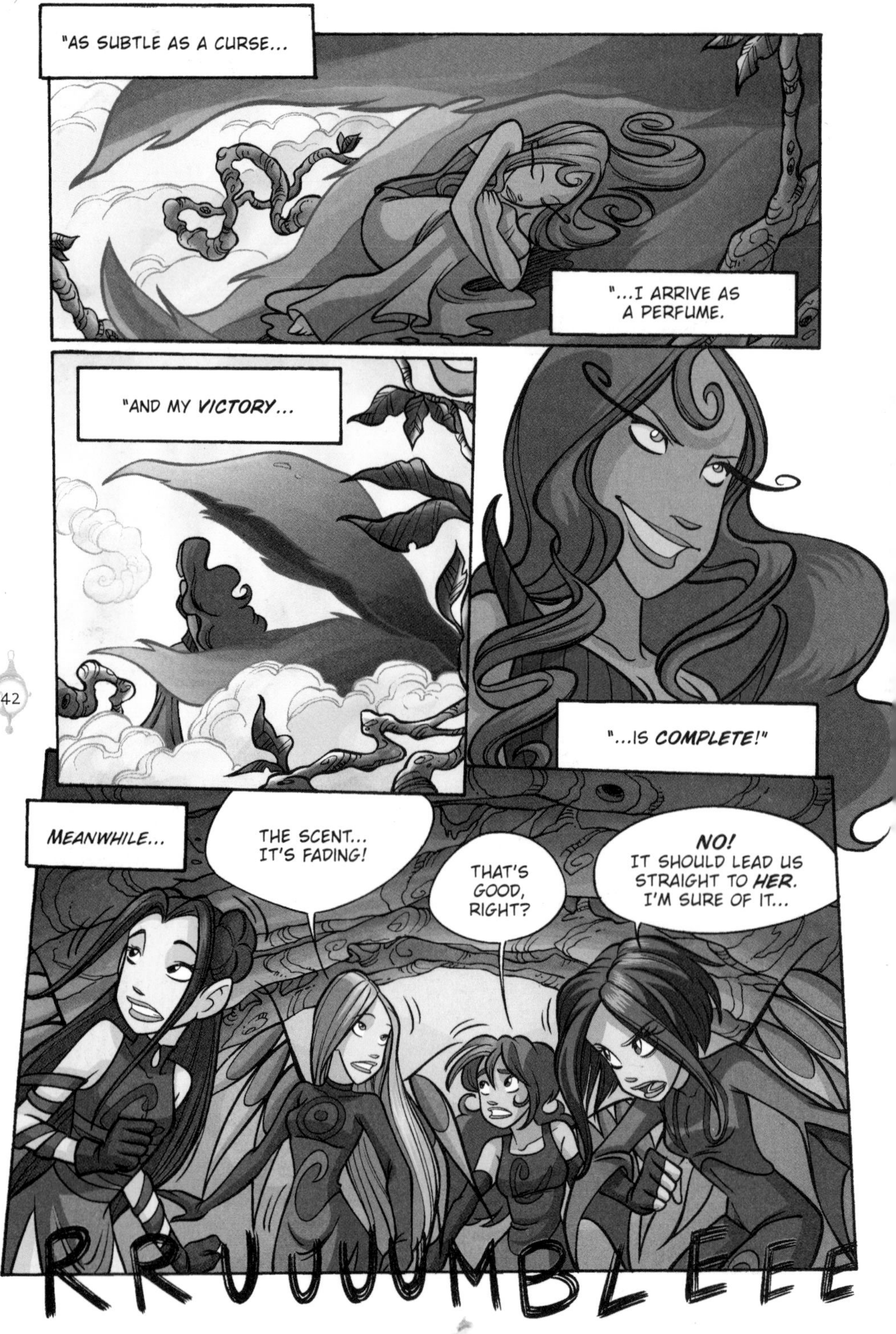
"AS SUBTLE AS A CURSE...
"...I ARRIVE AS A PERFUME.
"AND MY VICTORY...
"...IS COMPLETE!"
MEANWHILE...
THE SCENT... IT'S FADING!
THAT'S GOOD, RIGHT?
NO! IT SHOULD LEAD US STRAIGHT TO HER. I'M SURE OF IT...
RRUUUUMBLEEE

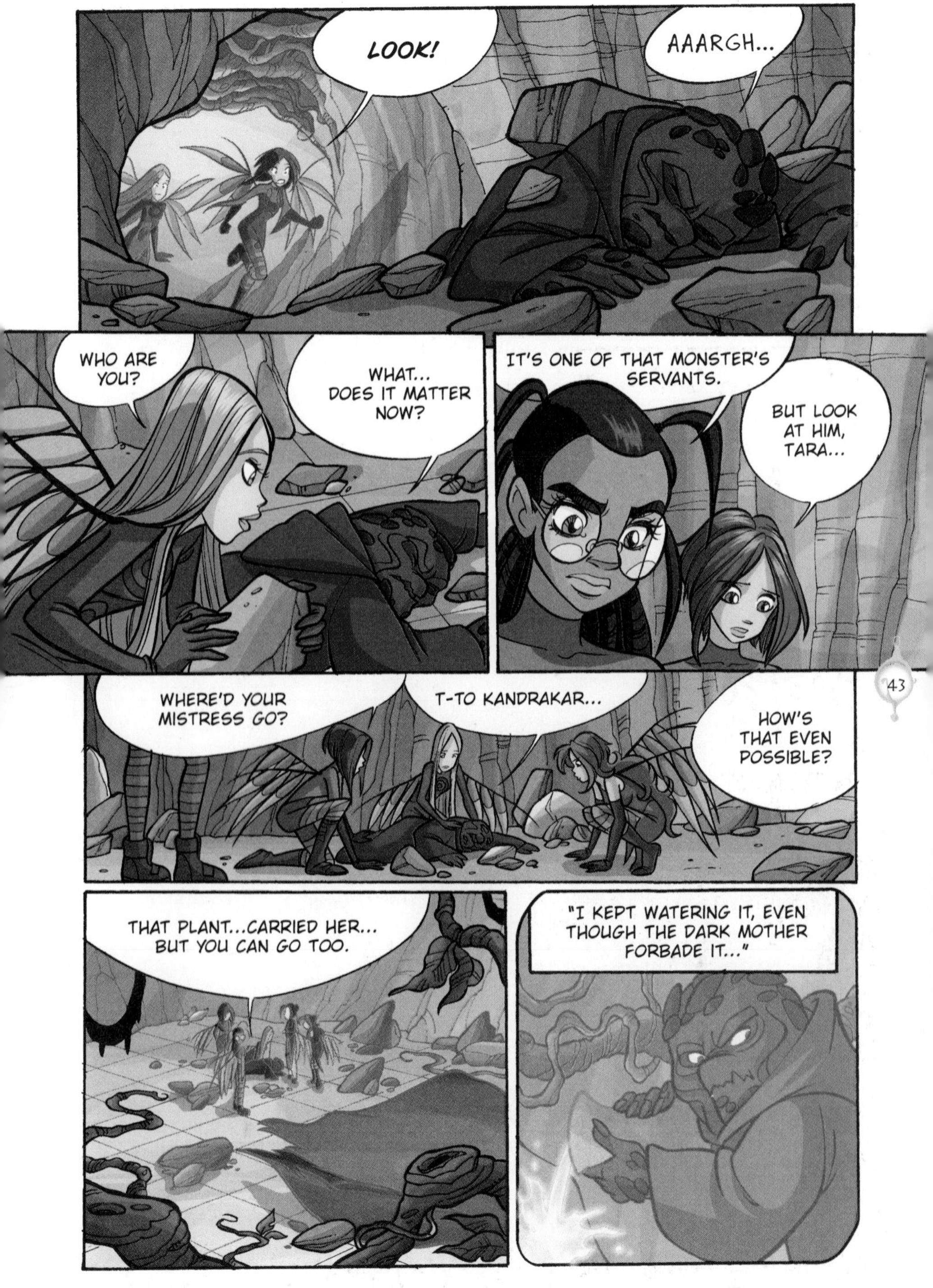
LOOK!
AAARGH...
WHO ARE YOU?
WHAT... DOES IT MATTER NOW?
IT'S ONE OF THAT MONSTER'S SERVANTS.
BUT LOOK AT HIM, TARA...
WHERE'D YOUR MISTRESS GO?
T-TO KANDRAKAR...
HOW'S THAT EVEN POSSIBLE?
THAT PLANT...CARRIED HER... BUT YOU CAN GO TOO.
"I KEPT WATERING IT, EVEN THOUGH THE DARK MOTHER FORBADE IT..."

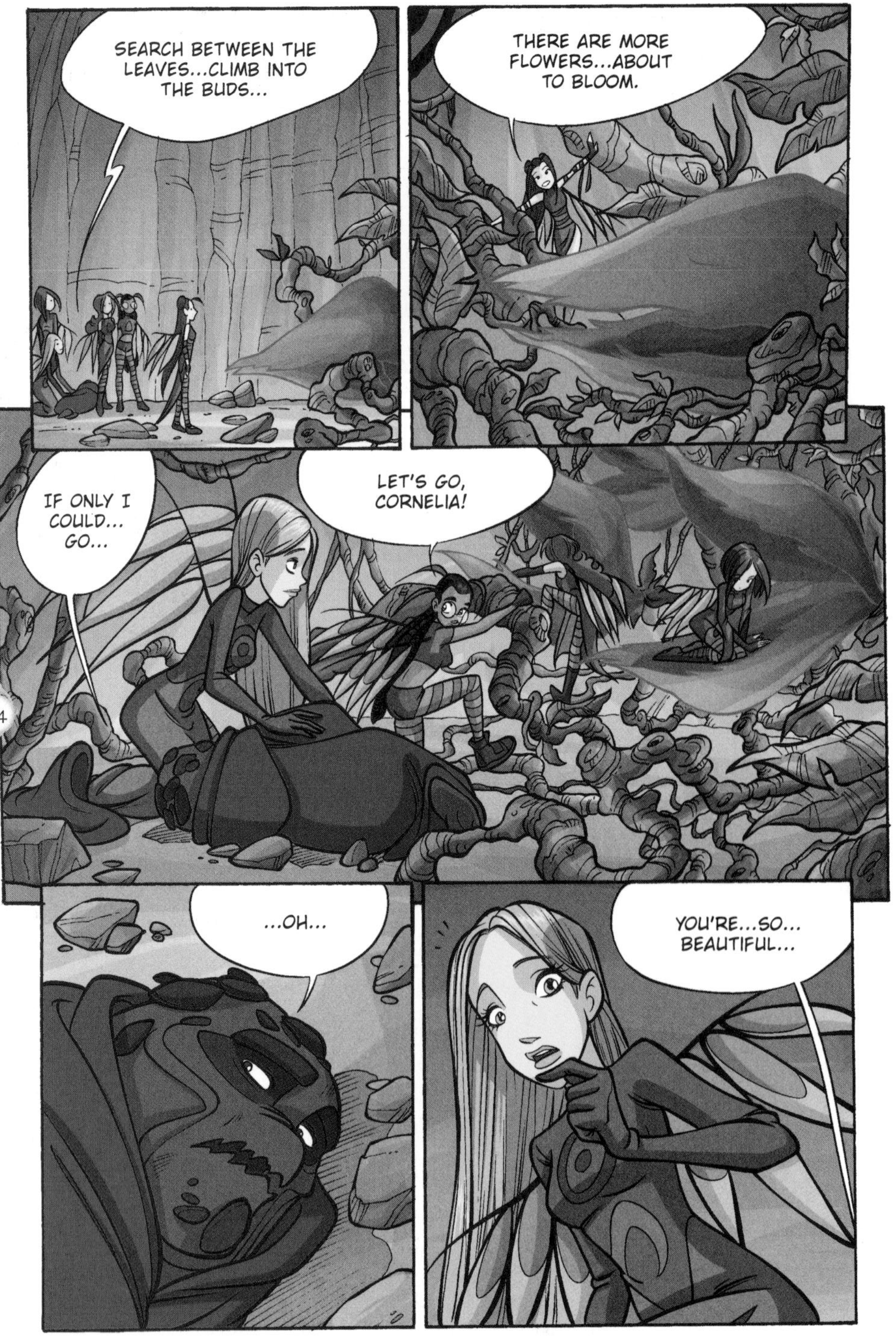
SEARCH BETWEEN THE LEAVES...CLIMB INTO THE BUDS...
THERE ARE MORE FLOWERS...ABOUT TO BLOOM.
IF ONLY I COULD... GO...
LET'S GO, CORNELIA!
...OH...
YOU'RE...SO... BEAUTIFUL...

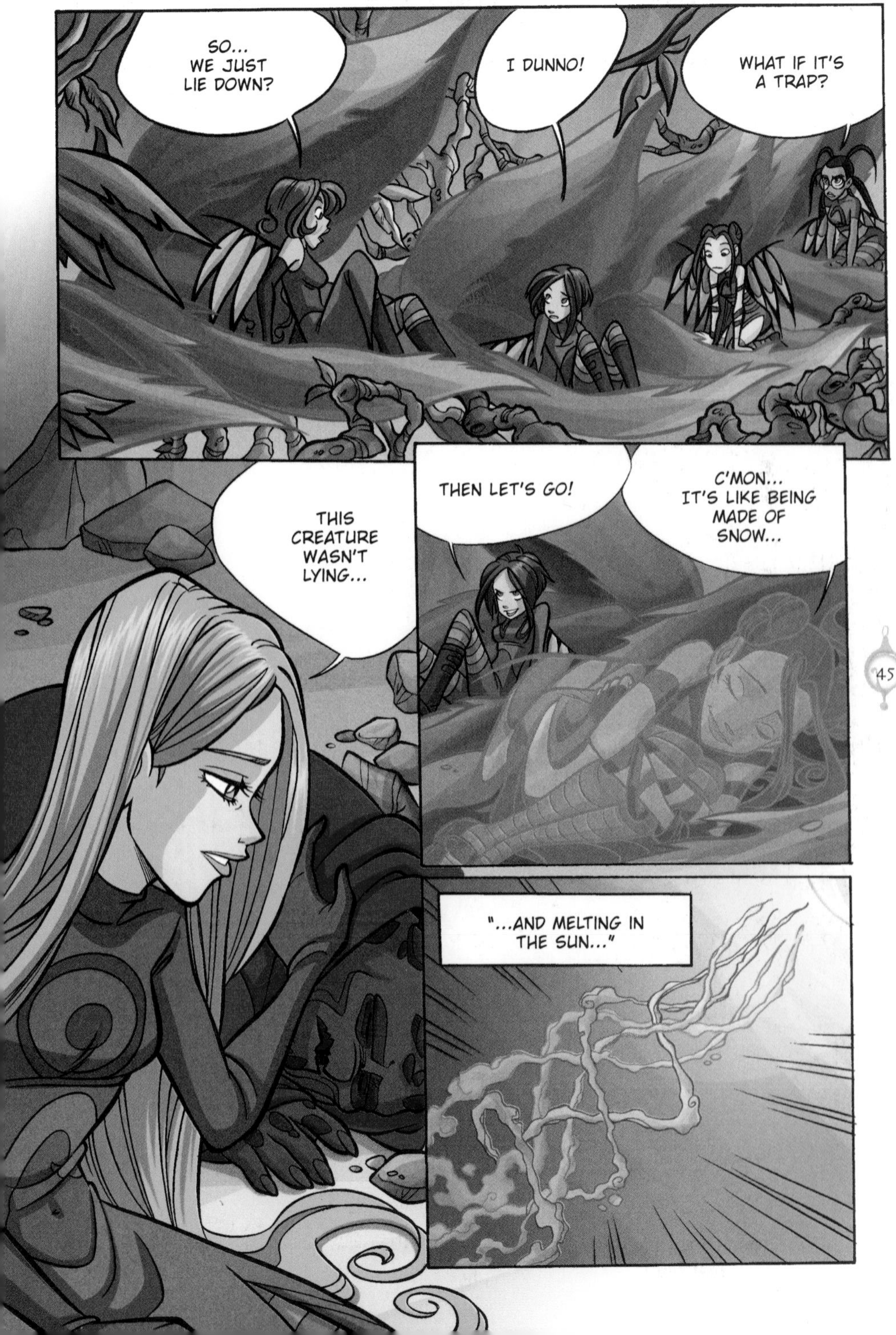
SO... WE JUST LIE DOWN?
I DUNNO!
WHAT IF IT'S A TRAP?
THIS CREATURE WASN'T LYING...
THEN LET'S GO!
C'MON... IT'S LIKE BEING MADE OF SNOW...
"...AND MELTING IN THE SUN..."

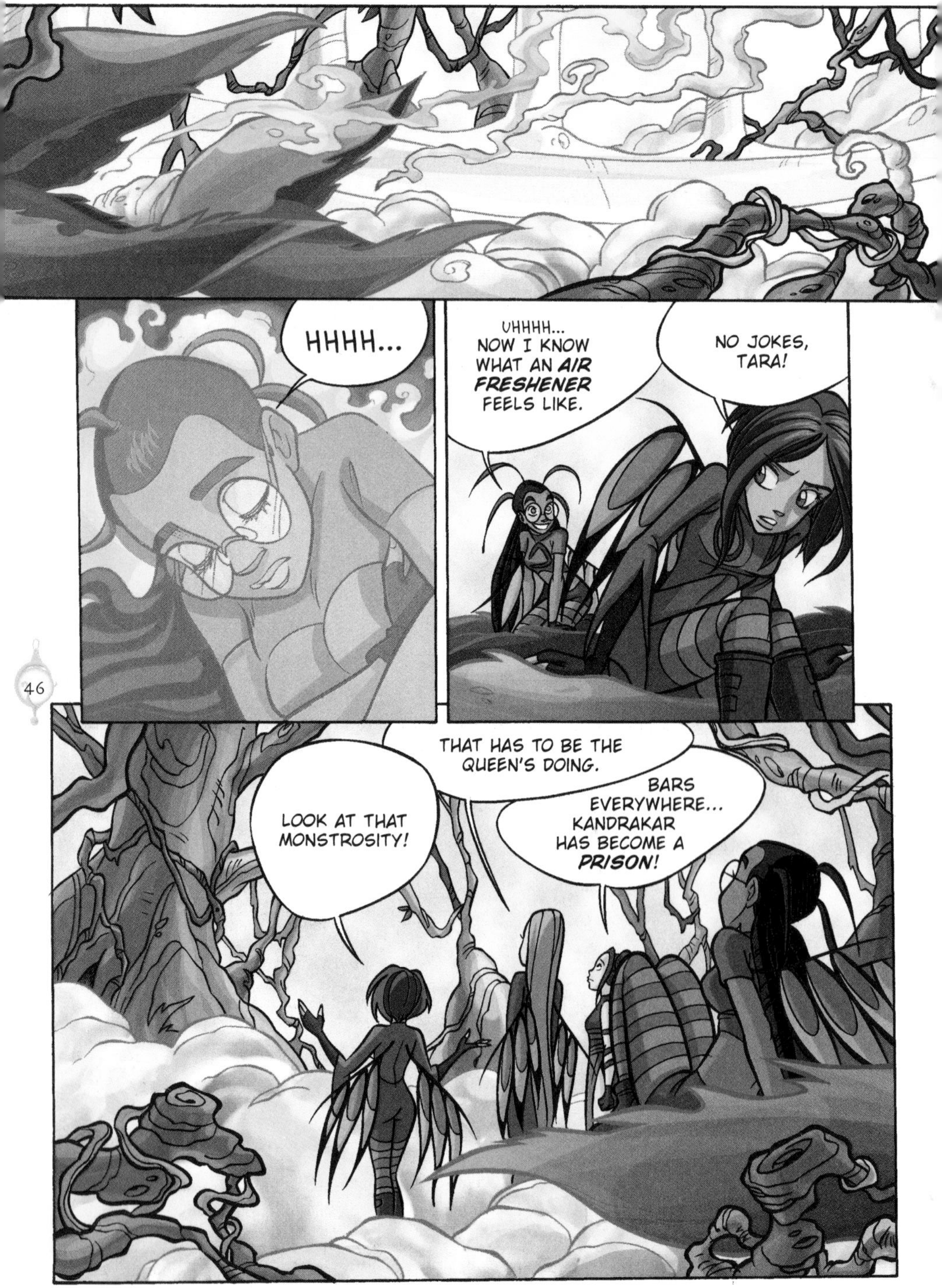
HHHH...
UHHHH... NOW I KNOW WHAT AN AIR FRESHENER FEELS LIKE.
NO JOKES, TARA!
THAT HAS TO BE THE QUEEN'S DOING.
LOOK AT THAT MONSTROSITY!
BARS EVERYWHERE... KANDRAKAR HAS BECOME A PRISON!

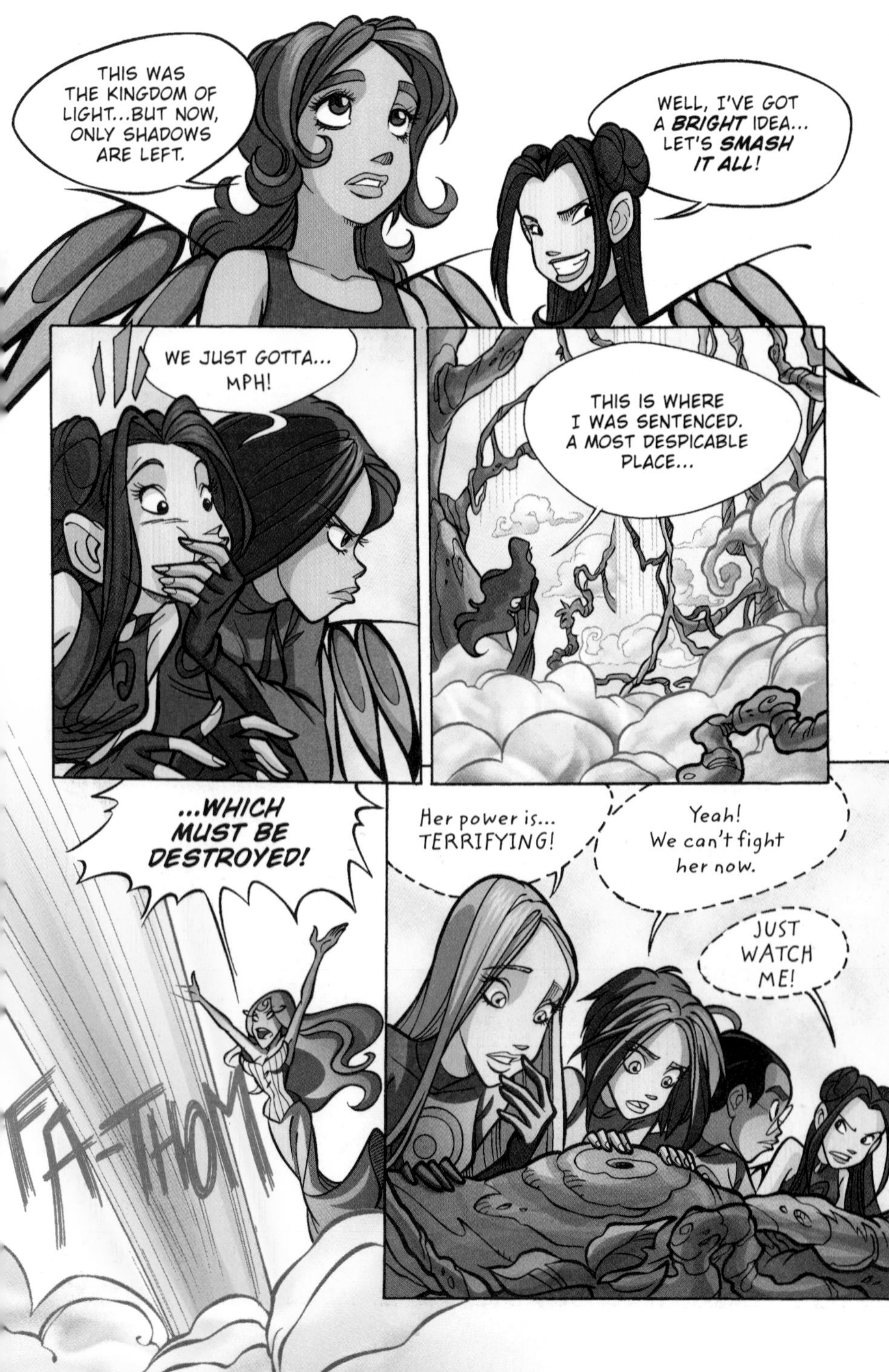
THIS WAS THE KINGDOM OF LIGHT...BUT NOW, ONLY SHADOWS ARE LEFT.
WELL, I'VE GOT A BRIGHT IDEA... LET'S SMASH IT ALL!
WE JUST GOTTA... MPH!
THIS IS WHERE I WAS SENTENCED. A MOST DESPICABLE PLACE...
...WHICH MUST BE DESTROYED!
FA-THOM
Her power is... TERRIFYING!
Yeah! We can't fight her now.
JUST WATCH ME!

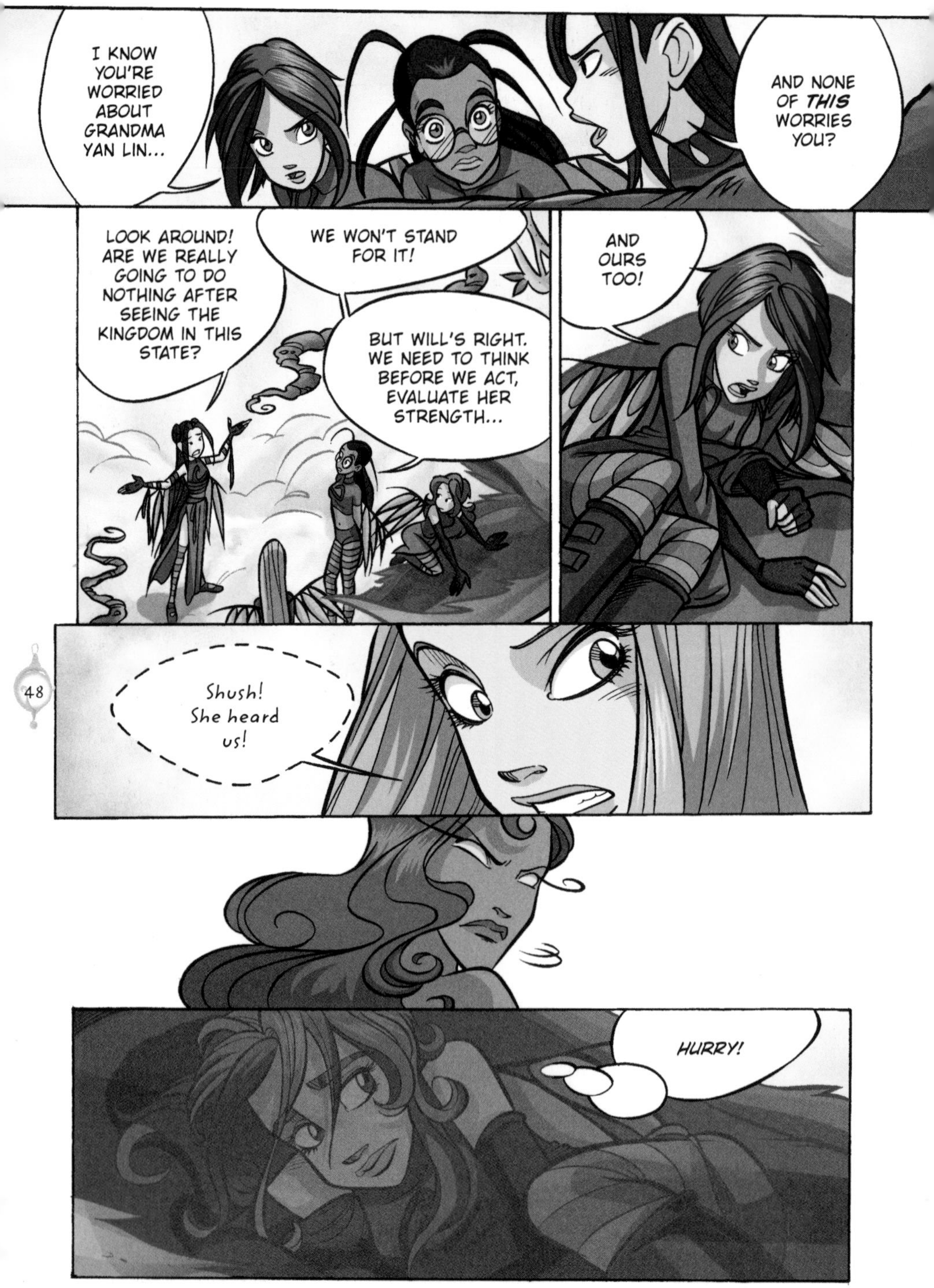
I KNOW YOU'RE WORRIED ABOUT GRANDMA YAN LIN...
AND NONE OF *THIS* WORRIES YOU?
LOOK AROUND! ARE WE REALLY GOING TO DO NOTHING AFTER SEEING THE KINGDOM IN THIS STATE?
WE WON'T STAND FOR IT!
BUT WILL'S RIGHT. WE NEED TO THINK BEFORE WE ACT, EVALUATE HER STRENGTH...
AND OURS TOO!
Shush! She heard us!
HURRY!

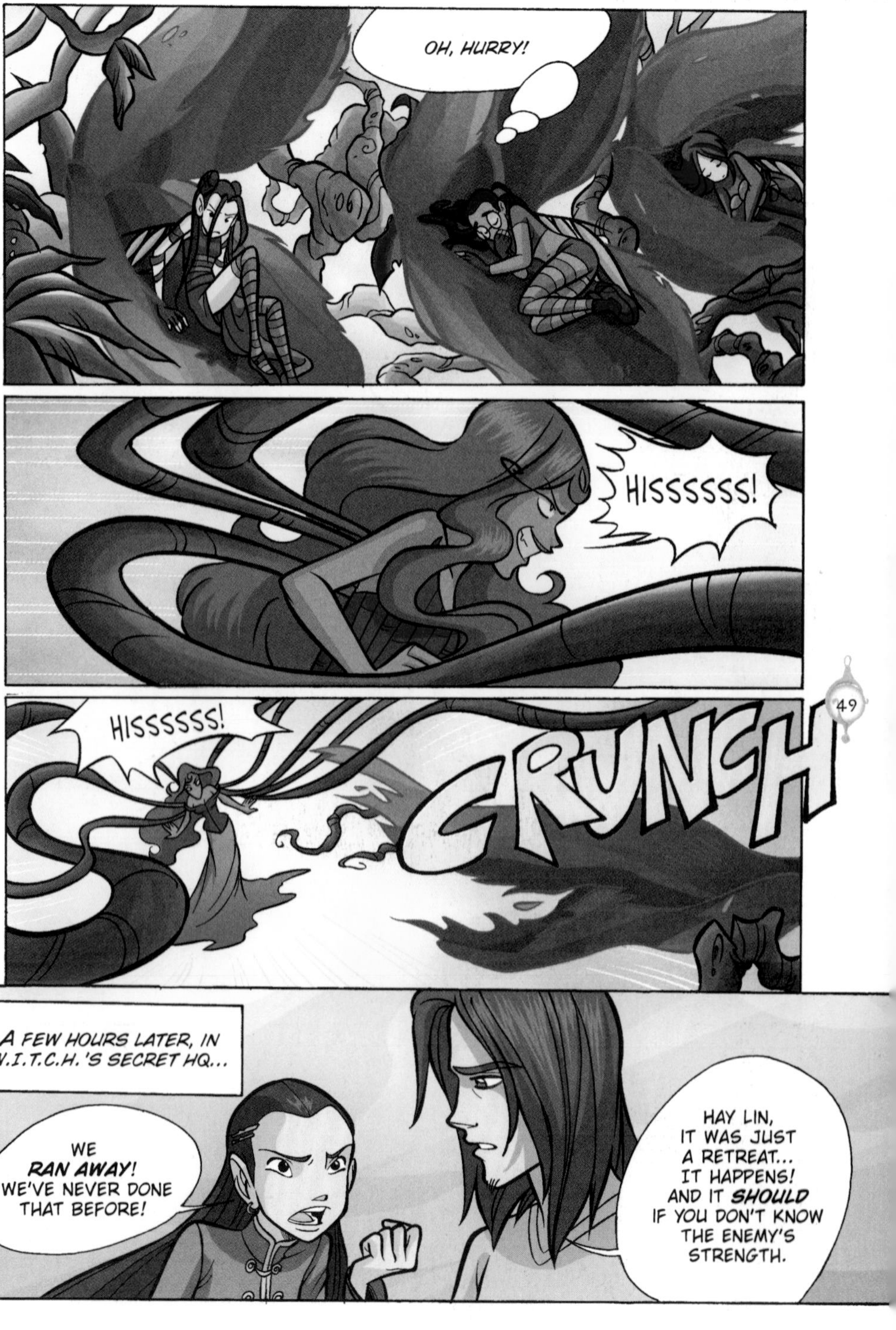
OH, HURRY!
HISSSSSS!
HISSSSSS!
CRUNCH
A FEW HOURS LATER, IN W.I.T.C.H.'S SECRET HQ...
WE RAN AWAY! WE'VE NEVER DONE THAT BEFORE!
HAY LIN, IT WAS JUST A RETREAT... IT HAPPENS! AND IT SHOULD IF YOU DON'T KNOW THE ENEMY'S STRENGTH.

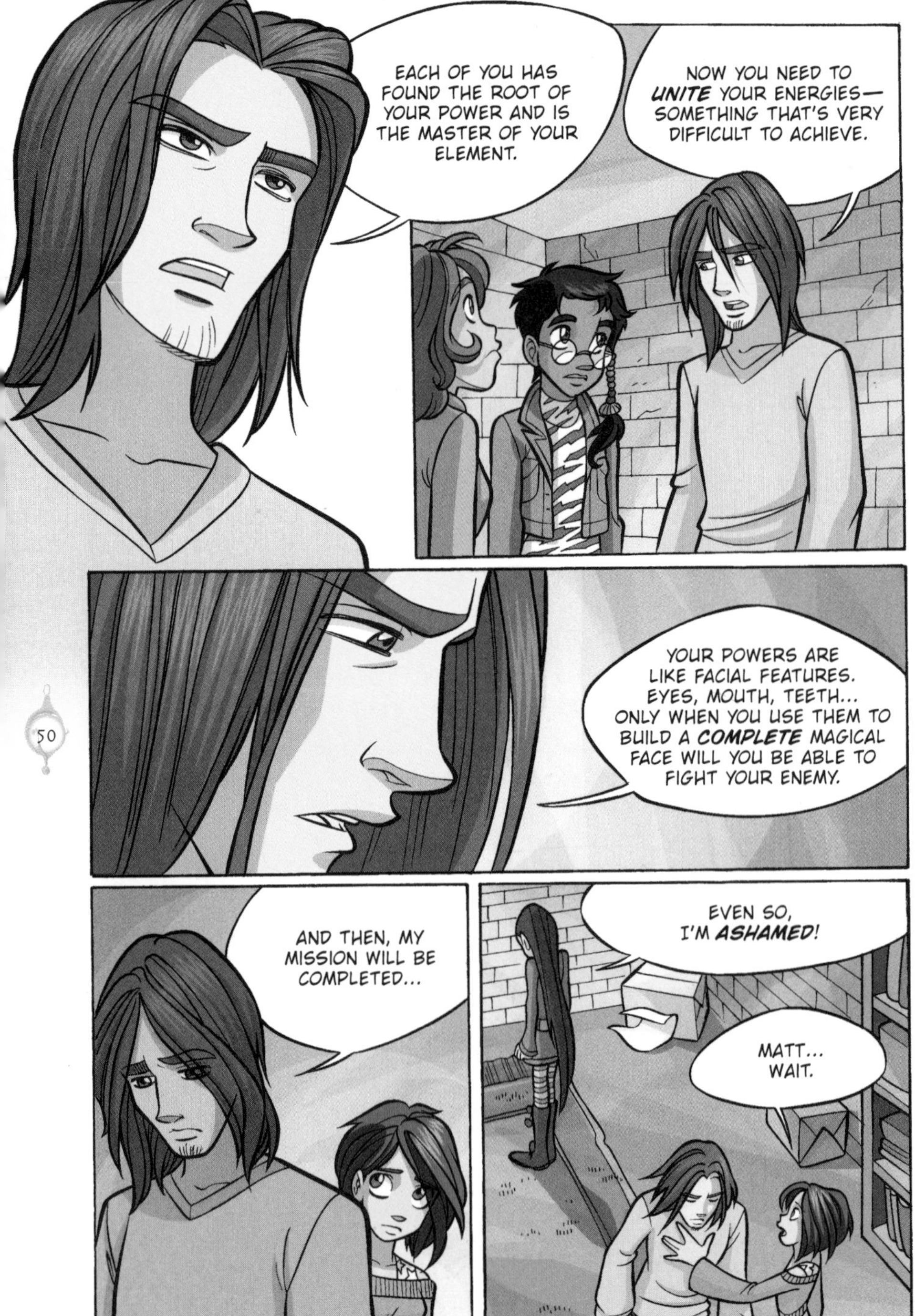
EACH OF YOU HAS FOUND THE ROOT OF YOUR POWER AND IS THE MASTER OF YOUR ELEMENT.
NOW YOU NEED TO ***UNITE*** YOUR ENERGIES—SOMETHING THAT'S VERY DIFFICULT TO ACHIEVE.
YOUR POWERS ARE LIKE FACIAL FEATURES. EYES, MOUTH, TEETH... ONLY WHEN YOU USE THEM TO BUILD A ***COMPLETE*** MAGICAL FACE WILL YOU BE ABLE TO FIGHT YOUR ENEMY.
AND THEN, MY MISSION WILL BE COMPLETED...
EVEN SO, I'M ***ASHAMED***!
MATT... WAIT.

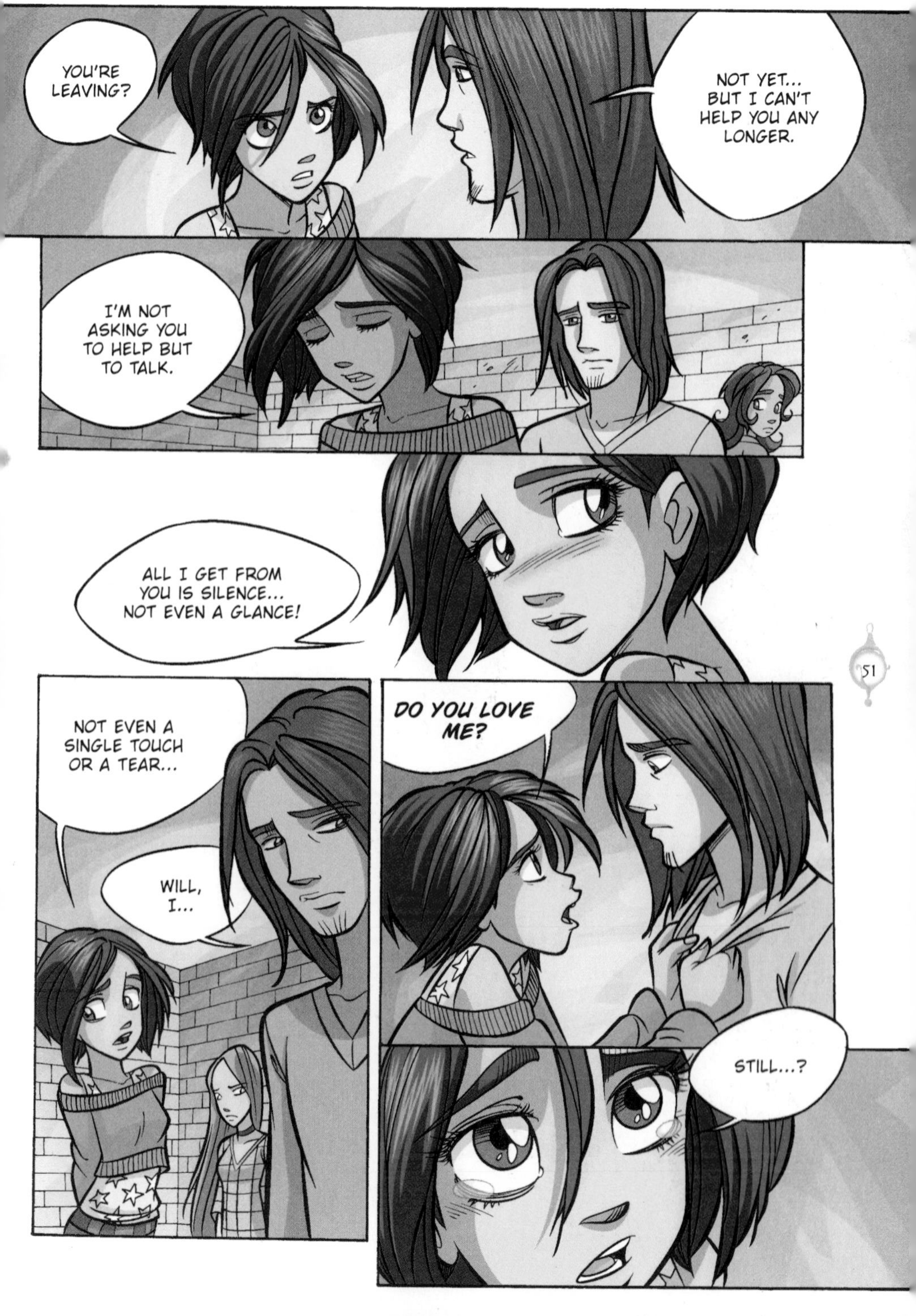

YOU'RE LEAVING?
NOT YET... BUT I CAN'T HELP YOU ANY LONGER.
I'M NOT ASKING YOU TO HELP BUT TO TALK.
ALL I GET FROM YOU IS SILENCE... NOT EVEN A GLANCE!
NOT EVEN A SINGLE TOUCH OR A TEAR...
WILL, I...
DO YOU LOVE ME?
STILL...?

SO MANY THINGS DIVIDED US AND KEPT US APART...

THAT'S NOT WHAT I WANNA HEAR...

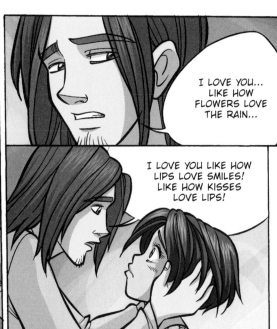

I LOVE YOU... LIKE HOW FLOWERS LOVE THE RAIN...

I LOVE YOU LIKE HOW LIPS LOVE SMILES! LIKE HOW KISSES LOVE LIPS!

LET ANYONE TRY AND SAY THEY HAVE LOVED SOMEONE MORE... I'LL LAUGH AT THEIR LIE!

IF ANYONE LAUGHS AT ME FOR HOW MUCH I LOVE YOU... I'LL LAUGH WITH THEM!

IT WAS THERE IN MY SILENCES. MY TEARS WERE HIDDEN AND MY TOUCHES TOO LIGHT FOR YOU TO FEEL, BUT THEY WERE ENDLESS...

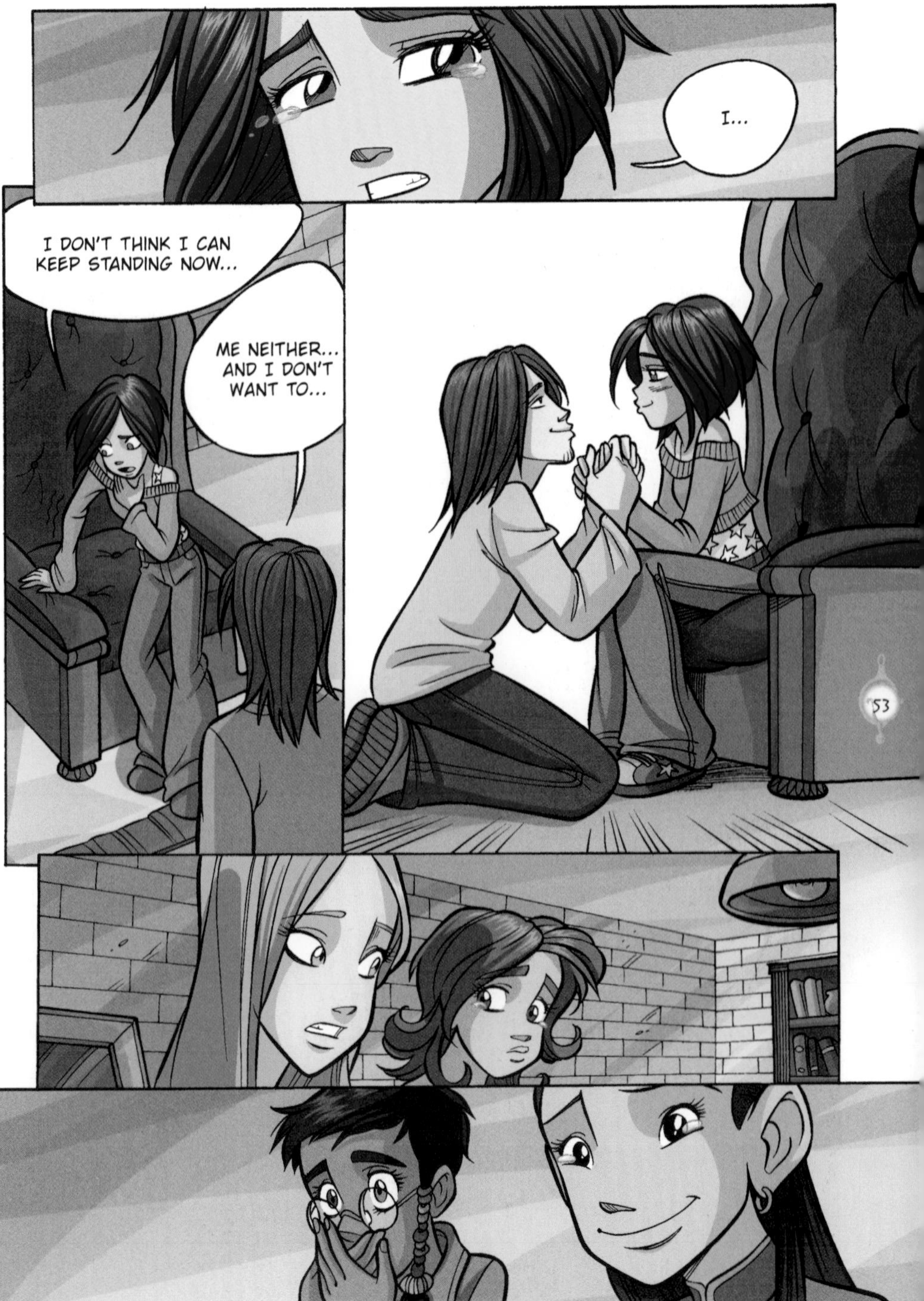
I...
I DON'T THINK I CAN KEEP STANDING NOW...
ME NEITHER... AND I DON'T WANT TO...

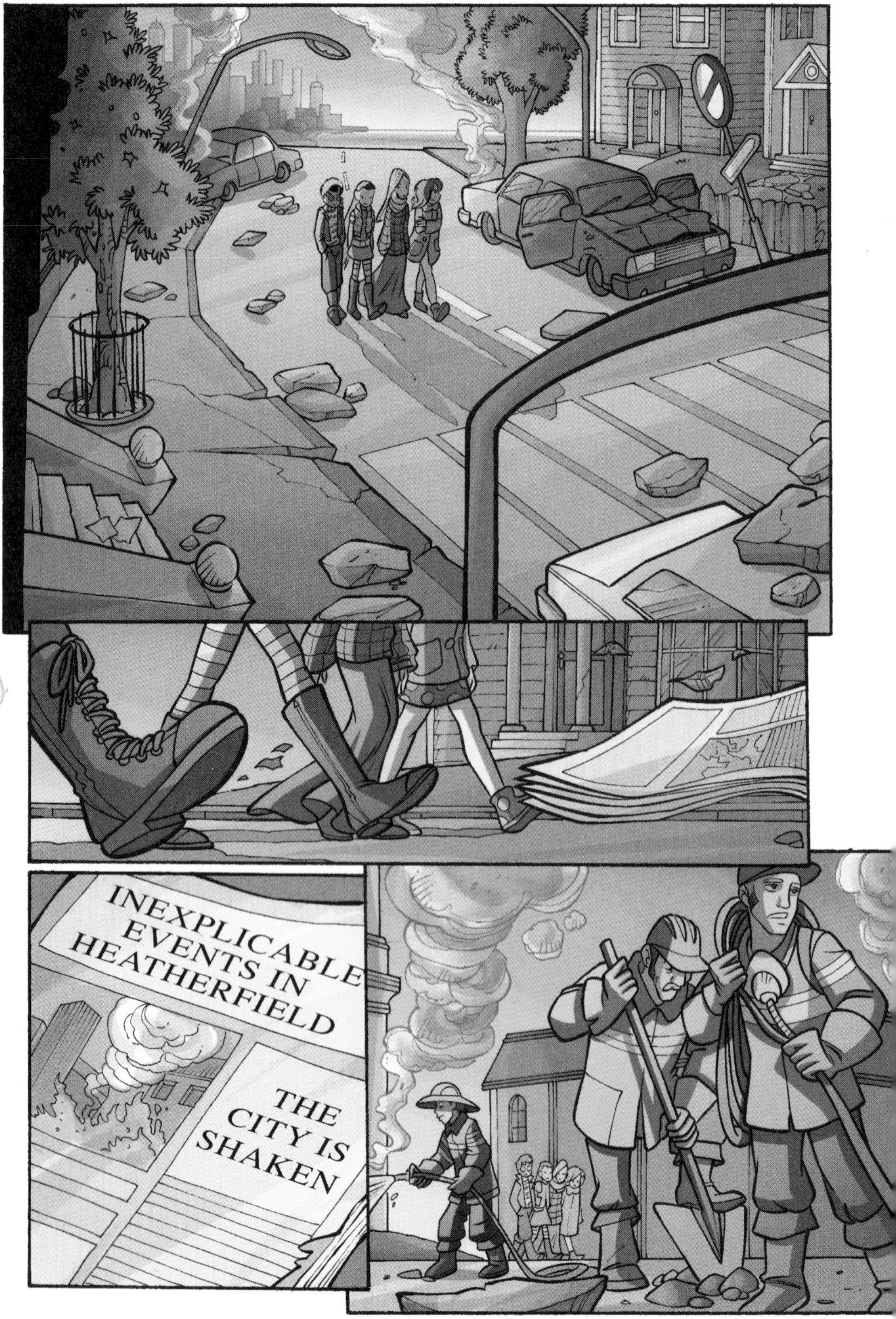
INEXPLICABLE EVENTS IN HEATHERFIELD
THE CITY IS SHAKEN

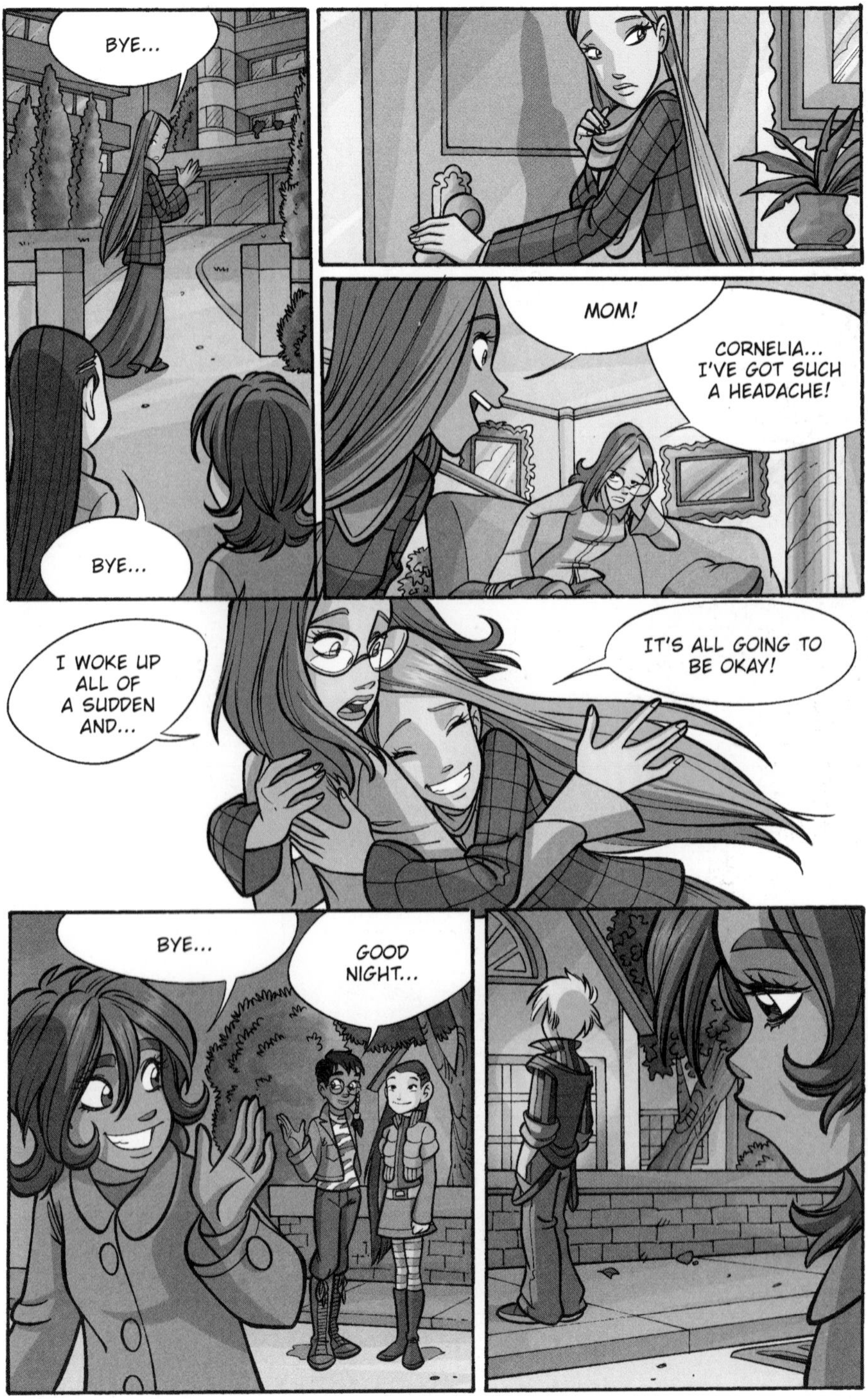
BYE...
BYE...
MOM!
CORNELIA... I'VE GOT SUCH A HEADACHE!
I WOKE UP ALL OF A SUDDEN AND...
IT'S ALL GOING TO BE OKAY!
BYE...
GOOD NIGHT...

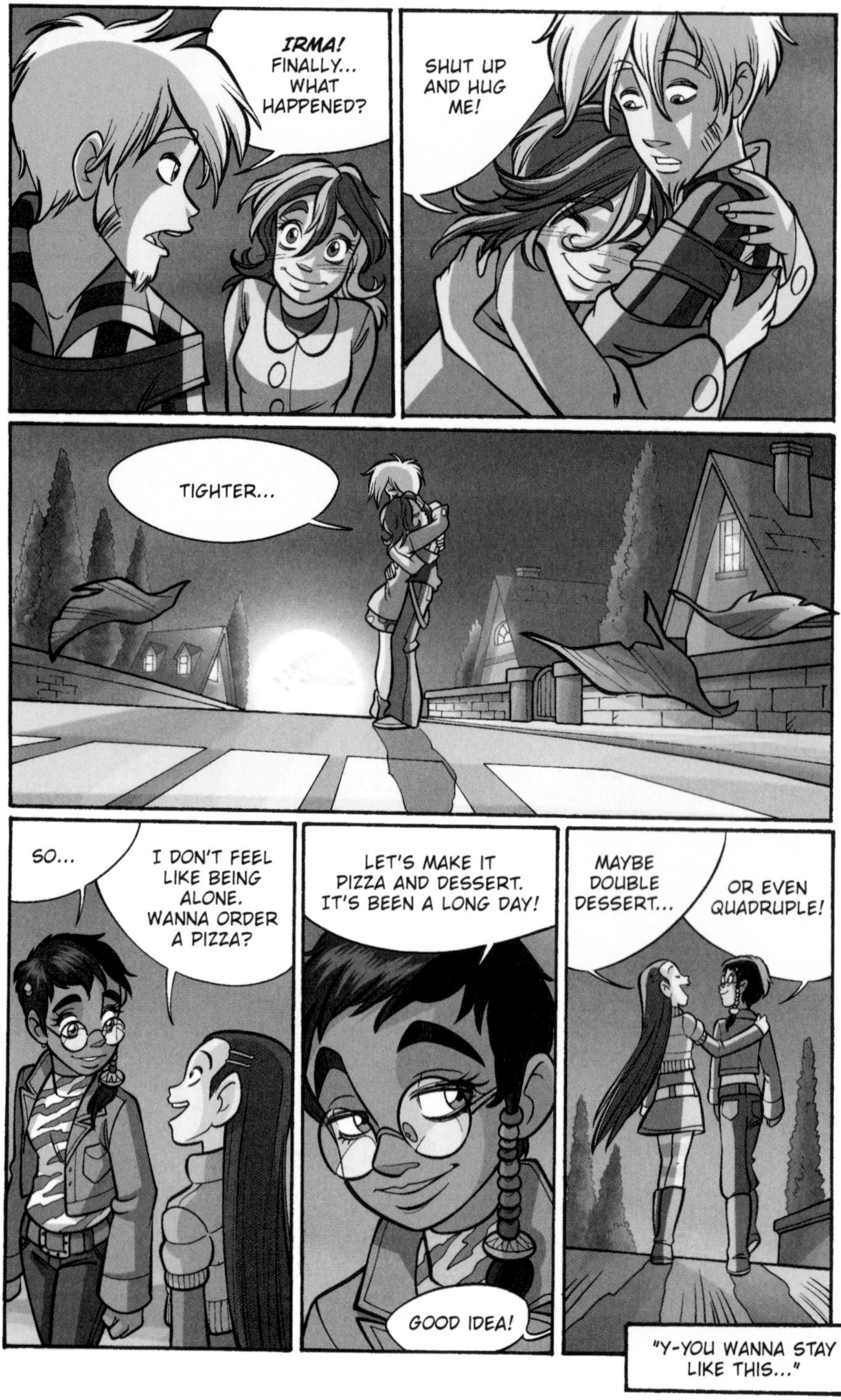
IRMA! FINALLY... WHAT HAPPENED?
SHUT UP AND HUG ME!
TIGHTER...
SO...
I DON'T FEEL LIKE BEING ALONE. WANNA ORDER A PIZZA?
LET'S MAKE IT PIZZA AND DESSERT. IT'S BEEN A LONG DAY!
GOOD IDEA!
MAYBE DOUBLE DESSERT...
OR EVEN QUADRUPLE!
"Y-YOU WANNA STAY LIKE THIS..."

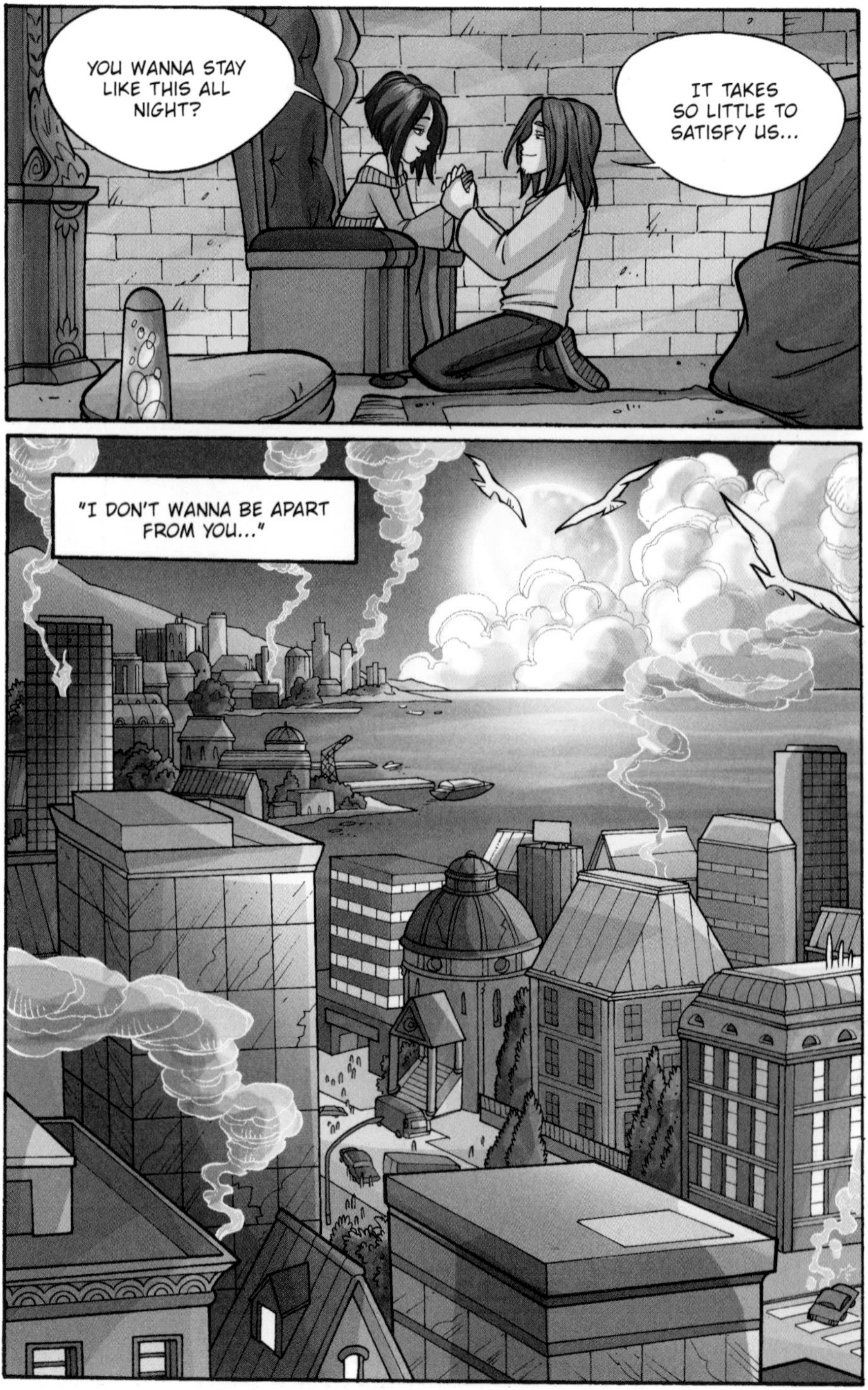
YOU WANNA STAY LIKE THIS ALL NIGHT?
IT TAKES SO LITTLE TO SATISFY US...
"I DON'T WANNA BE APART FROM YOU..."

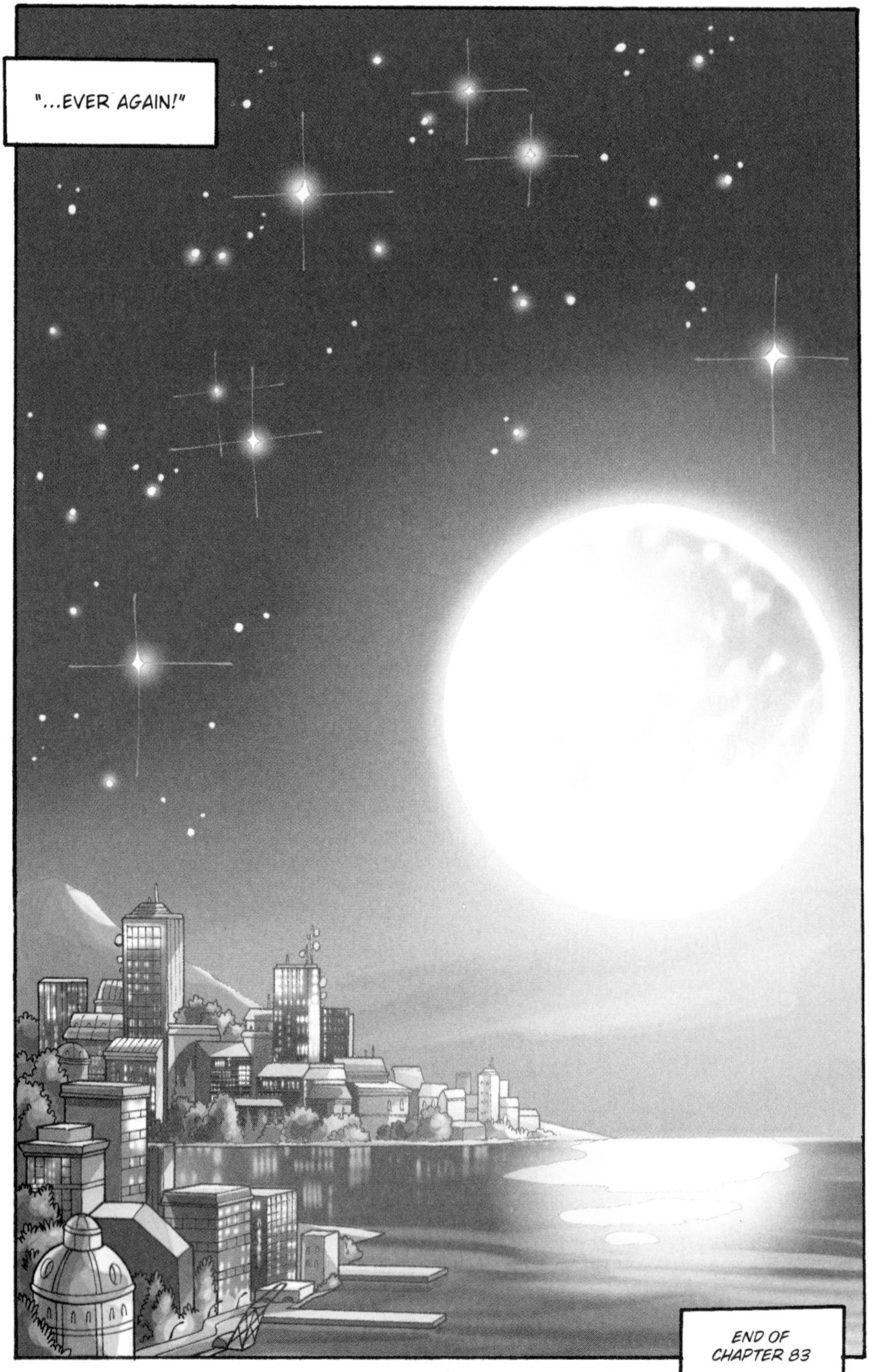
"...EVER AGAIN!"
END OF CHAPTER 83

84

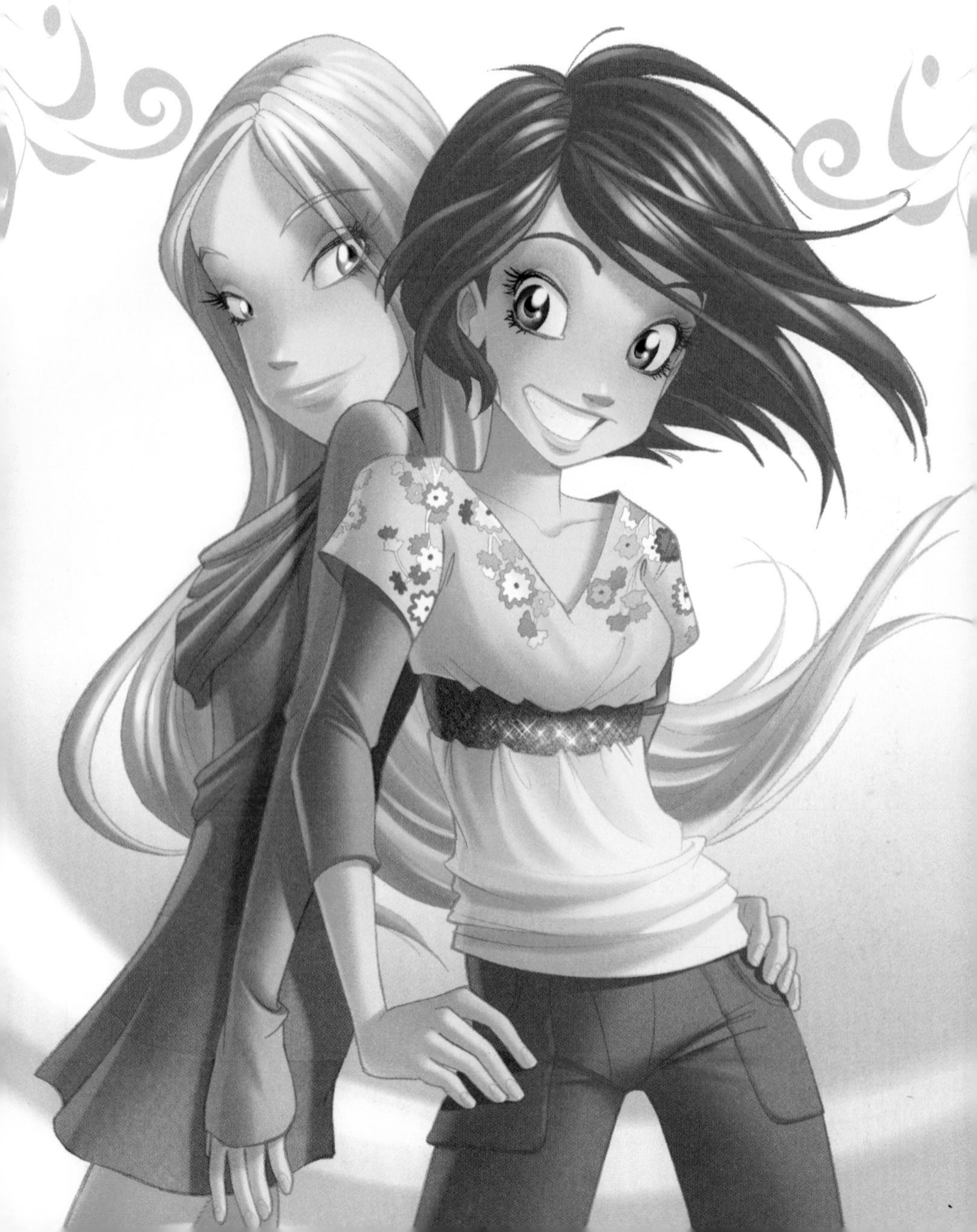

A Special Flow

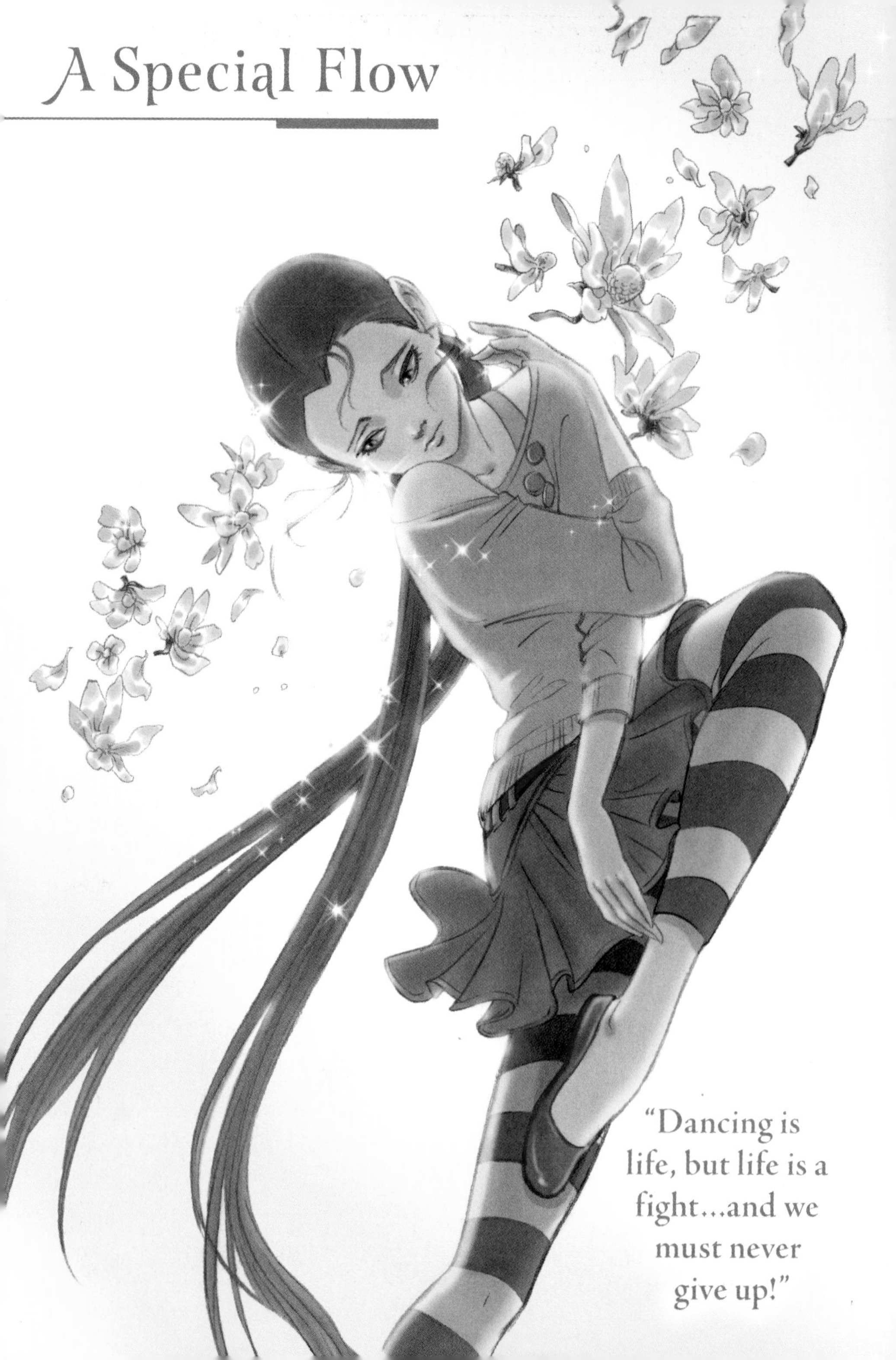
"Dancing is life, but life is a fight...and we must never give up!"

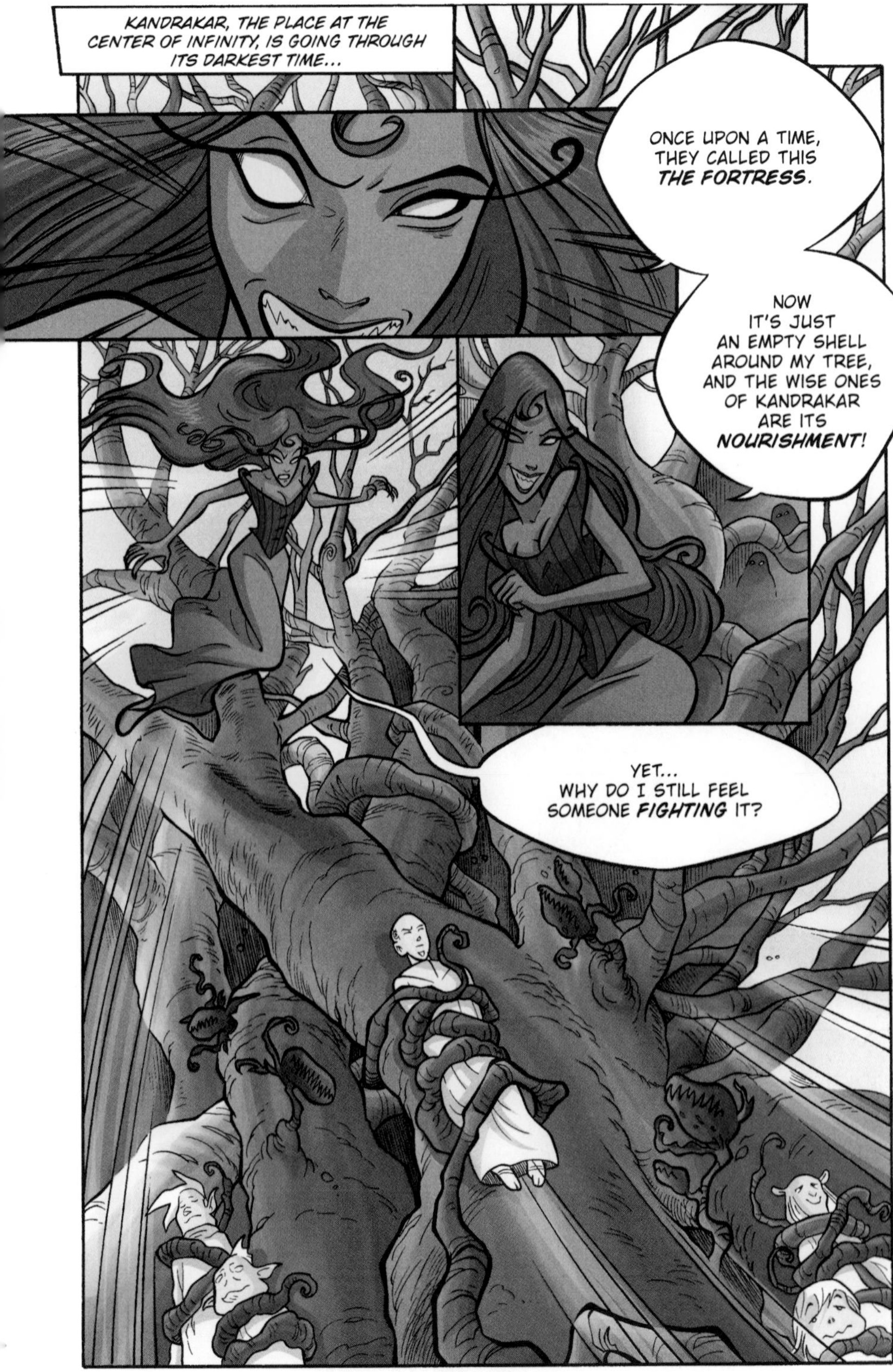
KANDRAKAR, THE PLACE AT THE CENTER OF INFINITY, IS GOING THROUGH ITS DARKEST TIME...
ONCE UPON A TIME, THEY CALLED THIS THE FORTRESS.
NOW IT'S JUST AN EMPTY SHELL AROUND MY TREE, AND THE WISE ONES OF KANDRAKAR ARE ITS NOURISHMENT!
YET... WHY DO I STILL FEEL SOMEONE FIGHTING IT?

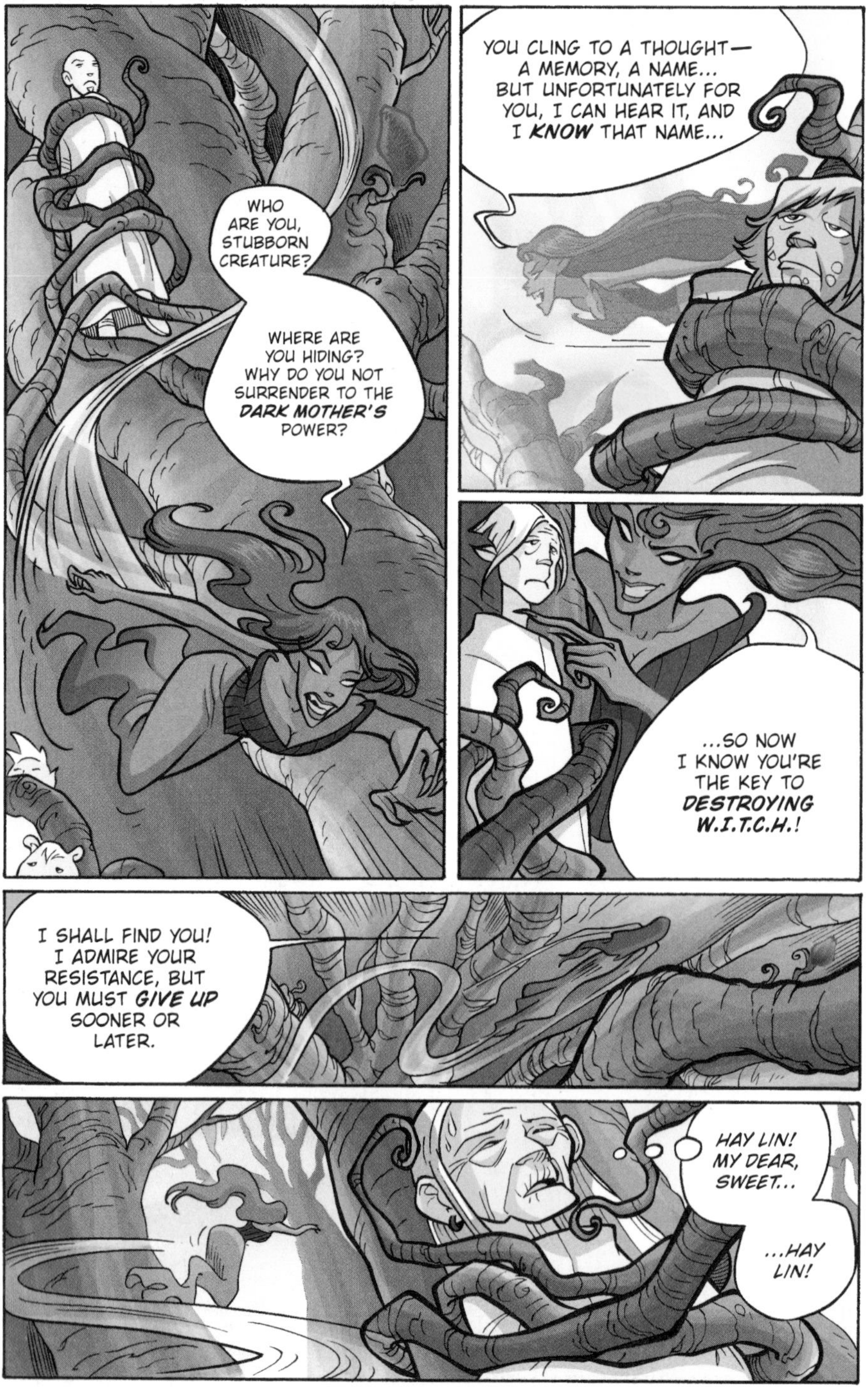
WHO ARE YOU, STUBBORN CREATURE?
WHERE ARE YOU HIDING? WHY DO YOU NOT SURRENDER TO THE DARK MOTHER'S POWER?
YOU CLING TO A THOUGHT— A MEMORY, A NAME... BUT UNFORTUNATELY FOR YOU, I CAN HEAR IT, AND I KNOW THAT NAME...
...SO NOW I KNOW YOU'RE THE KEY TO DESTROYING W.I.T.C.H.!
I SHALL FIND YOU! I ADMIRE YOUR RESISTANCE, BUT YOU MUST GIVE UP SOONER OR LATER.
HAY LIN! MY DEAR, SWEET...
...HAY LIN!

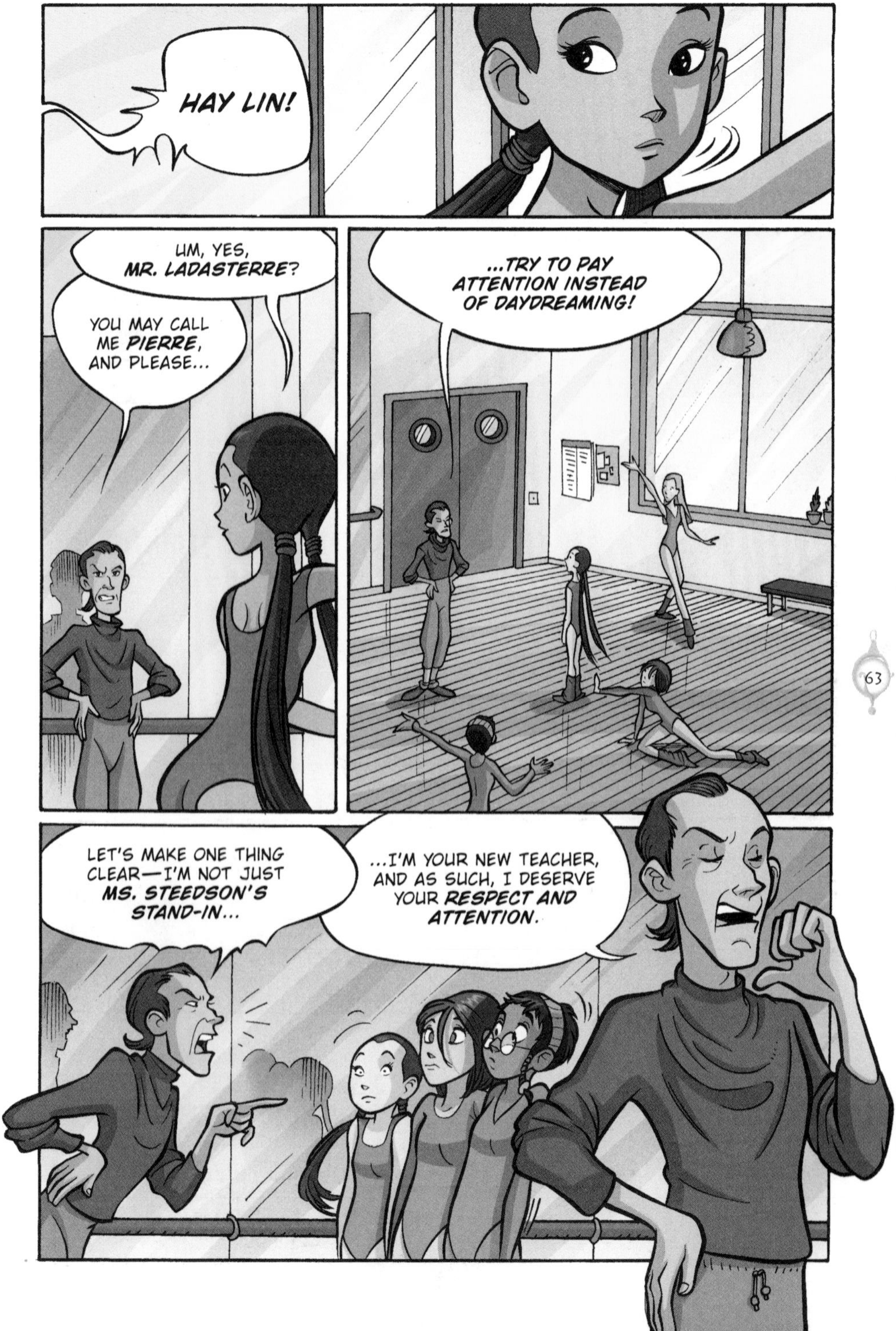
HAY LIN!
UM, YES, MR. LADASTERRE?
YOU MAY CALL ME PIERRE, AND PLEASE...
...TRY TO PAY ATTENTION INSTEAD OF DAYDREAMING!
LET'S MAKE ONE THING CLEAR—I'M NOT JUST MS. STEEDSON'S STAND-IN...
...I'M YOUR NEW TEACHER, AND AS SUCH, I DESERVE YOUR RESPECT AND ATTENTION.

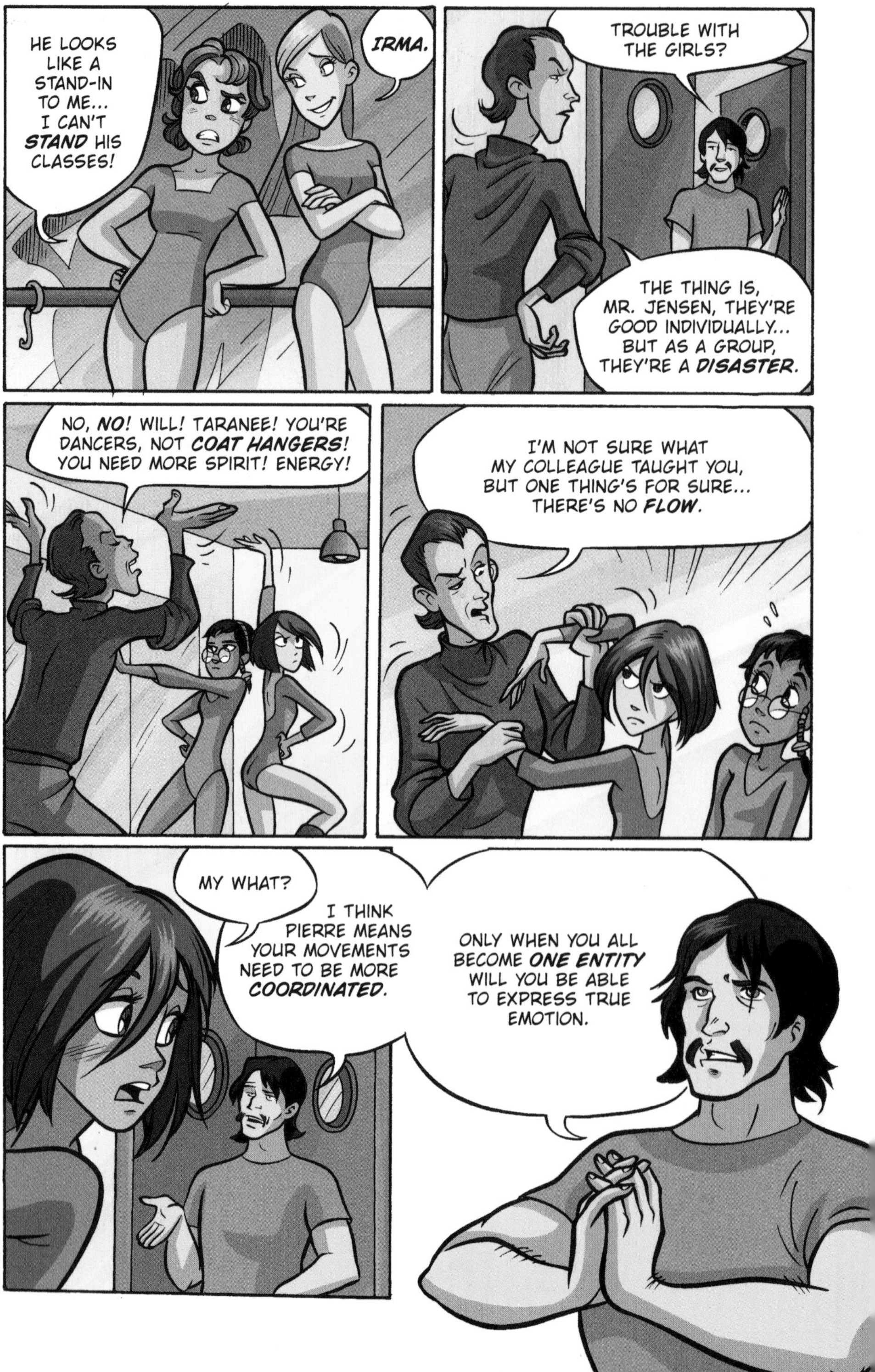
HE LOOKS LIKE A STAND-IN TO ME... I CAN'T STAND HIS CLASSES!
IRMA.
TROUBLE WITH THE GIRLS?
THE THING IS, MR. JENSEN, THEY'RE GOOD INDIVIDUALLY... BUT AS A GROUP, THEY'RE A DISASTER.
NO, NO! WILL! TARANEE! YOU'RE DANCERS, NOT COAT HANGERS! YOU NEED MORE SPIRIT! ENERGY!
I'M NOT SURE WHAT MY COLLEAGUE TAUGHT YOU, BUT ONE THING'S FOR SURE... THERE'S NO FLOW.
MY WHAT?
I THINK PIERRE MEANS YOUR MOVEMENTS NEED TO BE MORE COORDINATED.
ONLY WHEN YOU ALL BECOME ONE ENTITY WILL YOU BE ABLE TO EXPRESS TRUE EMOTION.

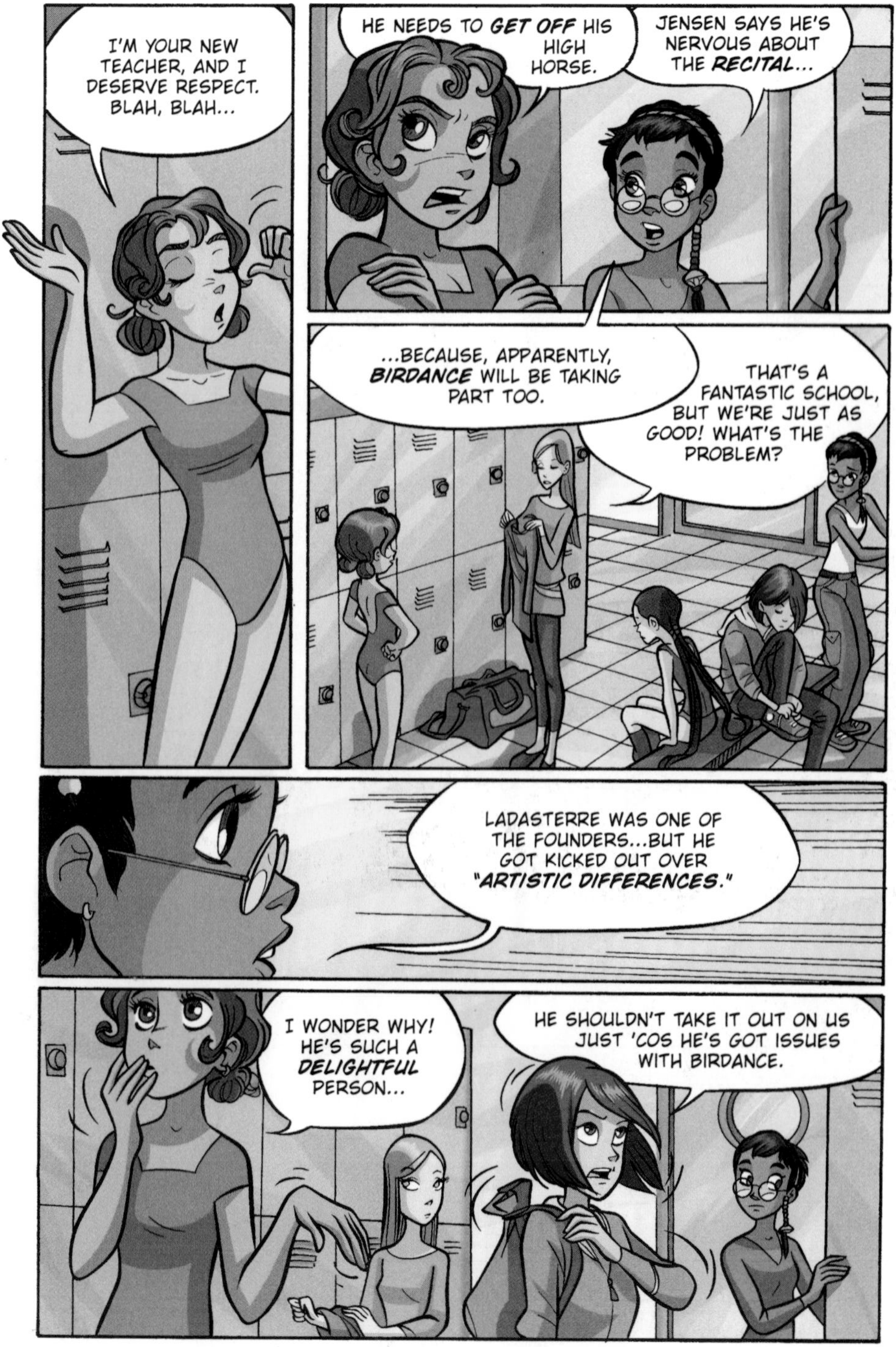

I'M YOUR NEW TEACHER, AND I DESERVE RESPECT. BLAH, BLAH...
HE NEEDS TO GET OFF HIS HIGH HORSE.
JENSEN SAYS HE'S NERVOUS ABOUT THE RECITAL...
...BECAUSE, APPARENTLY, BIRDANCE WILL BE TAKING PART TOO.
THAT'S A FANTASTIC SCHOOL, BUT WE'RE JUST AS GOOD! WHAT'S THE PROBLEM?
LADASTERRE WAS ONE OF THE FOUNDERS...BUT HE GOT KICKED OUT OVER "ARTISTIC DIFFERENCES."
I WONDER WHY! HE'S SUCH A DELIGHTFUL PERSON...
HE SHOULDN'T TAKE IT OUT ON US JUST 'COS HE'S GOT ISSUES WITH BIRDANCE.

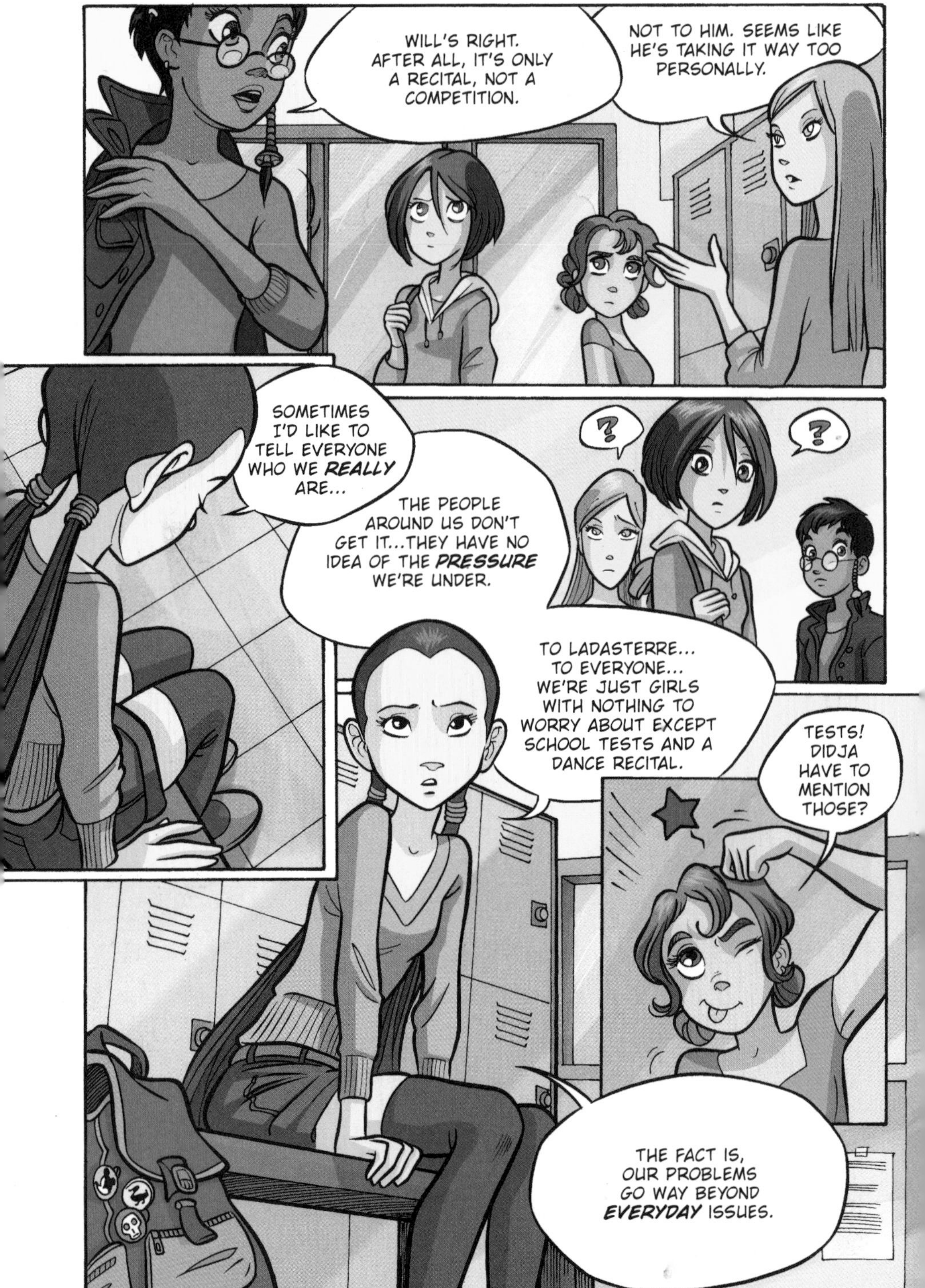
WILL'S RIGHT. AFTER ALL, IT'S ONLY A RECITAL, NOT A COMPETITION.
NOT TO HIM. SEEMS LIKE HE'S TAKING IT WAY TOO PERSONALLY.
SOMETIMES I'D LIKE TO TELL EVERYONE WHO WE REALLY ARE...
THE PEOPLE AROUND US DON'T GET IT...THEY HAVE NO IDEA OF THE PRESSURE WE'RE UNDER.
?
?
TO LADASTERRE... TO EVERYONE... WE'RE JUST GIRLS WITH NOTHING TO WORRY ABOUT EXCEPT SCHOOL TESTS AND A DANCE RECITAL.
TESTS! DIDJA HAVE TO MENTION THOSE?
THE FACT IS, OUR PROBLEMS GO WAY BEYOND EVERYDAY ISSUES.

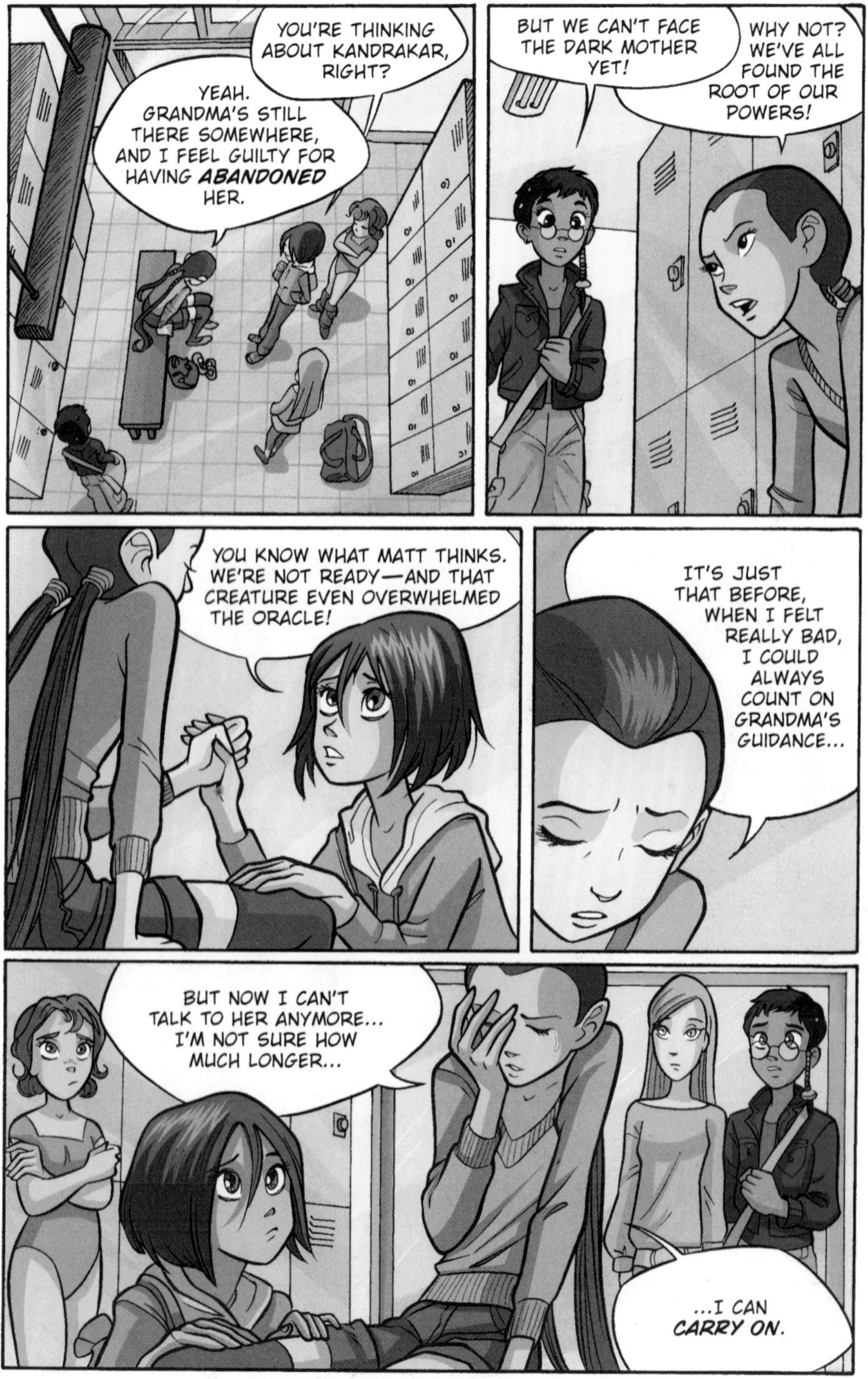
YOU'RE THINKING ABOUT KANDRAKAR, RIGHT?
YEAH. GRANDMA'S STILL THERE SOMEWHERE, AND I FEEL GUILTY FOR HAVING ***ABANDONED*** HER.
BUT WE CAN'T FACE THE DARK MOTHER YET!
WHY NOT? WE'VE ALL FOUND THE ROOT OF OUR POWERS!
YOU KNOW WHAT MATT THINKS. WE'RE NOT READY—AND THAT CREATURE EVEN OVERWHELMED THE ORACLE!
IT'S JUST THAT BEFORE, WHEN I FELT REALLY BAD, I COULD ALWAYS COUNT ON GRANDMA'S GUIDANCE...
BUT NOW I CAN'T TALK TO HER ANYMORE... I'M NOT SURE HOW MUCH LONGER...
...I CAN ***CARRY ON.***

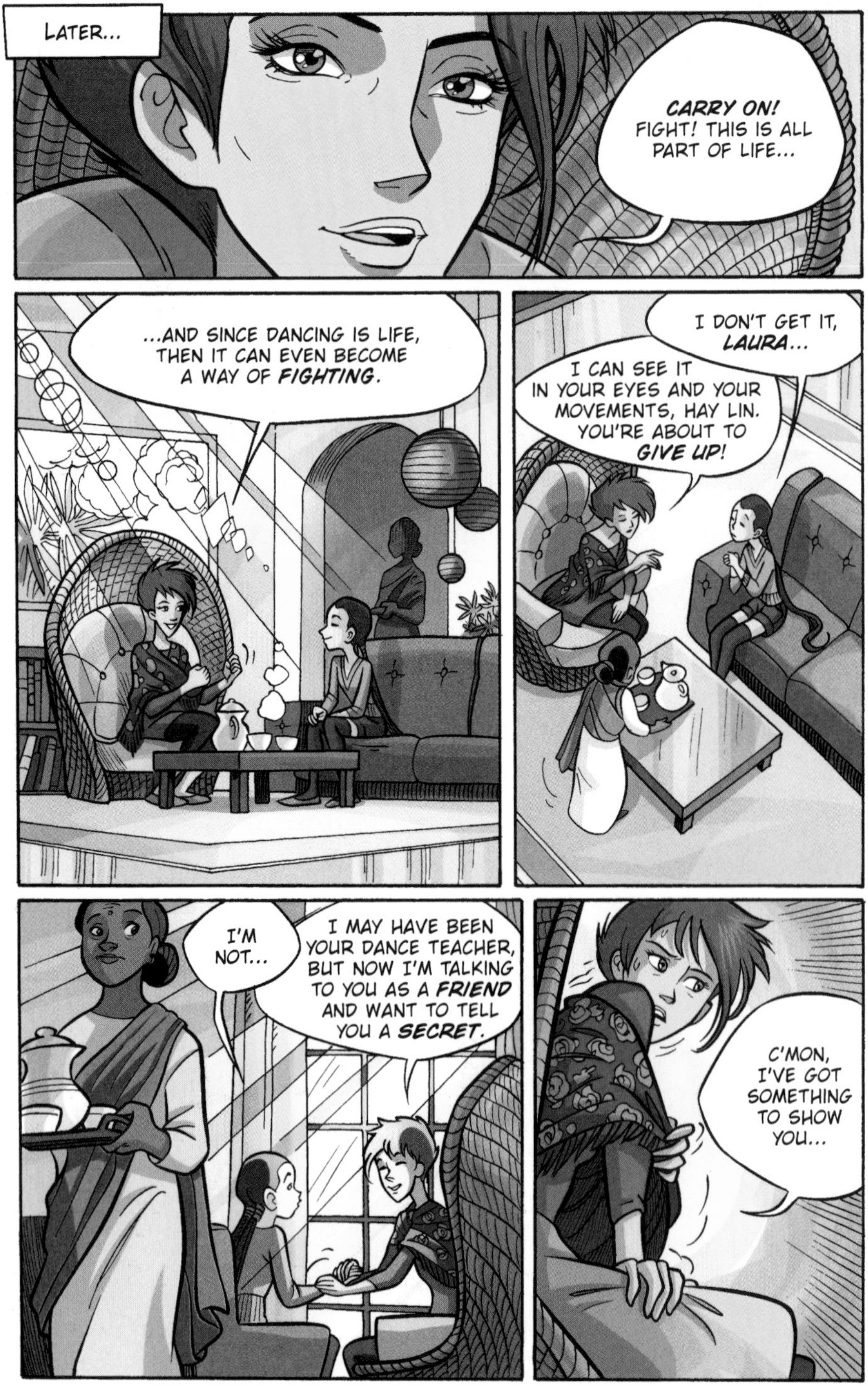
LATER...
CARRY ON! FIGHT! THIS IS ALL PART OF LIFE...
...AND SINCE DANCING IS LIFE, THEN IT CAN EVEN BECOME A WAY OF FIGHTING.
I DON'T GET IT, LAURA...
I CAN SEE IT IN YOUR EYES AND YOUR MOVEMENTS, HAY LIN. YOU'RE ABOUT TO GIVE UP!
I'M NOT...
I MAY HAVE BEEN YOUR DANCE TEACHER, BUT NOW I'M TALKING TO YOU AS A FRIEND AND WANT TO TELL YOU A SECRET.
C'MON, I'VE GOT SOMETHING TO SHOW YOU...

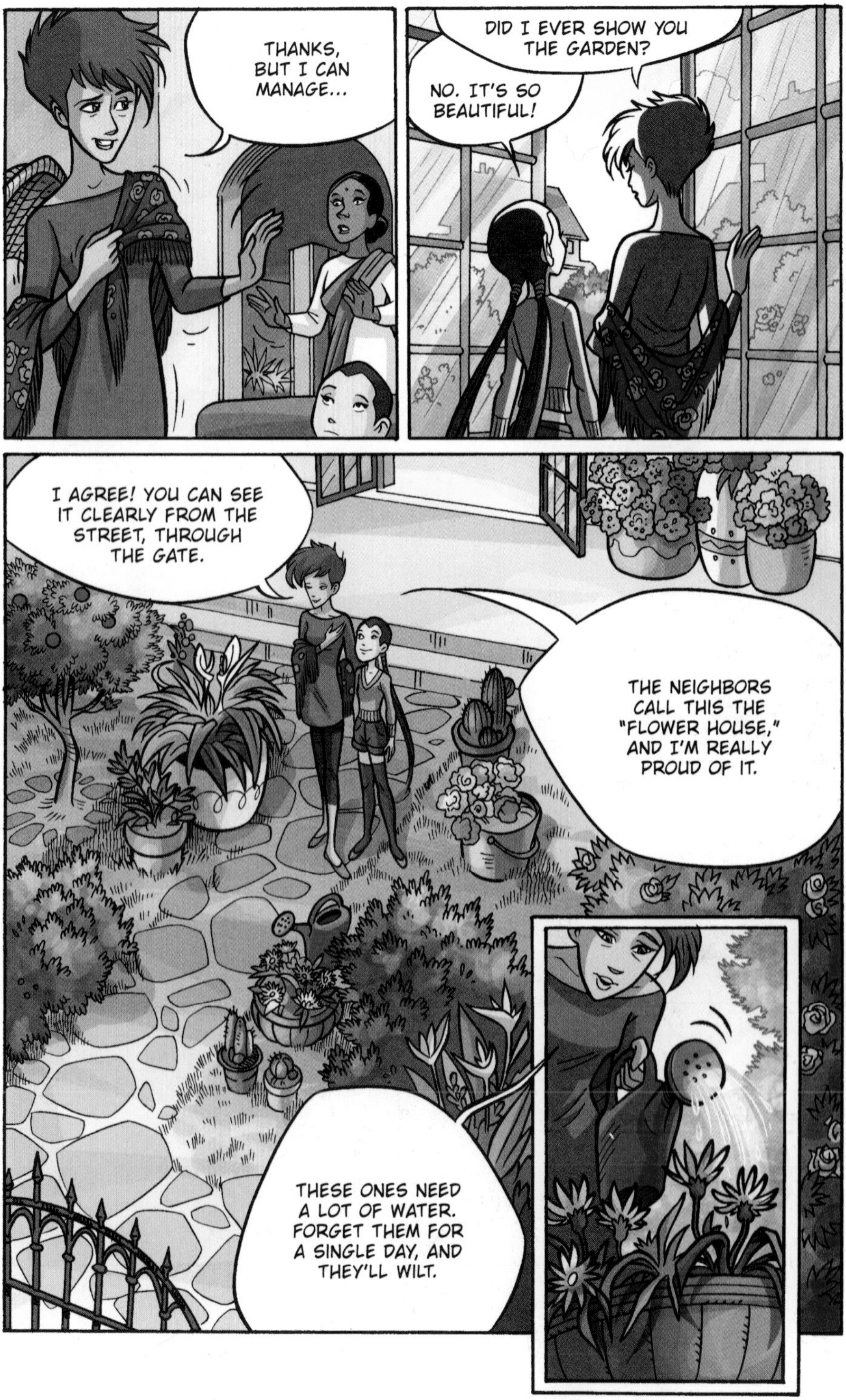
THANKS, BUT I CAN MANAGE...
DID I EVER SHOW YOU THE GARDEN?
NO. IT'S SO BEAUTIFUL!
I AGREE! YOU CAN SEE IT CLEARLY FROM THE STREET, THROUGH THE GATE.
THE NEIGHBORS CALL THIS THE "FLOWER HOUSE," AND I'M REALLY PROUD OF IT.
THESE ONES NEED A LOT OF WATER. FORGET THEM FOR A SINGLE DAY, AND THEY'LL WILT.

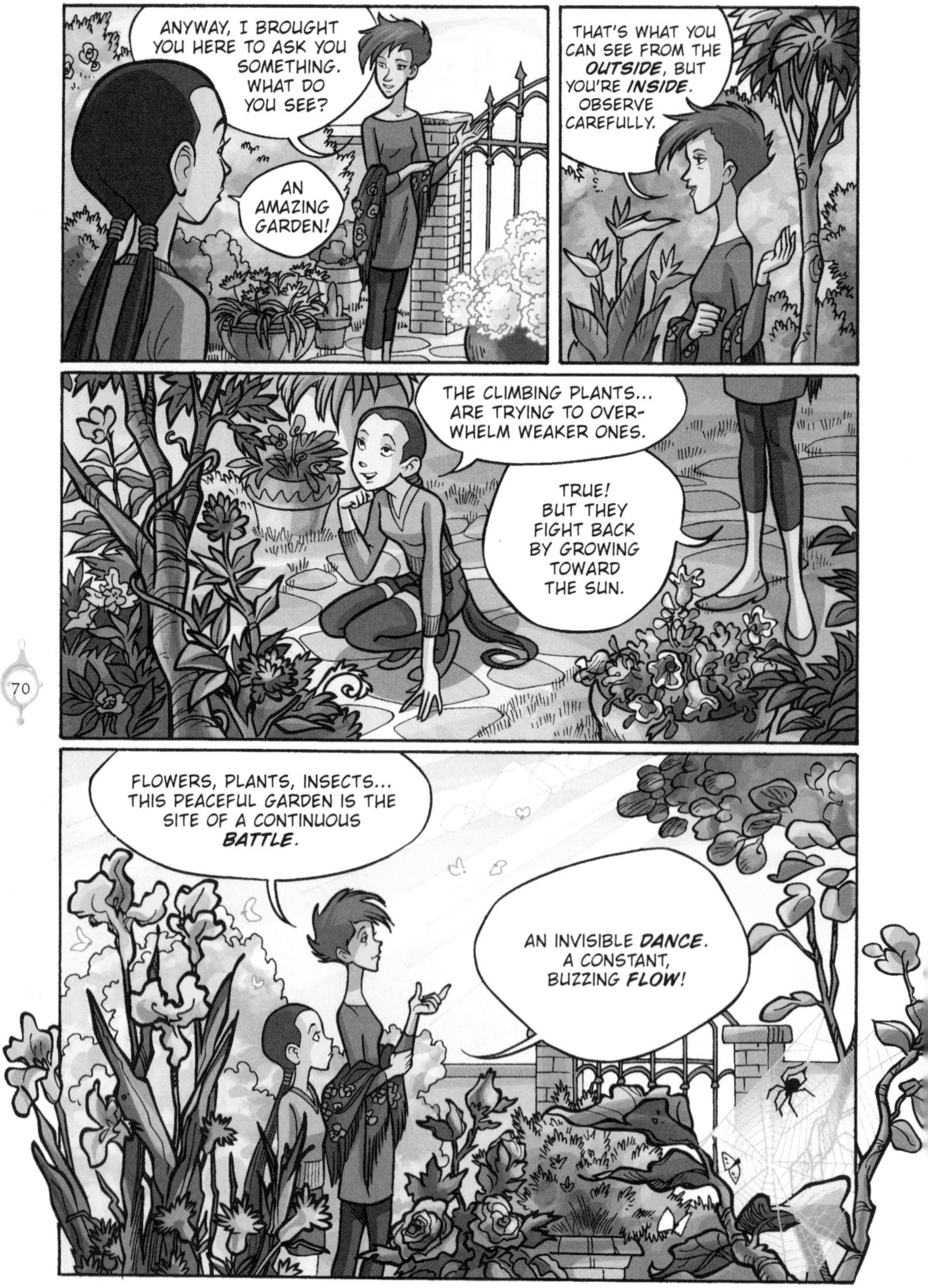
ANYWAY, I BROUGHT YOU HERE TO ASK YOU SOMETHING. WHAT DO YOU SEE?
AN AMAZING GARDEN!
THAT'S WHAT YOU CAN SEE FROM THE **OUTSIDE**, BUT YOU'RE **INSIDE**. OBSERVE CAREFULLY.
THE CLIMBING PLANTS... ARE TRYING TO OVER-WHELM WEAKER ONES.
TRUE! BUT THEY FIGHT BACK BY GROWING TOWARD THE SUN.
FLOWERS, PLANTS, INSECTS... THIS PEACEFUL GARDEN IS THE SITE OF A CONTINUOUS **BATTLE**.
AN INVISIBLE **DANCE**. A CONSTANT, BUZZING **FLOW**!

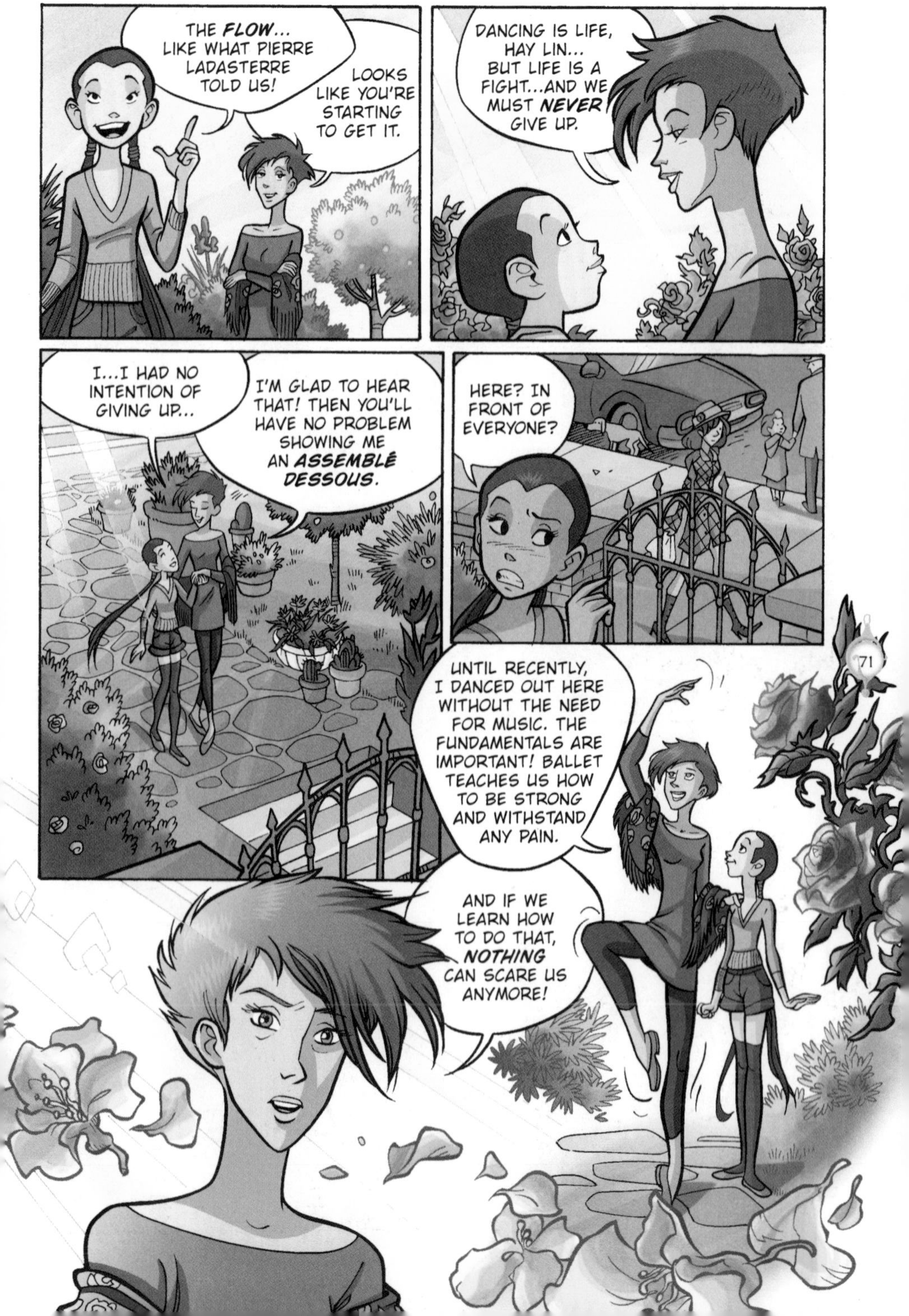
THE FLOW... LIKE WHAT PIERRE LADASTERRE TOLD US!
LOOKS LIKE YOU'RE STARTING TO GET IT.
DANCING IS LIFE, HAY LIN... BUT LIFE IS A FIGHT...AND WE MUST NEVER GIVE UP.
I...I HAD NO INTENTION OF GIVING UP...
I'M GLAD TO HEAR THAT! THEN YOU'LL HAVE NO PROBLEM SHOWING ME AN ASSEMBLÉ DESSOUS.
HERE? IN FRONT OF EVERYONE?
UNTIL RECENTLY, I DANCED OUT HERE WITHOUT THE NEED FOR MUSIC. THE FUNDAMENTALS ARE IMPORTANT! BALLET TEACHES US HOW TO BE STRONG AND WITHSTAND ANY PAIN.
AND IF WE LEARN HOW TO DO THAT, NOTHING CAN SCARE US ANYMORE!

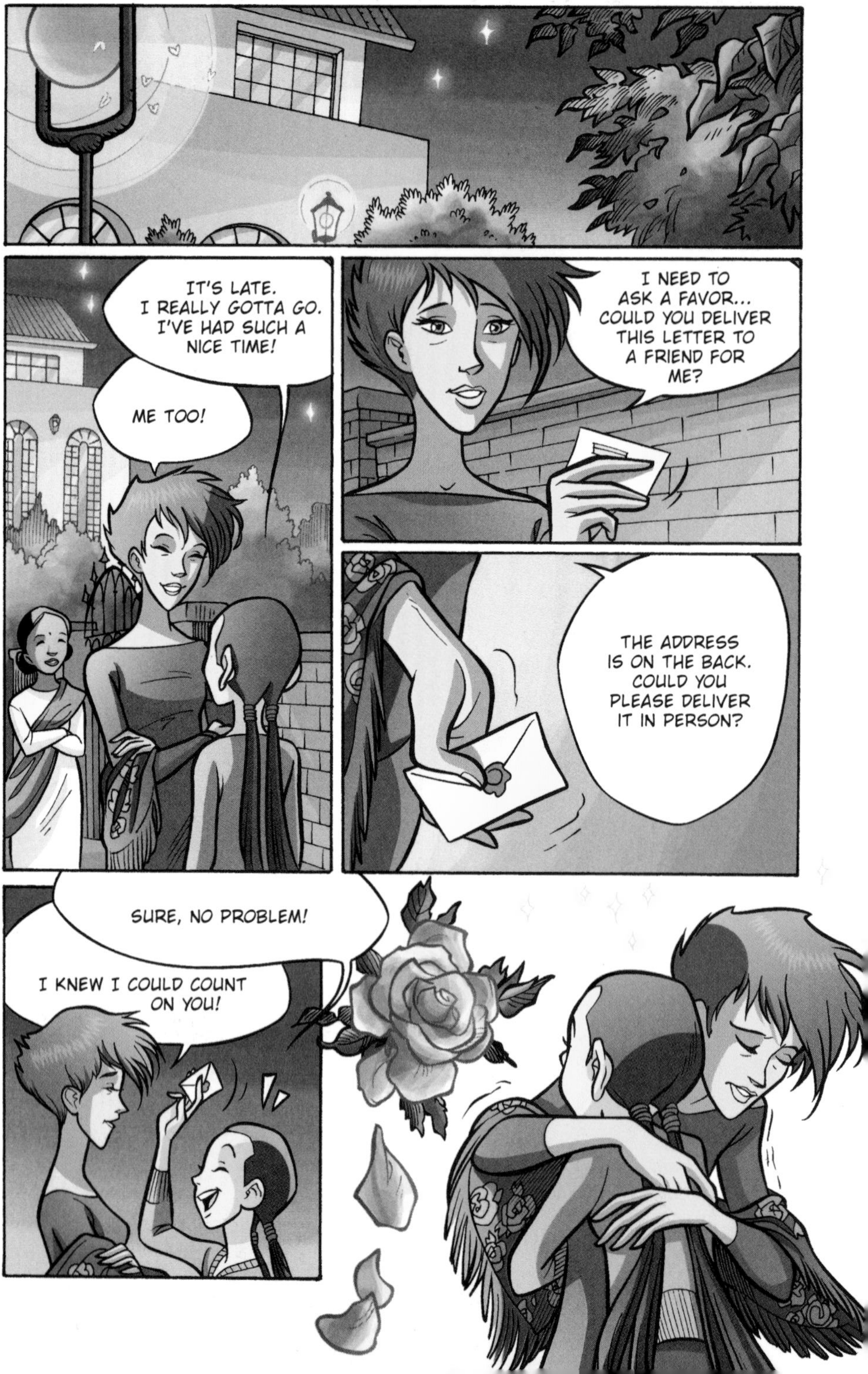
IT'S LATE. I REALLY GOTTA GO. I'VE HAD SUCH A NICE TIME!
ME TOO!
I NEED TO ASK A FAVOR... COULD YOU DELIVER THIS LETTER TO A FRIEND FOR ME?
THE ADDRESS IS ON THE BACK. COULD YOU PLEASE DELIVER IT IN PERSON?
SURE, NO PROBLEM!
I KNEW I COULD COUNT ON YOU!

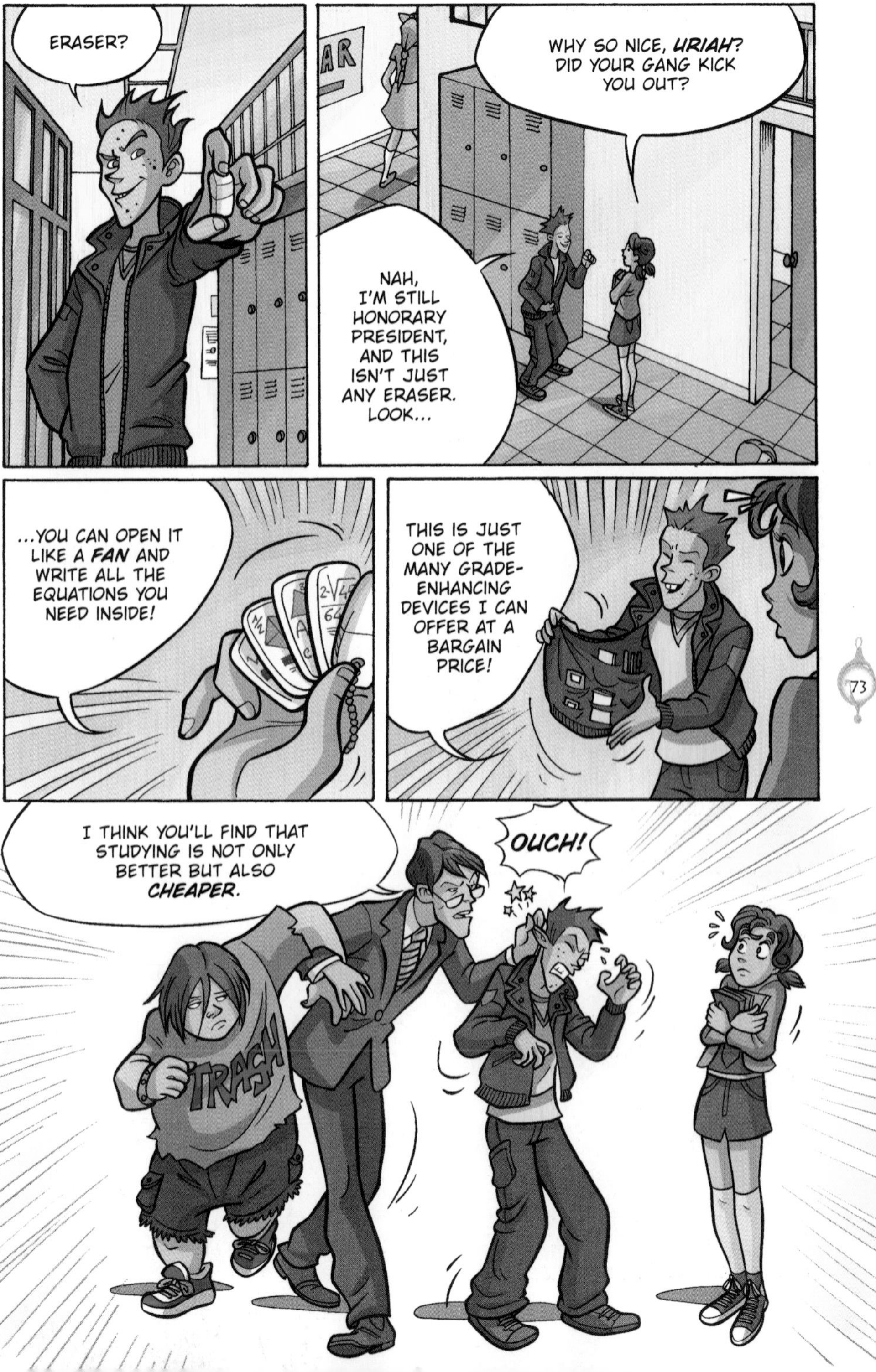
ERASER?
WHY SO NICE, URIAH? DID YOUR GANG KICK YOU OUT?
NAH, I'M STILL HONORARY PRESIDENT, AND THIS ISN'T JUST ANY ERASER. LOOK...
...YOU CAN OPEN IT LIKE A FAN AND WRITE ALL THE EQUATIONS YOU NEED INSIDE!
THIS IS JUST ONE OF THE MANY GRADE-ENHANCING DEVICES I CAN OFFER AT A BARGAIN PRICE!
I THINK YOU'LL FIND THAT STUDYING IS NOT ONLY BETTER BUT ALSO CHEAPER.
OUCH!
TRASH

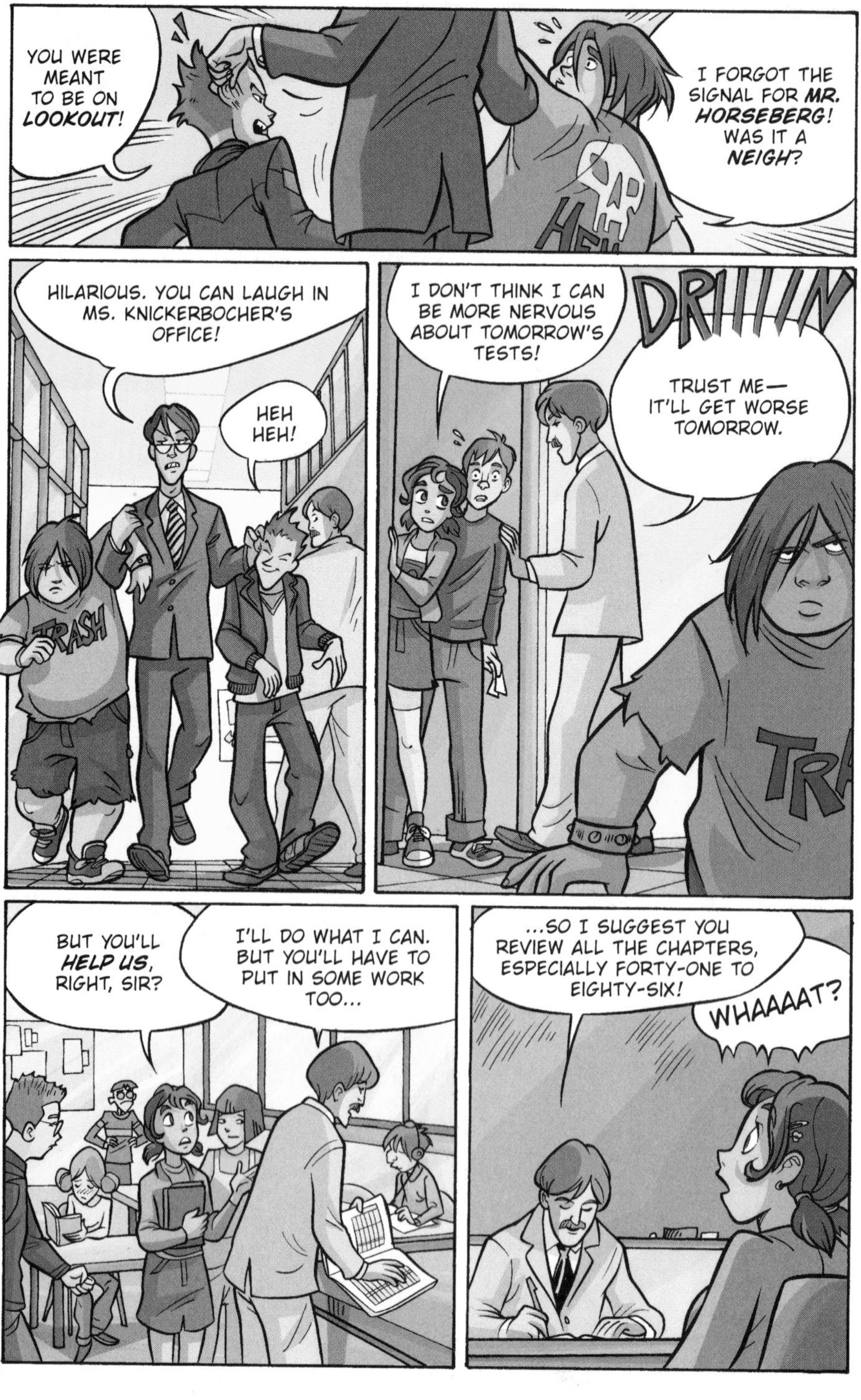

YOU WERE MEANT TO BE ON LOOKOUT!
I FORGOT THE SIGNAL FOR MR. HORSEBERG! WAS IT A NEIGH?
HILARIOUS. YOU CAN LAUGH IN MS. KNICKERBOCHER'S OFFICE!
HEH HEH!
TRASH
I DON'T THINK I CAN BE MORE NERVOUS ABOUT TOMORROW'S TESTS!
DRIIIIN
TRUST ME— IT'LL GET WORSE TOMORROW.
TRA
BUT YOU'LL HELP US, RIGHT, SIR?
I'LL DO WHAT I CAN. BUT YOU'LL HAVE TO PUT IN SOME WORK TOO...
...SO I SUGGEST YOU REVIEW ALL THE CHAPTERS, ESPECIALLY FORTY-ONE TO EIGHTY-SIX!
WHAAAAT?

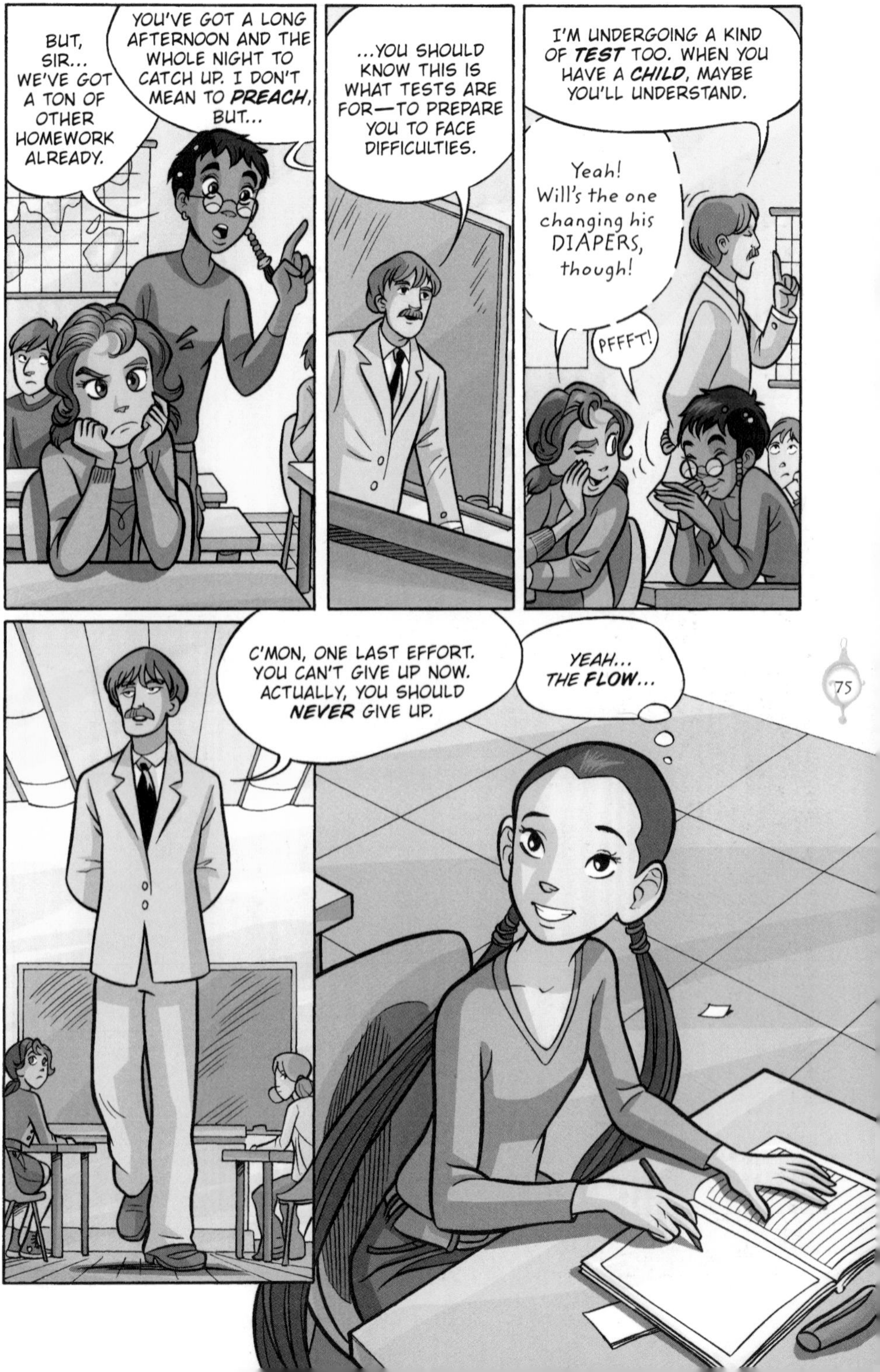
BUT, SIR... WE'VE GOT A TON OF OTHER HOMEWORK ALREADY.
YOU'VE GOT A LONG AFTERNOON AND THE WHOLE NIGHT TO CATCH UP. I DON'T MEAN TO PREACH, BUT...
...YOU SHOULD KNOW THIS IS WHAT TESTS ARE FOR—TO PREPARE YOU TO FACE DIFFICULTIES.
I'M UNDERGOING A KIND OF TEST TOO. WHEN YOU HAVE A CHILD, MAYBE YOU'LL UNDERSTAND.
Yeah! Will's the one changing his DIAPERS, though!
PFFFT!
C'MON, ONE LAST EFFORT. YOU CAN'T GIVE UP NOW. ACTUALLY, YOU SHOULD NEVER GIVE UP.
YEAH... THE FLOW...

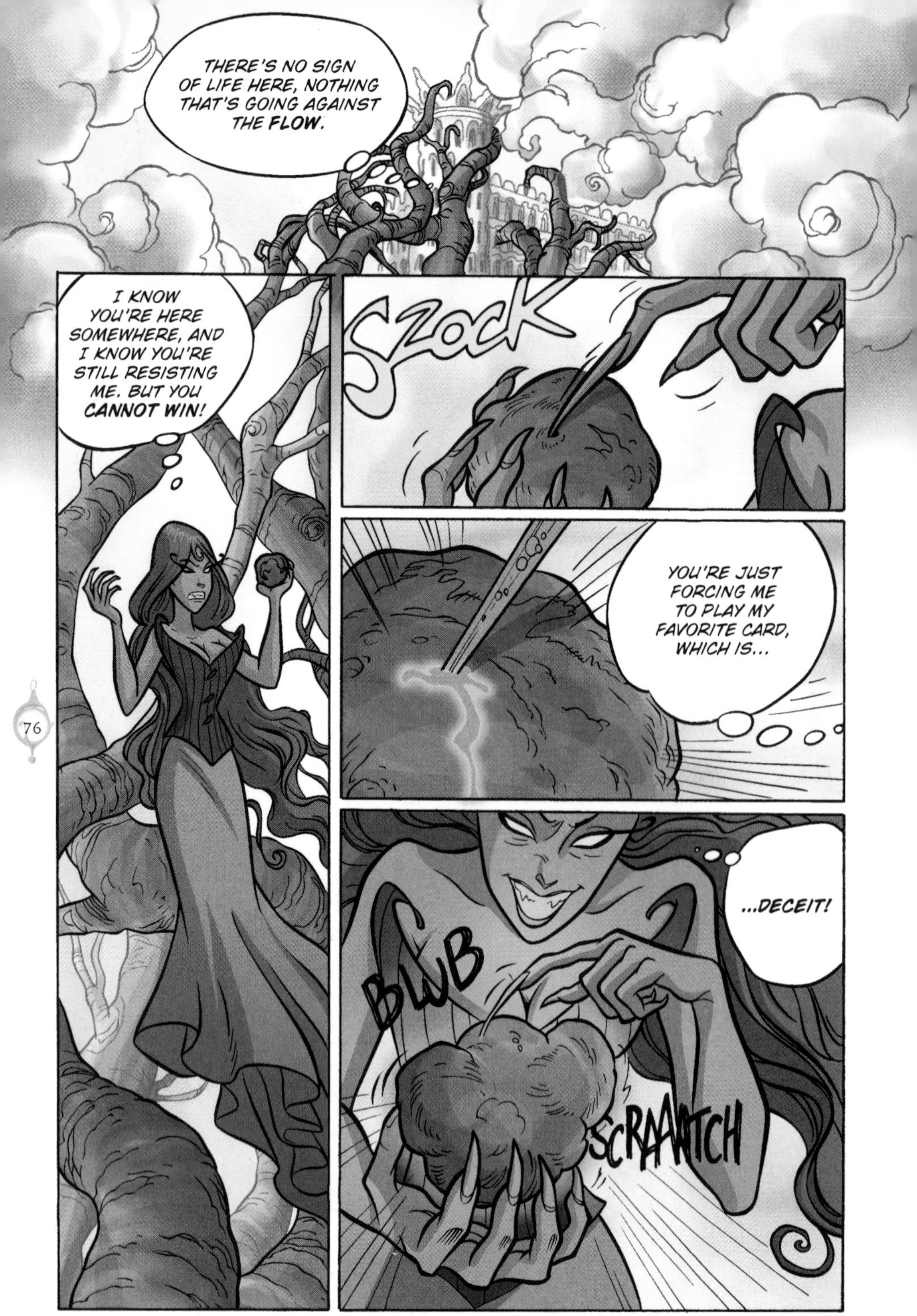
THERE'S NO SIGN OF LIFE HERE, NOTHING THAT'S GOING AGAINST THE FLOW.
I KNOW YOU'RE HERE SOMEWHERE, AND I KNOW YOU'RE STILL RESISTING ME. BUT YOU CANNOT WIN!
SZOCK
YOU'RE JUST FORCING ME TO PLAY MY FAVORITE CARD, WHICH IS...
...DECEIT!
BWB
SCRAAWTCH

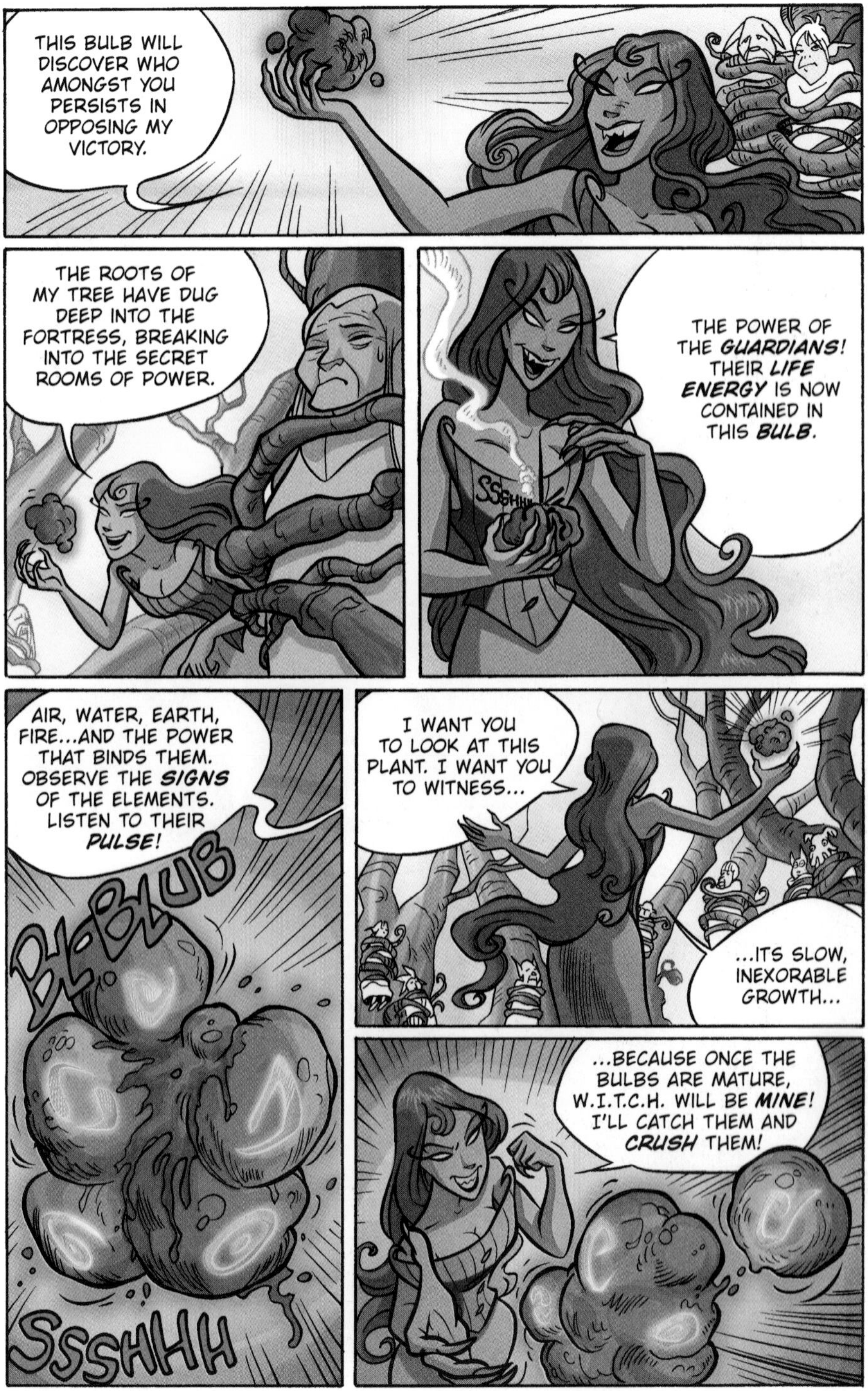

THIS BULB WILL DISCOVER WHO AMONGST YOU PERSISTS IN OPPOSING MY VICTORY.
THE ROOTS OF MY TREE HAVE DUG DEEP INTO THE FORTRESS, BREAKING INTO THE SECRET ROOMS OF POWER.
THE POWER OF THE GUARDIANS! THEIR LIFE ENERGY IS NOW CONTAINED IN THIS BULB.
SSSHHH
AIR, WATER, EARTH, FIRE...AND THE POWER THAT BINDS THEM. OBSERVE THE SIGNS OF THE ELEMENTS. LISTEN TO THEIR PULSE!
BL-BLUB
SSSHHH
I WANT YOU TO LOOK AT THIS PLANT. I WANT YOU TO WITNESS...
...ITS SLOW, INEXORABLE GROWTH...
...BECAUSE ONCE THE BULBS ARE MATURE, W.I.T.C.H. WILL BE MINE! I'LL CATCH THEM AND CRUSH THEM!

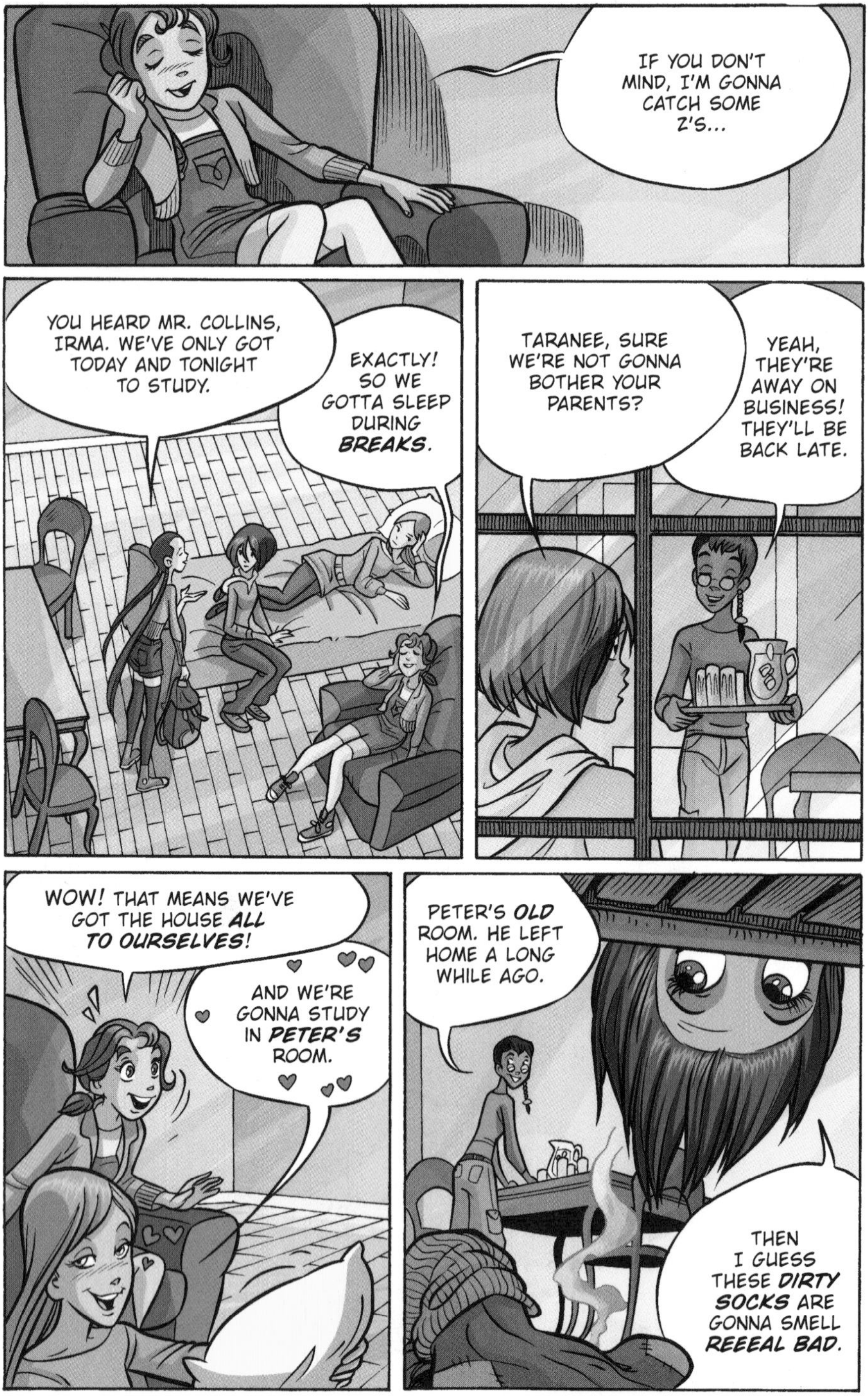
IF YOU DON'T MIND, I'M GONNA CATCH SOME Z'S...
YOU HEARD MR. COLLINS, IRMA. WE'VE ONLY GOT TODAY AND TONIGHT TO STUDY.
EXACTLY! SO WE GOTTA SLEEP DURING **BREAKS**.
TARANEE, SURE WE'RE NOT GONNA BOTHER YOUR PARENTS?
YEAH, THEY'RE AWAY ON BUSINESS! THEY'LL BE BACK LATE.
WOW! THAT MEANS WE'VE GOT THE HOUSE **ALL TO OURSELVES**!
AND WE'RE GONNA STUDY IN **PETER'S** ROOM.
PETER'S **OLD** ROOM. HE LEFT HOME A LONG WHILE AGO.
THEN I GUESS THESE **DIRTY SOCKS** ARE GONNA SMELL **REEEAL BAD**.

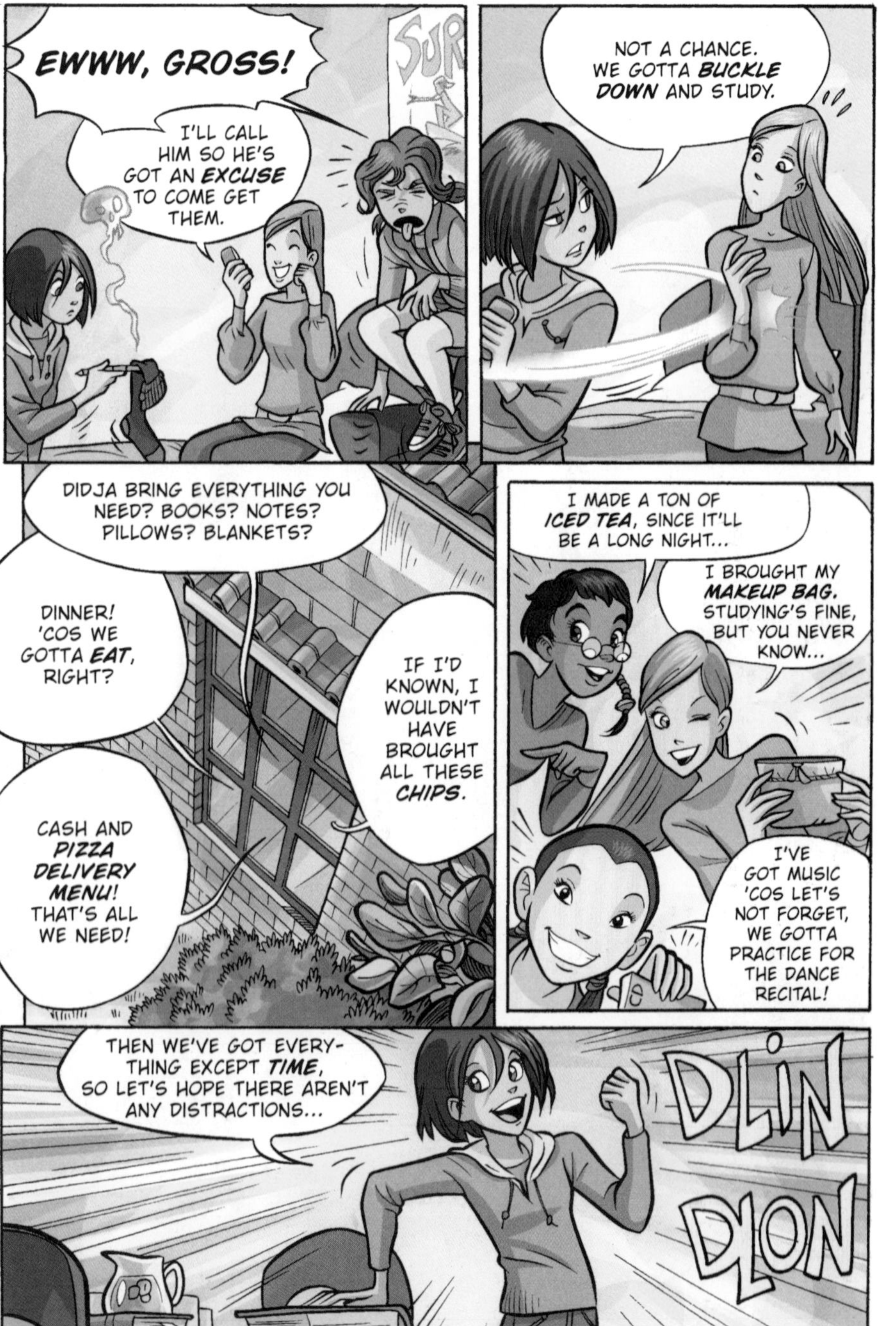
EWWW, GROSS!
I'LL CALL HIM SO HE'S GOT AN EXCUSE TO COME GET THEM.
NOT A CHANCE. WE GOTTA BUCKLE DOWN AND STUDY.
DIDJA BRING EVERYTHING YOU NEED? BOOKS? NOTES? PILLOWS? BLANKETS?
DINNER! 'COS WE GOTTA EAT, RIGHT?
IF I'D KNOWN, I WOULDN'T HAVE BROUGHT ALL THESE CHIPS.
CASH AND PIZZA DELIVERY MENU! THAT'S ALL WE NEED!
I MADE A TON OF ICED TEA, SINCE IT'LL BE A LONG NIGHT...
I BROUGHT MY MAKEUP BAG. STUDYING'S FINE, BUT YOU NEVER KNOW...
I'VE GOT MUSIC 'COS LET'S NOT FORGET, WE GOTTA PRACTICE FOR THE DANCE RECITAL!
THEN WE'VE GOT EVERY-THING EXCEPT TIME, SO LET'S HOPE THERE AREN'T ANY DISTRACTIONS...
DLIN
DLON

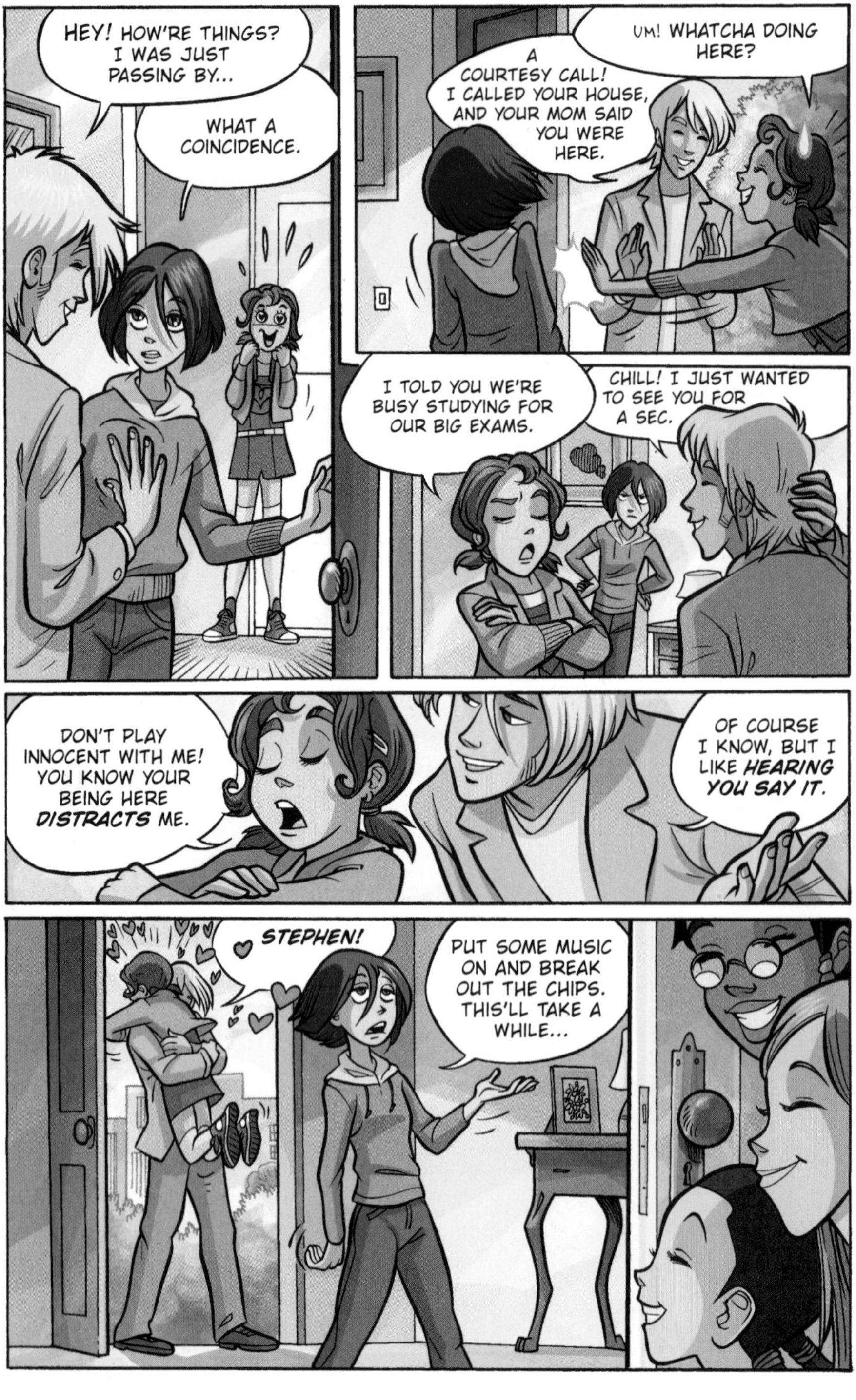
HEY! HOW'RE THINGS? I WAS JUST PASSING BY...
WHAT A COINCIDENCE.
UM! WHATCHA DOING HERE?
A COURTESY CALL! I CALLED YOUR HOUSE, AND YOUR MOM SAID YOU WERE HERE.
I TOLD YOU WE'RE BUSY STUDYING FOR OUR BIG EXAMS.
CHILL! I JUST WANTED TO SEE YOU FOR A SEC.
DON'T PLAY INNOCENT WITH ME! YOU KNOW YOUR BEING HERE *DISTRACTS* ME.
OF COURSE I KNOW, BUT I LIKE *HEARING YOU SAY IT*.
STEPHEN!
PUT SOME MUSIC ON AND BREAK OUT THE CHIPS. THIS'LL TAKE A WHILE...

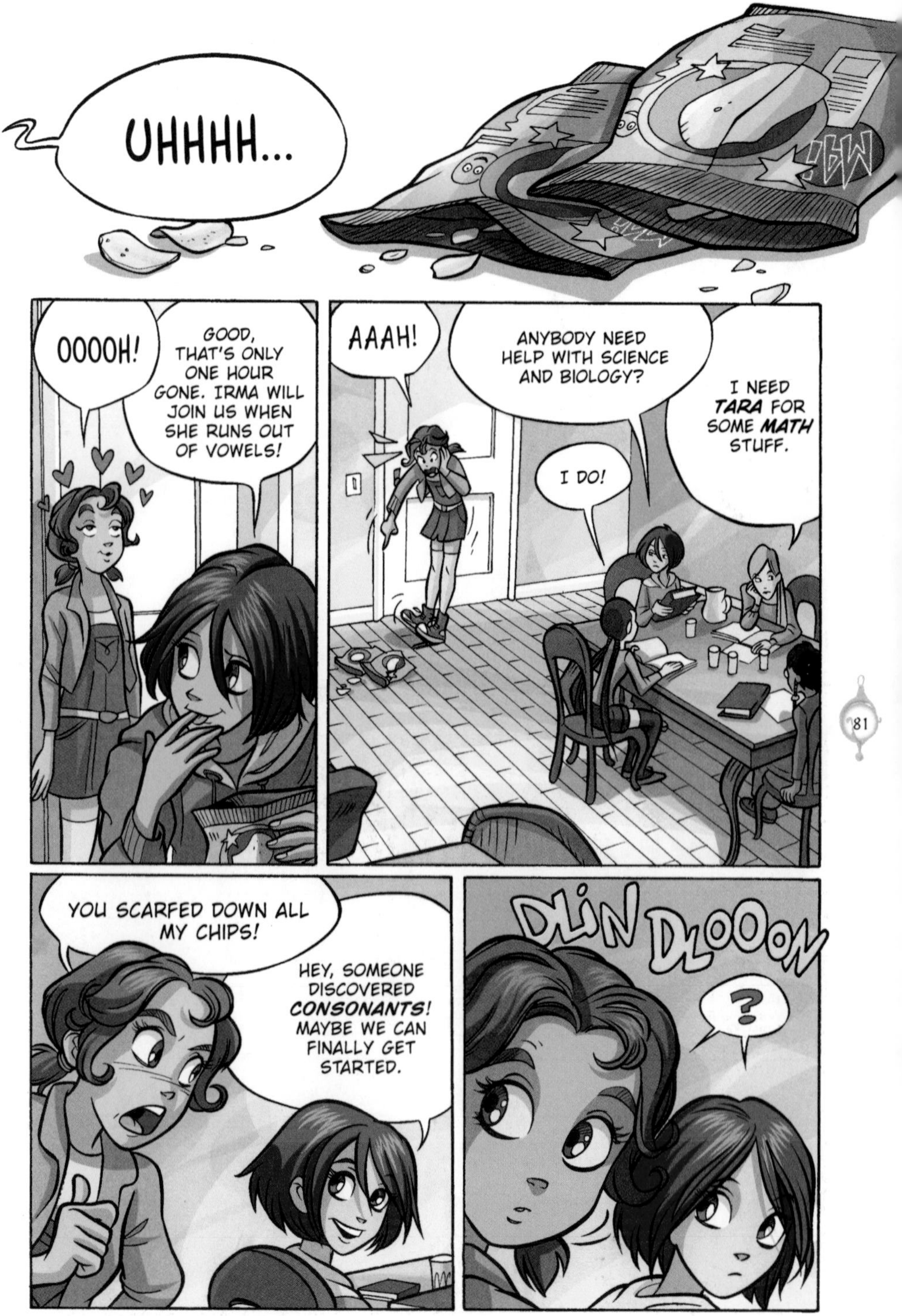
UHHHH...
OOOOH!
GOOD, THAT'S ONLY ONE HOUR GONE. IRMA WILL JOIN US WHEN SHE RUNS OUT OF VOWELS!
AAAH!
ANYBODY NEED HELP WITH SCIENCE AND BIOLOGY?
I DO!
I NEED TARA FOR SOME MATH STUFF.
YOU SCARFED DOWN ALL MY CHIPS!
HEY, SOMEONE DISCOVERED CONSONANTS! MAYBE WE CAN FINALLY GET STARTED.
DLIN DLOOON
?

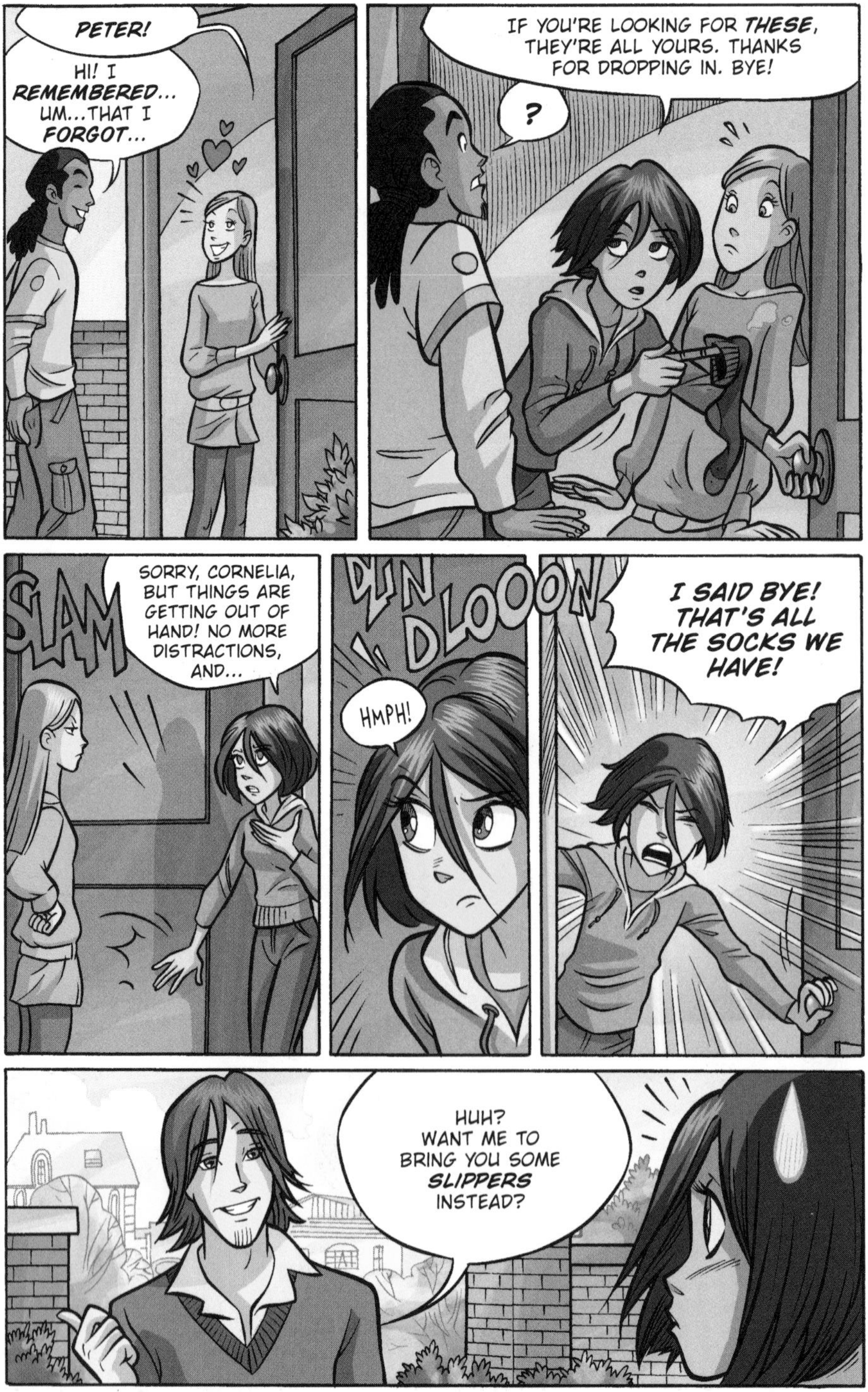
PETER!
HI! I REMEMBERED... UM...THAT I FORGOT...
IF YOU'RE LOOKING FOR THESE, THEY'RE ALL YOURS. THANKS FOR DROPPING IN. BYE!
?
SLAM
SORRY, CORNELIA, BUT THINGS ARE GETTING OUT OF HAND! NO MORE DISTRACTIONS, AND...
DIN
DLOOON
HMPH!
I SAID BYE! THAT'S ALL THE SOCKS WE HAVE!
HUH? WANT ME TO BRING YOU SOME SLIPPERS INSTEAD?

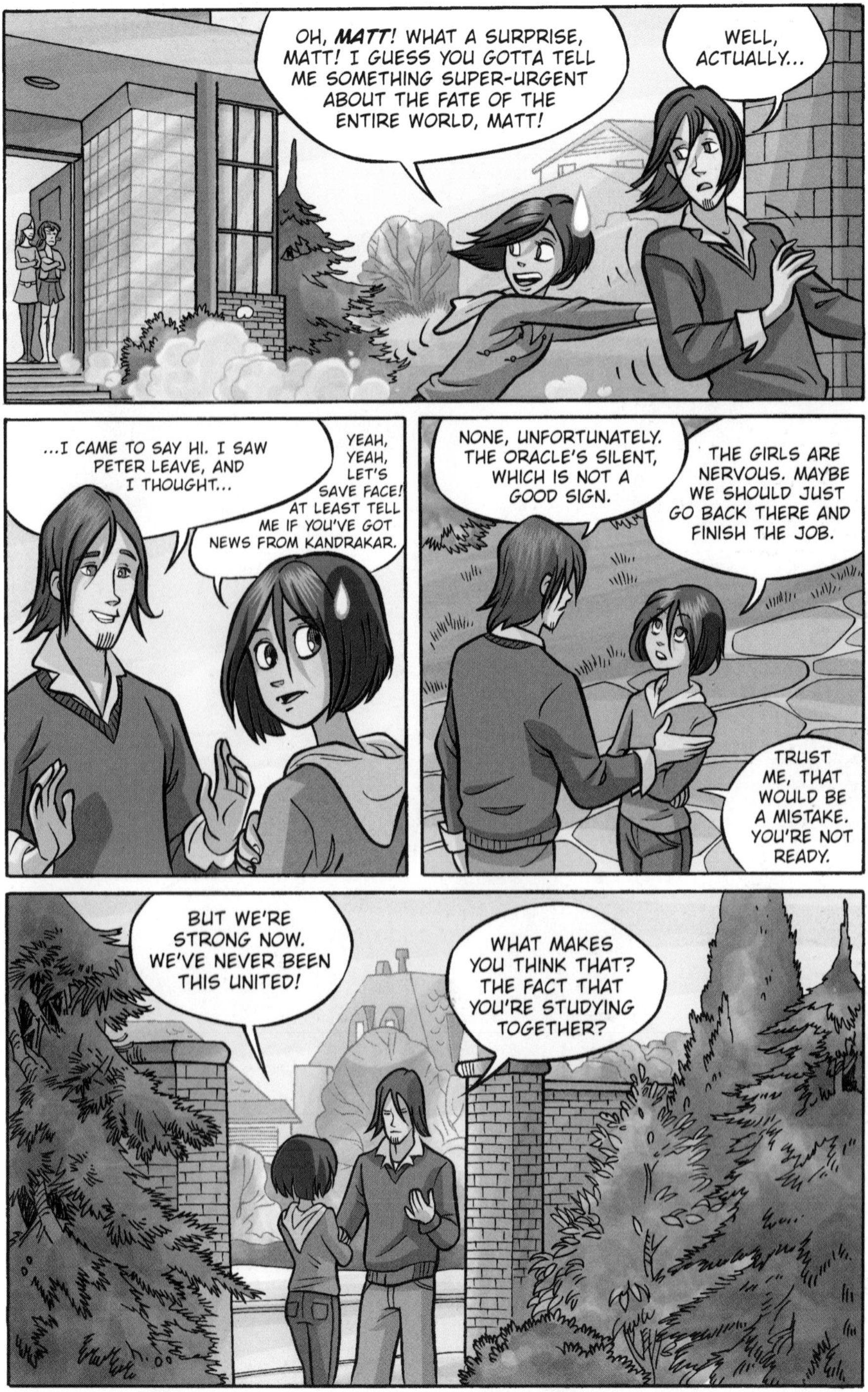
OH, MATT! WHAT A SURPRISE, MATT! I GUESS YOU GOTTA TELL ME SOMETHING SUPER-URGENT ABOUT THE FATE OF THE ENTIRE WORLD, MATT!
WELL, ACTUALLY...
...I CAME TO SAY HI. I SAW PETER LEAVE, AND I THOUGHT...
YEAH, YEAH, LET'S SAVE FACE! AT LEAST TELL ME IF YOU'VE GOT NEWS FROM KANDRAKAR.
NONE, UNFORTUNATELY. THE ORACLE'S SILENT, WHICH IS NOT A GOOD SIGN.
THE GIRLS ARE NERVOUS. MAYBE WE SHOULD JUST GO BACK THERE AND FINISH THE JOB.
TRUST ME, THAT WOULD BE A MISTAKE. YOU'RE NOT READY.
BUT WE'RE STRONG NOW. WE'VE NEVER BEEN THIS UNITED!
WHAT MAKES YOU THINK THAT? THE FACT THAT YOU'RE STUDYING TOGETHER?

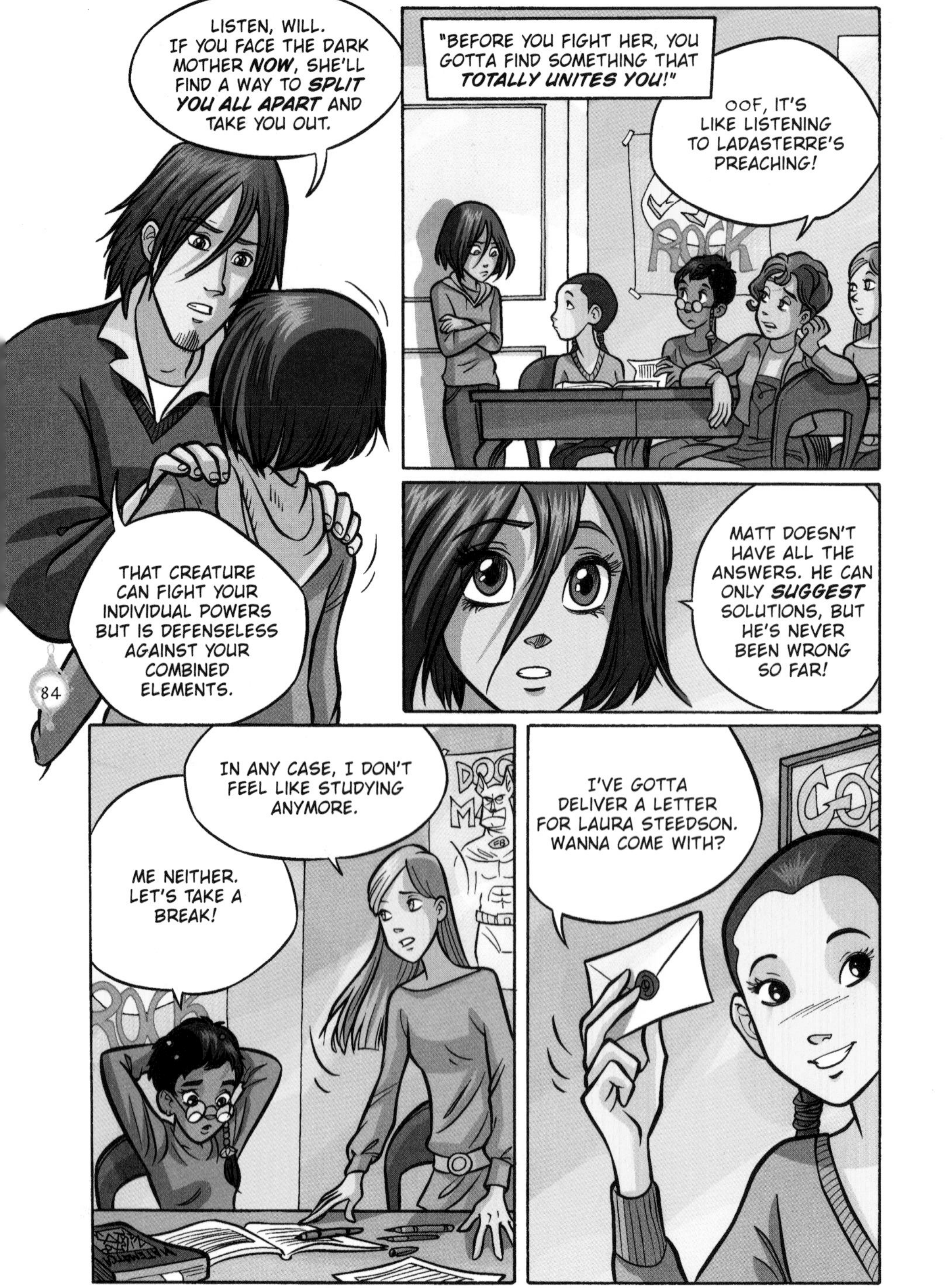
LISTEN, WILL. IF YOU FACE THE DARK MOTHER NOW, SHE'LL FIND A WAY TO SPLIT YOU ALL APART AND TAKE YOU OUT.
THAT CREATURE CAN FIGHT YOUR INDIVIDUAL POWERS BUT IS DEFENSELESS AGAINST YOUR COMBINED ELEMENTS.
"BEFORE YOU FIGHT HER, YOU GOTTA FIND SOMETHING THAT TOTALLY UNITES YOU!"
OOF, IT'S LIKE LISTENING TO LADASTERRE'S PREACHING!
ROCK
MATT DOESN'T HAVE ALL THE ANSWERS. HE CAN ONLY SUGGEST SOLUTIONS, BUT HE'S NEVER BEEN WRONG SO FAR!
IN ANY CASE, I DON'T FEEL LIKE STUDYING ANYMORE.
ME NEITHER. LET'S TAKE A BREAK!
I'VE GOTTA DELIVER A LETTER FOR LAURA STEEDSON. WANNA COME WITH?

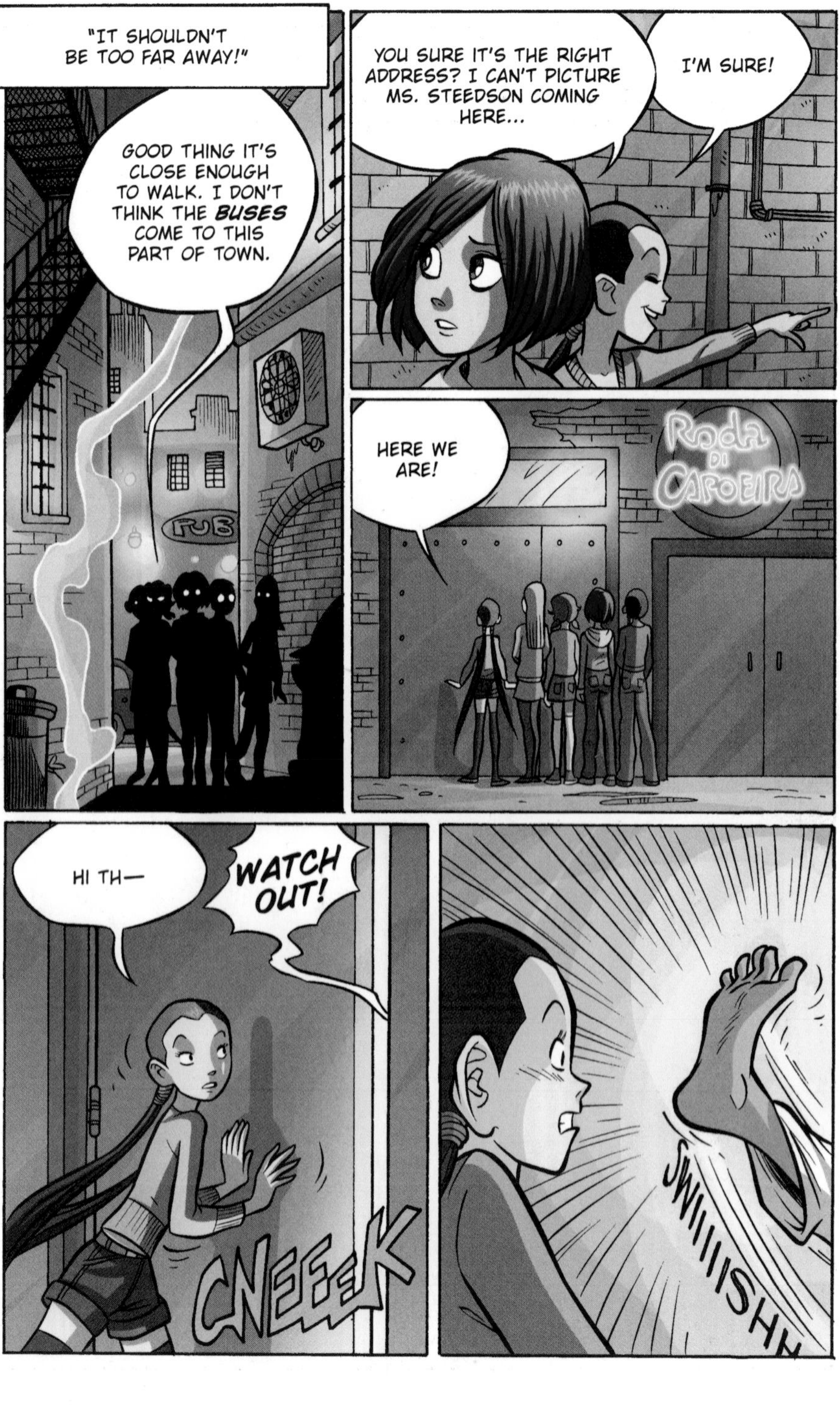
"IT SHOULDN'T BE TOO FAR AWAY!"
GOOD THING IT'S CLOSE ENOUGH TO WALK. I DON'T THINK THE BUSES COME TO THIS PART OF TOWN.
PUB
YOU SURE IT'S THE RIGHT ADDRESS? I CAN'T PICTURE MS. STEEDSON COMING HERE...
I'M SURE!
HERE WE ARE!
Roda di Capoeira
HI TH—
WATCH OUT!
CNEEEK
SWIIIIISHH

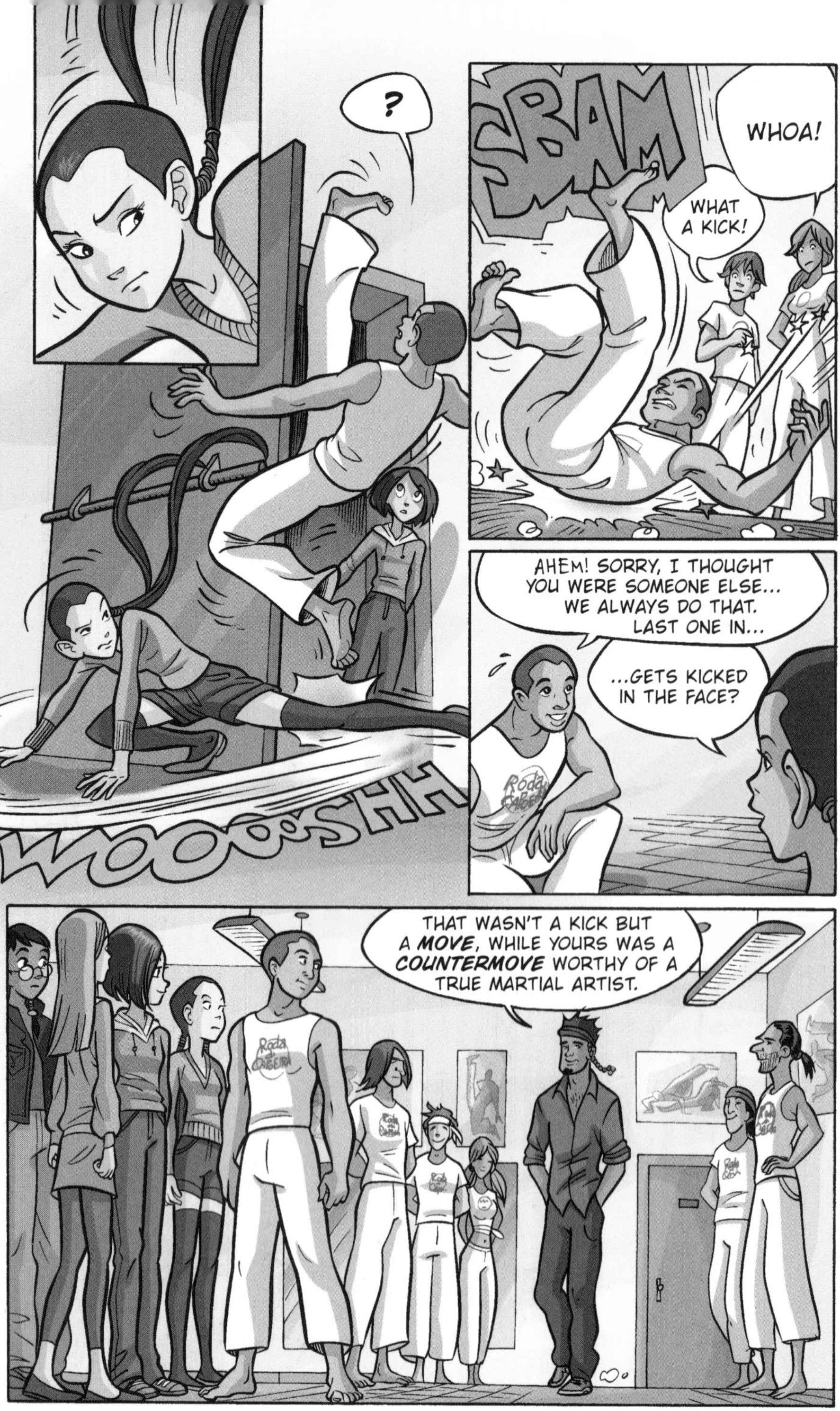
?
SBAM
WHOA!
WHAT A KICK!
WOOOSHH
AHEM! SORRY, I THOUGHT YOU WERE SOMEONE ELSE... WE ALWAYS DO THAT. LAST ONE IN...
...GETS KICKED IN THE FACE?
THAT WASN'T A KICK BUT A **MOVE**, WHILE YOURS WAS A **COUNTERMOVE** WORTHY OF A TRUE MARTIAL ARTIST.

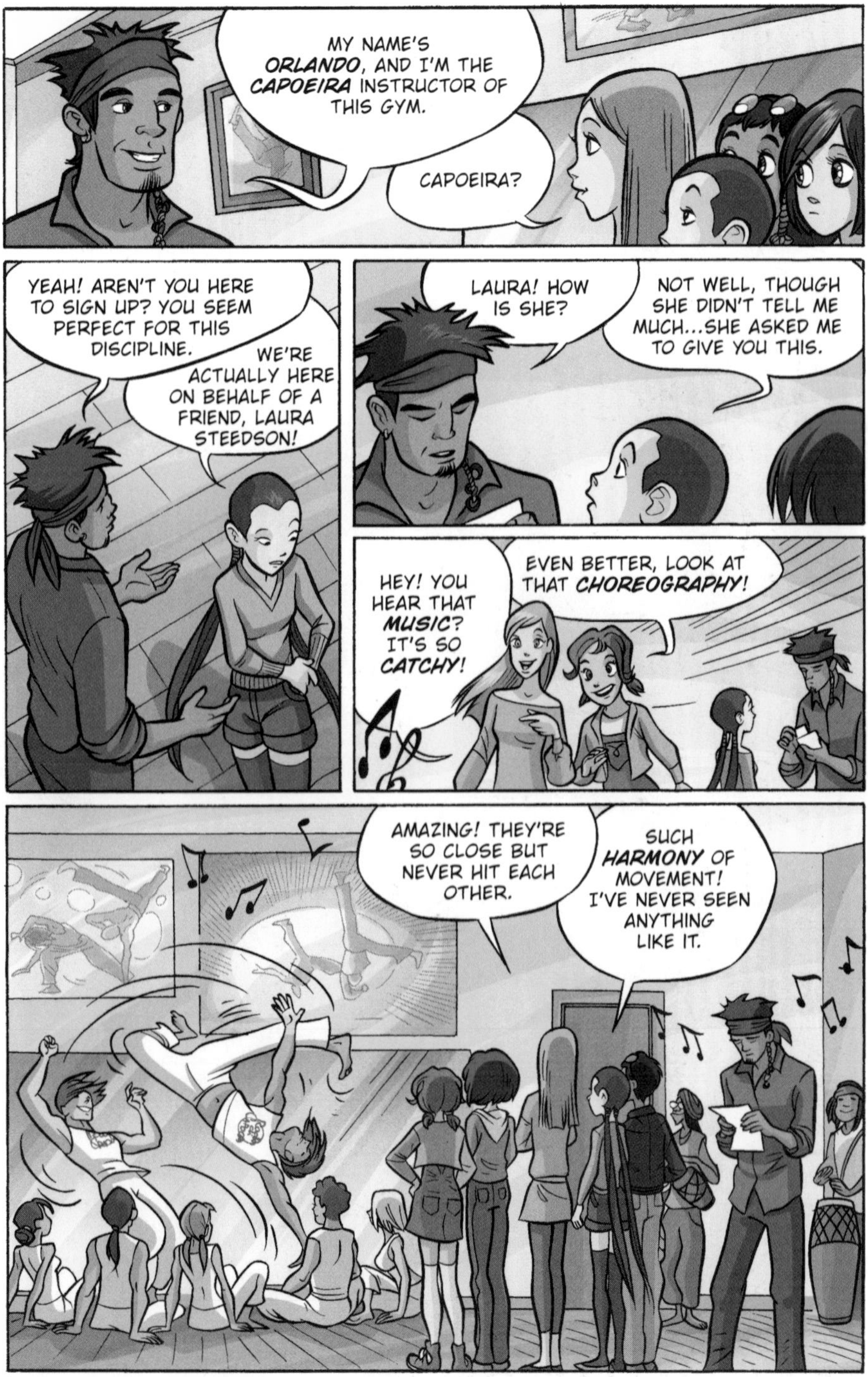
MY NAME'S ORLANDO, AND I'M THE CAPOEIRA INSTRUCTOR OF THIS GYM.
CAPOEIRA?
YEAH! AREN'T YOU HERE TO SIGN UP? YOU SEEM PERFECT FOR THIS DISCIPLINE.
WE'RE ACTUALLY HERE ON BEHALF OF A FRIEND, LAURA STEEDSON!
LAURA! HOW IS SHE?
NOT WELL, THOUGH SHE DIDN'T TELL ME MUCH...SHE ASKED ME TO GIVE YOU THIS.
HEY! YOU HEAR THAT MUSIC? IT'S SO CATCHY!
EVEN BETTER, LOOK AT THAT CHOREOGRAPHY!
AMAZING! THEY'RE SO CLOSE BUT NEVER HIT EACH OTHER.
SUCH HARMONY OF MOVEMENT! I'VE NEVER SEEN ANYTHING LIKE IT.

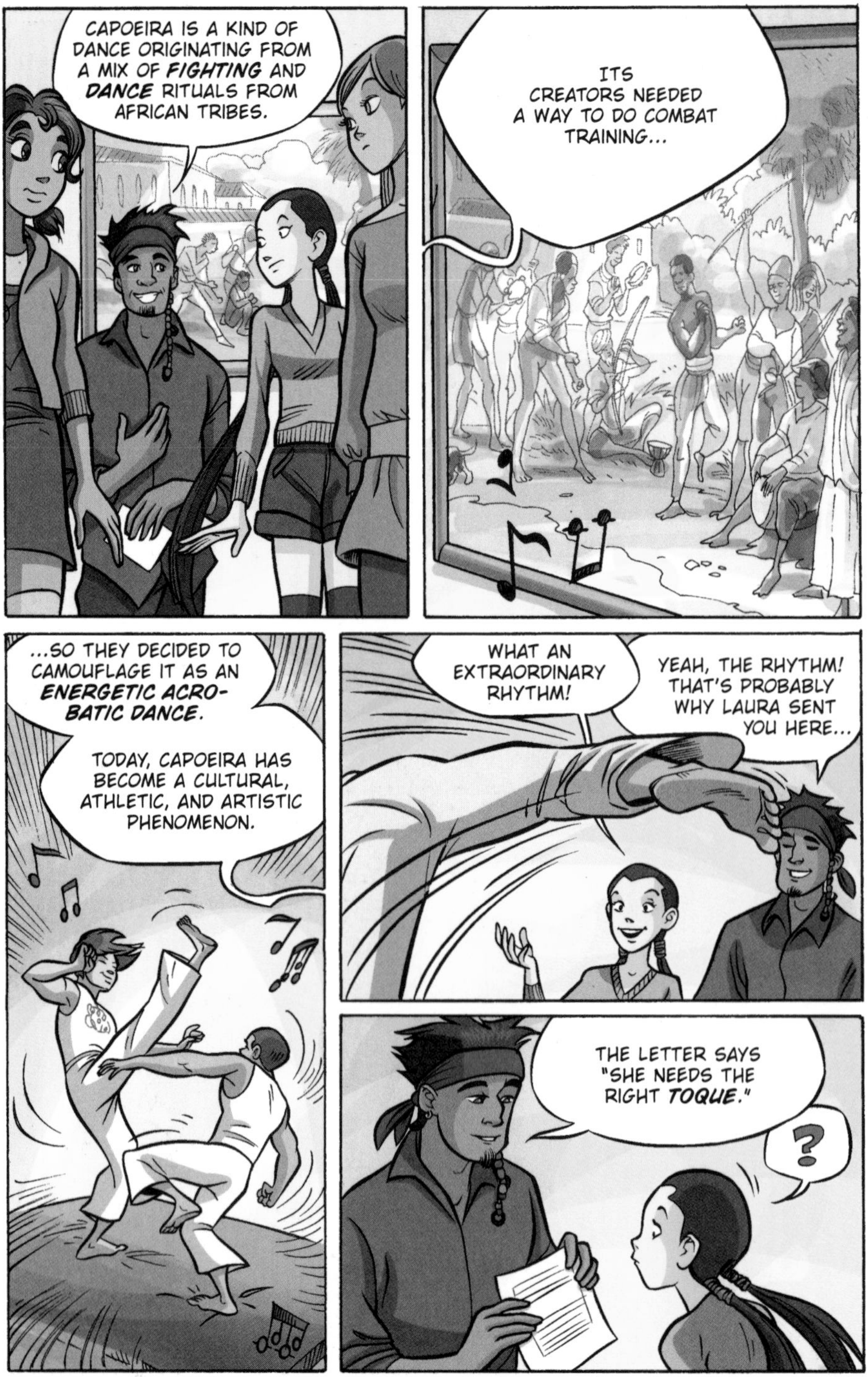
CAPOEIRA IS A KIND OF DANCE ORIGINATING FROM A MIX OF FIGHTING AND DANCE RITUALS FROM AFRICAN TRIBES.
ITS CREATORS NEEDED A WAY TO DO COMBAT TRAINING...
...SO THEY DECIDED TO CAMOUFLAGE IT AS AN ENERGETIC ACRO-BATIC DANCE.
TODAY, CAPOEIRA HAS BECOME A CULTURAL, ATHLETIC, AND ARTISTIC PHENOMENON.
WHAT AN EXTRAORDINARY RHYTHM!
YEAH, THE RHYTHM! THAT'S PROBABLY WHY LAURA SENT YOU HERE...
THE LETTER SAYS "SHE NEEDS THE RIGHT TOQUE."
?

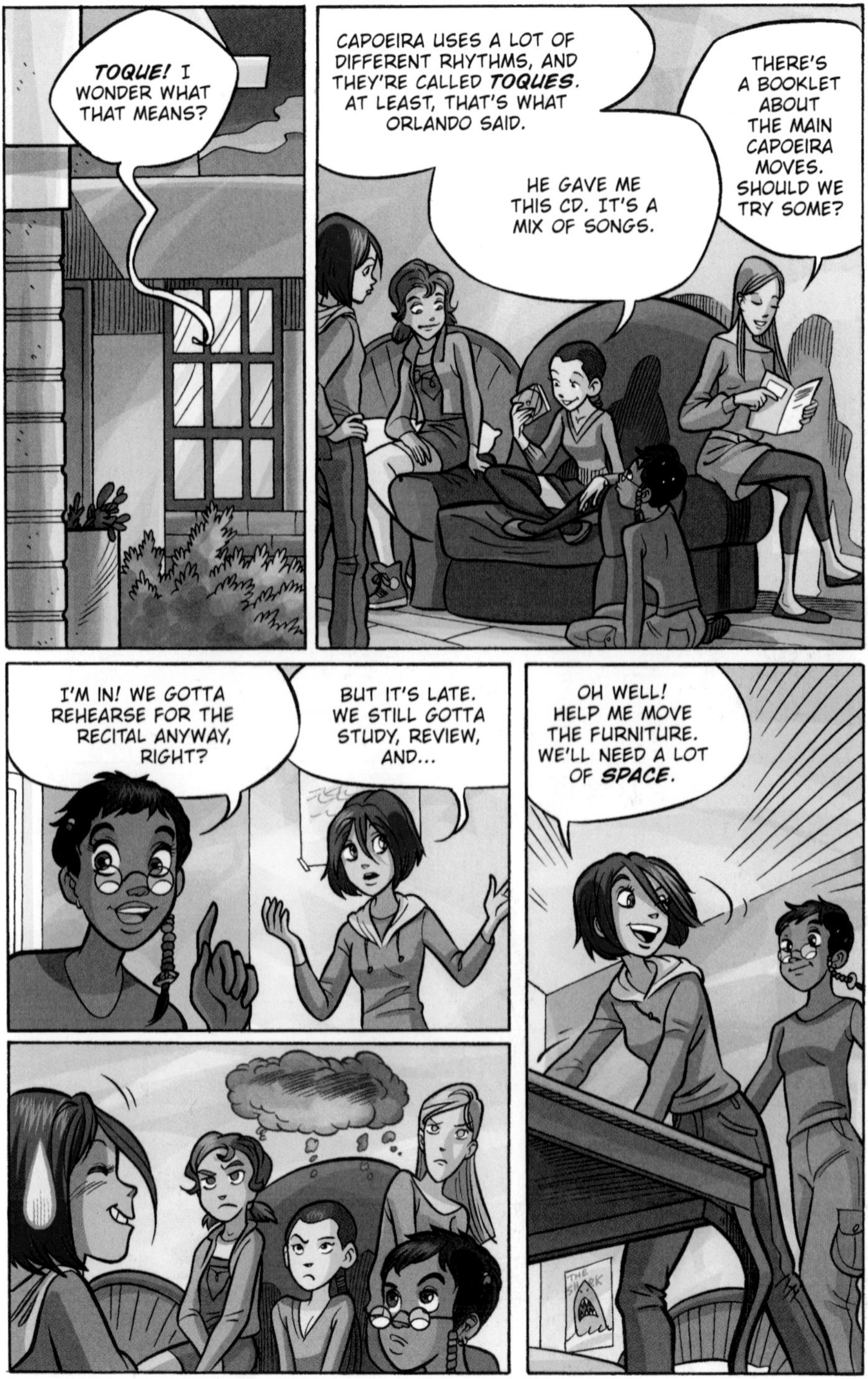
TOQUE! I WONDER WHAT THAT MEANS?
CAPOEIRA USES A LOT OF DIFFERENT RHYTHMS, AND THEY'RE CALLED TOQUES. AT LEAST, THAT'S WHAT ORLANDO SAID.
HE GAVE ME THIS CD. IT'S A MIX OF SONGS.
THERE'S A BOOKLET ABOUT THE MAIN CAPOEIRA MOVES. SHOULD WE TRY SOME?
I'M IN! WE GOTTA REHEARSE FOR THE RECITAL ANYWAY, RIGHT?
BUT IT'S LATE. WE STILL GOTTA STUDY, REVIEW, AND...
OH WELL! HELP ME MOVE THE FURNITURE. WE'LL NEED A LOT OF SPACE.

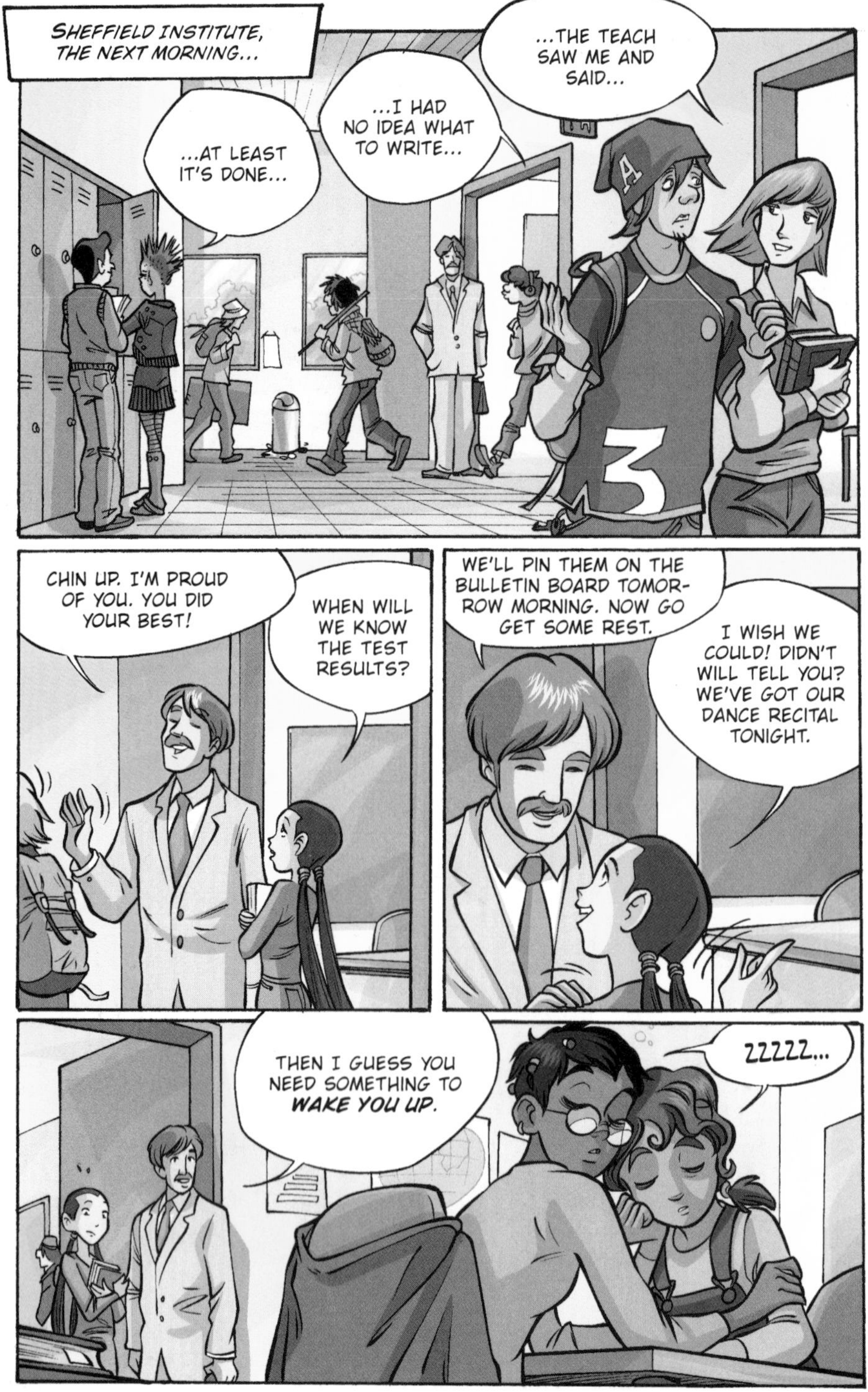
SHEFFIELD INSTITUTE, THE NEXT MORNING...
...AT LEAST IT'S DONE...
...I HAD NO IDEA WHAT TO WRITE...
...THE TEACH SAW ME AND SAID...
CHIN UP. I'M PROUD OF YOU. YOU DID YOUR BEST!
WHEN WILL WE KNOW THE TEST RESULTS?
WE'LL PIN THEM ON THE BULLETIN BOARD TOMORROW MORNING. NOW GO GET SOME REST.
I WISH WE COULD! DIDN'T WILL TELL YOU? WE'VE GOT OUR DANCE RECITAL TONIGHT.
THEN I GUESS YOU NEED SOMETHING TO ***WAKE YOU UP***.
ZZZZZ...

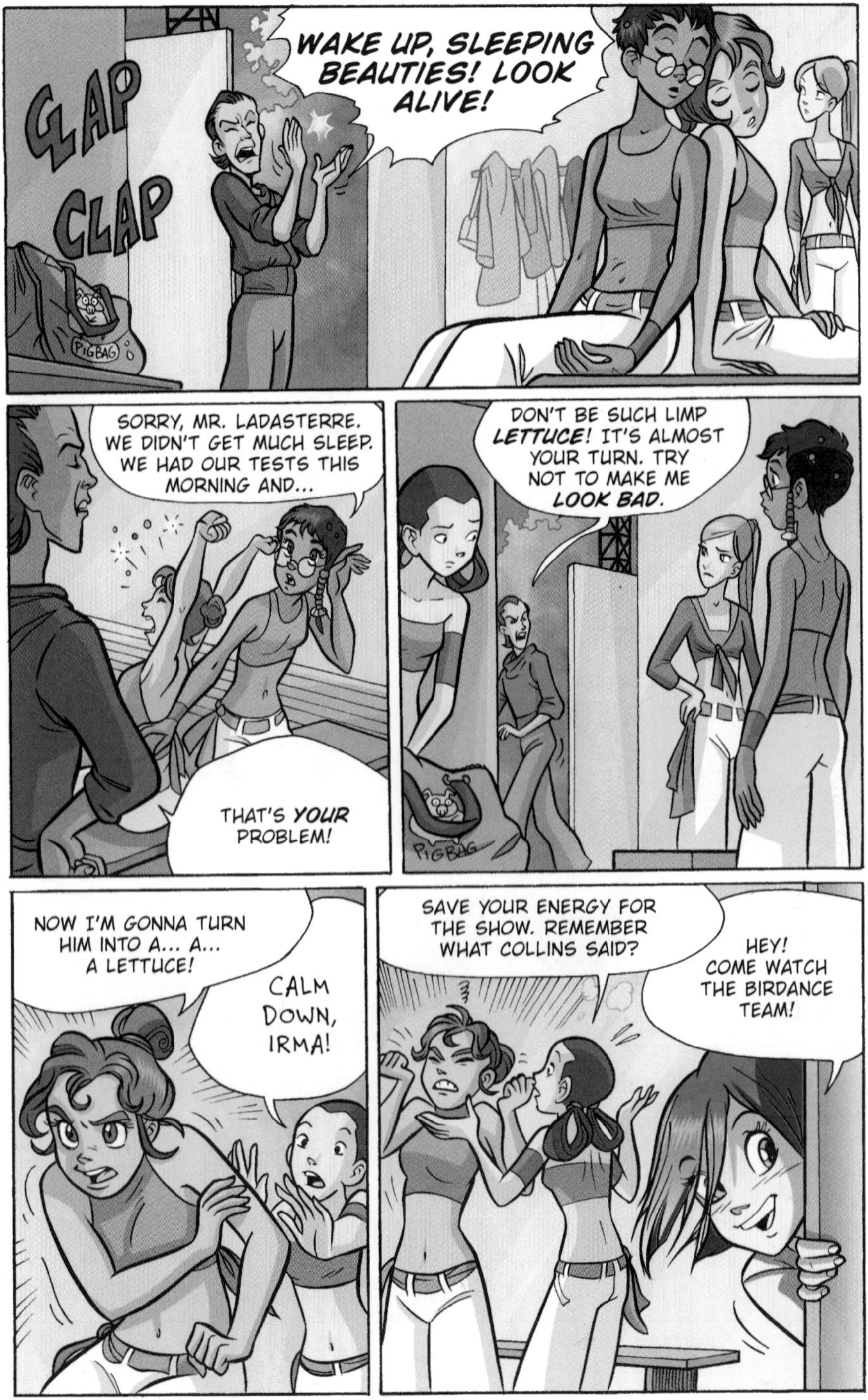
CLAP
CLAP
WAKE UP, SLEEPING BEAUTIES! LOOK ALIVE!
PIGBAG
SORRY, MR. LADASTERRE. WE DIDN'T GET MUCH SLEEP. WE HAD OUR TESTS THIS MORNING AND...
THAT'S YOUR PROBLEM!
DON'T BE SUCH LIMP LETTUCE! IT'S ALMOST YOUR TURN. TRY NOT TO MAKE ME LOOK BAD.
PIGBAG
NOW I'M GONNA TURN HIM INTO A... A... A LETTUCE!
CALM DOWN, IRMA!
SAVE YOUR ENERGY FOR THE SHOW. REMEMBER WHAT COLLINS SAID?
HEY! COME WATCH THE BIRDANCE TEAM!

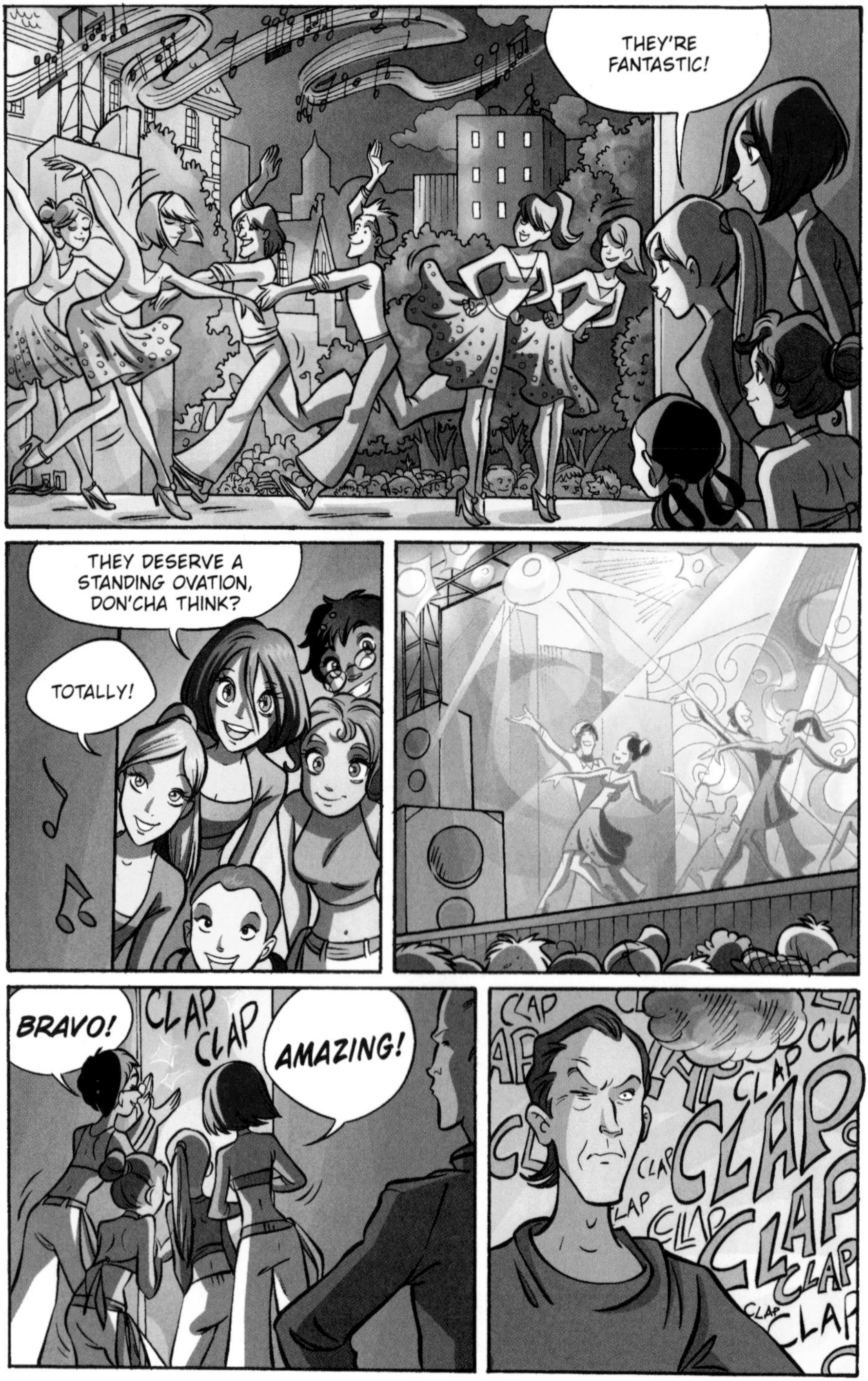
THEY'RE FANTASTIC!
THEY DESERVE A STANDING OVATION, DON'CHA THINK?
TOTALLY!
BRAVO!
CLAP CLAP
AMAZING!
CLAP
CLAP
CLAP
CLAP
CLAP
CLAP
CLAP
CLAP
CLAP

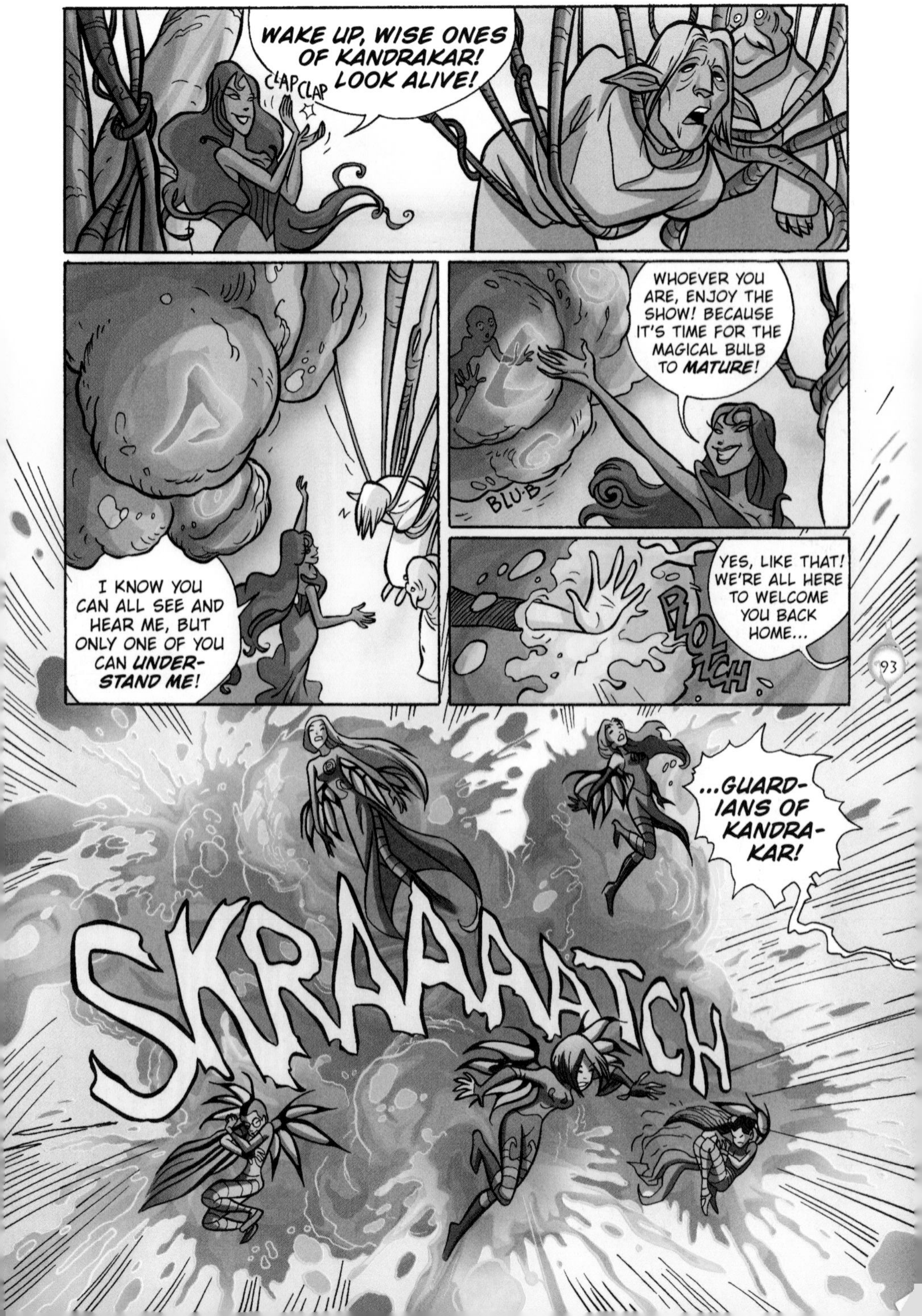
WAKE UP, WISE ONES OF KANDRAKAR! LOOK ALIVE!
CLAP CLAP
I KNOW YOU CAN ALL SEE AND HEAR ME, BUT ONLY ONE OF YOU CAN UNDER-STAND ME!
WHOEVER YOU ARE, ENJOY THE SHOW! BECAUSE IT'S TIME FOR THE MAGICAL BULB TO MATURE!
BLUB
YES, LIKE THAT! WE'RE ALL HERE TO WELCOME YOU BACK HOME...
BLOTCH
...GUARD-IANS OF KANDRA-KAR!
SKRAAAATCH

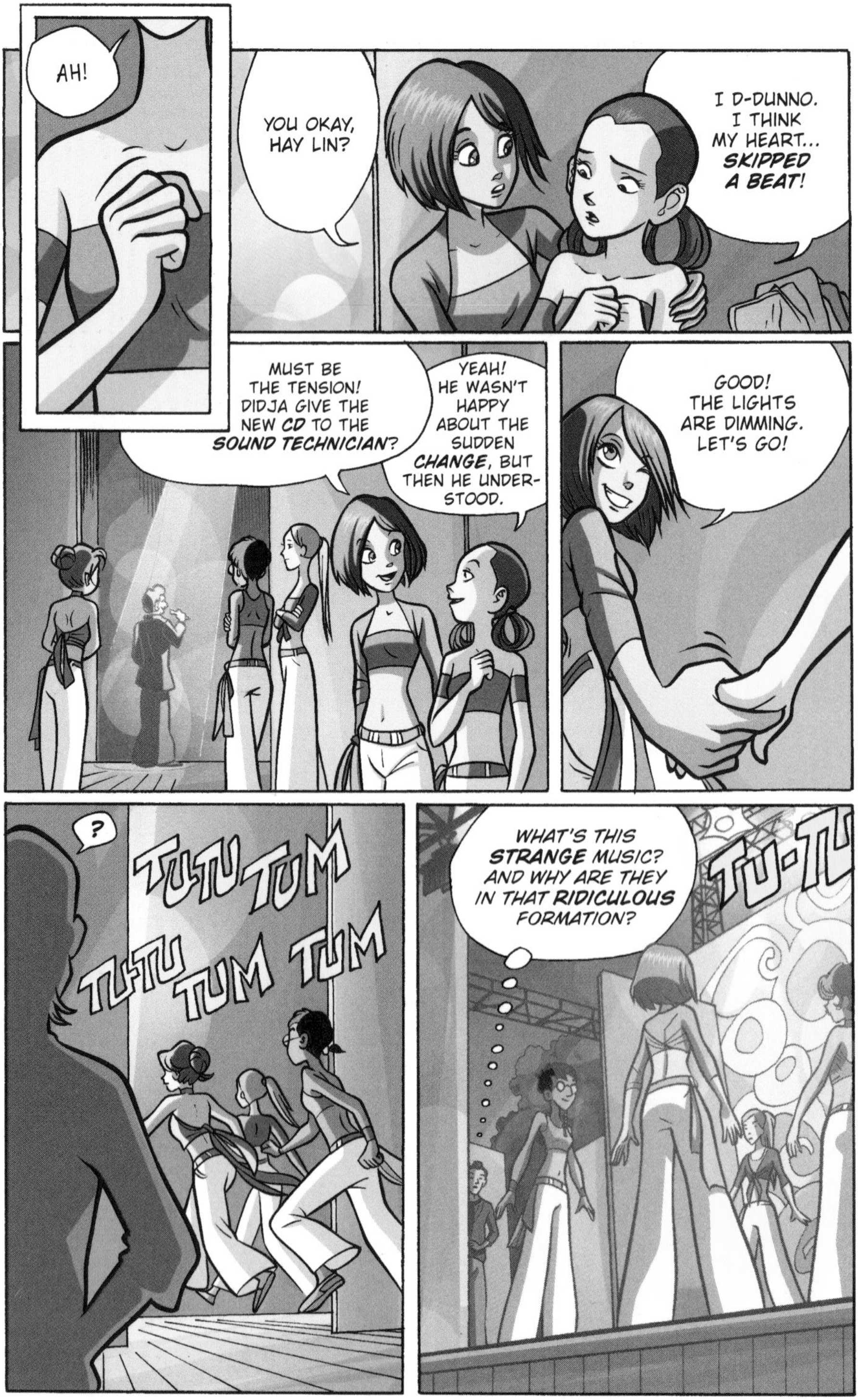
AH!
YOU OKAY, HAY LIN?
I D-DUNNO. I THINK MY HEART... SKIPPED A BEAT!
MUST BE THE TENSION! DIDJA GIVE THE NEW CD TO THE SOUND TECHNICIAN?
YEAH! HE WASN'T HAPPY ABOUT THE SUDDEN CHANGE, BUT THEN HE UNDER-STOOD.
GOOD! THE LIGHTS ARE DIMMING. LET'S GO!
?
TUTU TUM
TUTU TUM TUM
WHAT'S THIS STRANGE MUSIC? AND WHY ARE THEY IN THAT RIDICULOUS FORMATION?
TU-TU

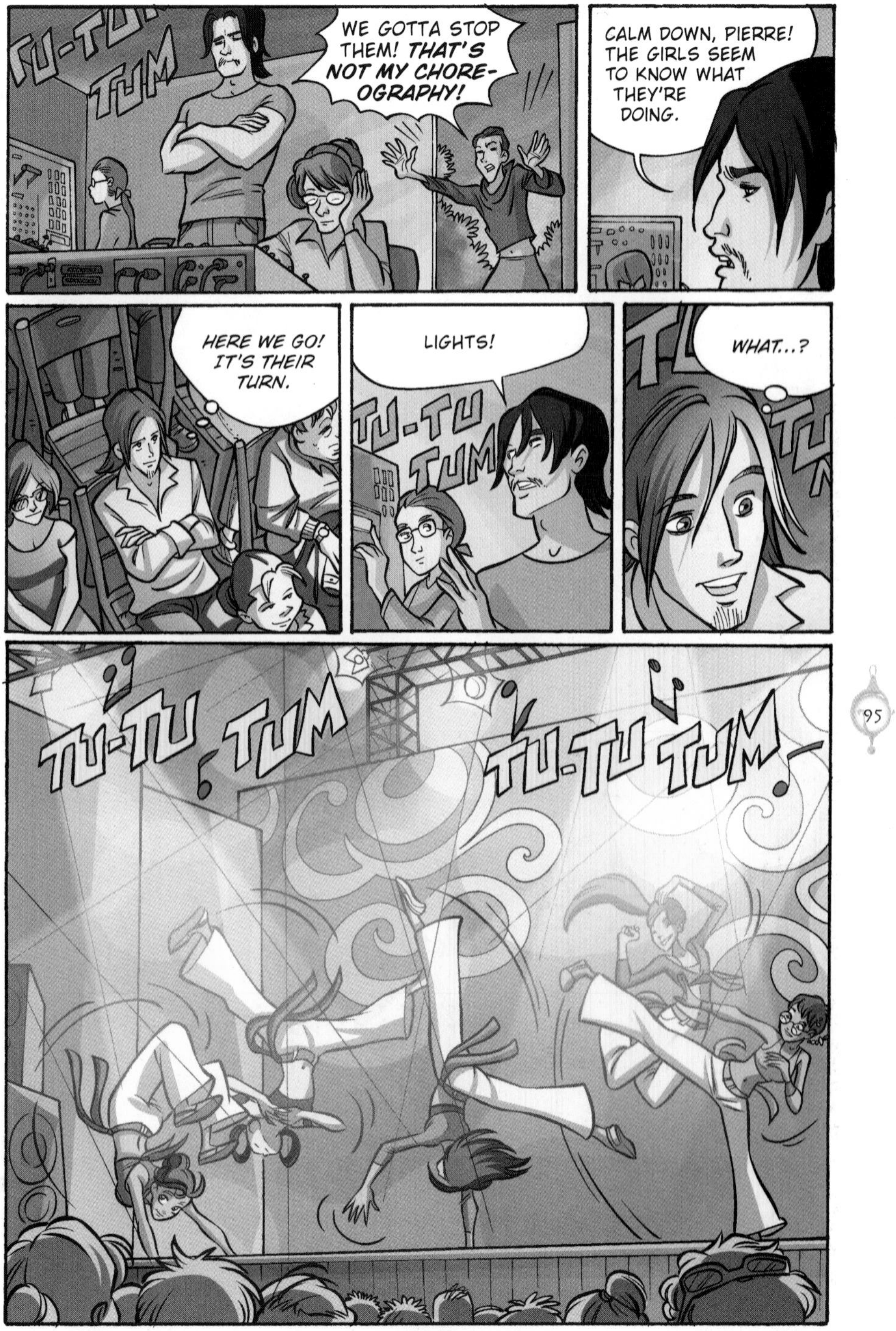
TUM
WE GOTTA STOP THEM! THAT'S NOT MY CHOREOGRAPHY!
CALM DOWN, PIERRE! THE GIRLS SEEM TO KNOW WHAT THEY'RE DOING.
HERE WE GO! IT'S THEIR TURN.
LIGHTS!
TU-TU TUM
WHAT...?
TU-TU TUM
TU-TU TUM

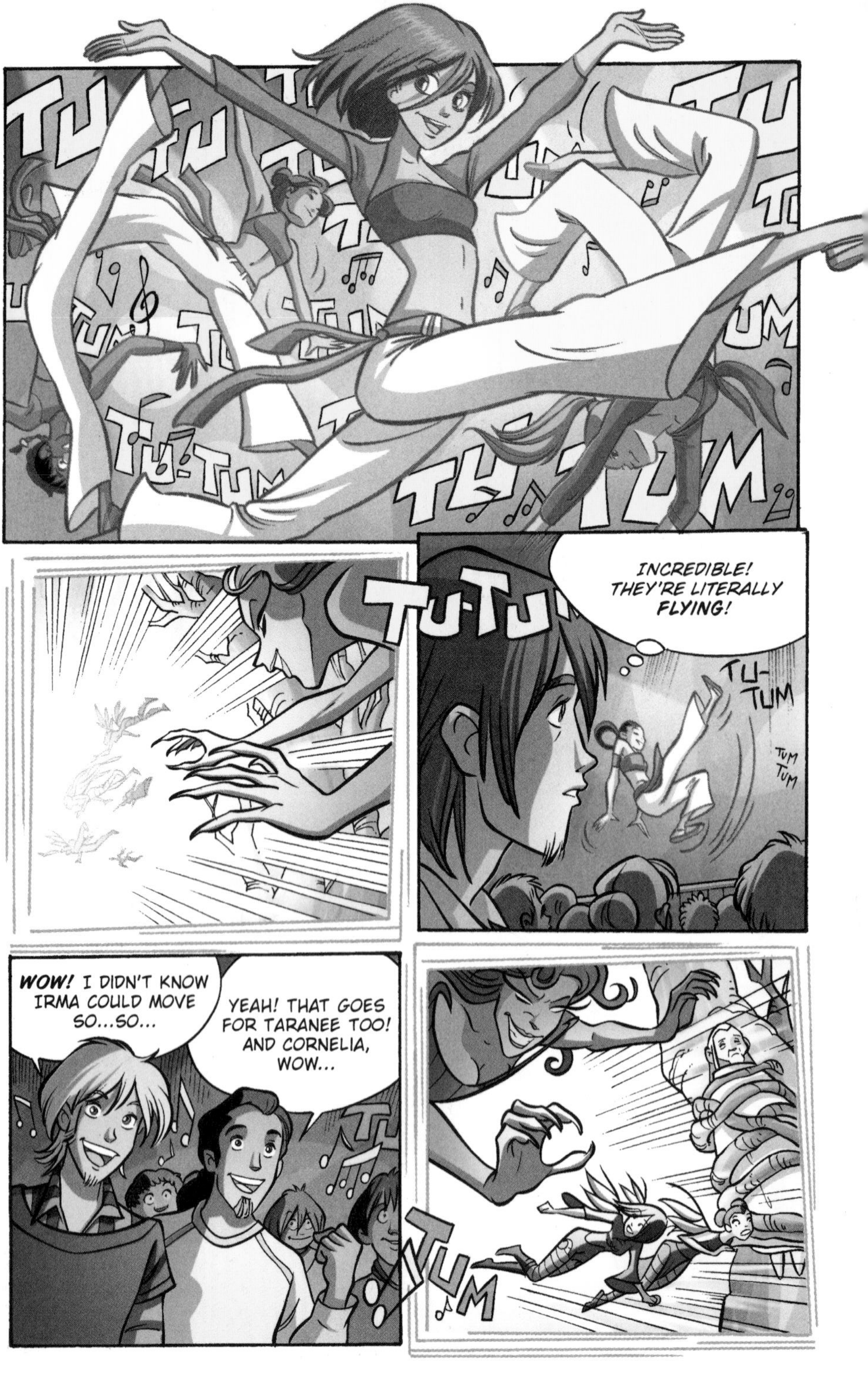
TU-TU
TUM
TU-TUM
TU-TUM
TU-TUM
INCREDIBLE! THEY'RE LITERALLY FLYING!
TU-TUM
TUM TUM
WOW! I DIDN'T KNOW IRMA COULD MOVE SO...SO...
YEAH! THAT GOES FOR TARANEE TOO! AND CORNELIA, WOW...
TUM

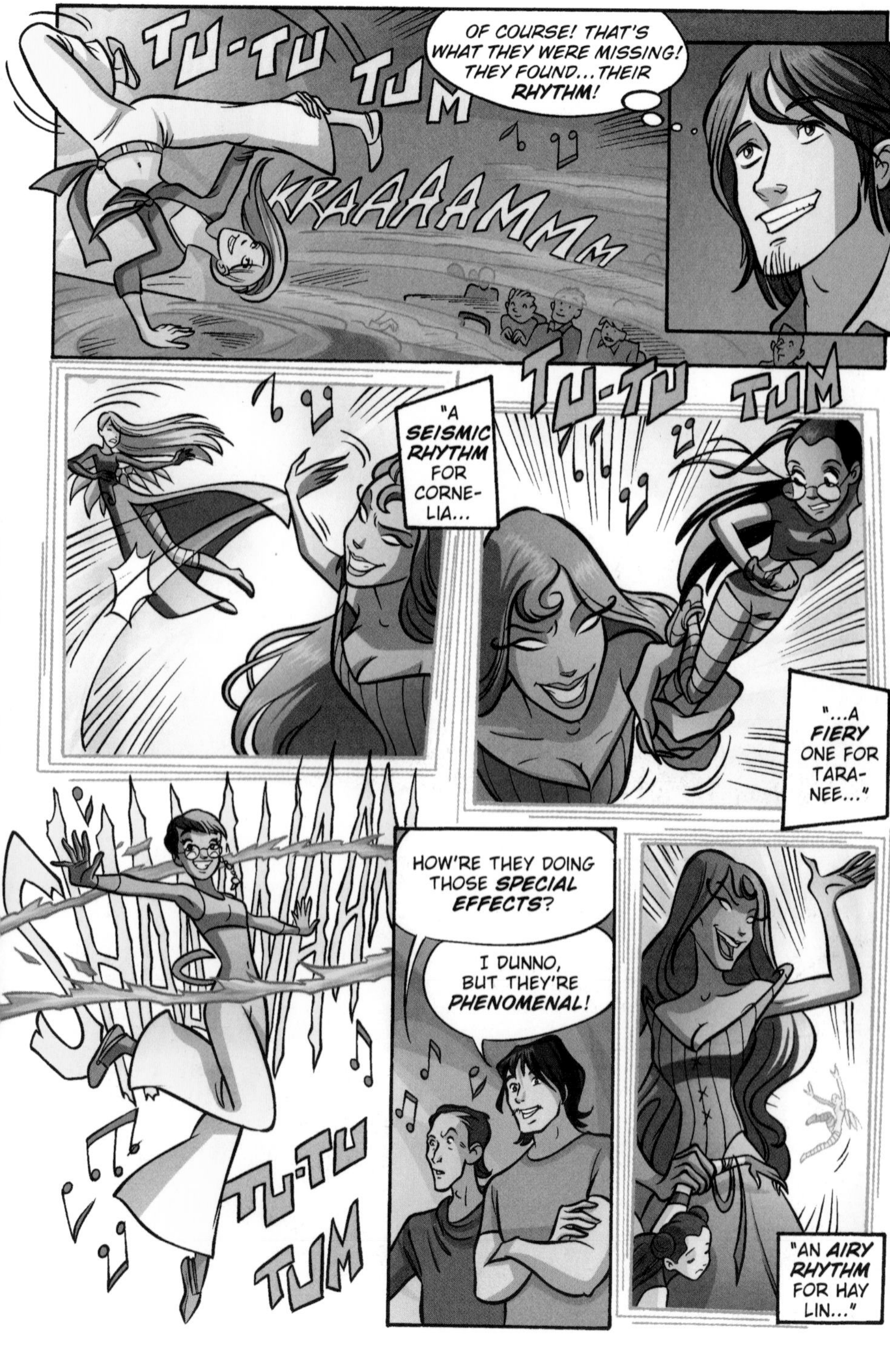
TU-TU
TUM
OF COURSE! THAT'S WHAT THEY WERE MISSING! THEY FOUND... THEIR RHYTHM!
KRAAAAAMMMM
TU-TU
TUM
"A SEISMIC RHYTHM FOR CORNE-LIA...
"...A FIERY ONE FOR TARA-NEE..."
TU-TU
TUM
HOW'RE THEY DOING THOSE SPECIAL EFFECTS?
I DUNNO, BUT THEY'RE PHENOMENAL!
"AN AIRY RHYTHM FOR HAY LIN..."

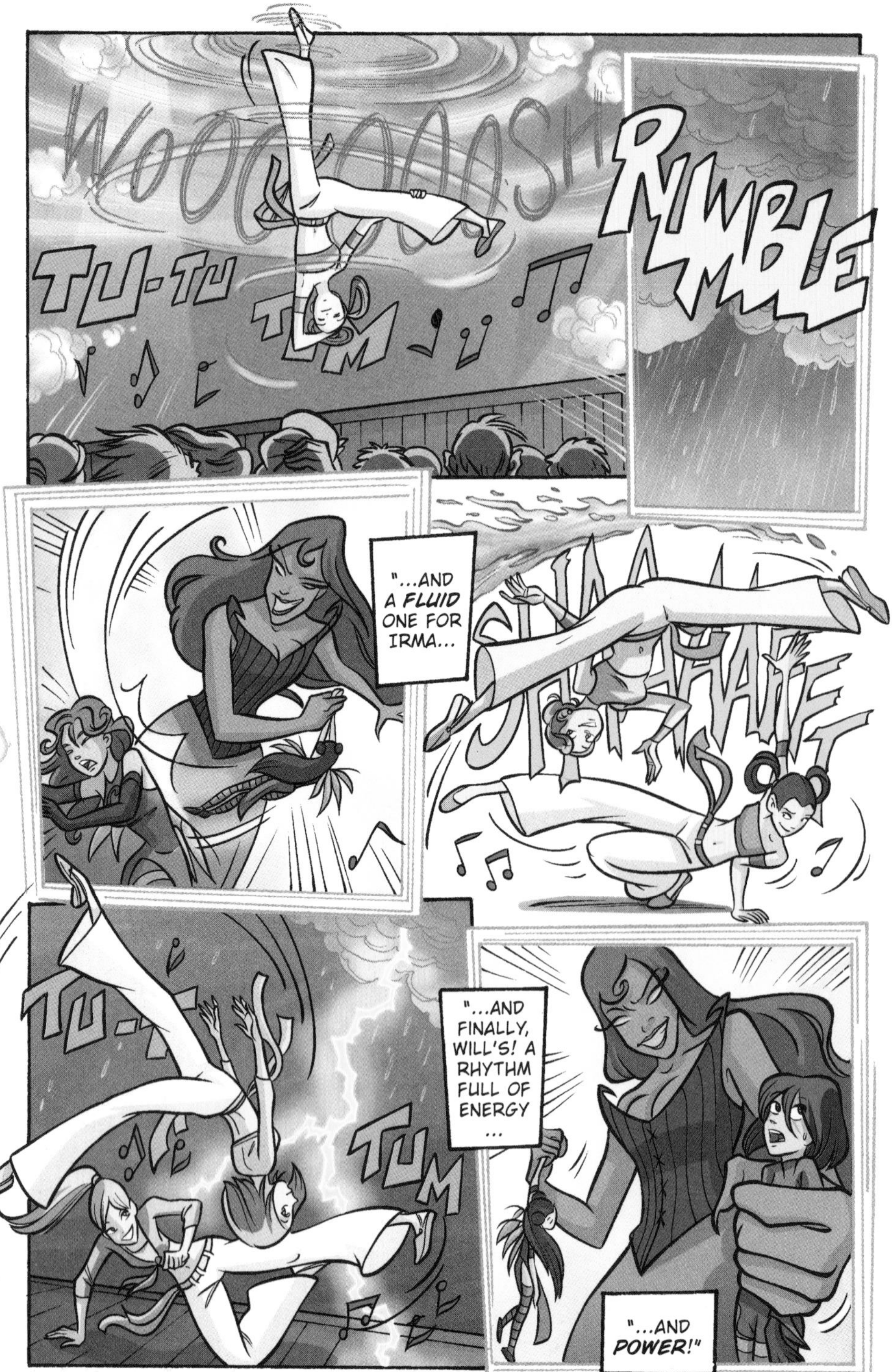
WOOOOOOOSH
TU-TU
TUM
RUMBLE
"...AND A FLUID ONE FOR IRMA..."
SHAAAAAFFF
"...AND FINALLY, WILL'S! A RHYTHM FULL OF ENERGY ..."
TUM
"...AND POWER!"

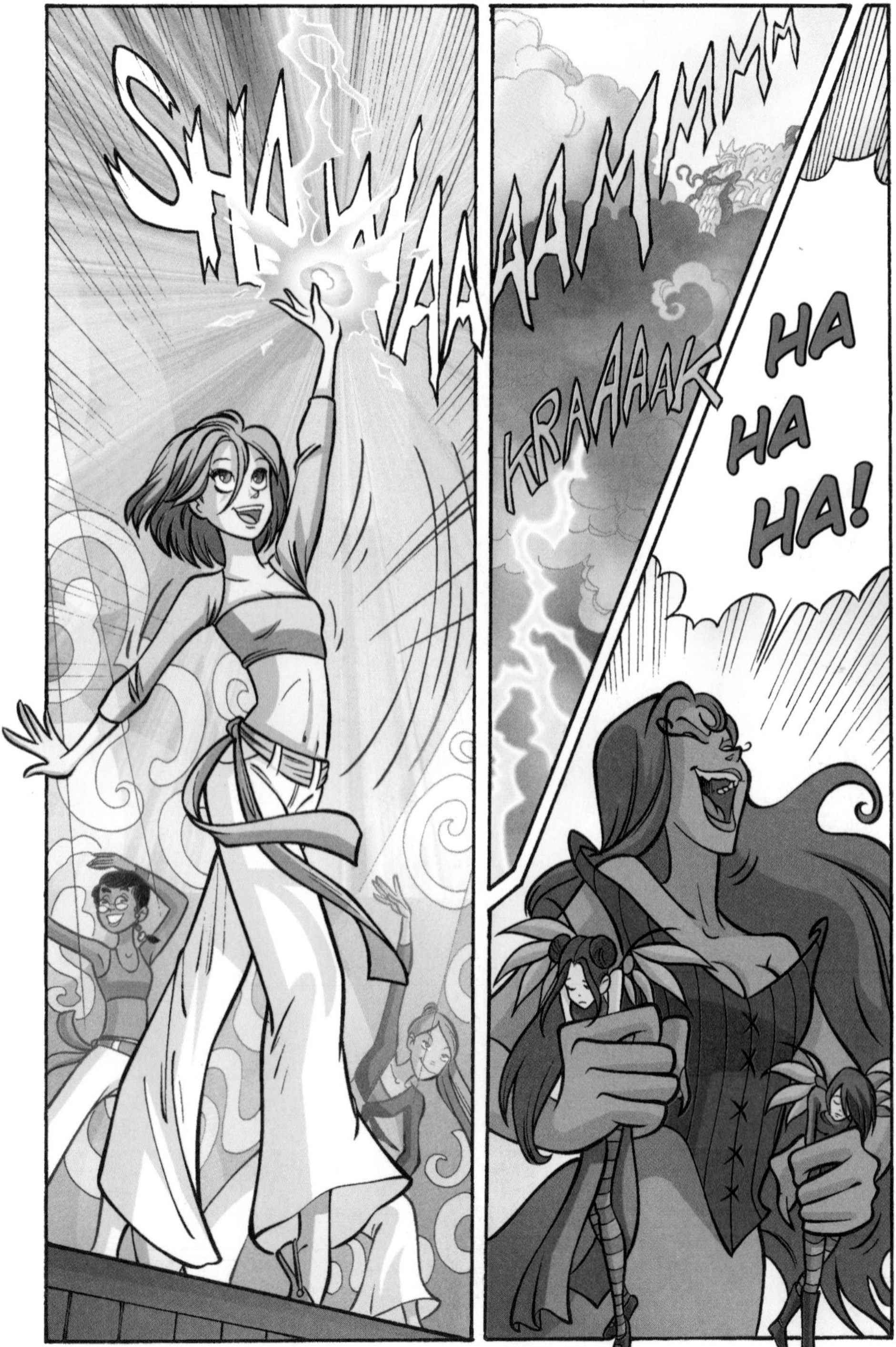
SHAAAAAAMMMMM
KRAAAAK
HA
HA
HA!

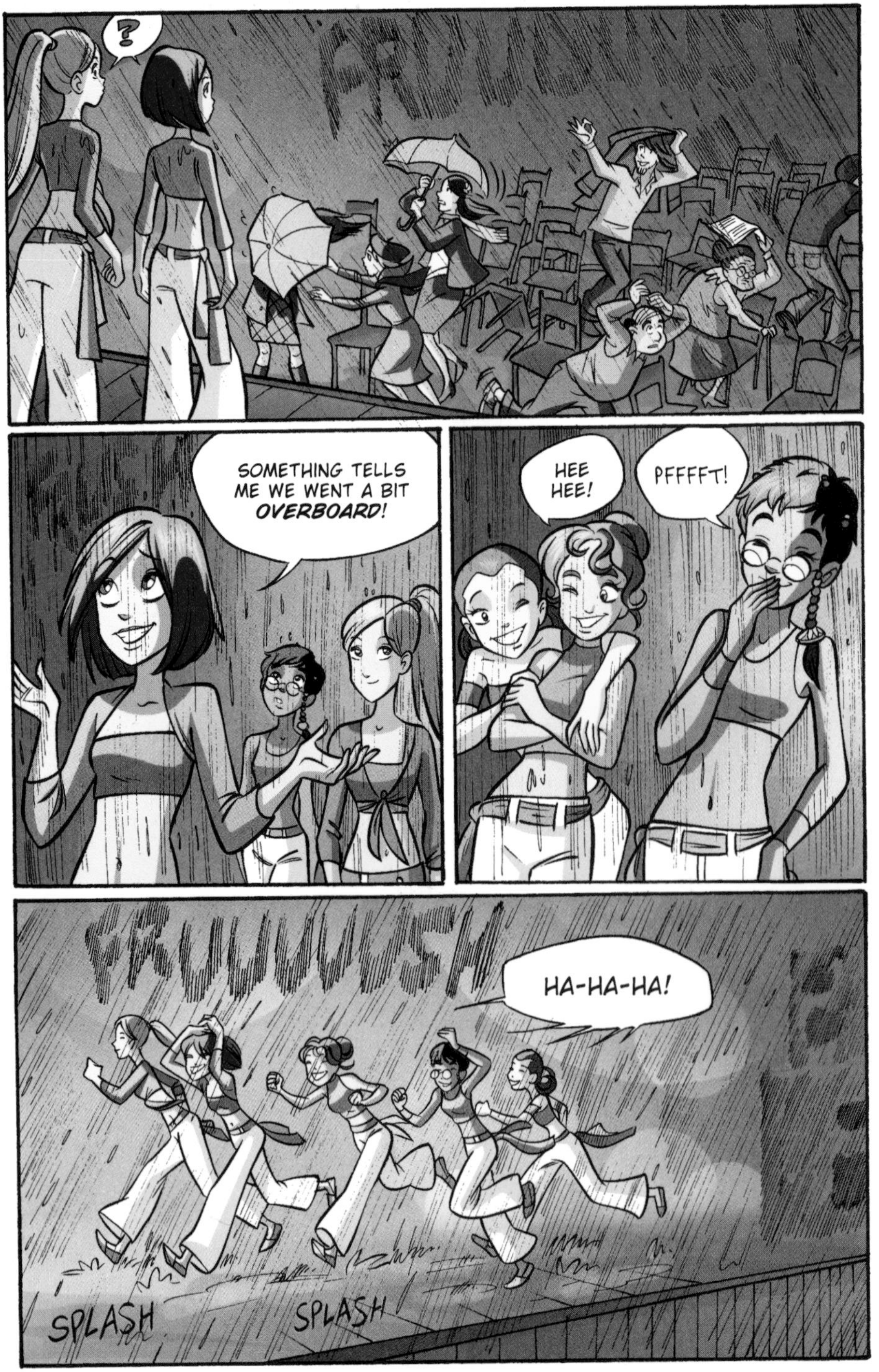
?
SOMETHING TELLS ME WE WENT A BIT *OVERBOARD*!
HEE HEE!
PFFFFT!
FRUUUUSH
HA-HA-HA!
SPLASH
SPLASH

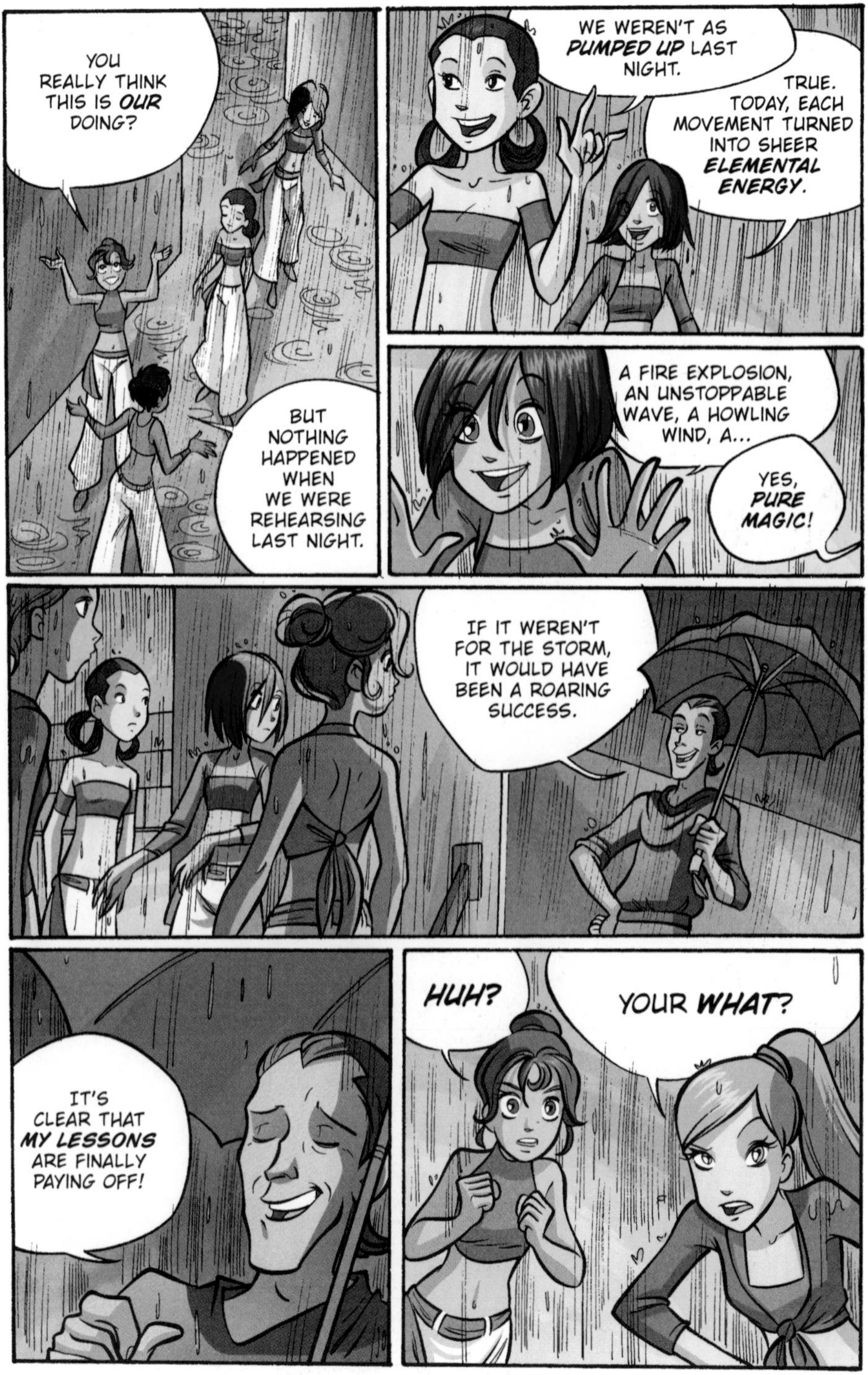
YOU REALLY THINK THIS IS OUR DOING?
BUT NOTHING HAPPENED WHEN WE WERE REHEARSING LAST NIGHT.
WE WEREN'T AS PUMPED UP LAST NIGHT.
TRUE. TODAY, EACH MOVEMENT TURNED INTO SHEER ELEMENTAL ENERGY.
A FIRE EXPLOSION, AN UNSTOPPABLE WAVE, A HOWLING WIND, A...
YES, PURE MAGIC!
IF IT WEREN'T FOR THE STORM, IT WOULD HAVE BEEN A ROARING SUCCESS.
IT'S CLEAR THAT MY LESSONS ARE FINALLY PAYING OFF!
HUH?
YOUR WHAT?

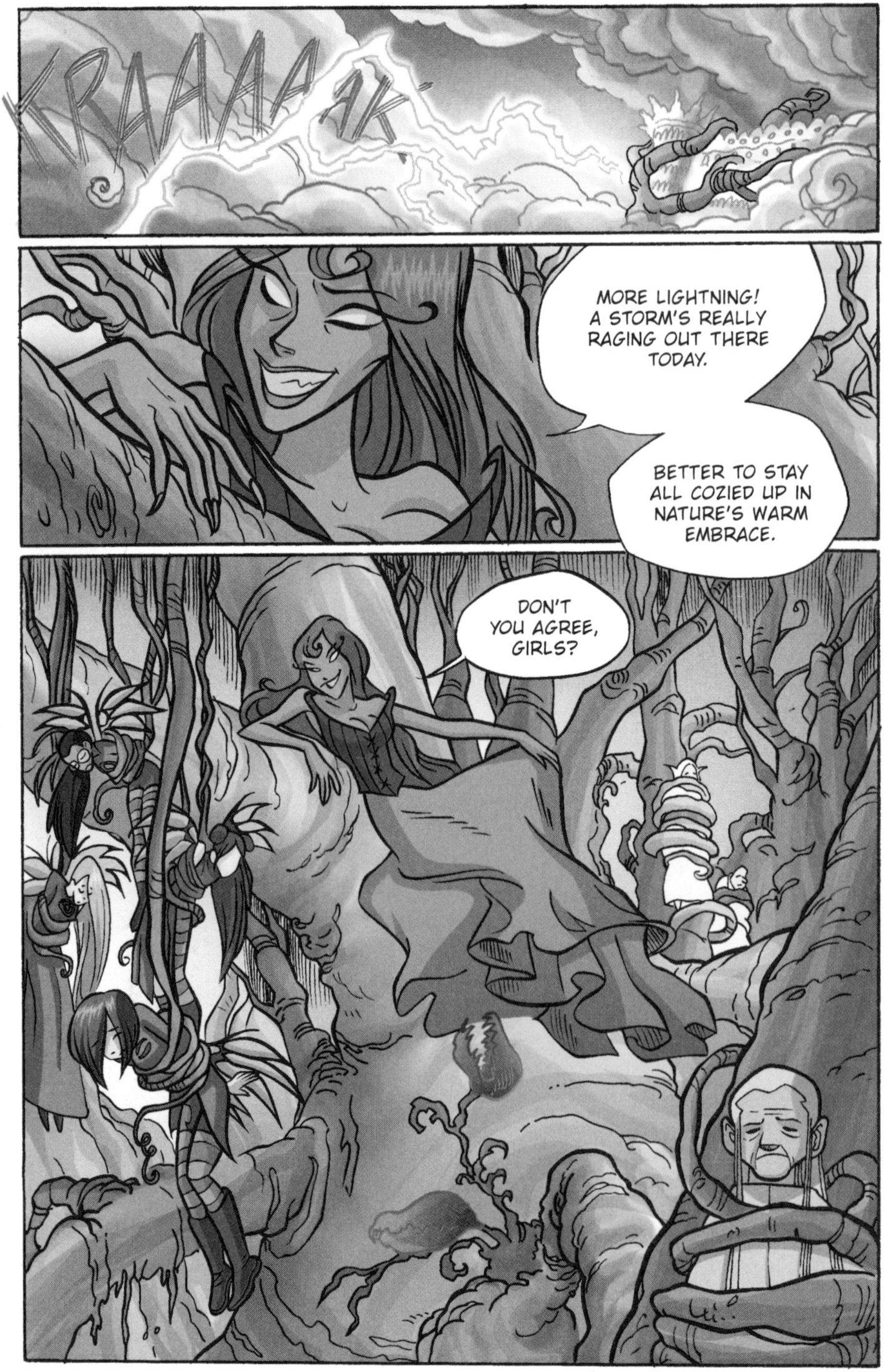
KRAAAAAK
MORE LIGHTNING! A STORM'S REALLY RAGING OUT THERE TODAY.
BETTER TO STAY ALL COZIED UP IN NATURE'S WARM EMBRACE.
DON'T YOU AGREE, GIRLS?

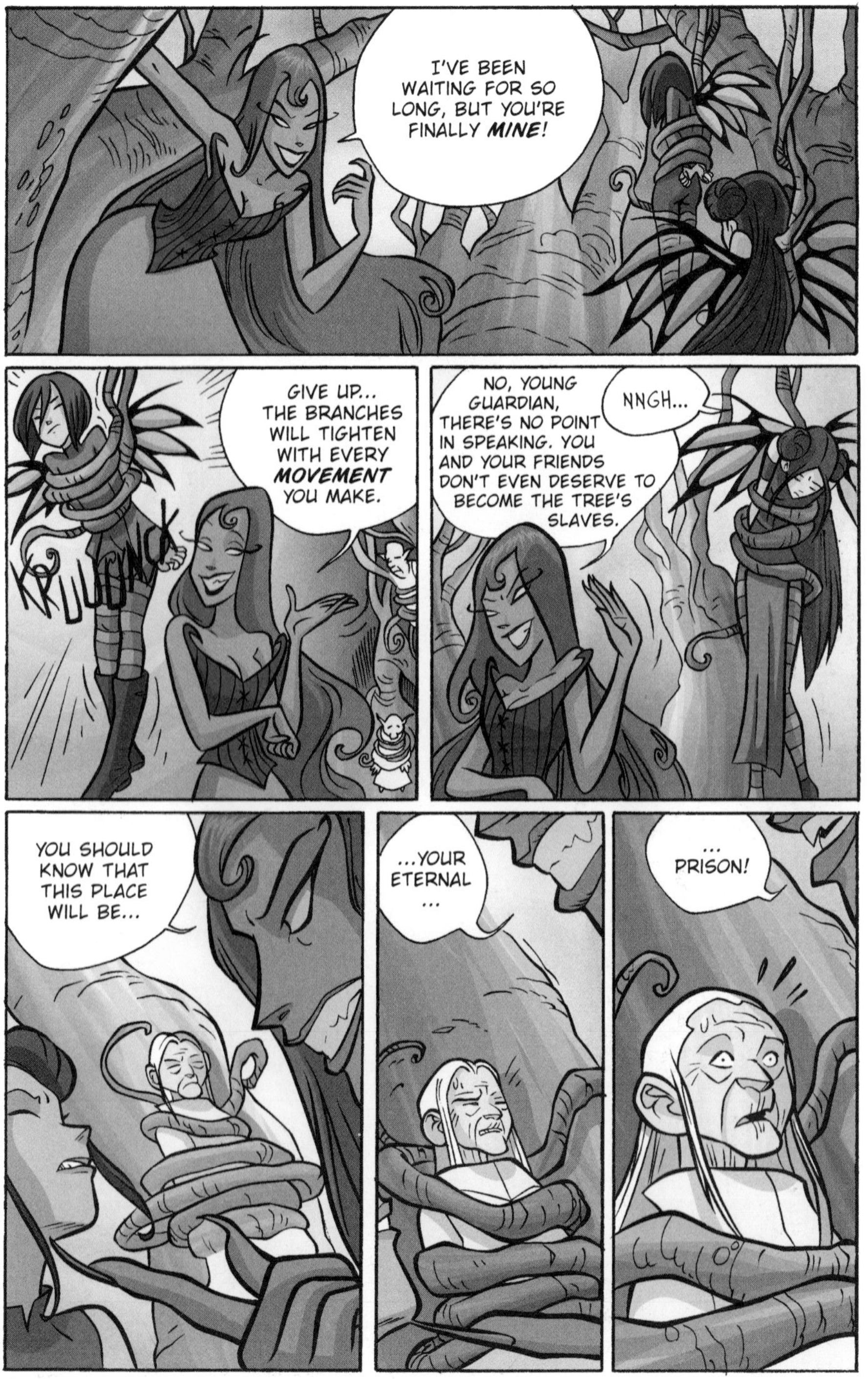
I'VE BEEN WAITING FOR SO LONG, BUT YOU'RE FINALLY ***MINE***!
GIVE UP... THE BRANCHES WILL TIGHTEN WITH EVERY ***MOVEMENT*** YOU MAKE.
KRUUUNCK
NNGH...
NO, YOUNG GUARDIAN, THERE'S NO POINT IN SPEAKING. YOU AND YOUR FRIENDS DON'T EVEN DESERVE TO BECOME THE TREE'S SLAVES.
YOU SHOULD KNOW THAT THIS PLACE WILL BE...
...YOUR ETERNAL ...
... PRISON!

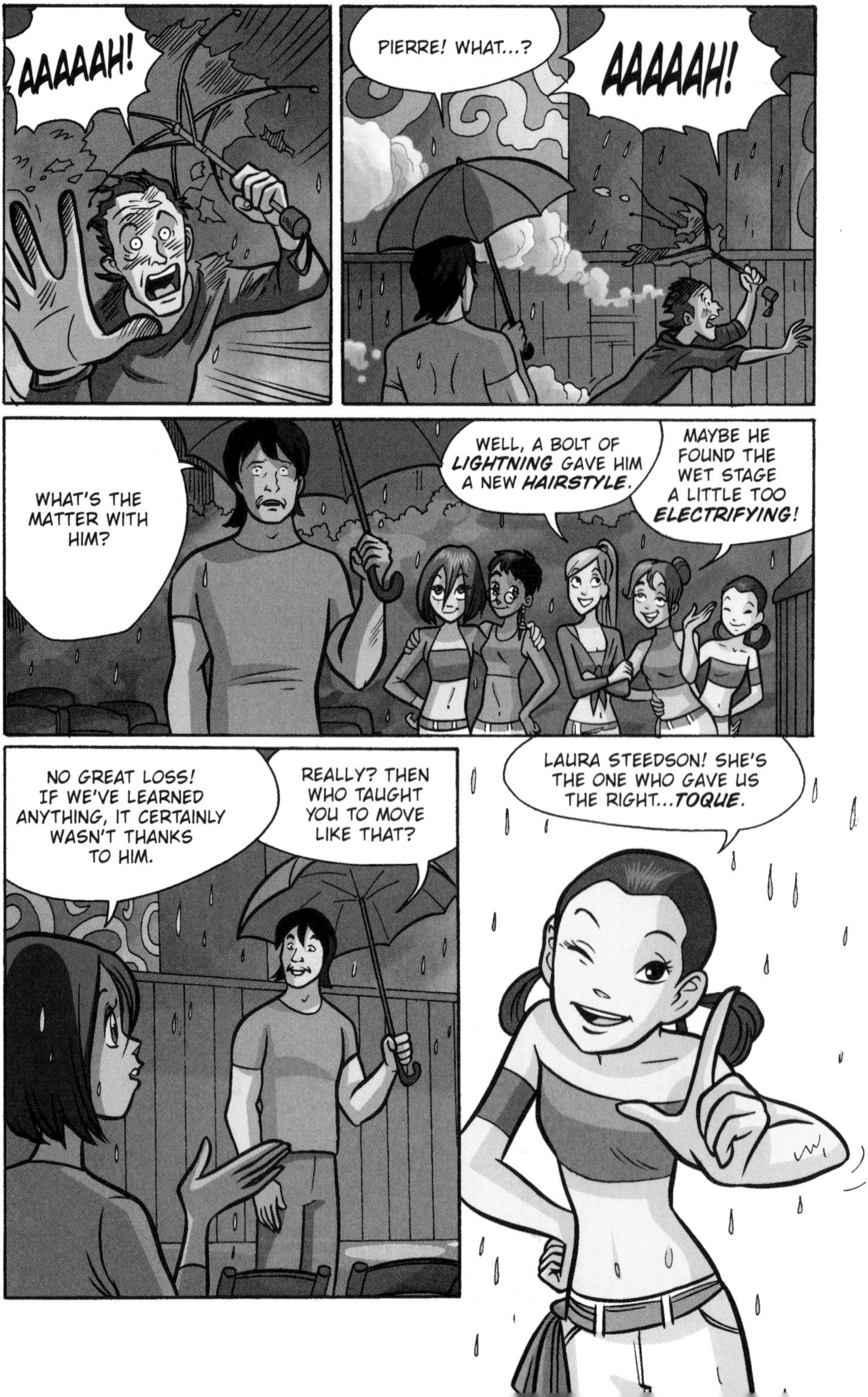
AAAAAH!
PIERRE! WHAT...?
AAAAAH!
WHAT'S THE MATTER WITH HIM?
WELL, A BOLT OF LIGHTNING GAVE HIM A NEW HAIRSTYLE.
MAYBE HE FOUND THE WET STAGE A LITTLE TOO ELECTRIFYING!
NO GREAT LOSS! IF WE'VE LEARNED ANYTHING, IT CERTAINLY WASN'T THANKS TO HIM.
REALLY? THEN WHO TAUGHT YOU TO MOVE LIKE THAT?
LAURA STEEDSON! SHE'S THE ONE WHO GAVE US THE RIGHT...TOQUE.

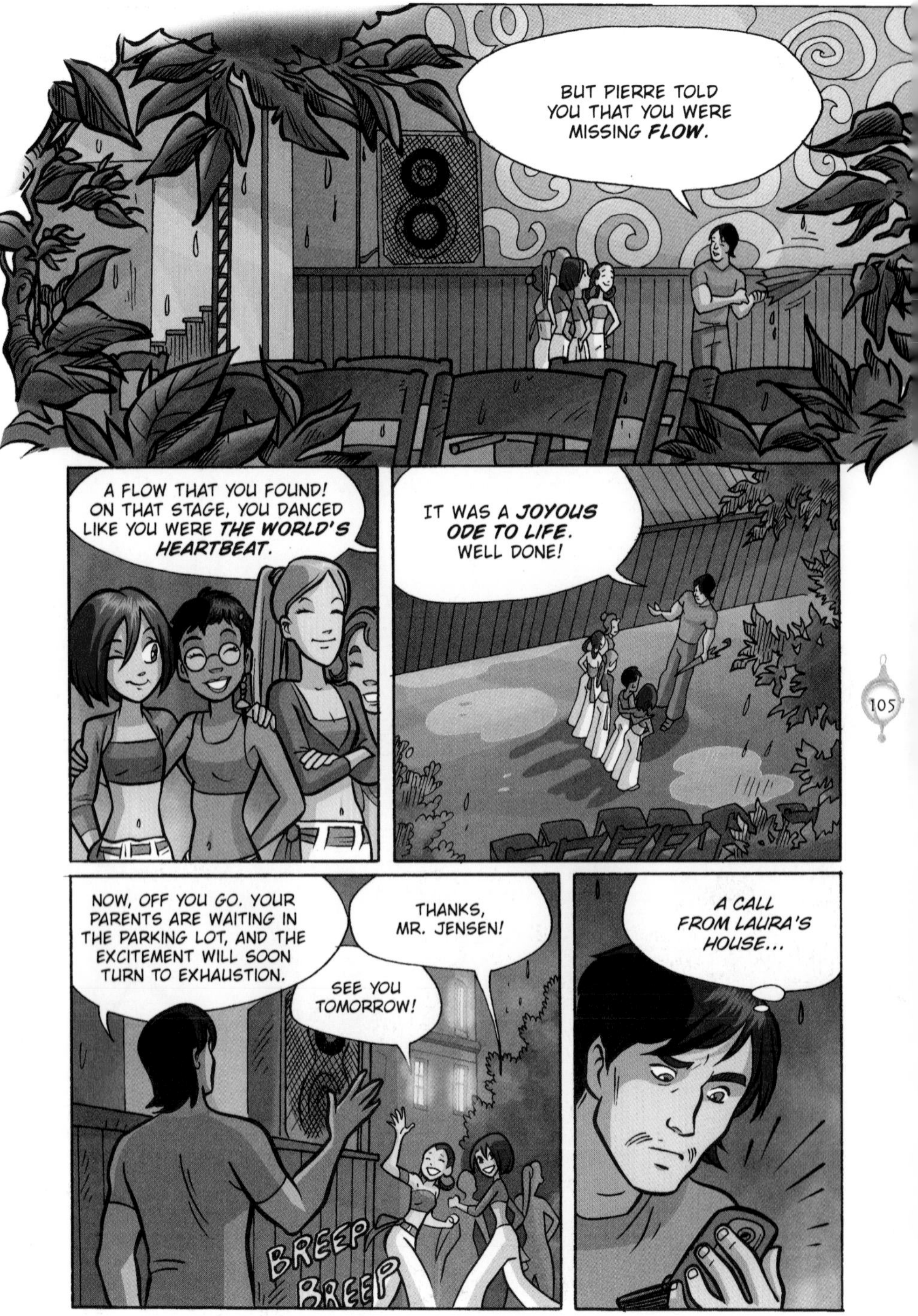
BUT PIERRE TOLD YOU THAT YOU WERE MISSING FLOW.
A FLOW THAT YOU FOUND! ON THAT STAGE, YOU DANCED LIKE YOU WERE THE WORLD'S HEARTBEAT.
IT WAS A JOYOUS ODE TO LIFE. WELL DONE!
NOW, OFF YOU GO. YOUR PARENTS ARE WAITING IN THE PARKING LOT, AND THE EXCITEMENT WILL SOON TURN TO EXHAUSTION.
THANKS, MR. JENSEN!
SEE YOU TOMORROW!
BREEP
BREEP
A CALL FROM LAURA'S HOUSE...

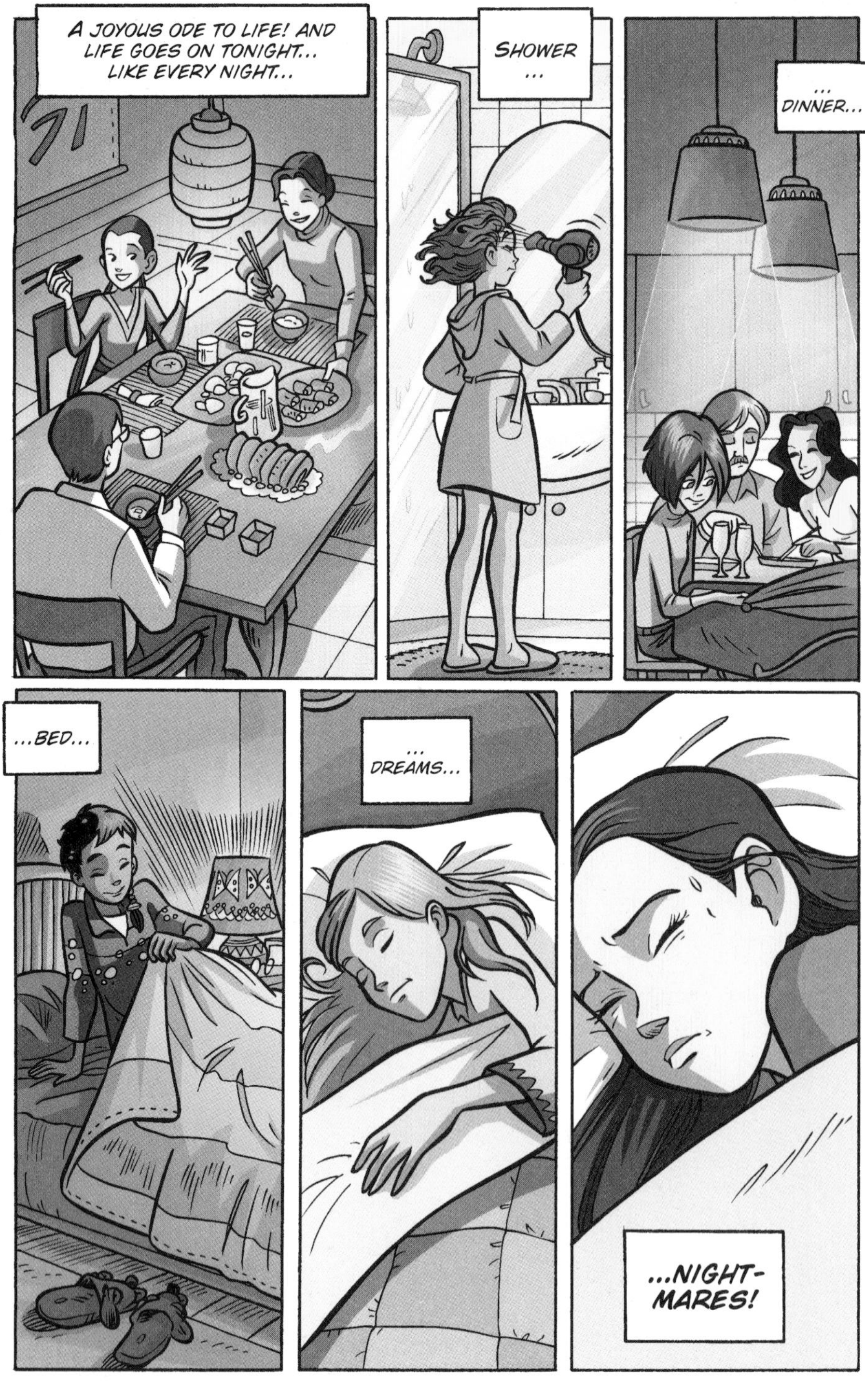
A JOYOUS ODE TO LIFE! AND LIFE GOES ON TONIGHT... LIKE EVERY NIGHT...
SHOWER ...
... DINNER...
...BED...
... DREAMS...
...NIGHT-MARES!

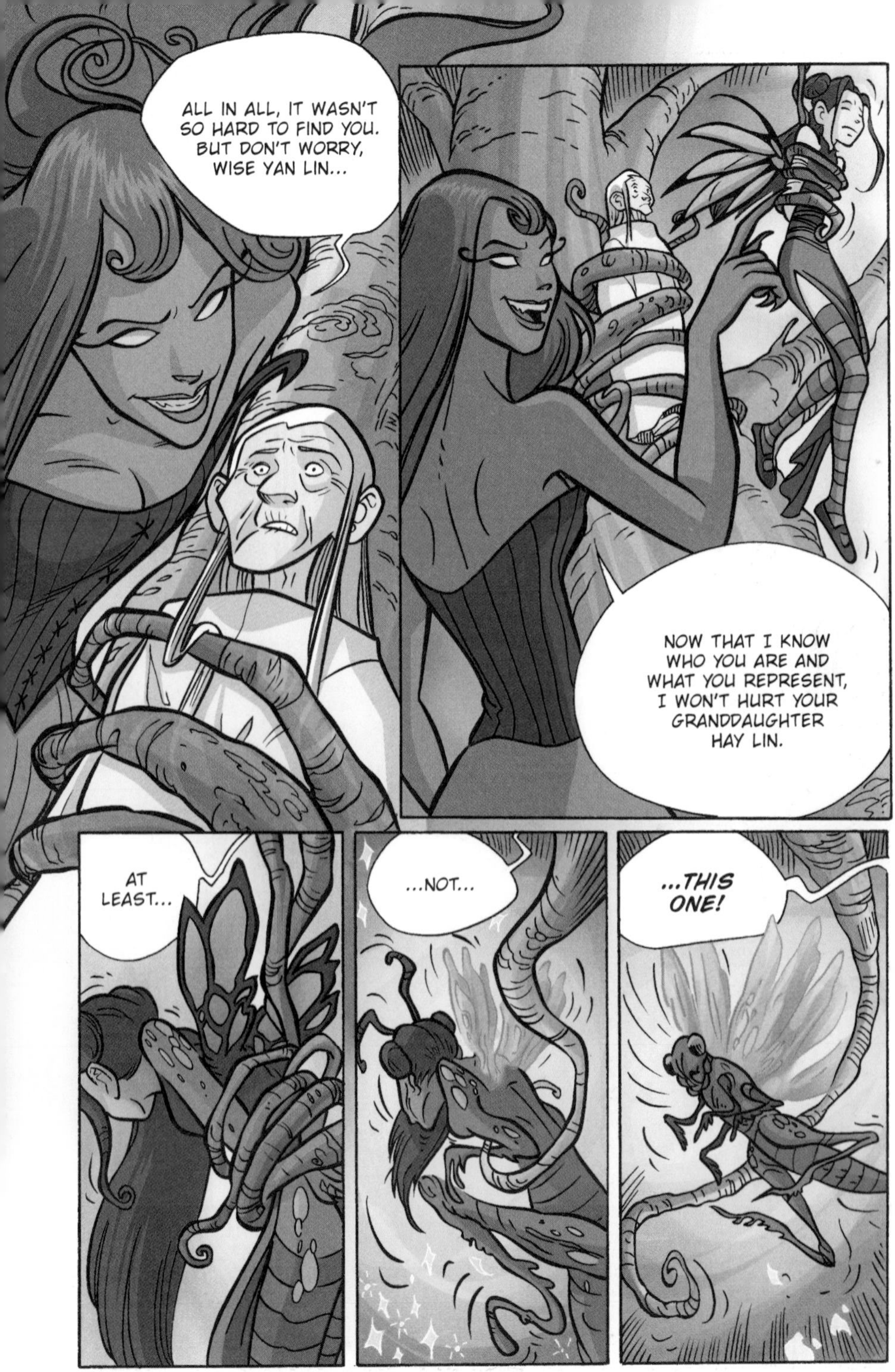

ALL IN ALL, IT WASN'T SO HARD TO FIND YOU. BUT DON'T WORRY, WISE YAN LIN...
NOW THAT I KNOW WHO YOU ARE AND WHAT YOU REPRESENT, I WON'T HURT YOUR GRANDDAUGHTER HAY LIN.
AT LEAST...
...NOT...
...THIS ONE!

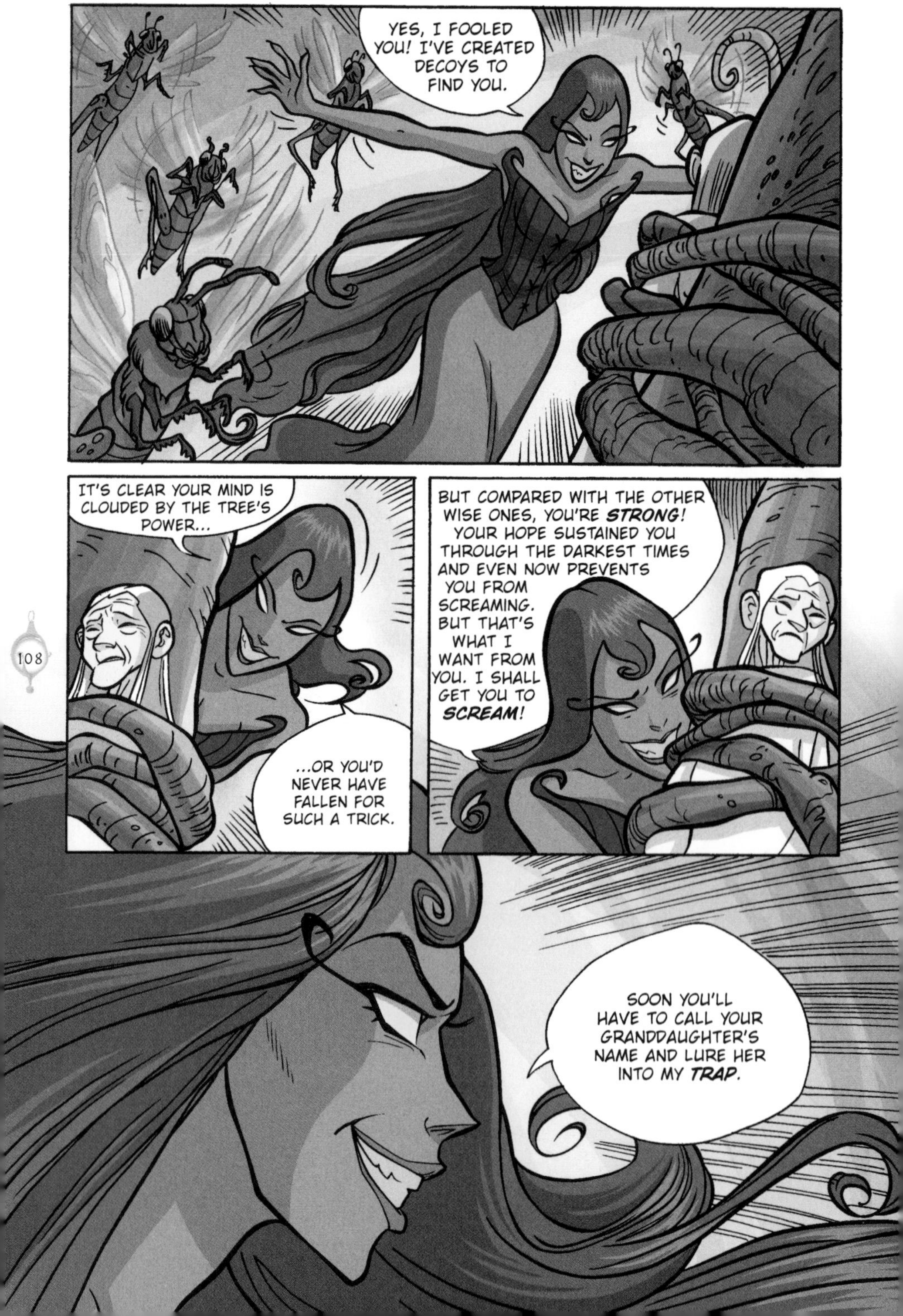
YES, I FOOLED YOU! I'VE CREATED DECOYS TO FIND YOU.
IT'S CLEAR YOUR MIND IS CLOUDED BY THE TREE'S POWER...
...OR YOU'D NEVER HAVE FALLEN FOR SUCH A TRICK.
BUT COMPARED WITH THE OTHER WISE ONES, YOU'RE *STRONG*! YOUR HOPE SUSTAINED YOU THROUGH THE DARKEST TIMES AND EVEN NOW PREVENTS YOU FROM SCREAMING. BUT THAT'S WHAT I WANT FROM YOU. I SHALL GET YOU TO *SCREAM*!
SOON YOU'LL HAVE TO CALL YOUR GRANDDAUGHTER'S NAME AND LURE HER INTO MY *TRAP*.

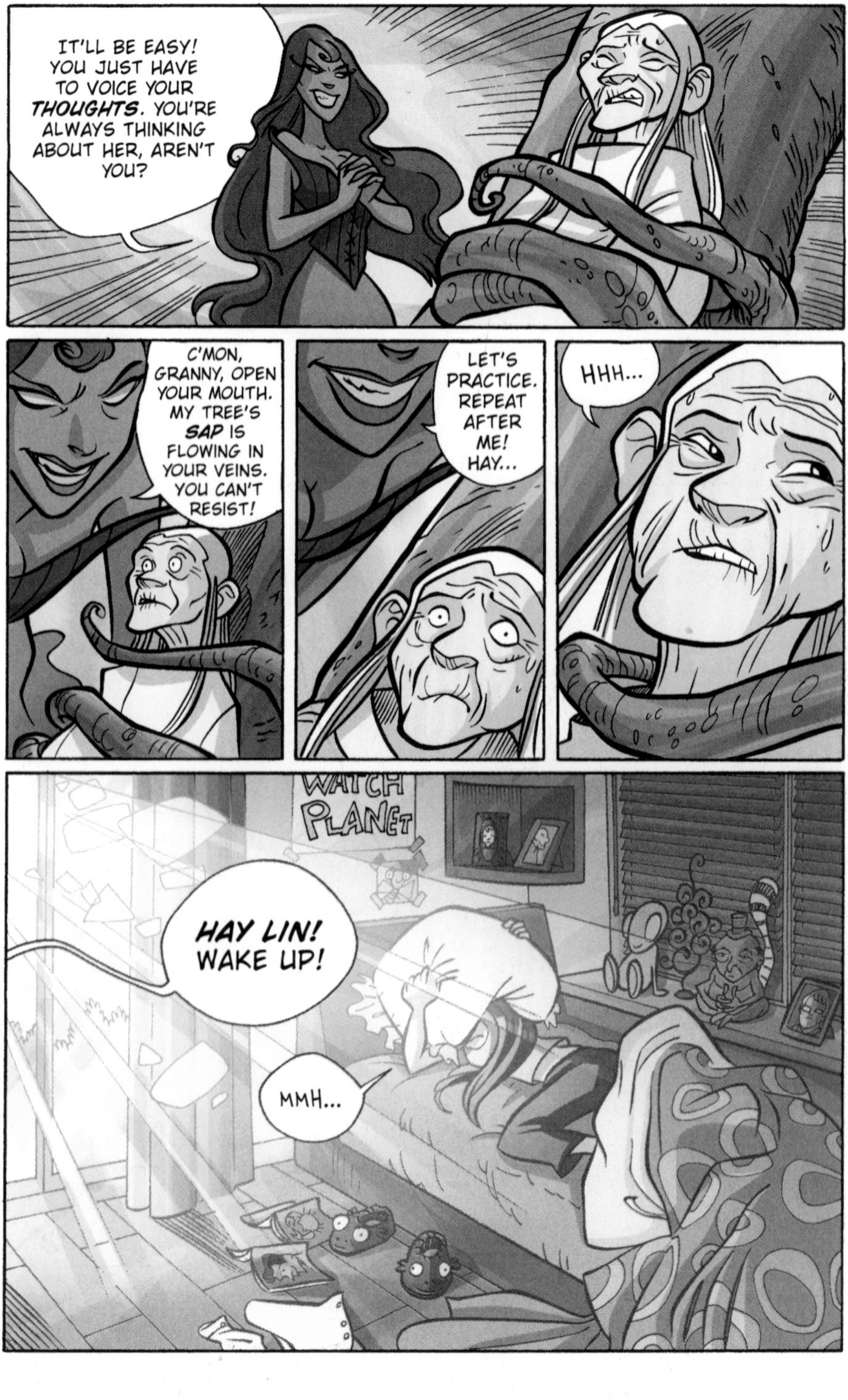
IT'LL BE EASY! YOU JUST HAVE TO VOICE YOUR THOUGHTS. YOU'RE ALWAYS THINKING ABOUT HER, AREN'T YOU?
C'MON, GRANNY, OPEN YOUR MOUTH. MY TREE'S SAP IS FLOWING IN YOUR VEINS. YOU CAN'T RESIST!
LET'S PRACTICE. REPEAT AFTER ME! HAY...
HHH...
WATCH PLANET
HAY LIN! WAKE UP!
MMH...

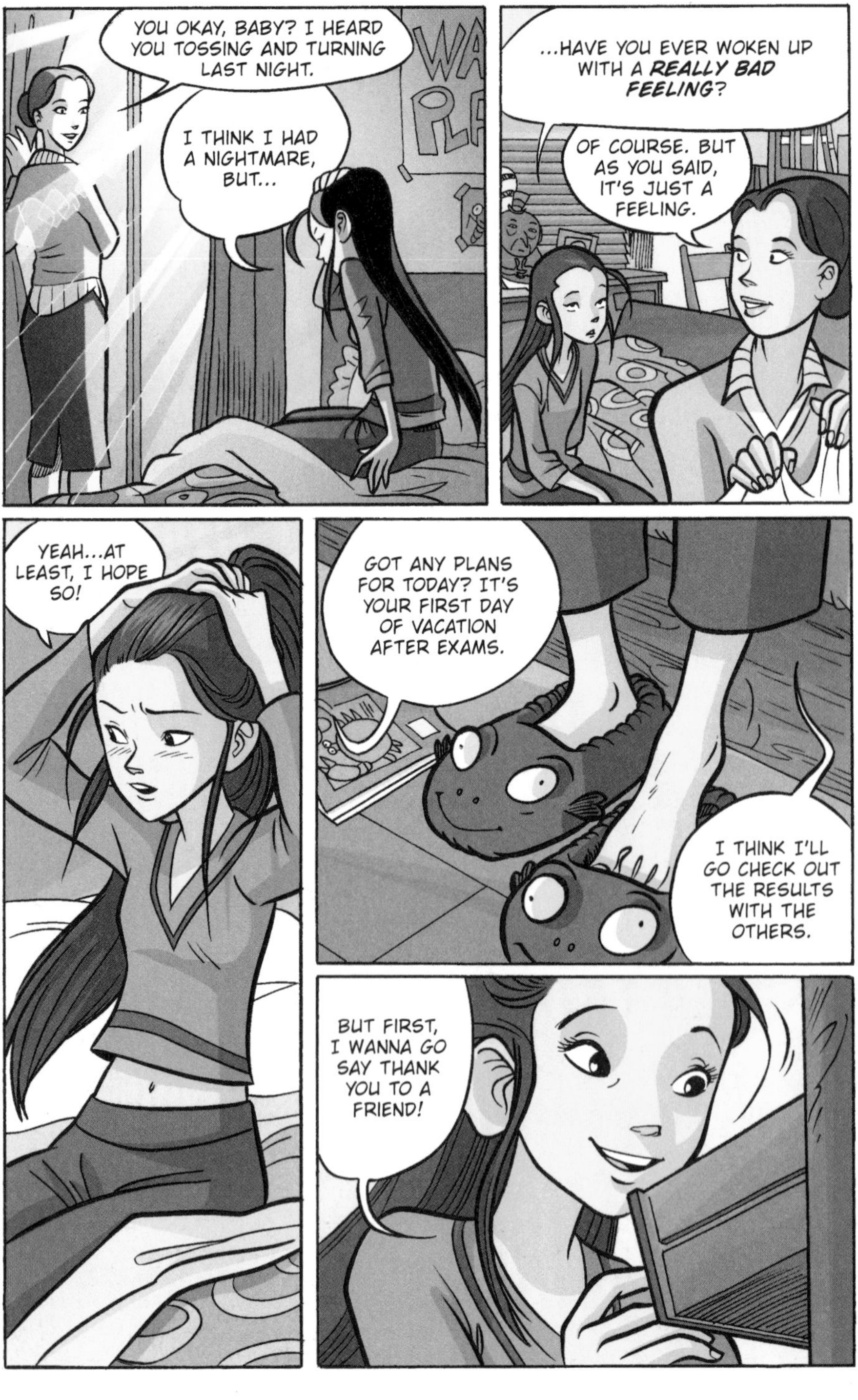

YOU OKAY, BABY? I HEARD YOU TOSSING AND TURNING LAST NIGHT.
I THINK I HAD A NIGHTMARE, BUT...
...HAVE YOU EVER WOKEN UP WITH A ***REALLY BAD FEELING***?
OF COURSE. BUT AS YOU SAID, IT'S JUST A FEELING.
YEAH...AT LEAST, I HOPE SO!
GOT ANY PLANS FOR TODAY? IT'S YOUR FIRST DAY OF VACATION AFTER EXAMS.
I THINK I'LL GO CHECK OUT THE RESULTS WITH THE OTHERS.
BUT FIRST, I WANNA GO SAY THANK YOU TO A FRIEND!

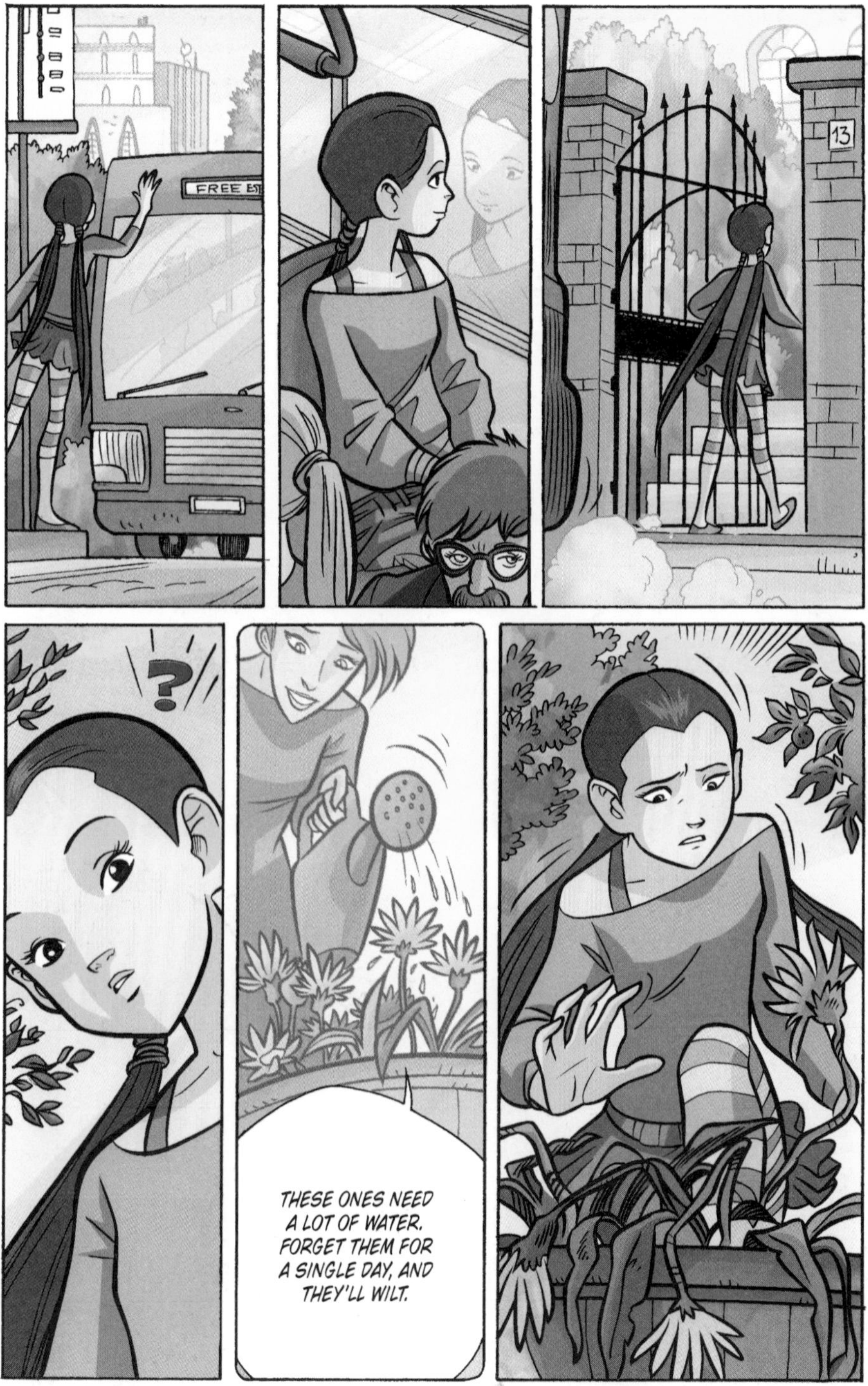
FREE
13
?
THESE ONES NEED A LOT OF WATER. FORGET THEM FOR A SINGLE DAY, AND THEY'LL WILT.

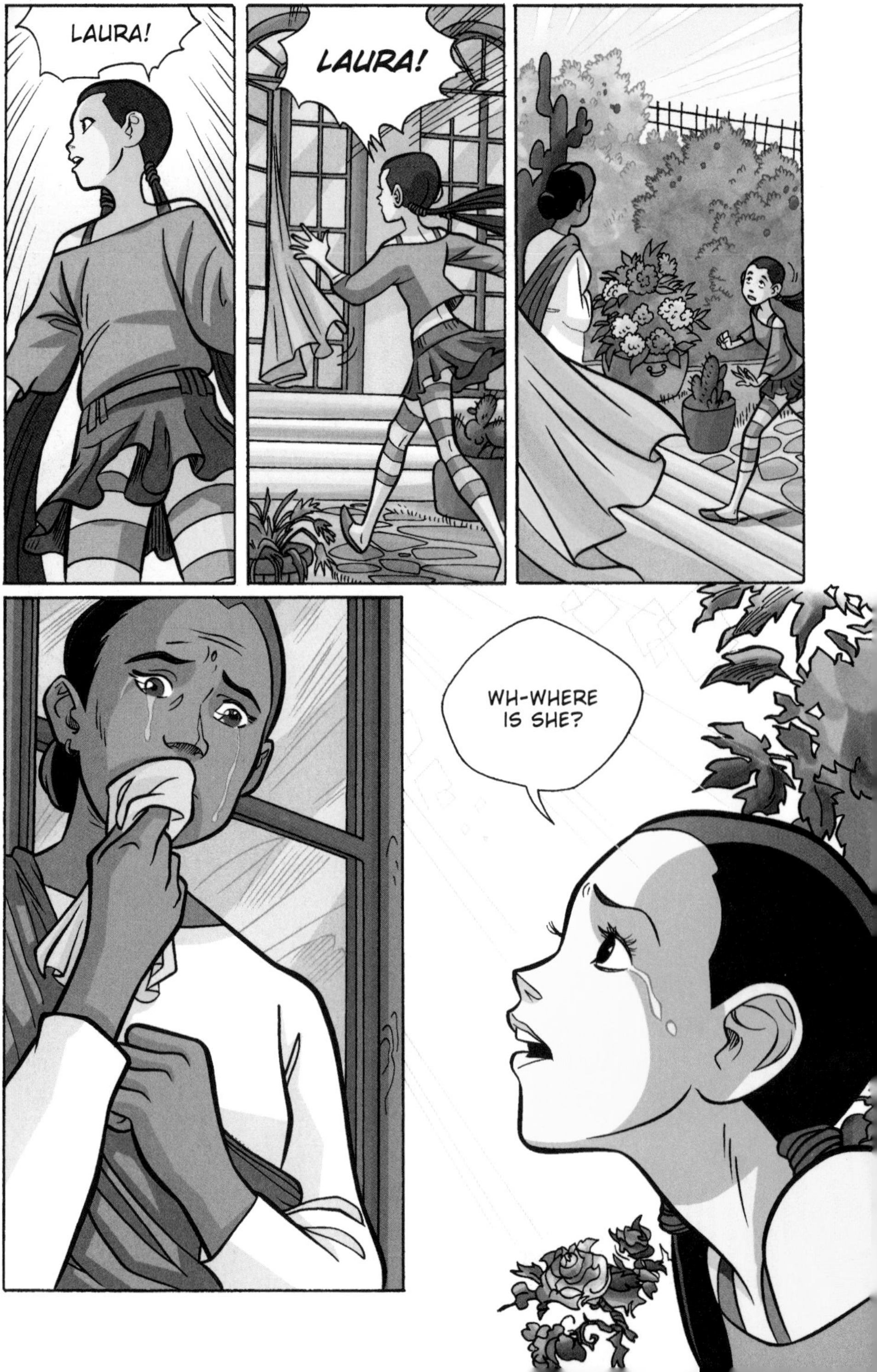
LAURA!
LAURA!
WH-WHERE IS SHE?

WHERE IS IT? IT'S NOT... AH, **FOUND IT!**

Andrea Lee ✓
Irma Lair ✓
Jessica Smith ✗
Cora Bloom ✓
Jerry
Danilo
Car...
Silvio

YAAAY! I ALMOST GOT STRAIGHT A'S!

UNBELIEVABLE!

WHAT? THE FACT THAT I ACED IT FOR ONCE?

NO, THE FACT THAT, DESPITE EVERYTHING, **WE MADE IT!**

MR. JENSEN! WHAT'RE YOU DOING HERE?

I WAS LOOKING FOR YOU. I'M AFRAID I'VE GOT BAD NEWS.

LAURA STEEDSON ...SHE...

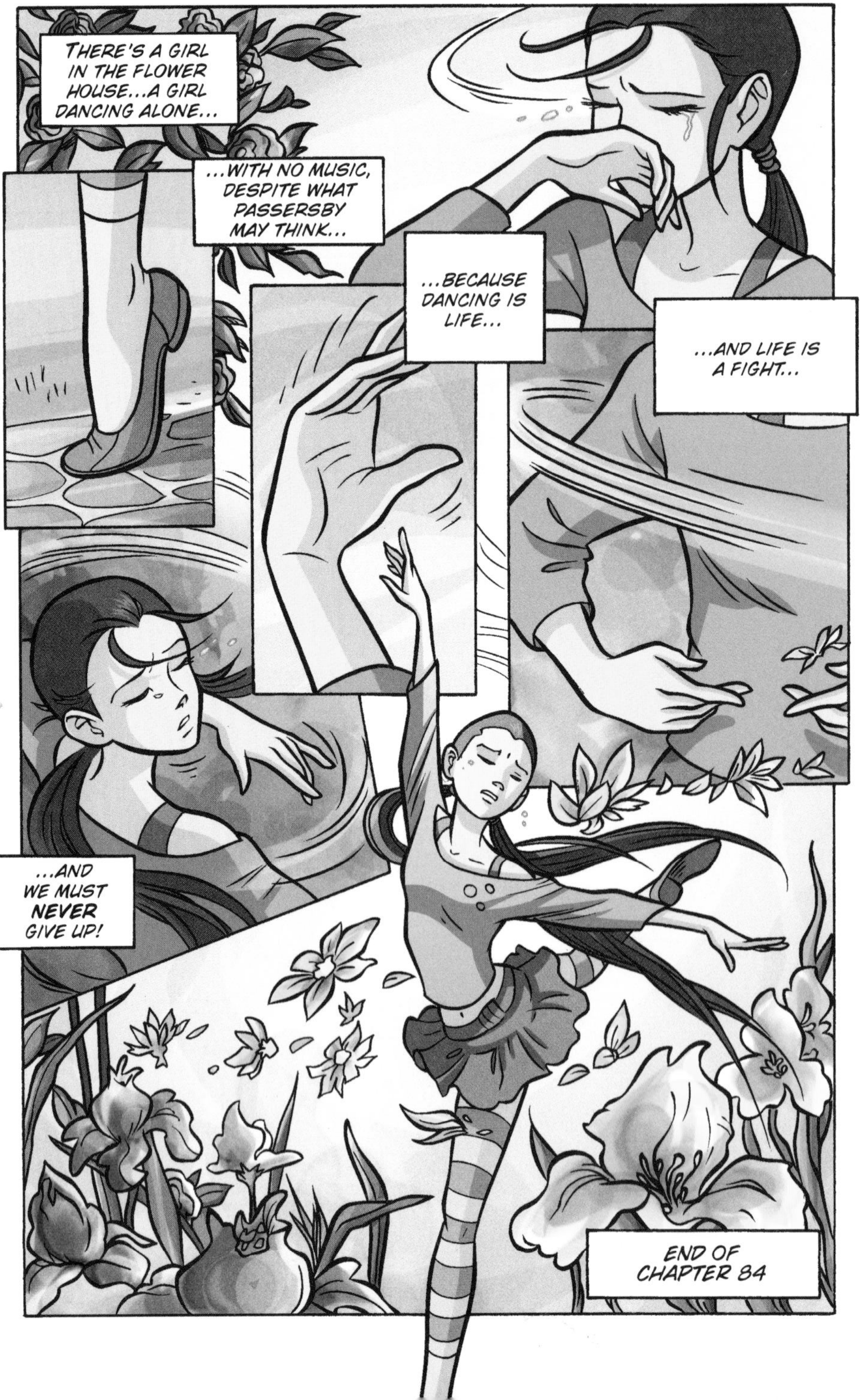
THERE'S A GIRL IN THE FLOWER HOUSE...A GIRL DANCING ALONE...
...WITH NO MUSIC, DESPITE WHAT PASSERSBY MAY THINK...
...BECAUSE DANCING IS LIFE...
...AND LIFE IS A FIGHT...
...AND WE MUST **NEVER** GIVE UP!
END OF CHAPTER 84

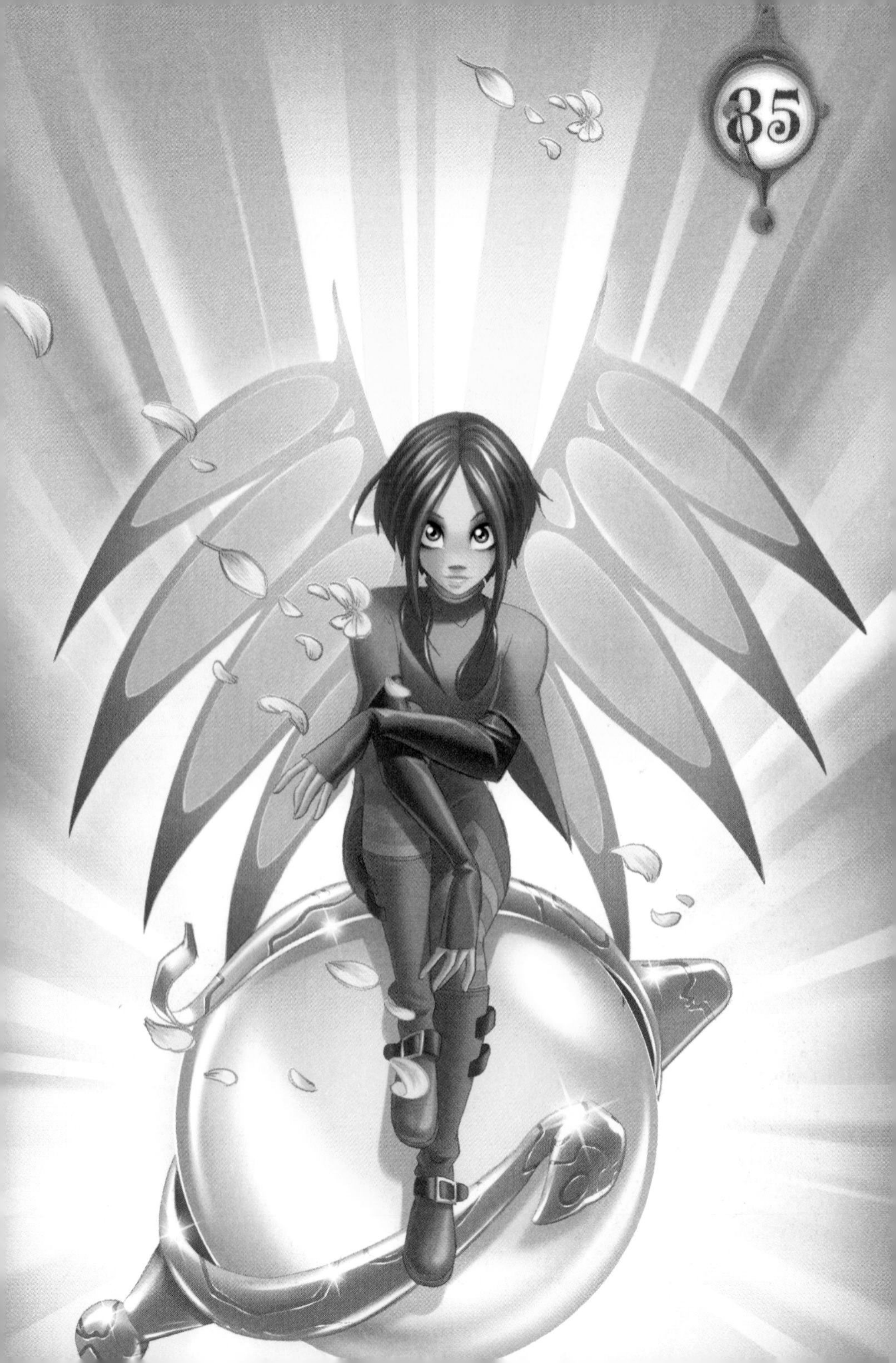
35

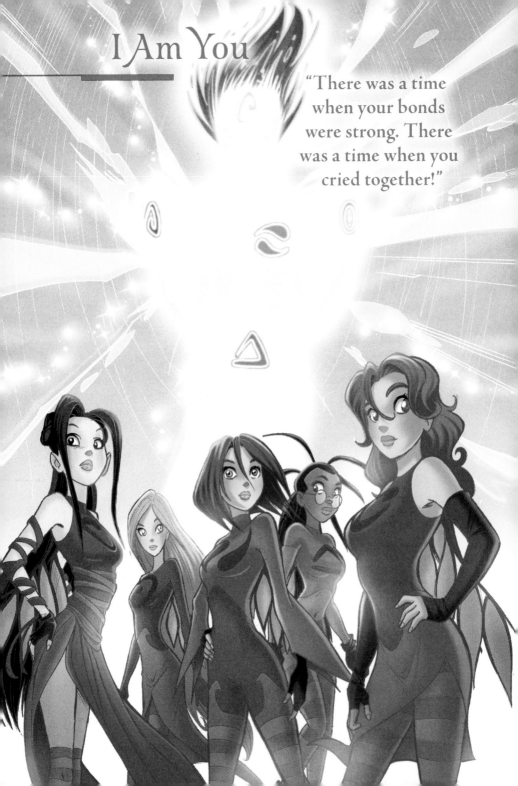

I Am You

"There was a time when your bonds were strong. There was a time when you cried together!"

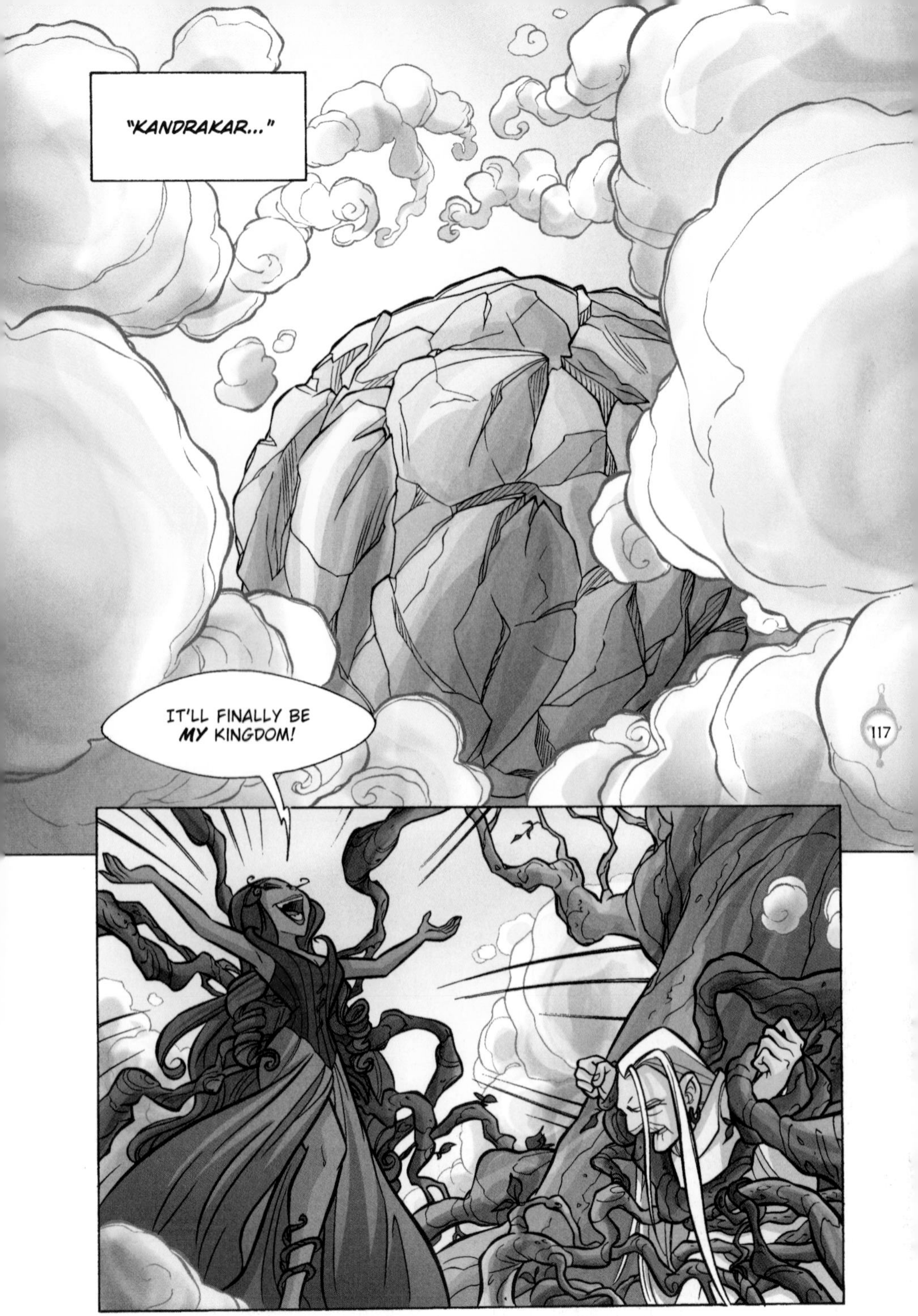
"KANDRAKAR..."
IT'LL FINALLY BE *MY* KINGDOM!

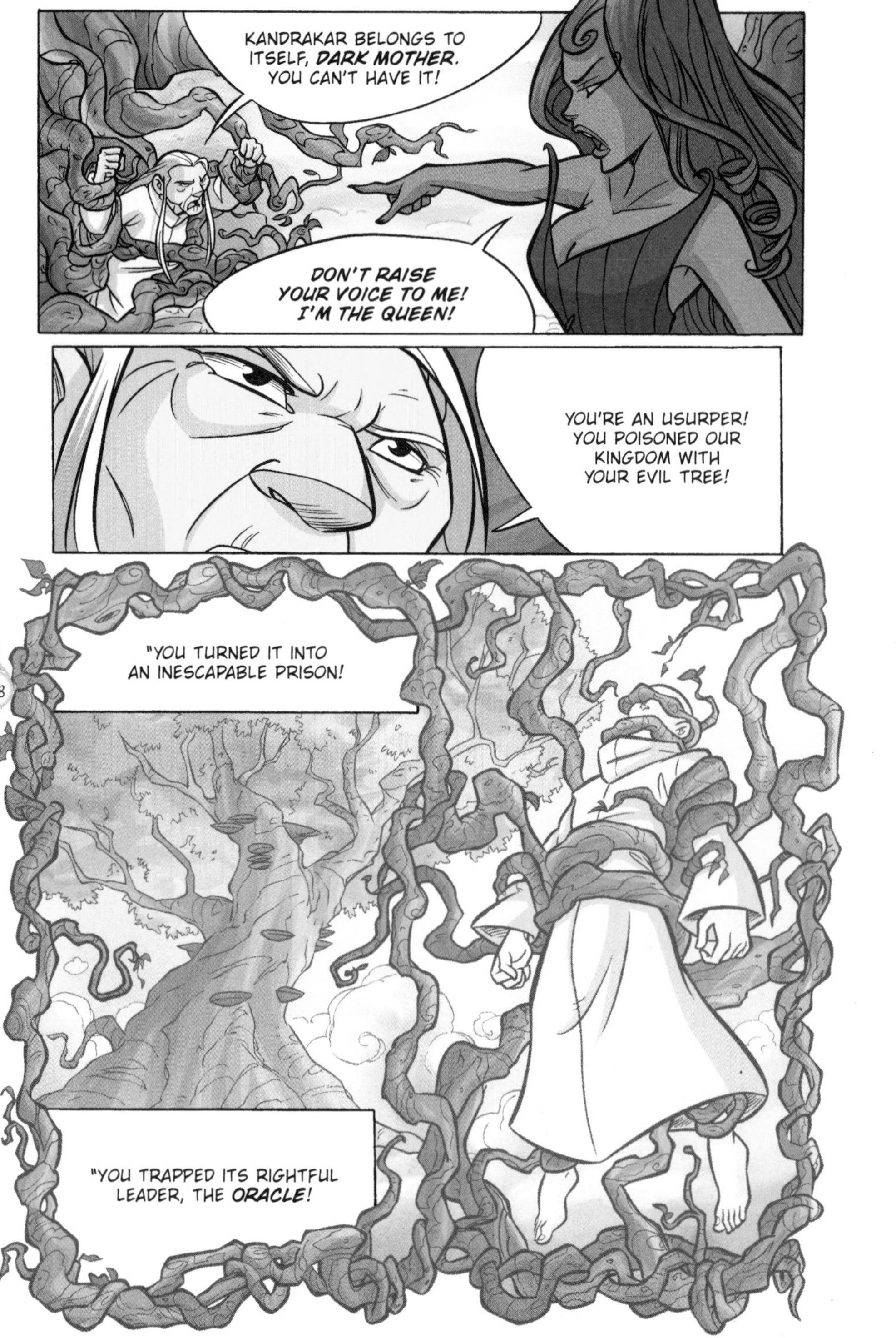
KANDRAKAR BELONGS TO ITSELF, ***DARK MOTHER***. YOU CAN'T HAVE IT!
DON'T RAISE YOUR VOICE TO ME! I'M THE QUEEN!
YOU'RE AN USURPER! YOU POISONED OUR KINGDOM WITH YOUR EVIL TREE!
"YOU TURNED IT INTO AN INESCAPABLE PRISON!
"YOU TRAPPED ITS RIGHTFUL LEADER, THE ***ORACLE***!

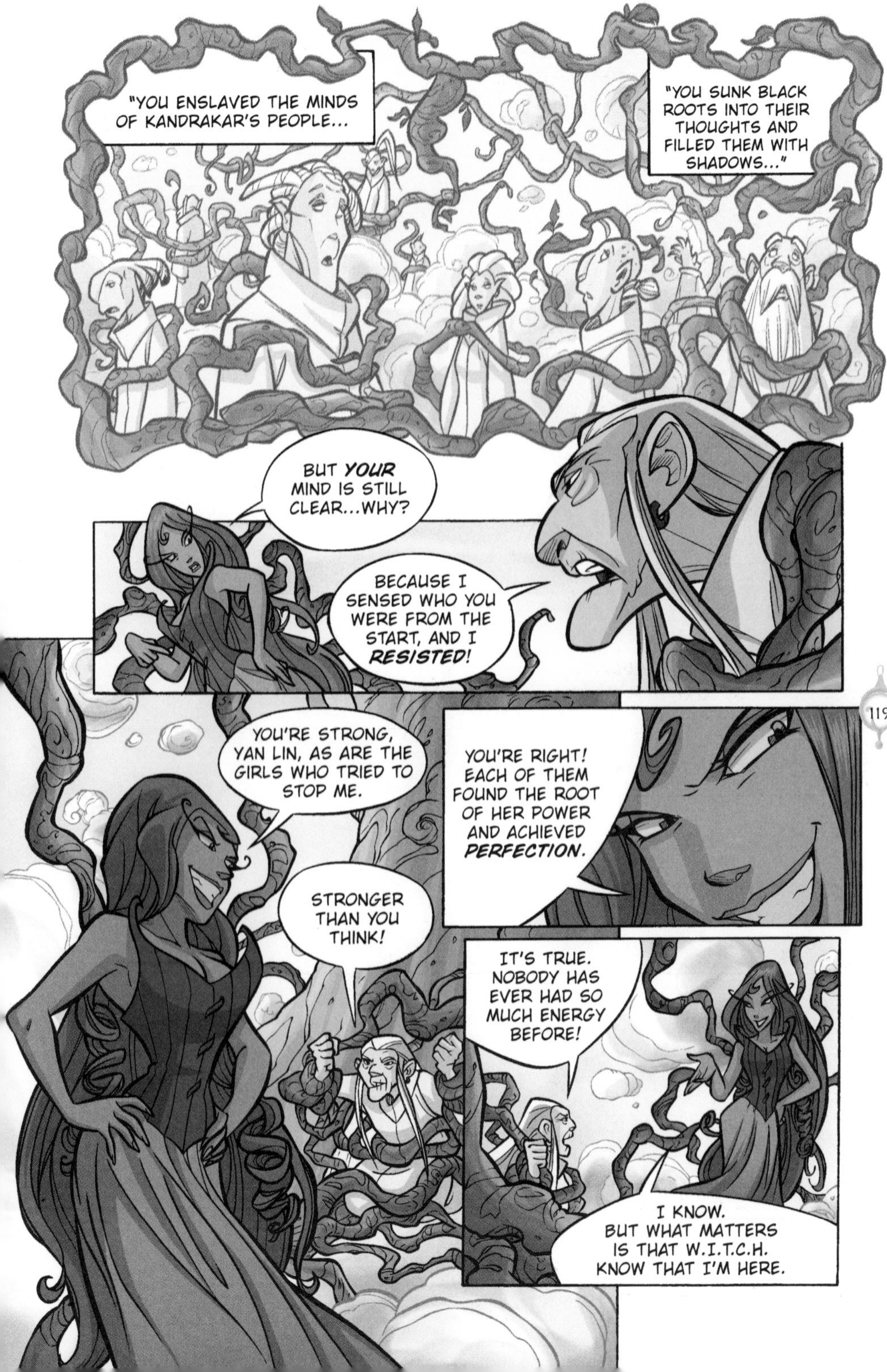
"YOU ENSLAVED THE MINDS OF KANDRAKAR'S PEOPLE...
"YOU SUNK BLACK ROOTS INTO THEIR THOUGHTS AND FILLED THEM WITH SHADOWS..."
BUT *YOUR* MIND IS STILL CLEAR...WHY?
BECAUSE I SENSED WHO YOU WERE FROM THE START, AND I *RESISTED*!
YOU'RE STRONG, YAN LIN, AS ARE THE GIRLS WHO TRIED TO STOP ME.
YOU'RE RIGHT! EACH OF THEM FOUND THE ROOT OF HER POWER AND ACHIEVED *PERFECTION*.
STRONGER THAN YOU THINK!
IT'S TRUE. NOBODY HAS EVER HAD SO MUCH ENERGY BEFORE!
I KNOW. BUT WHAT MATTERS IS THAT W.I.T.C.H. KNOW THAT I'M HERE.

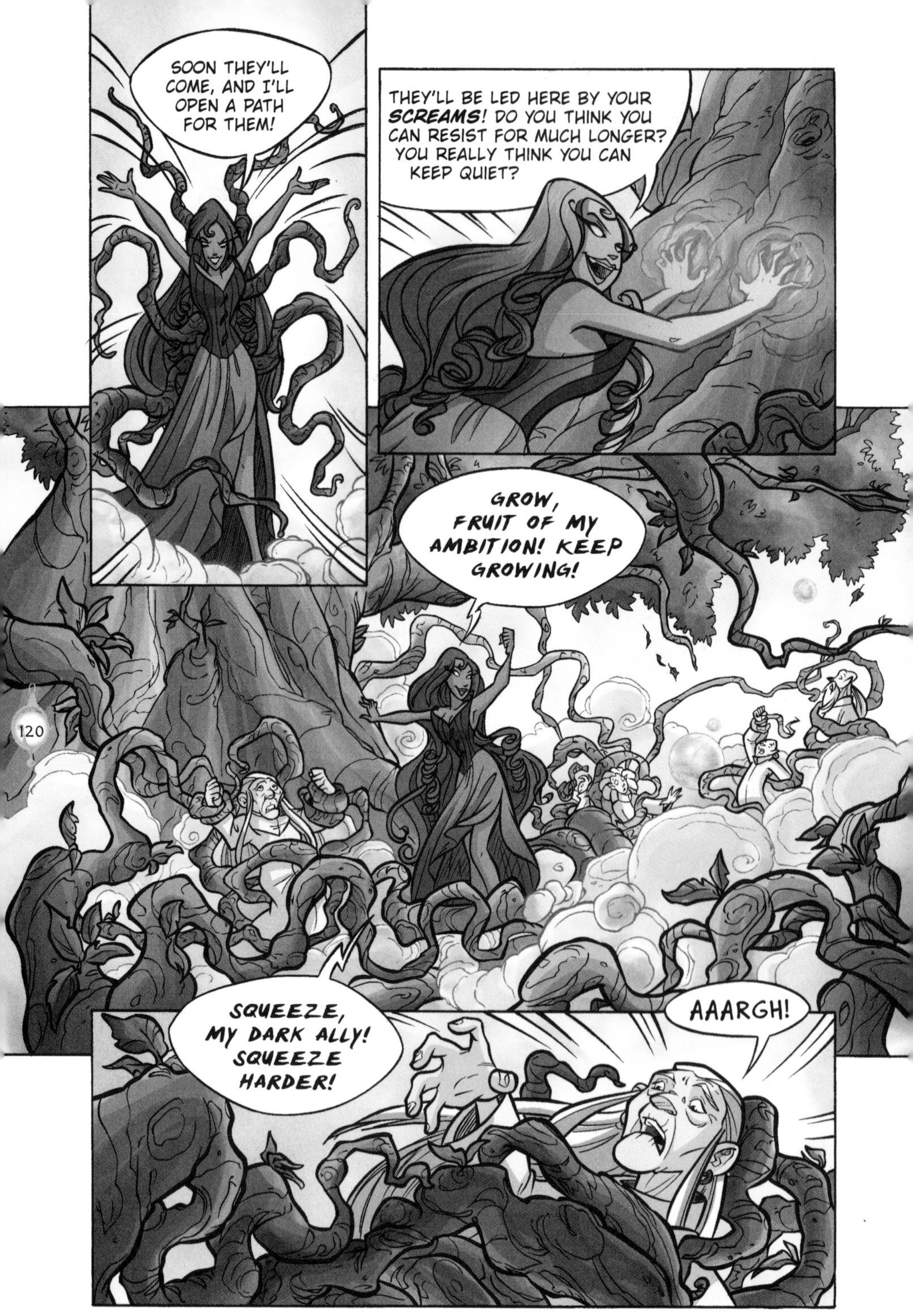
SOON THEY'LL COME, AND I'LL OPEN A PATH FOR THEM!
THEY'LL BE LED HERE BY YOUR SCREAMS! DO YOU THINK YOU CAN RESIST FOR MUCH LONGER? YOU REALLY THINK YOU CAN KEEP QUIET?
GROW, FRUIT OF MY AMBITION! KEEP GROWING!
SQUEEZE, MY DARK ALLY! SQUEEZE HARDER!
AAARGH!

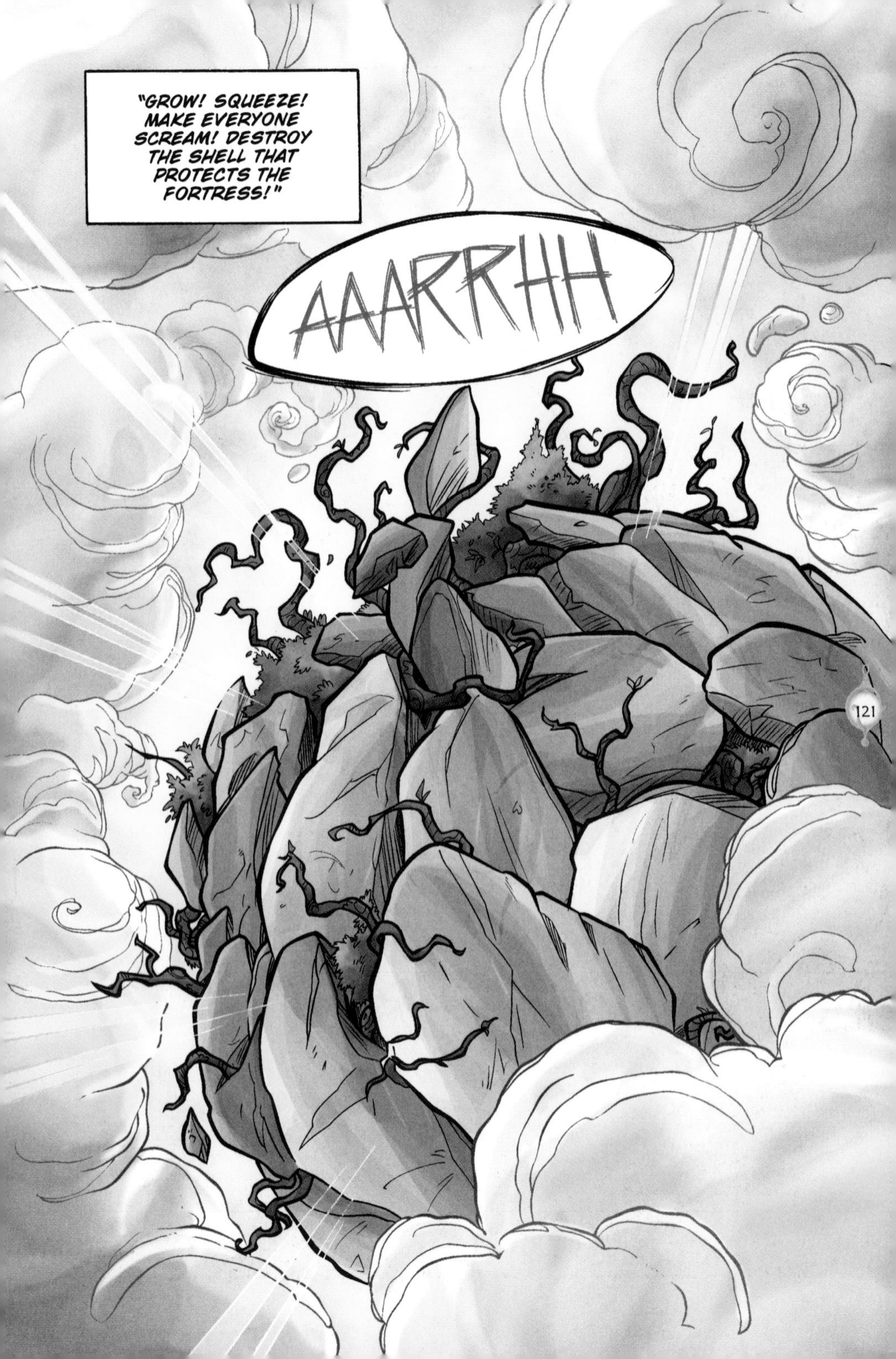
"GROW! SQUEEZE! MAKE EVERYONE SCREAM! DESTROY THE SHELL THAT PROTECTS THE FORTRESS!"
AAARRHH

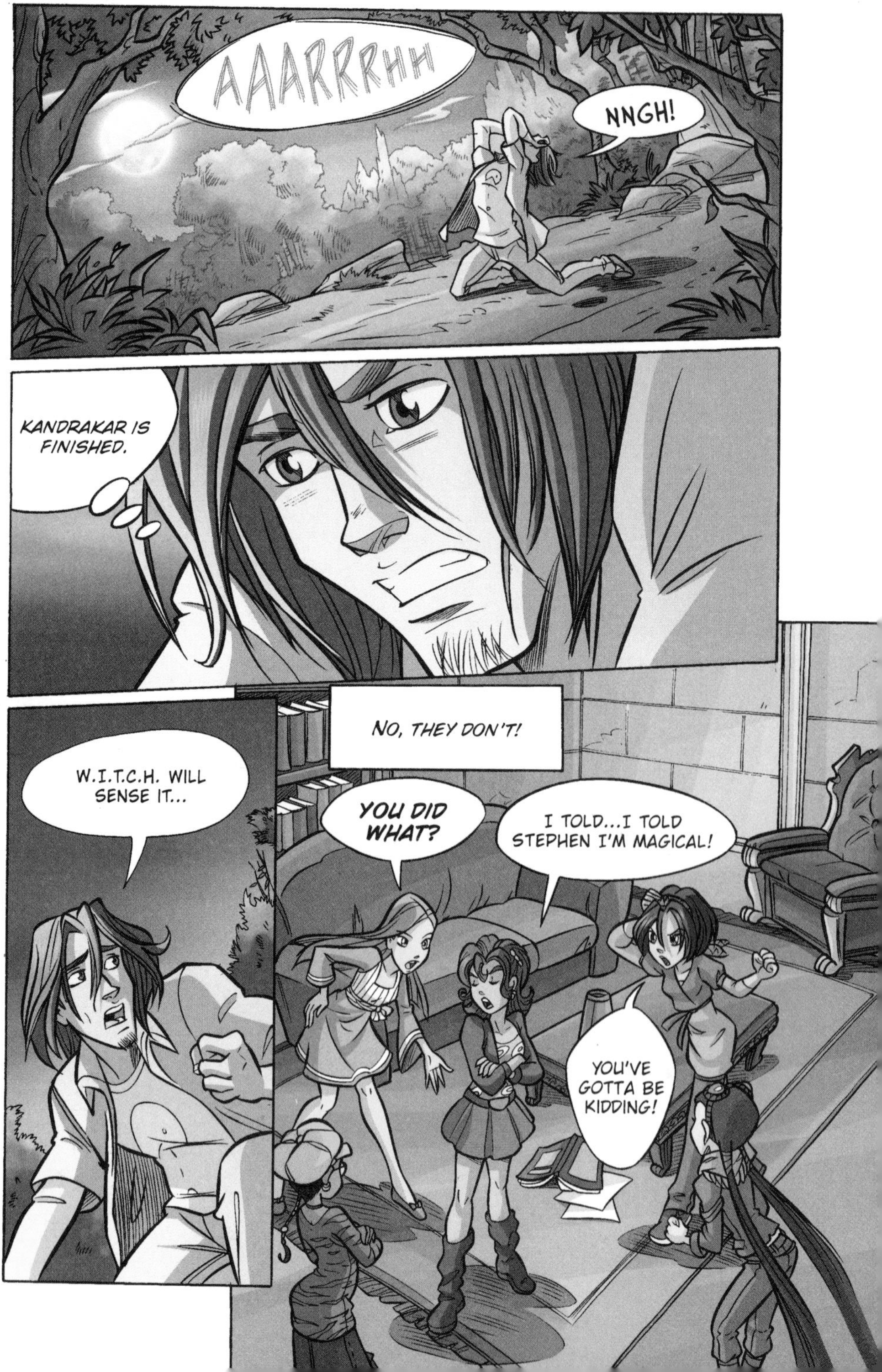
AAARRRHH
NNGH!
KANDRAKAR IS FINISHED.
W.I.T.C.H. WILL SENSE IT...
NO, THEY DON'T!
YOU DID WHAT?
I TOLD...I TOLD STEPHEN I'M MAGICAL!
YOU'VE GOTTA BE KIDDING!

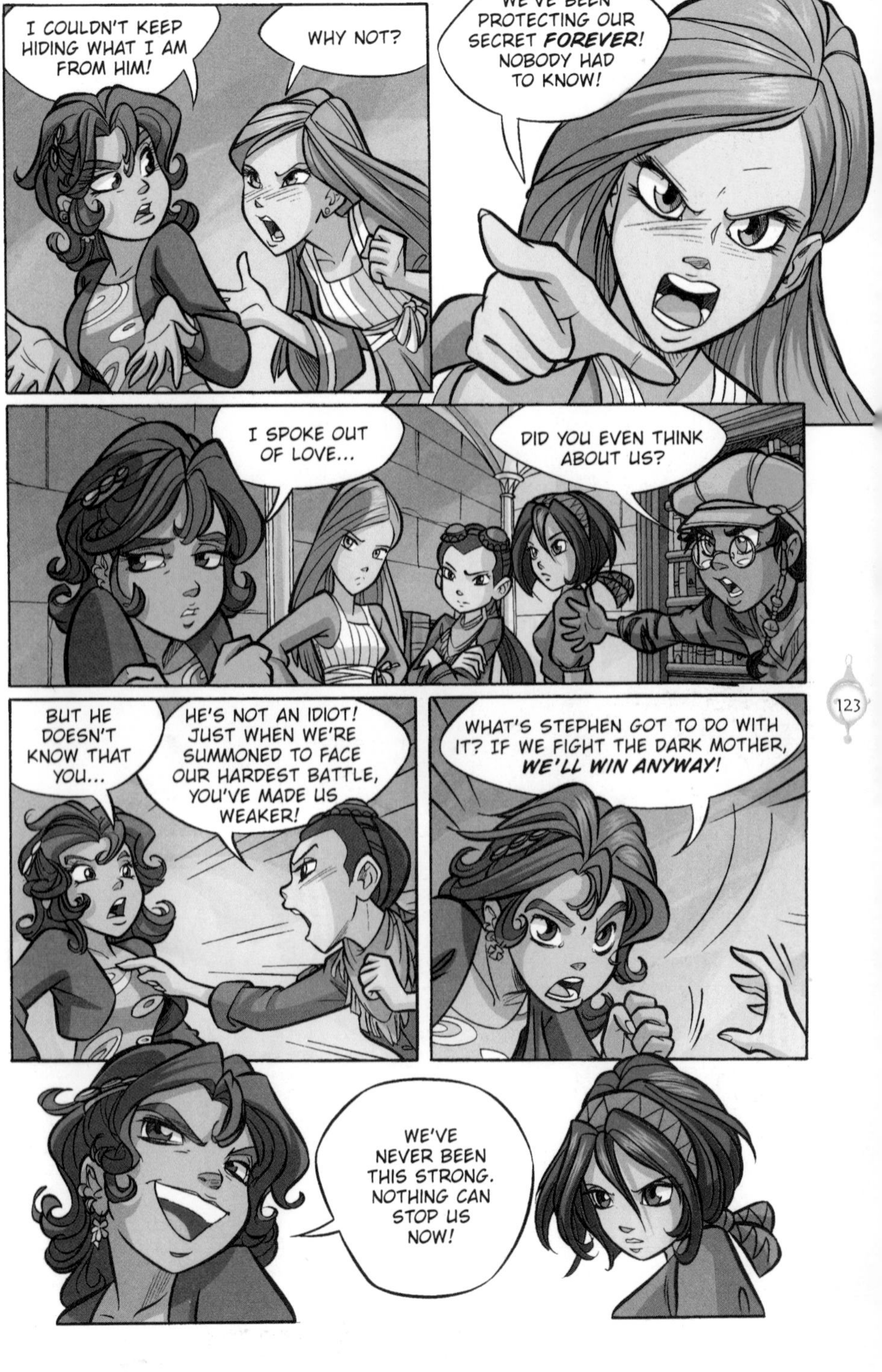
I COULDN'T KEEP HIDING WHAT I AM FROM HIM!
WHY NOT?
WE'VE BEEN PROTECTING OUR SECRET **FOREVER**! NOBODY HAD TO KNOW!
I SPOKE OUT OF LOVE...
DID YOU EVEN THINK ABOUT US?
BUT HE DOESN'T KNOW THAT YOU...
HE'S NOT AN IDIOT! JUST WHEN WE'RE SUMMONED TO FACE OUR HARDEST BATTLE, YOU'VE MADE US WEAKER!
WHAT'S STEPHEN GOT TO DO WITH IT? IF WE FIGHT THE DARK MOTHER, **WE'LL WIN ANYWAY**!
WE'VE NEVER BEEN THIS STRONG. NOTHING CAN STOP US NOW!

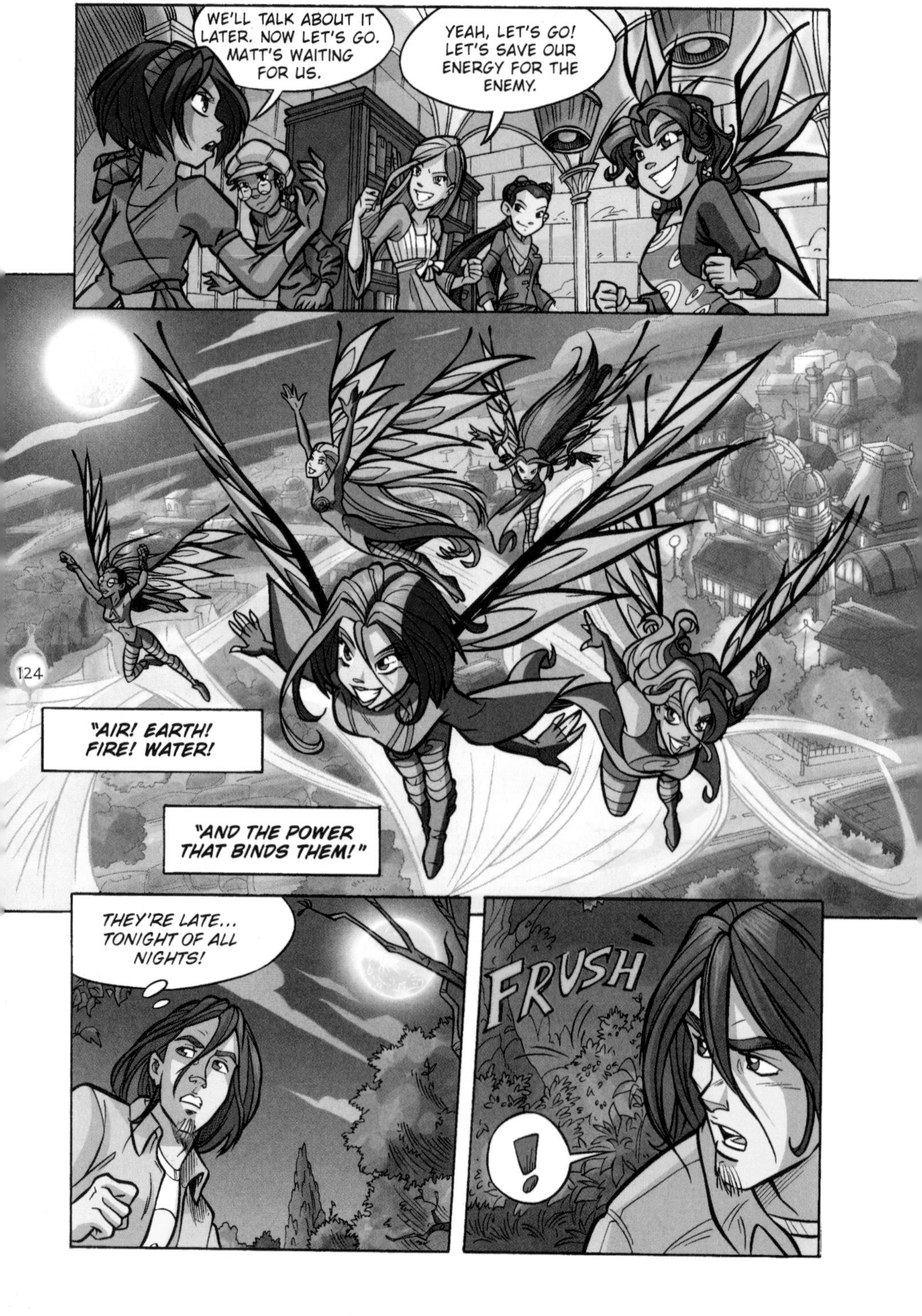

WE'LL TALK ABOUT IT LATER. NOW LET'S GO. MATT'S WAITING FOR US.
YEAH, LET'S GO! LET'S SAVE OUR ENERGY FOR THE ENEMY.
"AIR! EARTH! FIRE! WATER!
"AND THE POWER THAT BINDS THEM!"
THEY'RE LATE... TONIGHT OF ALL NIGHTS!
FRUSH
!

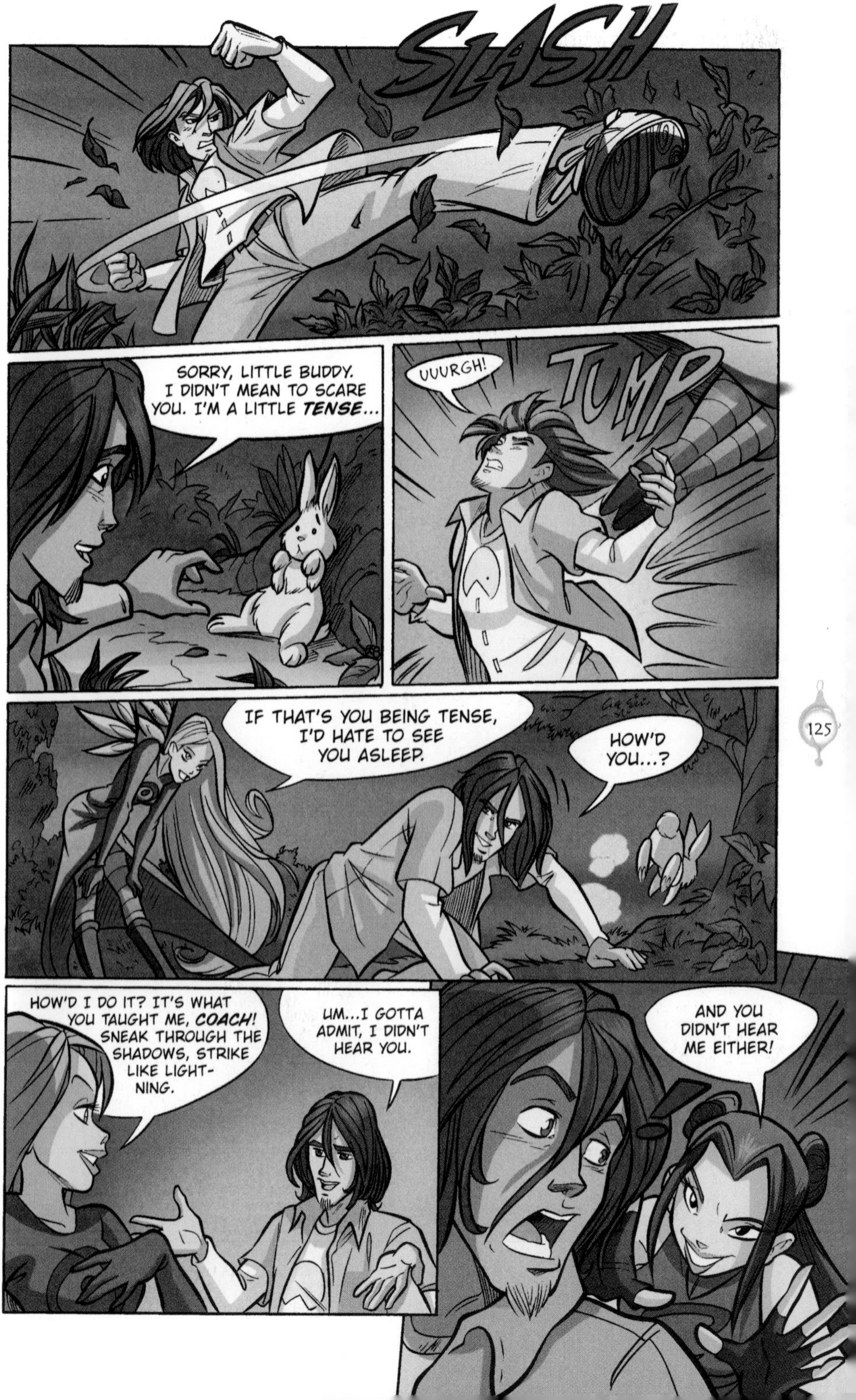

SLASH
SORRY, LITTLE BUDDY. I DIDN'T MEAN TO SCARE YOU. I'M A LITTLE TENSE...
UUURGH!
TUMP
IF THAT'S YOU BEING TENSE, I'D HATE TO SEE YOU ASLEEP.
HOW'D YOU...?
HOW'D I DO IT? IT'S WHAT YOU TAUGHT ME, COACH! SNEAK THROUGH THE SHADOWS, STRIKE LIKE LIGHT-NING.
UM...I GOTTA ADMIT, I DIDN'T HEAR YOU.
AND YOU DIDN'T HEAR ME EITHER!

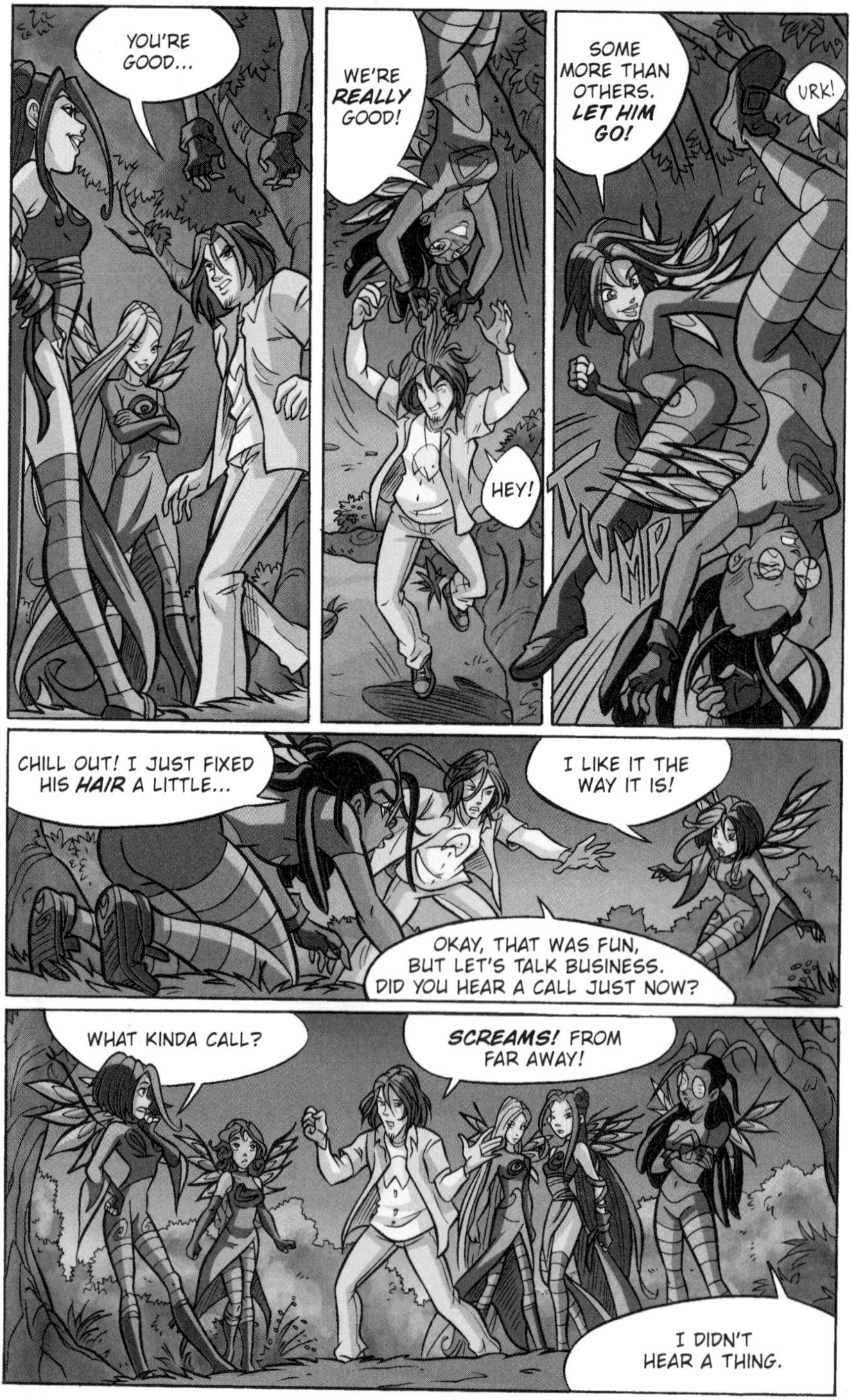
YOU'RE GOOD...
WE'RE *REALLY* GOOD!
HEY!
SOME MORE THAN OTHERS. *LET HIM GO!*
URK!
TUMP
CHILL OUT! I JUST FIXED HIS *HAIR* A LITTLE...
I LIKE IT THE WAY IT IS!
OKAY, THAT WAS FUN, BUT LET'S TALK BUSINESS. DID YOU HEAR A CALL JUST NOW?
WHAT KINDA CALL?
SCREAMS! FROM FAR AWAY!
I DIDN'T HEAR A THING.

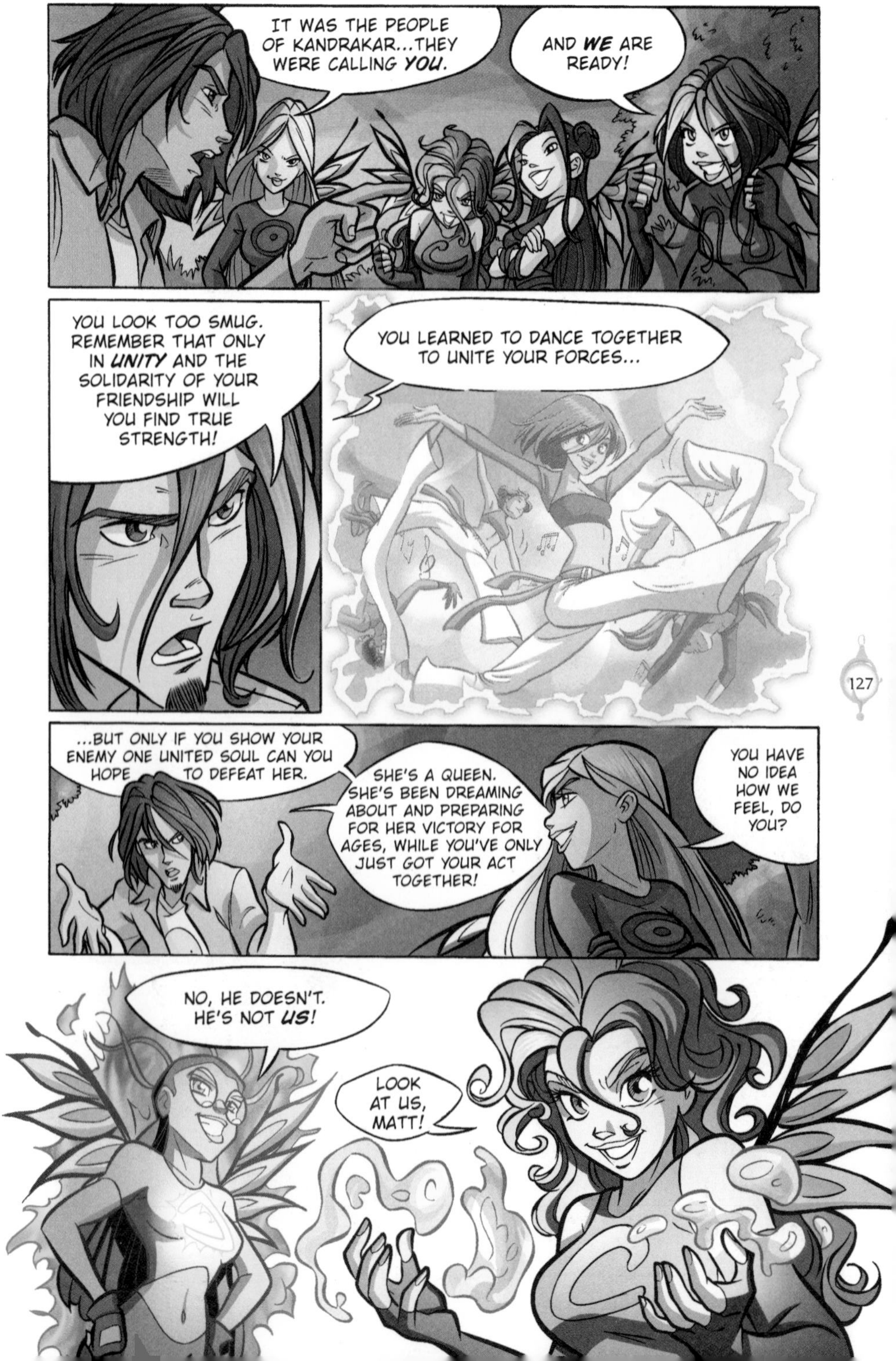
IT WAS THE PEOPLE OF KANDRAKAR...THEY WERE CALLING YOU.
AND WE ARE READY!
YOU LOOK TOO SMUG. REMEMBER THAT ONLY IN UNITY AND THE SOLIDARITY OF YOUR FRIENDSHIP WILL YOU FIND TRUE STRENGTH!
YOU LEARNED TO DANCE TOGETHER TO UNITE YOUR FORCES...
...BUT ONLY IF YOU SHOW YOUR ENEMY ONE UNITED SOUL CAN YOU HOPE TO DEFEAT HER.
SHE'S A QUEEN. SHE'S BEEN DREAMING ABOUT AND PREPARING FOR HER VICTORY FOR AGES, WHILE YOU'VE ONLY JUST GOT YOUR ACT TOGETHER!
YOU HAVE NO IDEA HOW WE FEEL, DO YOU?
NO, HE DOESN'T. HE'S NOT US!
LOOK AT US, MATT!

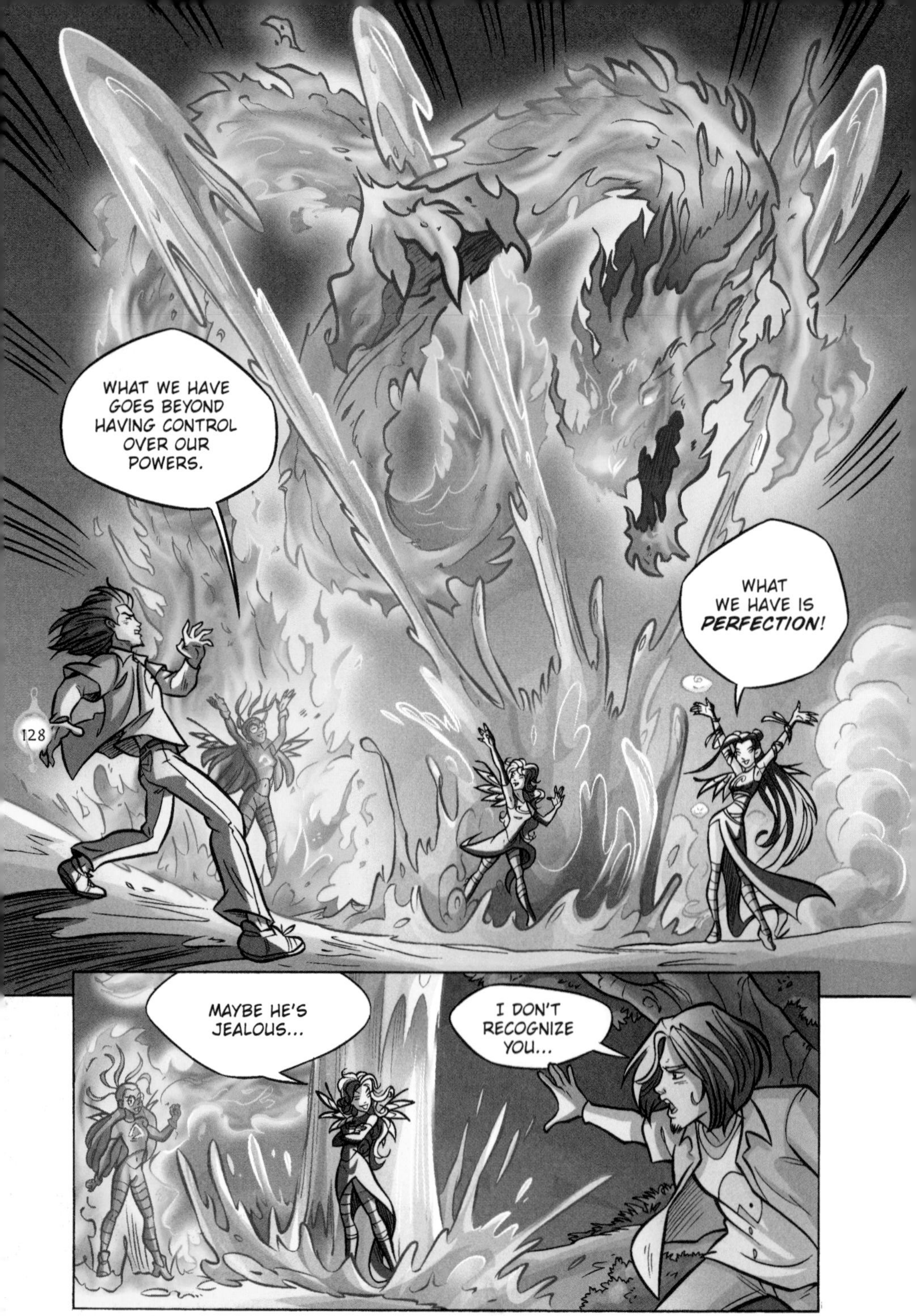
WHAT WE HAVE GOES BEYOND HAVING CONTROL OVER OUR POWERS.
WHAT WE HAVE IS *PERFECTION!*
MAYBE HE'S JEALOUS...
I DON'T RECOGNIZE YOU...

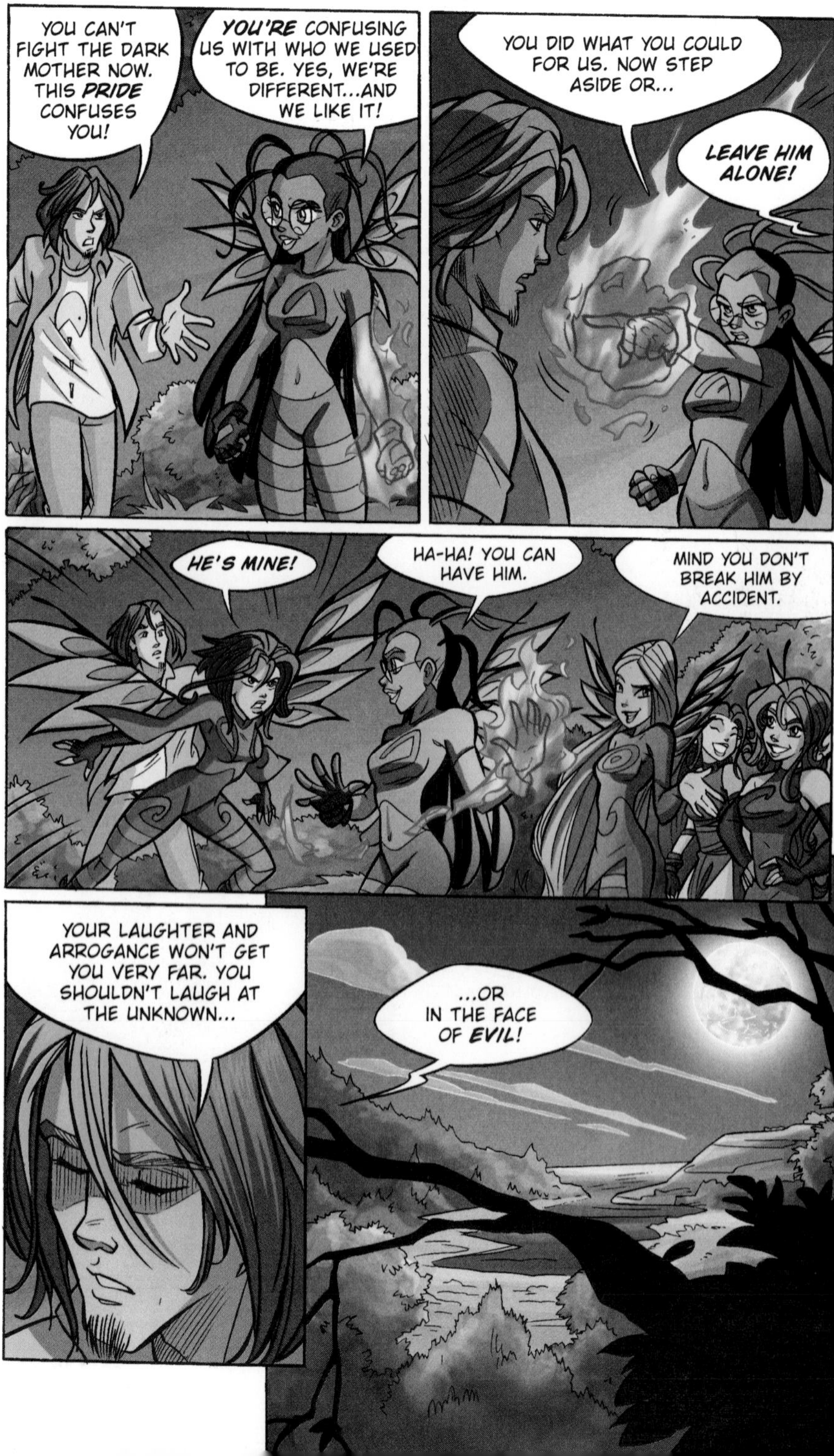
YOU CAN'T FIGHT THE DARK MOTHER NOW. THIS PRIDE CONFUSES YOU!
YOU'RE CONFUSING US WITH WHO WE USED TO BE. YES, WE'RE DIFFERENT...AND WE LIKE IT!
YOU DID WHAT YOU COULD FOR US. NOW STEP ASIDE OR...
LEAVE HIM ALONE!
HE'S MINE!
HA-HA! YOU CAN HAVE HIM.
MIND YOU DON'T BREAK HIM BY ACCIDENT.
YOUR LAUGHTER AND ARROGANCE WON'T GET YOU VERY FAR. YOU SHOULDN'T LAUGH AT THE UNKNOWN...
...OR IN THE FACE OF EVIL!

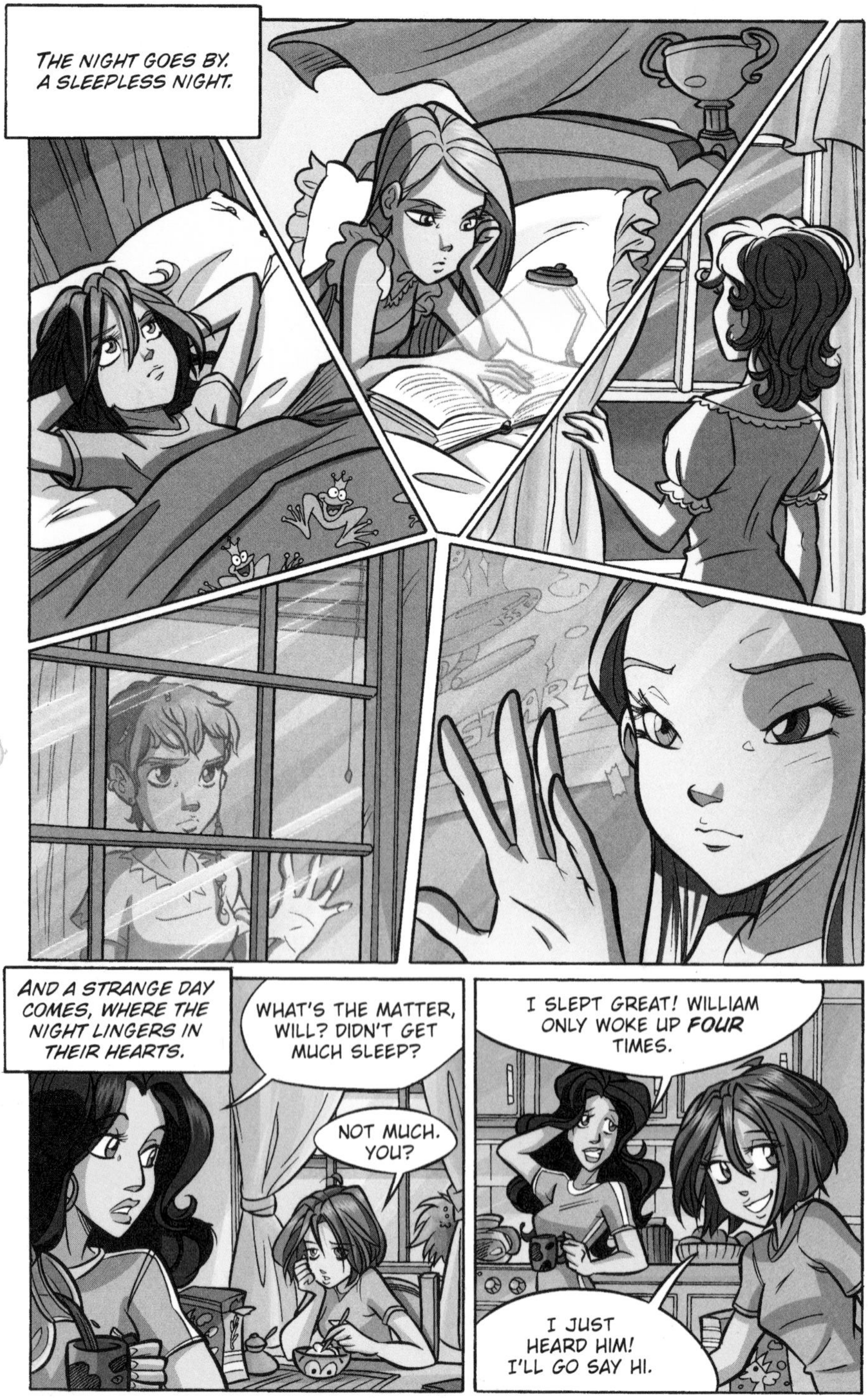
THE NIGHT GOES BY. A SLEEPLESS NIGHT.
AND A STRANGE DAY COMES, WHERE THE NIGHT LINGERS IN THEIR HEARTS.
WHAT'S THE MATTER, WILL? DIDN'T GET MUCH SLEEP?
NOT MUCH. YOU?
I SLEPT GREAT! WILLIAM ONLY WOKE UP FOUR TIMES.
I JUST HEARD HIM! I'LL GO SAY HI.

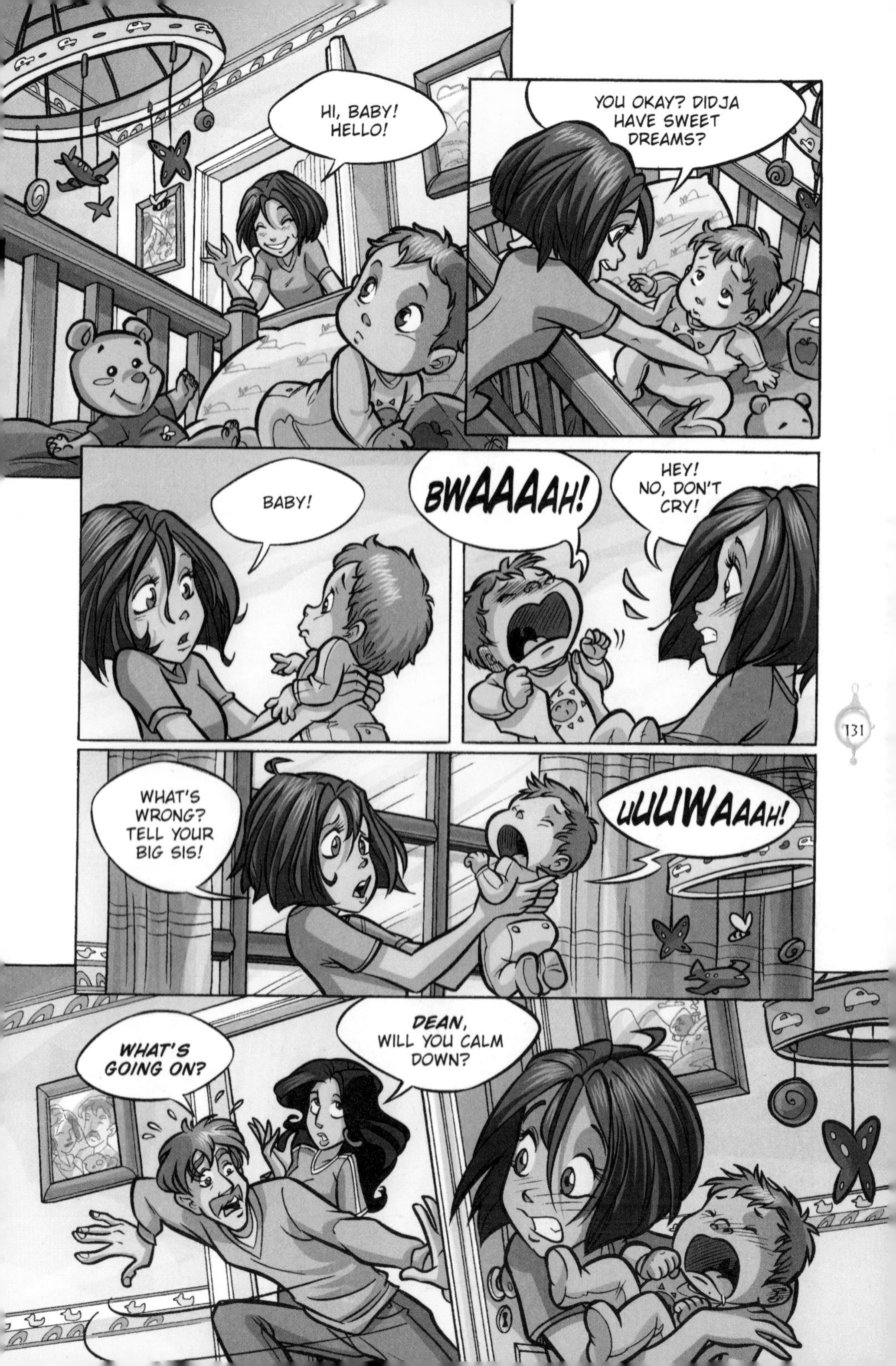
HI, BABY! HELLO!
YOU OKAY? DIDJA HAVE SWEET DREAMS?
BABY!
BWAAAAH!
HEY! NO, DON'T CRY!
WHAT'S WRONG? TELL YOUR BIG SIS!
uUUWAAAH!
WHAT'S GOING ON?
DEAN, WILL YOU CALM DOWN?

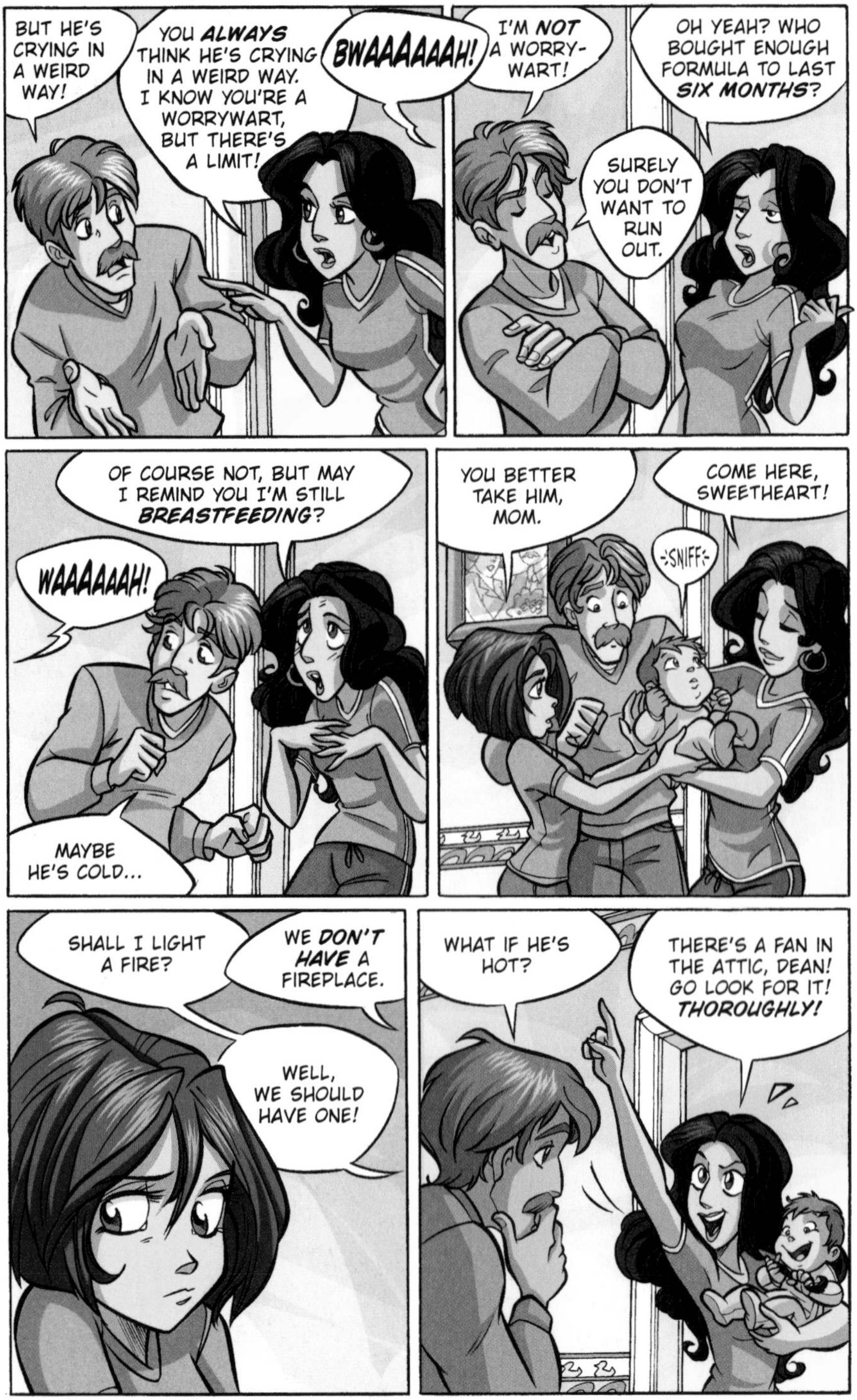
BUT HE'S CRYING IN A WEIRD WAY!
YOU ALWAYS THINK HE'S CRYING IN A WEIRD WAY. I KNOW YOU'RE A WORRYWART, BUT THERE'S A LIMIT!
BWAAAAAAAH!
I'M NOT A WORRY-WART!
OH YEAH? WHO BOUGHT ENOUGH FORMULA TO LAST SIX MONTHS?
SURELY YOU DON'T WANT TO RUN OUT.
OF COURSE NOT, BUT MAY I REMIND YOU I'M STILL BREASTFEEDING?
WAAAAAAH!
MAYBE HE'S COLD...
YOU BETTER TAKE HIM, MOM.
COME HERE, SWEETHEART!
SNIFF
SHALL I LIGHT A FIRE?
WE DON'T HAVE A FIREPLACE.
WELL, WE SHOULD HAVE ONE!
WHAT IF HE'S HOT?
THERE'S A FAN IN THE ATTIC, DEAN! GO LOOK FOR IT! THOROUGHLY!

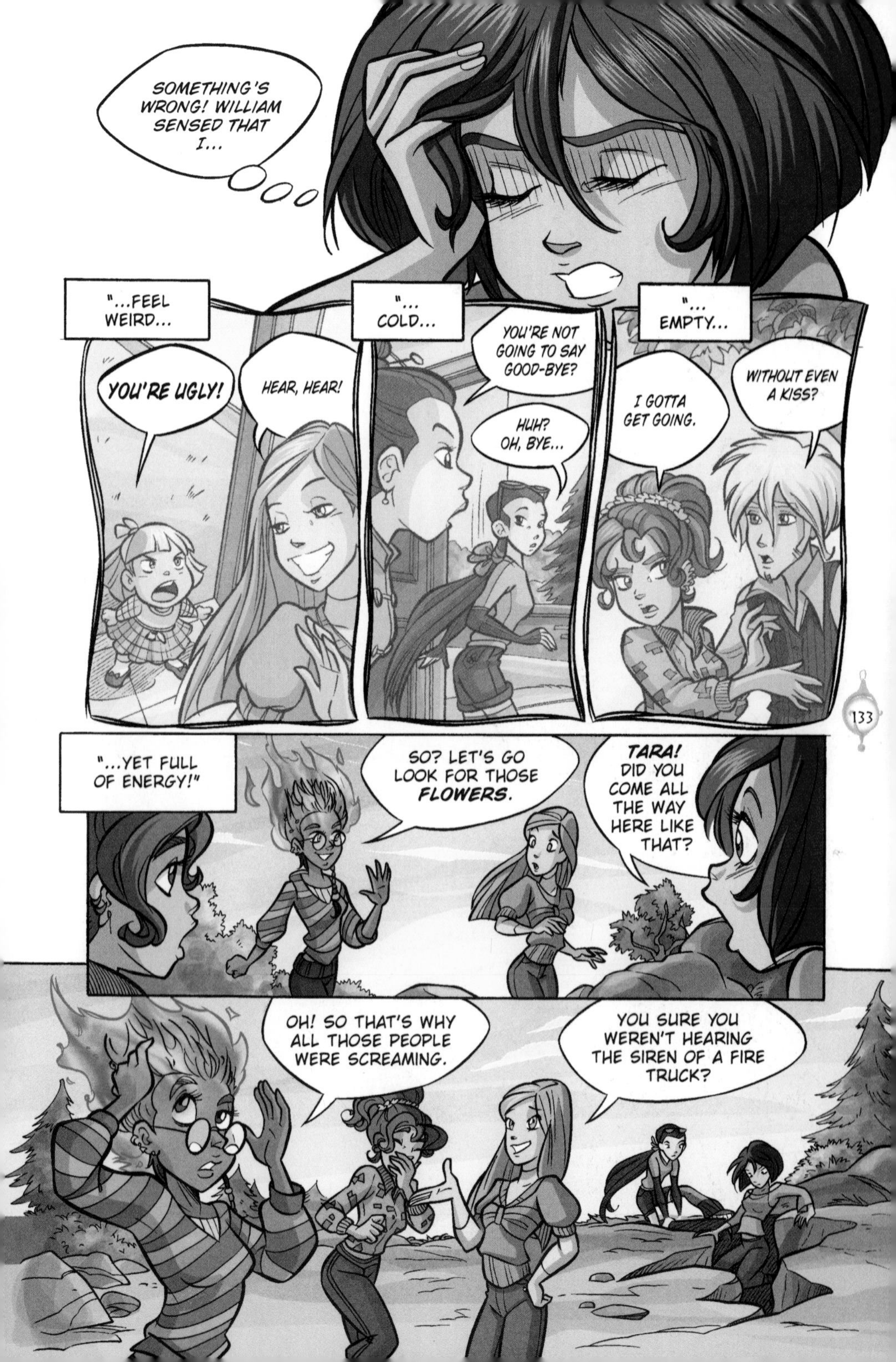
SOMETHING'S WRONG! WILLIAM SENSED THAT I...
"...FEEL WEIRD...
YOU'RE UGLY!
HEAR, HEAR!
"... COLD...
YOU'RE NOT GOING TO SAY GOOD-BYE?
HUH? OH, BYE...
"... EMPTY...
I GOTTA GET GOING.
WITHOUT EVEN A KISS?
"...YET FULL OF ENERGY!"
SO? LET'S GO LOOK FOR THOSE **FLOWERS**.
TARA! DID YOU COME ALL THE WAY HERE LIKE THAT?
OH! SO THAT'S WHY ALL THOSE PEOPLE WERE SCREAMING.
YOU SURE YOU WEREN'T HEARING THE SIREN OF A FIRE TRUCK?

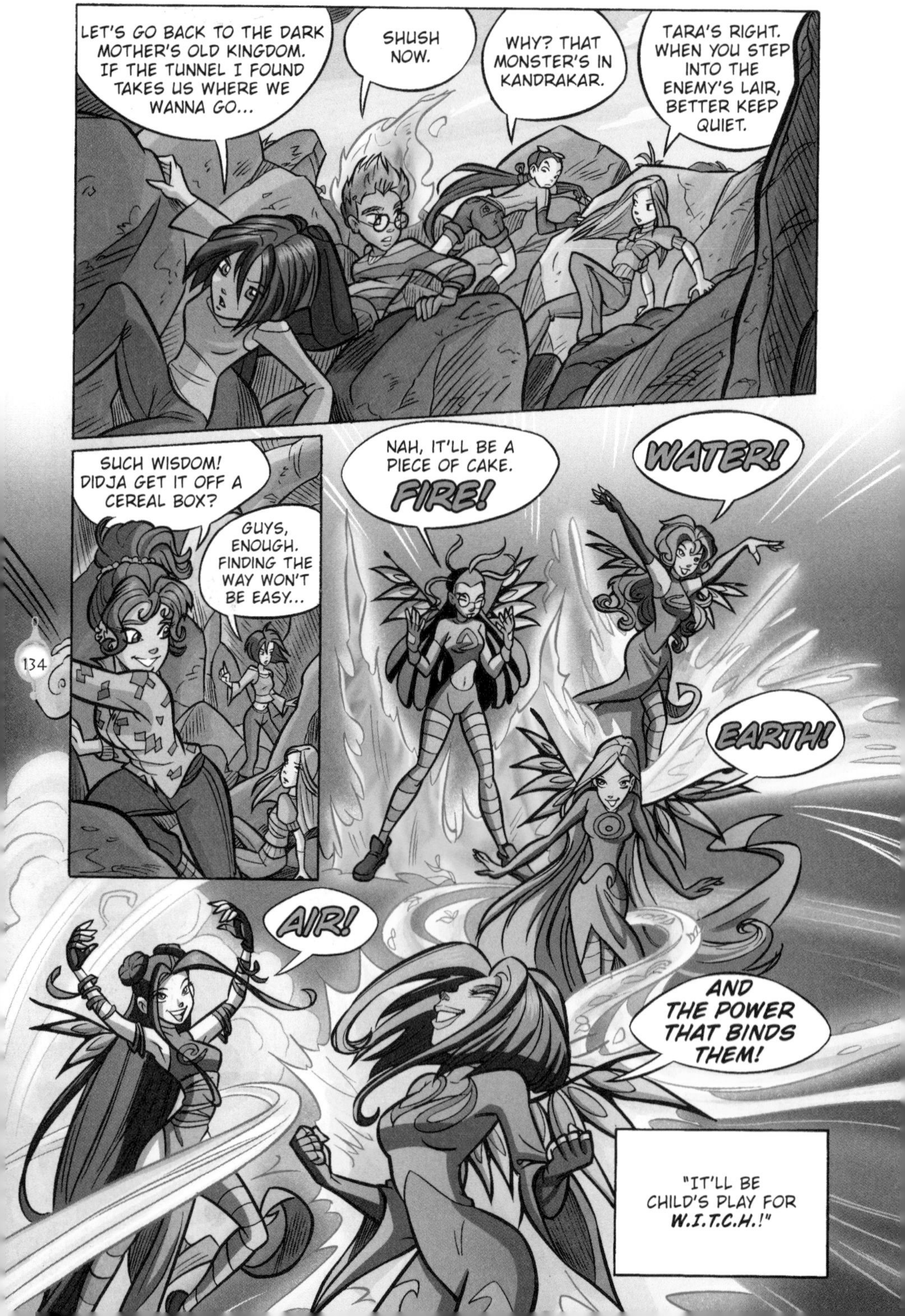
LET'S GO BACK TO THE DARK MOTHER'S OLD KINGDOM. IF THE TUNNEL I FOUND TAKES US WHERE WE WANNA GO...
SHUSH NOW.
WHY? THAT MONSTER'S IN KANDRAKAR.
TARA'S RIGHT. WHEN YOU STEP INTO THE ENEMY'S LAIR, BETTER KEEP QUIET.
SUCH WISDOM! DIDJA GET IT OFF A CEREAL BOX?
GUYS, ENOUGH. FINDING THE WAY WON'T BE EASY...
NAH, IT'LL BE A PIECE OF CAKE. FIRE!
WATER!
EARTH!
AIR!
AND THE POWER THAT BINDS THEM!
"IT'LL BE CHILD'S PLAY FOR W.I.T.C.H.!"

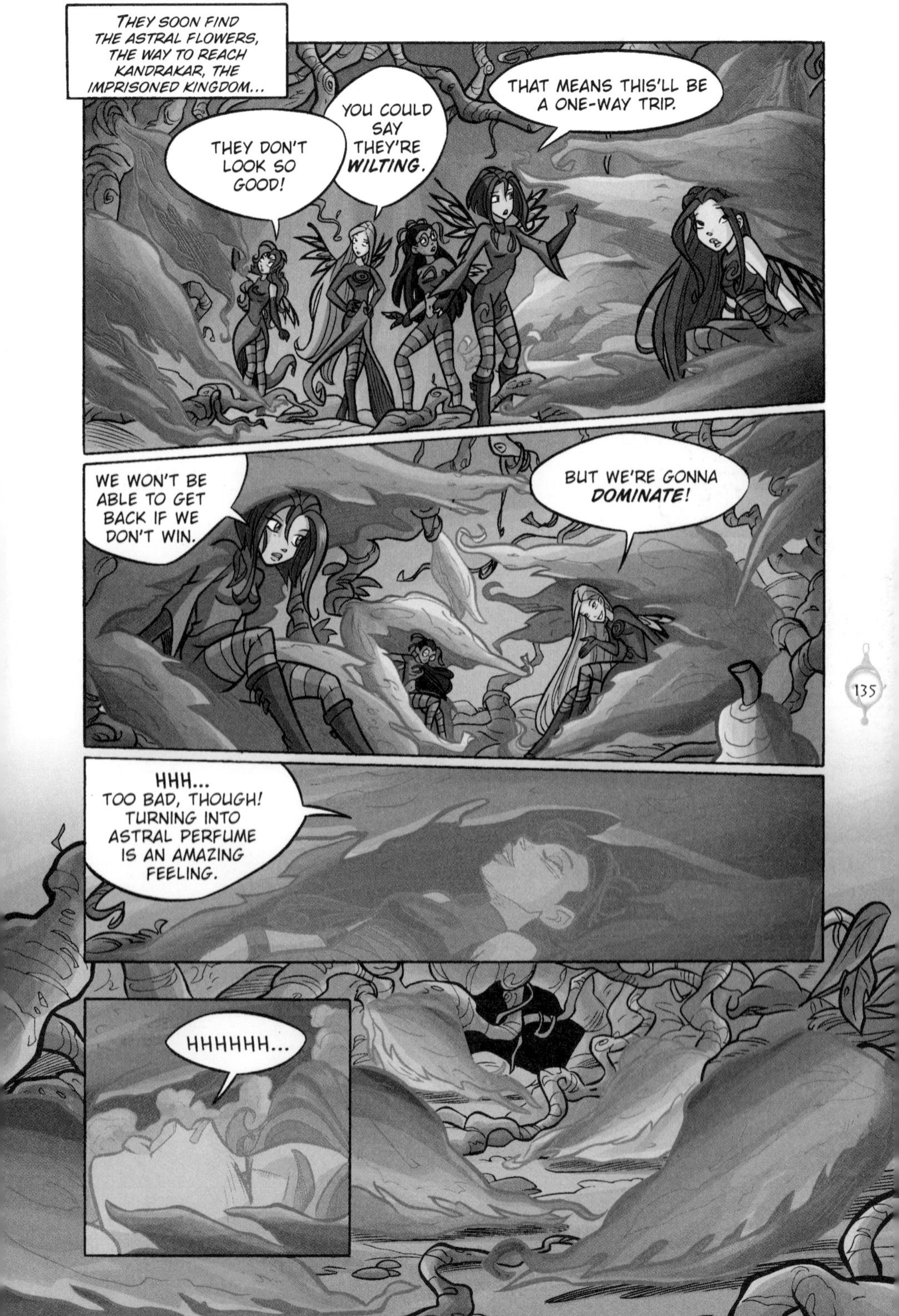
THEY SOON FIND THE ASTRAL FLOWERS, THE WAY TO REACH KANDRAKAR, THE IMPRISONED KINGDOM...
THEY DON'T LOOK SO GOOD!
YOU COULD SAY THEY'RE WILTING.
THAT MEANS THIS'LL BE A ONE-WAY TRIP.
WE WON'T BE ABLE TO GET BACK IF WE DON'T WIN.
BUT WE'RE GONNA DOMINATE!
HHH... TOO BAD, THOUGH! TURNING INTO ASTRAL PERFUME IS AN AMAZING FEELING.
HHHHHH...

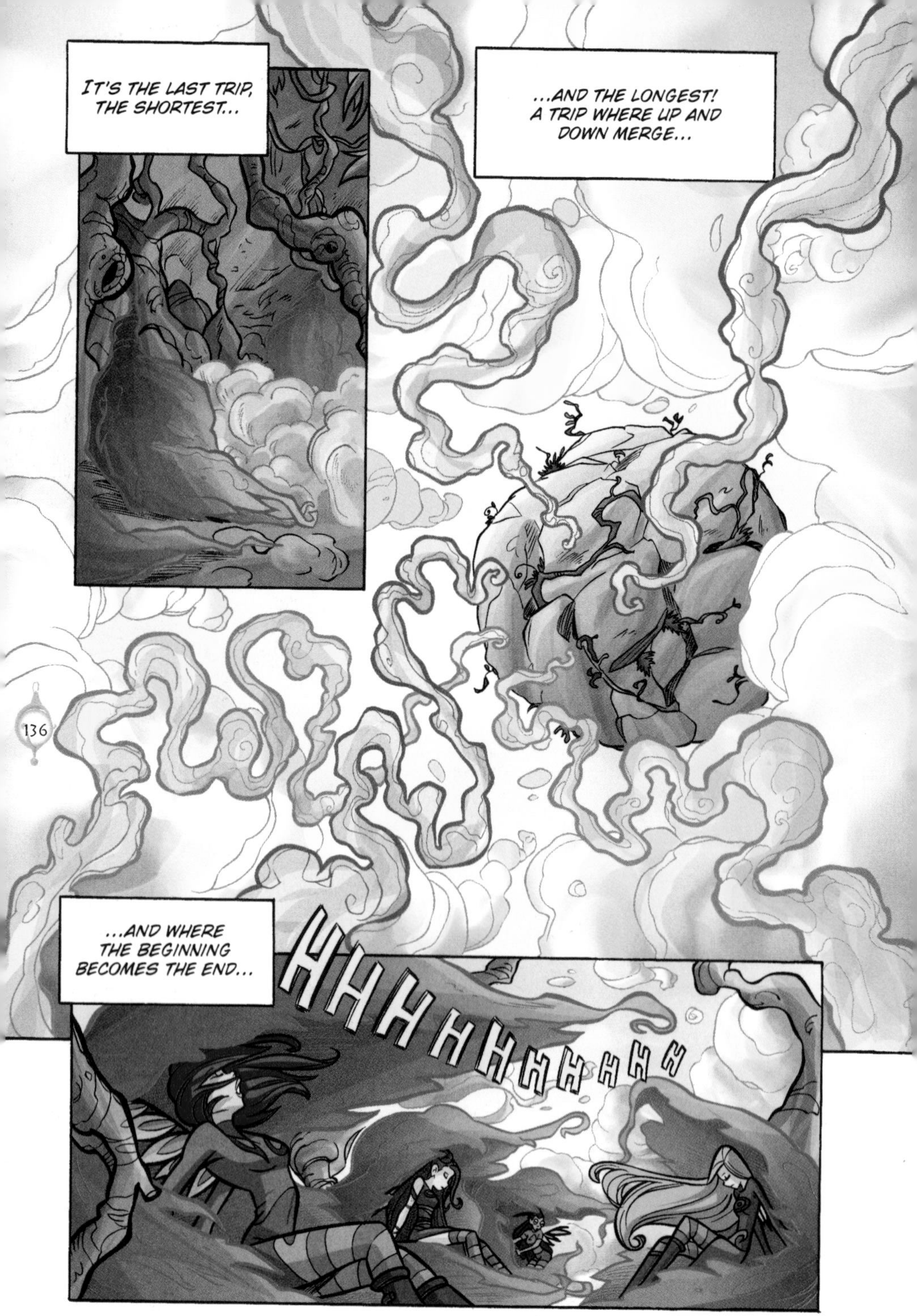
IT'S THE LAST TRIP, THE SHORTEST...
...AND THE LONGEST! A TRIP WHERE UP AND DOWN MERGE...
...AND WHERE THE BEGINNING BECOMES THE END...
HHHHHHHHHHHHH

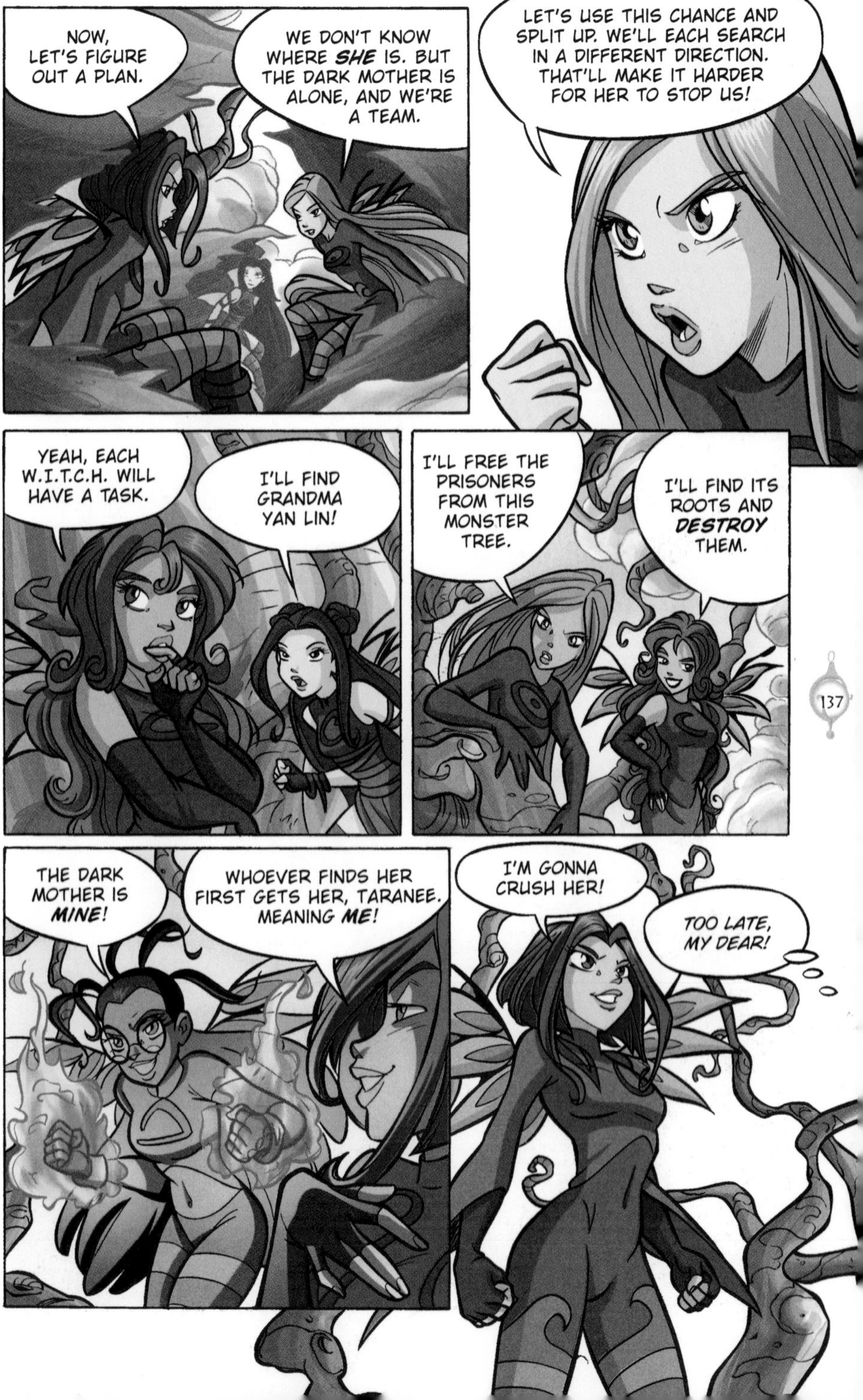
NOW, LET'S FIGURE OUT A PLAN.
WE DON'T KNOW WHERE SHE IS. BUT THE DARK MOTHER IS ALONE, AND WE'RE A TEAM.
LET'S USE THIS CHANCE AND SPLIT UP. WE'LL EACH SEARCH IN A DIFFERENT DIRECTION. THAT'LL MAKE IT HARDER FOR HER TO STOP US!
YEAH, EACH W.I.T.C.H. WILL HAVE A TASK.
I'LL FIND GRANDMA YAN LIN!
I'LL FREE THE PRISONERS FROM THIS MONSTER TREE.
I'LL FIND ITS ROOTS AND DESTROY THEM.
THE DARK MOTHER IS MINE!
WHOEVER FINDS HER FIRST GETS HER, TARANEE. MEANING ME!
I'M GONNA CRUSH HER!
TOO LATE, MY DEAR!

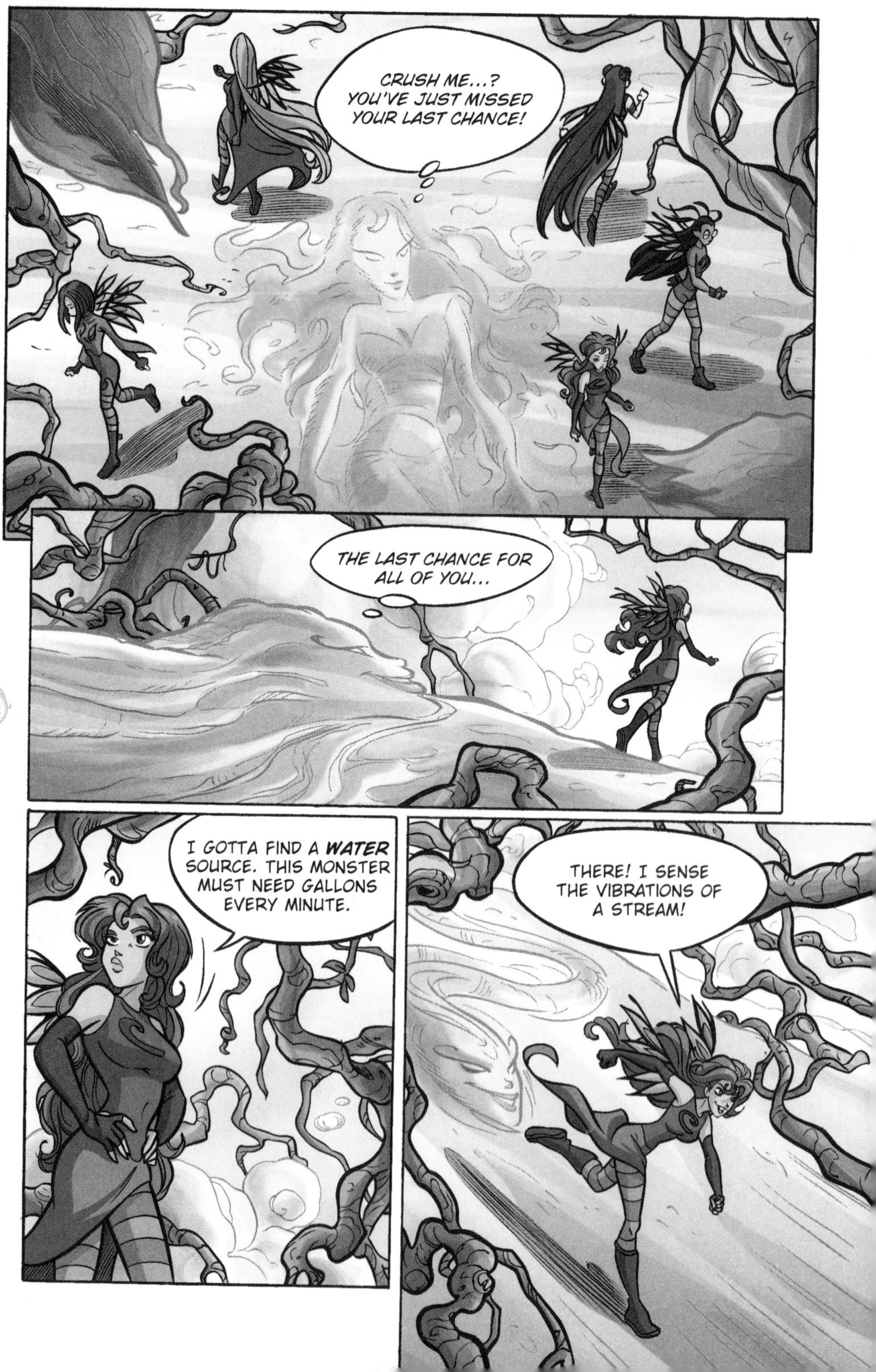
CRUSH ME...? YOU'VE JUST MISSED YOUR LAST CHANCE!
THE LAST CHANCE FOR ALL OF YOU...
I GOTTA FIND A **WATER** SOURCE. THIS MONSTER MUST NEED GALLONS EVERY MINUTE.
THERE! I SENSE THE VIBRATIONS OF A STREAM!

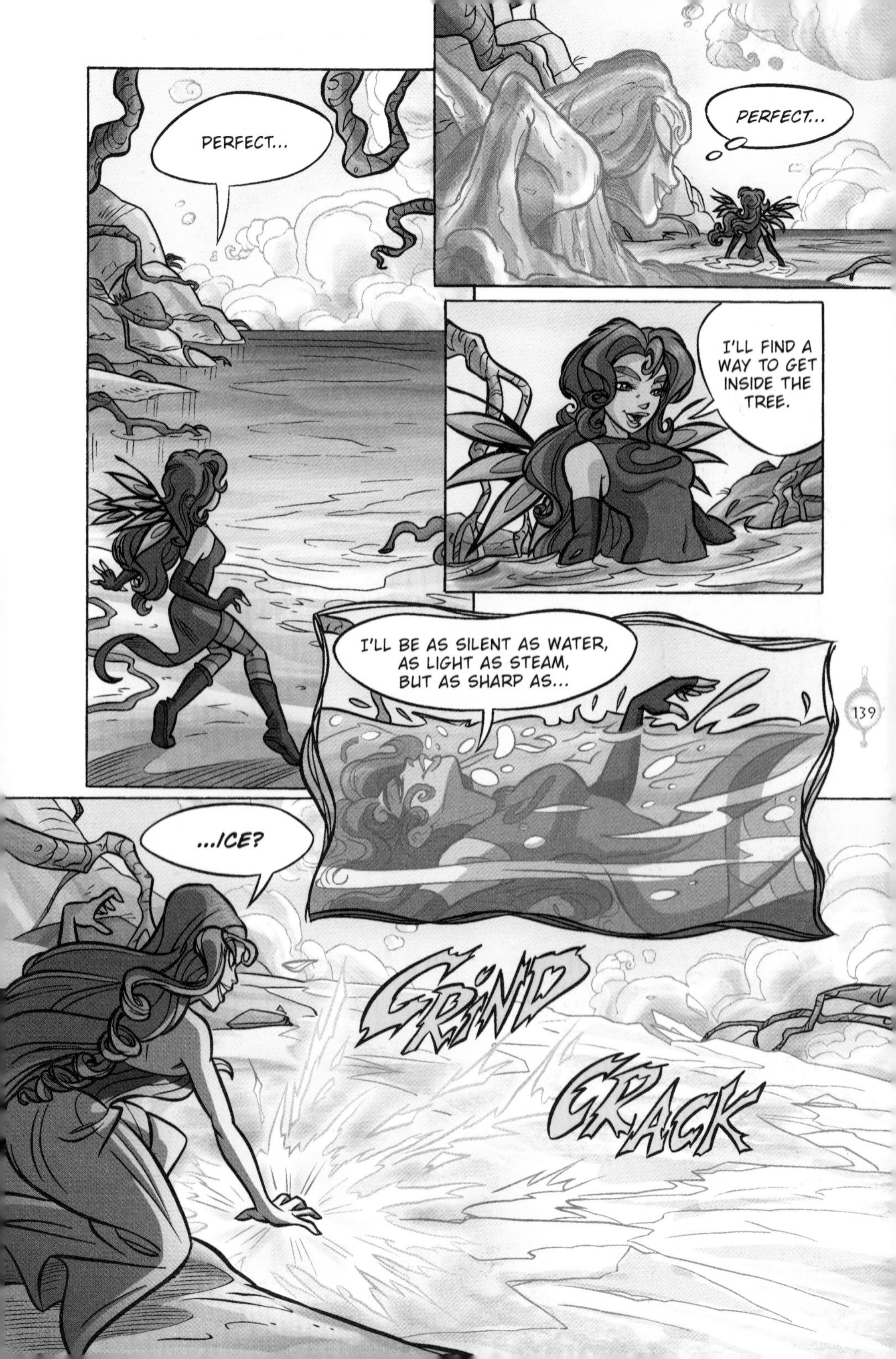
PERFECT...
PERFECT...
I'LL FIND A WAY TO GET INSIDE THE TREE.
I'LL BE AS SILENT AS WATER, AS LIGHT AS STEAM, BUT AS SHARP AS...
...ICE?
GRIND
CRACK

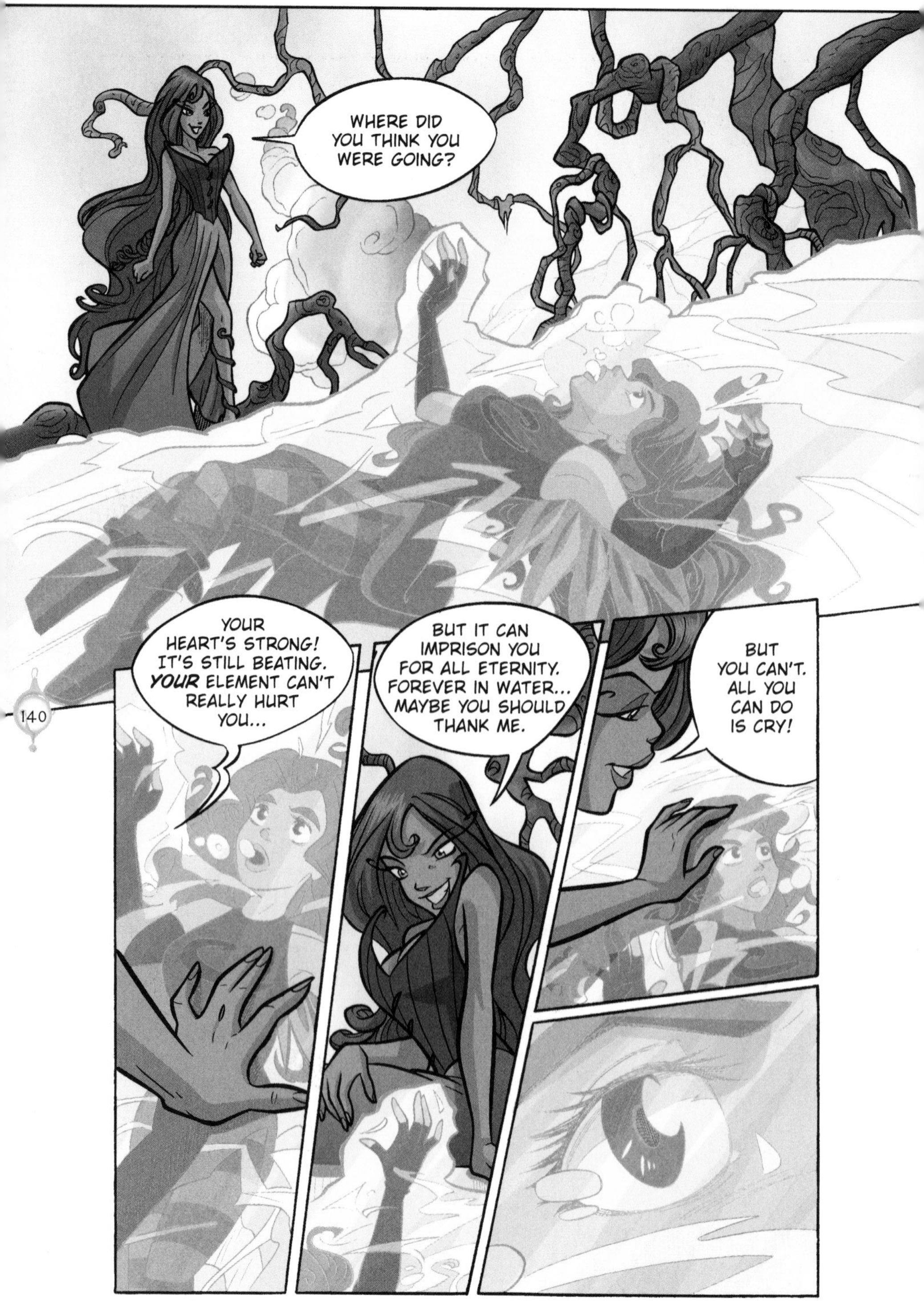

WHERE DID YOU THINK YOU WERE GOING?
YOUR HEART'S STRONG! IT'S STILL BEATING. **YOUR** ELEMENT CAN'T REALLY HURT YOU...
BUT IT CAN IMPRISON YOU FOR ALL ETERNITY. FOREVER IN WATER... MAYBE YOU SHOULD THANK ME.
BUT YOU CAN'T. ALL YOU CAN DO IS CRY!

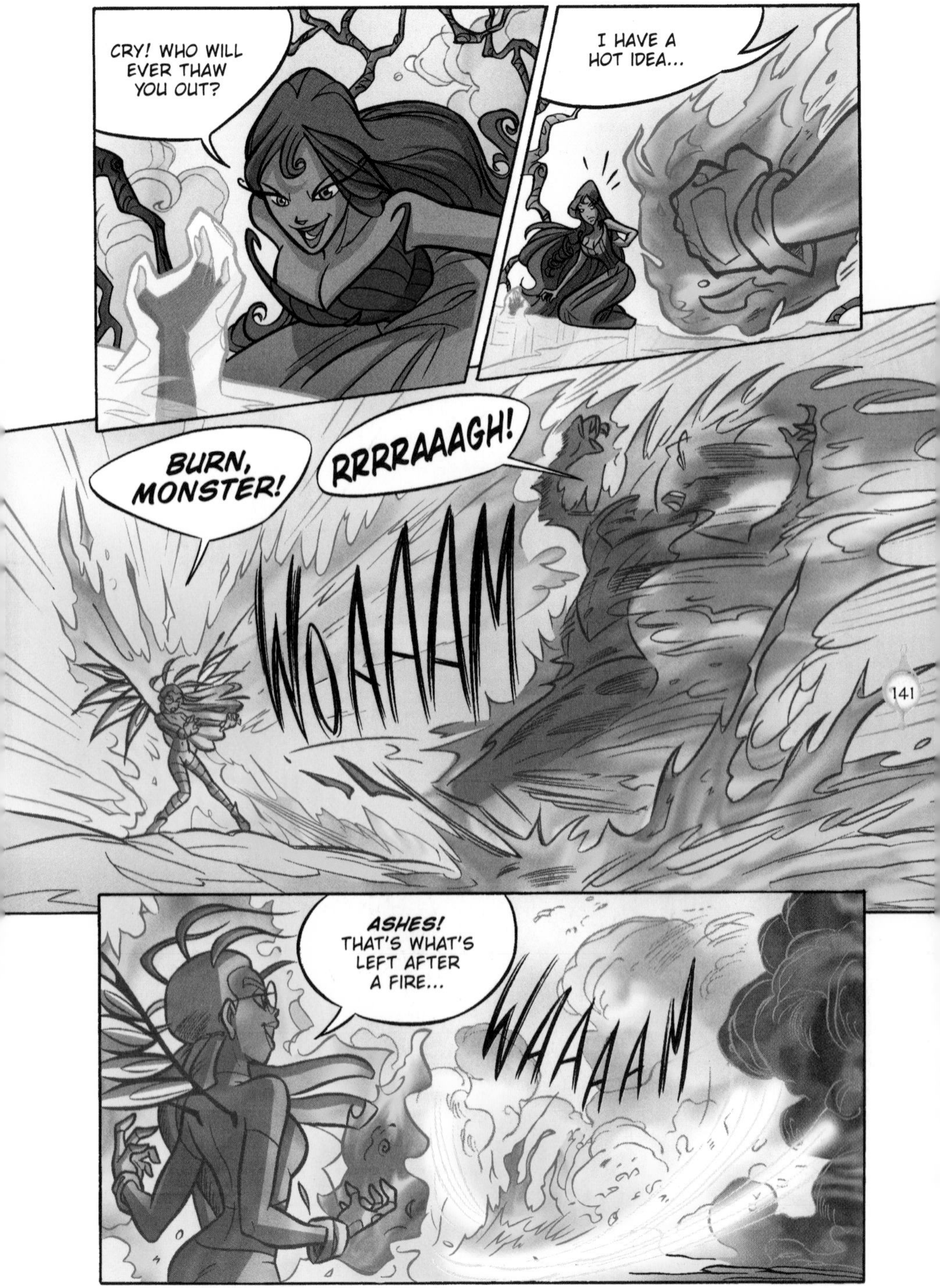
CRY! WHO WILL EVER THAW YOU OUT?
I HAVE A HOT IDEA...
BURN, MONSTER!
RRRRAAAGH!
WOAAAM
ASHES! THAT'S WHAT'S LEFT AFTER A FIRE...
WAAAAM

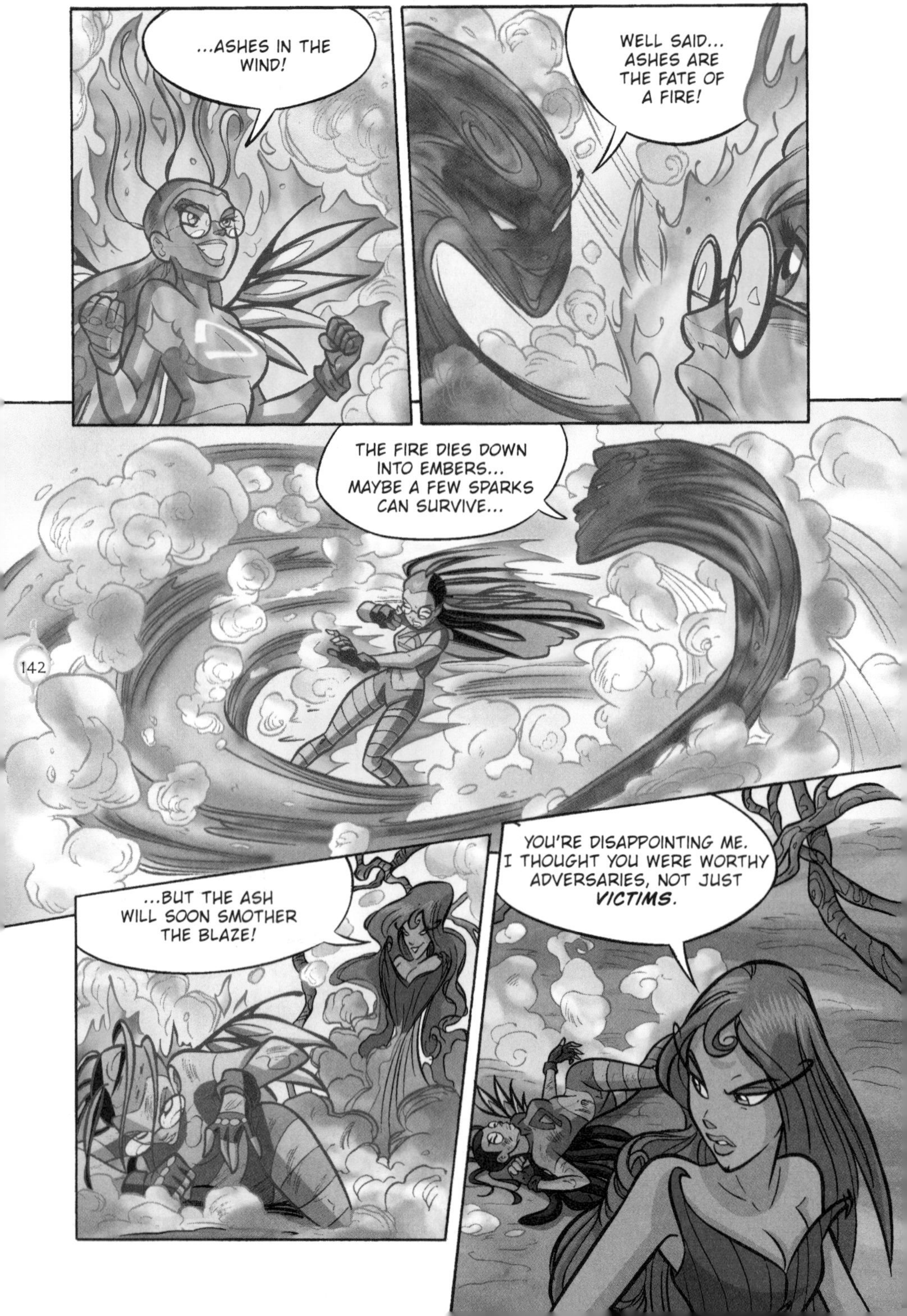

...ASHES IN THE WIND!
WELL SAID... ASHES ARE THE FATE OF A FIRE!
THE FIRE DIES DOWN INTO EMBERS... MAYBE A FEW SPARKS CAN SURVIVE...
...BUT THE ASH WILL SOON SMOTHER THE BLAZE!
YOU'RE DISAPPOINTING ME. I THOUGHT YOU WERE WORTHY ADVERSARIES, NOT JUST VICTIMS.

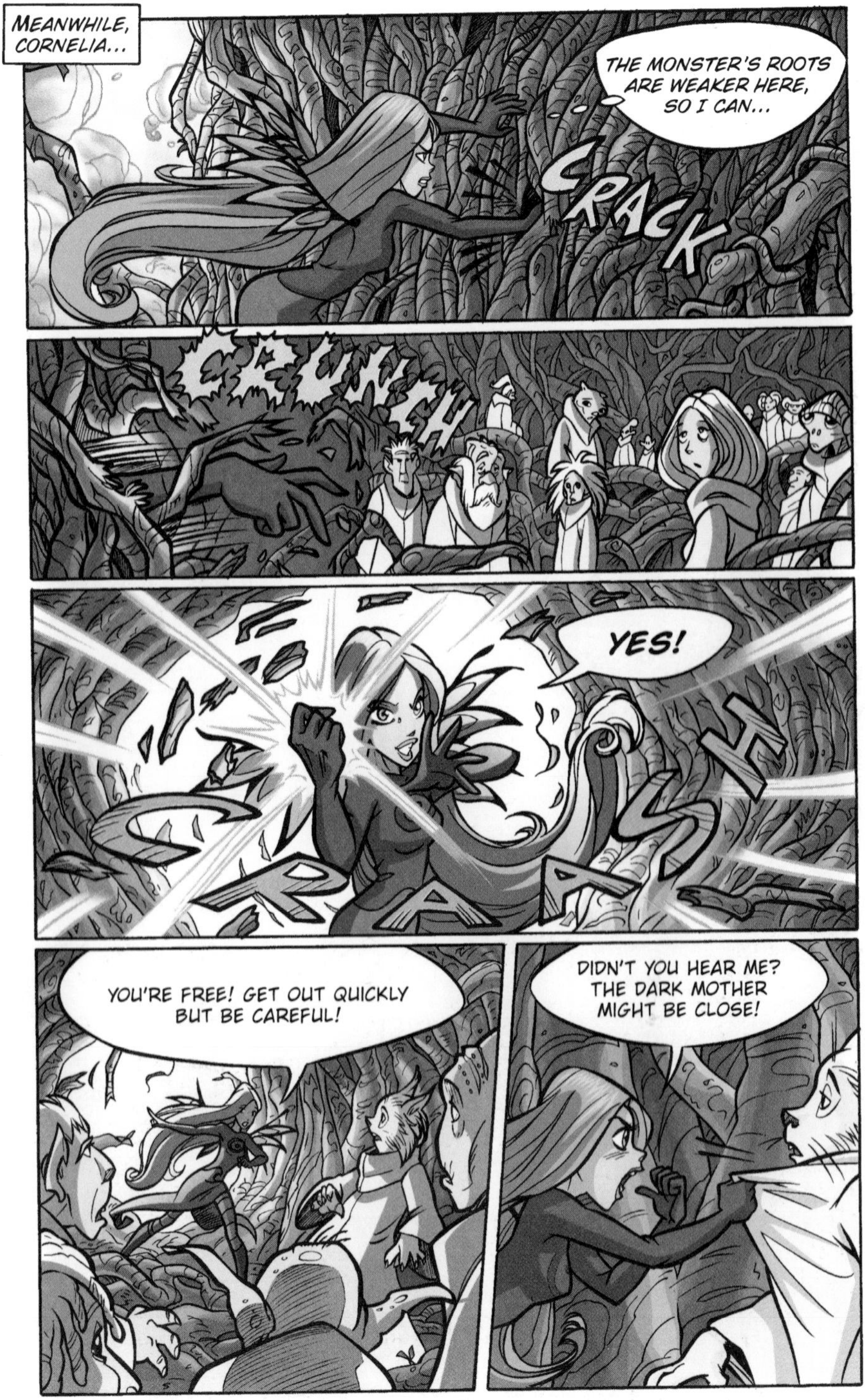
MEANWHILE, CORNELIA...
THE MONSTER'S ROOTS ARE WEAKER HERE, SO I CAN...
CRACK
CRUNCH
YES!
CRAASH
YOU'RE FREE! GET OUT QUICKLY BUT BE CAREFUL!
DIDN'T YOU HEAR ME? THE DARK MOTHER MIGHT BE CLOSE!

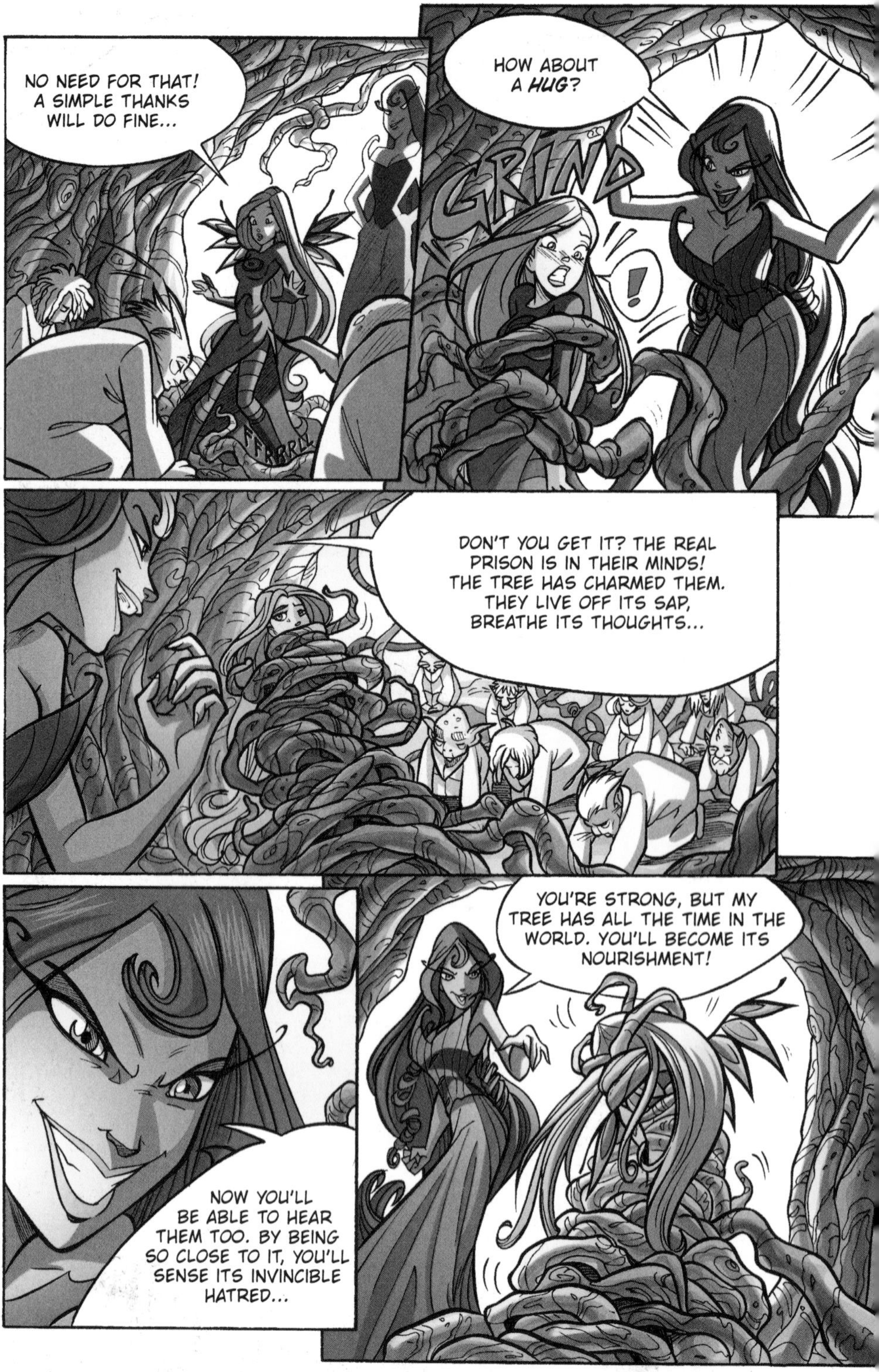
NO NEED FOR THAT! A SIMPLE THANKS WILL DO FINE...
FFRRRLL
HOW ABOUT A HUG?
GRIND
!
DON'T YOU GET IT? THE REAL PRISON IS IN THEIR MINDS! THE TREE HAS CHARMED THEM. THEY LIVE OFF ITS SAP, BREATHE ITS THOUGHTS...
NOW YOU'LL BE ABLE TO HEAR THEM TOO. BY BEING SO CLOSE TO IT, YOU'LL SENSE ITS INVINCIBLE HATRED...
YOU'RE STRONG, BUT MY TREE HAS ALL THE TIME IN THE WORLD. YOU'LL BECOME ITS NOURISHMENT!

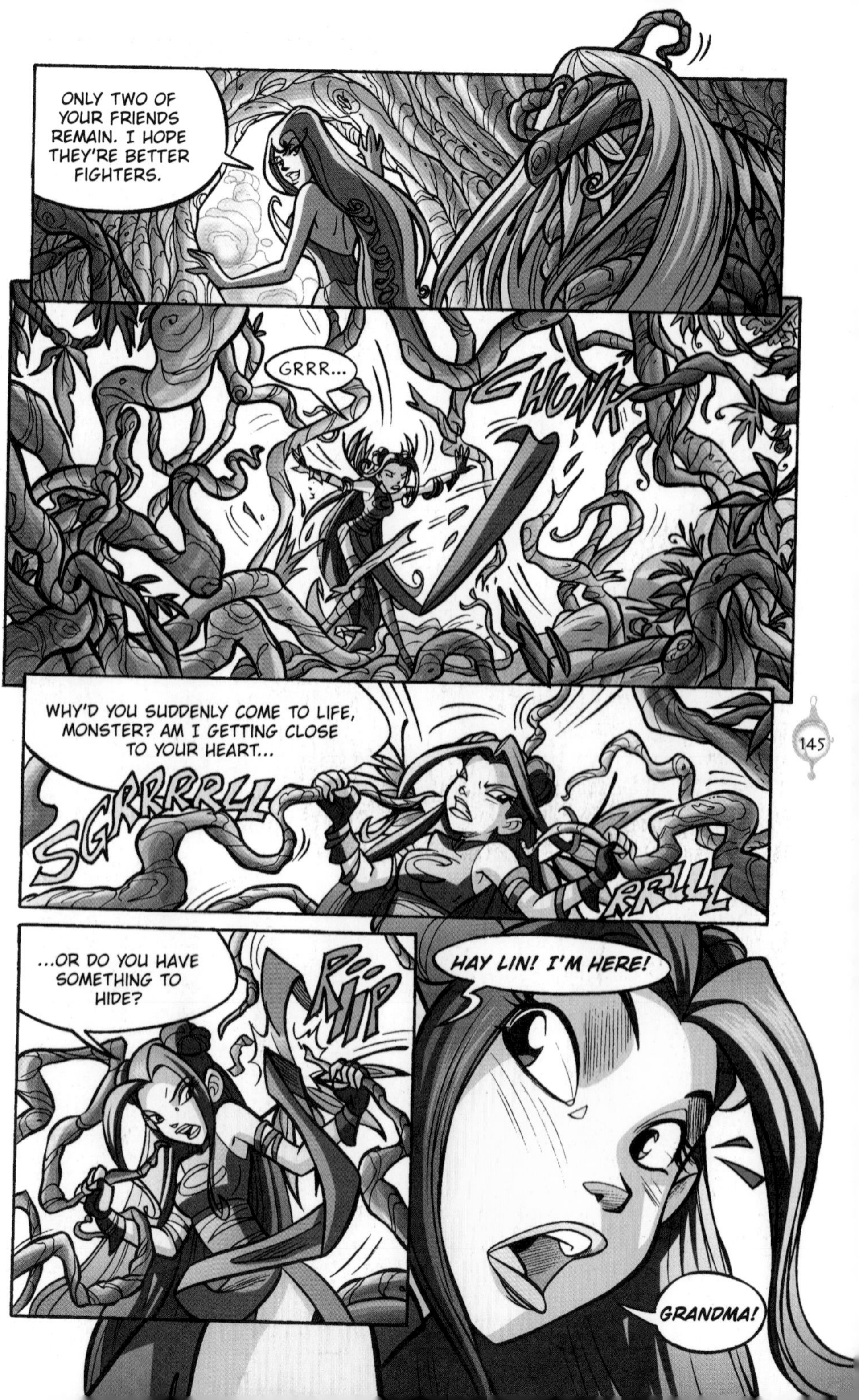
ONLY TWO OF YOUR FRIENDS REMAIN. I HOPE THEY'RE BETTER FIGHTERS.
GRRR...
CHONK
WHY'D YOU SUDDENLY COME TO LIFE, MONSTER? AM I GETTING CLOSE TO YOUR HEART...
SGRRRRLL
RRLL
...OR DO YOU HAVE SOMETHING TO HIDE?
POOMIP
HAY LIN! I'M HERE!
GRANDMA!

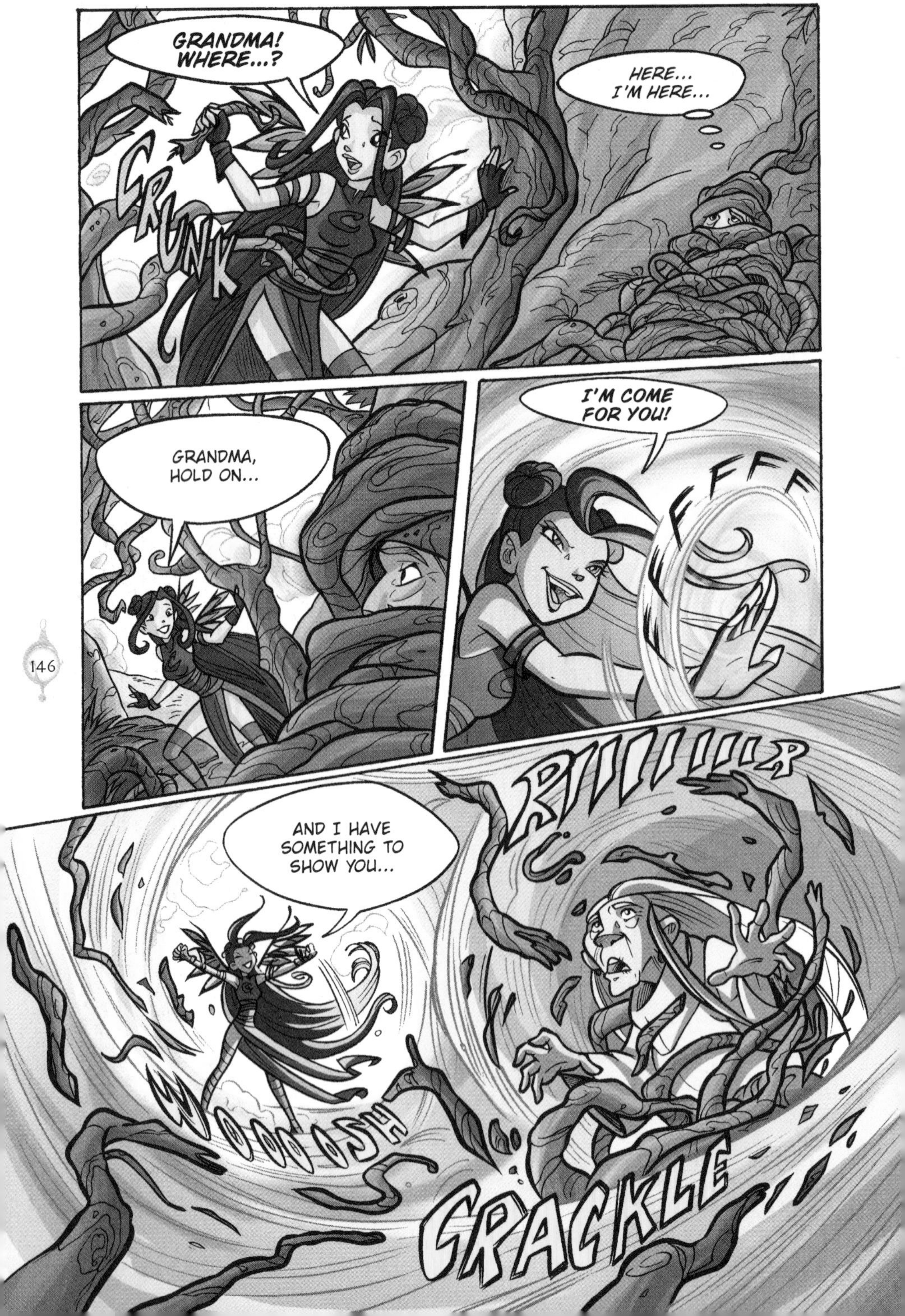
GRANDMA! WHERE...?
CRUNK
HERE... I'M HERE...
GRANDMA, HOLD ON...
I'M COME FOR YOU!
FFFF
AND I HAVE SOMETHING TO SHOW YOU...
RIIIIIIR
WOOOOSH
CRACKLE

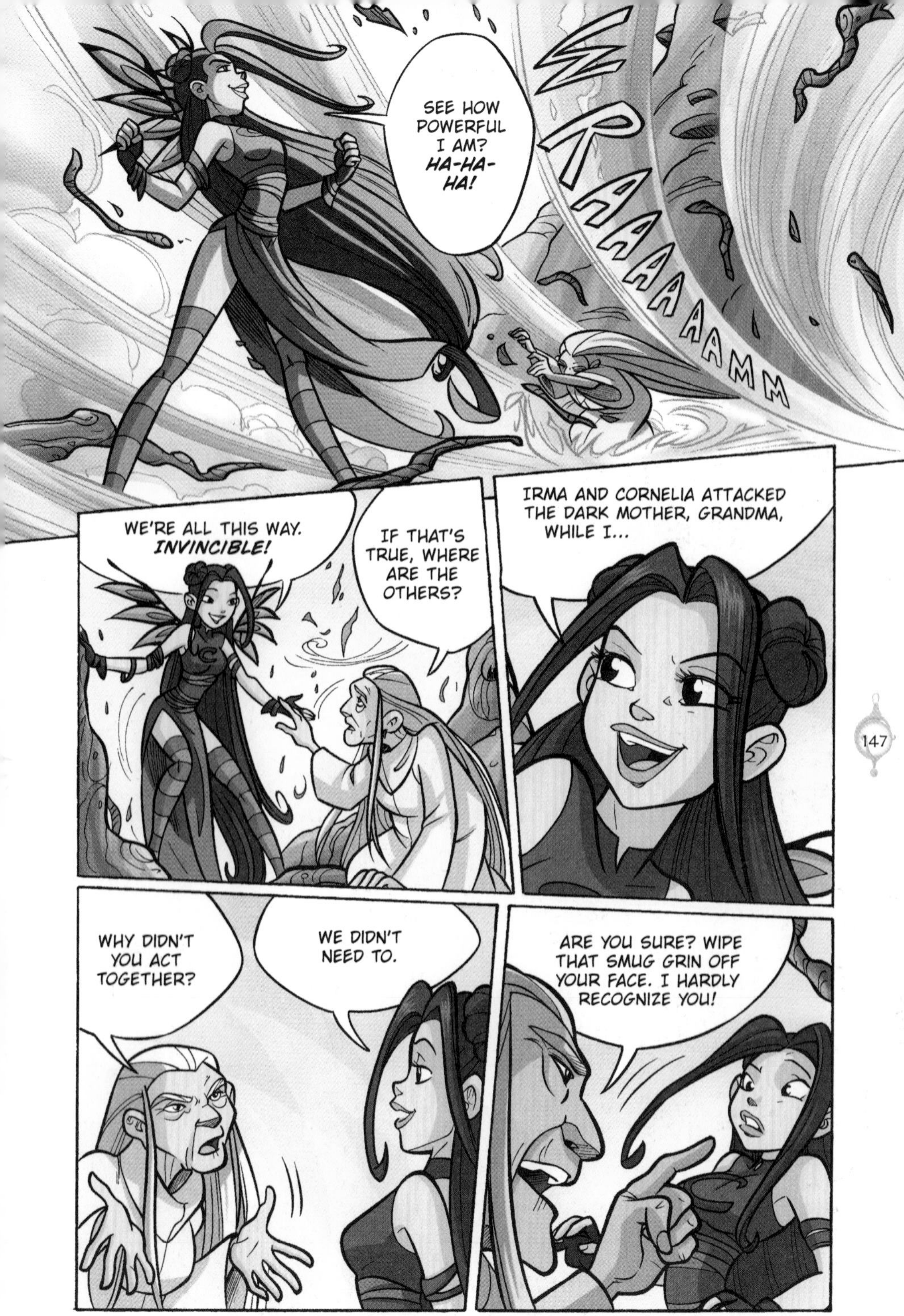

SEE HOW POWERFUL I AM? HA-HA-HA!
ZRAAAAAAAAMM
WE'RE ALL THIS WAY. INVINCIBLE!
IF THAT'S TRUE, WHERE ARE THE OTHERS?
IRMA AND CORNELIA ATTACKED THE DARK MOTHER, GRANDMA, WHILE I...
WHY DIDN'T YOU ACT TOGETHER?
WE DIDN'T NEED TO.
ARE YOU SURE? WIPE THAT SMUG GRIN OFF YOUR FACE. I HARDLY RECOGNIZE YOU!

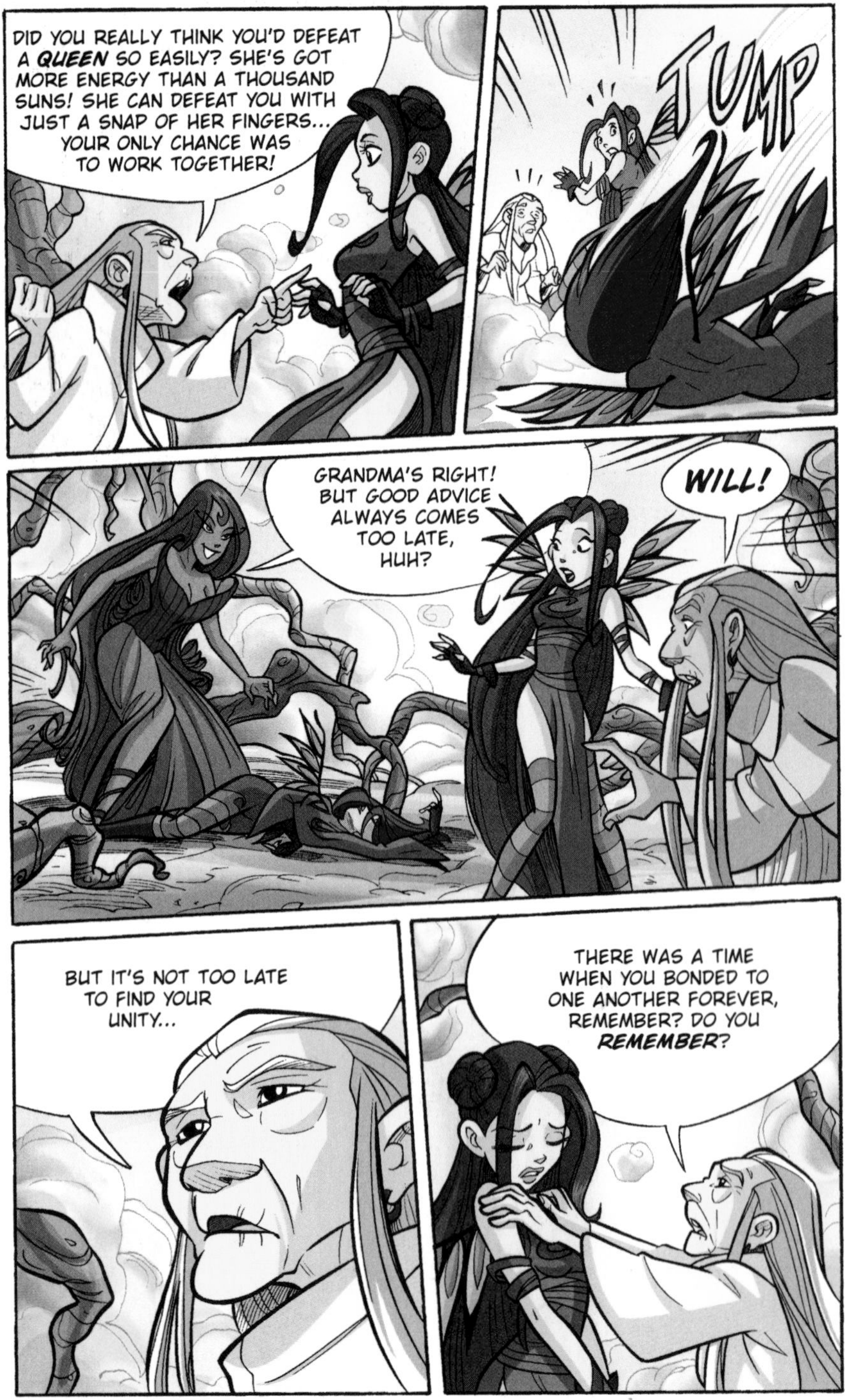
DID YOU REALLY THINK YOU'D DEFEAT A QUEEN SO EASILY? SHE'S GOT MORE ENERGY THAN A THOUSAND SUNS! SHE CAN DEFEAT YOU WITH JUST A SNAP OF HER FINGERS... YOUR ONLY CHANCE WAS TO WORK TOGETHER!
TUMP
GRANDMA'S RIGHT! BUT GOOD ADVICE ALWAYS COMES TOO LATE, HUH?
WILL!
BUT IT'S NOT TOO LATE TO FIND YOUR UNITY...
THERE WAS A TIME WHEN YOU BONDED TO ONE ANOTHER FOREVER, REMEMBER? DO YOU REMEMBER?

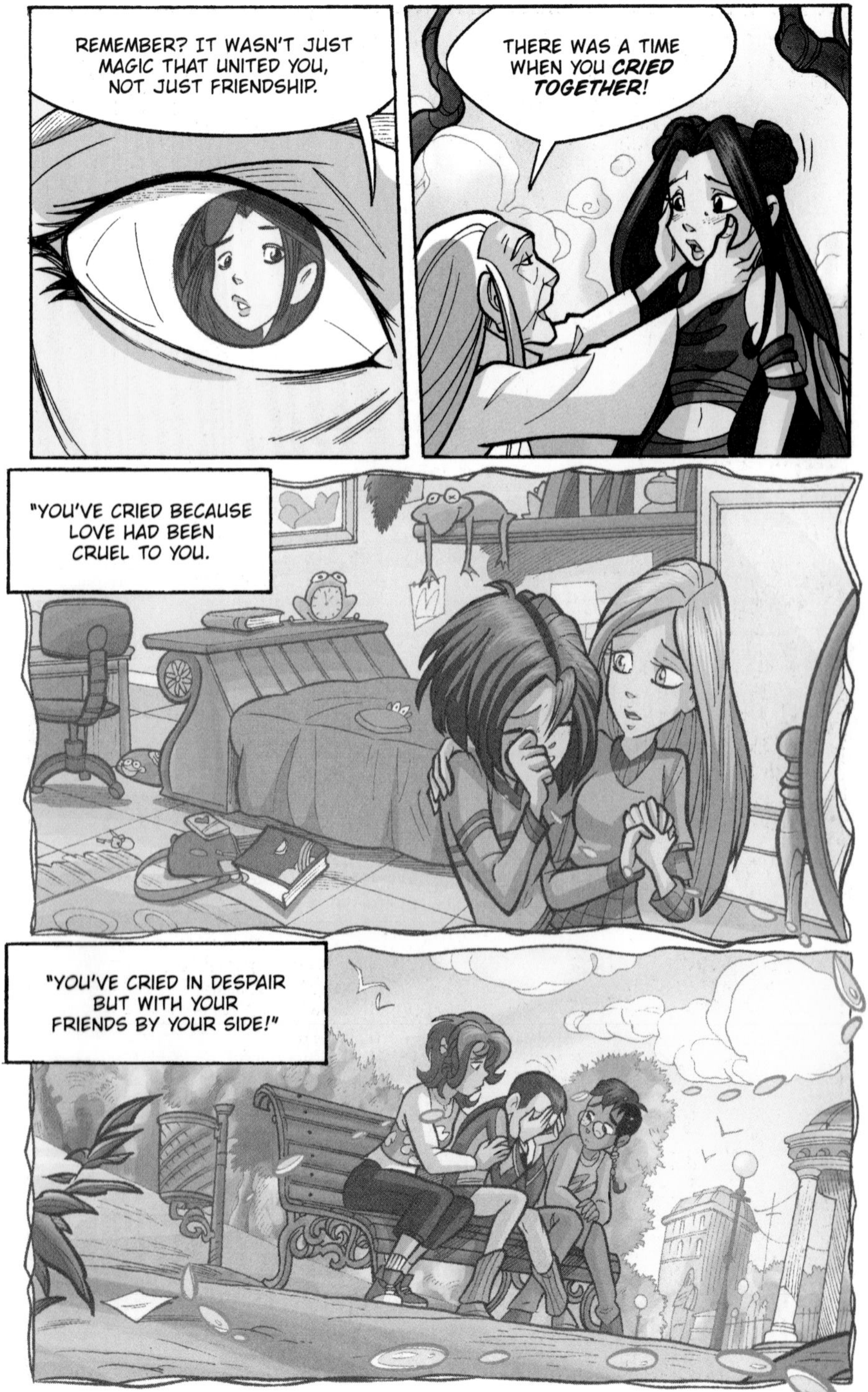
REMEMBER? IT WASN'T JUST MAGIC THAT UNITED YOU, NOT JUST FRIENDSHIP.
THERE WAS A TIME WHEN YOU **CRIED TOGETHER**!
"YOU'VE CRIED BECAUSE LOVE HAD BEEN CRUEL TO YOU.
"YOU'VE CRIED IN DESPAIR BUT WITH YOUR FRIENDS BY YOUR SIDE!"

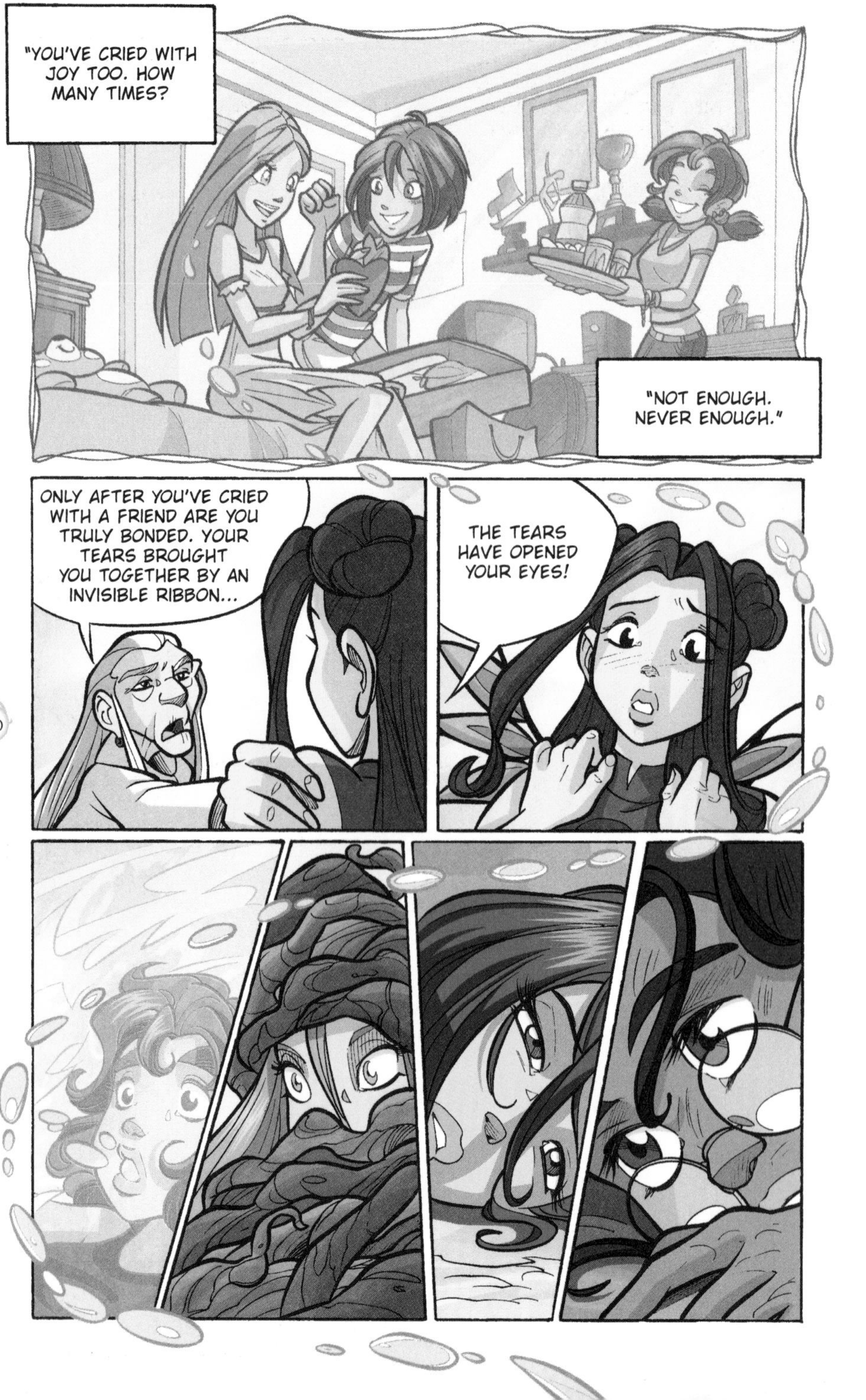
"YOU'VE CRIED WITH JOY TOO. HOW MANY TIMES?
"NOT ENOUGH. NEVER ENOUGH."
ONLY AFTER YOU'VE CRIED WITH A FRIEND ARE YOU TRULY BONDED. YOUR TEARS BROUGHT YOU TOGETHER BY AN INVISIBLE RIBBON...
THE TEARS HAVE OPENED YOUR EYES!

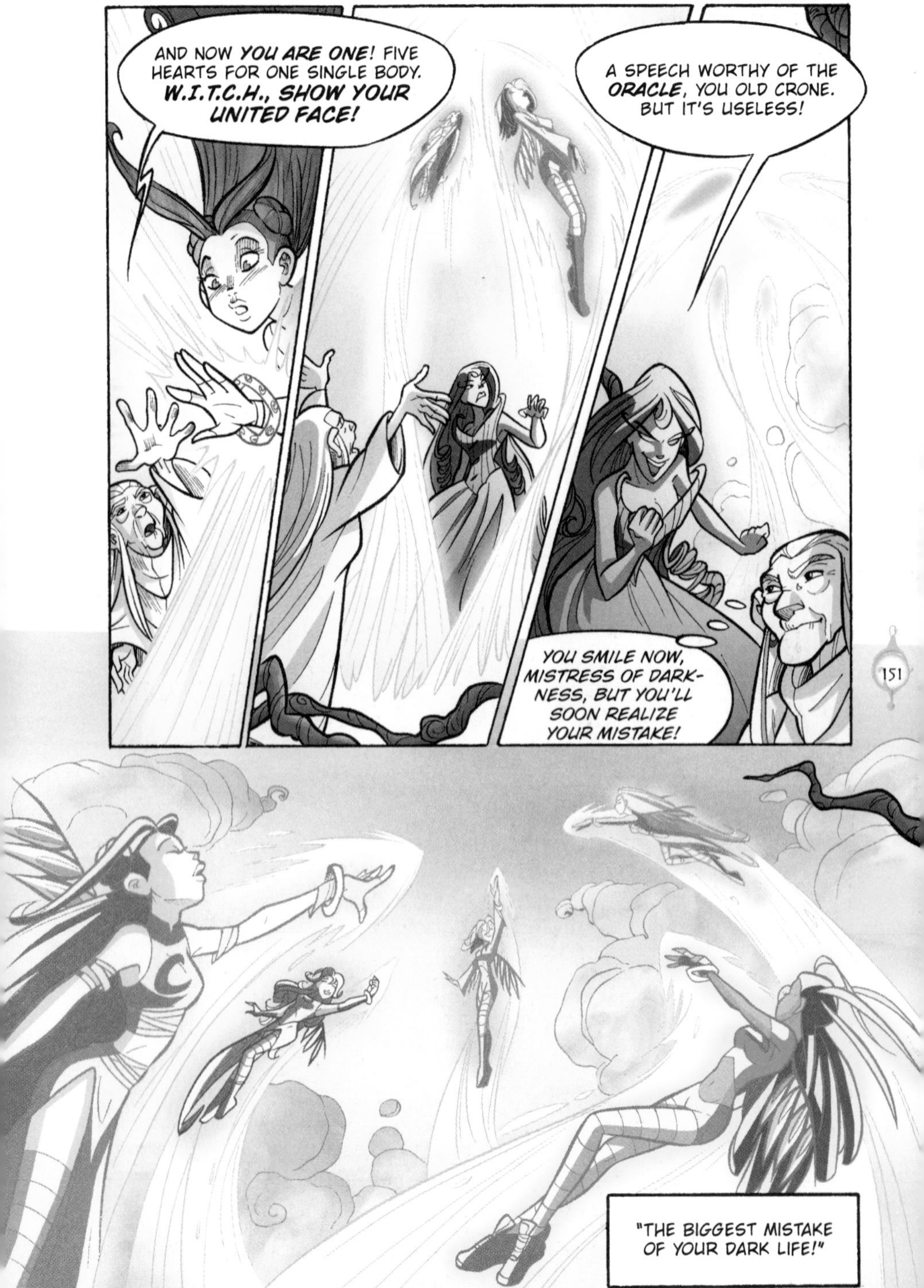
AND NOW YOU ARE ONE! FIVE HEARTS FOR ONE SINGLE BODY. W.I.T.C.H., SHOW YOUR UNITED FACE!
A SPEECH WORTHY OF THE ORACLE, YOU OLD CRONE. BUT IT'S USELESS!
YOU SMILE NOW, MISTRESS OF DARKNESS, BUT YOU'LL SOON REALIZE YOUR MISTAKE!
"THE BIGGEST MISTAKE OF YOUR DARK LIFE!"

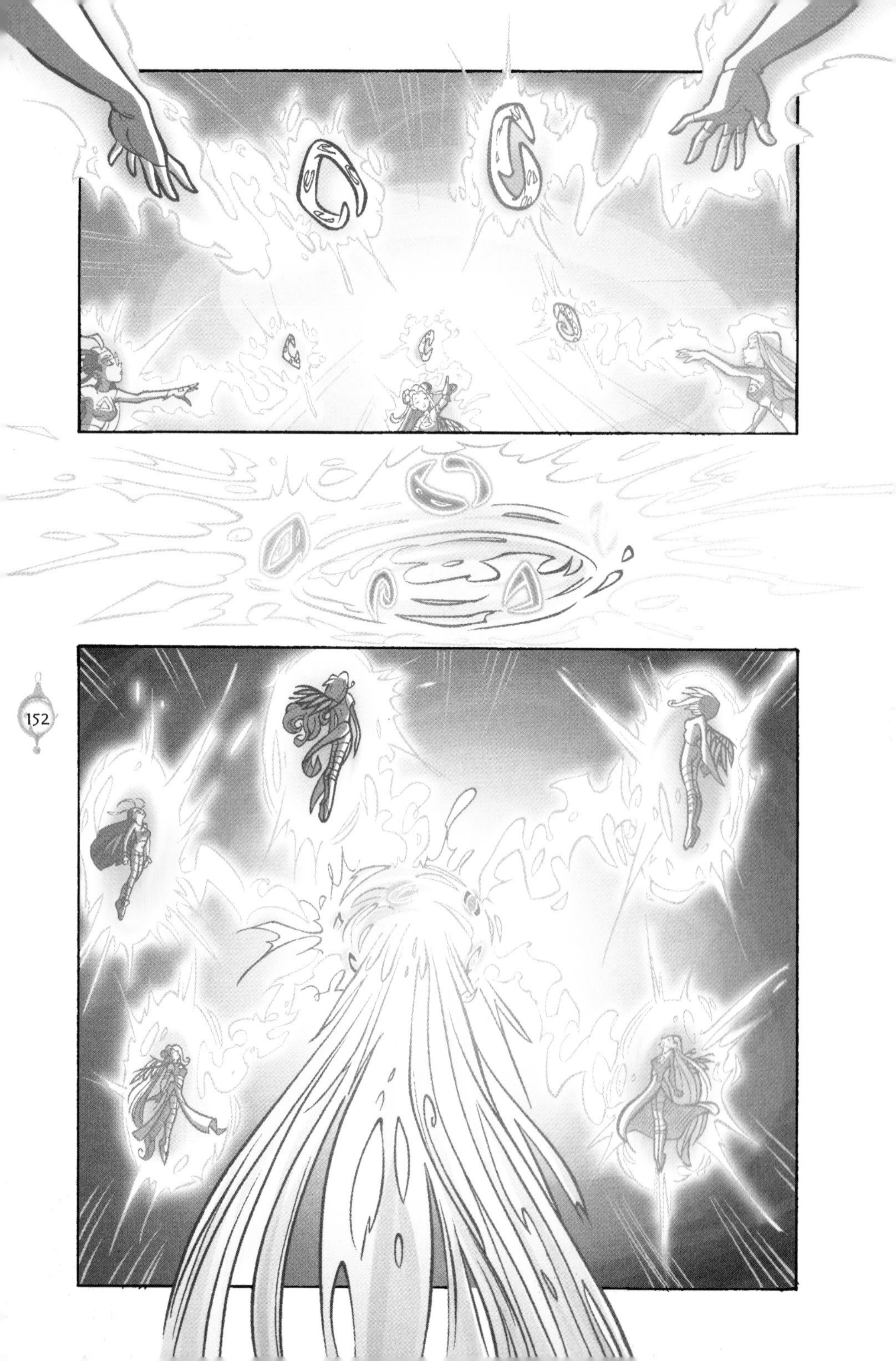

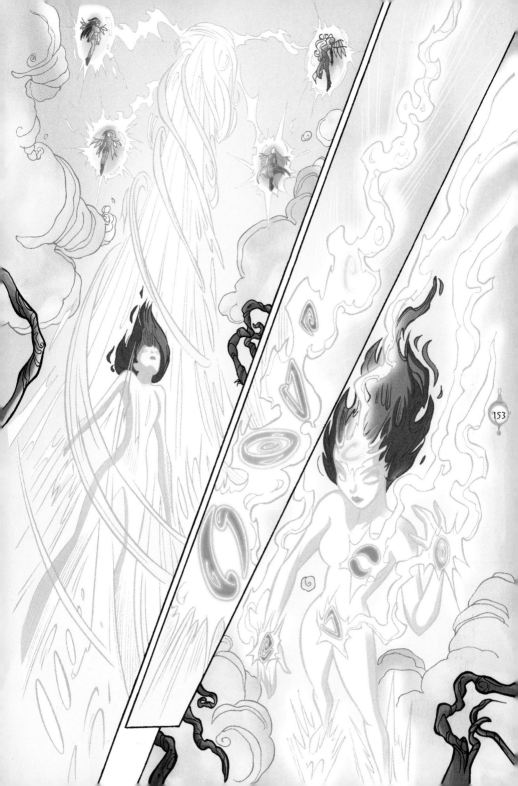

153

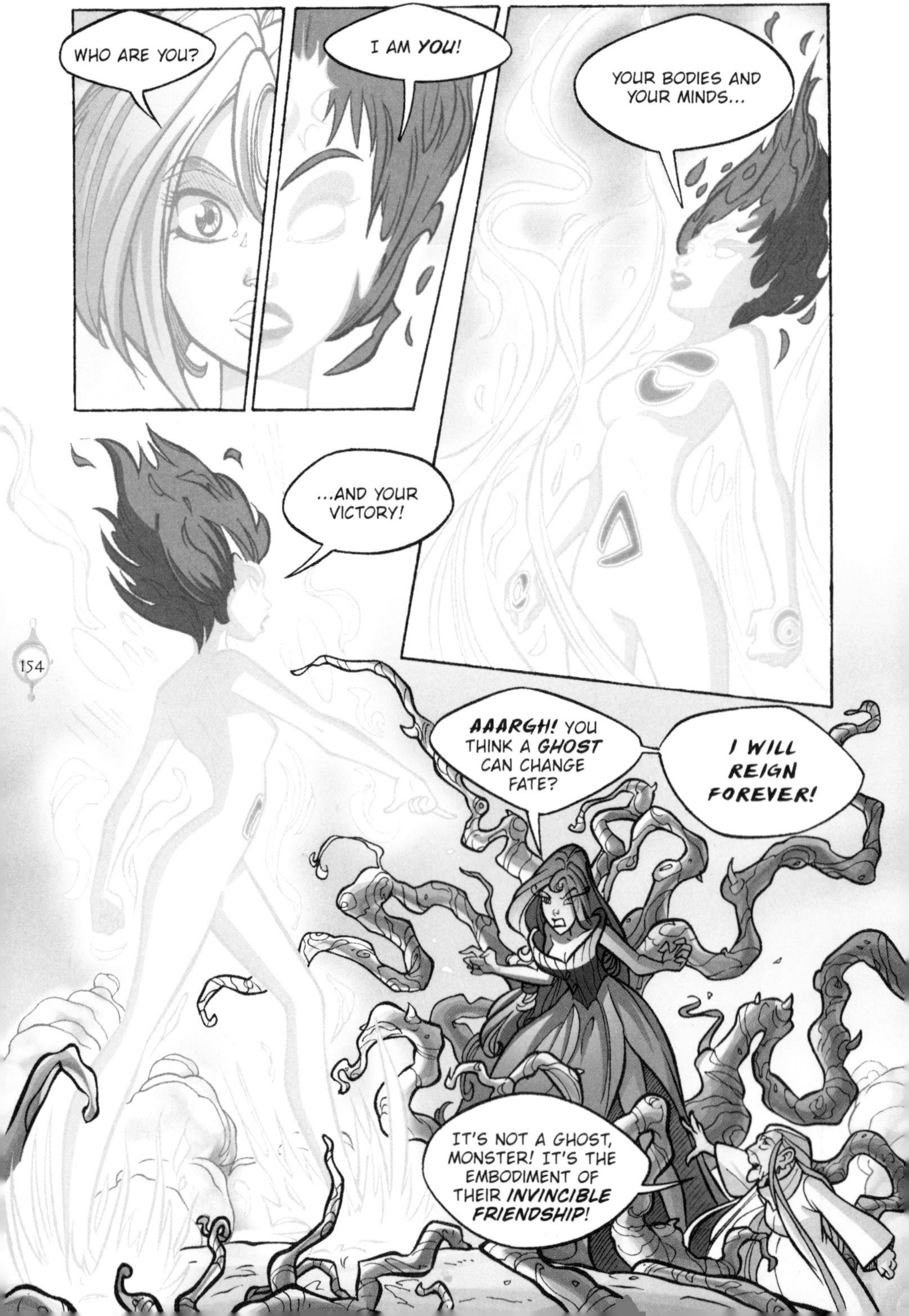
WHO ARE YOU?
I AM YOU!
YOUR BODIES AND YOUR MINDS...
...AND YOUR VICTORY!
AAARGH! YOU THINK A GHOST CAN CHANGE FATE?
I WILL REIGN FOREVER!
IT'S NOT A GHOST, MONSTER! IT'S THE EMBODIMENT OF THEIR INVINCIBLE FRIENDSHIP!

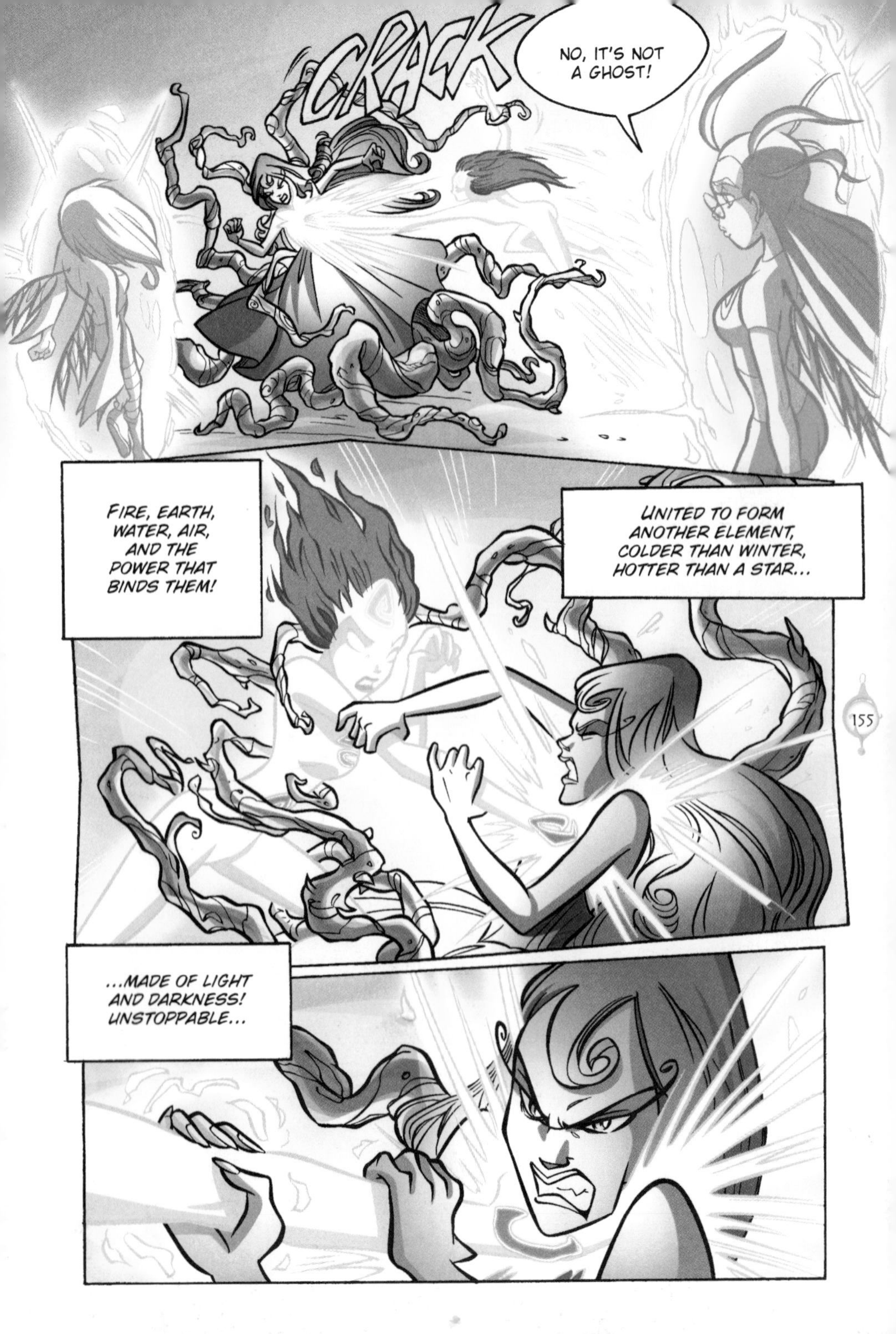
CRACK
NO, IT'S NOT A GHOST!
FIRE, EARTH, WATER, AIR, AND THE POWER THAT BINDS THEM!
UNITED TO FORM ANOTHER ELEMENT, COLDER THAN WINTER, HOTTER THAN A STAR...
...MADE OF LIGHT AND DARKNESS! UNSTOPPABLE...

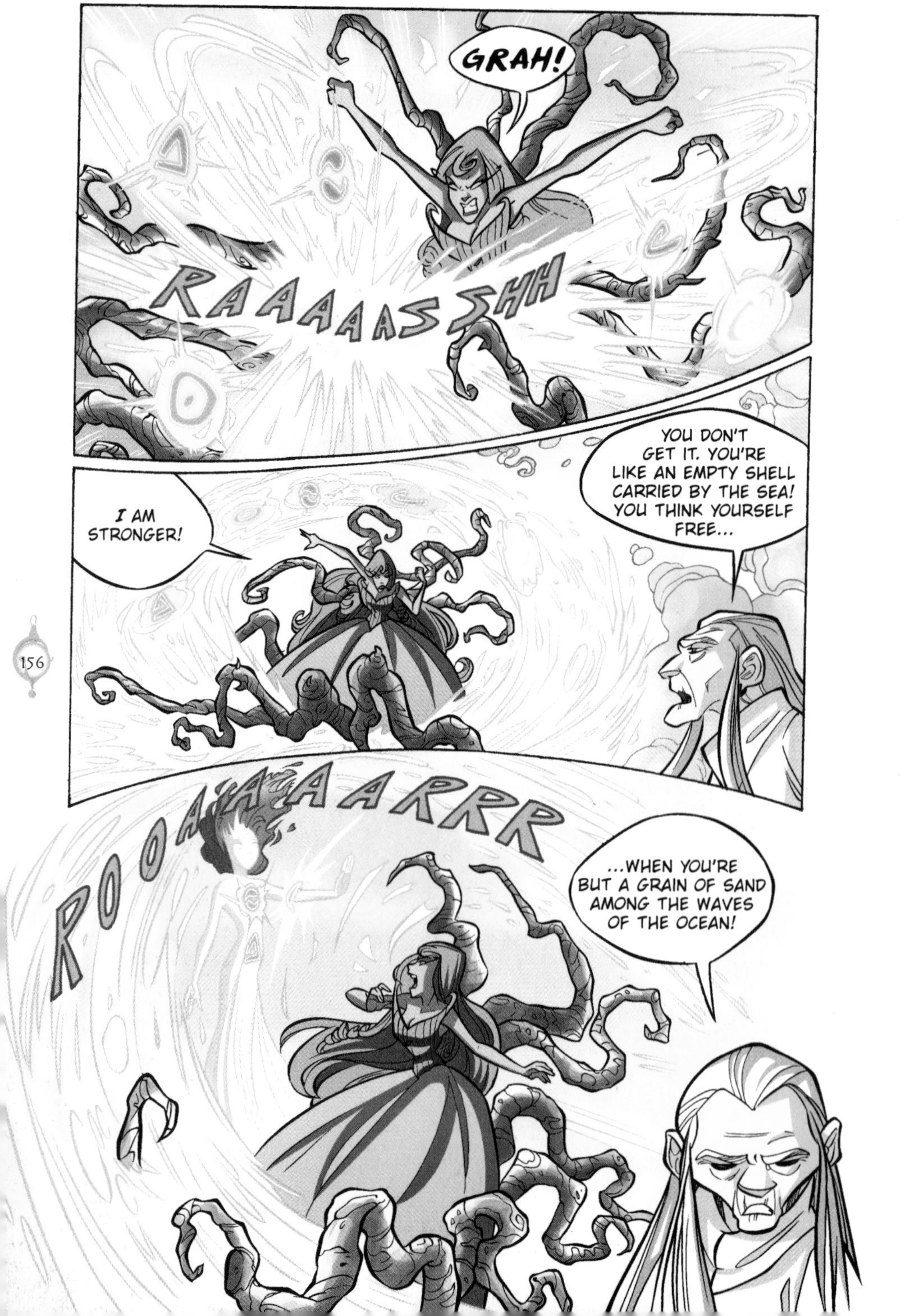
GRAH!
RAAAAASSHH
I AM STRONGER!
YOU DON'T GET IT. YOU'RE LIKE AN EMPTY SHELL CARRIED BY THE SEA! YOU THINK YOURSELF FREE...
ROOAAAAARRR
...WHEN YOU'RE BUT A GRAIN OF SAND AMONG THE WAVES OF THE OCEAN!

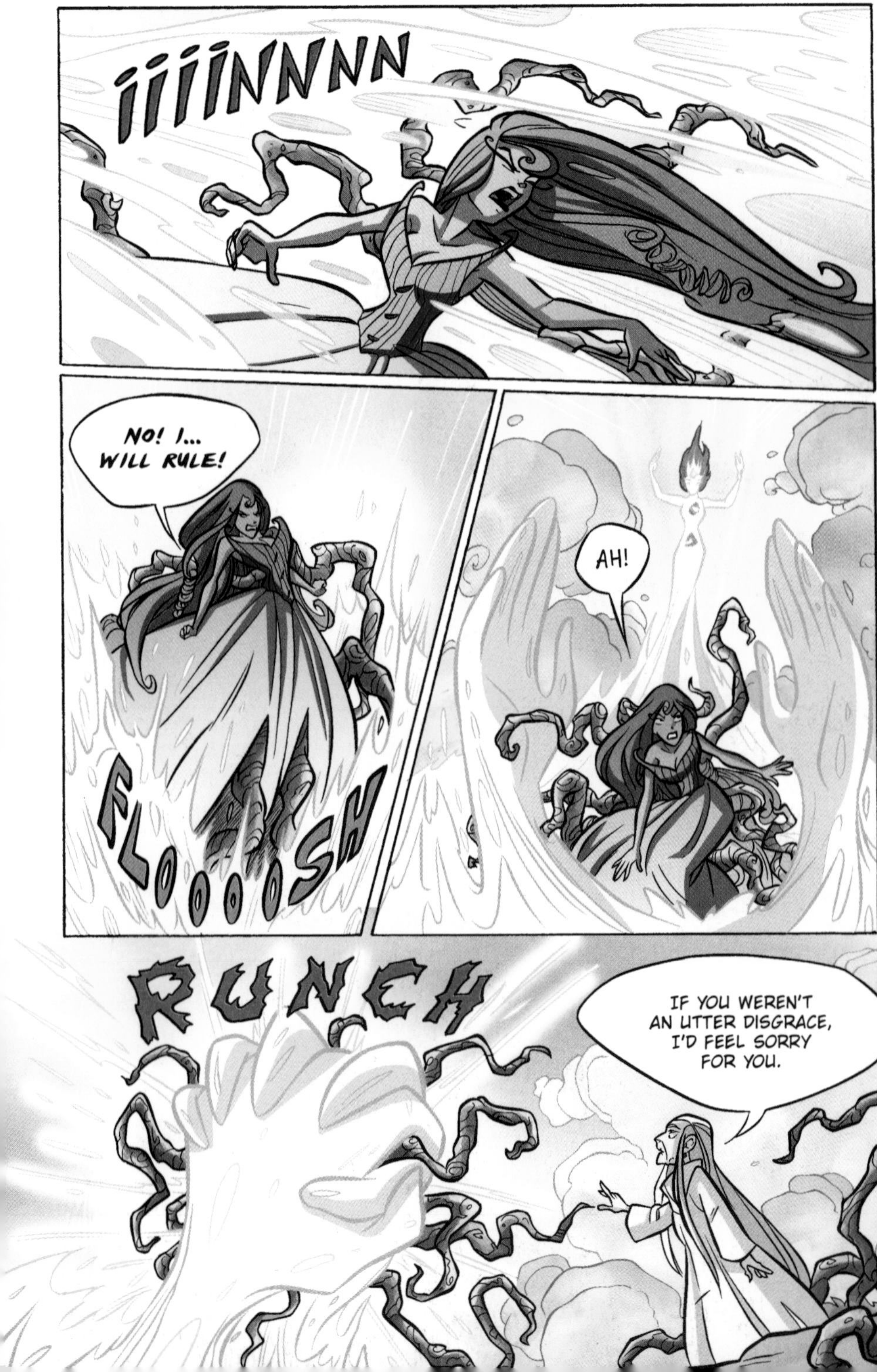
IIIINNNN
NO! I... WILL RULE!
FLOOOOSH
AH!
RUNCH
IF YOU WEREN'T AN UTTER DISGRACE, I'D FEEL SORRY FOR YOU.

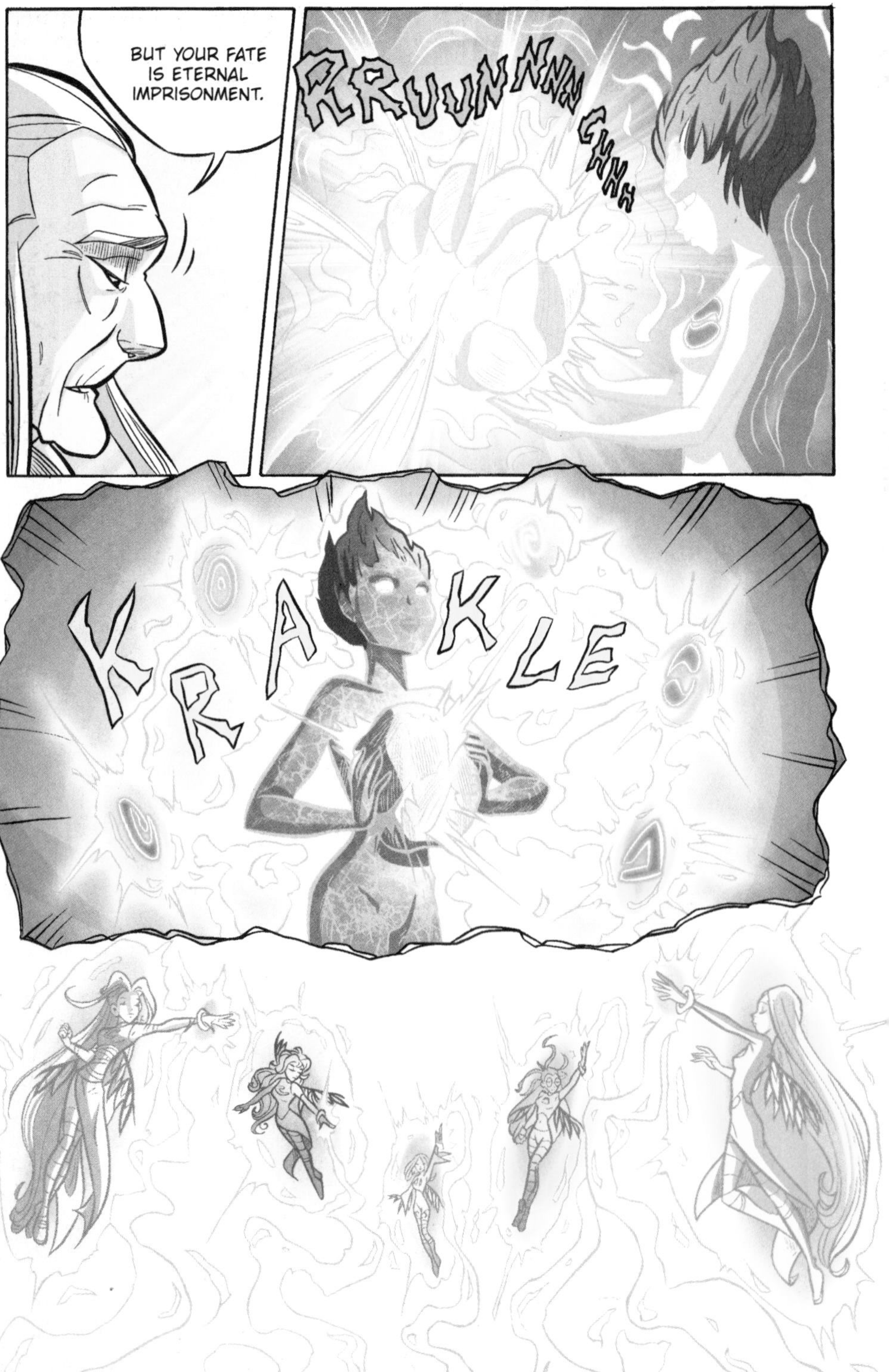
BUT YOUR FATE IS ETERNAL IMPRISONMENT.
RRUUNNNNGHHH
KRAKLE

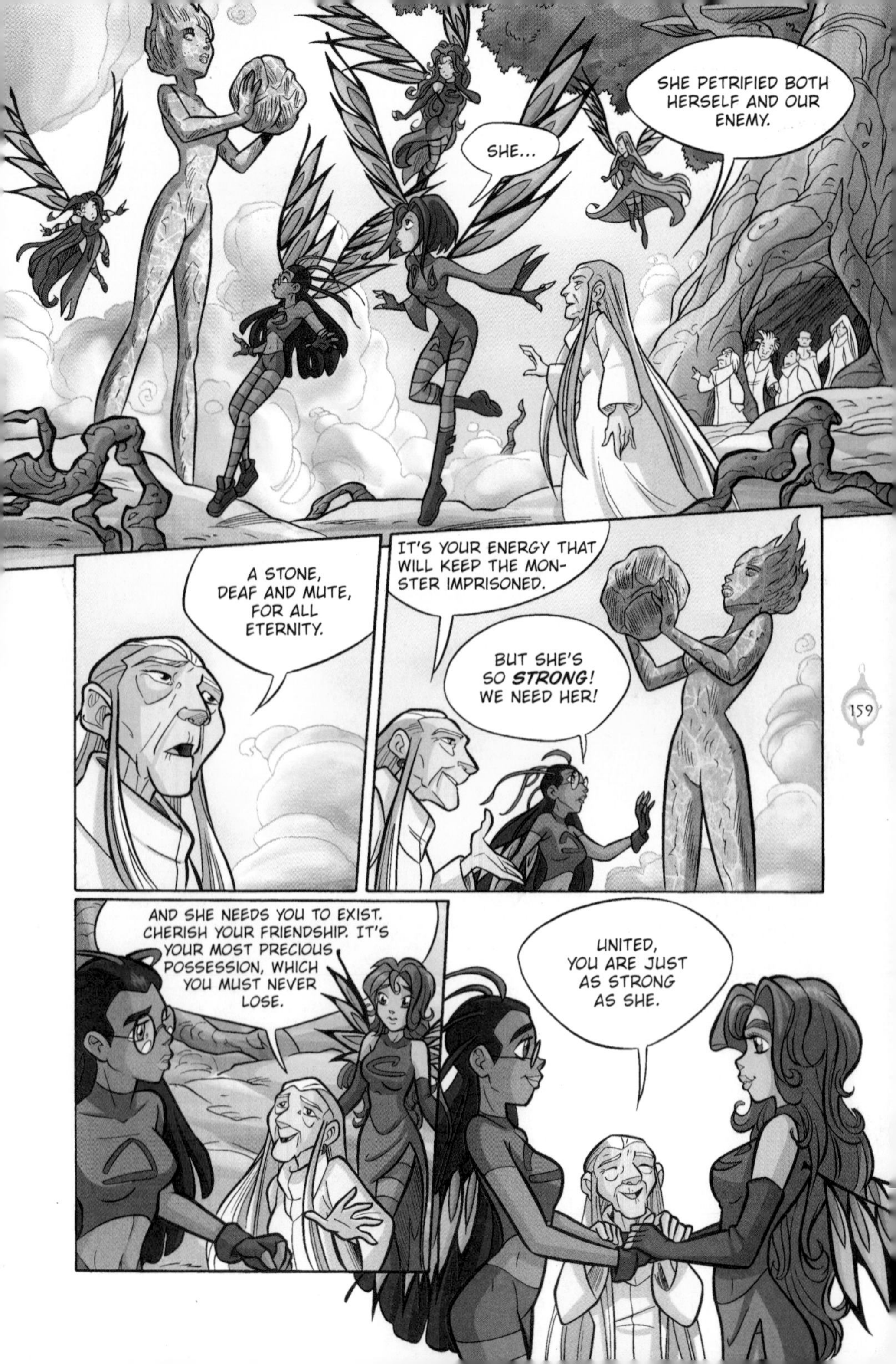
SHE...
SHE PETRIFIED BOTH HERSELF AND OUR ENEMY.
A STONE, DEAF AND MUTE, FOR ALL ETERNITY.
IT'S YOUR ENERGY THAT WILL KEEP THE MON-STER IMPRISONED.
BUT SHE'S SO **STRONG**! WE NEED HER!
AND SHE NEEDS YOU TO EXIST. CHERISH YOUR FRIENDSHIP. IT'S YOUR MOST PRECIOUS POSSESSION, WHICH YOU MUST NEVER LOSE.
UNITED, YOU ARE JUST AS STRONG AS SHE.

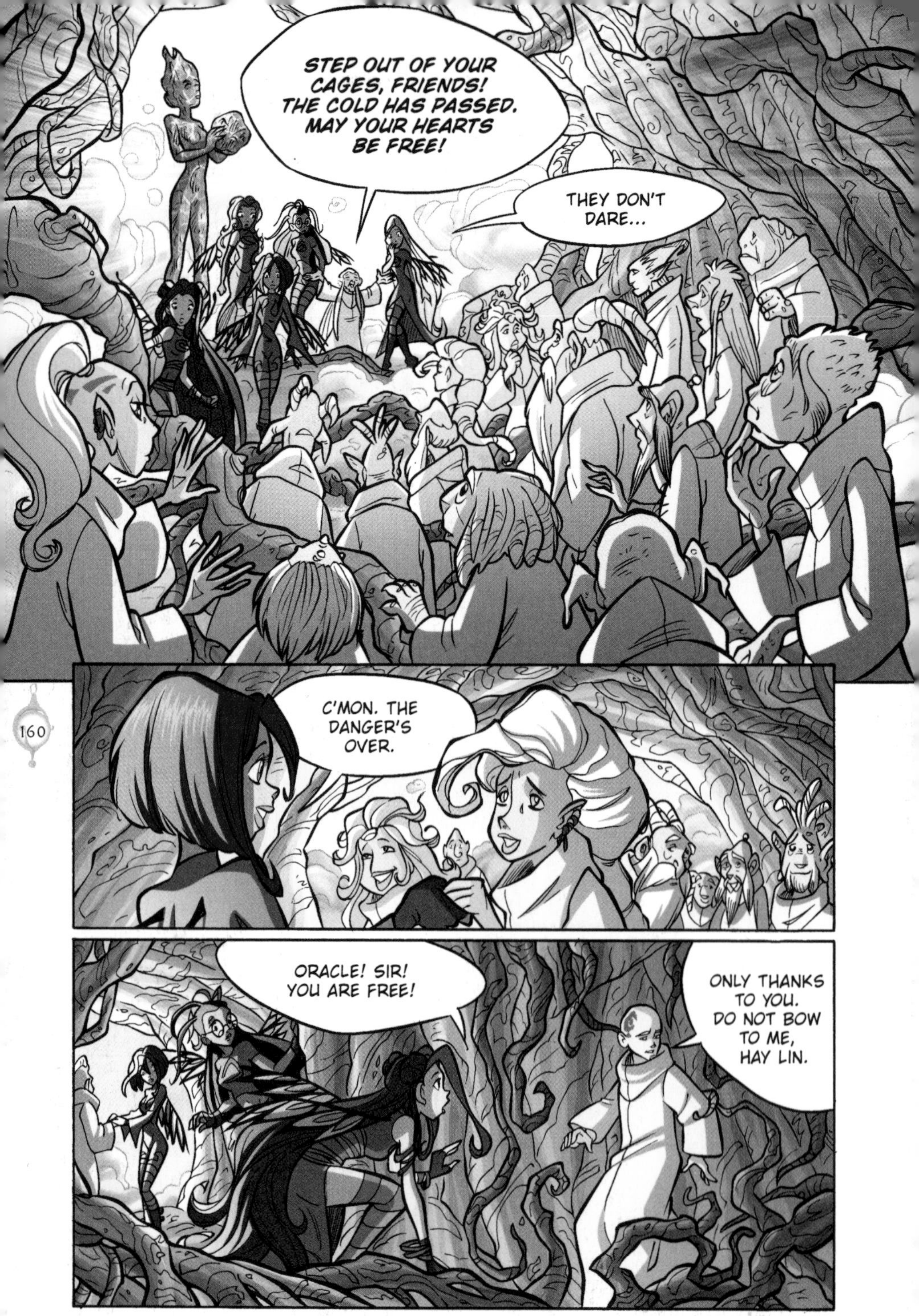
STEP OUT OF YOUR CAGES, FRIENDS! THE COLD HAS PASSED. MAY YOUR HEARTS BE FREE!
THEY DON'T DARE...
C'MON. THE DANGER'S OVER.
ORACLE! SIR! YOU ARE FREE!
ONLY THANKS TO YOU. DO NOT BOW TO ME, HAY LIN.

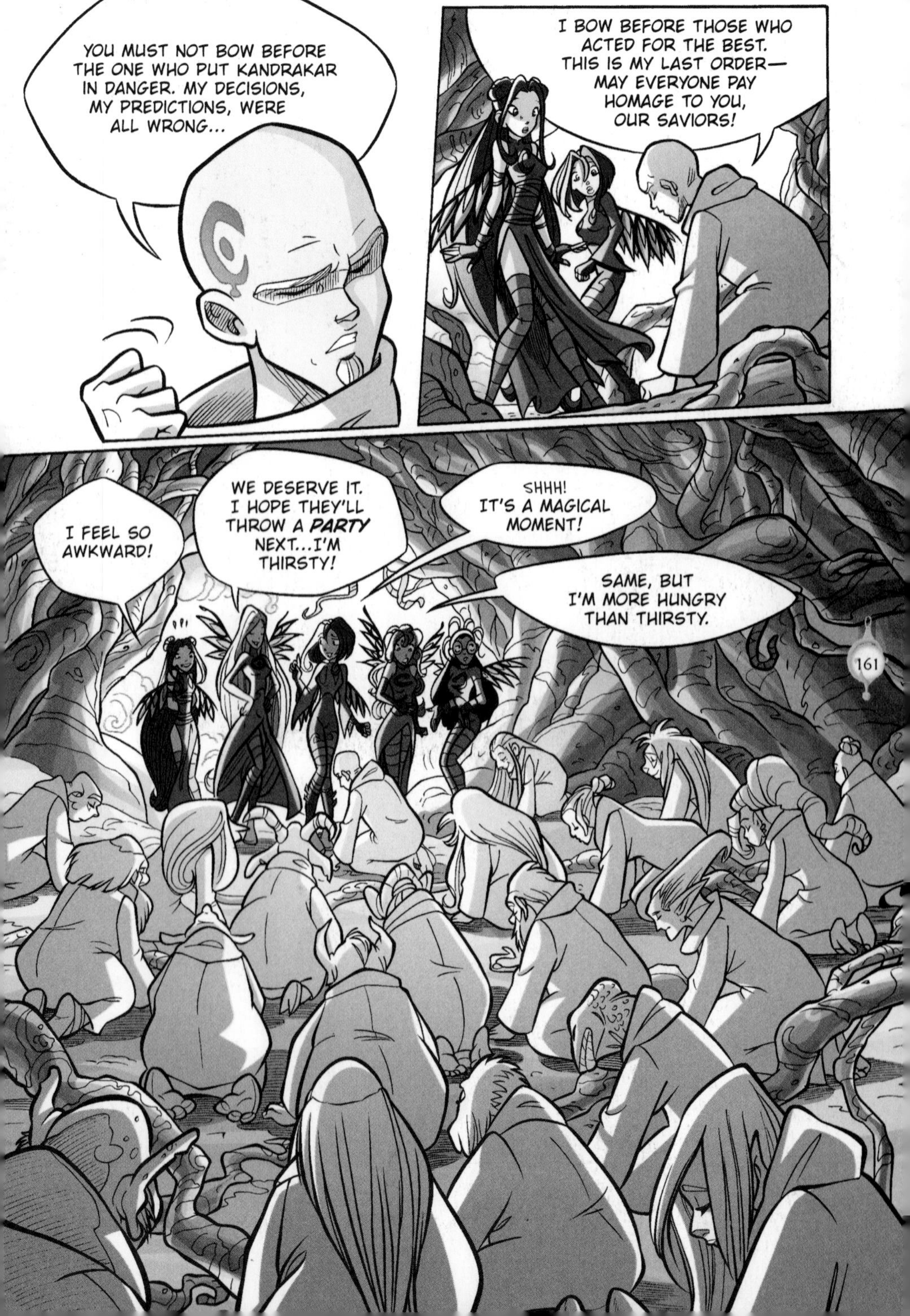
YOU MUST NOT BOW BEFORE THE ONE WHO PUT KANDRAKAR IN DANGER. MY DECISIONS, MY PREDICTIONS, WERE ALL WRONG...
I BOW BEFORE THOSE WHO ACTED FOR THE BEST. THIS IS MY LAST ORDER— MAY EVERYONE PAY HOMAGE TO YOU, OUR SAVIORS!
I FEEL SO AWKWARD!
WE DESERVE IT. I HOPE THEY'LL THROW A PARTY NEXT...I'M THIRSTY!
SHHH! IT'S A MAGICAL MOMENT!
SAME, BUT I'M MORE HUNGRY THAN THIRSTY.

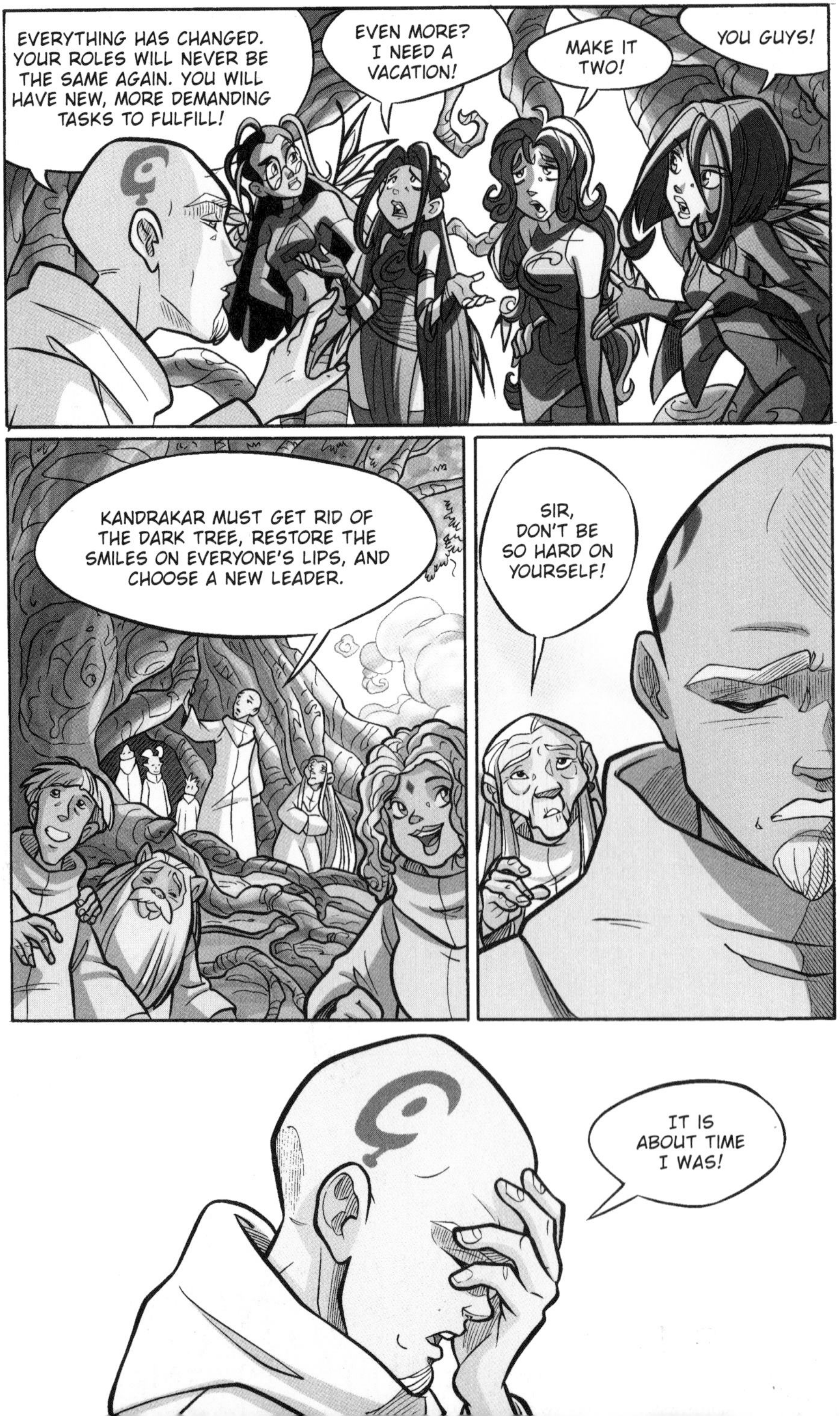
EVERYTHING HAS CHANGED. YOUR ROLES WILL NEVER BE THE SAME AGAIN. YOU WILL HAVE NEW, MORE DEMANDING TASKS TO FULFILL!
EVEN MORE? I NEED A VACATION!
MAKE IT TWO!
YOU GUYS!
KANDRAKAR MUST GET RID OF THE DARK TREE, RESTORE THE SMILES ON EVERYONE'S LIPS, AND CHOOSE A NEW LEADER.
SIR, DON'T BE SO HARD ON YOURSELF!
IT IS ABOUT TIME I WAS!

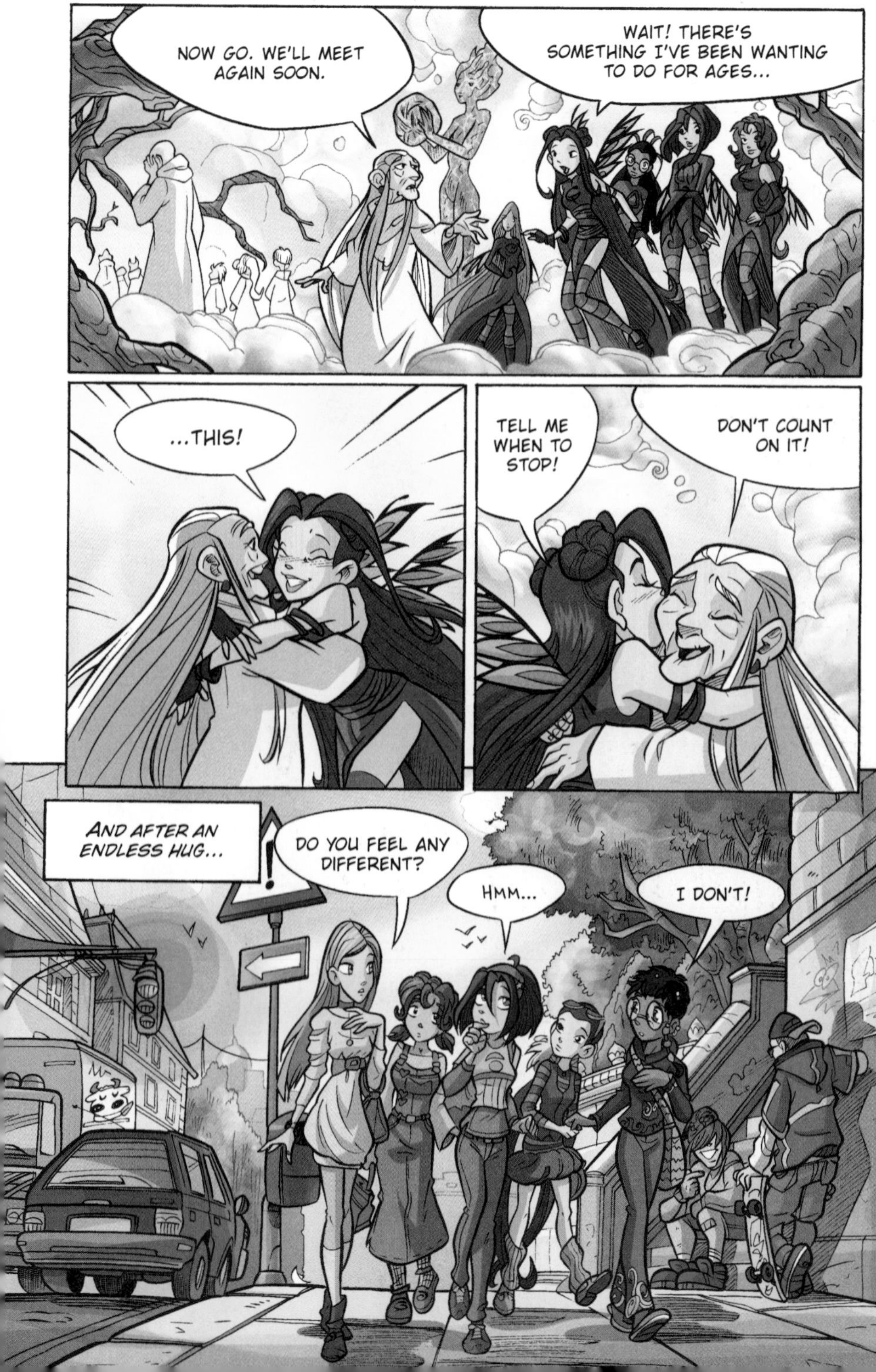
NOW GO. WE'LL MEET AGAIN SOON.
WAIT! THERE'S SOMETHING I'VE BEEN WANTING TO DO FOR AGES...
...THIS!
TELL ME WHEN TO STOP!
DON'T COUNT ON IT!
AND AFTER AN ENDLESS HUG...
DO YOU FEEL ANY DIFFERENT?
HMM...
I DON'T!

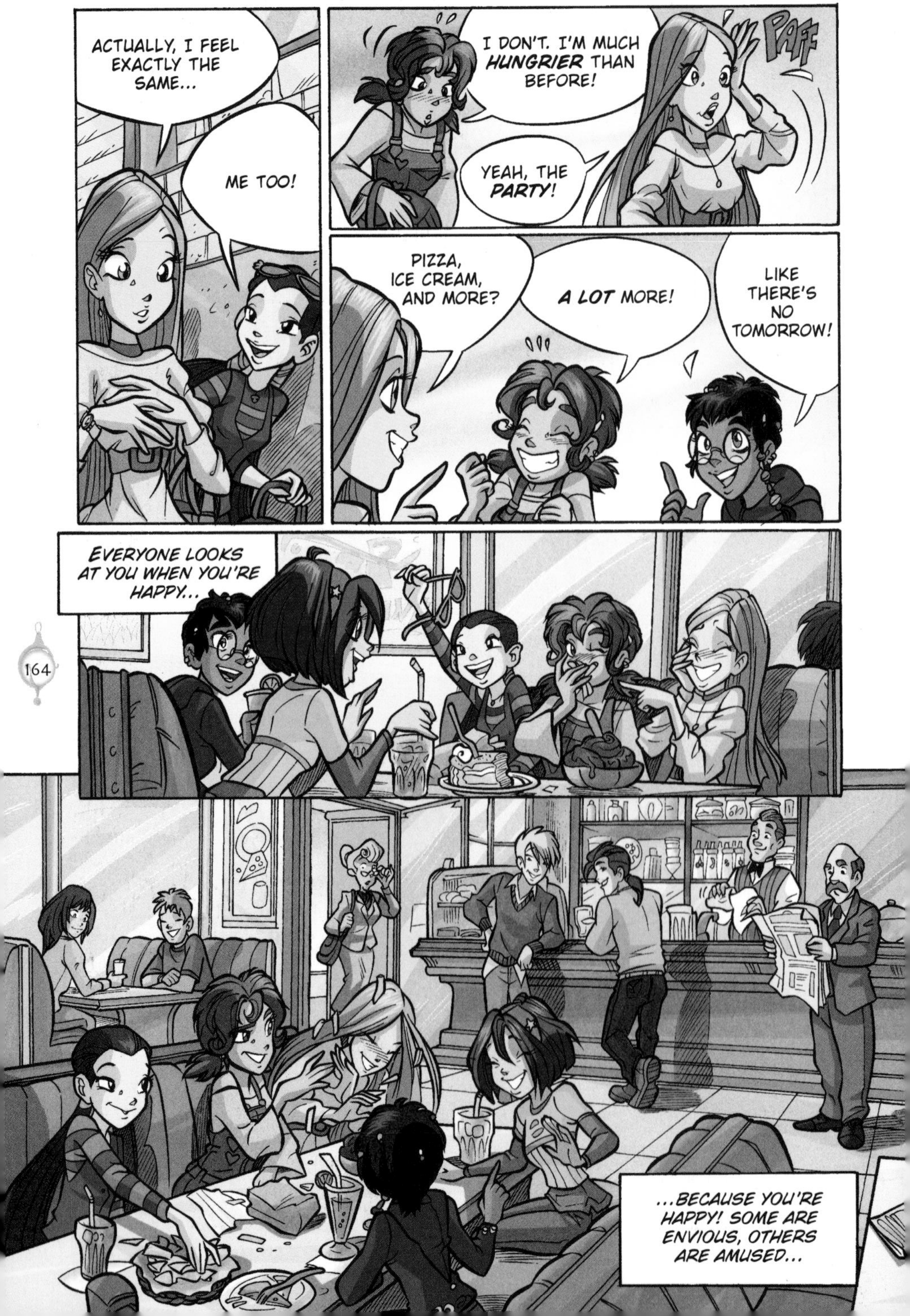
ACTUALLY, I FEEL EXACTLY THE SAME...
ME TOO!
I DON'T. I'M MUCH *HUNGRIER* THAN BEFORE!
PAFF
YEAH, THE *PARTY*!
PIZZA, ICE CREAM, AND MORE?
A LOT MORE!
LIKE THERE'S NO TOMORROW!
EVERYONE LOOKS AT YOU WHEN YOU'RE HAPPY...
...BECAUSE YOU'RE HAPPY! SOME ARE ENVIOUS, OTHERS ARE AMUSED...

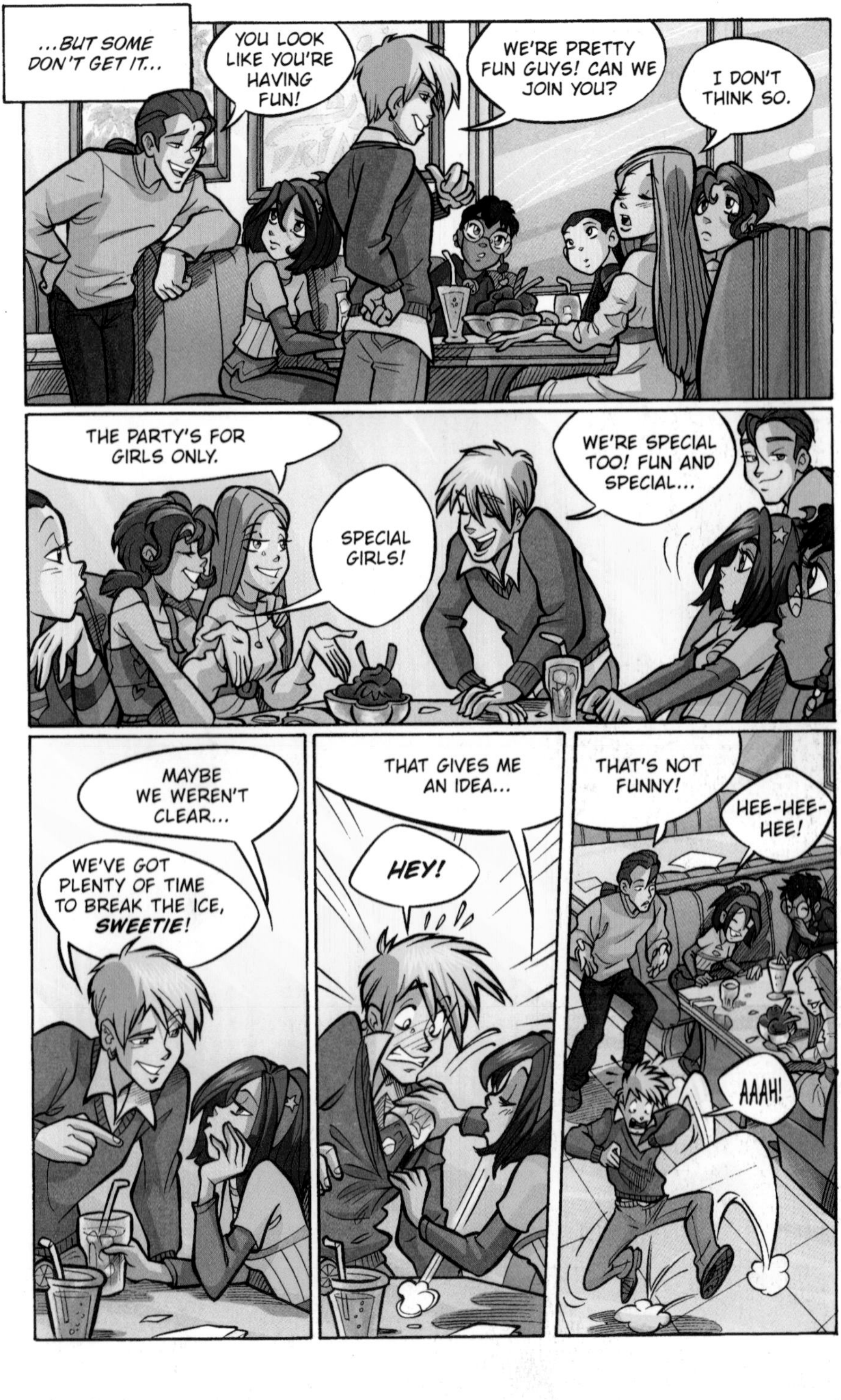
...BUT SOME DON'T GET IT...
YOU LOOK LIKE YOU'RE HAVING FUN!
WE'RE PRETTY FUN GUYS! CAN WE JOIN YOU?
I DON'T THINK SO.
THE PARTY'S FOR GIRLS ONLY.
SPECIAL GIRLS!
WE'RE SPECIAL TOO! FUN AND SPECIAL...
MAYBE WE WEREN'T CLEAR...
WE'VE GOT PLENTY OF TIME TO BREAK THE ICE, **SWEETIE!**
THAT GIVES ME AN IDEA...
HEY!
THAT'S NOT FUNNY!
HEE-HEE-HEE!
AAAH!

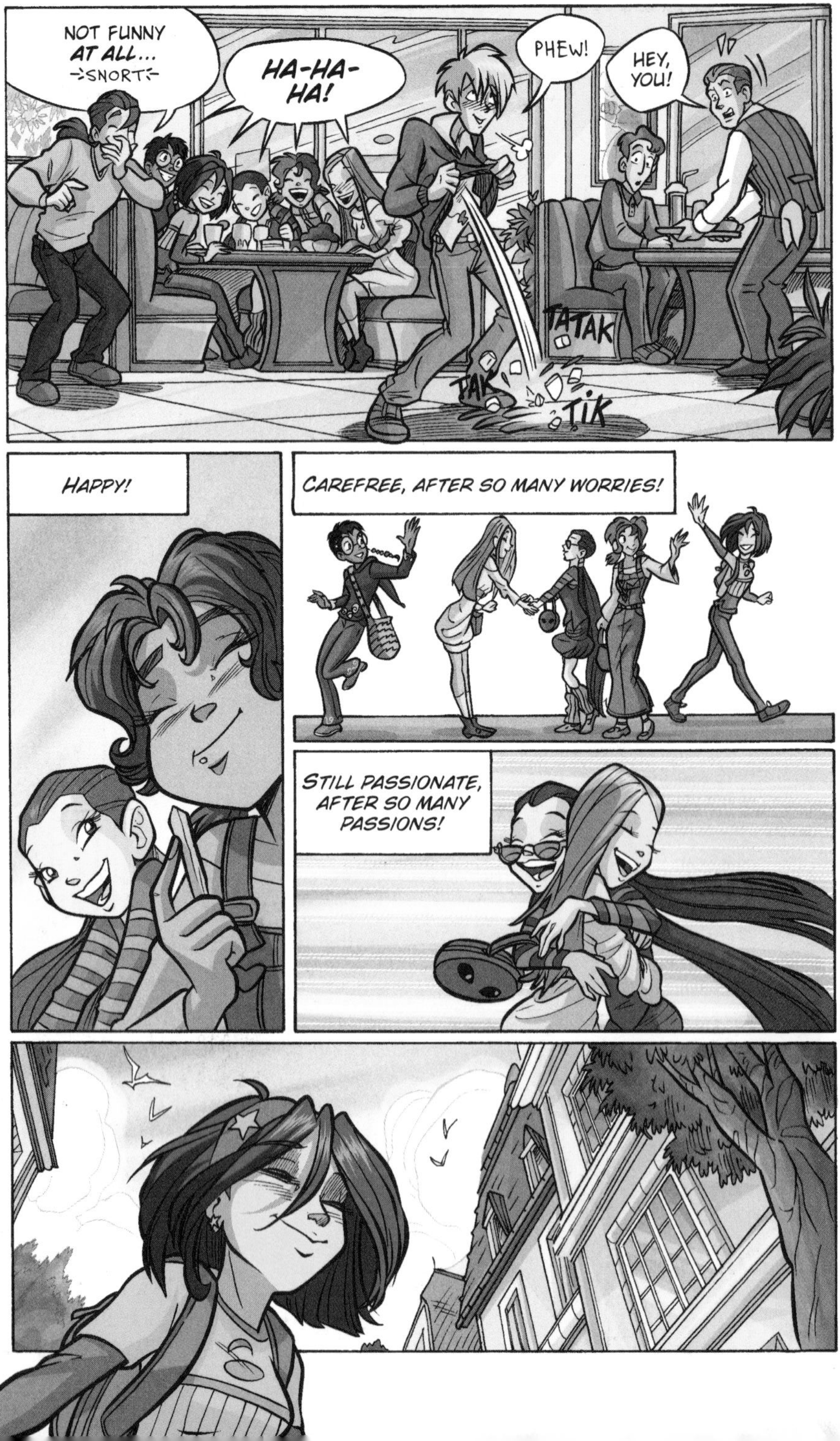

NOT FUNNY AT ALL... -SNORT-
HA-HA-HA!
PHEW!
HEY, YOU!
TATAK
TAK
TIK
HAPPY!
CAREFREE, AFTER SO MANY WORRIES!
STILL PASSIONATE, AFTER SO MANY PASSIONS!

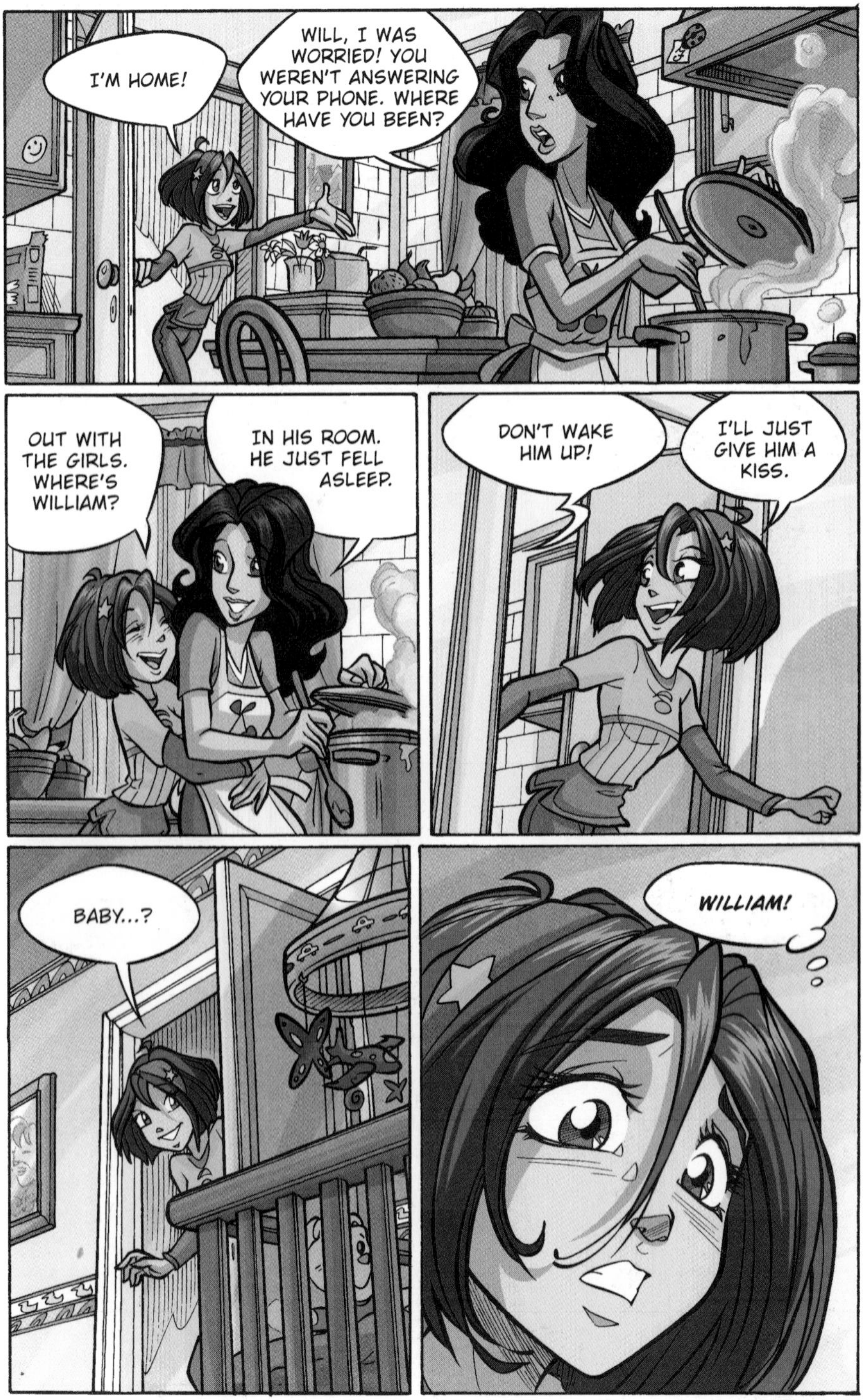
I'M HOME!
WILL, I WAS WORRIED! YOU WEREN'T ANSWERING YOUR PHONE. WHERE HAVE YOU BEEN?
OUT WITH THE GIRLS. WHERE'S WILLIAM?
IN HIS ROOM. HE JUST FELL ASLEEP.
DON'T WAKE HIM UP!
I'LL JUST GIVE HIM A KISS.
BABY...?
WILLIAM!

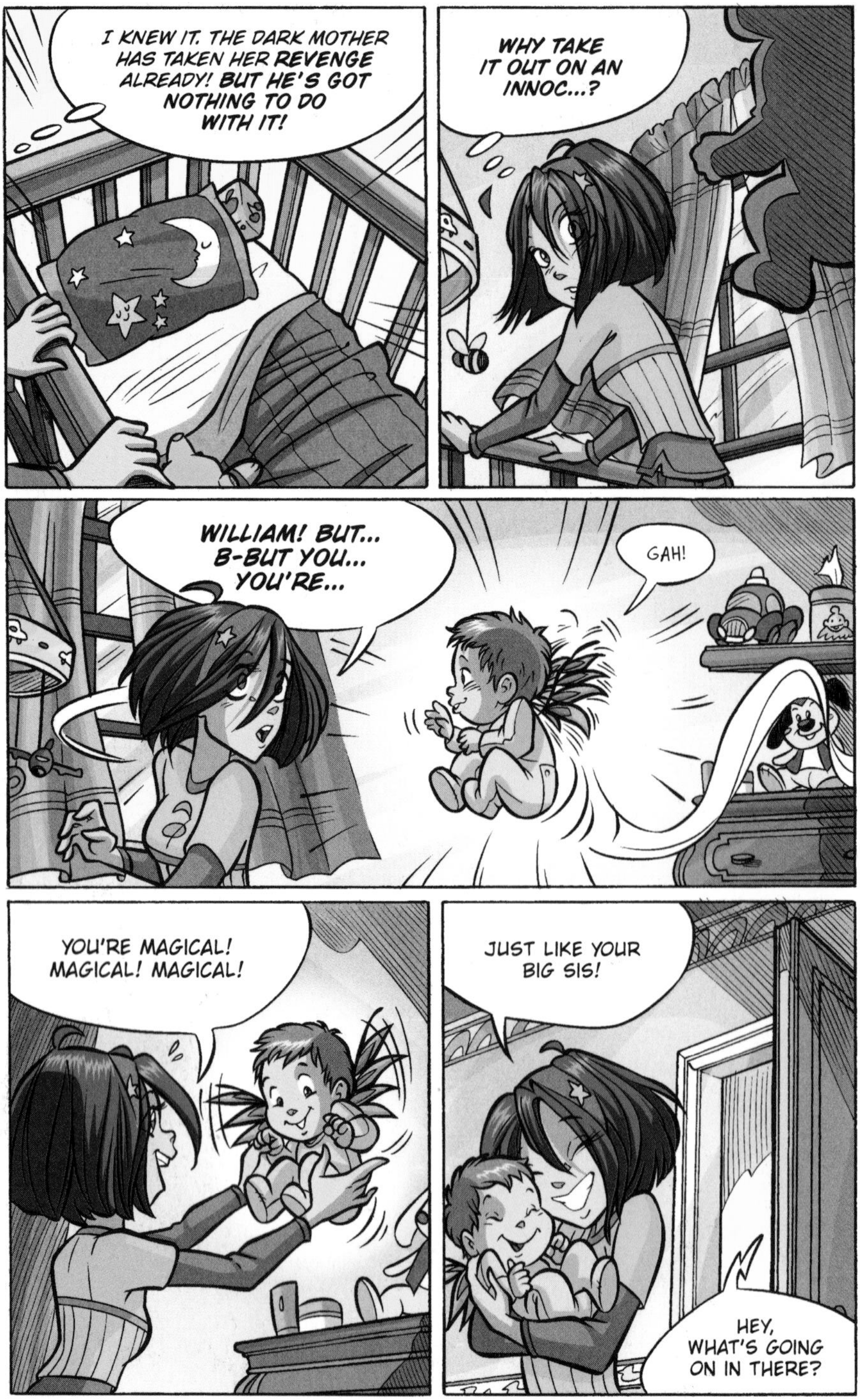
I KNEW IT. THE DARK MOTHER HAS TAKEN HER REVENGE ALREADY! BUT HE'S GOT NOTHING TO DO WITH IT!
WHY TAKE IT OUT ON AN INNOC...?
WILLIAM! BUT... B-BUT YOU... YOU'RE...
GAH!
YOU'RE MAGICAL! MAGICAL! MAGICAL!
JUST LIKE YOUR BIG SIS!
HEY, WHAT'S GOING ON IN THERE?

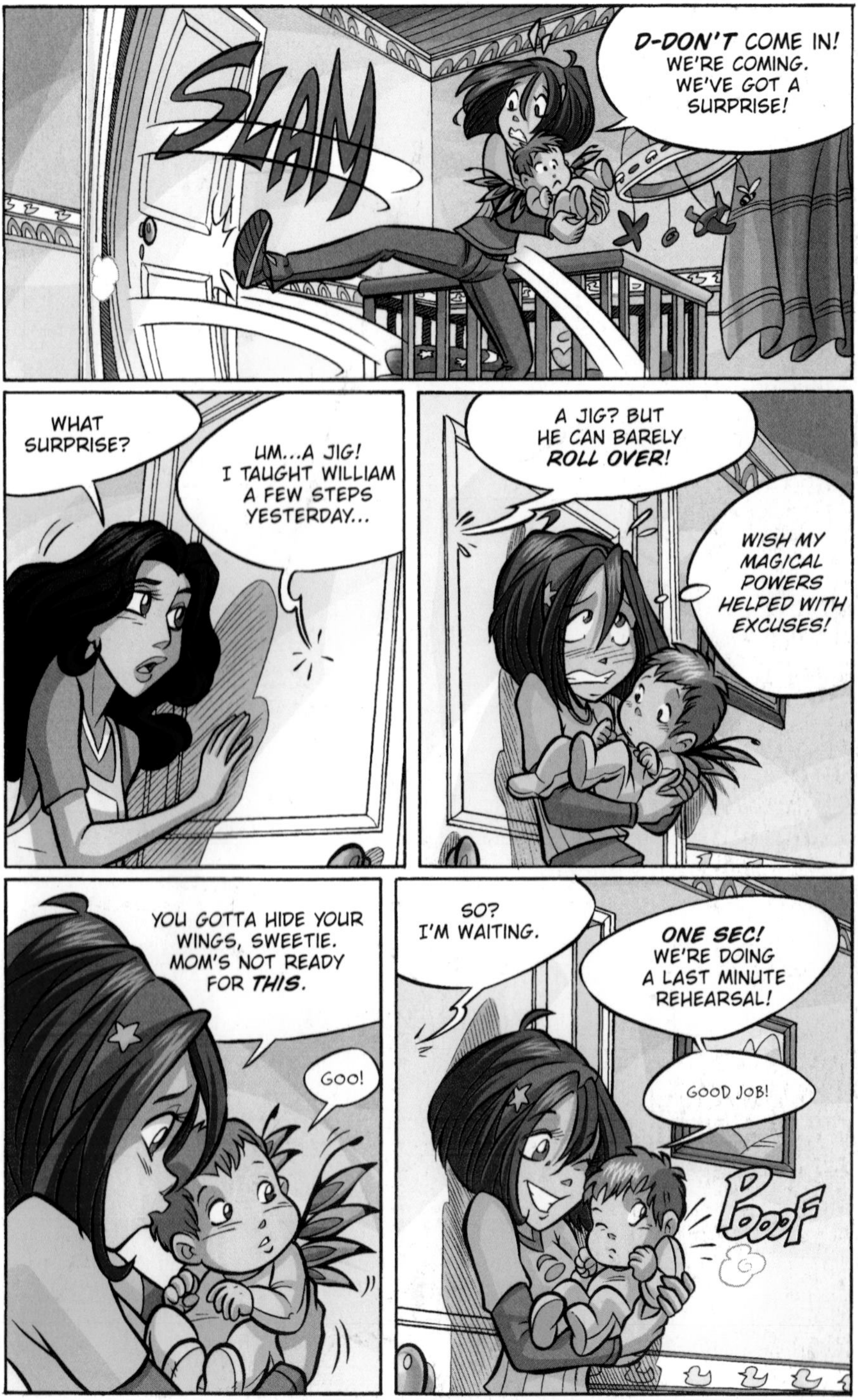
SLAM
D-DON'T COME IN! WE'RE COMING. WE'VE GOT A SURPRISE!
WHAT SURPRISE?
UM...A JIG! I TAUGHT WILLIAM A FEW STEPS YESTERDAY...
A JIG? BUT HE CAN BARELY ROLL OVER!
WISH MY MAGICAL POWERS HELPED WITH EXCUSES!
YOU GOTTA HIDE YOUR WINGS, SWEETIE. MOM'S NOT READY FOR THIS.
GOO!
SO? I'M WAITING.
ONE SEC! WE'RE DOING A LAST MINUTE REHEARSAL!
GOOD JOB!
POOOF

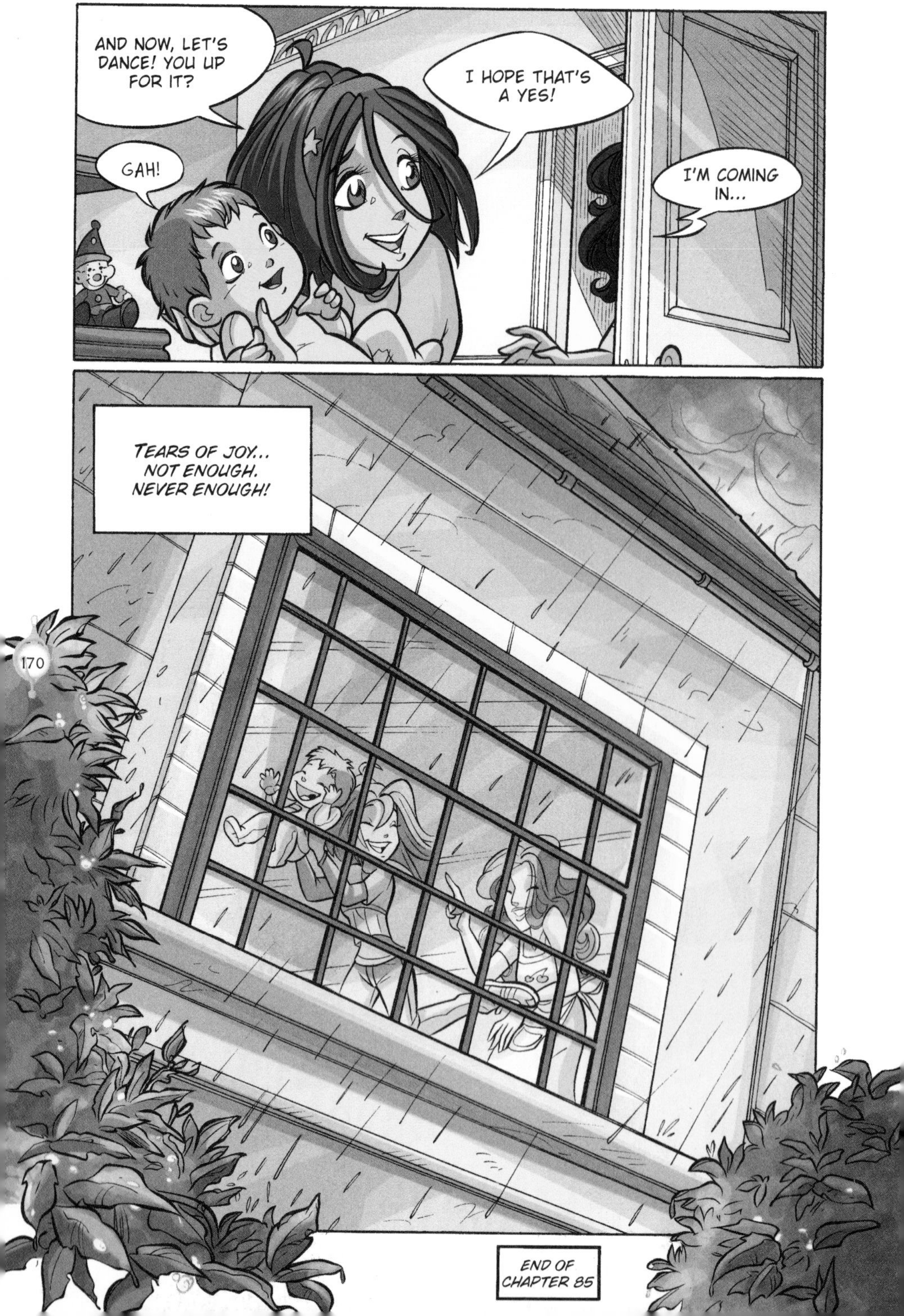
AND NOW, LET'S DANCE! YOU UP FOR IT?
I HOPE THAT'S A YES!
GAH!
I'M COMING IN...
TEARS OF JOY... NOT ENOUGH. NEVER ENOUGH!
END OF CHAPTER 85

36

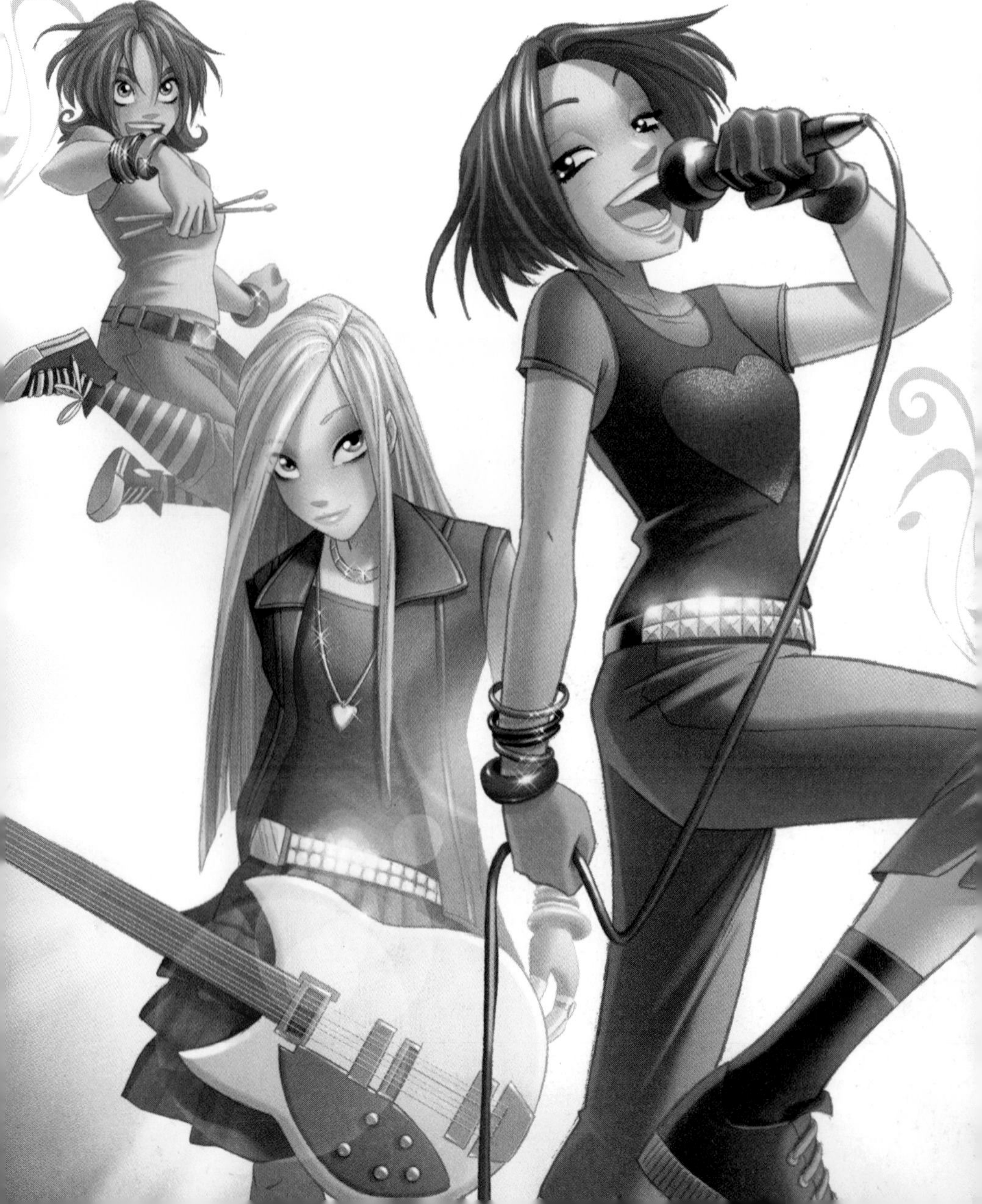

The Heart of It All

"Once, I would have fixed everything myself in the blink of an eye. But today, my eyes are only full of bitter tears."

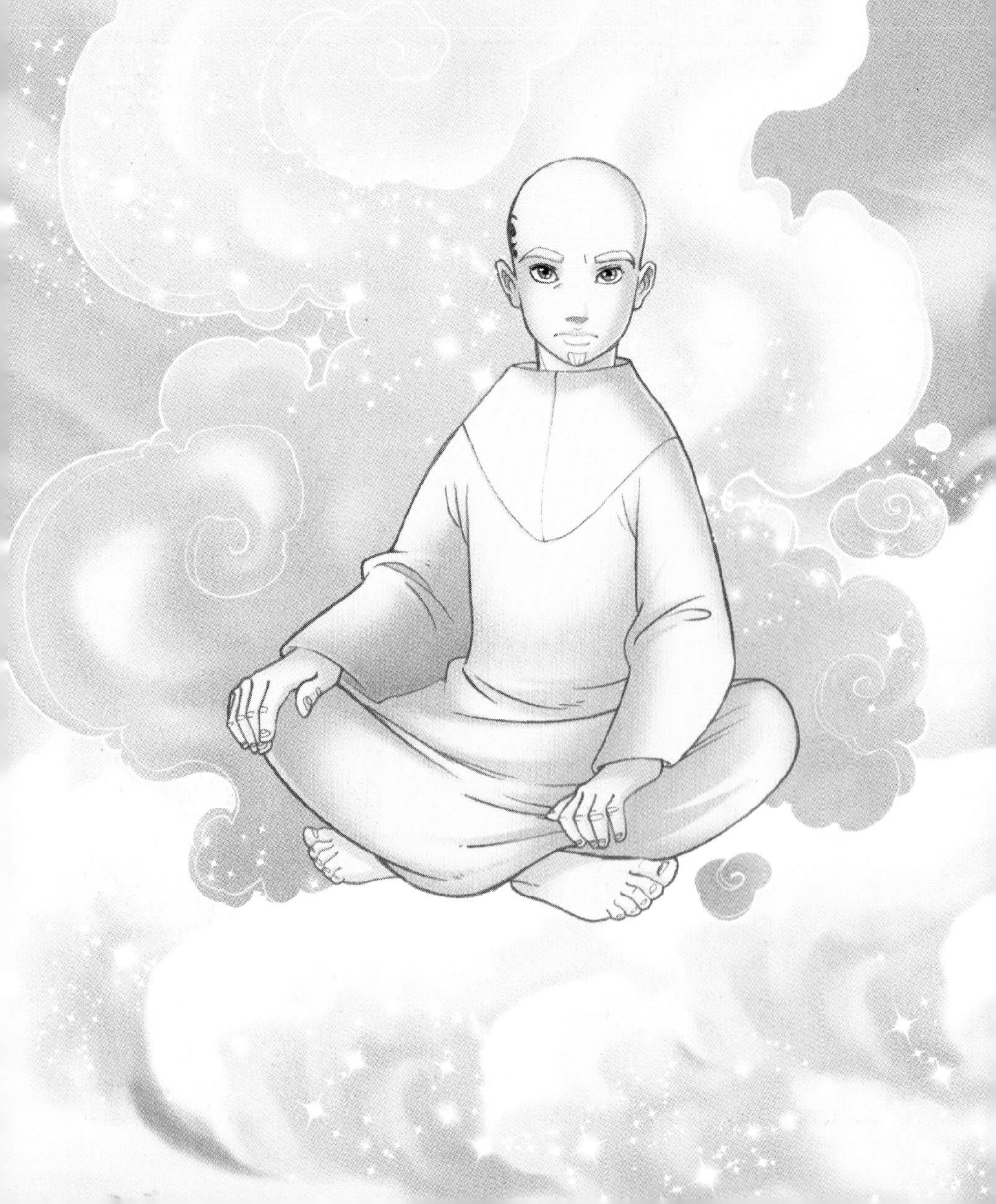

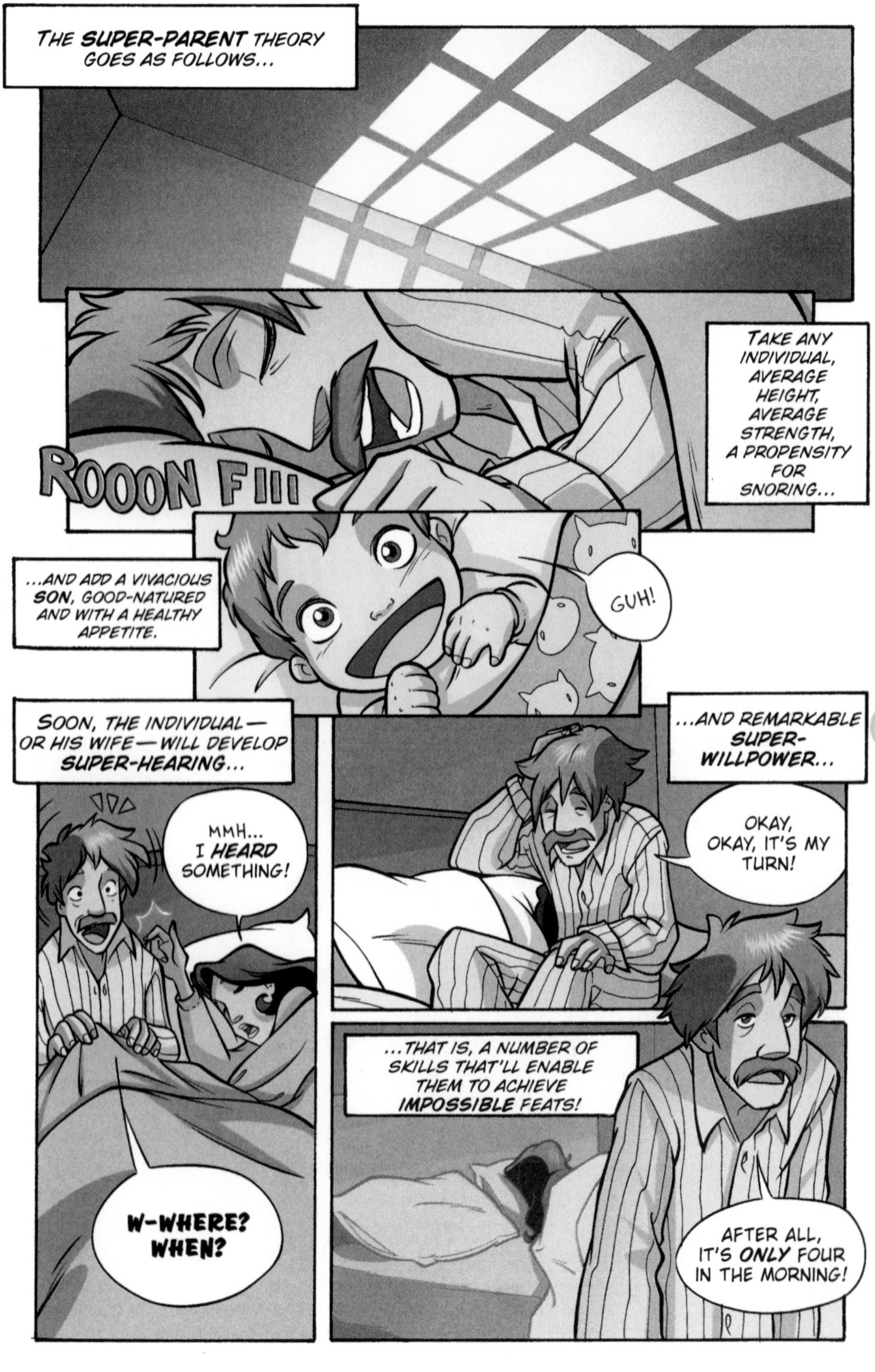
THE SUPER-PARENT THEORY GOES AS FOLLOWS...
TAKE ANY INDIVIDUAL, AVERAGE HEIGHT, AVERAGE STRENGTH, A PROPENSITY FOR SNORING...
ROOON FIII
...AND ADD A VIVACIOUS SON, GOOD-NATURED AND WITH A HEALTHY APPETITE.
GUH!
SOON, THE INDIVIDUAL— OR HIS WIFE—WILL DEVELOP SUPER-HEARING...
MMH... I HEARD SOMETHING!
W-WHERE? WHEN?
...AND REMARKABLE SUPER-WILLPOWER...
OKAY, OKAY, IT'S MY TURN!
...THAT IS, A NUMBER OF SKILLS THAT'LL ENABLE THEM TO ACHIEVE IMPOSSIBLE FEATS!
AFTER ALL, IT'S ONLY FOUR IN THE MORNING!

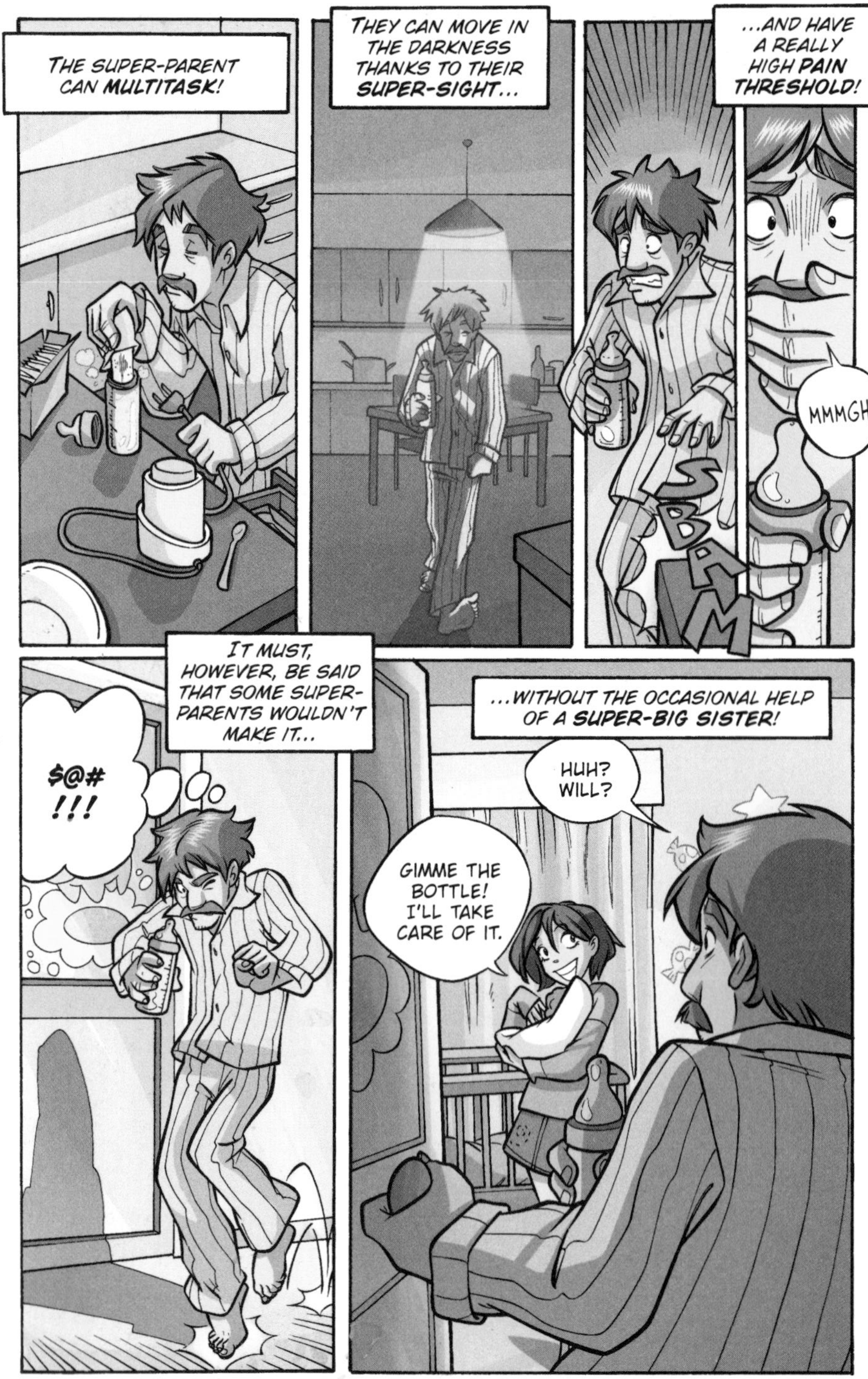
THE SUPER-PARENT CAN MULTITASK!
THEY CAN MOVE IN THE DARKNESS THANKS TO THEIR SUPER-SIGHT...
...AND HAVE A REALLY HIGH PAIN THRESHOLD!
SBAM
MMMGH!
IT MUST, HOWEVER, BE SAID THAT SOME SUPER-PARENTS WOULDN'T MAKE IT...
$@# !!!
...WITHOUT THE OCCASIONAL HELP OF A SUPER-BIG SISTER!
HUH? WILL?
GIMME THE BOTTLE! I'LL TAKE CARE OF IT.

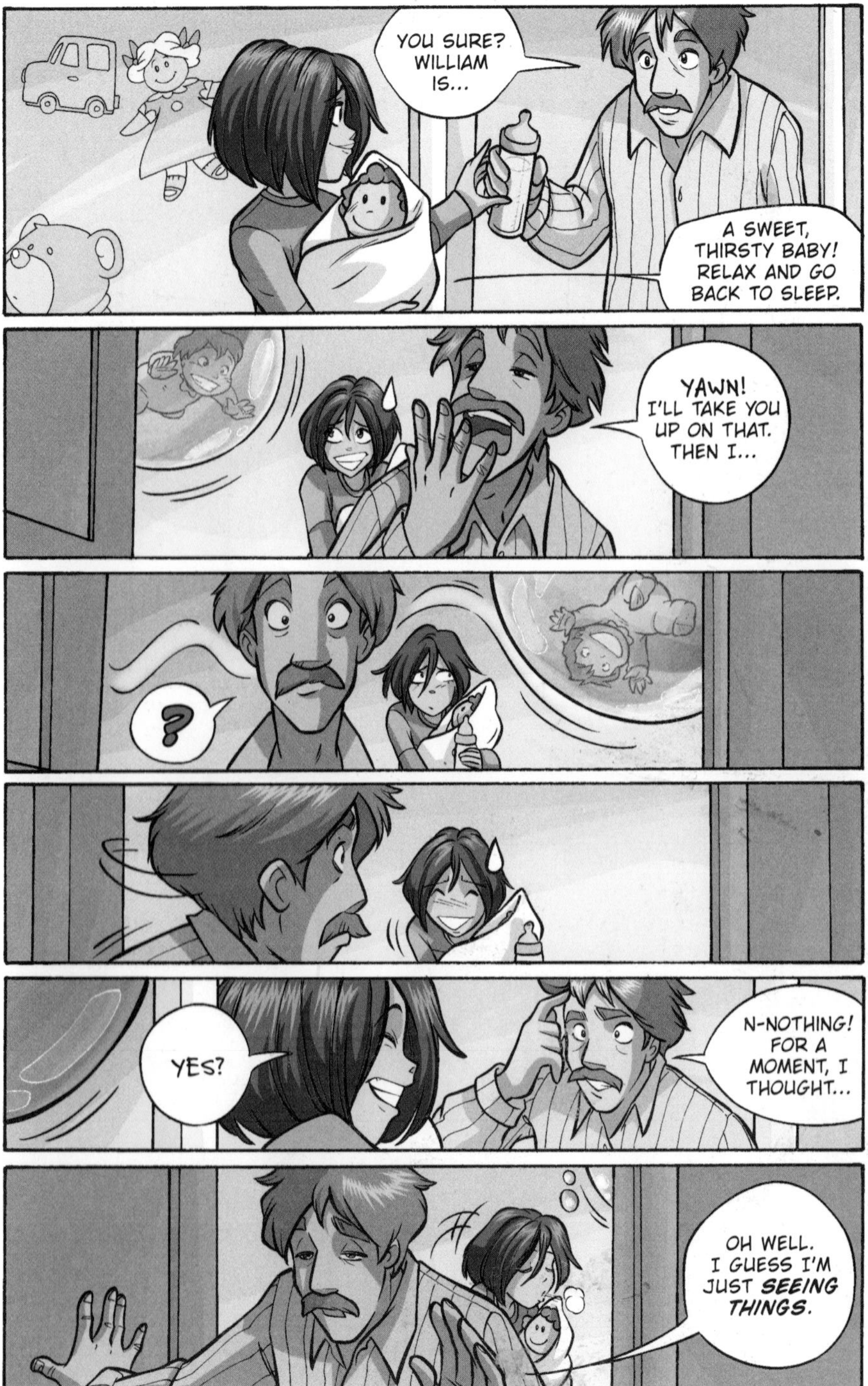
YOU SURE? WILLIAM IS...
A SWEET, THIRSTY BABY! RELAX AND GO BACK TO SLEEP.
YAWN! I'LL TAKE YOU UP ON THAT. THEN I...
?
YES?
N-NOTHING! FOR A MOMENT, I THOUGHT...
OH WELL. I GUESS I'M JUST SEEING THINGS.

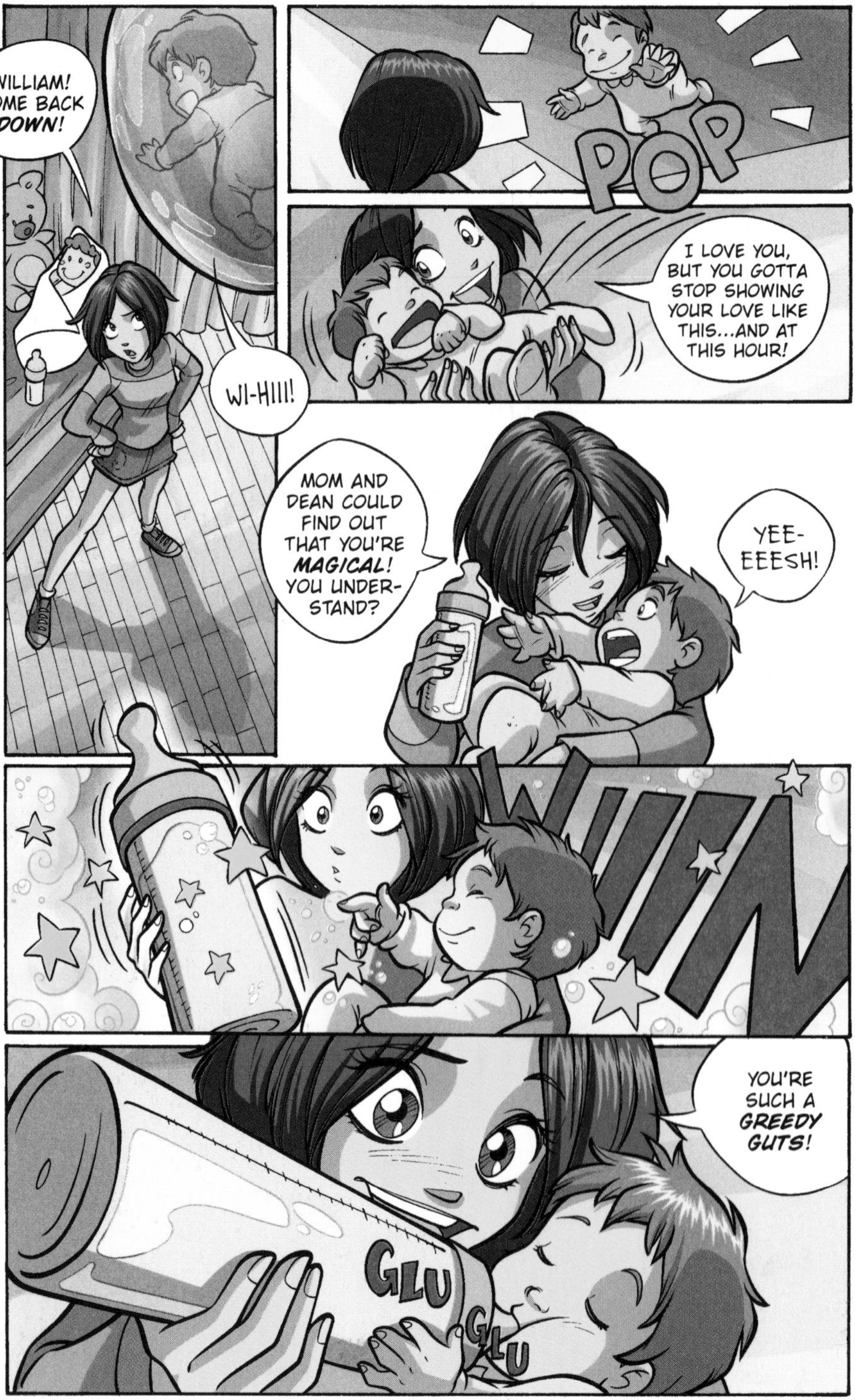
WILLIAM! COME BACK DOWN!
WI-HIII!
POP
I LOVE YOU, BUT YOU GOTTA STOP SHOWING YOUR LOVE LIKE THIS...AND AT THIS HOUR!
MOM AND DEAN COULD FIND OUT THAT YOU'RE MAGICAL! YOU UNDERSTAND?
YEE-EEESH!
YOU'RE SUCH A GREEDY GUTS!
GLU
GLU
GLU

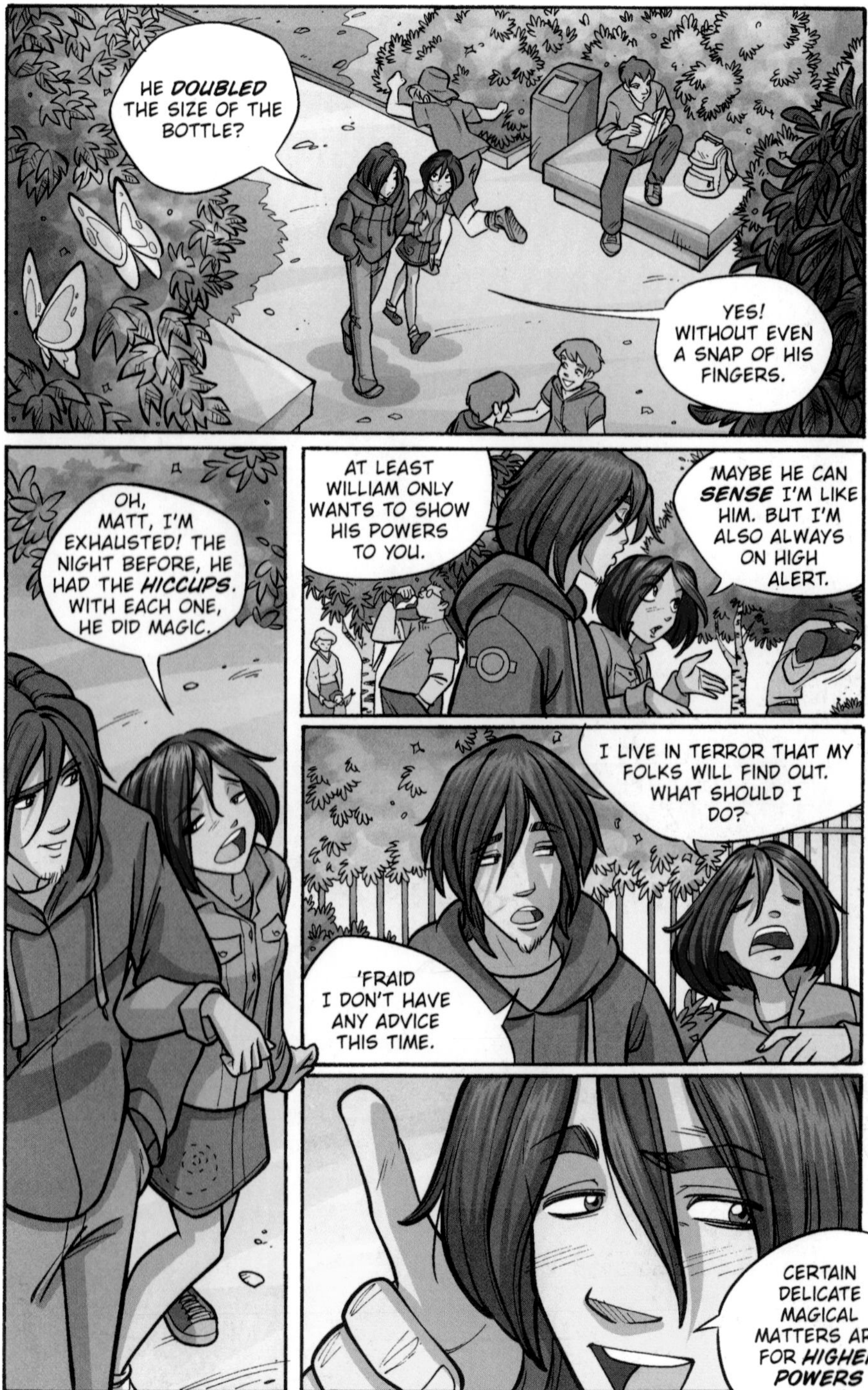
HE *DOUBLED* THE SIZE OF THE BOTTLE?
YES! WITHOUT EVEN A SNAP OF HIS FINGERS.
OH, MATT, I'M EXHAUSTED! THE NIGHT BEFORE, HE HAD THE *HICCUPS*. WITH EACH ONE, HE DID MAGIC.
AT LEAST WILLIAM ONLY WANTS TO SHOW HIS POWERS TO YOU.
MAYBE HE CAN *SENSE* I'M LIKE HIM. BUT I'M ALSO ALWAYS ON HIGH ALERT.
I LIVE IN TERROR THAT MY FOLKS WILL FIND OUT. WHAT SHOULD I DO?
'FRAID I DON'T HAVE ANY ADVICE THIS TIME.
CERTAIN DELICATE MAGICAL MATTERS ARE FOR *HIGHER POWERS* ONLY!

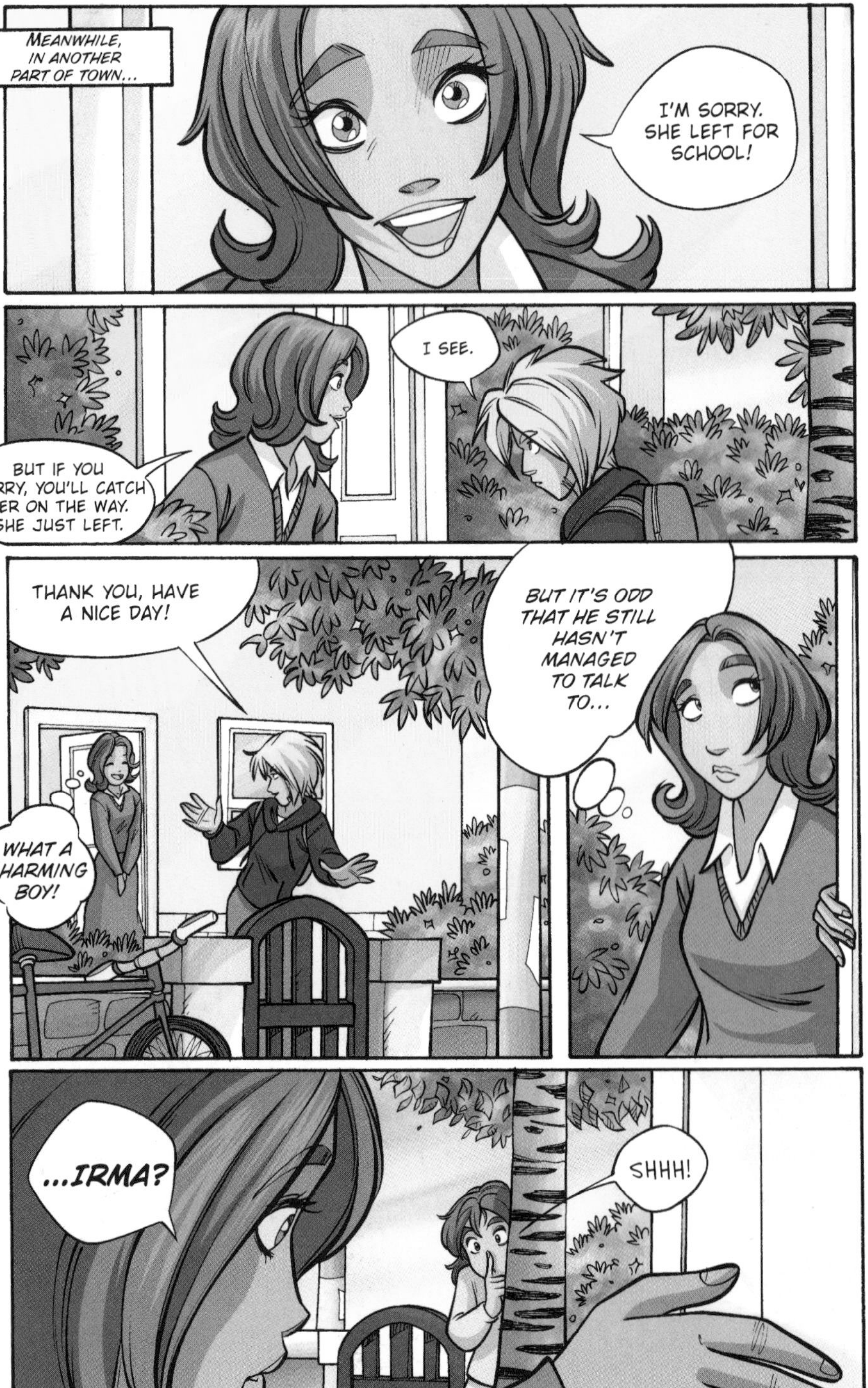
MEANWHILE, IN ANOTHER PART OF TOWN...
I'M SORRY. SHE LEFT FOR SCHOOL!
I SEE.
BUT IF YOU HURRY, YOU'LL CATCH HER ON THE WAY. SHE JUST LEFT.
THANK YOU, HAVE A NICE DAY!
WHAT A CHARMING BOY!
BUT IT'S ODD THAT HE STILL HASN'T MANAGED TO TALK TO...
...IRMA?
SHHH!

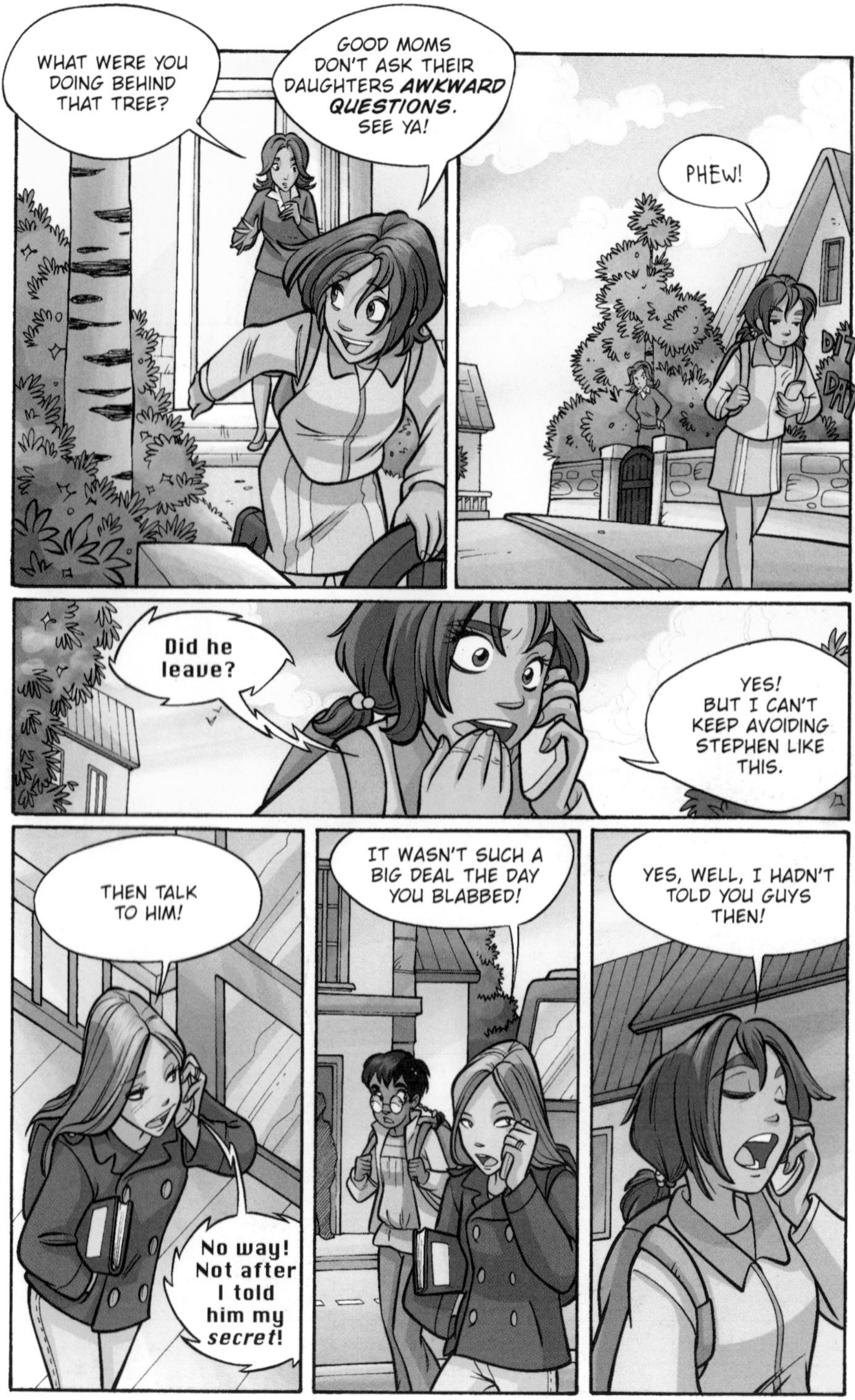
WHAT WERE YOU DOING BEHIND THAT TREE?
GOOD MOMS DON'T ASK THEIR DAUGHTERS **AWKWARD QUESTIONS**. SEE YA!
PHEW!
DIT DAT
Did he leave?
YES! BUT I CAN'T KEEP AVOIDING STEPHEN LIKE THIS.
THEN TALK TO HIM!
No way! Not after I told him my *secret*!
IT WASN'T SUCH A BIG DEAL THE DAY YOU BLABBED!
YES, WELL, I HADN'T TOLD YOU GUYS THEN!

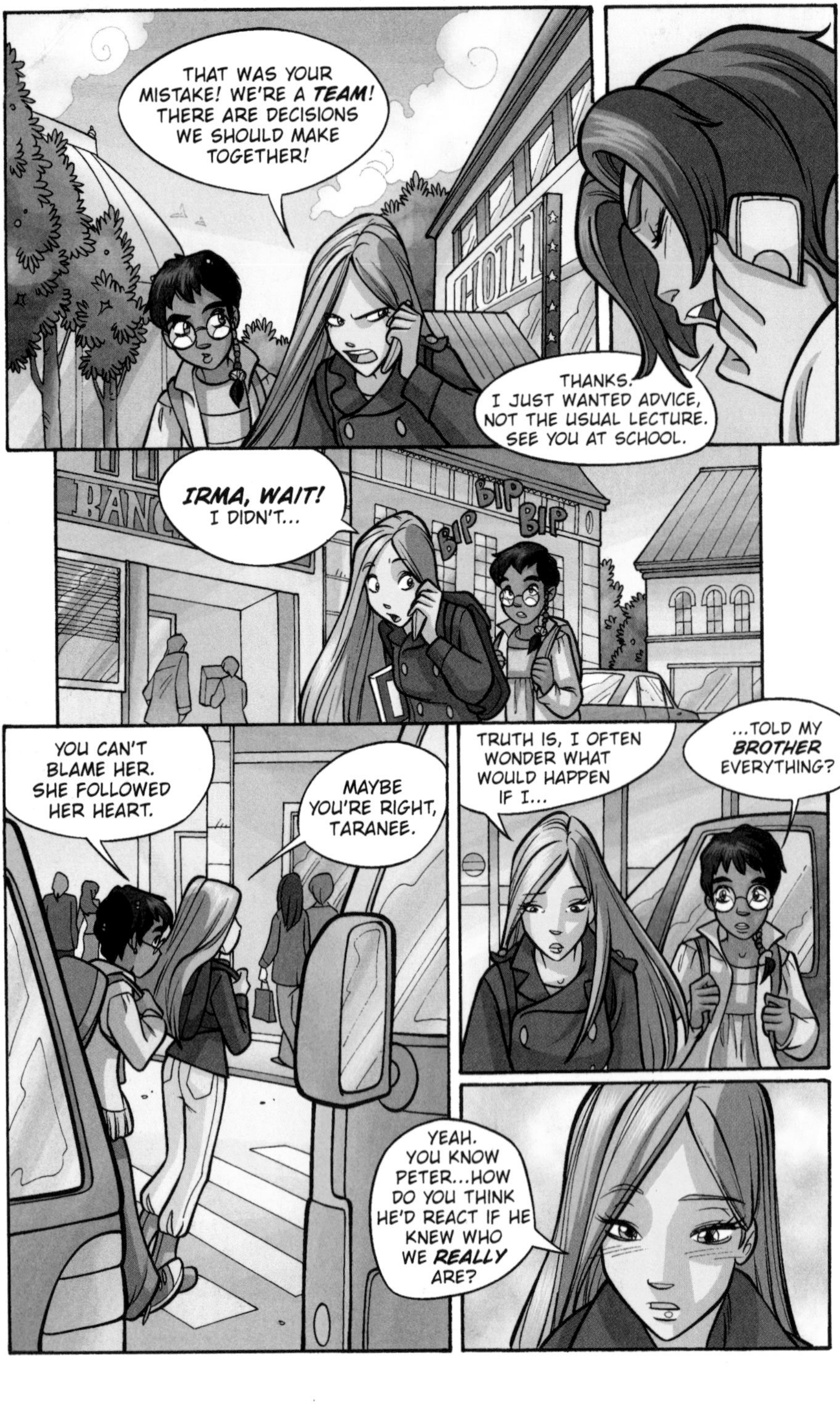
THAT WAS YOUR MISTAKE! WE'RE A **TEAM**! THERE ARE DECISIONS WE SHOULD MAKE TOGETHER!
HOTEL
THANKS. I JUST WANTED ADVICE, NOT THE USUAL LECTURE. SEE YOU AT SCHOOL.
IRMA, WAIT! I DIDN'T...
BIP BIP BIP
YOU CAN'T BLAME HER. SHE FOLLOWED HER HEART.
MAYBE YOU'RE RIGHT, TARANEE.
TRUTH IS, I OFTEN WONDER WHAT WOULD HAPPEN IF I...
...TOLD MY **BROTHER** EVERYTHING?
YEAH. YOU KNOW PETER...HOW DO YOU THINK HE'D REACT IF HE KNEW WHO WE **REALLY** ARE?

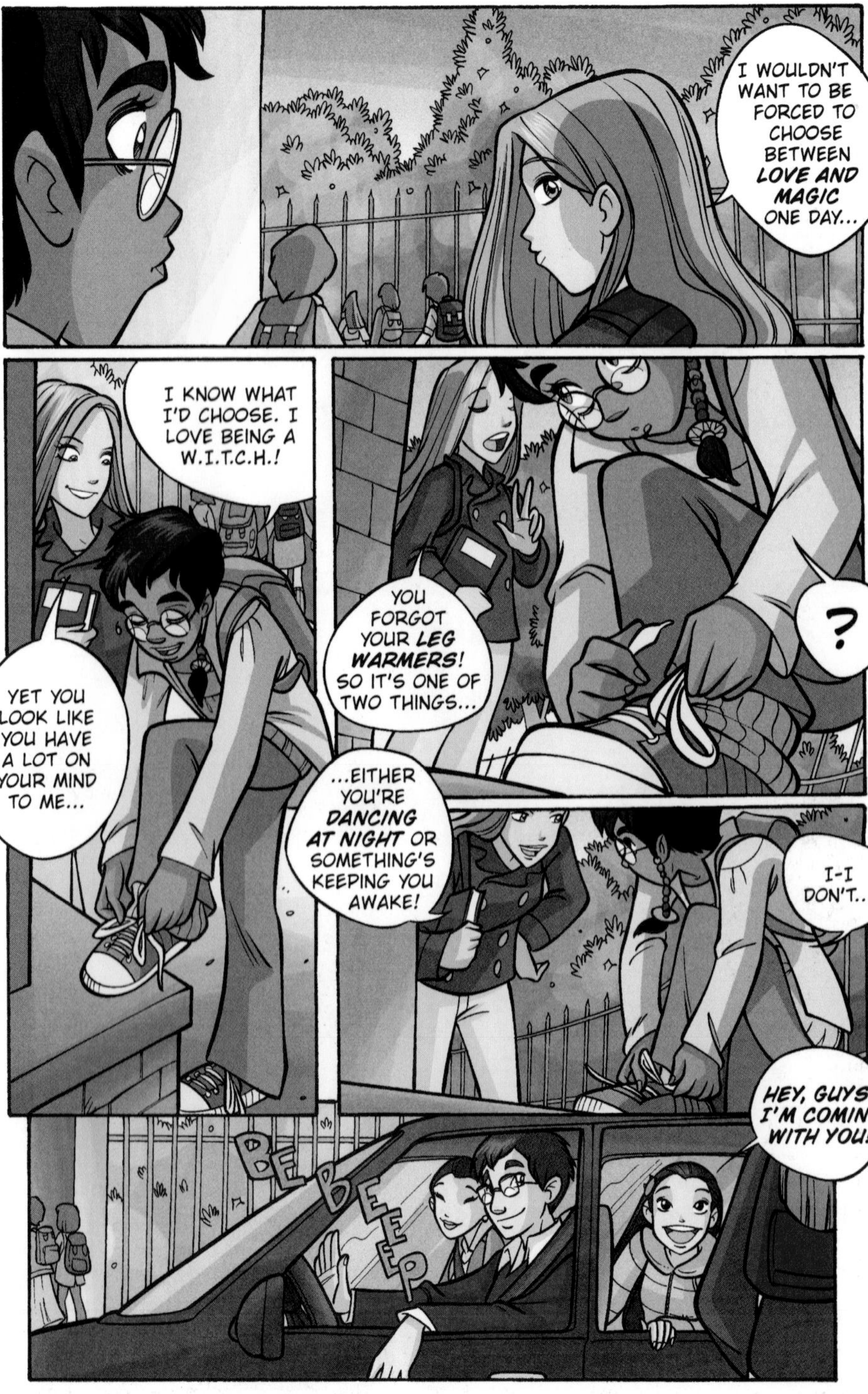

I WOULDN'T WANT TO BE FORCED TO CHOOSE BETWEEN **LOVE AND MAGIC** ONE DAY...
I KNOW WHAT I'D CHOOSE. I LOVE BEING A W.I.T.C.H.!
YET YOU LOOK LIKE YOU HAVE A LOT ON YOUR MIND TO ME...
YOU FORGOT YOUR **LEG WARMERS**! SO IT'S ONE OF TWO THINGS...
?
...EITHER YOU'RE **DANCING AT NIGHT** OR SOMETHING'S KEEPING YOU AWAKE!
I-I DON'T...
HEY, GUYS! I'M COMING WITH YOU!
BEBEEEP

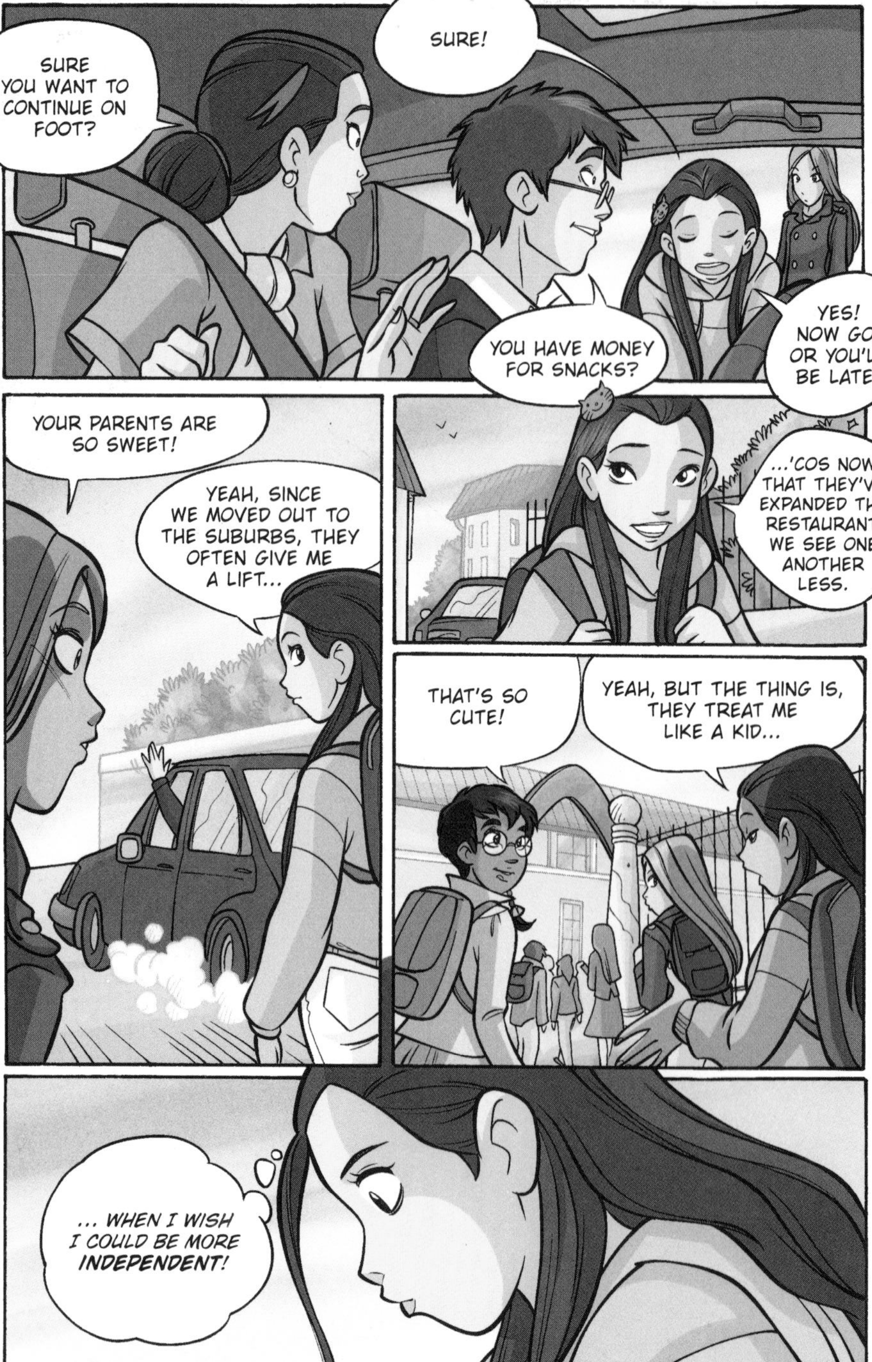
SURE YOU WANT TO CONTINUE ON FOOT?
SURE!
YOU HAVE MONEY FOR SNACKS?
YES! NOW GO, OR YOU'LL BE LATE!
YOUR PARENTS ARE SO SWEET!
YEAH, SINCE WE MOVED OUT TO THE SUBURBS, THEY OFTEN GIVE ME A LIFT...
...'COS NOW THAT THEY'VE EXPANDED THE RESTAURANT, WE SEE ONE ANOTHER LESS.
THAT'S SO CUTE!
YEAH, BUT THE THING IS, THEY TREAT ME LIKE A KID...
... WHEN I WISH I COULD BE MORE INDEPENDENT!

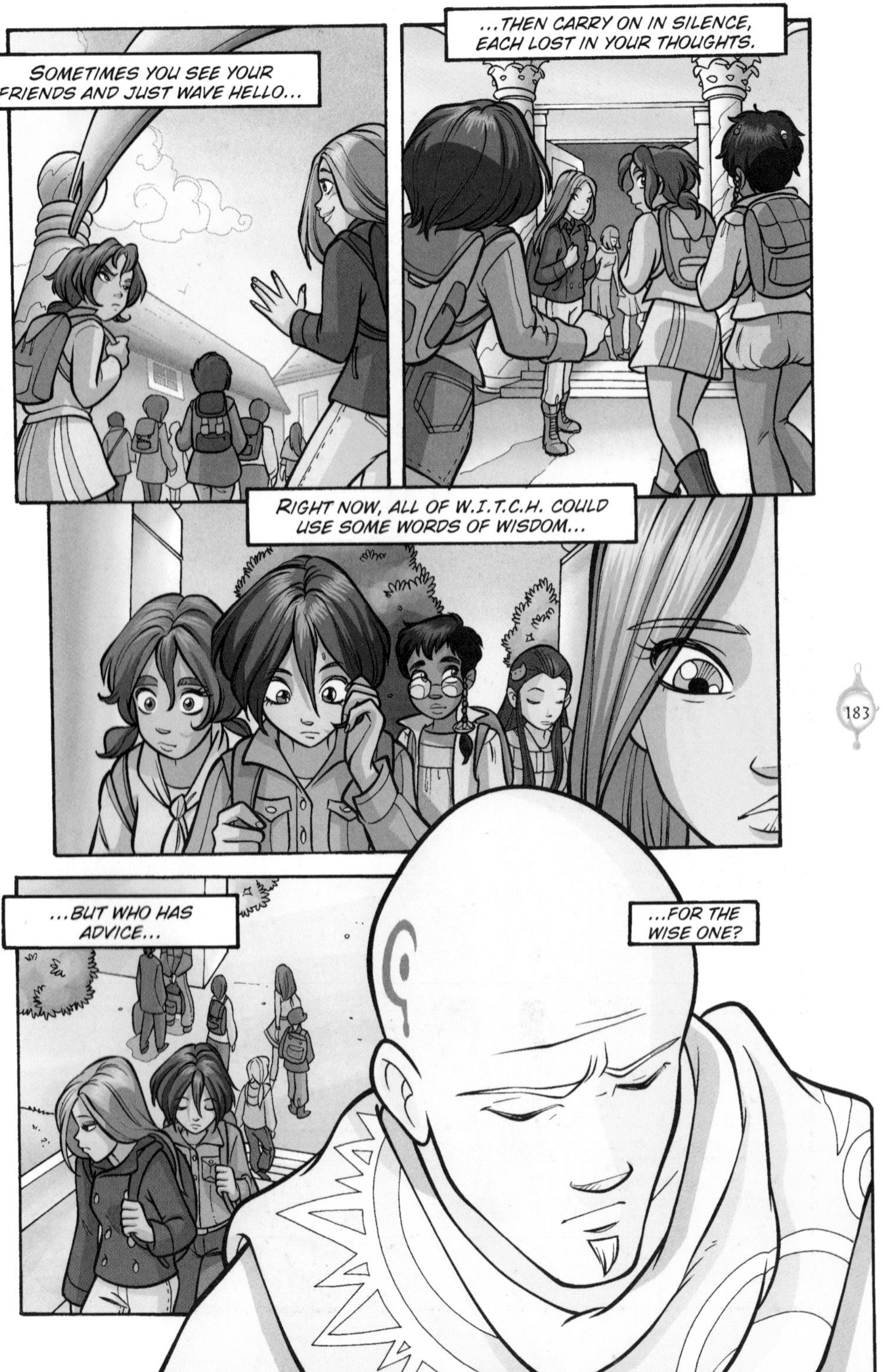
SOMETIMES YOU SEE YOUR FRIENDS AND JUST WAVE HELLO...
...THEN CARRY ON IN SILENCE, EACH LOST IN YOUR THOUGHTS.
RIGHT NOW, ALL OF W.I.T.C.H. COULD USE SOME WORDS OF WISDOM...
...BUT WHO HAS ADVICE...
...FOR THE WISE ONE?

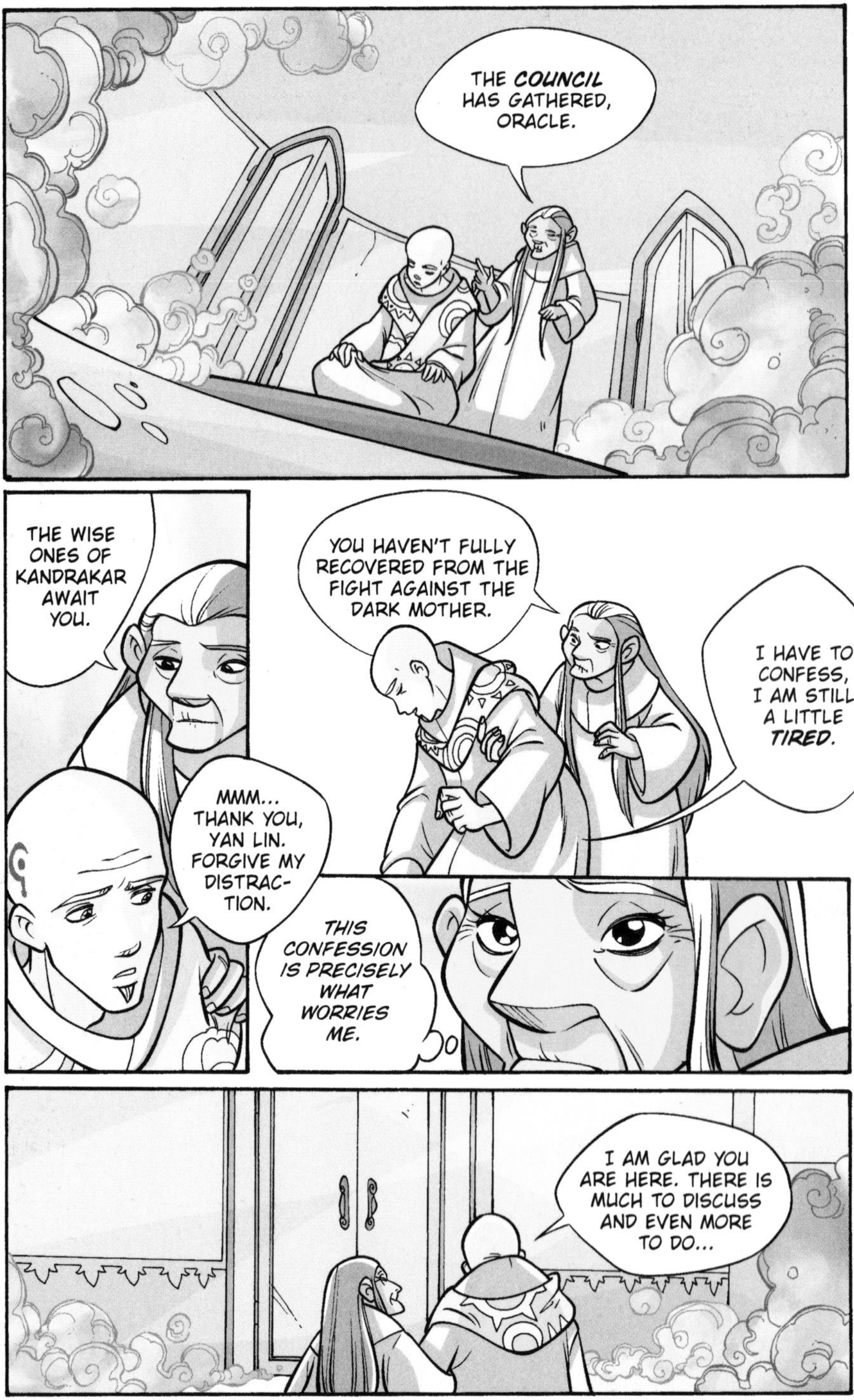
THE COUNCIL HAS GATHERED, ORACLE.
THE WISE ONES OF KANDRAKAR AWAIT YOU.
YOU HAVEN'T FULLY RECOVERED FROM THE FIGHT AGAINST THE DARK MOTHER.
I HAVE TO CONFESS, I AM STILL A LITTLE TIRED.
MMM... THANK YOU, YAN LIN. FORGIVE MY DISTRACTION.
THIS CONFESSION IS PRECISELY WHAT WORRIES ME.
I AM GLAD YOU ARE HERE. THERE IS MUCH TO DISCUSS AND EVEN MORE TO DO...

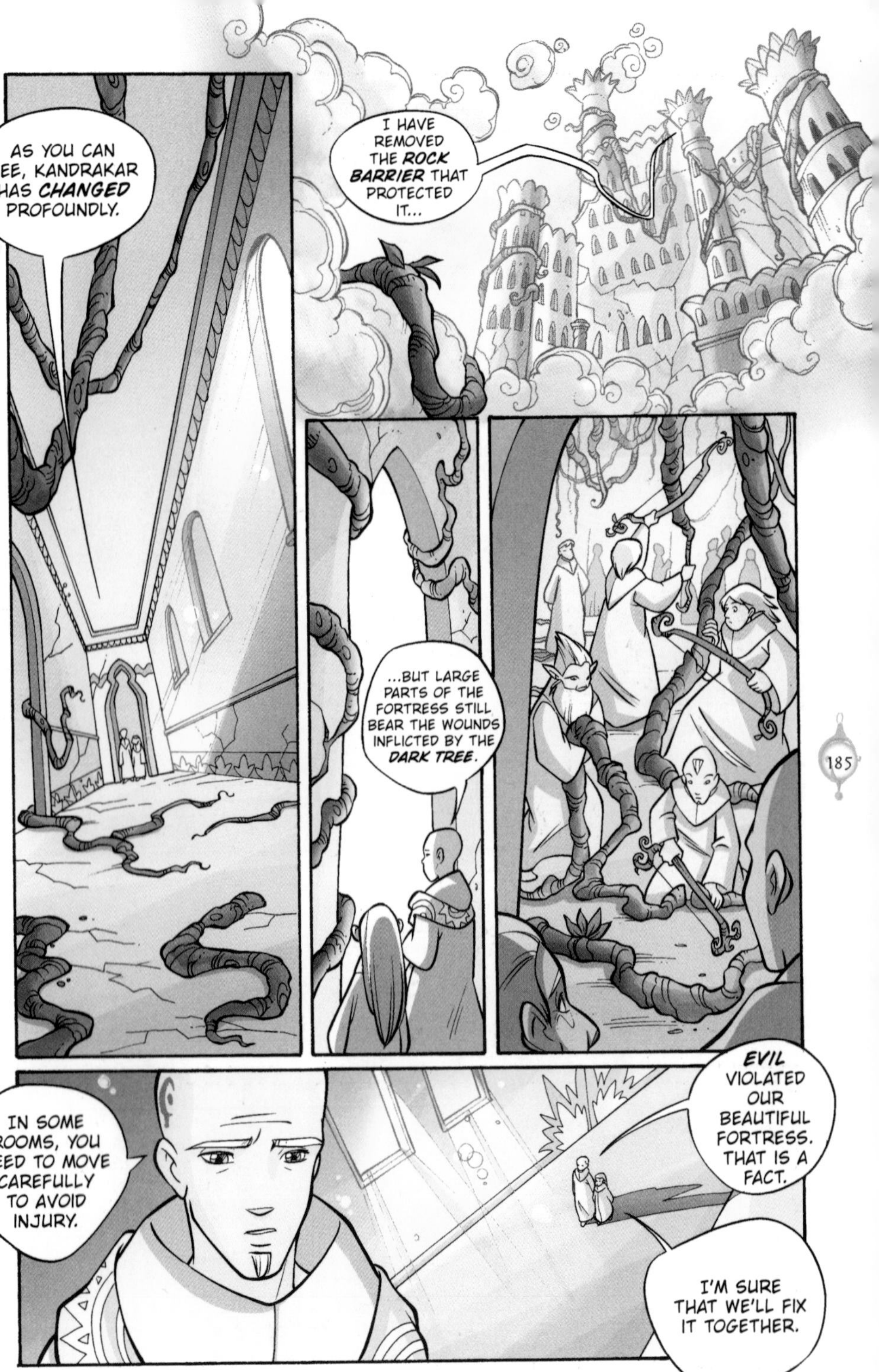
AS YOU CAN SEE, KANDRAKAR HAS CHANGED PROFOUNDLY.
I HAVE REMOVED THE ROCK BARRIER THAT PROTECTED IT...
...BUT LARGE PARTS OF THE FORTRESS STILL BEAR THE WOUNDS INFLICTED BY THE DARK TREE.
IN SOME ROOMS, YOU NEED TO MOVE CAREFULLY TO AVOID INJURY.
EVIL VIOLATED OUR BEAUTIFUL FORTRESS. THAT IS A FACT.
I'M SURE THAT WE'LL FIX IT TOGETHER.

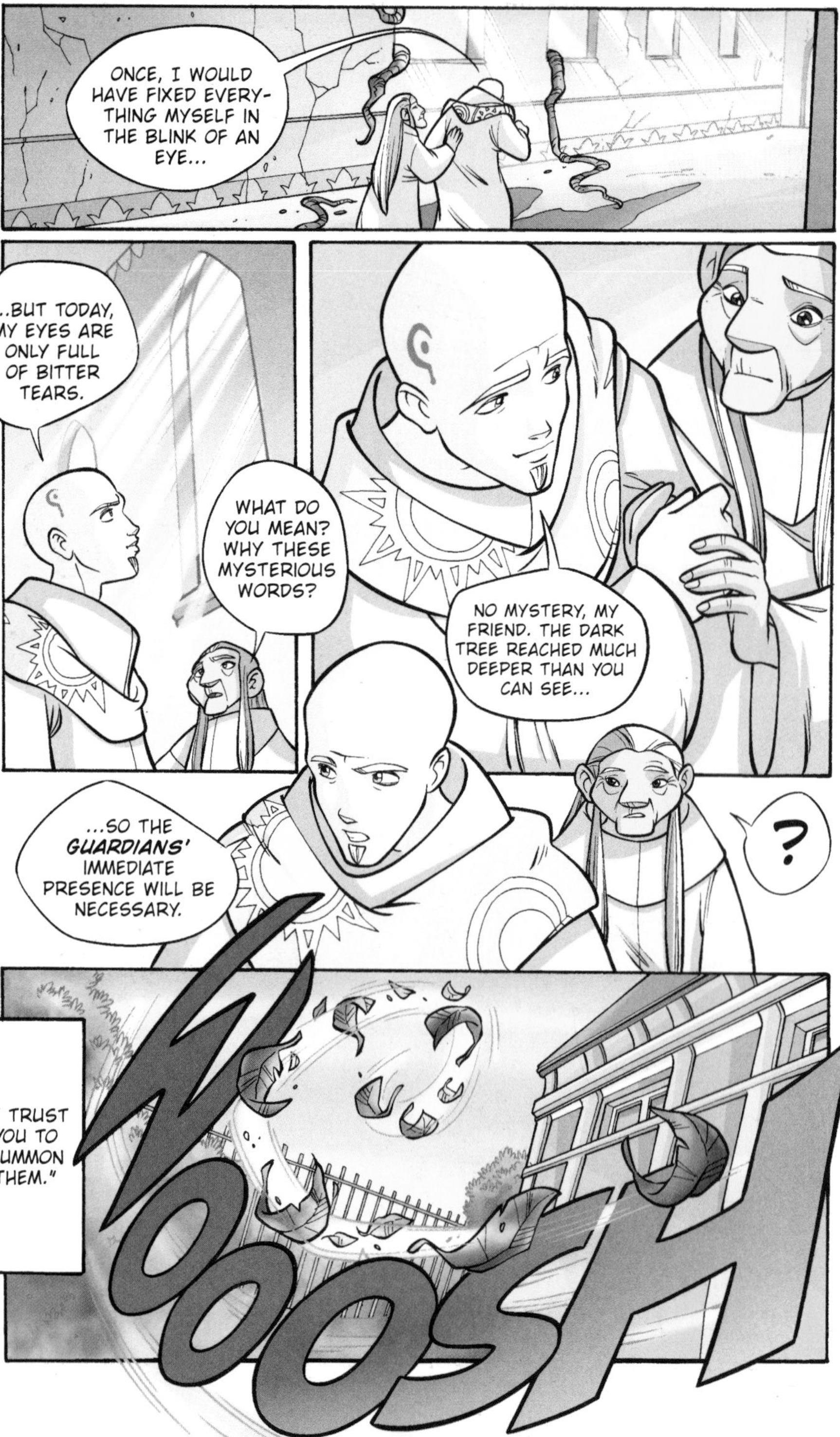
ONCE, I WOULD HAVE FIXED EVERY-THING MYSELF IN THE BLINK OF AN EYE...
...BUT TODAY, MY EYES ARE ONLY FULL OF BITTER TEARS.
WHAT DO YOU MEAN? WHY THESE MYSTERIOUS WORDS?
NO MYSTERY, MY FRIEND. THE DARK TREE REACHED MUCH DEEPER THAN YOU CAN SEE...
...SO THE *GUARDIANS'* IMMEDIATE PRESENCE WILL BE NECESSARY.
?
"I TRUST YOU TO SUMMON THEM."
WHOOSH

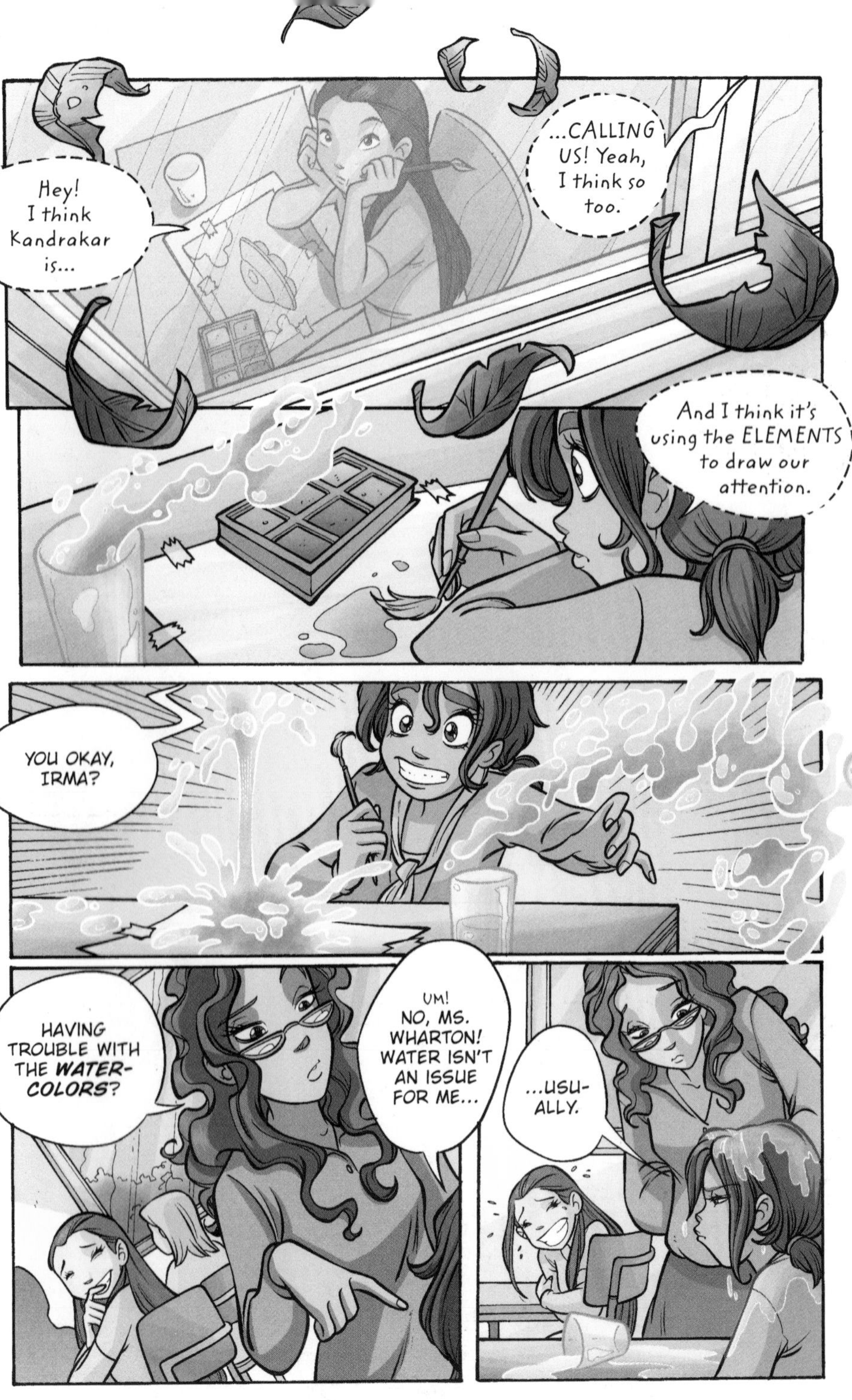
Hey! I think Kandrakar is...
...CALLING US! Yeah, I think so too.
And I think it's using the ELEMENTS to draw our attention.
YOU OKAY, IRMA?
HAVING TROUBLE WITH THE ***WATER-COLORS***?
UM! NO, MS. WHARTON! WATER ISN'T AN ISSUE FOR ME...
...USU-ALLY.

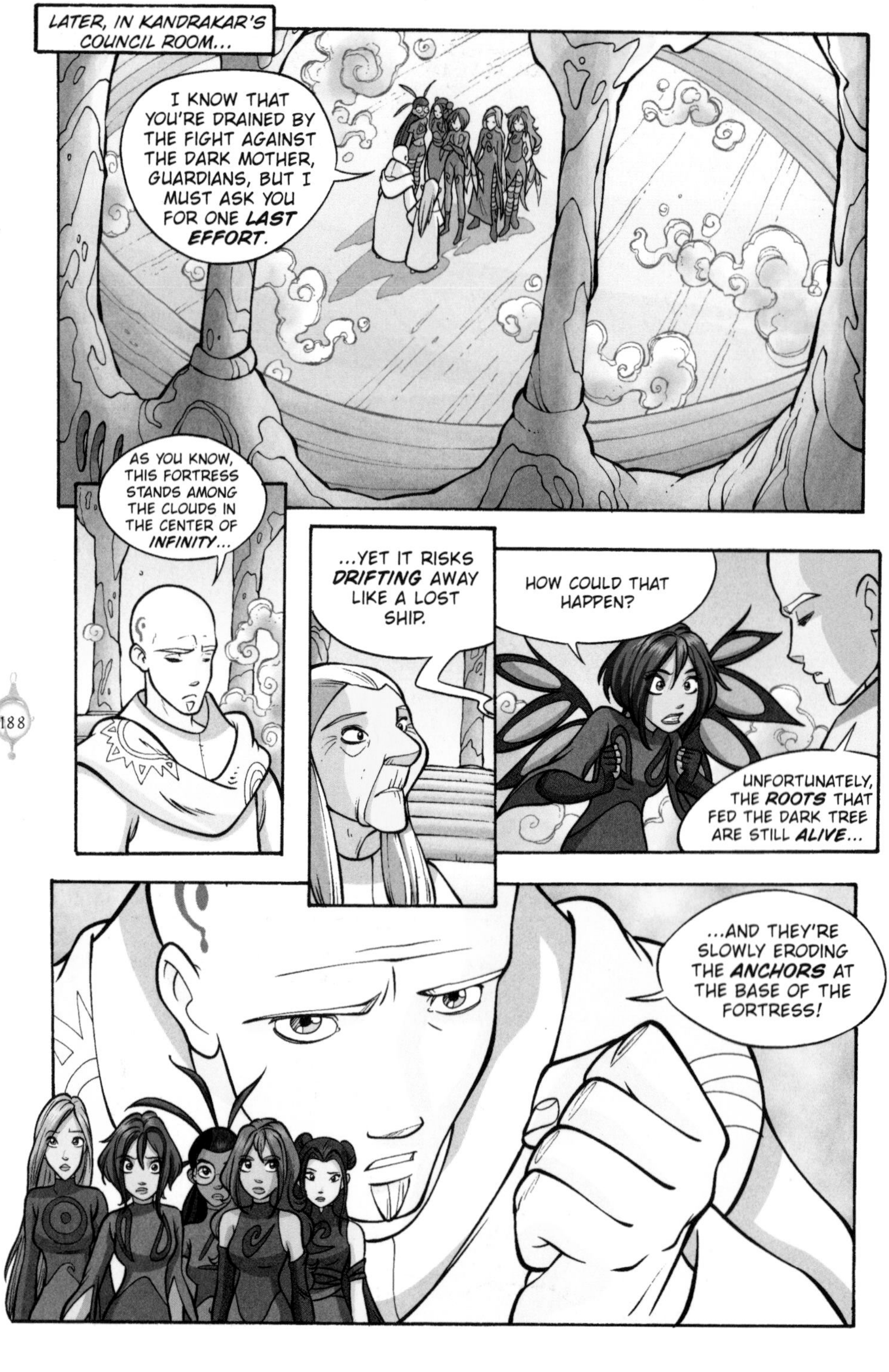
LATER, IN KANDRAKAR'S COUNCIL ROOM...
I KNOW THAT YOU'RE DRAINED BY THE FIGHT AGAINST THE DARK MOTHER, GUARDIANS, BUT I MUST ASK YOU FOR ONE LAST EFFORT.
AS YOU KNOW, THIS FORTRESS STANDS AMONG THE CLOUDS IN THE CENTER OF INFINITY...
...YET IT RISKS DRIFTING AWAY LIKE A LOST SHIP.
HOW COULD THAT HAPPEN?
UNFORTUNATELY, THE ROOTS THAT FED THE DARK TREE ARE STILL ALIVE...
...AND THEY'RE SLOWLY ERODING THE ANCHORS AT THE BASE OF THE FORTRESS!

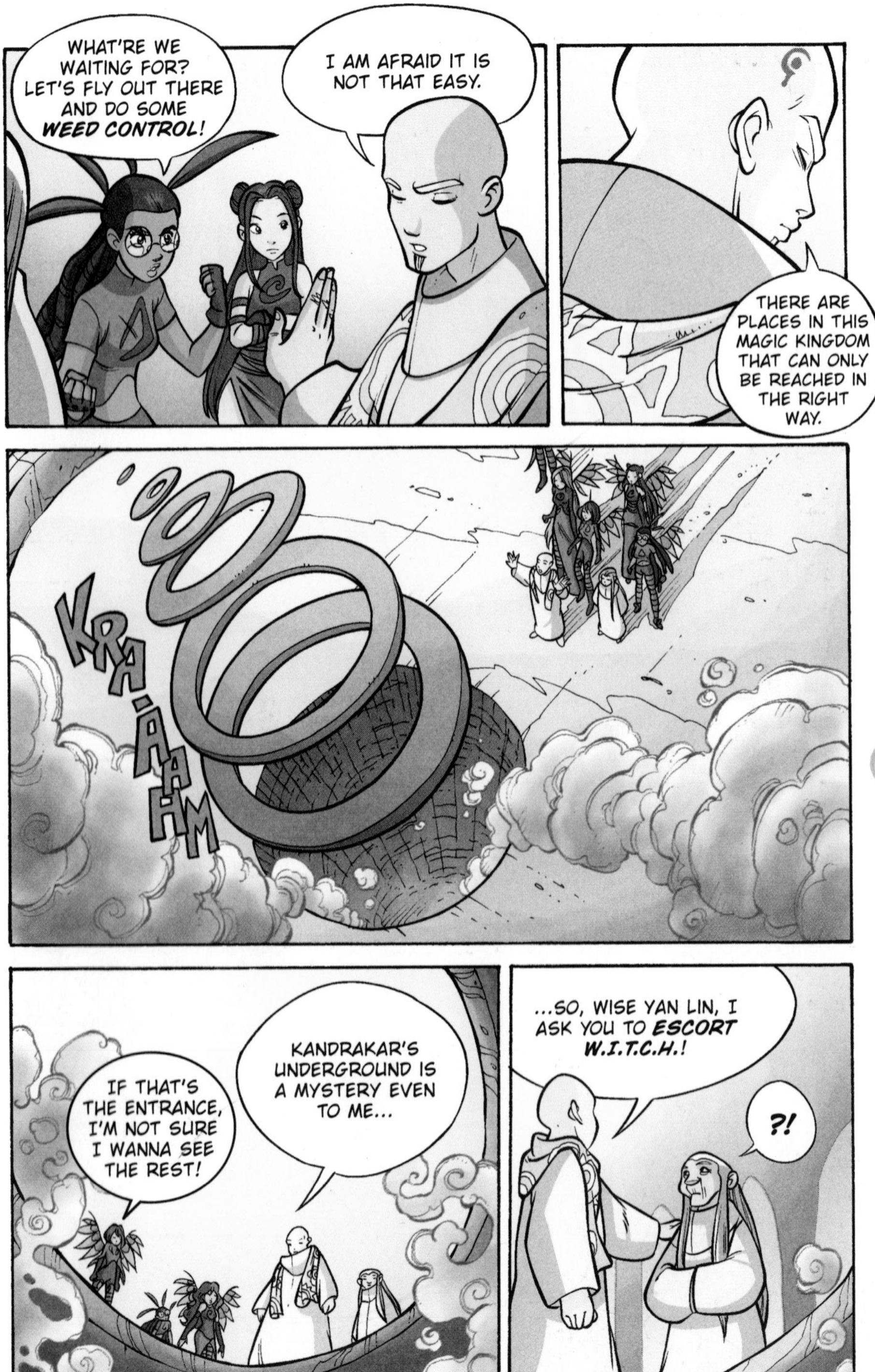
WHAT'RE WE WAITING FOR? LET'S FLY OUT THERE AND DO SOME **WEED CONTROL**!
I AM AFRAID IT IS NOT THAT EASY.
THERE ARE PLACES IN THIS MAGIC KINGDOM THAT CAN ONLY BE REACHED IN THE RIGHT WAY.
KRA-AAAHM
IF THAT'S THE ENTRANCE, I'M NOT SURE I WANNA SEE THE REST!
KANDRAKAR'S UNDERGROUND IS A MYSTERY EVEN TO ME...
...SO, WISE YAN LIN, I ASK YOU TO **ESCORT W.I.T.C.H.**!
?!

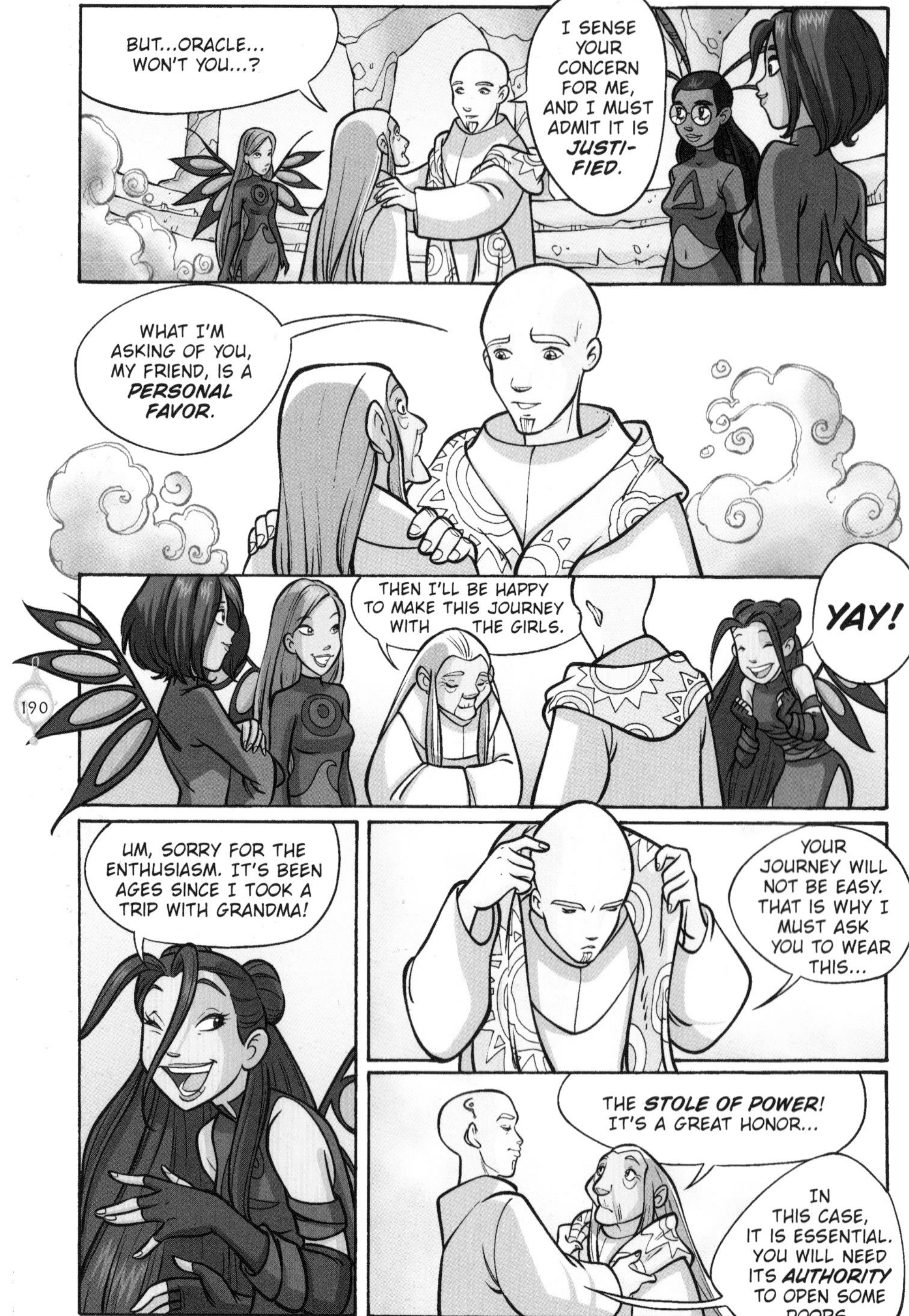
BUT...ORACLE... WON'T YOU...?
I SENSE YOUR CONCERN FOR ME, AND I MUST ADMIT IT IS JUSTIFIED.
WHAT I'M ASKING OF YOU, MY FRIEND, IS A PERSONAL FAVOR.
THEN I'LL BE HAPPY TO MAKE THIS JOURNEY WITH THE GIRLS.
YAY!
UM, SORRY FOR THE ENTHUSIASM. IT'S BEEN AGES SINCE I TOOK A TRIP WITH GRANDMA!
YOUR JOURNEY WILL NOT BE EASY. THAT IS WHY I MUST ASK YOU TO WEAR THIS...
THE STOLE OF POWER! IT'S A GREAT HONOR...
IN THIS CASE, IT IS ESSENTIAL. YOU WILL NEED ITS AUTHORITY TO OPEN SOME DOORS.

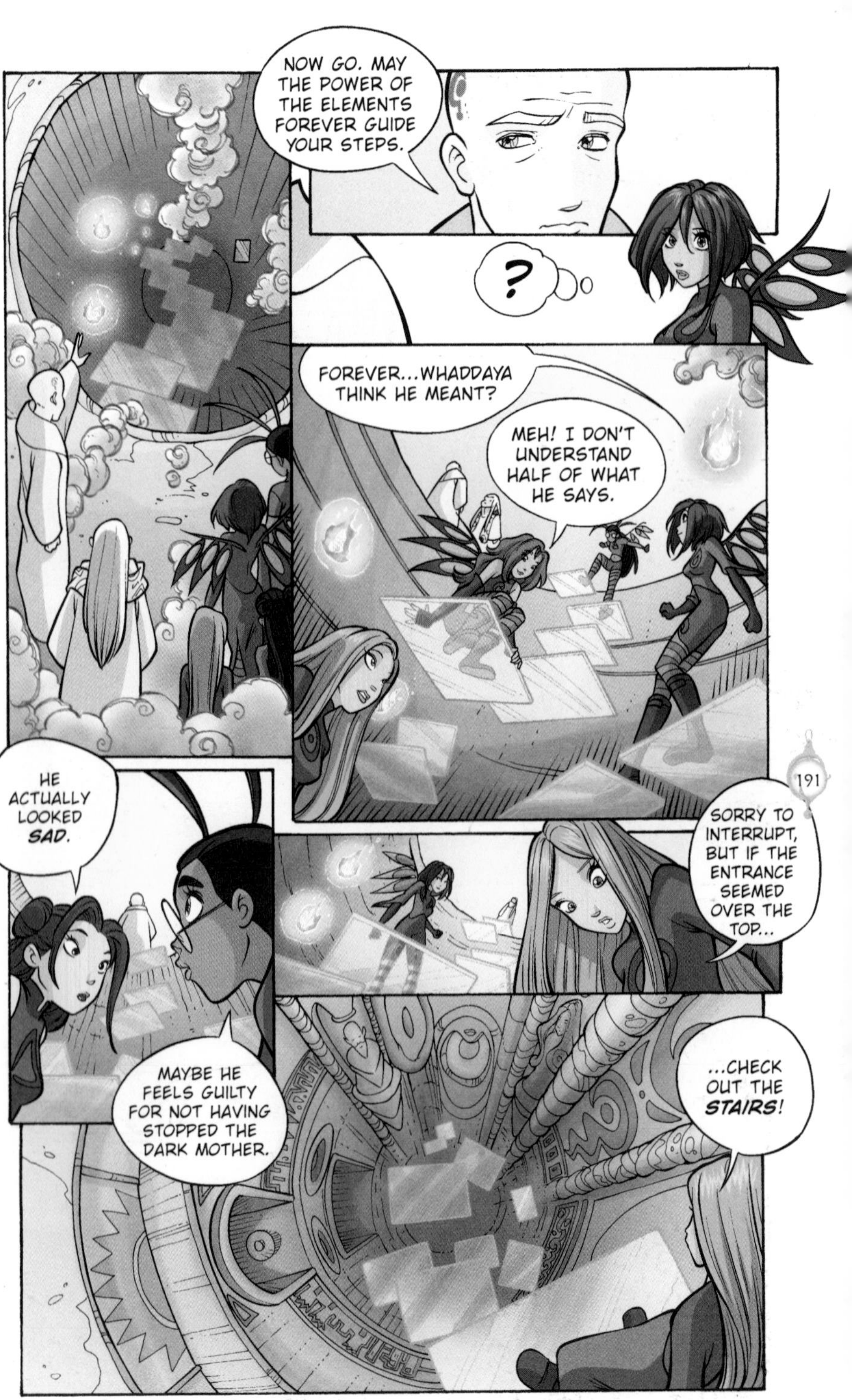
NOW GO. MAY THE POWER OF THE ELEMENTS FOREVER GUIDE YOUR STEPS.
?
FOREVER...WHADDAYA THINK HE MEANT?
MEH! I DON'T UNDERSTAND HALF OF WHAT HE SAYS.
HE ACTUALLY LOOKED **SAD**.
SORRY TO INTERRUPT, BUT IF THE ENTRANCE SEEMED OVER THE TOP...
MAYBE HE FEELS GUILTY FOR NOT HAVING STOPPED THE DARK MOTHER.
...CHECK OUT THE **STAIRS**!

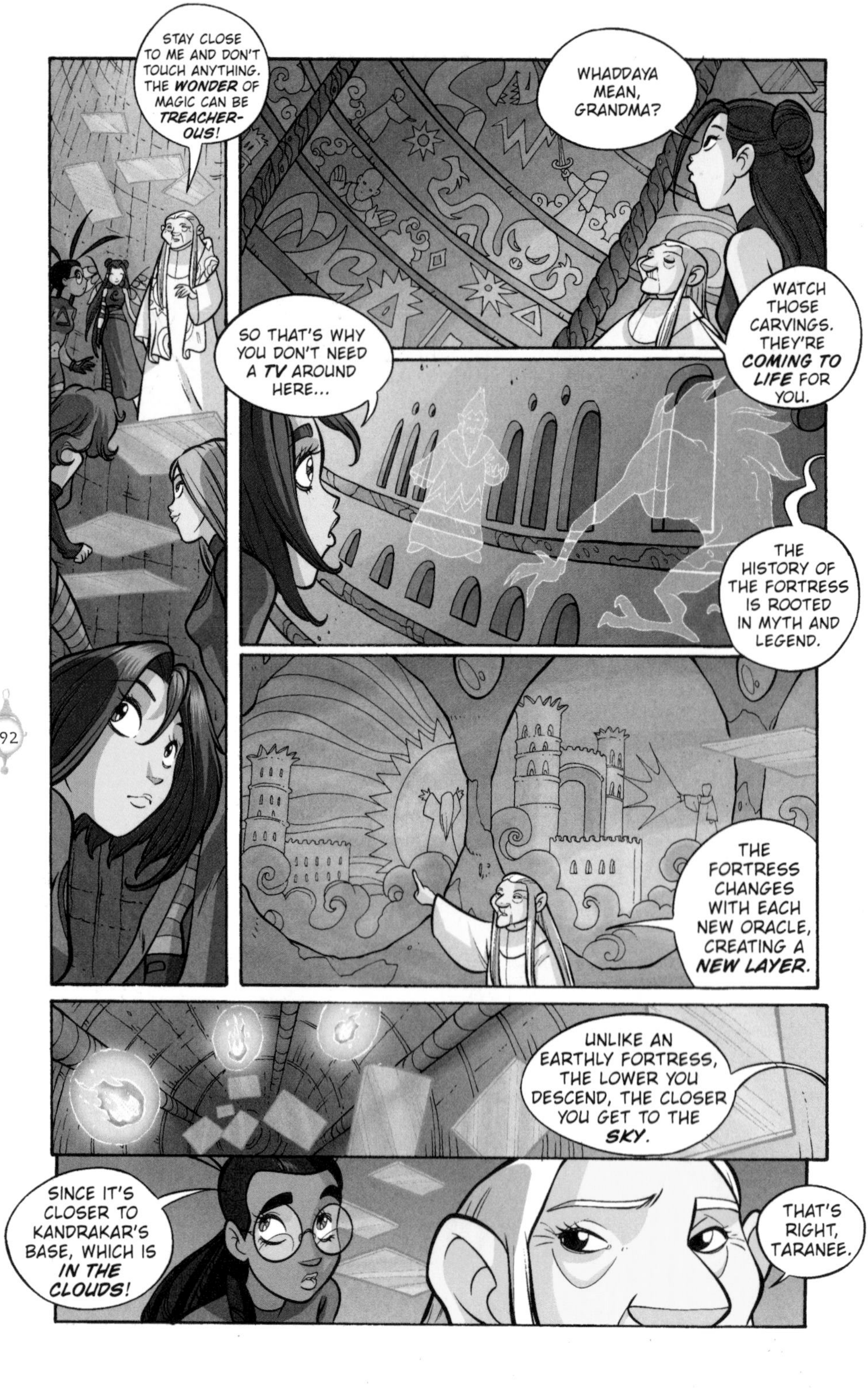

STAY CLOSE TO ME AND DON'T TOUCH ANYTHING. THE WONDER OF MAGIC CAN BE TREACHEROUS!
WHADDAYA MEAN, GRANDMA?
WATCH THOSE CARVINGS. THEY'RE COMING TO LIFE FOR YOU.
SO THAT'S WHY YOU DON'T NEED A TV AROUND HERE...
THE HISTORY OF THE FORTRESS IS ROOTED IN MYTH AND LEGEND.
THE FORTRESS CHANGES WITH EACH NEW ORACLE, CREATING A NEW LAYER.
UNLIKE AN EARTHLY FORTRESS, THE LOWER YOU DESCEND, THE CLOSER YOU GET TO THE SKY.
SINCE IT'S CLOSER TO KANDRAKAR'S BASE, WHICH IS IN THE CLOUDS!
THAT'S RIGHT, TARANEE.

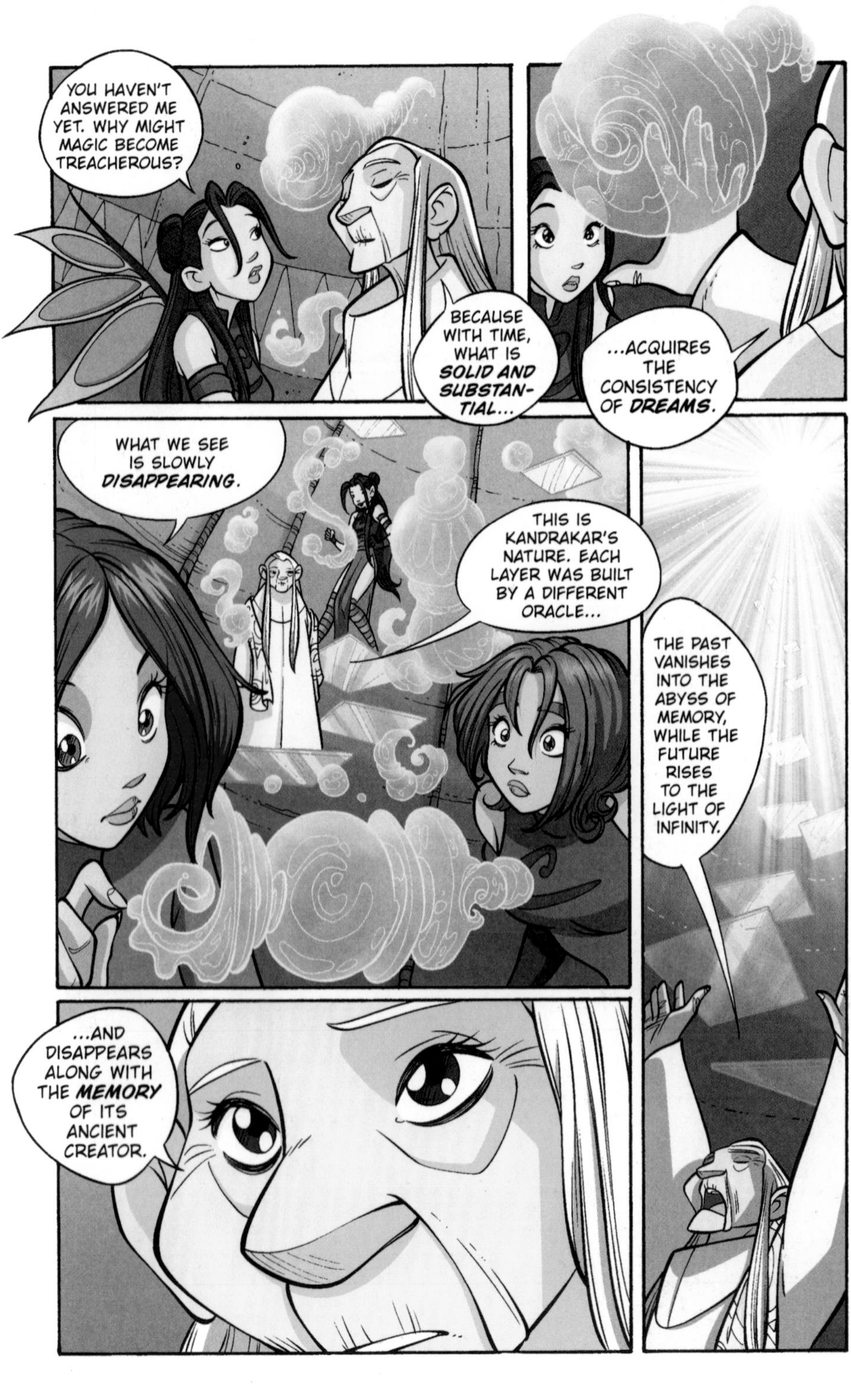
YOU HAVEN'T ANSWERED ME YET. WHY MIGHT MAGIC BECOME TREACHEROUS?
BECAUSE WITH TIME, WHAT IS ***SOLID AND SUBSTAN-TIAL***...
...ACQUIRES THE CONSISTENCY OF ***DREAMS***.
WHAT WE SEE IS SLOWLY ***DISAPPEARING***.
THIS IS KANDRAKAR'S NATURE. EACH LAYER WAS BUILT BY A DIFFERENT ORACLE...
THE PAST VANISHES INTO THE ABYSS OF MEMORY, WHILE THE FUTURE RISES TO THE LIGHT OF INFINITY.
...AND DISAPPEARS ALONG WITH THE ***MEMORY*** OF ITS ANCIENT CREATOR.

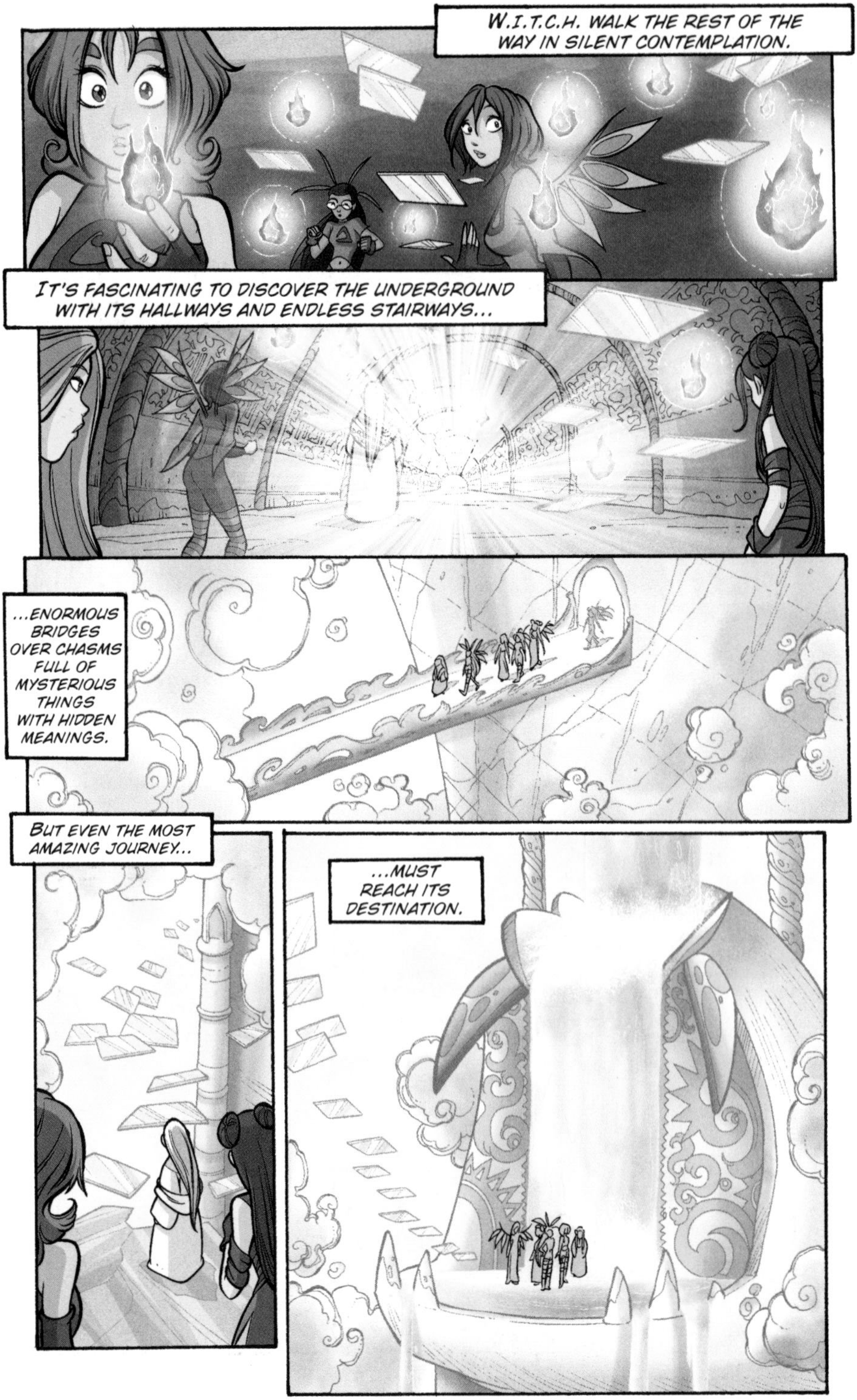
W.I.T.C.H. WALK THE REST OF THE WAY IN SILENT CONTEMPLATION.
IT'S FASCINATING TO DISCOVER THE UNDERGROUND WITH ITS HALLWAYS AND ENDLESS STAIRWAYS...
...ENORMOUS BRIDGES OVER CHASMS FULL OF MYSTERIOUS THINGS WITH HIDDEN MEANINGS.
BUT EVEN THE MOST AMAZING JOURNEY...
...MUST REACH ITS DESTINATION.

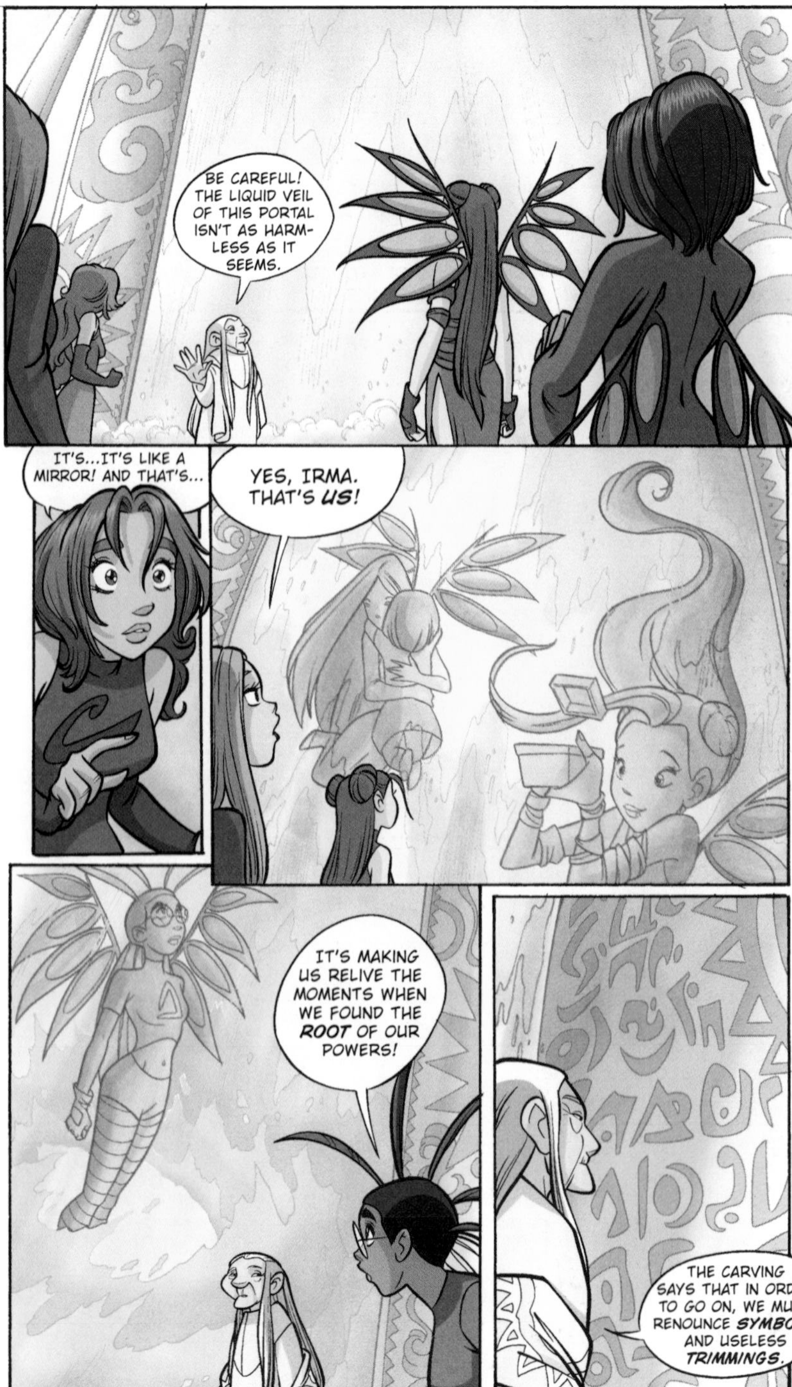
BE CAREFUL! THE LIQUID VEIL OF THIS PORTAL ISN'T AS HARM-LESS AS IT SEEMS.
IT'S...IT'S LIKE A MIRROR! AND THAT'S...
YES, IRMA. THAT'S *US*!
IT'S MAKING US RELIVE THE MOMENTS WHEN WE FOUND THE *ROOT* OF OUR POWERS!
THE CARVING SAYS THAT IN ORDER TO GO ON, WE MUST RENOUNCE *SYMBOLS* AND USELESS *TRIMMINGS*.

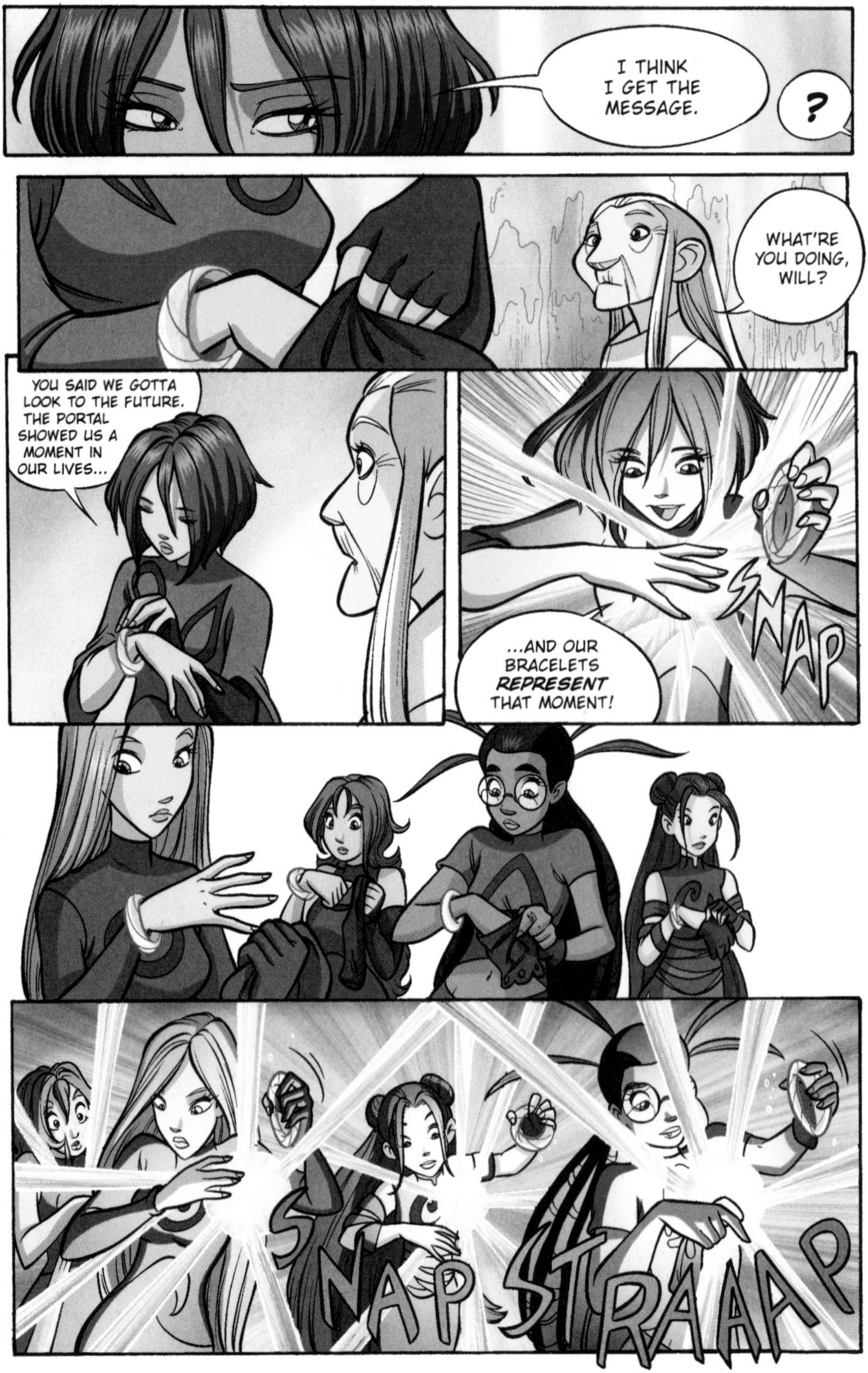
I THINK I GET THE MESSAGE.
?
WHAT'RE YOU DOING, WILL?
YOU SAID WE GOTTA LOOK TO THE FUTURE. THE PORTAL SHOWED US A MOMENT IN OUR LIVES...
...AND OUR BRACELETS **REPRESENT** THAT MOMENT!
SNAP
SNAP
STRAAAP

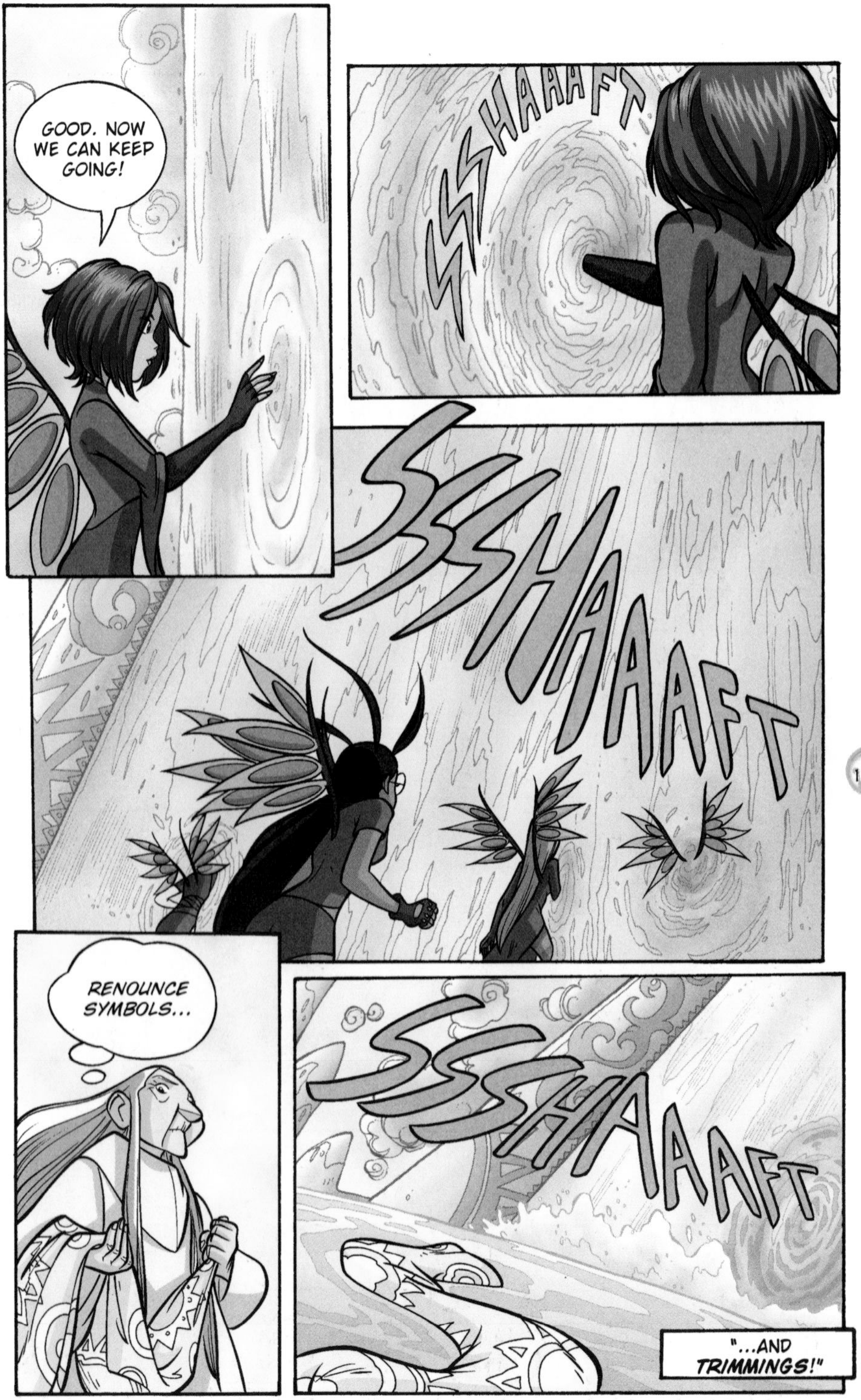
GOOD. NOW WE CAN KEEP GOING!
SSSHAAAFT
SSSHAAAFT
RENOUNCE SYMBOLS...
SSSHAAAFT
"...AND TRIMMINGS!"

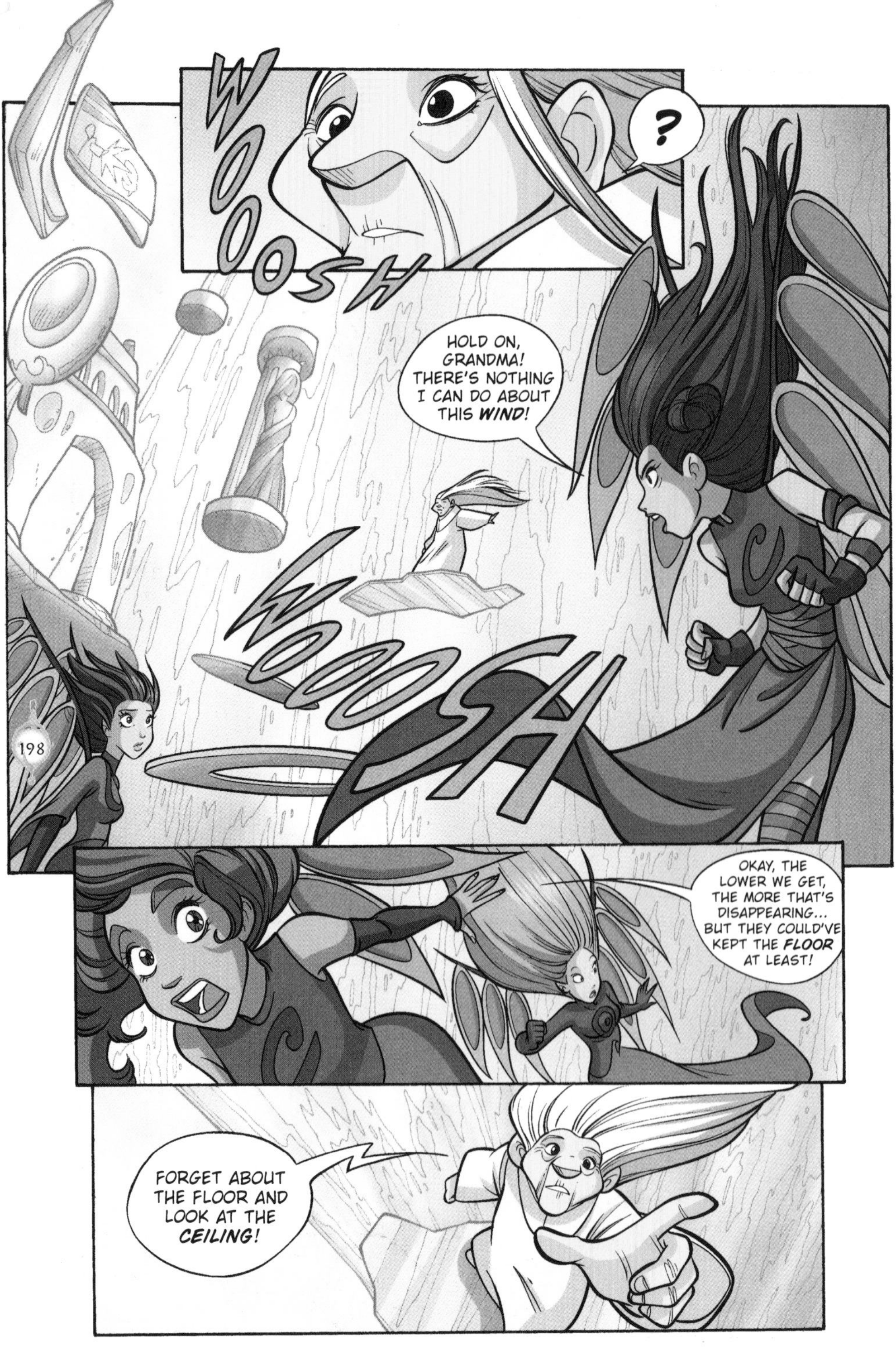
WOOOSH
?
HOLD ON, GRANDMA! THERE'S NOTHING I CAN DO ABOUT THIS *WIND*!
WOOOSH
OKAY, THE LOWER WE GET, THE MORE THAT'S DISAPPEARING... BUT THEY COULD'VE KEPT THE *FLOOR* AT LEAST!
FORGET ABOUT THE FLOOR AND LOOK AT THE *CEILING*!

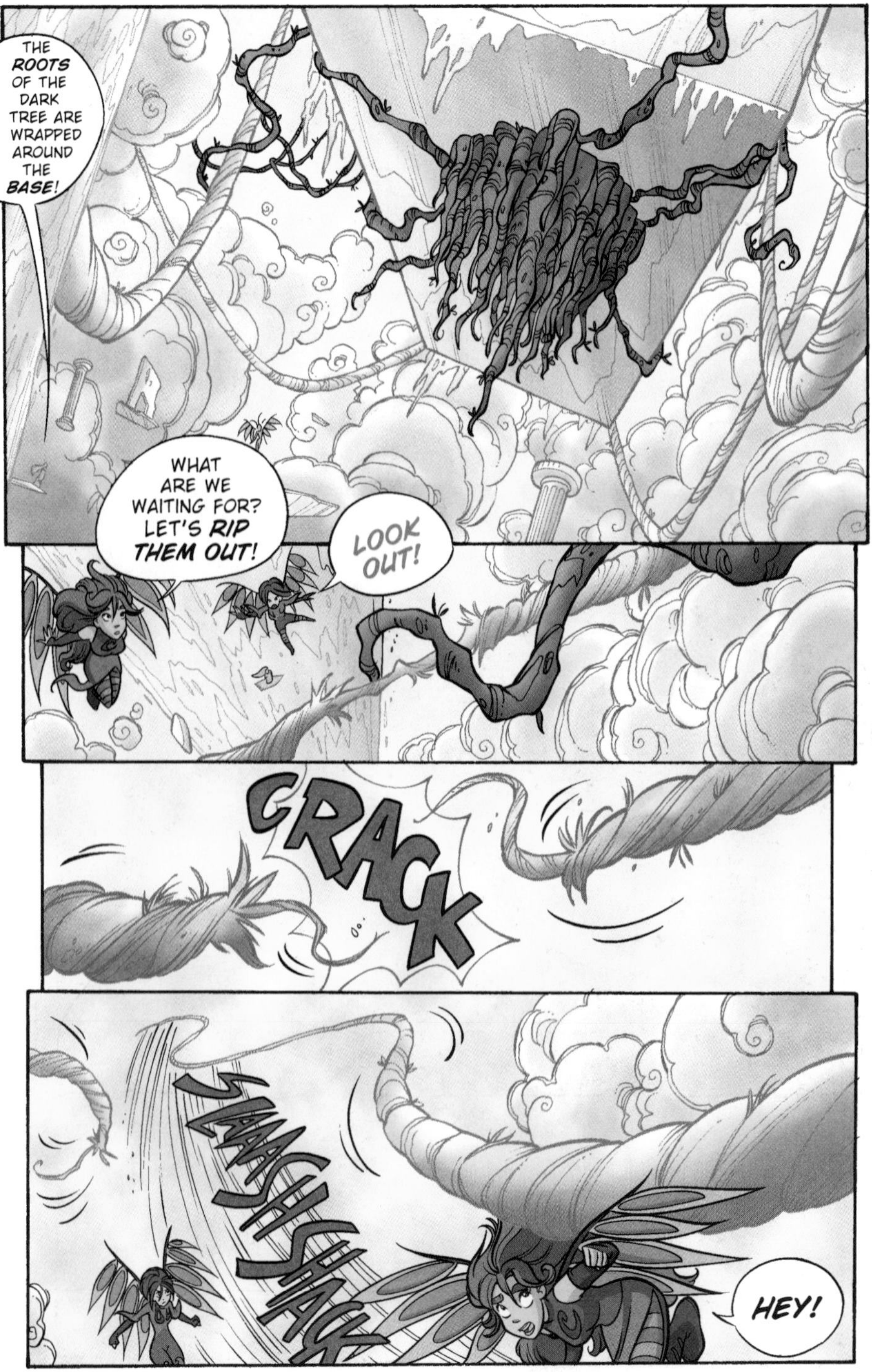
THE ROOTS OF THE DARK TREE ARE WRAPPED AROUND THE BASE!
WHAT ARE WE WAITING FOR? LET'S RIP THEM OUT!
LOOK OUT!
CRACK
SHAASH SHACK
HEY!

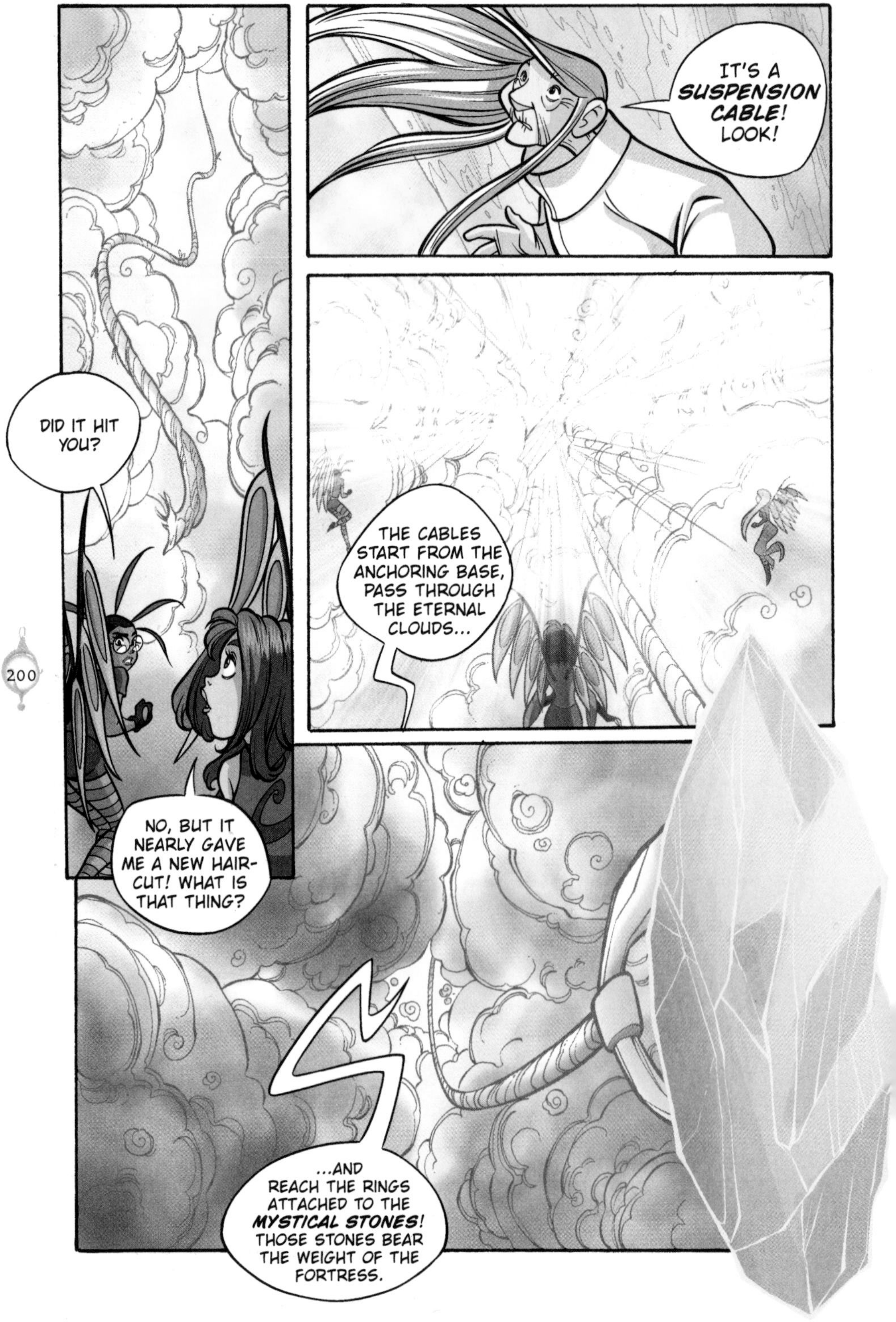

DID IT HIT YOU?
NO, BUT IT NEARLY GAVE ME A NEW HAIR-CUT! WHAT IS THAT THING?
IT'S A SUSPENSION CABLE! LOOK!
THE CABLES START FROM THE ANCHORING BASE, PASS THROUGH THE ETERNAL CLOUDS...
...AND REACH THE RINGS ATTACHED TO THE MYSTICAL STONES! THOSE STONES BEAR THE WEIGHT OF THE FORTRESS.

200

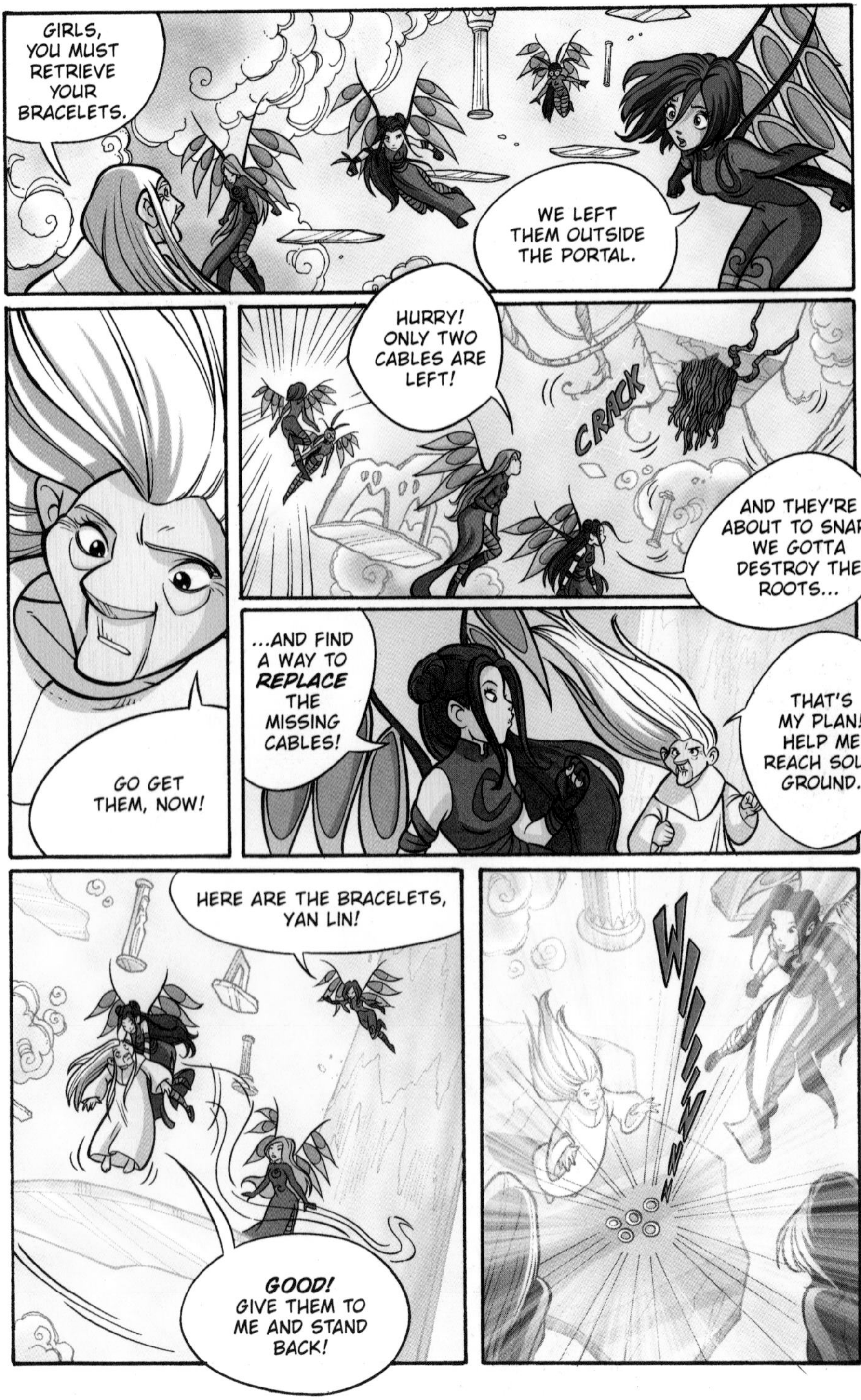
GIRLS, YOU MUST RETRIEVE YOUR BRACELETS.
WE LEFT THEM OUTSIDE THE PORTAL.
GO GET THEM, NOW!
HURRY! ONLY TWO CABLES ARE LEFT!
CRACK
AND THEY'RE ABOUT TO SNAP! WE GOTTA DESTROY THE ROOTS...
...AND FIND A WAY TO REPLACE THE MISSING CABLES!
THAT'S MY PLAN! HELP ME REACH SOLID GROUND.
HERE ARE THE BRACELETS, YAN LIN!
GOOD! GIVE THEM TO ME AND STAND BACK!

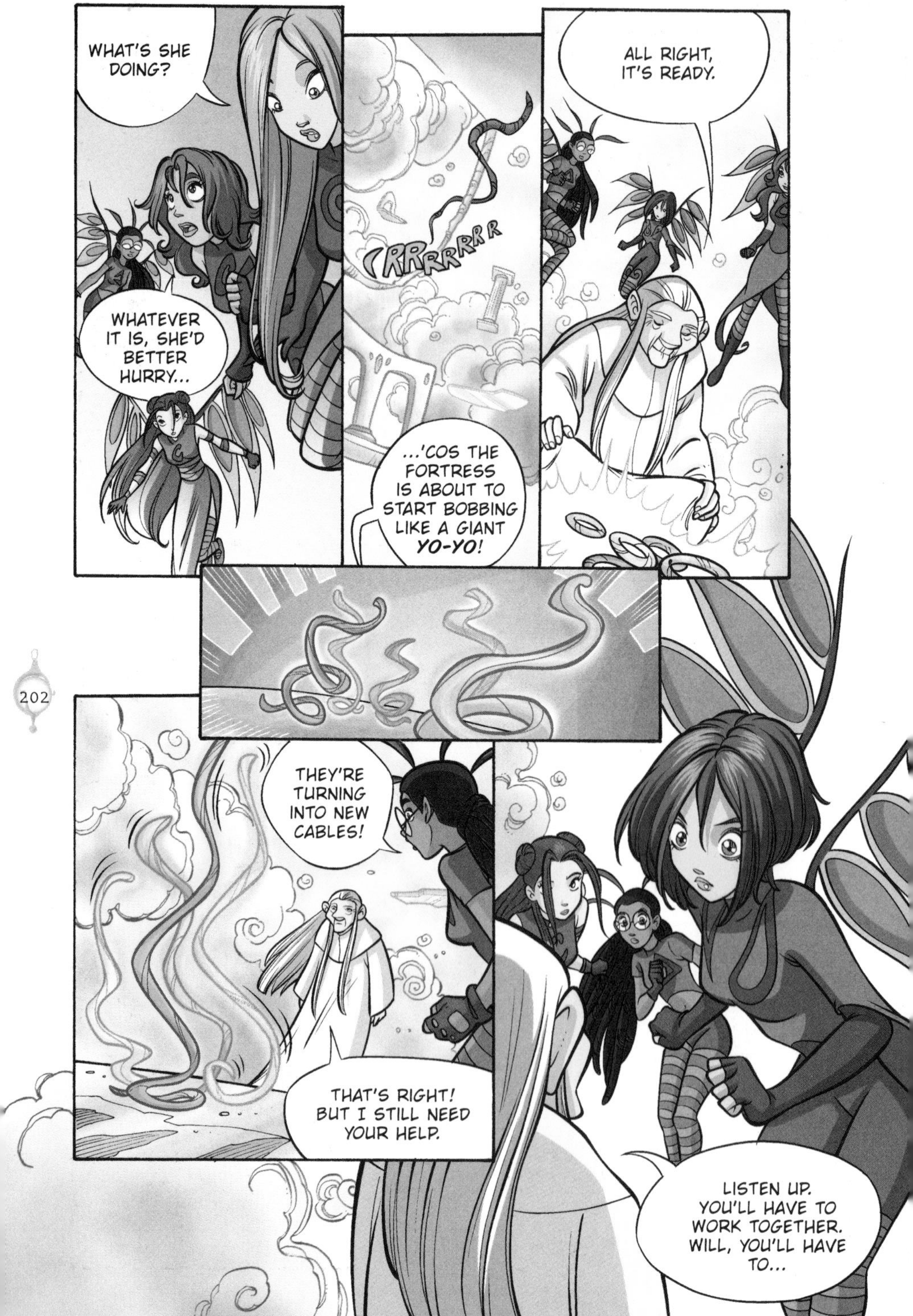
WHAT'S SHE DOING?
WHATEVER IT IS, SHE'D BETTER HURRY...
CRRRRRRRR
...'COS THE FORTRESS IS ABOUT TO START BOBBING LIKE A GIANT YO-YO!
ALL RIGHT, IT'S READY.
THEY'RE TURNING INTO NEW CABLES!
THAT'S RIGHT! BUT I STILL NEED YOUR HELP.
LISTEN UP. YOU'LL HAVE TO WORK TOGETHER. WILL, YOU'LL HAVE TO...

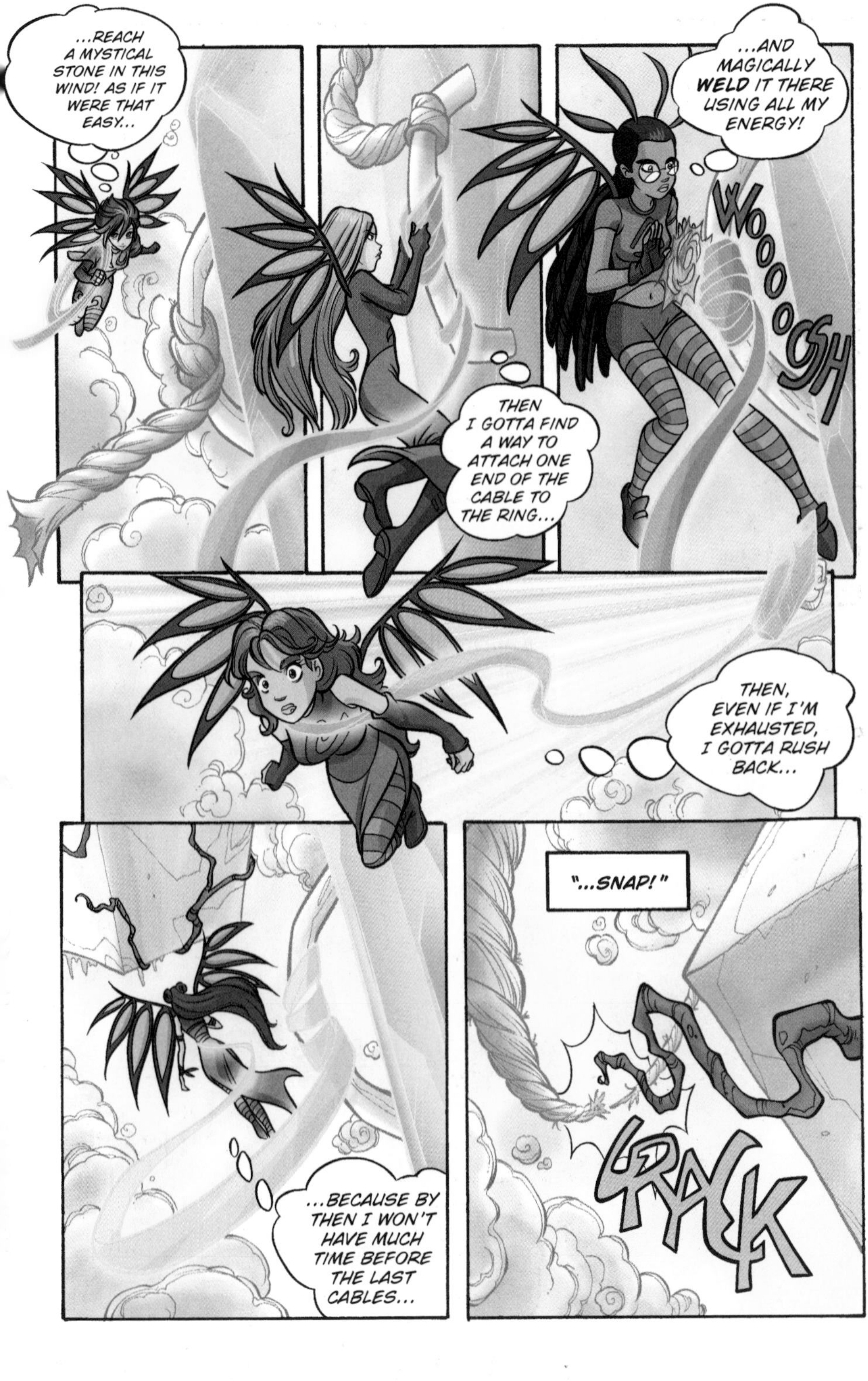
...REACH A MYSTICAL STONE IN THIS WIND! AS IF IT WERE THAT EASY...
THEN I GOTTA FIND A WAY TO ATTACH ONE END OF THE CABLE TO THE RING...
...AND MAGICALLY WELD IT THERE USING ALL MY ENERGY!
WOOOOOSH
THEN, EVEN IF I'M EXHAUSTED, I GOTTA RUSH BACK...
...BECAUSE BY THEN I WON'T HAVE MUCH TIME BEFORE THE LAST CABLES...
"...SNAP!"
CRACK

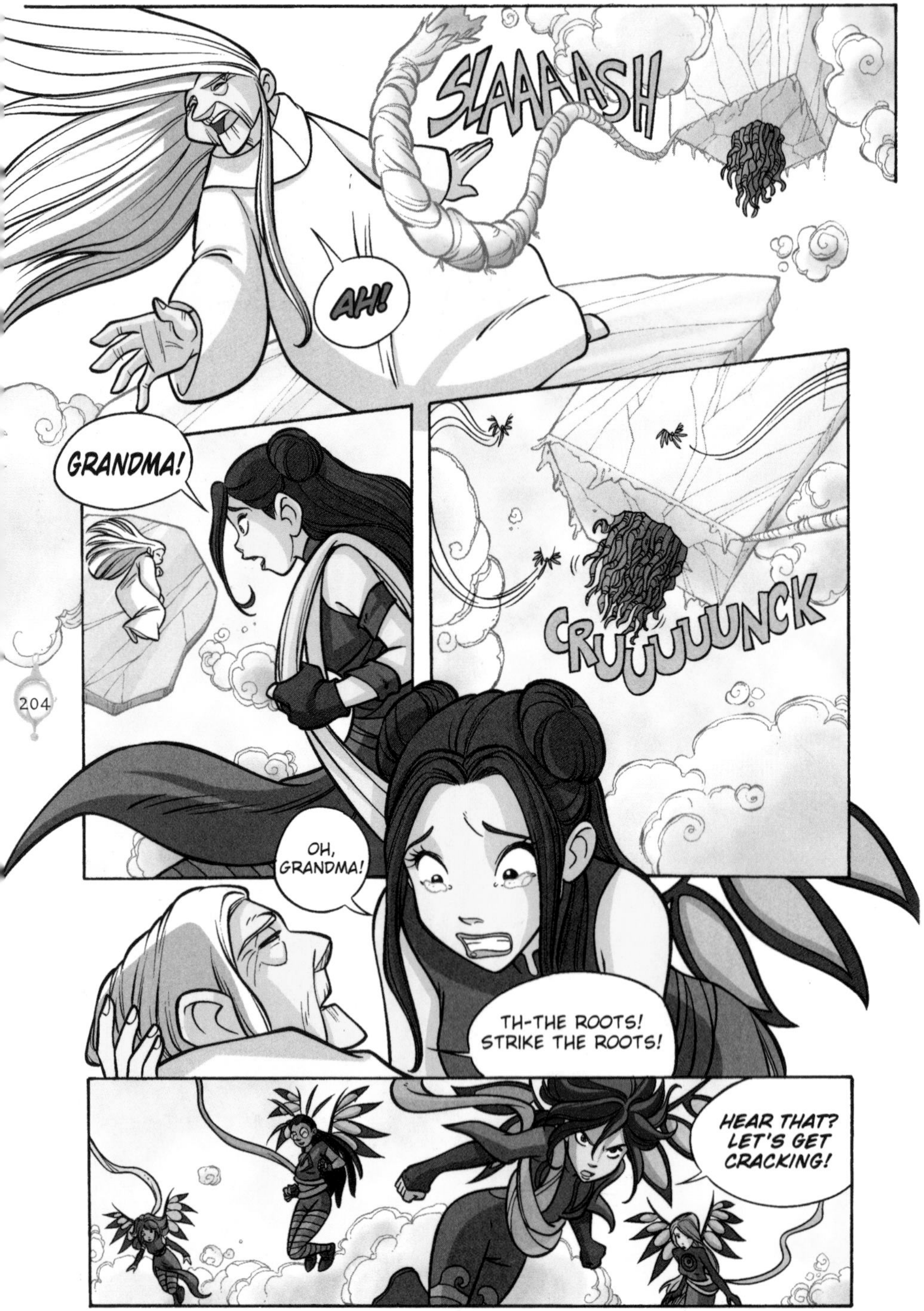
SLAAAASH
AH!
GRANDMA!
CRUUUUUNCK
OH, GRANDMA!
TH-THE ROOTS! STRIKE THE ROOTS!
HEAR THAT? LET'S GET CRACKING!

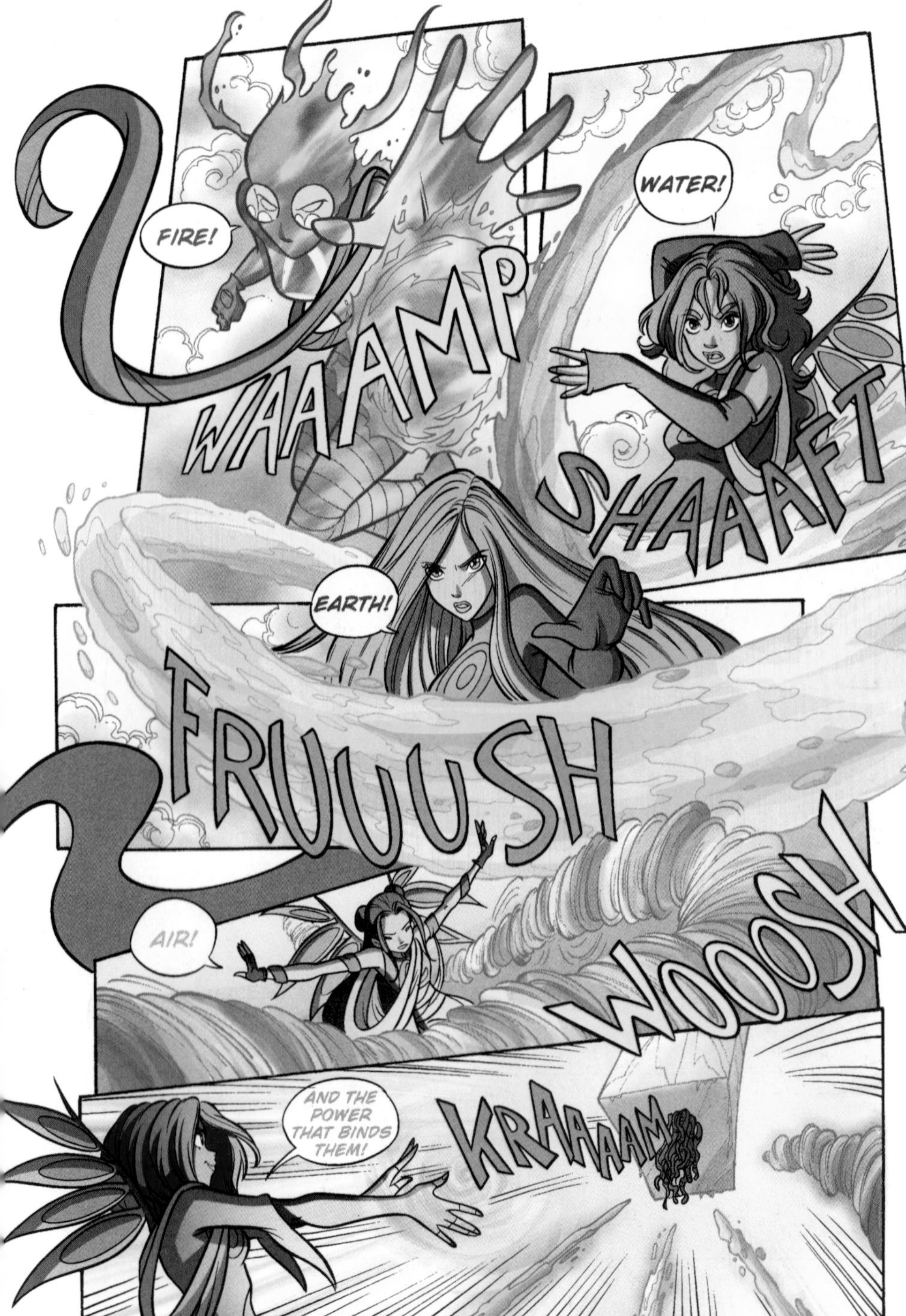
FIRE!
WAAAMP
WATER!
SHAAAFT
EARTH!
FRUUUSH
AIR!
WOOOSH
AND THE POWER THAT BINDS THEM!
KRAAAAM

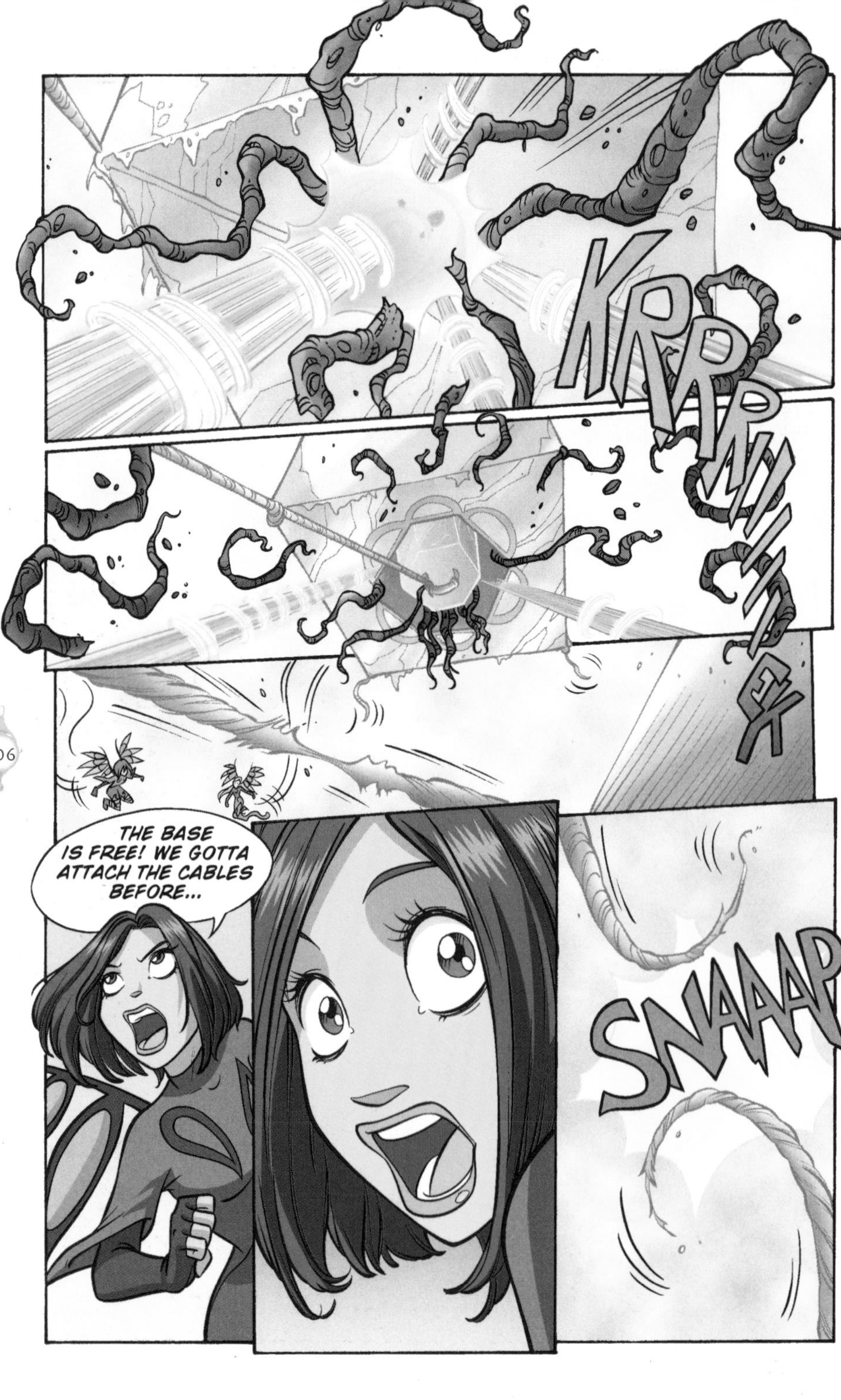
KRRRRIIIIIEK
THE BASE IS FREE! WE GOTTA ATTACH THE CABLES BEFORE...
SNAAAP

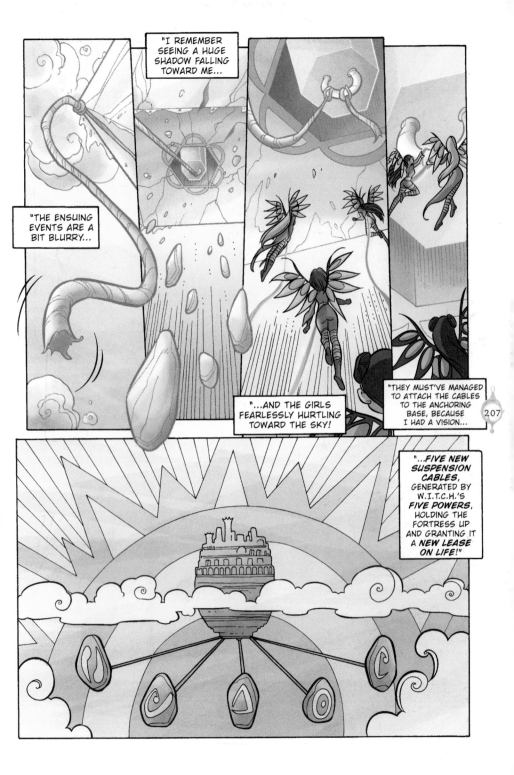

"I REMEMBER SEEING A HUGE SHADOW FALLING TOWARD ME..."

"THE ENSUING EVENTS ARE A BIT BLURRY..."

"...AND THE GIRLS FEARLESSLY HURTLING TOWARD THE SKY!"

"THEY MUST'VE MANAGED TO ATTACH THE CABLES TO THE ANCHORING BASE, BECAUSE I HAD A VISION...

207

"...FIVE NEW SUSPENSION CABLES, GENERATED BY W.I.T.C.H.'S FIVE POWERS, HOLDING THE FORTRESS UP AND GRANTING IT A NEW LEASE ON LIFE!"

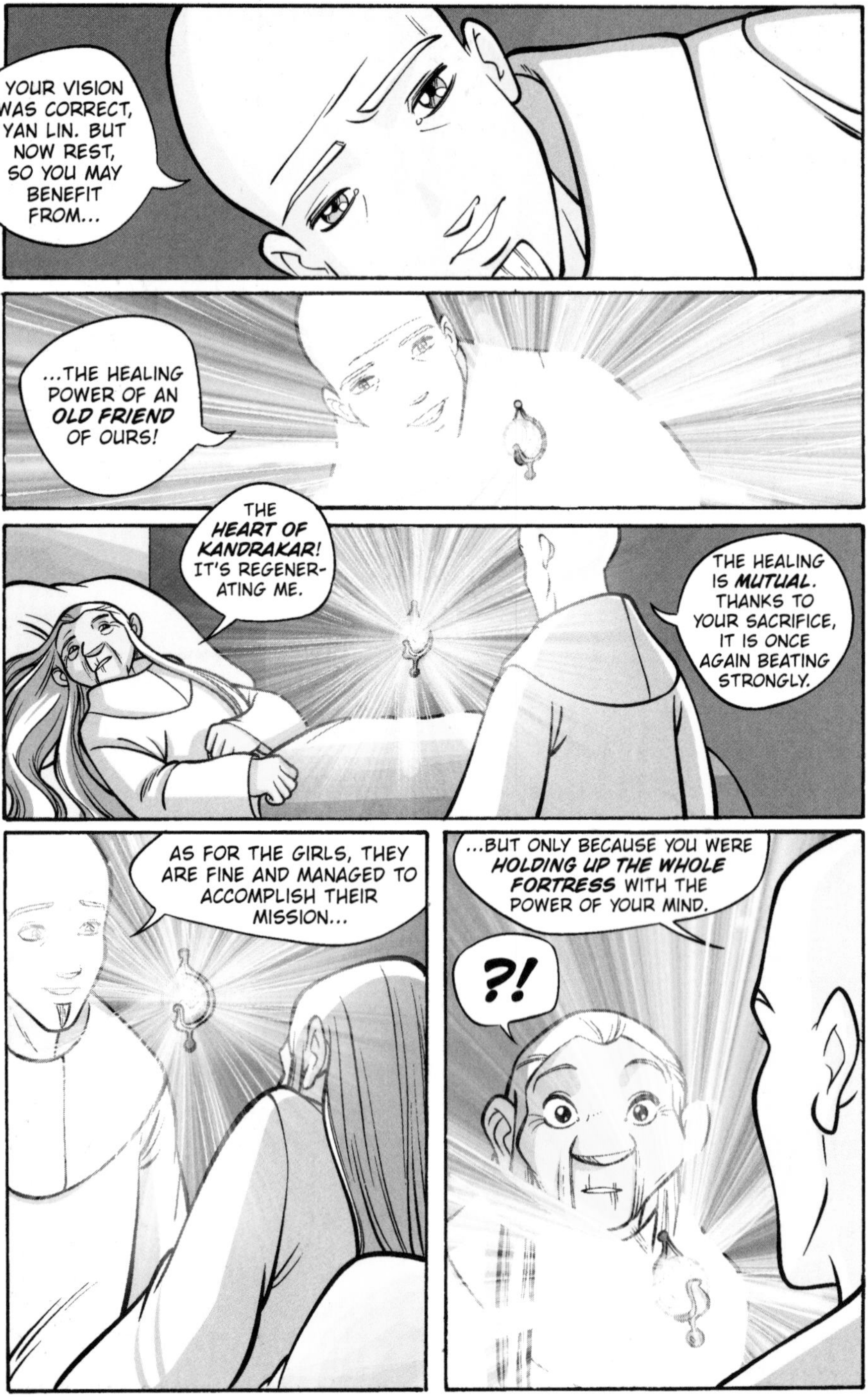
YOUR VISION WAS CORRECT, YAN LIN. BUT NOW REST, SO YOU MAY BENEFIT FROM...
...THE HEALING POWER OF AN OLD FRIEND OF OURS!
THE HEART OF KANDRAKAR! IT'S REGENERATING ME.
THE HEALING IS MUTUAL. THANKS TO YOUR SACRIFICE, IT IS ONCE AGAIN BEATING STRONGLY.
AS FOR THE GIRLS, THEY ARE FINE AND MANAGED TO ACCOMPLISH THEIR MISSION...
...BUT ONLY BECAUSE YOU WERE HOLDING UP THE WHOLE FORTRESS WITH THE POWER OF YOUR MIND.
?!

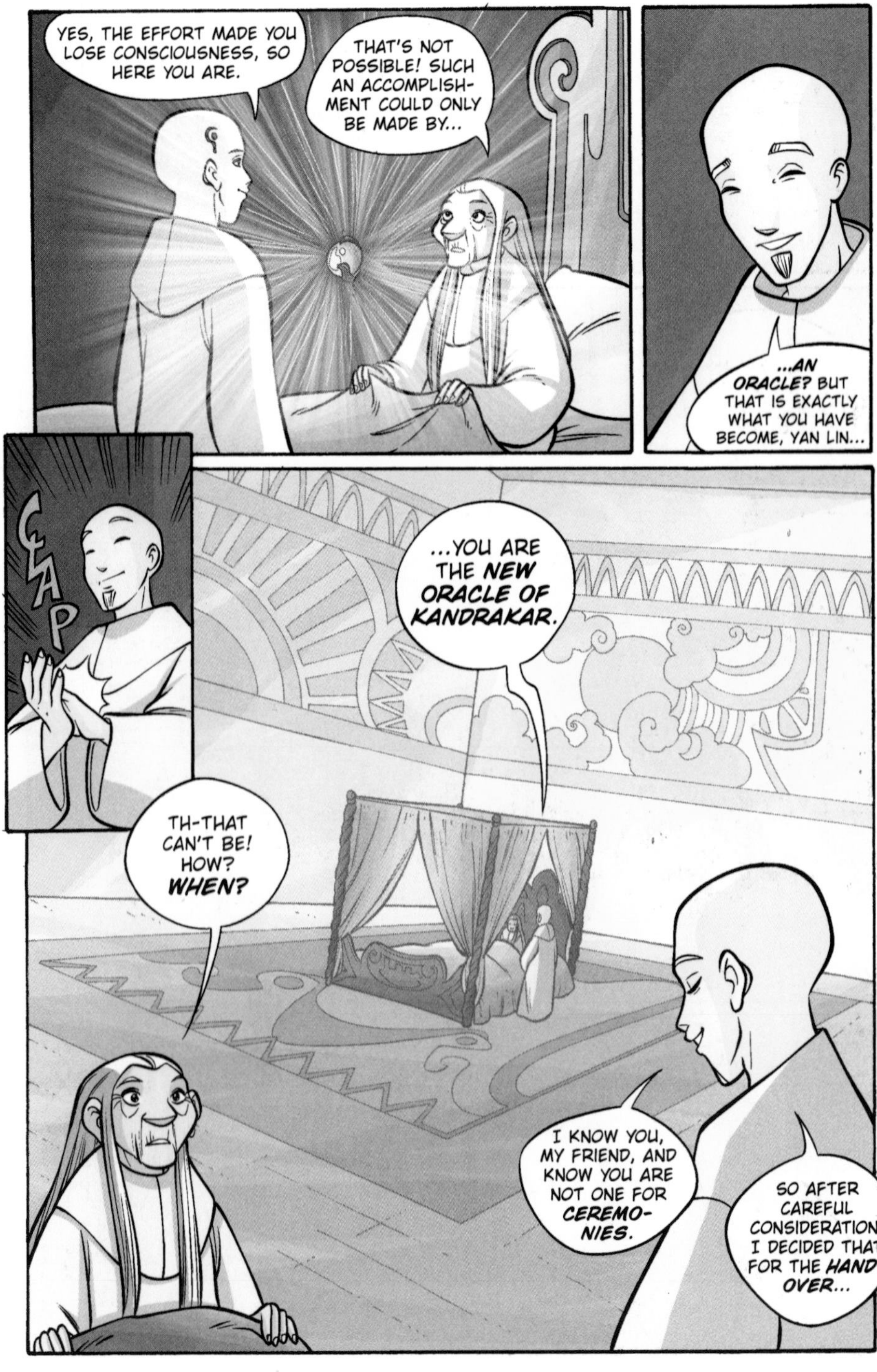

YES, THE EFFORT MADE YOU LOSE CONSCIOUSNESS, SO HERE YOU ARE.
THAT'S NOT POSSIBLE! SUCH AN ACCOMPLISHMENT COULD ONLY BE MADE BY...
...AN ORACLE? BUT THAT IS EXACTLY WHAT YOU HAVE BECOME, YAN LIN...
CLAP
...YOU ARE THE NEW ORACLE OF KANDRAKAR.
TH-THAT CAN'T BE! HOW? WHEN?
I KNOW YOU, MY FRIEND, AND KNOW YOU ARE NOT ONE FOR CEREMONIES.
SO AFTER CAREFUL CONSIDERATION, I DECIDED THAT FOR THE HAND-OVER...

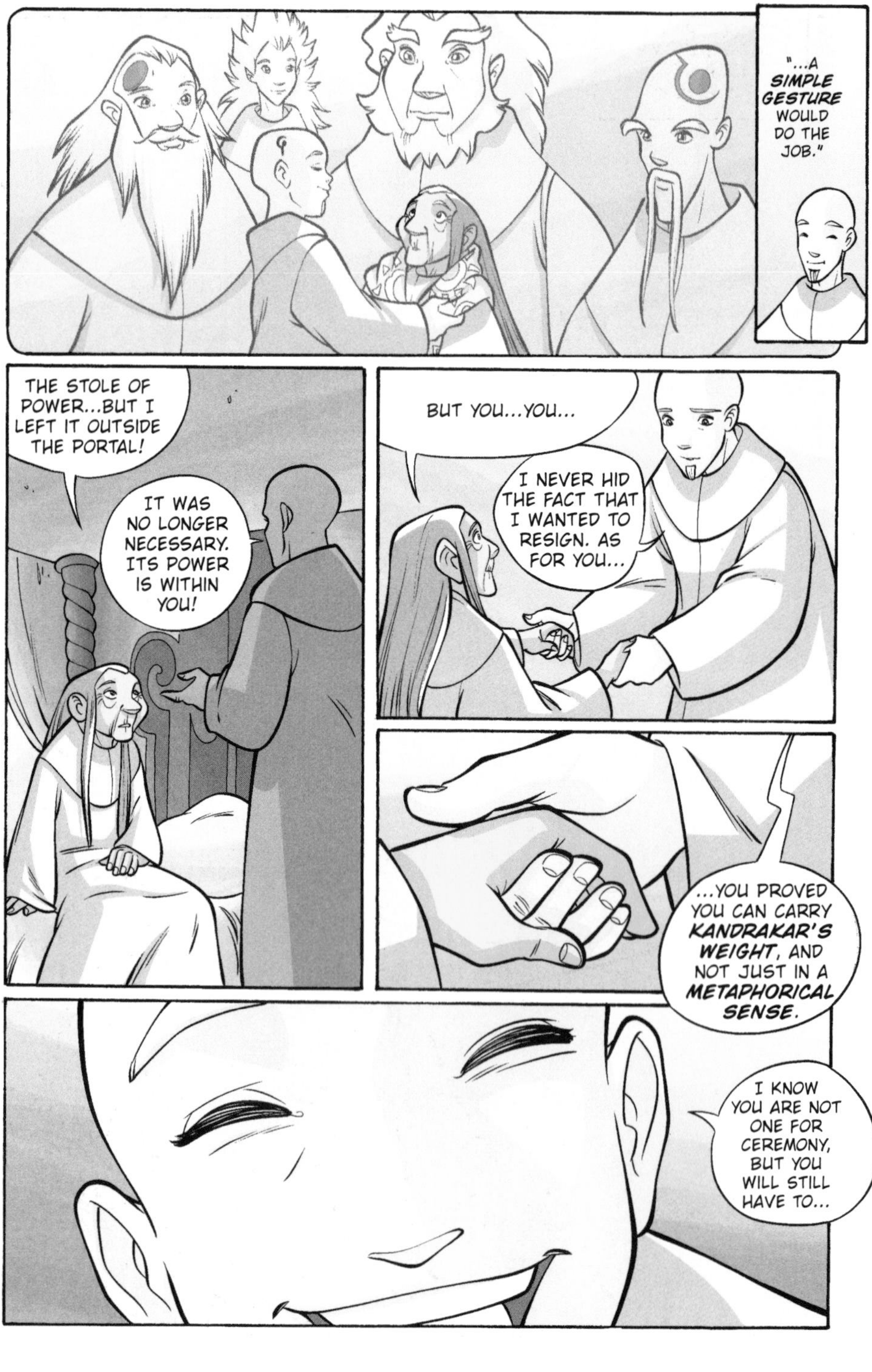
"...A SIMPLE GESTURE WOULD DO THE JOB."
THE STOLE OF POWER...BUT I LEFT IT OUTSIDE THE PORTAL!
IT WAS NO LONGER NECESSARY. ITS POWER IS WITHIN YOU!
BUT YOU...YOU...
I NEVER HID THE FACT THAT I WANTED TO RESIGN. AS FOR YOU...
...YOU PROVED YOU CAN CARRY KANDRAKAR'S WEIGHT, AND NOT JUST IN A METAPHORICAL SENSE.
I KNOW YOU ARE NOT ONE FOR CEREMONY, BUT YOU WILL STILL HAVE TO...

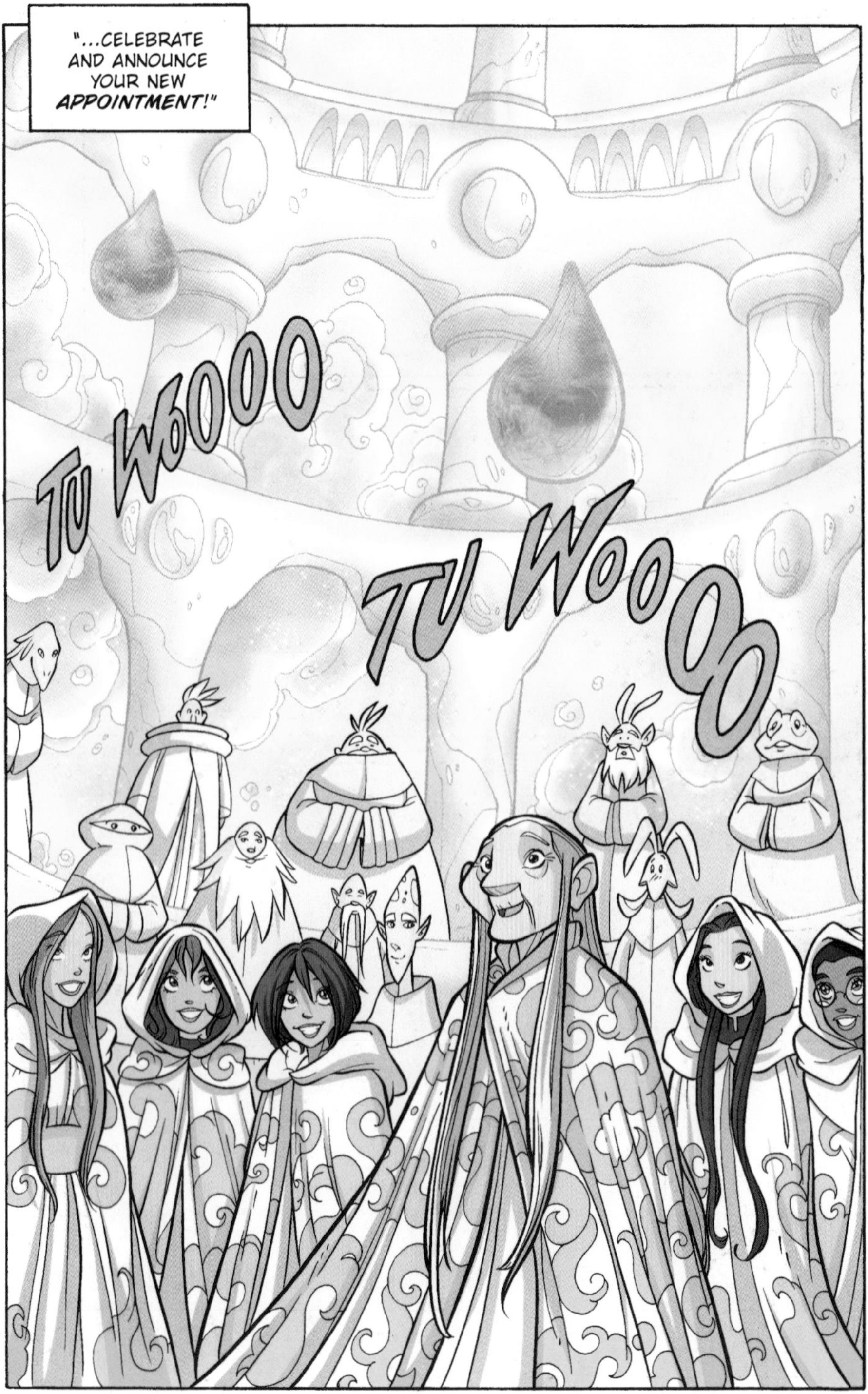
"...CELEBRATE AND ANNOUNCE YOUR NEW APPOINTMENT!"
TU WOOO
TU WOOOO

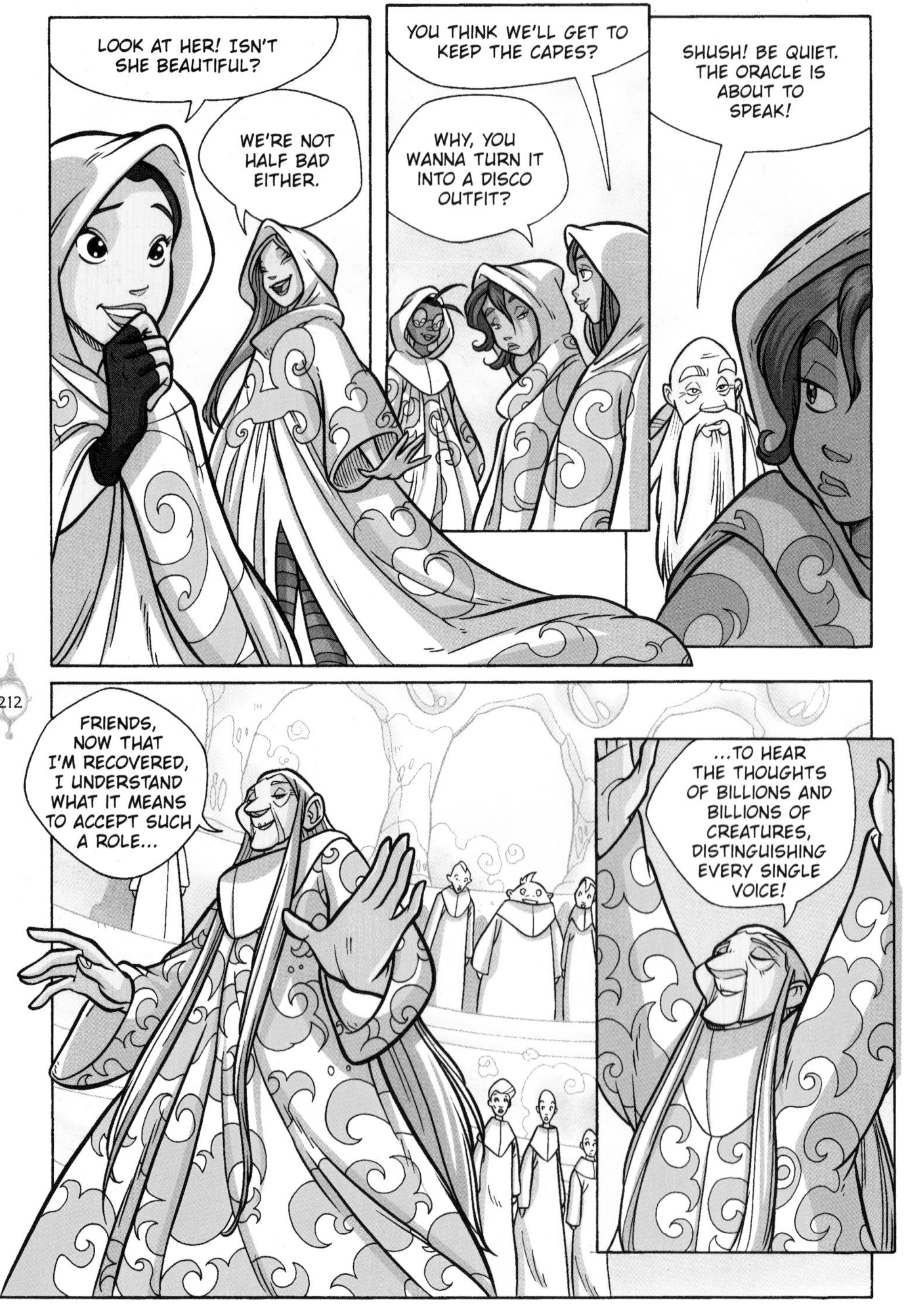
LOOK AT HER! ISN'T SHE BEAUTIFUL?
WE'RE NOT HALF BAD EITHER.
YOU THINK WE'LL GET TO KEEP THE CAPES?
WHY, YOU WANNA TURN IT INTO A DISCO OUTFIT?
SHUSH! BE QUIET. THE ORACLE IS ABOUT TO SPEAK!
FRIENDS, NOW THAT I'M RECOVERED, I UNDERSTAND WHAT IT MEANS TO ACCEPT SUCH A ROLE...
...TO HEAR THE THOUGHTS OF BILLIONS AND BILLIONS OF CREATURES, DISTINGUISHING EVERY SINGLE VOICE!

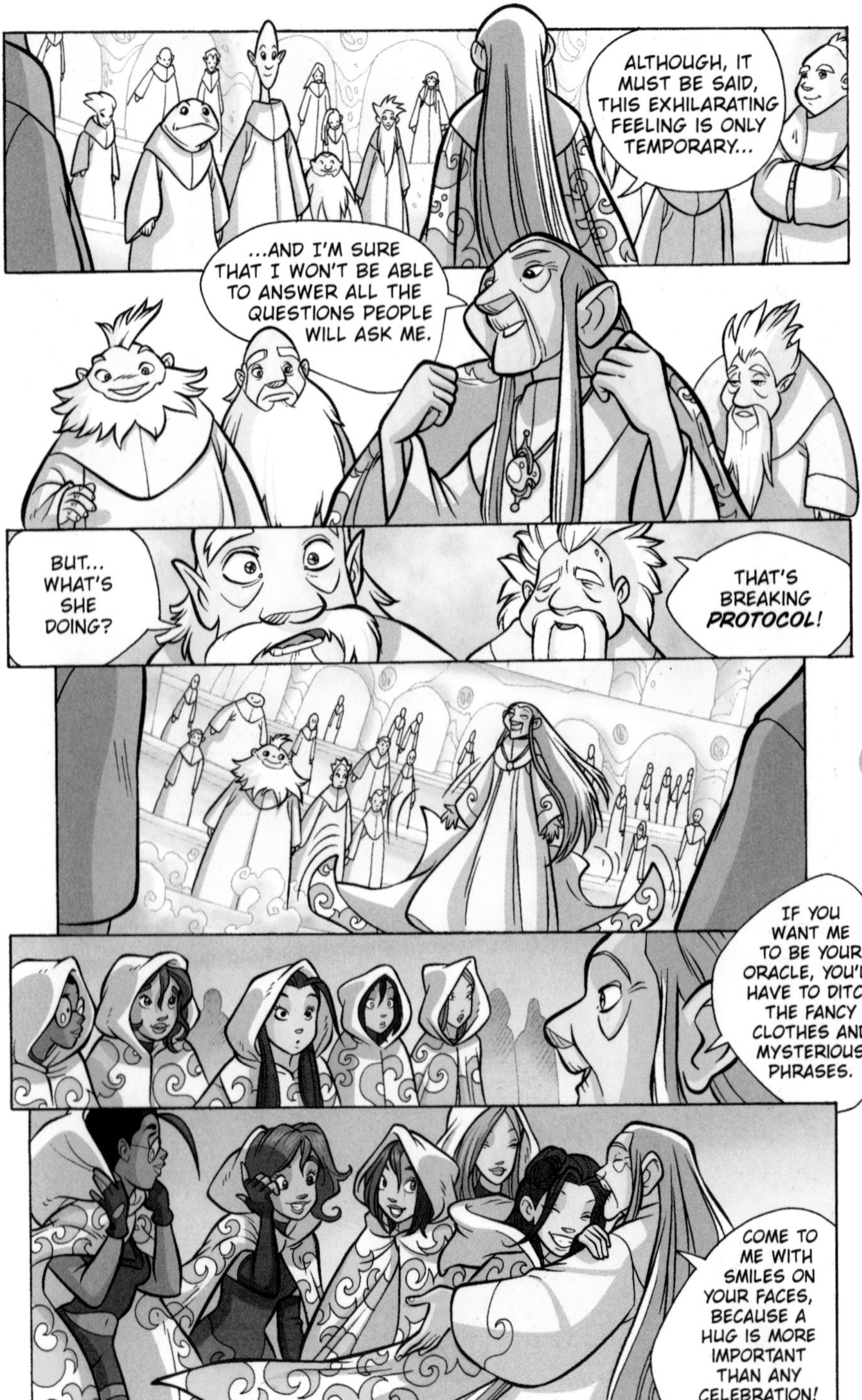
ALTHOUGH, IT MUST BE SAID, THIS EXHILARATING FEELING IS ONLY TEMPORARY...
...AND I'M SURE THAT I WON'T BE ABLE TO ANSWER ALL THE QUESTIONS PEOPLE WILL ASK ME.
BUT... WHAT'S SHE DOING?
THAT'S BREAKING PROTOCOL!
IF YOU WANT ME TO BE YOUR ORACLE, YOU'LL HAVE TO DITCH THE FANCY CLOTHES AND MYSTERIOUS PHRASES.
COME TO ME WITH SMILES ON YOUR FACES, BECAUSE A HUG IS MORE IMPORTANT THAN ANY CELEBRATION!

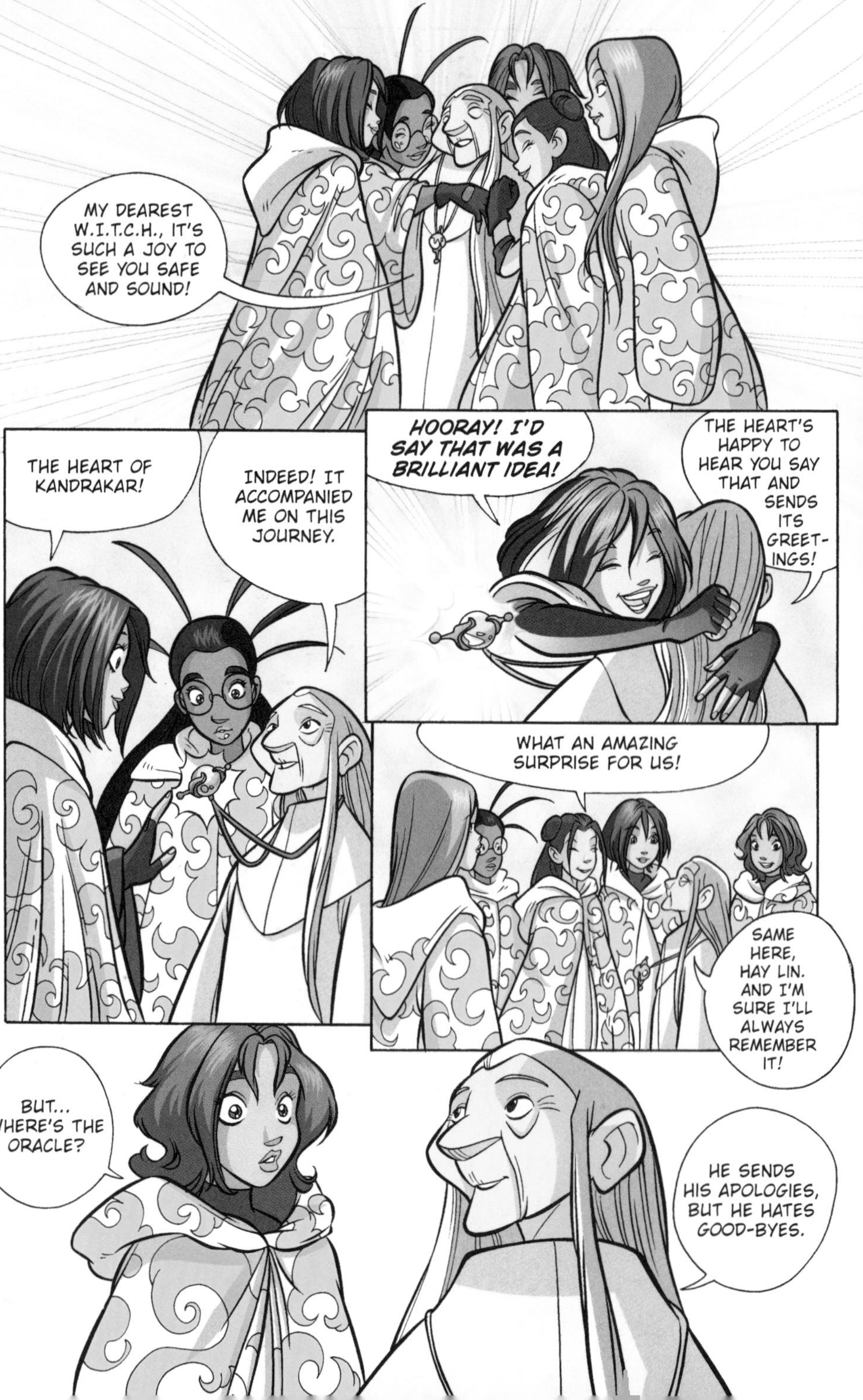
MY DEAREST W.I.T.C.H., IT'S SUCH A JOY TO SEE YOU SAFE AND SOUND!
THE HEART OF KANDRAKAR!
INDEED! IT ACCOMPANIED ME ON THIS JOURNEY.
HOORAY! I'D SAY THAT WAS A BRILLIANT IDEA!
THE HEART'S HAPPY TO HEAR YOU SAY THAT AND SENDS ITS GREET-INGS!
WHAT AN AMAZING SURPRISE FOR US!
SAME HERE, HAY LIN. AND I'M SURE I'LL ALWAYS REMEMBER IT!
BUT... WHERE'S THE ORACLE?
HE SENDS HIS APOLOGIES, BUT HE HATES GOOD-BYES.

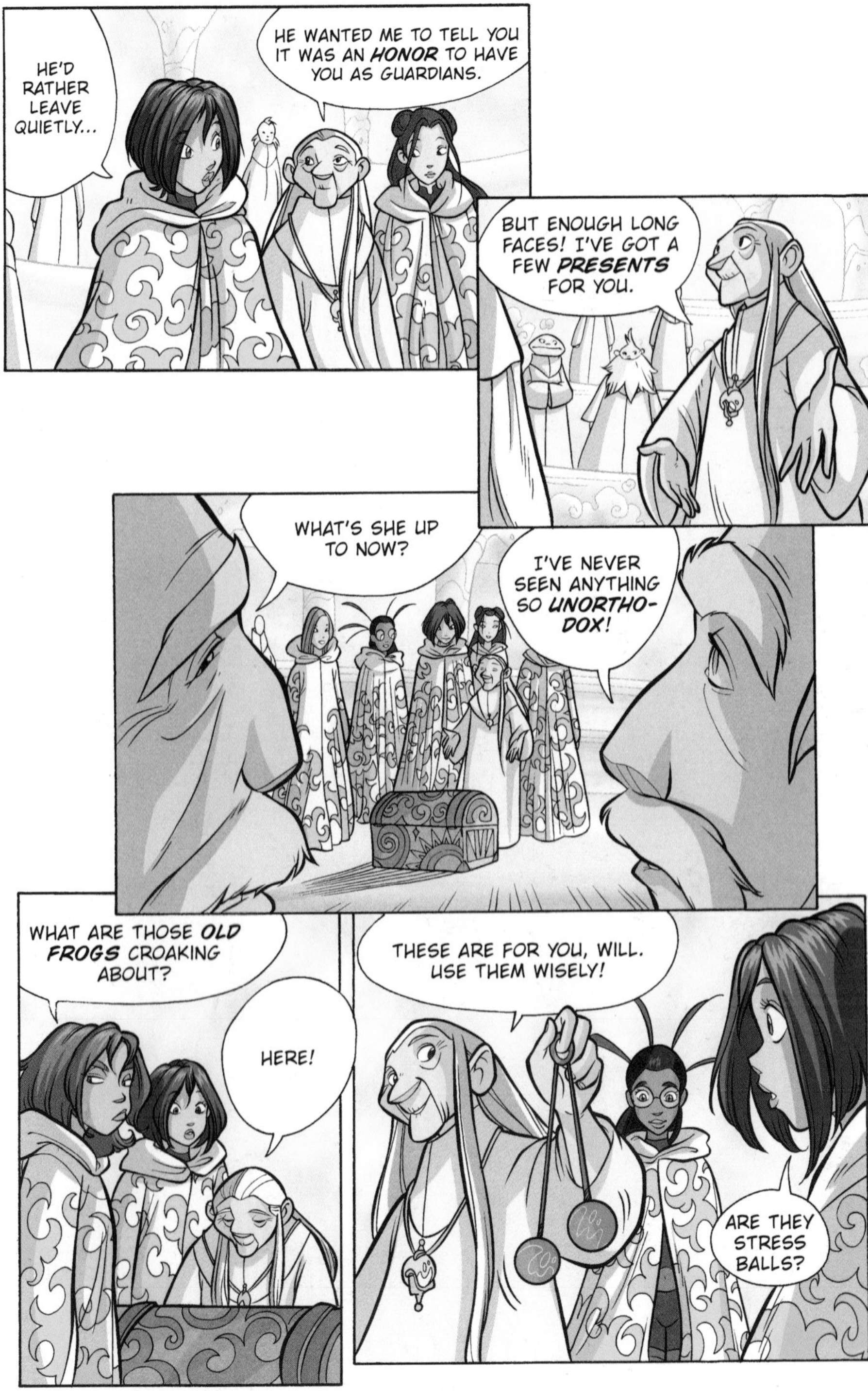
HE'D RATHER LEAVE QUIETLY...
HE WANTED ME TO TELL YOU IT WAS AN *HONOR* TO HAVE YOU AS GUARDIANS.
BUT ENOUGH LONG FACES! I'VE GOT A FEW *PRESENTS* FOR YOU.
WHAT'S SHE UP TO NOW?
I'VE NEVER SEEN ANYTHING SO *UNORTHO-DOX*!
WHAT ARE THOSE *OLD FROGS* CROAKING ABOUT?
HERE!
THESE ARE FOR YOU, WILL. USE THEM WISELY!
ARE THEY STRESS BALLS?

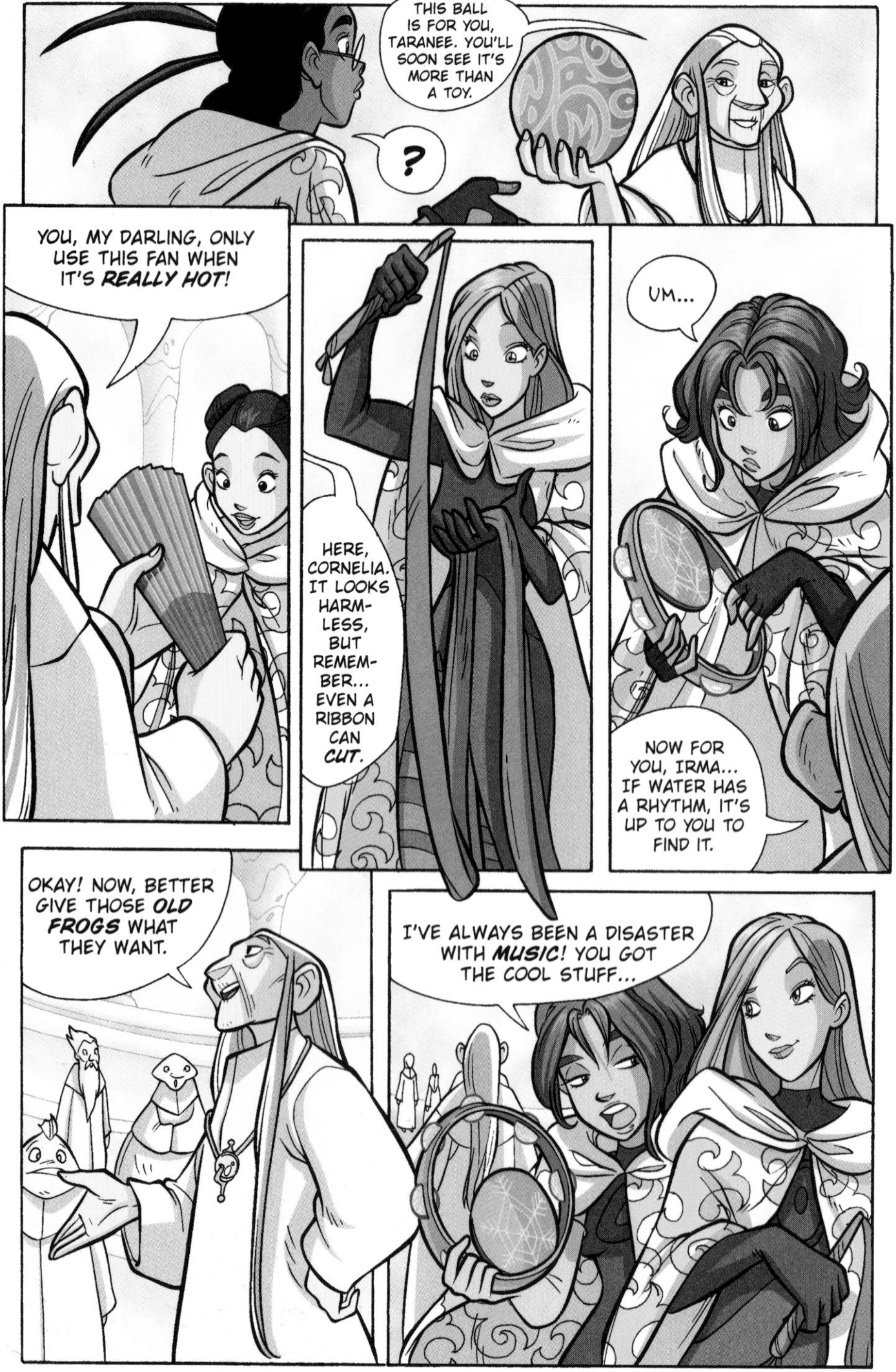

THIS BALL IS FOR YOU, TARANEE. YOU'LL SOON SEE IT'S MORE THAN A TOY.
?
YOU, MY DARLING, ONLY USE THIS FAN WHEN IT'S *REALLY HOT*!
HERE, CORNELIA. IT LOOKS HARMLESS, BUT REMEMBER... EVEN A RIBBON CAN *CUT*.
UM...
NOW FOR YOU, IRMA... IF WATER HAS A RHYTHM, IT'S UP TO YOU TO FIND IT.
OKAY! NOW, BETTER GIVE THOSE *OLD FROGS* WHAT THEY WANT.
I'VE ALWAYS BEEN A DISASTER WITH *MUSIC*! YOU GOT THE COOL STUFF...

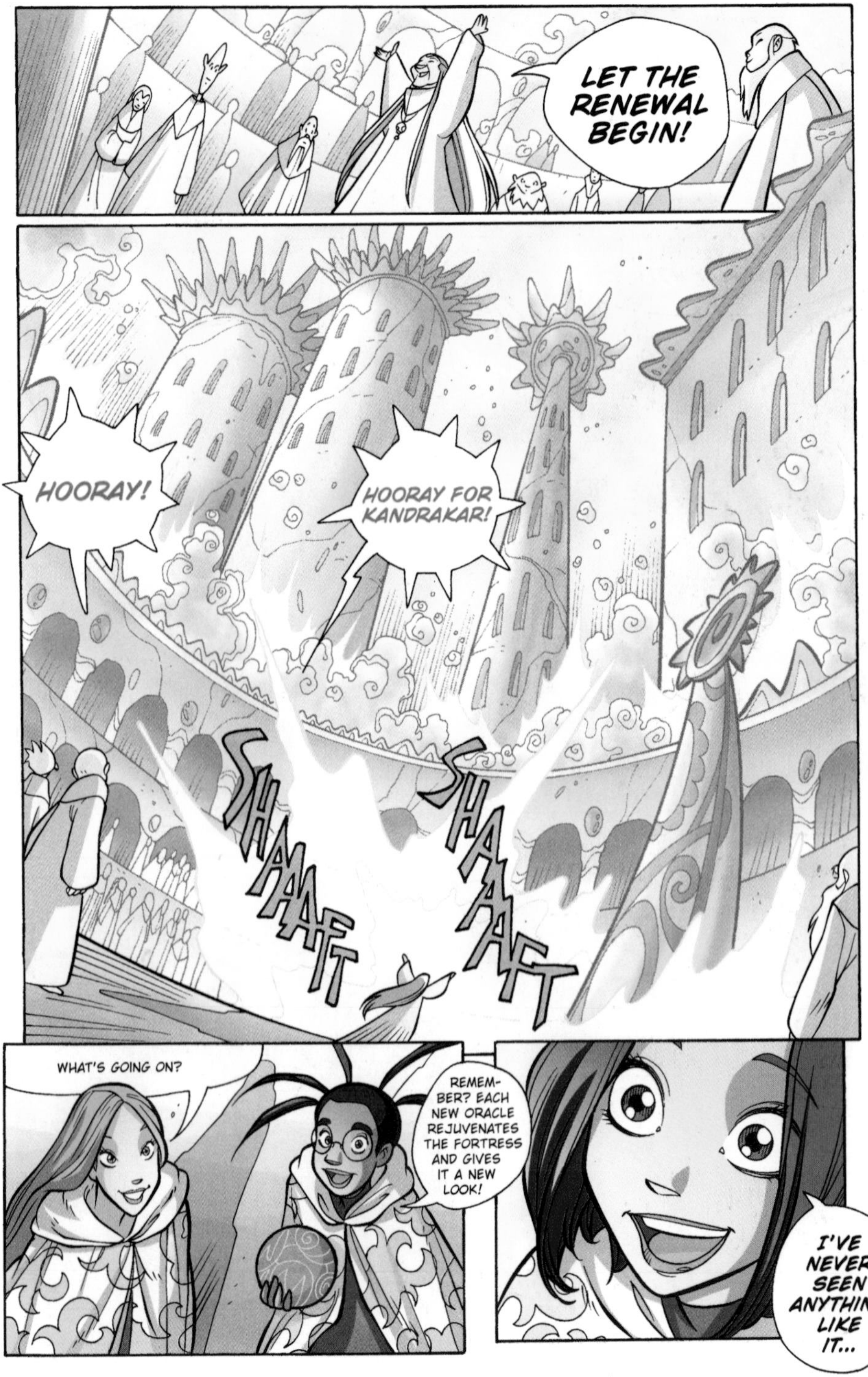
LET THE RENEWAL BEGIN!
HOORAY!
HOORAY FOR KANDRAKAR!
SHAAAFT
SHAAAFT
WHAT'S GOING ON?
REMEMBER? EACH NEW ORACLE REJUVENATES THE FORTRESS AND GIVES IT A NEW LOOK!
I'VE NEVER SEEN ANYTHING LIKE IT...

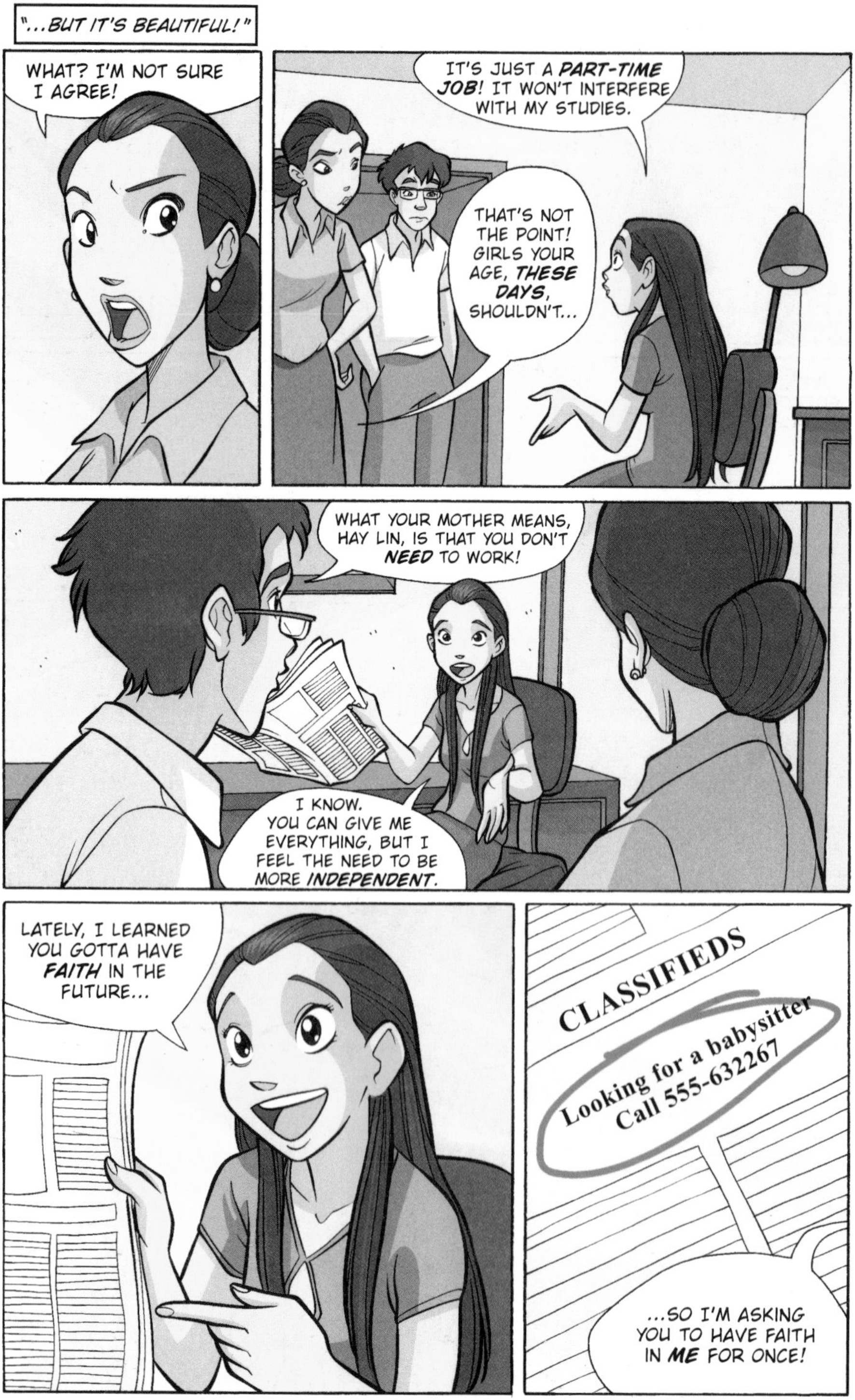
"...BUT IT'S BEAUTIFUL!"
WHAT? I'M NOT SURE I AGREE!
IT'S JUST A PART-TIME JOB! IT WON'T INTERFERE WITH MY STUDIES.
THAT'S NOT THE POINT! GIRLS YOUR AGE, THESE DAYS, SHOULDN'T...
WHAT YOUR MOTHER MEANS, HAY LIN, IS THAT YOU DON'T NEED TO WORK!
I KNOW. YOU CAN GIVE ME EVERYTHING, BUT I FEEL THE NEED TO BE MORE INDEPENDENT.
LATELY, I LEARNED YOU GOTTA HAVE FAITH IN THE FUTURE...
CLASSIFIEDS
Looking for a babysitter
Call 555-632267
...SO I'M ASKING YOU TO HAVE FAITH IN ME FOR ONCE!

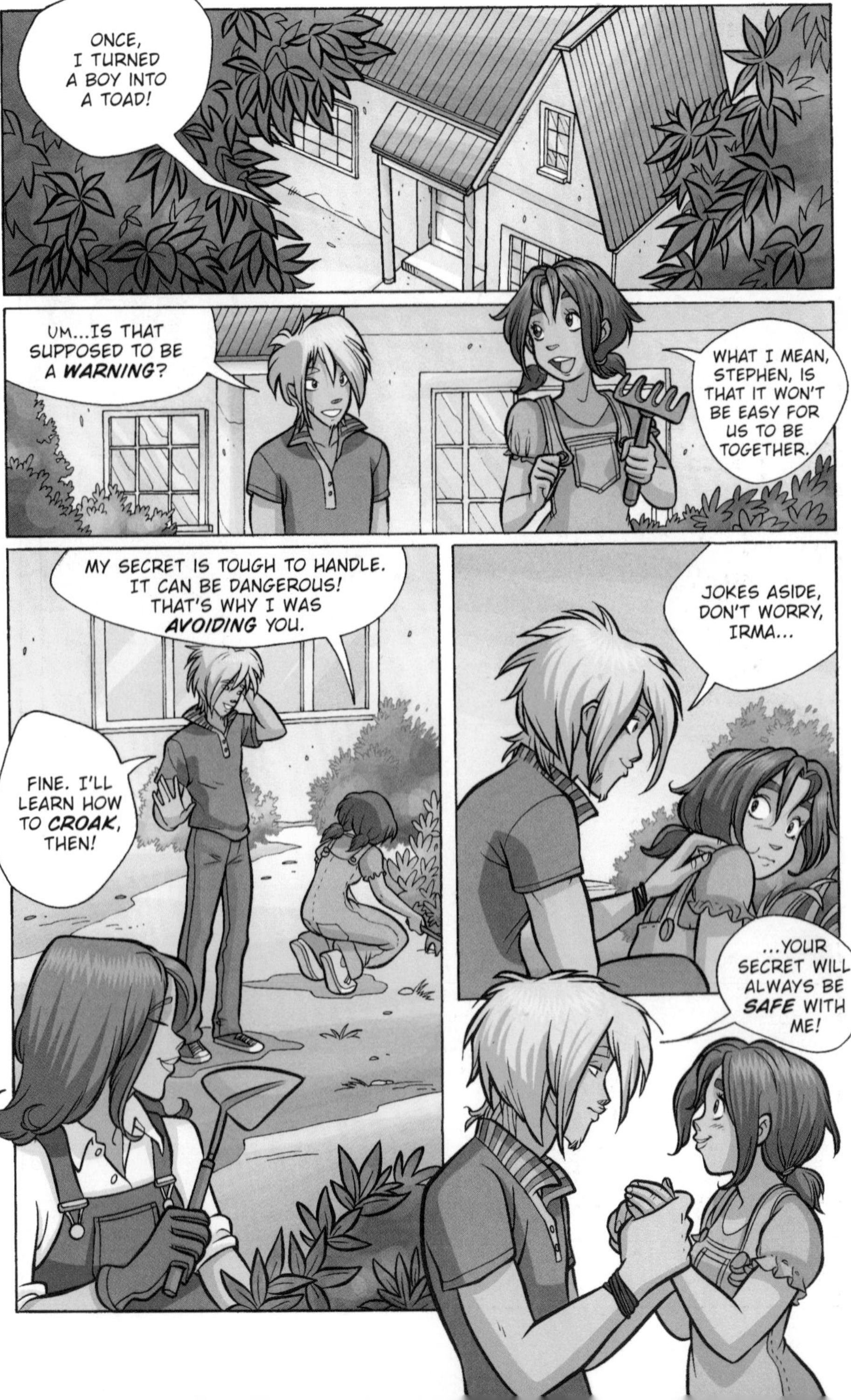
ONCE, I TURNED A BOY INTO A TOAD!
UM...IS THAT SUPPOSED TO BE A **WARNING**?
WHAT I MEAN, STEPHEN, IS THAT IT WON'T BE EASY FOR US TO BE TOGETHER.
MY SECRET IS TOUGH TO HANDLE. IT CAN BE DANGEROUS! THAT'S WHY I WAS **AVOIDING** YOU.
FINE. I'LL LEARN HOW TO **CROAK**, THEN!
JOKES ASIDE, DON'T WORRY, IRMA...
...YOUR SECRET WILL ALWAYS BE **SAFE** WITH ME!

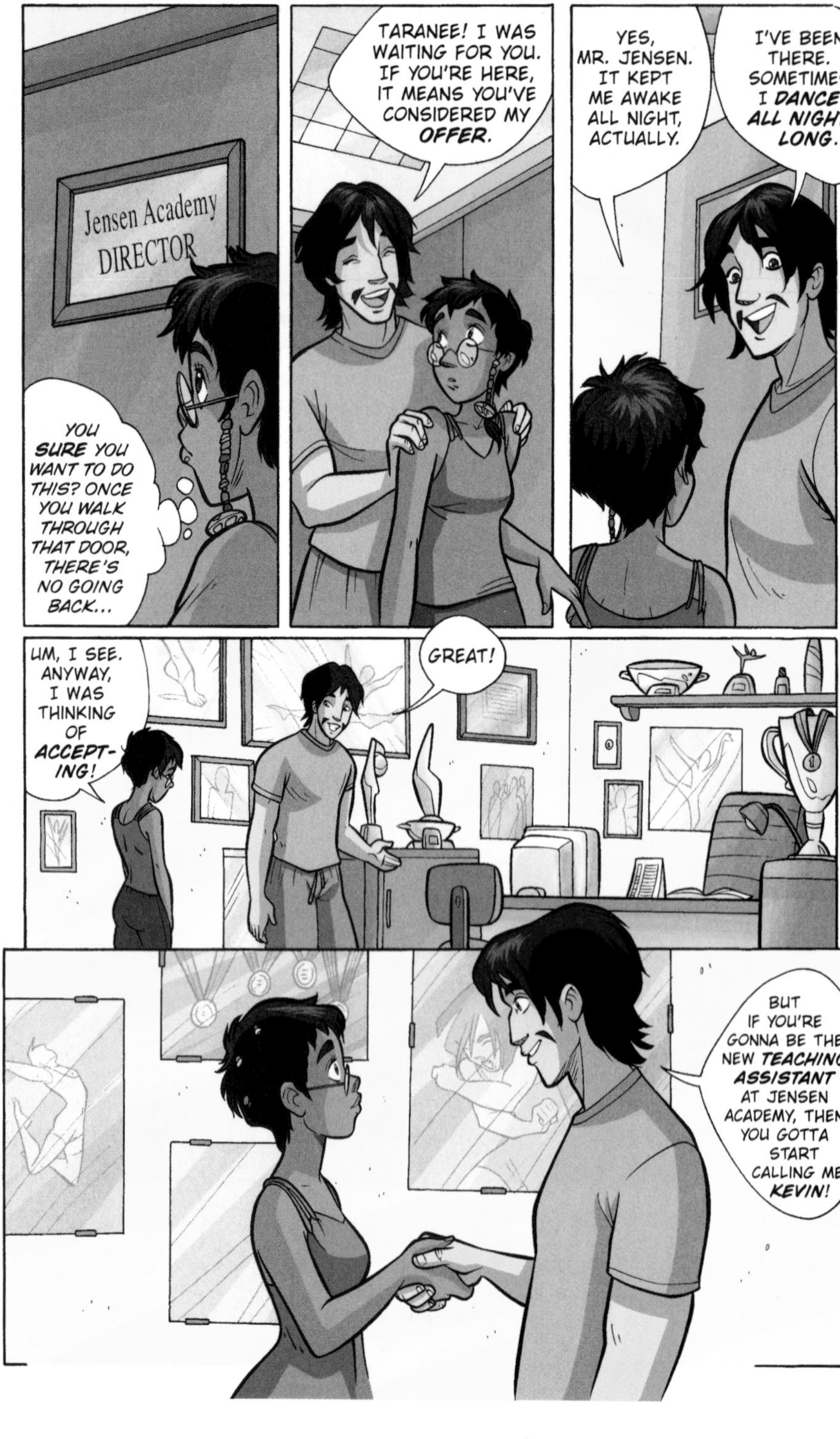
Jensen Academy DIRECTOR
YOU SURE YOU WANT TO DO THIS? ONCE YOU WALK THROUGH THAT DOOR, THERE'S NO GOING BACK...
TARANEE! I WAS WAITING FOR YOU. IF YOU'RE HERE, IT MEANS YOU'VE CONSIDERED MY OFFER.
YES, MR. JENSEN. IT KEPT ME AWAKE ALL NIGHT, ACTUALLY.
I'VE BEEN THERE. SOMETIMES I DANCE ALL NIGHT LONG.
UM, I SEE. ANYWAY, I WAS THINKING OF ACCEPTING!
GREAT!
BUT IF YOU'RE GONNA BE THE NEW TEACHING ASSISTANT AT JENSEN ACADEMY, THEN YOU GOTTA START CALLING ME KEVIN!

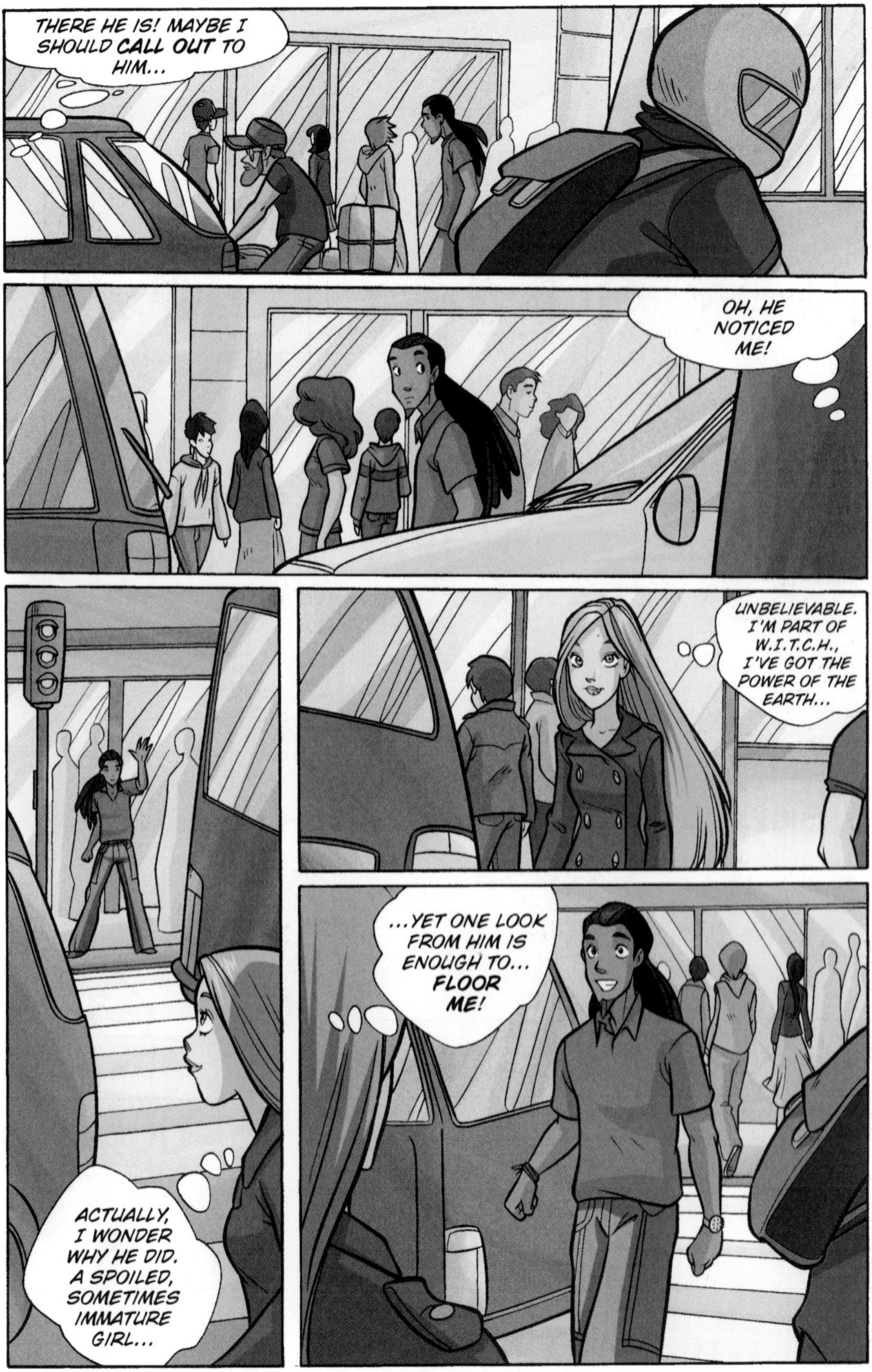
THERE HE IS! MAYBE I SHOULD CALL OUT TO HIM...
OH, HE NOTICED ME!
UNBELIEVABLE. I'M PART OF W.I.T.C.H., I'VE GOT THE POWER OF THE EARTH...
ACTUALLY, I WONDER WHY HE DID. A SPOILED, SOMETIMES IMMATURE GIRL...
...YET ONE LOOK FROM HIM IS ENOUGH TO... FLOOR ME!

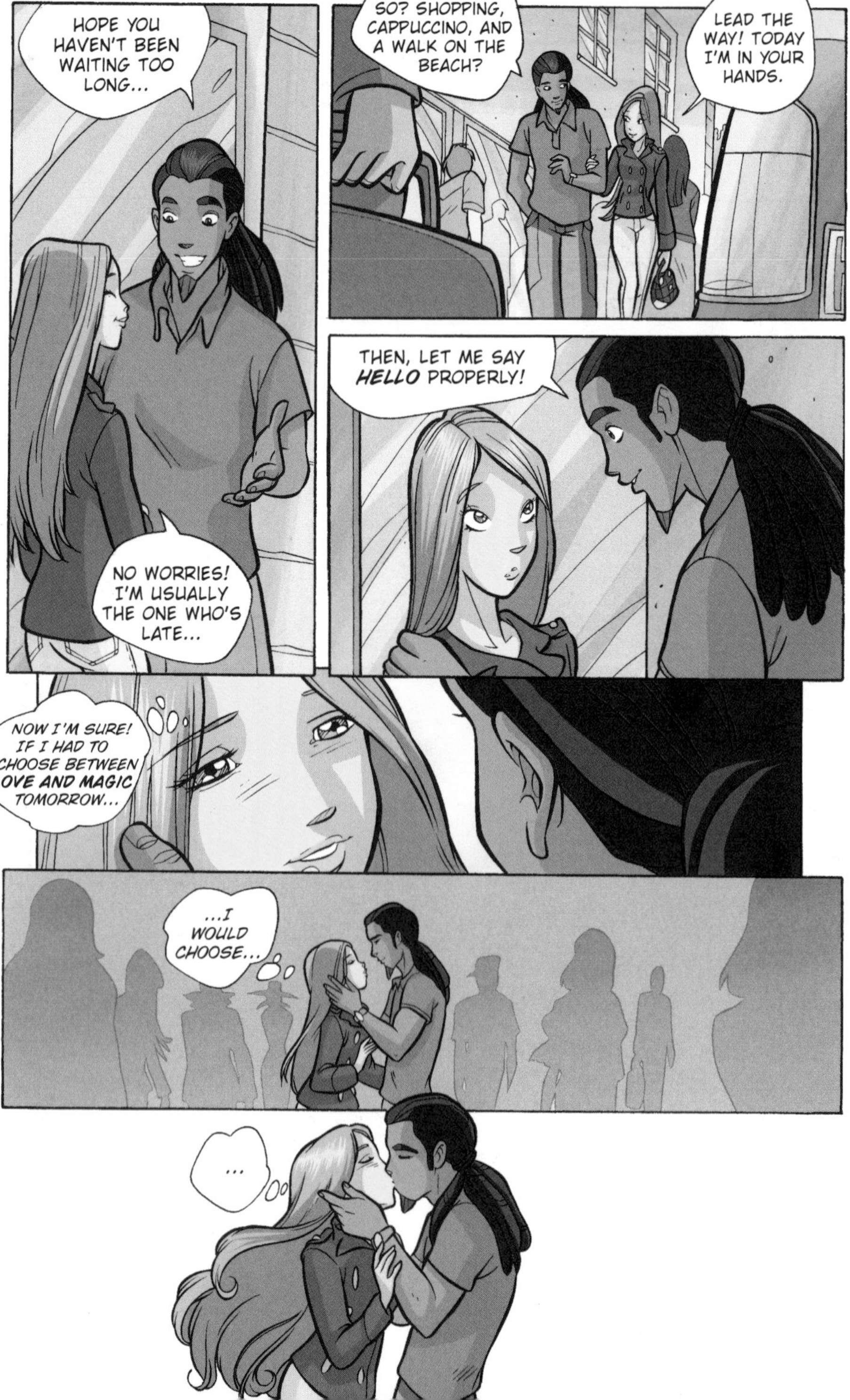
HOPE YOU HAVEN'T BEEN WAITING TOO LONG...
NO WORRIES! I'M USUALLY THE ONE WHO'S LATE...
SO? SHOPPING, CAPPUCCINO, AND A WALK ON THE BEACH?
LEAD THE WAY! TODAY I'M IN YOUR HANDS.
THEN, LET ME SAY *HELLO* PROPERLY!
NOW I'M SURE! IF I HAD TO CHOOSE BETWEEN **LOVE AND MAGIC** TOMORROW...
...I WOULD CHOOSE...
...

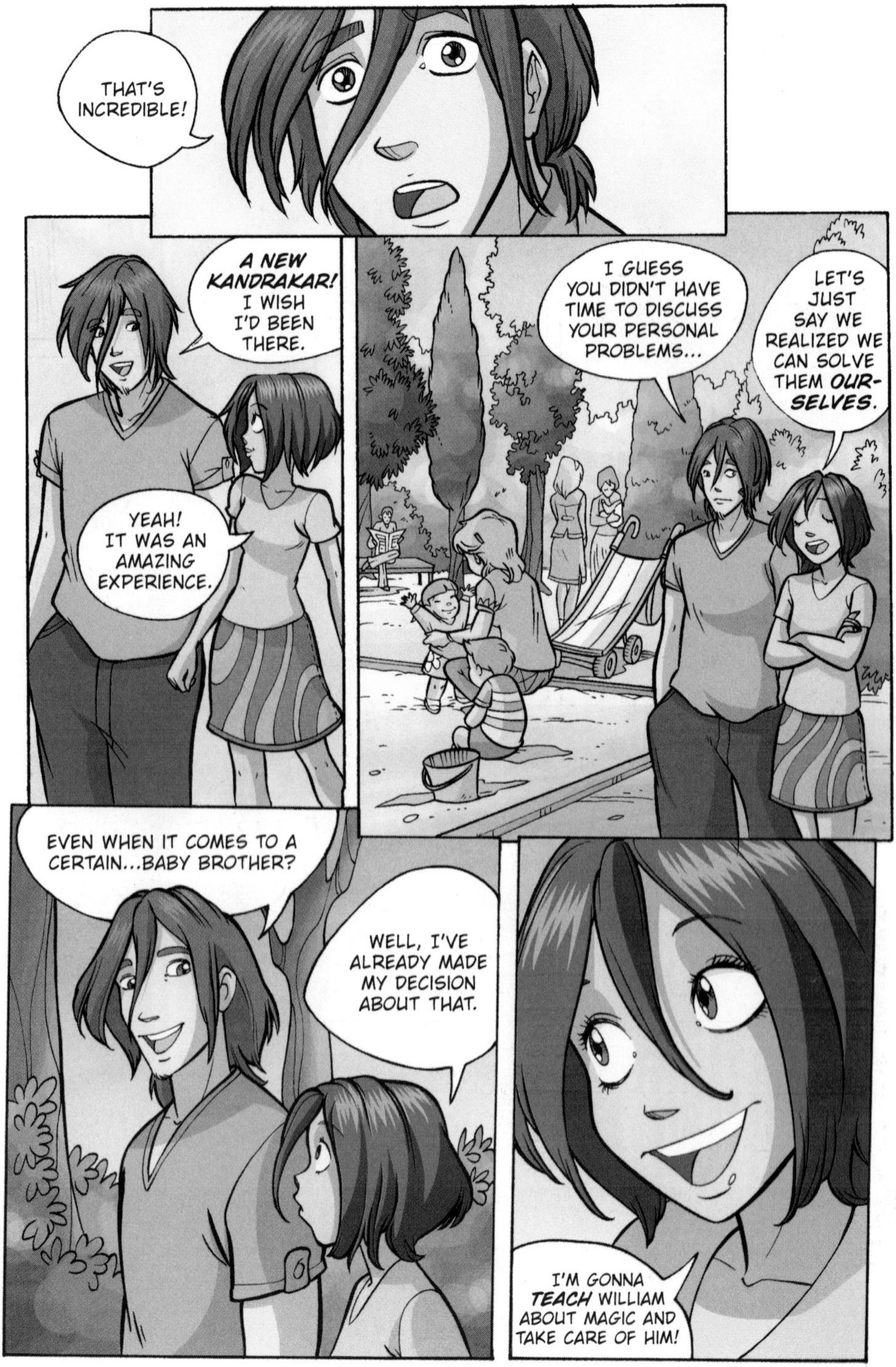
THAT'S INCREDIBLE!
A NEW KANDRAKAR! I WISH I'D BEEN THERE.
YEAH! IT WAS AN AMAZING EXPERIENCE.
I GUESS YOU DIDN'T HAVE TIME TO DISCUSS YOUR PERSONAL PROBLEMS...
LET'S JUST SAY WE REALIZED WE CAN SOLVE THEM OURSELVES.
EVEN WHEN IT COMES TO A CERTAIN...BABY BROTHER?
WELL, I'VE ALREADY MADE MY DECISION ABOUT THAT.
I'M GONNA TEACH WILLIAM ABOUT MAGIC AND TAKE CARE OF HIM!

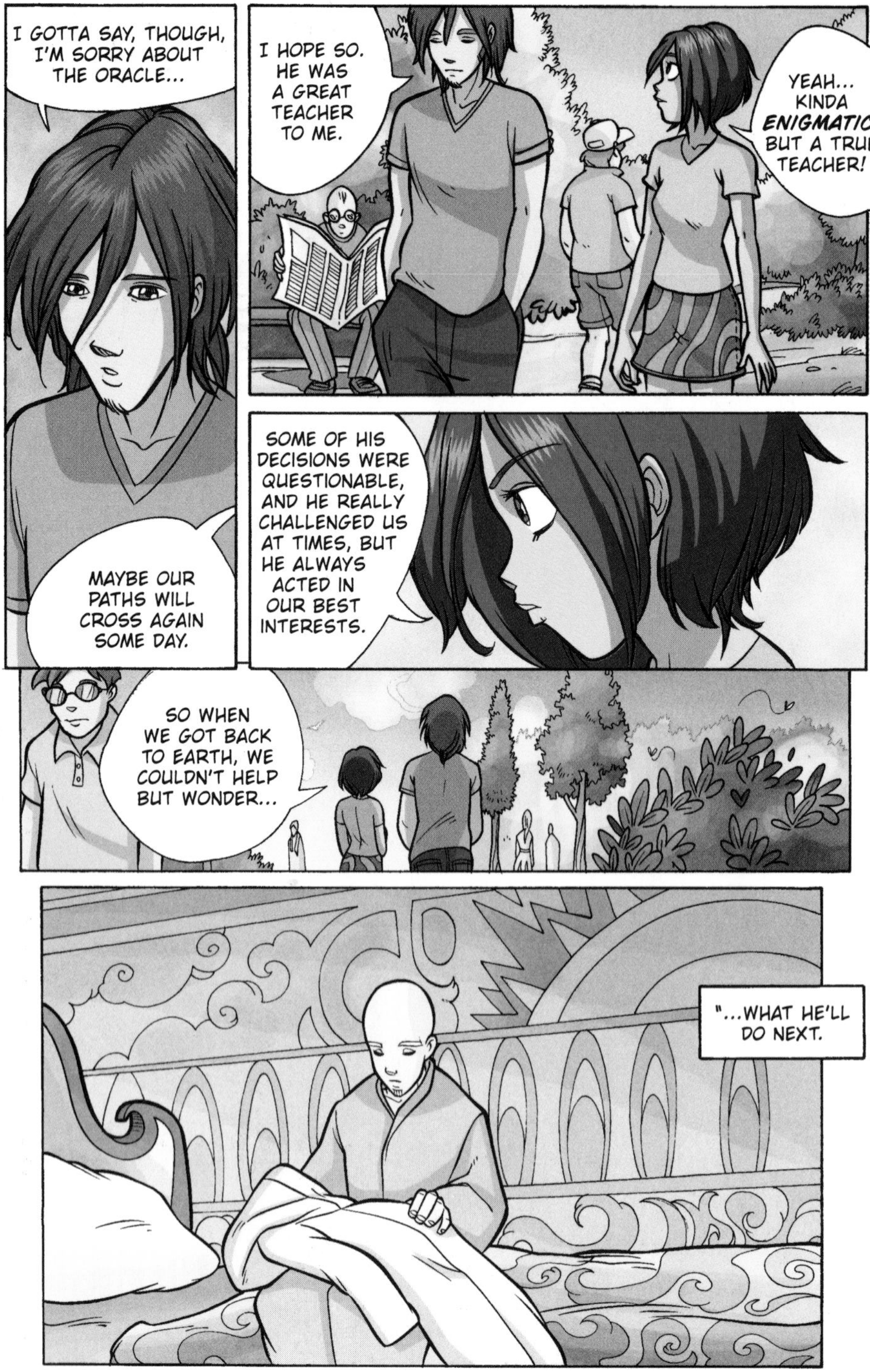

I GOTTA SAY, THOUGH, I'M SORRY ABOUT THE ORACLE...
I HOPE SO. HE WAS A GREAT TEACHER TO ME.
YEAH... KINDA ENIGMATIC, BUT A TRUE TEACHER!
MAYBE OUR PATHS WILL CROSS AGAIN SOME DAY.
SOME OF HIS DECISIONS WERE QUESTIONABLE, AND HE REALLY CHALLENGED US AT TIMES, BUT HE ALWAYS ACTED IN OUR BEST INTERESTS.
SO WHEN WE GOT BACK TO EARTH, WE COULDN'T HELP BUT WONDER...
"...WHAT HE'LL DO NEXT.

"...OR WILL HE GO BACK TO HIS HOME WORLD AND GROW OLD, LIKE THE REST OF US?

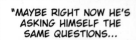

"WILL HE TRAVEL TO THOSE WORLDS THAT HE WATCHED FROM AFAR FOR YEARS...

"MAYBE RIGHT NOW HE'S ASKING HIMSELF THE SAME QUESTIONS...

"...AND REALIZING THAT, FOR THE FIRST TIME, HE DOESN'T KNOW THE *ANSWERS*.

"HE'S SO USED TO FORESEEING EVERYTHING, THIS NEW FEELING MUST BE ODD FOR HIM, BUT AT THE SAME TIME..."

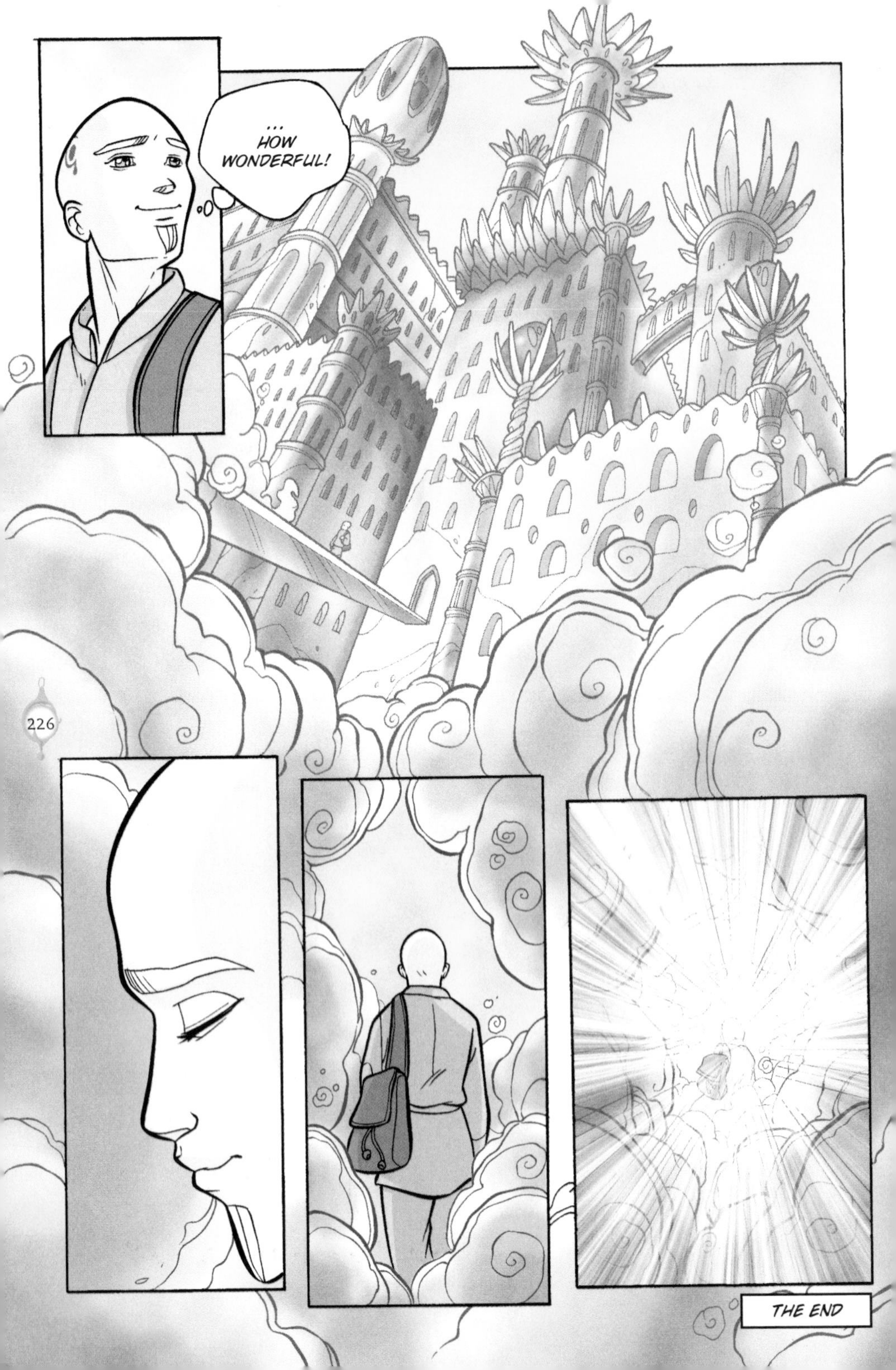

... HOW WONDERFUL!
THE END

W.i.t.c.h.

Will Irma Taranee Cornelia Hay Lin

Read on in Volume 23!

Will's family

WILL

Will Vandom, W.I.T.C.H.'s leader, introduces us to her family!

A family snapshot! The Vandom/Collinses' school life!

SUSAN

Attentive and practical, this mom knows what really matters to her daughter! She loves geography and traveling!

WILLIAM

The newest addition is little William! His favorite subjects are naps and snacks!

DEAN

Mr. Collins is a wonderful and caring dad, but don't tell him Will doesn't like history, the subject he teaches!

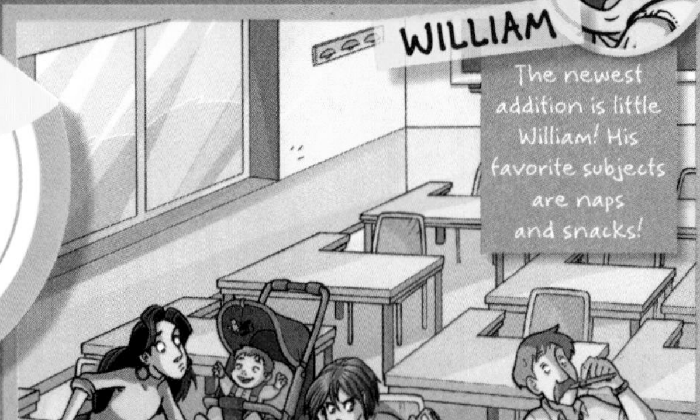

Will and her family in class as they take a test!

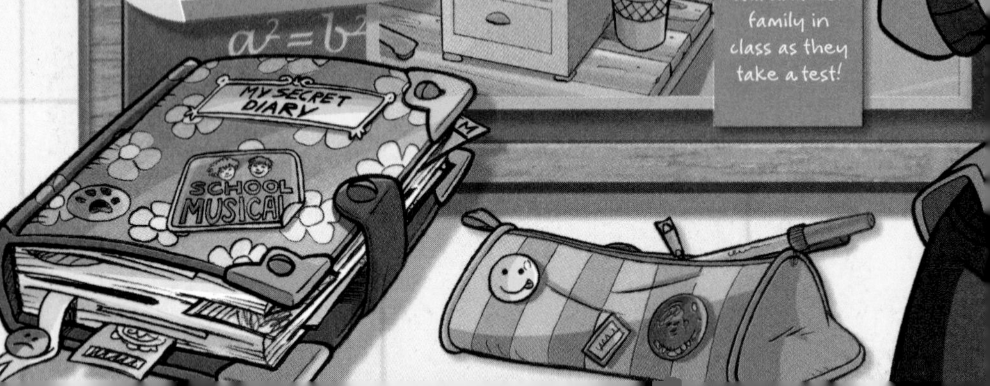
MY SECRET DIARY
SCHOOL MUSICAL

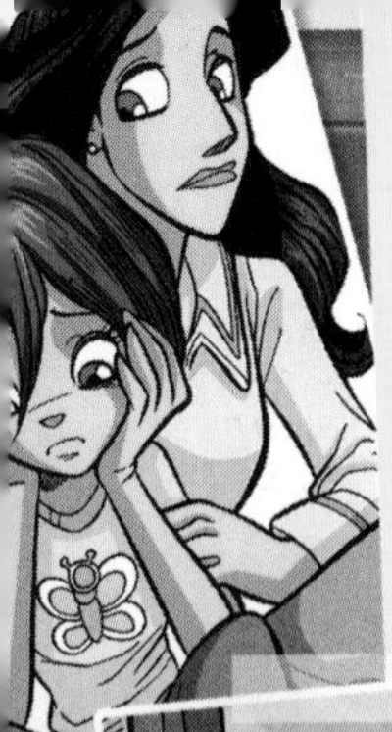

The Vandom family has rules and a strict schedule...which nobody can stick to! During breakfast, lunch, and dinner, things are always chaotic, especially since little William was born. But they're such a loving family, always ready to support one another. Nobody knows what their secret is!

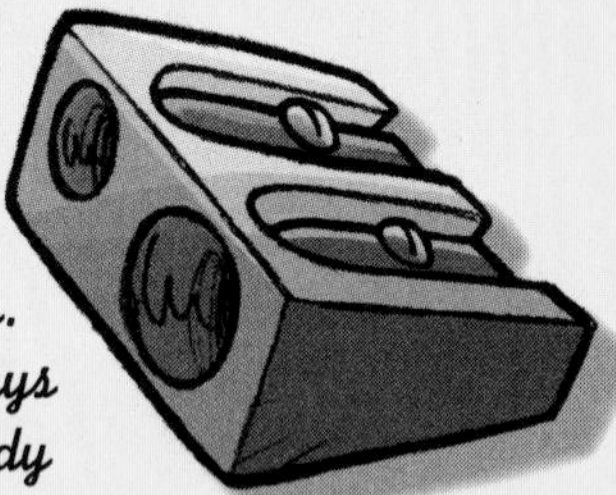

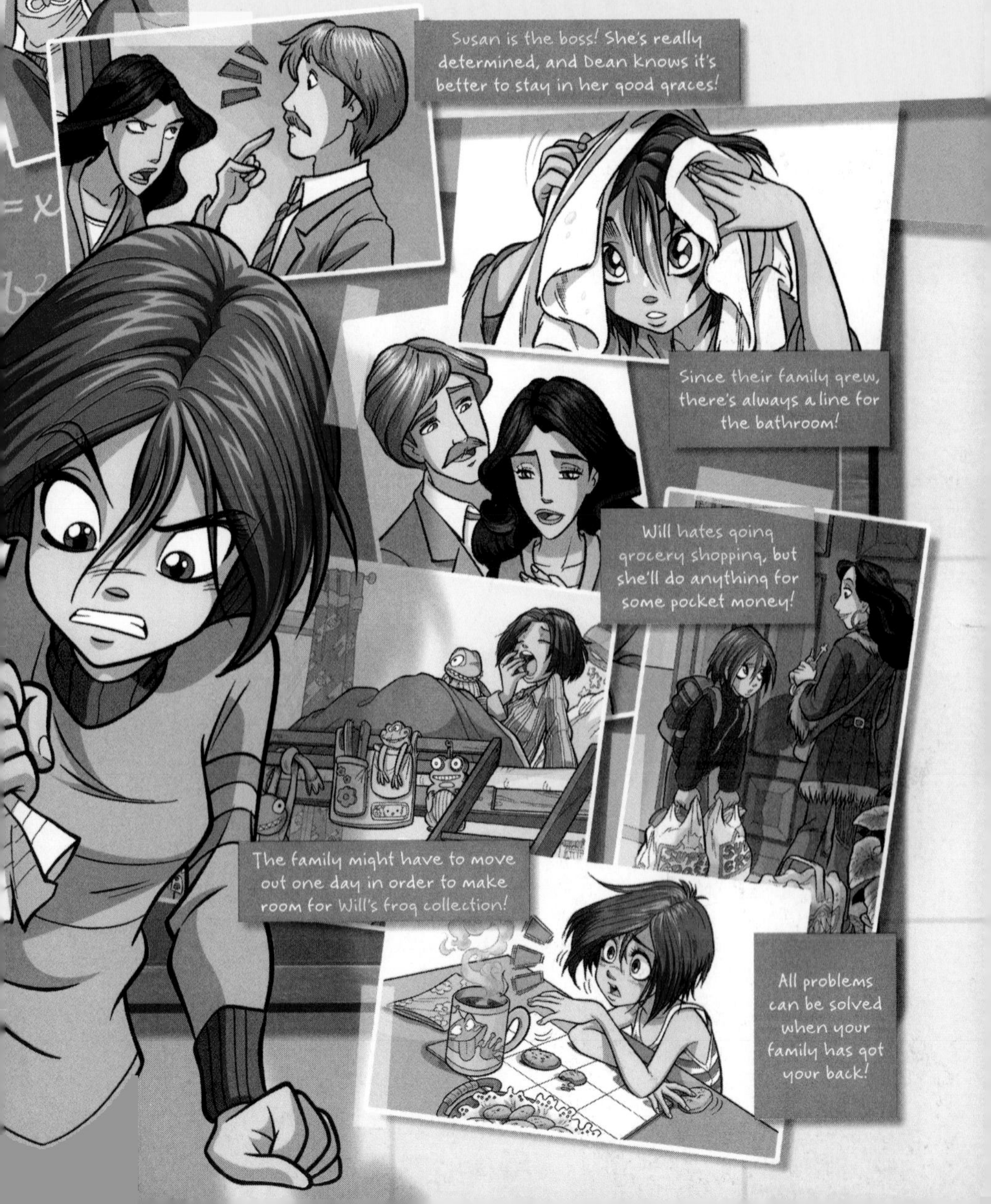

Susan is the boss! She's really determined, and Dean knows it's better to stay in her good graces!
Since their family grew, there's always a line for the bathroom!
Will hates going grocery shopping, but she'll do anything for some pocket money!
The family might have to move out one day in order to make room for Will's frog collection!
All problems can be solved when your family has got your back!

Taranee's family

A family snapshot!
The truth about the Cooks!

TARANEE

Taranee was authorized to snap some photos in court for a school project, so she involved her whole family!

THERESA

Judge Cook might seem like a stern woman, but she's a sweet, wise mom who loves cooking for her family!

PETER

He loves sports, especially surfing and basketball! Charming and fun, he recently moved out with a bunch of friends!

LIONEL

He looks a bit grumpy, but Lionel is a friendly dad, always ready to chat, laugh, and joke around with Tara and Peter.

SURPRISE PHOTO OF THE COOKS

Taranee's family on the stand!

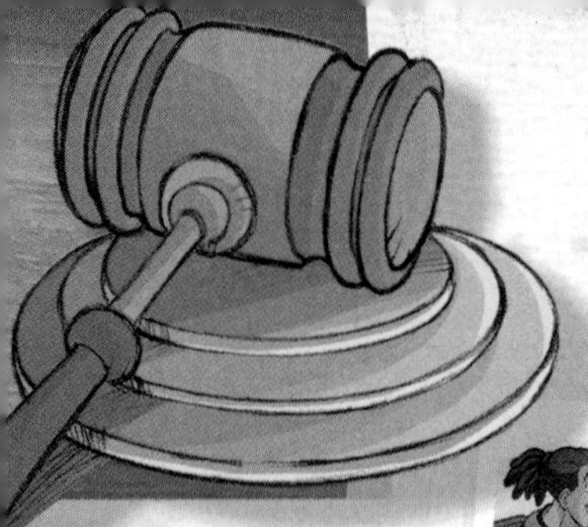

The Cook family never has a boring day! They're always busy with something important: work, school, sports...sometimes they don't see one another until the sun's gone down! But they always gather around the dinner table, eating Theresa's delicious cooking as they talk about their day!

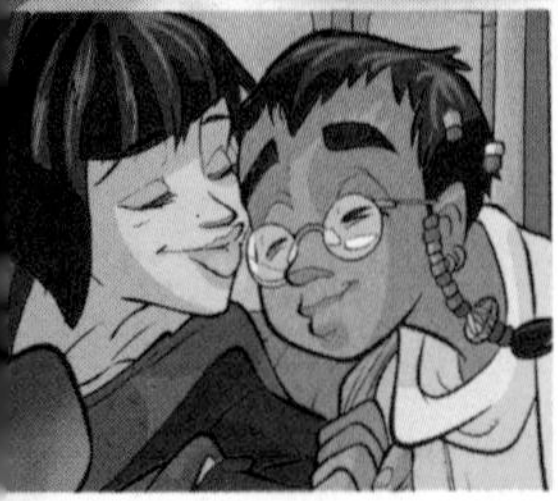

Mom and daughter sometimes argue—it happens! But they always make up!

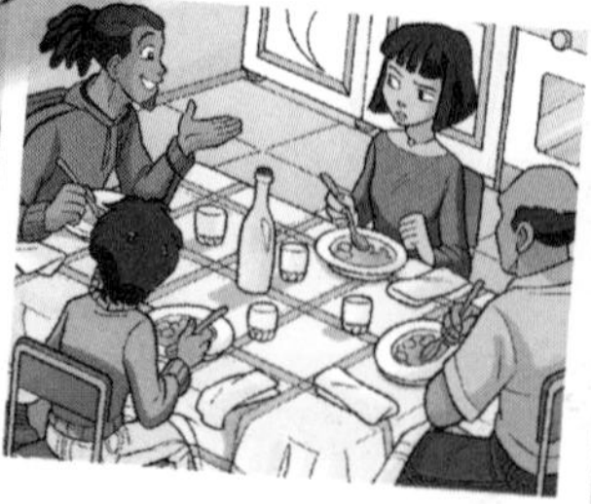

At dinner, the family enjoys Theresa's cooking while chatting about their day!

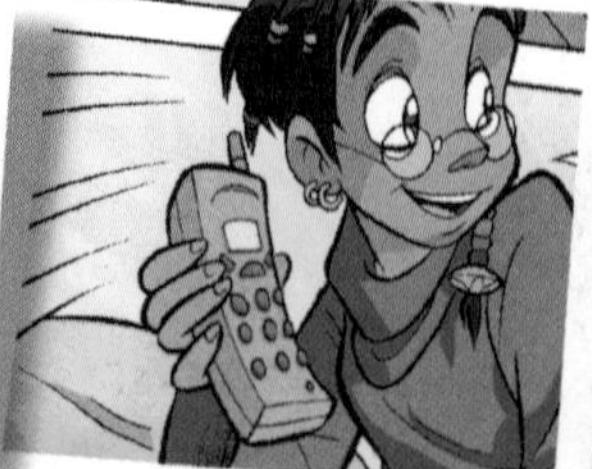

The phone is always in high demand...but since Peter moved out, it's available more often!

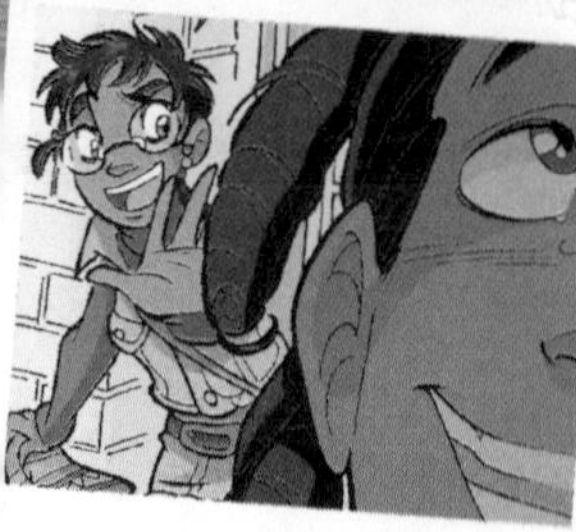

Tara and Peter bicker often, but they know they can rely on each other!

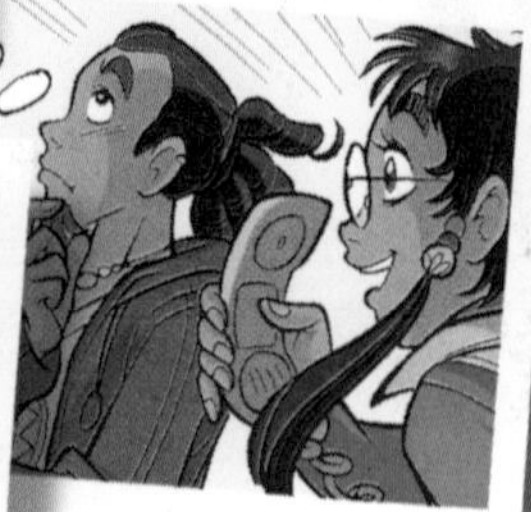

Taranee knows her brother has a crush on Cornelia, and she likes ribbing him about it!

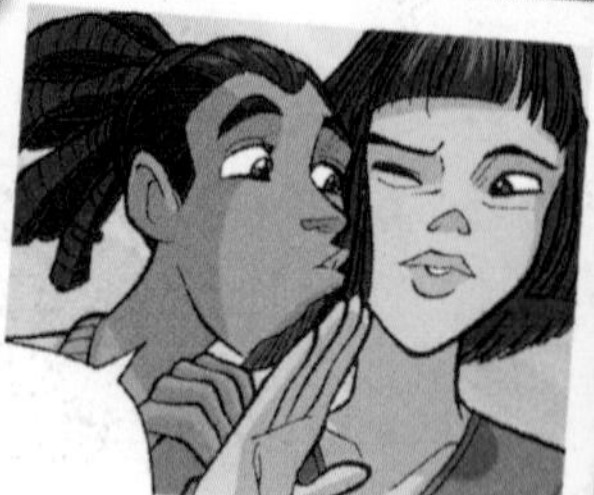

A surprise kiss on the cheek: the secret weapon to ask Mom for a favor!

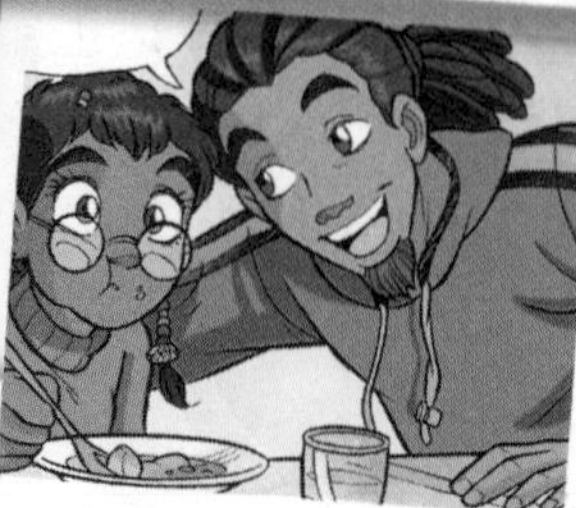

And promising Tara to drive her wherever she wants is the secret weapon to guarantee her silence!

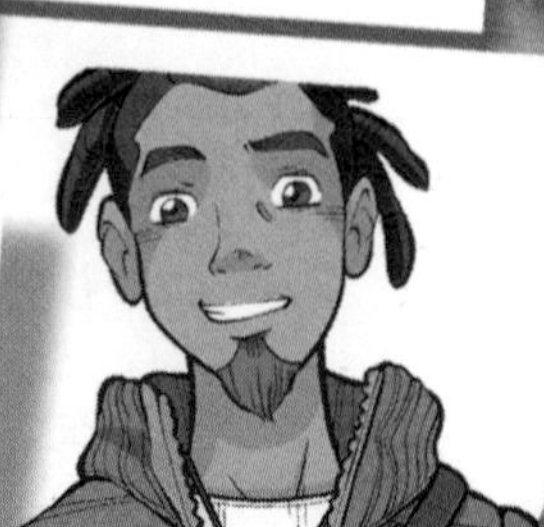

Peter has a great relationship with his sister and continues to give great advice!

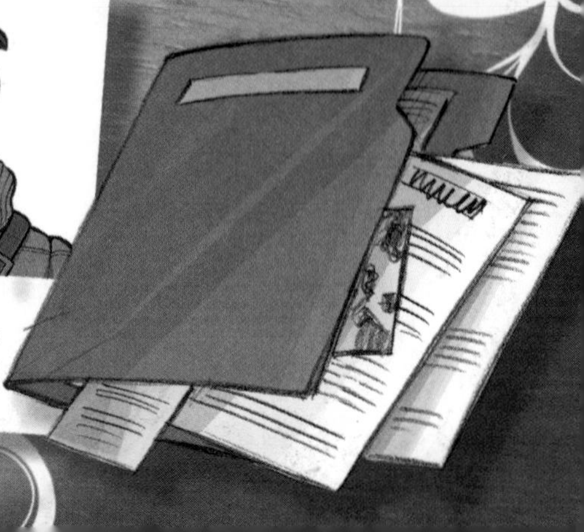

A family snapshot! The Hales' family portrait is pinned to their fridge!

Cornelia's family

CORNELIA

The Guardian of the Earth introduces us to her family!

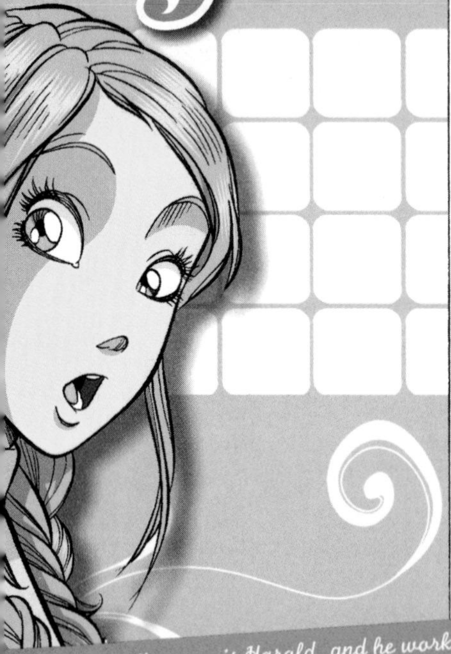

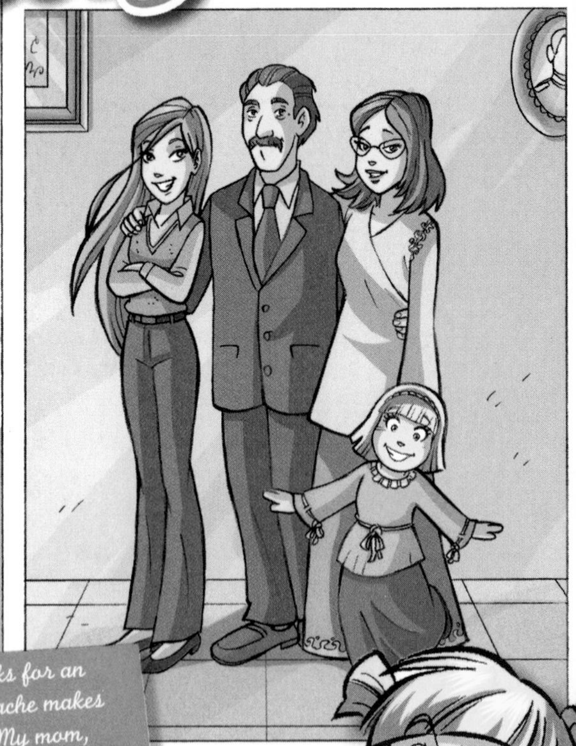

"My dad's name is Harold, and he works for an important bank in Heatherfield. His mustache makes him look serious, but he's super-sweet. My mom, Elizabeth, is so beautiful—I think she looks a lot like me! And Lilian is my lovely baby sister!"

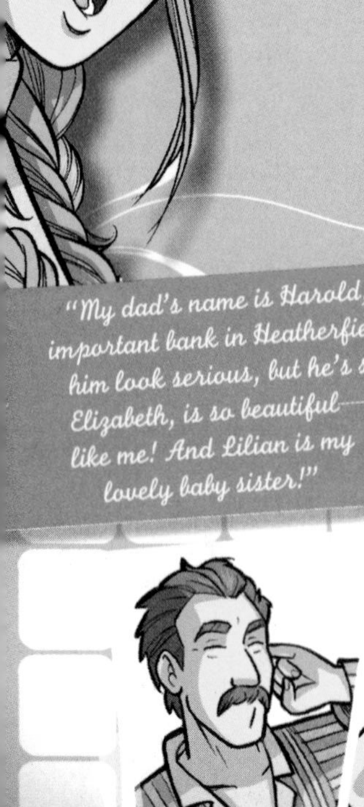

HAROLD

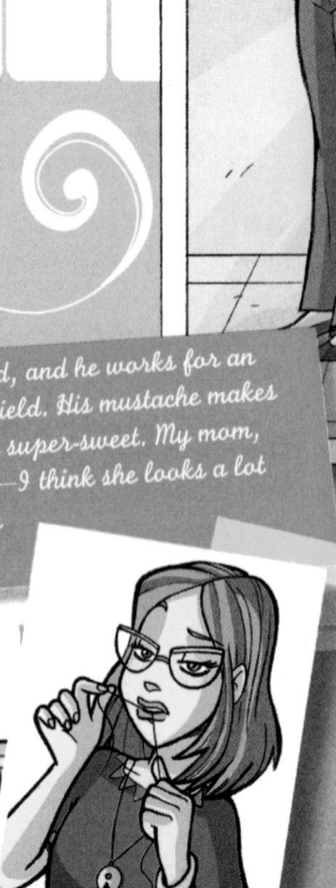

ELIZABETH

A message from Lilian: "My sister is a witch, but I'm a fairy! Don't tell anyone—it's my secret!"

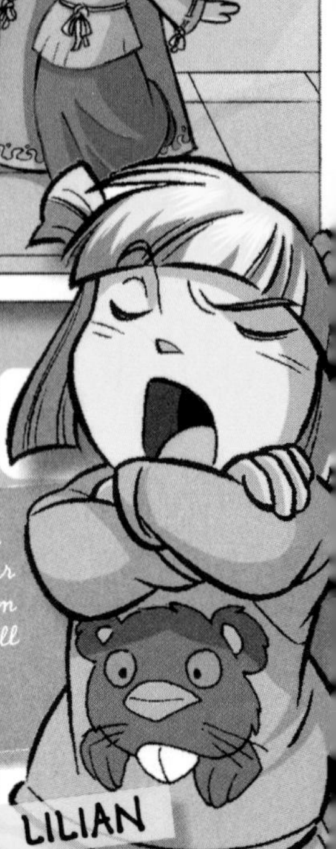

LILIAN

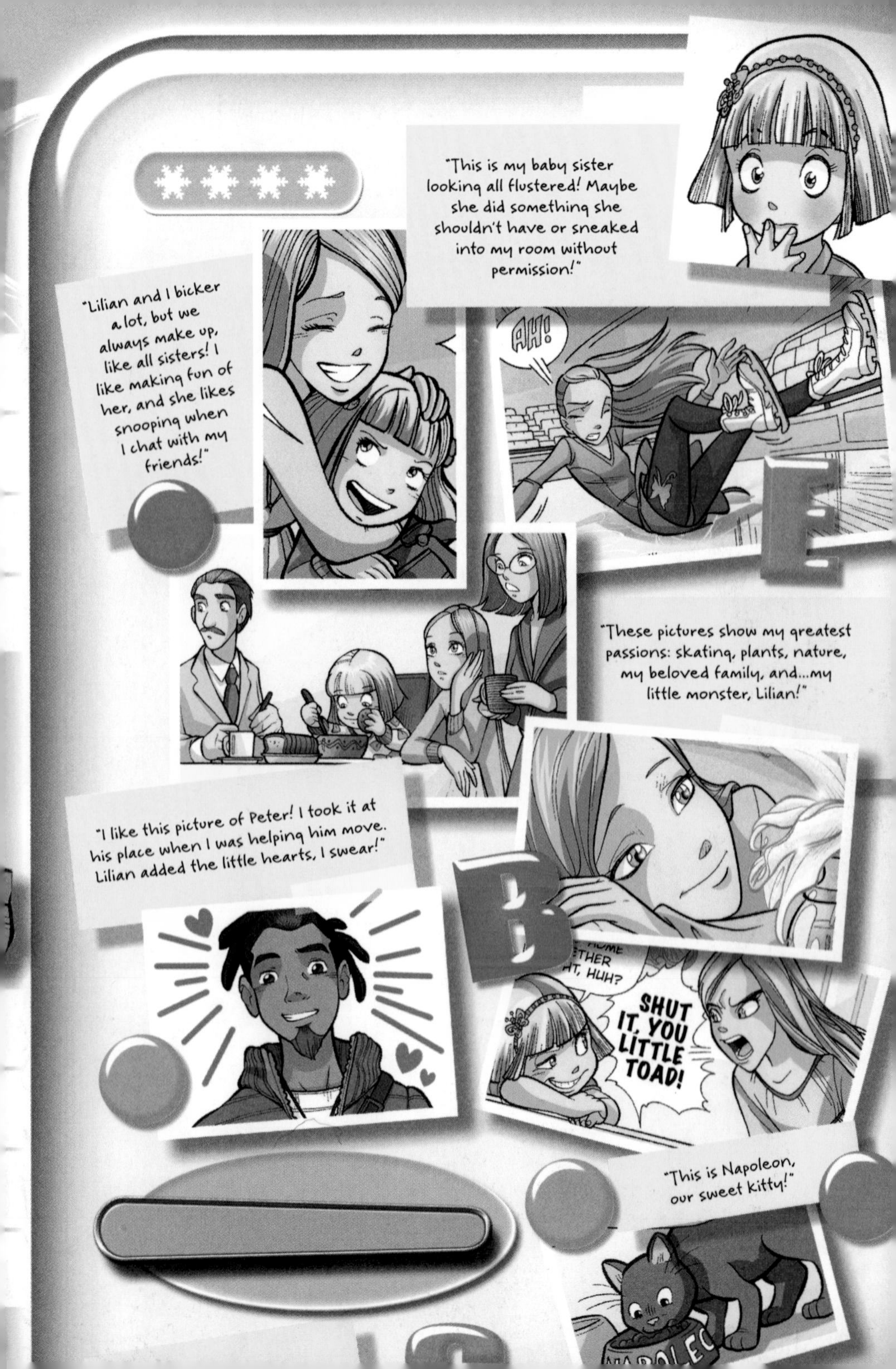
"This is my baby sister looking all flustered! Maybe she did something she shouldn't have or sneaked into my room without permission!"
"Lilian and I bicker a lot, but we always make up, like all sisters! I like making fun of her, and she likes snooping when I chat with my friends!"
AH!
"These pictures show my greatest passions: skating, plants, nature, my beloved family, and...my little monster, Lilian!"
"I like this picture of Peter! I took it at his place when I was helping him move. Lilian added the little hearts, I swear!"
SHUT IT, YOU LITTLE TOAD!
"This is Napoleon, our sweet kitty!"

With hip clothes and a new lookbook, W.I.T.C.H. are changing their style!

W.I.T.C.H. Style!

A SPECIAL FASHION PREVIEW!

Let's switch on the spotlight: Here's W.I.T.C.H.'s new look! Some young fashion designers from Milan, Italy, designed five collections, custom-tailored for each of W.I.T.C.H. with plenty of accessories! Check out some of the beautiful designs from those collections!

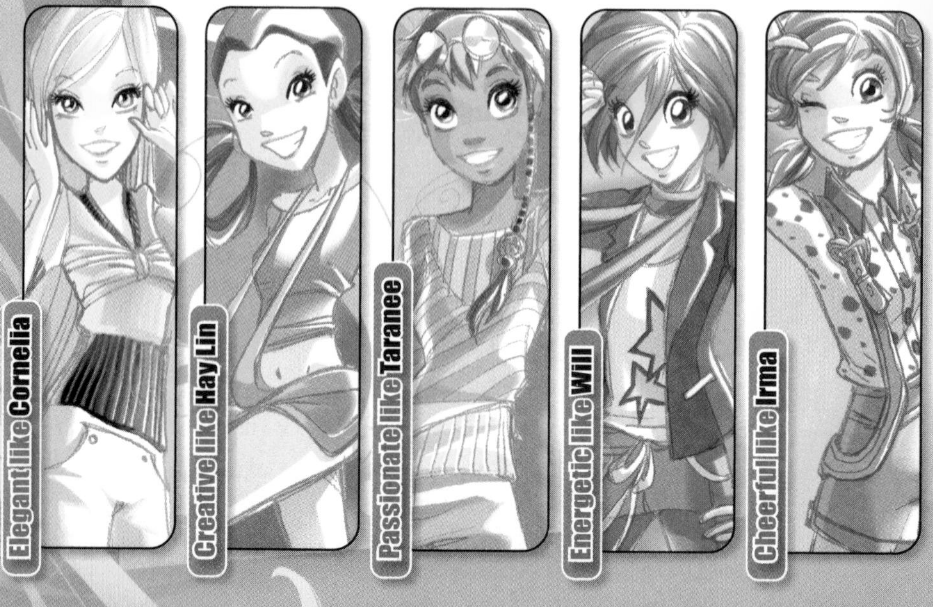
Elegant like Cornelia
Creative like Hay Lin
Passionate like Taranee
Energetic like Will
Cheerful like Irma

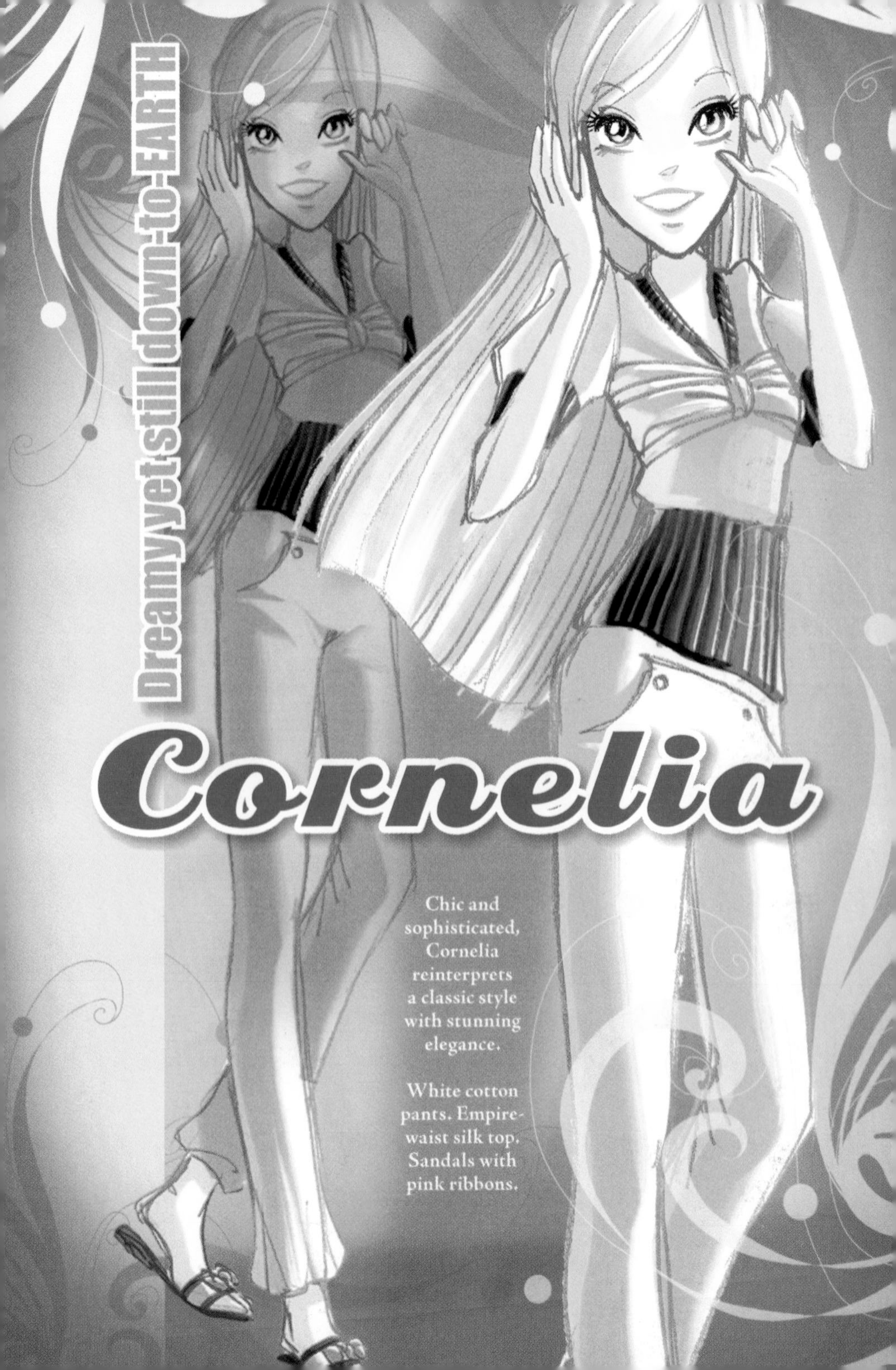
Dreamy yet still down-to-EARTH
Cornelia
Chic and sophisticated, Cornelia reinterprets a classic style with stunning elegance.
White cotton pants. Empire-waist silk top. Sandals with pink ribbons.

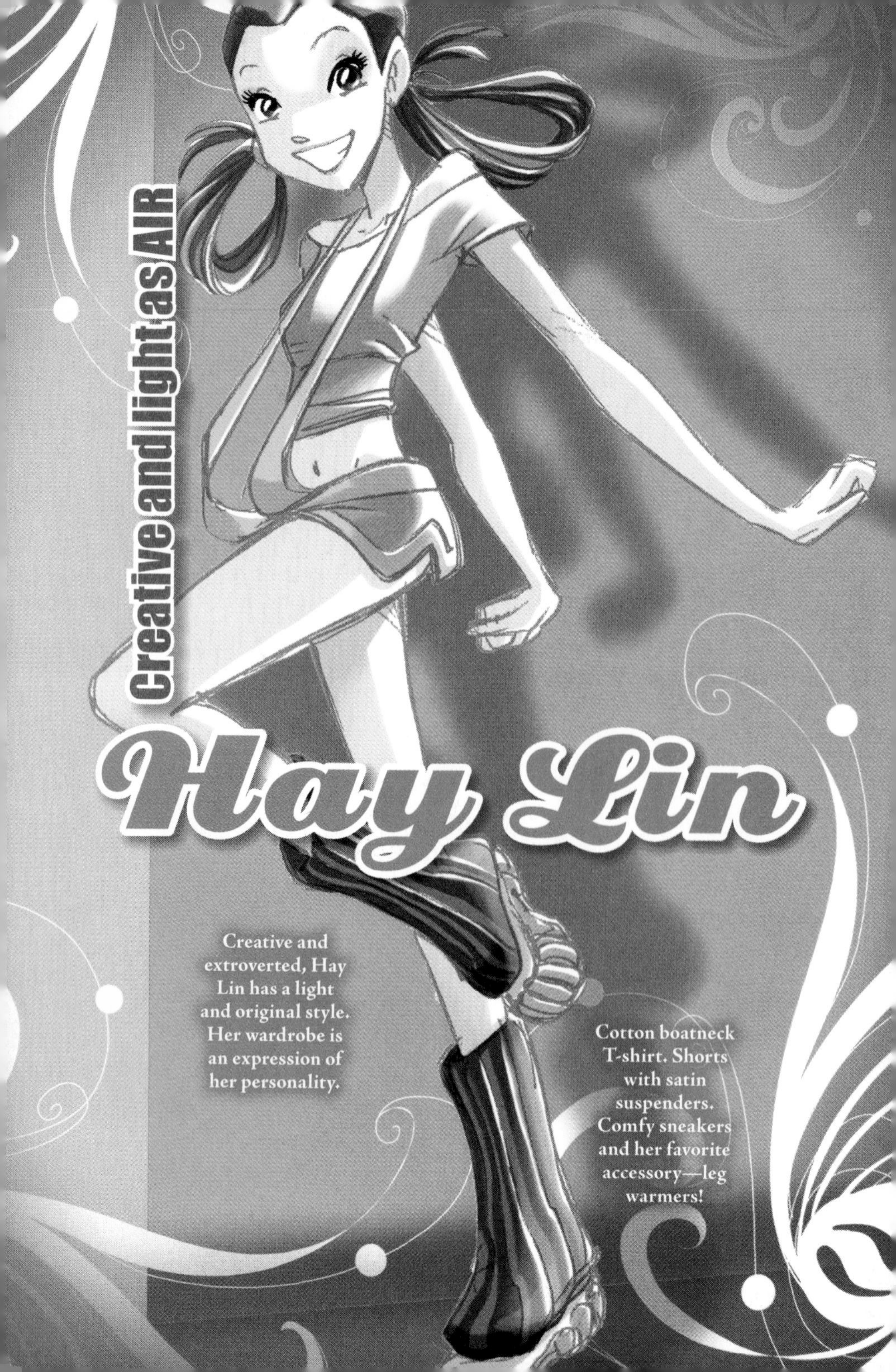
Creative and light as AIR
Hay Lin
Creative and extroverted, Hay Lin has a light and original style. Her wardrobe is an expression of her personality.
Cotton boatneck T-shirt. Shorts with satin suspenders. Comfy sneakers and her favorite accessory—leg warmers!

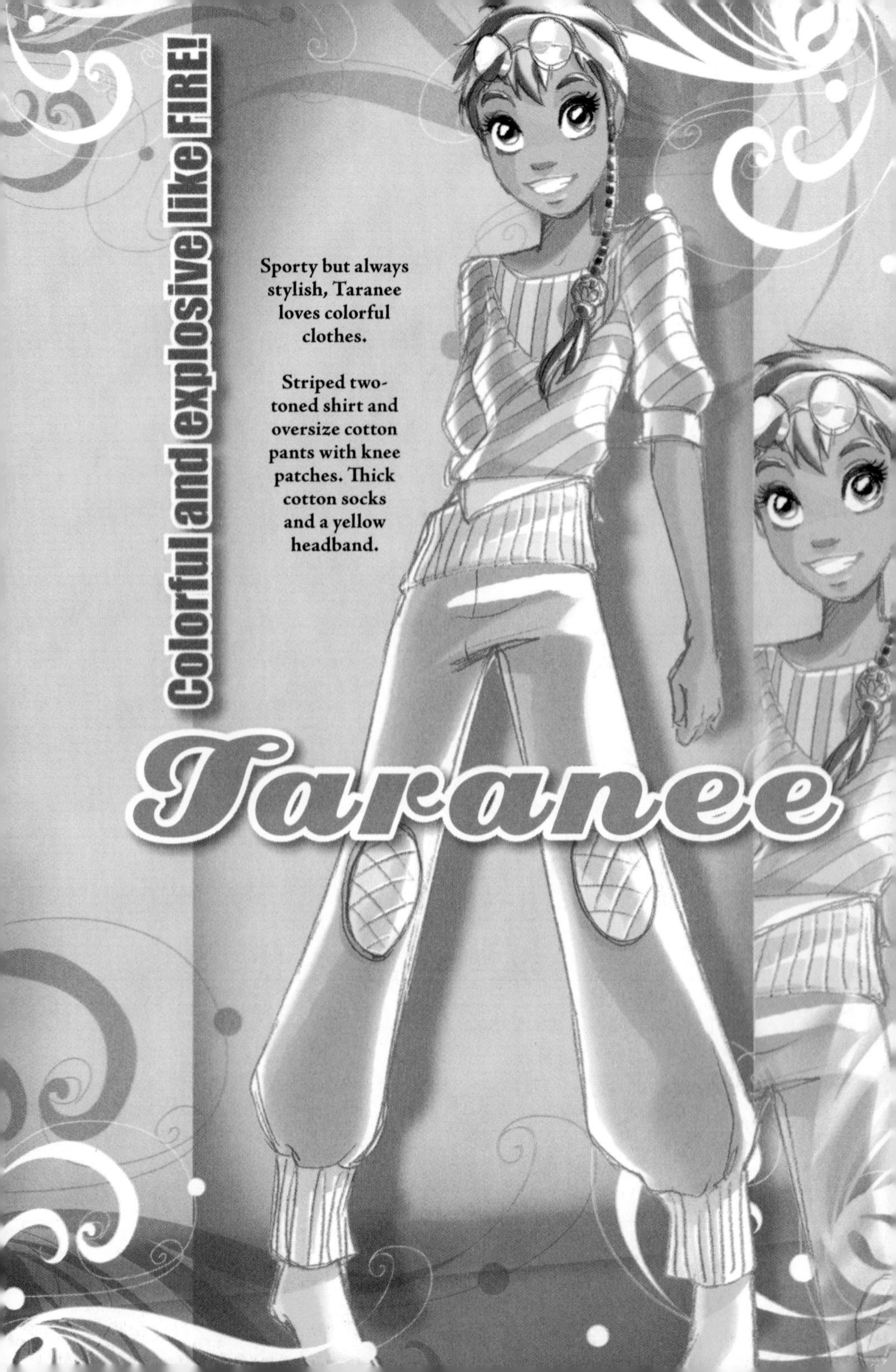
Colorful and explosive like FIRE!
Sporty but always stylish, Taranee loves colorful clothes.
Striped two-toned shirt and oversize cotton pants with knee patches. Thick cotton socks and a yellow headband.
Taranee

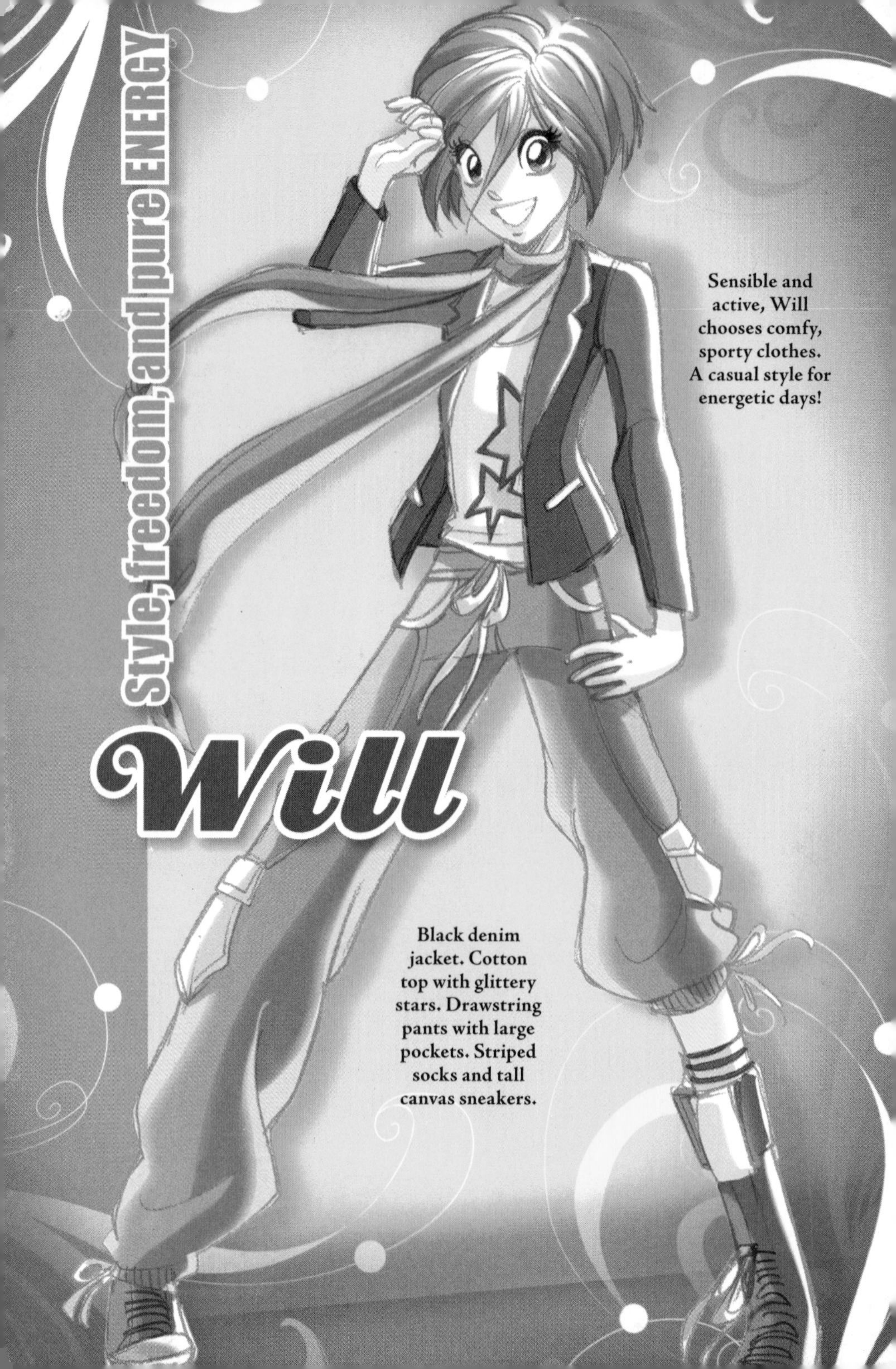
Style, freedom, and pure ENERGY
Will
Sensible and active, Will chooses comfy, sporty clothes. A casual style for energetic days!
Black denim jacket. Cotton top with glittery stars. Drawstring pants with large pockets. Striped socks and tall canvas sneakers.

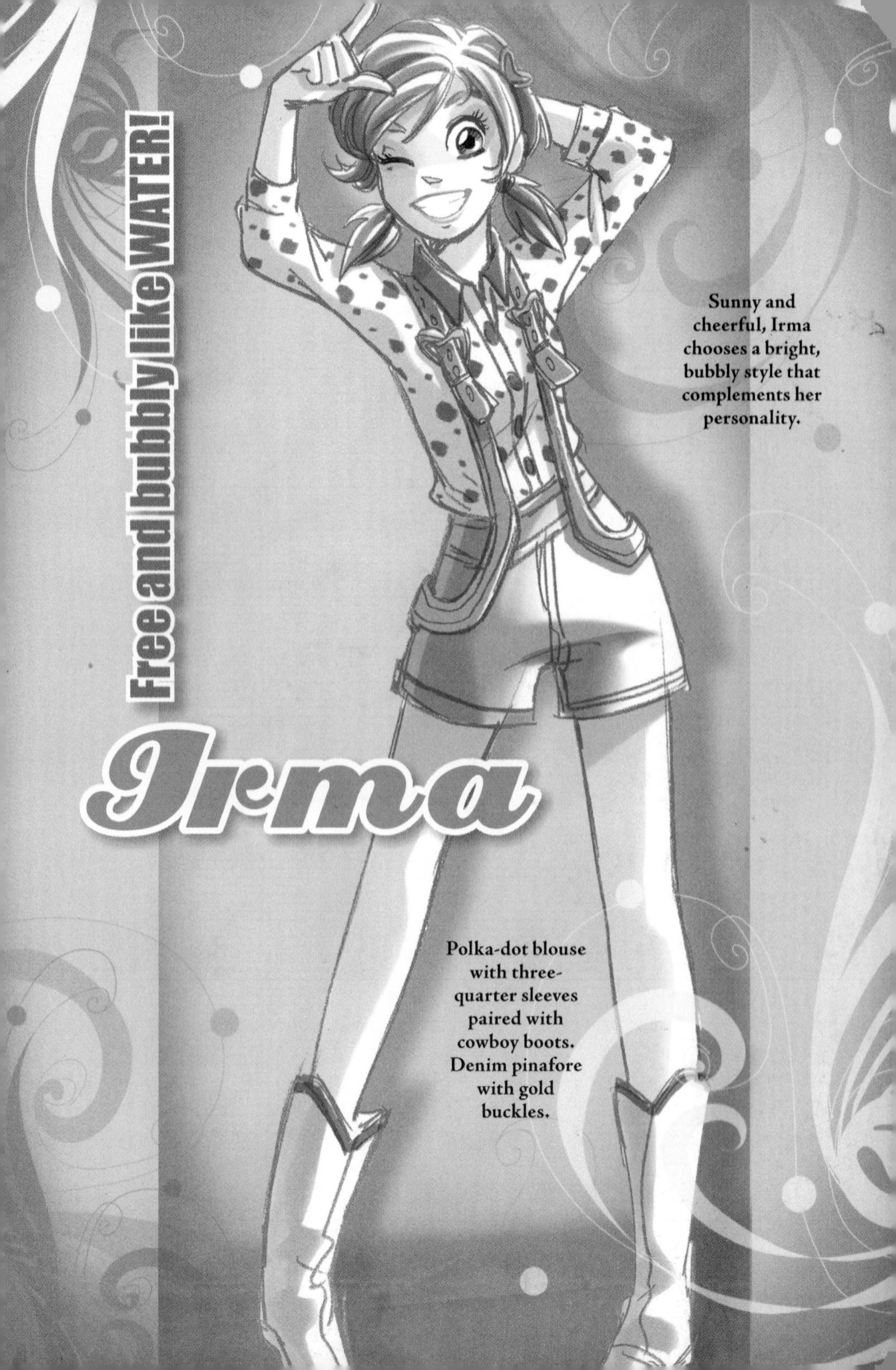
Free and bubbly like WATER!
Irma
Sunny and cheerful, Irma chooses a bright, bubbly style that complements her personality.
Polka-dot blouse with three-quarter sleeves paired with cowboy boots. Denim pinafore with gold buckles.

Part VII. New Power • Volume 3

Series Created by Elisabetta Gnone
Comic Art Direction: Alessandro Barbucci, Barbara Canepa

W.I.T.C.H.: The Graphic Novel, Part VII: New Power
© Disney Enterprises, Inc.

English translation © 2021 by Disney Enterprises, Inc.

JY
150 West 30th Street, 19th Floor
New York, NY 10001

Visit us at jyforkids.com
facebook.com/jyforkids
twitter.com/jyforkids
jyforkids.tumblr.com
instagram.com/jyforkids

First JY Edition: March 2021

JY is an imprint of Yen Press, LLC.
The JY name and logo are trademarks of Yen Press, LLC.

The publisher is not responsible for websites (or their content) that are not owned by the publisher.

Library of Congress Control Number: 2017950917

ISBNs:
978-1-9753-3300-3 (paperback)
978-1-9753-3316-4 (ebook)

10 9 8 7 6 5 4 3 2 1

LSC-C

Printed in the United States of America

Cover Art by Alessia Martusciello
Colors by Andrea Cagol

Translation by Linda Ghio and Stephanie Dagg at Editing Zone
Lettering by Katie Blakeslee

BACK TO KANDRAKAR

Concept and Script by Augusto Macchetto
Layout by Ettore Gula
Pencils by Giada Perissinotto
Inks by Marina Baggio and Roberta Zanotta
Color and Light Direction by Francesco Legramandi
Title Page Art by Daniela Vetro

A SPECIAL FLOW

Concept and Script by Bruno Enna
Layout by Daniela Vetro
Pencils by Federico Bertolucci
Inks by Marina Baggio and Roberta Zanotta
Color and Light Direction by Francesco Legramandi
Title Page Art by Giada Perissinotto
with colors by Francesco Legramandi

I AM YOU

Concept and Script by Augusto Macchetto
Layout by Lucio Leoni
Pencils by Flavia Scuderi
Inks by Marina Baggio
Color and Light Direction by Francesco Legramandi
Title Page Art by Paolo Campinoti
with colors by Francesco Legramandi

THE HEART OF IT ALL

Concept and Script by Bruno Enna
Layout by Alberto Zanon
Pencils by Caterina Giorgetti
Inks by Marina Baggio and Roberta Zanotta
Color and Light Direction by Francesco Legramandi
Title Page Art by Caterina Giorgetti
with colors by Francesco Legramandi